Bjørnstjerne Bjørnson,
Collection novels

In this book:
A Happy Boy
Arne: Early Tales and Sketches
Magnhild Dust

Translator: Rasmus B. Anderson

Three Comedies
Translator: R. Farquharson Sharp

Mary
Translator: Mary Morison

Bjørnstjerne Martinius Bjørnson (1832 –1910) was a Norwegian writer who received the 1903 Nobel Prize in Literature "as a tribute to his noble, magnificent and versatile poetry, which has always been distinguished by both the freshness of its inspiration and the rare purity of its spirit". Bjørnson is considered to be one of The Four Greats (De Fire Store) among Norwegian writers, the others being Henrik Ibsen, Jonas Lie, and Alexander Kielland.

In this book:
A Happy Boy……………………….Pag. 3
Arne: Early Tales and Sketches…….Pag. 41
Three Comedies…………………….Pag. 109
Mary………………………..……...Pag. 178
Magnhild Dust………………….....Pag. 233

A Happy Boy

CHAPTER I.

His name was Oyvind, and he cried when he was born. But no sooner did he sit up on his mother's lap than he laughed, and when the candle was lit in the evening the room rang with his laughter, but he cried when he was not allowed to reach it.

"Something remarkable will come of that boy!" said the mother.

A barren cliff, not a very high one, though, overhung the house where he was born; fir and birch looked down upon the roof, the bird-cherry strewed flowers over it. And on the roof was a little goat belonging to Oyvind; it was kept there that it might not wander away, and Oyvind bore leaves and grass up to it. One fine day the goat leaped down and was off to the cliff; it went straight up and soon stood where it had never been before. Oyvind did not see the goat when he came out in the afternoon, and thought at once of the fox. He grew hot all over, and gazing about him, cried,—

"Killy-killy-killy-killy-goat!"

"Ba-a-a-a!" answered the goat, from the brow of the hill, putting its head on one side and peering down.

At the side of the goat there was kneeling a little girl.

"Is this goat yours?" asked she.

Oyvind opened wide his mouth and eyes, thrust both hands into his pants and said,—

"Who are you?"

"I am Marit, mother's young one, father's fiddle, the hulder of the house, granddaughter to Ola Nordistuen of the Heidegards, four years old in the autumn, two days after the frost nights—I am!"

"Is that who you are?" cried he, drawing a long breath, for he had not ventured to take one while she was speaking.

"Is this goat yours?" she again inquired.

"Ye-es!" replied he, raising his eyes.

"I have taken such a liking to the goat;—you will not give it to me?"

"No, indeed I will not."

She lay kicking up her heels and staring down at him, and presently she said: "But if I give you a twisted bun for the goat, can I have it then?"

Oyvind was the son of poor people; he had tasted twisted bun only once in his life, that was when grandfather came to his house, and he had never eaten anything equal to it before or since. He fixed his eyes on the girl.

"Let me see the bun first?" said he.

She was not slow in producing a large twisted bun that she held in her hand.

"Here it is!" cried she, and tossed it down to him.

"Oh! it broke in pieces!" exclaimed the boy, picking up every fragment with the utmost care. He could not help tasting of the very smallest morsel, and it was so good that he had to try another piece, and before he knew it himself he had devoured the whole bun.

"Now the goat belongs to me," said the girl.

The boy paused with the last morsel in his mouth; the girl lay there laughing, and the goat stood by her side, with its white breast and shining brown hair, giving sidelong glances down.

"Could you not wait a while," begged the boy,—his heart beginning to throb. Then the girl laughed more than ever, and hurriedly got up on her knees.

"No, the goat is mine," said she, and threw her arms about it, then loosening one of her garters she fastened it around its neck. Oyvind watched her. She rose to her feet and began to tug at the goat; it would not go along with her, and stretched its neck over the edge of the cliff toward Oyvind.

"Ba-a-a-a!" said the goat.

Then the little girl took hold of its hair with one hand, pulled at the garter with the other, and said prettily: "Come, now, goat, you shall go into the sitting-room and eat from mother's dish and my apron."

And then she sang,—

> "Come, boy's pretty goatie,
> Come, calf, my delight,
> Come here, mewing pussie,
> In shoes snowy white,
> Yellow ducks, from your shelter,
> Come forth, helter-skelter.

> Come, doves, ever beaming,
> With soft feathers gleaming!
> The grass is still wet,
> But sun 't will soon get;
> Now call, though early 't is in the summer,
> And autumn will be the new-comer."

Footnote 1: Auber Forestier's translation.

There the boy stood.

He had taken care of the goat ever since winter, when it was born, and it had never occurred to him that he could lose it; but now it was gone in an instant, and he would never see it again.

The mother came trolling up from the beach, with some wooden pails she had been scouring; she saw the boy sitting on the grass, with his legs crossed under him, crying, and went to him.

"What makes you cry?"

"Oh, my goat—my goat!"

"Why, where is the goat?" asked the mother, glancing up at the roof.

"It will never come back any more," said the boy.

"Dear me! how can *that* be?"

Oyvind would not confess at once.

"Has the fox carried it off?"

"Oh, I wish it were the fox!"

"You must have lost your senses!" cried the mother. "What has become of the goat?"

"Oh—oh—oh! I was so unlucky. I sold it for a twisted bun!"

The moment he uttered the words he realized what it was to sell the goat for a bun; he had not thought about it before. The mother said,—

"What do you imagine the little goat thinks of you now, since you were willing to sell it for a twisted bun?"

The boy reflected upon this himself, and felt perfectly sure that he never could know happiness more in *this* world—nor in heaven either, he thought, afterwards.

He was so overwhelmed with sorrow that he promised himself that he would never do anything wrong again,—neither cut the cord of the spinning-wheel, nor let the sheep loose, nor go down to the sea alone. He fell asleep lying there, and he dreamed that the goat had reached heaven. There the Lord was sitting, with a long beard, as in the Catechism, and the goat stood munching at the leaves of a shining tree; but Oyvind sat alone on the roof, and, could get no higher. Then something wet was thrust right against his ear, and he started up. "Ba-a-a-a!" he heard, and it was the goat that had returned to him.

"What! have you come back again?" With these words he sprang up, seized it by the two fore-legs, and danced about with it as if it were a brother. He pulled it by the beard, and was on the point of going in to his mother with it, when he heard some one behind him, and saw the little girl sitting on the greensward beside him. Now he understood the whole thing, and he let go of the goat.

"Is it you who have brought the goat?"

She sat tearing up the grass with her hands, and said, "I was not allowed to keep it; grandfather is up there waiting."

While the boy stood staring at her, a sharp voice from the road above called, "Well!"

Then she remembered what she had to do: she rose, walked up to Oyvind, thrust one of her dirt-covered hands into his, and, turning her face away, said, "I beg your pardon."

But then her courage forsook her, and, flinging herself on the goat, she burst into tears.

"I believe you had better keep the goat," faltered Oyvind, looking away.

"Make haste, now!" said her grandfather, from the hill; and Marit got up and walked, with hesitating feet, upward.

"You have forgotten your garter," Oyvind shouted after her. She turned and bestowed a glance, first on the garter, then on him. Finally she formed a great resolve, and replied, in a choked voice, "You may keep it."

He walked up to her, took her by the hand, and said, "I thank you!"

"Oh, there is nothing to thank me for," she answered, and, drawing a piteous sigh, went on.

Oyvind sat down on the grass again, the goat roaming about near him; but he was no longer as happy with it as before.

CHAPTER II.

The goat was tethered near the house, but Oyvind wandered off, with his eyes fixed on the cliff. The mother came and sat down beside him; he asked her to tell him stories about things that were far away, for now the goat was no longer enough to content him. So his mother told him how once everything could talk: the mountain talked to the brook, and the brook to the river, and the river to the sea, and the sea to the sky; he asked if the sky did not talk to any one, and was told that it talked to the clouds, and the clouds to the trees, the trees to the grass, the grass to the flies, the flies to the beasts, and the beasts to the children, but the children to grown people; and thus it continued until it had gone round in a circle, and neither knew where it had begun. Oyvind gazed at the cliff, the trees, the sea, and the sky, and he had never truly seen them before. The cat came out just then, and stretched itself out on the door-step, in the sunshine.

"What does the cat say?" asked Oyvind, and pointed.

The mother sang,—

> "Evening sunshine softly is dying,
> On the door-step lazy puss is lying.
> 'Two small mice,
> Cream so thick and nice;
> Four small bits of fish
> Stole I from a dish;
> Well-filled am I and sleek,
> Am very languid and meek,'
> Says the pussie."

Footnote 1: Auber Forestier's translation.

Then the cock came strutting up with all the hens.

"What does the cock say?" asked Oyvind, clapping his hands.

The mother sang,—

> "Mother-hen her wings now are sinking,
> Chanticleer on one leg stands thinking:
> 'High, indeed,
> You gray goose can speed;
> Never, surely though, she
> Clever as a cock can be.
> Seek your shelter, hens, I pray,
> Gone is the sun to his rest for to-day,'—
> Says the rooster."

Footnote 1: Auber Forestier's translation.

Two small birds sat singing on the gable.

"What are the birds saying?" asked Oyvind, and laughed.

> "'Dear Lord, how pleasant is life,
> For those who have neither toil nor strife,'—
> Say the birds."

—was the answer.

Footnote 2: Translated by H.R.G.

Thus he learned what all were saying, even to the ant crawling in the moss and the worm working in the bark.

The same summer his mother undertook to teach him to read. He had had books for a long time, and wondered how it would be when they, too, should begin to talk. Now the letters were transformed into beasts and birds and all living creatures; and soon they began to move about together, two and two; *a* stood resting beneath a tree called *b*, *c* came and joined it; but when three or four were grouped together they seemed to get angry with one another, and nothing would then go right. The farther he advanced the more completely he found himself forgetting what the letters were; he longest remembered *a*, which he liked best; it was a little black lamb and was on friendly terms with all the rest; but soon *a*, too, was forgotten, the books no longer contained stories, only lessons.

Then one day his mother came in and said to him,—

"To-morrow school begins again, and you are going with me up to the gard."

Oyvind had heard that school was a place where many boys played together, and he had nothing against that. He was greatly pleased; he had often been to the gard, but not when there was school there, and he walked faster than his mother up the hill-side, so eager was he. When they came to the house of the old people, who lived on their annuity, a loud buzzing, like that from the mill at home, met them, and he asked his mother what it was.

"It is the children reading," answered she, and he was delighted, for thus it was that he had read before he learned the letters.

On entering he saw so many children round a table that there could not be more at church; others sat on their dinner-pails along the wall, some stood in little knots about an arithmetic table; the school-master, an old, gray-haired man, sat on a stool by the hearth, filling his pipe. They all looked up when Oyvind and his mother came in, and the clatter ceased as if the mill-stream had been turned off. Every eye was fixed on the new-comers; the mother saluted the school-master, who returned her greeting.

"I have come here to bring a little boy who wants to learn to read," said the mother.

"What is the fellow's name?" inquired the school-master, fumbling down in his leathern pouch after tobacco.

"Oyvind," replied the mother, "he knows his letters and he can spell."

"You do not say so!" exclaimed the school-master. "Come here, you white-head!"

"Oyvind walked up to him, the school-master took him up on his knee and removed his cap.

"What a nice little boy!" said he, stroking the child's hair. Oyvind looked up into his eyes and laughed.

"Are you laughing at me!" The old man knit his brow, as he spoke.

"Yes, I am," replied Oyvind, with a merry peal of laughter.

Then the school-master laughed, too; the mother laughed; the children knew now that they had permission to laugh, and so they all laughed together.

With this Oyvind was initiated into school.

When he was to take his seat, all the scholars wished to make room for him; he on his part looked about for a long time; while the other children whispered and pointed, he turned in every direction, his cap in his hand, his book under his arm.

"Well, what now?" asked the school-master, who was again busied with his pipe.

Just as the boy was about turning toward the school-master, he espied, near the hearthstone close beside him, sitting on a little red-painted box, Marit with the many names; she had hidden her face behind both hands and sat peeping out at him.

"I will sit here!" cried Oyvind, promptly, and seizing a lunch-box he seated himself at her side. Now she raised the arm nearest him a little and peered at him from under her elbow; forthwith he, too, covered his face with both hands and looked at her from under his elbow. Thus they sat cutting up capers until she laughed, and then he laughed also; the other little folks noticed this, and they joined in the laughter; suddenly a voice which was frightfully strong, but which grew milder as it spoke, interposed with,—

"Silence, troll-children, wretches, chatter-boxes!—hush, and be good to me, sugar-pigs!"

It was the school-master, who had a habit of flaring up, but becoming good-natured again before he was through. Immediately there was quiet in the school, until the pepper grinders again began to go; they read aloud, each from his book; the most delicate trebles piped up, the rougher voices drumming louder and louder in order to gain the ascendency, and here and there one chimed in, louder than the others. In all his life Oyvind had never had such fun.

"Is it always so here?" he whispered to Marit.

"Yes, always," said she.

Later they had to go forward to the school-master and read; a little boy was afterwards appointed to teach them to read, and then they were allowed to go and sit quietly down again.

"I have a goat now myself," said Marit.

"Have you?"

"Yes, but it is not as pretty as yours."

"Why do you never come up to the cliff again?"

"Grandfather is afraid I might fall over."

"Why, it is not so very high."

"Grandfather will not let me, nevertheless."

"Mother knows a great many songs," said Oyvind.

"Grandfather does, too, I can tell you."

"Yes, but he does not know mother's songs."

"Grandfather knows one about a dance. Do you want to hear it?"

"Yes, very much."

"Well, then, come nearer this way, that the school-master may not see us."

He moved close to her, and then she recited a little snatch of a song, four or five times, until the boy learned it, and it was the first thing he learned at school.

"Dance!" cried the fiddle;
Its strings all were quaking,
The lensmand's son making
Spring up and say "Ho!"
"Stay!" called out Ola,

>   And tripped him up lightly;
>   The girls laughed out brightly,
>   The lensmand lay low.
>   "Hop!" said then Erik,
>   His heel upward flinging;
>   The beams fell to ringing,
>   The walls gave a shriek.
>   "Stop!" shouted Elling,
>   His collar then grasping,
>   And held him up, gasping:
>   "Why, you're far too weak!"
>   "Hey!" spoke up Rasmus,
>   Fair Randi then seizing;
>   "Come, give without teasing
>   That kiss. Oh! you know!"
>   "Nay!" answered Randi,
>   And boxing him smartly,
>   Dashed off, crying tartly:
>   "Take that now and go!"
>
>   Footnote 1: Auber Forestier's translation.

"Up, youngsters!" cried the school-master; "this is the first day, so you shall be let off early; but first we must say a prayer and sing."

The whole school was now alive; the little folks jumped down from the benches, ran across the floor and all spoke at once.

"Silence, little gypsies, young rascals, yearlings!—be still and walk nicely across the floor, little children!" said the school-master, and they quietly took their places, after which the school-master stood in front of them and made a short prayer. Then they sang; the school-master started the tune, in a deep bass; all the children, folding their hands, joined in. Oyvind stood at the foot, near the door, with Marit, looking on; they also clasped their hands, but they could not sing.

This was the first day at school.

CHAPTER III.

Oyvind grew and became a clever boy; he was among the first scholars at school, and at home he was faithful in all his tasks. This was because at home he loved his mother and at school the school-master; he saw but little of his father, who was always either off fishing or was attending to the mill, where half the parish had their grinding done.

What had the most influence on his mind in these days was the school-master's history, which his mother related to him one evening as they sat by the hearth. It sank into his books, it thrust itself beneath every word the school-master spoke, it lurked in the school-room when all was still. It caused him to be obedient and reverent, and to have an easier apprehension as it were of everything that was taught him.

The history ran thus:—

The school-master's name was Baard, and he once had a brother whose name was Anders. They thought a great deal of each other; they both enlisted; they lived together in the town, and took part in the war, both being made corporals, and serving in the same company. On their return home after the war, every one thought they were two splendid fellows. Now their father died; he had a good deal of personal property, which was not easy to divide, but the brothers decided, in order that this should be no cause of disagreement between them, to put the things up at auction, so that each might buy what he wanted, and the proceeds could be divided between them. No sooner said than done. Their father had owned a large gold watch, which had a wide-spread fame, because it was the only gold watch people in that part of the country had seen, and when it was put up many a rich man tried to get it until the two brothers began to take part in the bidding; then the rest ceased. Now, Baard expected Anders to let him have the watch, and Anders expected the same of Baard; each bid in his turn to put the other to the test, and they looked hard at each other while bidding. When the watch had been run up to twenty dollars, it seemed to Baard that his brother was not acting rightly, and he continued to bid until he got it almost up to thirty; as Anders kept on, it struck Baard that his brother could not remember how kind he had always been to him, nor that he was the elder of the two, and the watch went up to over thirty dollars. Anders still kept on. Then Baard suddenly bid forty dollars, and ceased to look at his brother. It grew very still in the auction-room, the voice of the lensmand one was heard calmly naming the price. Anders, standing there, thought if Baard could afford to give forty dollars he could also, and if Baard grudged him the watch, he might as well take it. He bid higher. This Baard felt to be the greatest disgrace that had ever befallen him; he bid fifty dollars, in a very low tone. Many people stood around, and Anders did not see how his brother could so mock at him in the hearing of all; he bid higher. At length Baard laughed.

"A hundred dollars and my brotherly affection in the bargain," said he, and turning left the room. A little later, some one came out to him, just as he was engaged in saddling the horse he had bought a short time before.

"The watch is yours," said the man; "Anders has withdrawn."

The moment Baard heard this there passed through him a feeling of compunction; he thought of his brother, and not of the watch. The horse was saddled, but Baard paused with his hand on its back, uncertain whether to ride away or no. Now many people came out, among them Anders, who when he saw his brother standing beside the saddled horse, not knowing what Baard was reflecting on, shouted out to him:—

"Thank you for the watch, Baard! You will not see it run the day your brother treads on your heels."

"Nor the day I ride to the gard again," replied Baard, his face very white, swinging himself into the saddle.

Neither of them ever again set foot in the house where they had lived with their father.

A short time after, Anders married into a houseman's family; but Baard was not invited to the wedding, nor was he even at church. The first year of Anders' marriage the only cow he owned was found dead beyond the north side of the house, where it was tethered, and no one could find out what had killed it. Several misfortunes followed, and he kept going downhill; but the worst of all was when his barn, with all that it contained, burned down in the middle of the winter; no one knew how the fire had originated.

"This has been done by some one who wishes me ill," said Anders,—and he wept that night. He was now a poor man and had lost all ambition for work.

The next evening Baard appeared in his room. Anders was in bed when he entered, but sprang directly up.

"What do you want here?" he cried, then stood silent, staring fixedly at his brother.

Baard waited a little before he answered,—

"I wish to offer you help, Anders; things are going badly for you."

"I am faring as you meant I should, Baard! Go, I am not sure that I can control myself."

"You mistake, Anders; I repent"—

"Go, Baard, or God be merciful to us both!"

Baard fell back a few steps, and with quivering voice he murmured,—

"If you want the watch you shall have it."

"Go, Baard!" shrieked the other, and Baard left, not daring to linger longer.

Now with Baard it had been as follows: As soon as he had heard of his brother's misfortunes, his heart melted; but pride held him back. He felt impelled to go to church, and there he made good resolves, but he was not able to carry them out. Often he got far enough to see Anders' house; but now some one came out of the door; now there was a stranger there; again Anders was outside chopping wood, so there was always something in the way. But one Sunday, late in the winter, he went to church again, and Anders was there too. Baard saw him; he had grown pale and thin; he wore the same clothes as in former days when the brothers were constant companions, but now they were old and patched. During the sermon Anders kept his eyes fixed on the priest, and Baard thought he looked good and kind; he remembered their childhood and what a good boy Anders had been. Baard went to communion that day, and he made a solemn vow to his God that he would be reconciled with his brother whatever might happen. This determination passed through his soul while he was drinking the wine, and when he rose he wanted to go right to him and sit down beside him; but some one was in the way and Anders did not look up. After service, too, there was something in the way; there were too many people; Anders' wife was walking at his side, and Baard was not acquainted with her; he concluded that it would be best to go to his brother's house and have a serious talk with him. When evening came he set forth. He went straight to the sitting-room door and listened, then he heard his name spoken; it was by the wife.

"He took the sacrament to-day," said she; "he surely thought of you."

"No; he did not think of me," said Anders. "I know him; he thinks only of himself."

For a long time there was silence; the sweat poured from Baard as he stood there, although it was a cold evening. The wife inside was busied with a kettle that crackled and hissed on the hearth; a little infant cried now and then, and Anders rocked it. At last the wife spoke these few words:—

"I believe you both think of each other without being willing to admit it."

"Let us talk of something else," replied Anders.

After a while he got up and moved towards the door. Baard was forced to hide in the wood-shed; but to that very place Anders came to get an armful of wood. Baard stood in the corner and saw him distinctly; he had put off his threadbare Sunday clothes and wore the uniform he had brought home with him from the war, the match to Baard's, and which he had promised his brother never to touch but to leave for an heirloom, Baard having given him a similar promise. Anders' uniform was now patched and worn; his strong, well-built frame was encased, as it were, in a bundle of rags; and, at the same time, Baard heard the gold watch ticking in his own pocket. Anders walked to where the fagots lay; instead of stooping at once to pick them up, he paused, leaned back against the wood-pile and gazed up at the sky, which glittered brightly with stars. Then he drew a sigh and muttered,—

"Yes—yes—yes;—O Lord! O Lord!"

As long as Baard lived he heard these words. He wanted to step forward, but just then his brother coughed, and it seemed so difficult, more was not required to hold him back. Anders took up his armful of wood, and brushed past Baard, coming so close to him that the twigs struck his face, making it smart.

For fully ten minutes he stood as if riveted to the spot, and it is doubtful when he would have left, had he not, after his great emotion, been seized with a shivering fit that shook him through and through. Then he moved away; he frankly confessed to himself that he was too cowardly to go in, and so he now formed a new plan. From an ash-box which stood in the corner he had just left, he took some bits of charcoal, found a resinous pine-splint, went up to the barn, closed the door and struck a light. When he had lit the pine-splint, he held it up to find the wooden peg where Anders hung his lantern when he came early in the morning to thresh. Baard took his gold watch and hung it on the peg, blew out his light and left; and then he felt so relieved that he bounded over the snow like a young boy.

The next day he heard that the barn had burned to the ground during the night. No doubt sparks had fallen from the torch that had lit him while he was hanging up his watch.

This so overwhelmed him that he kept his room all day like a sick man, brought out his hymn-book, and sang until the people in the house thought he had gone mad. But in the evening he went out; it was bright moonlight. He walked to his brother's place, dug in the ground where the fire had been, and found, as he had expected, a little melted lump of gold. It was the watch.

It was with this in his tightly closed hand that he went in to his brother, imploring peace, and was about to explain everything.

A little girl had seen him digging in the ashes, some boys on their way to a dance had noticed him going down toward the place the preceding Sunday evening; the people in the house where he lived testified how curiously he had acted on Monday, and as every one knew that he and his brother were bitter enemies, information was given and a suit instituted.

No one could prove anything against Baard, but suspicion rested on him. Less than ever, now, did he feel able to approach his brother.

Anders had thought of Baard when the barn was burned, but had spoken of it to no one. When he saw him enter his room, the following evening, pale and excited, he immediately thought: "Now he is smitten with remorse, but for such a terrible crime against his brother he shall have no forgiveness." Afterwards he heard how people had seen Baard go down to the barn the evening of the fire, and, although nothing was brought to light at the trial, Anders firmly believed his brother to be guilty.

They met at the trial; Baard in his good clothes, Anders in his patched ones. Baard looked at his brother as he entered, and his eyes wore so piteous an expression of entreaty that Anders felt it in the inmost depths of his heart. "He does not want me to say anything," thought Anders, and when he was asked if he suspected his brother of the deed, he said loudly and decidedly, "No!"

Anders took to hard drinking from that day, and was soon far on the road to ruin. Still worse was it with Baard; although he did not drink, he was scarcely to be recognized by those who had known him before.

Late one evening a poor woman entered the little room Baard rented, and begged him to accompany her a short distance. He knew her: it was his brother's wife. Baard understood forthwith what her errand was; he grew deathly pale, dressed himself, and went with her without a word. There was a glimmer of light from Anders' window, it twinkled and disappeared, and they were guided by this light, for there was no path across the snow. When Baard stood once more in the passage, a strange odor met him which made him feel ill. They entered. A little child stood by the fireplace eating charcoal; its whole face was black, but as it looked up and laughed it displayed white teeth,—it was the brother's child.

There on the bed, with a heap of clothes thrown over him, lay Anders, emaciated, with smooth, high forehead, and with his hollow eyes fixed on his brother. Baard's knees trembled; he sat down at the foot of the bed and burst into a violent fit of weeping. The sick man looked at him intently and said nothing. At length he asked his wife to go out, but Baard made a sign to her to remain; and now these two brothers began to talk together. They accounted for everything from the day they had bid for the watch up to the present moment. Baard concluded by producing the lump of gold he always carried about him, and it now became manifest to the brothers that in all these years neither had known a happy day.

Anders did not say much, for he was not able to do so, but Baard watched by his bed as long as he was ill.

"Now I am perfectly well," said Anders one morning on waking. "Now, my brother, we will live long together, and never leave each other, just as in the old days."

But that day he died.

Baard took charge of the wife and the child, and they fared well from that time. What the brothers had talked of together by the bed, burst through the walls and the night, and was soon known to all the people in the parish, and Baard became the most respected man among them. He was honored as one who had known great sorrow and found happiness again, or as one who had been absent for a very long time. Baard grew inwardly strong through all this friendliness about him; he became a truly pious man, and wanted to be useful, he said, and so the old corporal took to teaching school. What he impressed upon the children, first and last, was love, and he practiced it himself, so that the children clung to him as to a playmate and father in one.

Such was the history of the school-master, and so deeply did it root itself in Oyvind's mind that it became both religion and education for him. The school-master grew to be almost a supernatural being in his eyes, although he sat there so sociably, grumbling at the scholars. Not to know every lesson for him was impossible, and if Oyvind got a smile or a pat on his head after he had recited, he felt warm and happy for a whole day.

It always made the deepest impression on the children when the old school-master sometimes before singing made a little speech to them, and at least once a week read aloud some verses about loving one's neighbor. When he read the first of those verses, his voice always trembled, although he had been reading it now some twenty or thirty years. It ran thus:—

"Love thy neighbor with Christian zeal!
Crush him not with an iron heel,
Though he in dust be prostrated!
Love's all powerful, quickening hand
Guides, forever, with magic wand
All that it has created."

But when he had recited the whole poem and had paused a little, he would cry, and his eyes would twinkle,—

"Up, small trolls! and go nicely home without any noise,—go quietly, that I may only hear good of you, little toddlers!"

But when they were making the most noise in hunting up their books and dinner-pails, he shouted above it all,—

"Come again to-morrow, as soon as it is light, or I will give you a thrashing. Come again in good season, little girls and boys, and then we will be industrious."

CHAPTER IV.

Of Oyvind's further progress until a year before confirmation there is not much to report. He studied in the morning, worked through the day, and played in the evening.

As he had an unusually sprightly disposition, it was not long before the neighboring children fell into the habit of resorting in their playtime to where he was to be found. A large hill sloped down to the bay in front of the place, bordered by the cliff on one side and the wood on the other, as before described; and all winter long, on pleasant evenings and on Sundays, this served as coasting-ground for the parish young folks. Oyvind was master of the hill, and he owned two sleds, "Fleet-foot" and "Idler;" the latter he loaned out to larger parties, the former he managed himself, holding Marit on his lap.

The first thing Oyvind did in those days on awaking, was to look out and see whether it was thawing, and if it was gray and lowering over the bushes beyond the bay, or if he heard a dripping from the roof, he was long about dressing, as though there were nothing to be accomplished that day. But if he awoke, especially on a Sunday, to crisp, frosty, clear weather, to his best clothes and no work, only catechism or church in the morning, with the whole afternoon and evening free—heigh! then the boy made one spring out of bed, donned his clothes in a hurry as if for a fire, and could scarcely eat a mouthful. As soon as afternoon had come, and the first boy on skees drew in sight along the road-side, swinging his guide-pole above his head and shouting so that echoes resounded through the mountain-ridges about the lake; and then another on the road on a sled, and still another and another,—off started Oyvind with "Fleet-foot," bounded down the hill, and stopped among the last-comers, with a long, ringing shout that pealed from ridge to ridge all along the bay, and died away in the far distance.

Then he would look round for Marit, but when she had come he payed no further attention to her.

At last there came a Christmas, when Oyvind and Marit might be about sixteen or seventeen, and were both to be confirmed in the spring. The fourth day after Christmas there was a party at the upper Heidegards, at Marit's grandparents', by whom she had been brought up, and who had been promising her this party for three years, and now at last had to give it during the holidays. Oyvind was invited to it.

It was a somewhat cloudy evening but not cold; no stars could be seen; the next day must surely bring rain. There blew a sleepy wind over the snow, which was swept away here and there on the white Heidefields; elsewhere it had drifted. Along the part of the road where there was but little snow, were smooth sheets of ice of a blue-black hue, lying between the snow and the bare field, and glittering in patches as far as the eye could reach. Along the mountain-sides there had been avalanches; it was dark and bare in their track, but on either side light and snow-clad, except where the forest birch-trees put their heads together and made dark shadows. No water was visible, but half-naked heaths and bogs lay under the deeply-fissured, melancholy mountains. Gards were spread in thick clusters in the centre of the plain; in the gloom of the winter evening they resembled black clumps, from which light shot out over the fields, now from one window, now from another; from these lights it might be judged that those within were busy.

Young people, grown-up and half-grown-up, were flocking together from diverse directions; only a few of them came by the road, the others had left it at least when they approached the gards, and stole onward, one behind the stable, a couple near the store-house, some stayed for a long time behind the barn, screaming like foxes, others answered from afar like cats; one stood behind the smoke-house, barking like a cross old dog whose upper notes were cracked; and at last all joined in a general chase. The girls came sauntering along in large groups, having a few boys, mostly small ones, with them, who had gathered about them on the road in order to appear like young men. When such a bevy of girls arrived at the gard and one or two of the grown youths saw them, the girls parted, flew into the passages or down in the garden, and had to be dragged thence into the house, one by one. Some were so excessively bashful that Marit had to be sent for, and then she came out and insisted upon their entering. Sometimes, too, there appeared one who had had no invitation and who had by no means intended to go in, coming only to look on, until perhaps she might have a chance just to take one single dance. Those whom Marit liked well she invited into a small chamber, where her grandfather sat smoking his pipe, and her grandmother was walking about. The old people offered them something to drink and spoke kindly to them. Oyvind was not among those invited in, and this seemed to him rather strange.

The best fiddler of the parish could not come until later, so meanwhile they had to content themselves with the old one, a houseman, who went by the name of Gray-Knut. He knew four dances; as follows: two spring dances, a halling, and an old dance, called the Napoleon waltz; but gradually he had been compelled to transform the halling into a schottishe by altering the accent, and in the same manner a spring dance had to become a polka-mazurka. He now struck up and the dancing began. Oyvind did not dare join in at once, for there were too many grown folks here; but the half-grown-up ones soon united, thrust one another forward, drank a little strong ale to strengthen their courage, and then Oyvind came forward with them. The room grew warm to them; merriment and ale mounted to their heads. Marit was on the floor most of the time that evening, no doubt because the party was at her grandparents'; and this led Oyvind to look frequently at her; but she was always dancing with others. He longed to dance with her himself, and so he sat through one dance, in order to be able to hasten to her side the moment it was ended; and he did so, but a tall, swarthy fellow, with thick hair, threw himself in his way.

"Back, youngster!" he shouted, and gave Oyvind a push that nearly made him fall backwards over Marit.

Never before had such a thing occurred to Oyvind; never had any one been otherwise than kind to him; never had he been called "youngster" when he wanted to take part; he blushed crimson, but said nothing, and drew back to the place where the new fiddler, who had just arrived, had taken his seat and was tuning his instrument. There was silence in the crowd, every one was waiting to hear the first vigorous tones from "the chief fiddler." He tried his instrument and kept on tuning; this lasted a long time; but finally he began with a spring dance, the boys shouted and leaped, couple after couple coming into the circle. Oyvind watched Marit dancing with the thick-haired man; she laughed over the man's shoulder and her white teeth glistened. Oyvind felt a strange, sharp pain in his heart for the first time in his life.

He looked longer and longer at her, but however it might be, it seemed to him that Marit was now a young maiden. "It cannot be so, though," thought he, "for she still takes part with the rest of us in our coasting." But grown-up she was, nevertheless, and after the dance was ended, the dark-haired man pulled her down on his lap; she tore herself away, but still she sat down beside him.

Oyvind's eyes turned to the man, who wore a fine blue broadcloth suit, blue checked shirt, and a soft silk neckerchief; he had a small face, vigorous blue eyes, a laughing, defiant mouth. He was handsome. Oyvind looked more and more intently, finally scanned himself also; he had had new trousers for Christmas, which he had taken much delight in, but now he saw that they were only gray wadmal; his jacket was of the same material, but old and dark; his vest, of checked homespun, was also old, and had two bright buttons and a black one. He glanced around him and it seemed to him that very few were so poorly clad as he. Marit wore a black, close-fitting dress of a fine material, a silver brooch in her neckerchief and had a folded silk handkerchief in her hand. On the back of her head was perched a little black silk cap, which was tied under the chin with a broad, striped silk ribbon. She was fair and had rosy cheeks, and she was laughing; the man was talking to her and was laughing too. The fiddler started another tune, and the dancing was about to begin again. A comrade came and sat down beside Oyvind.

"Why are you not dancing, Oyvind?" he asked pleasantly.

"Dear me!" said Oyvind, "I do not look fit."

"Do not look fit?" cried his comrade; but before he could say more, Oyvind inquired,—

"Who is that in the blue broadcloth suit, dancing with Marit?"

"That is Jon Hatlen, he who has been away so long at an agricultural school and is now to take the gard."

At that moment Marit and Jon sat down.

"Who is that boy with light hair sitting yonder by the fiddler, staring at me?" asked Jon.

Then Marit laughed and said,—

"He is the son of the houseman at Pladsen."

Oyvind had always known that he was a houseman's son; but until now he had never realized it. It made him feel so very little, smaller than all the rest; in order to keep up he had to try and think of all that hitherto had made him happy and proud, from the coasting hill to each kind word. He thought, too, of his mother and his father, who were now sitting at home and thinking that he was having a good time, and he could scarcely hold back his tears. Around him all were laughing and joking, the fiddle rang right into his ear, it was a moment in which something black seemed to rise up before him, but then he remembered the school with all his companions, and the school-master who patted him, and the priest who at the last examination had given him a book and told him he was a clever boy. His father himself had sat by listening and had smiled on him.

"Be good now, dear Oyvind," he thought he heard the school-master say, taking him on his lap, as when he was a child. "Dear me! it all matters so little, and in fact all people are kind; it merely seems as if they were not. We two will be clever, Oyvind, just as clever as Jon Hatlen; we shall yet have good clothes, and dance with Marit in a light room, with a hundred people in it; we will smile and talk together; there will be a bride and bridegroom, a priest, and I will be in the choir smiling upon you, and mother will be at home, and there will be a large gard with twenty cows, three horses, and Marit as good and kind as at school."

The dancing ceased. Oyvind saw Marit on the bench in front of him, and Jon by her side with his face close up to hers; again there came that great burning pain in his breast, and he seemed to be saying to himself: "It is true, I am suffering."

Just then Marit rose, and she came straight to him. She stooped over him.

"You must not sit there staring so fixedly at me," said she; "you might know that people are noticing it. Take some one now and join the dancers."

He made no reply, but he could not keep back the tears that welled up to his eyes as he looked at her. Marit had already risen to go when she saw this, and paused; suddenly she grew as red as fire, turned and went back to her place, but having arrived there she turned again and took another seat. Jon followed her forthwith.

Oyvind got up from the bench, passed through the crowd, out in the grounds, sat down on a porch, and then, not knowing what he wanted there rose, but sat down again, thinking he might just as well sit there as anywhere else. He did not care about going home, nor did he desire to go in again, it was all one to him. He was not capable of considering what had happened; he did not want to think of it; neither did he wish to think of the future, for there was nothing to which he looked forward.

"But what, then, is it I am thinking of?" he queried, half aloud, and when he had heard his own voice, he thought: "You can still speak, can you laugh?" And then he tried it; yes, he could laugh, and so he laughed loud, still louder, and then it occurred to him that it was very amusing to be sitting laughing here all by himself, and he laughed again. But Hans, the comrade who had been sitting beside him, came out after him.

"Good gracious, what are you laughing at?" he asked, pausing in front of the porch. At this Oyvind was silent.

Hans remained standing, as if waiting to see what further might happen. Oyvind got up, looked cautiously about him and said in a low tone,—

"Now Hans, I will tell you why I have been so happy before: it was because I did not really love any one; from the day we love some one, we cease to be happy," and he burst into tears.

"Oyvind!" a voice whispered out in the court; "Oyvind!" He paused and listened. "Oyvind," was repeated once more, a little louder. "It must be she," he thought.

"Yes," he answered, also in a whisper; and hastily wiping his eyes he came forward.

A woman stole softly across the gard.

Transcriber's Note: The above sentence should read, "A woman stole softly across the yard." In other early translations, the words "yard" and "court-yard" are used here. "Gard" in this case is apparently a typo. The use of the word, "gard" throughout the rest of this story refers to "farm."

"Are you there?" she asked.

"Yes," he answered, standing still.

"Who is with you?"

"Hans."

But Hans wanted to go.

"No, no!" besought Oyvind.

She slowly drew near them, and it was Marit.

"You left so soon," said she to Oyvind.

He knew not what to reply; thereupon Marit, too, became embarrassed, and all three were silent. But Hans gradually managed to steal away. The two remained behind, neither looking at each other, nor stirring. Finally Marit whispered:—

"I have been keeping some Christmas goodies in my pocket for you, Oyvind, the whole evening, but I have had no chance to give them to you before."

She drew forth some apples, a slice of a cake from town, and a little half pint bottle, which she thrust into his hand, and said he might keep. Oyvind took them.

"Thank you!" said he, holding out his hand; hers was warm, and he dropped it at once as if it had burned him.

"You have danced a good deal this evening," he murmured.

"Yes, I have," she replied, "but *you* have not danced much," she added.

"I have not," he rejoined.

"Why did you not dance?"

"Oh"—

"Oyvind!"

"Yes."

"Why did you sit looking at me so?"

"Oh—Marit!"

"What!"

"Why did you dislike having me look at you?"

"There were so many people."

"You danced a great deal with Jon Hatlen this evening."

"I did."

"He dances well."

"Do you think so?"

"Oh, yes. I do not know how it is, but this evening I could not bear to have you dance with him, Marit."

He turned away,—it had cost him something to say this.

"I do not understand you, Oyvind."

"Nor do I understand myself; it is very stupid of me. Good-by, Marit; I will go now."

He made a step forward without looking round. Then she called after him.

"You make a mistake about what you saw."

He stopped.

"That you have already become a maiden is no mistake."

He did not say what she had expected, therefore she was silent; but at that moment she saw the light from a pipe right in front of her. It was her grandfather, who had just turned the corner and was coming that way. He stood still.

"Is it here you are, Marit?"

"Yes."

"With whom are you talking?"

"With Oyvind."

"Whom did you say?"

"Oyvind Pladsen."

"Oh! the son of the houseman at Pladsen. Come at once and go in with me."

CHAPTER V.

The next morning, when Oyvind opened his eyes, it was from a long, refreshing sleep and happy dreams. Marit had been lying on the cliff, throwing leaves down on him; he had caught them and tossed them back again, so they had gone up and down in a thousand colors and forms; the sun was shining, and the whole cliff glittered beneath its rays. On awaking Oyvind looked around to find them all gone; then he remembered the day before, and the burning, cruel pain in his heart began at once. "This, I shall never be rid of again," thought he; and there came over him a feeling of indifference, as though his whole future had dropped away from him.

"Why, you have slept a long time," said his mother, who sat beside him spinning. "Get up now and eat your breakfast; your father is already in the forest cutting wood."

Her voice seemed to help him; he rose with a little more courage. His mother was no doubt thinking of her own dancing days, for she sat singing to the sound of the spinning-wheel, while he dressed himself and ate his breakfast. Her humming finally made him rise from the table and go to the window; the same dullness and depression he had felt before took possession of him now, and he was forced to rouse himself, and think of work. The weather had changed, there had come a little frost into the air, so that what yesterday had threatened to fall in rain, to-day came down as sleet. Oyvind put on his snow-socks, a fur cap, his sailor's jacket and mittens, said farewell, and started off, with his axe on his shoulder.

Snow fell slowly, in great, wet flakes; he toiled up over the coasting hill, in order to turn into the forest on the left. Never before, winter or summer, had he climbed this hill without recalling something that made him happy, or to which he was looking forward. Now it was a dull, weary walk. He slipped in the damp snow, his knees were stiff, either from the party yesterday or from his low spirits; he felt that it was all over with the coasting-hill for that year, and with it, forever. He longed for something different as he threaded his way in among the tree-trunks, where the snow fell softly. A frightened ptarmigan screamed and fluttered a few yards away, but everything else stood as if awaiting a word which never was spoken. But what his aspirations were, he did not distinctly know, only they concerned nothing at home, nothing abroad, neither pleasure nor work; but rather something far above, soaring upward like a song. Soon all became concentrated in one defined desire, and this was to be confirmed in the spring, and on that occasion to be number one. His heart beat wildly as he thought of it, and before he could yet hear his father's axe in the quivering little trees, this wish throbbed within him with more intensity than anything he had known in all his life.

His father, as usual, did not have much to say to him; they chopped away together and both dragged the wood into heaps. Now and then they chanced to meet, and on one such occasion Oyvind remarked, in a melancholy tone, "A houseman has to work very hard."

"He as well as others," said the father, as he spit in the palm of his hand and took up the axe again.

When the tree was felled and the father had drawn it up to the pile, Oyvind said,—

"If you were a gardman you would not have to work so hard."

"Oh! then there would doubtless be other things to distress us," and he grasped his axe with both hands.

The mother came up with dinner for them; they sat down. The mother was in high spirits, she sat humming and beating time with her feet.

"What are you going to make of yourself when you are grown up, Oyvind?" said she, suddenly.

"For a houseman's son, there are not many openings," he replied.

"The school-master says you must go to the seminary," said she.

"Can people go there free?" inquired Oyvind.

"The school-fund pays," answered the father, who was eating.

"Would you like to go?" asked the mother.

"I should like to learn something, but not to become a school-master."

They were all silent for a time. The mother hummed again and gazed before her; but Oyvind went off and sat down by himself.

"We do not actually need to borrow of the school-fund," said the mother, when the boy was gone.

Her husband looked at her.

"Such poor folks as we?"

"It does not please me, Thore, to have you always passing yourself off for poor when you are not so."

They both stole glances down after the boy to find out if he could hear. The father looked sharply at his wife.

"You talk as though you were very wise."

She laughed.

"It is just the same as not thanking God that things have prospered with us," said she, growing serious.

"We can surely thank Him without wearing silver buttons," observed the father.

"Yes, but to let Oyvind go to the dance, dressed as he was yesterday, is not thanking Him either."

"Oyvind is a houseman's son."

"That is no reason why he should not wear suitable clothes when we can afford it."

"Talk about it so he can hear it himself!"

"He does not hear it; but I should like to have him do so," said she, and looked bravely at her husband, who was gloomy, and laid down his spoon to take his pipe.

"Such a poor houseman's place as we have!" said he.

"I have to laugh at you, always talking about the place, as you are. Why do you never speak of the mills?"

"Oh! you and the mills. I believe you cannot bear to hear them go."

"Yes, I can, thank God! might they but go night and day!"

"They have stood still now, since before Christmas."

"Folks do not grind here about Christmas time."

"They grind when there is water; but since there has been a mill at New Stream, we have fared badly here."

"The school-master did not say so to-day."

"I shall get a more discreet fellow than the school-master to manage our money."

"Yes, he ought least of all to talk with your own wife."

Thore made no reply to this; he had just lit his pipe, and now, leaning up against a bundle of fagots, he let his eyes wander, first from his wife, then from his son, and fixed them on an old crow's-nest which hung, half overturned, from a fir-branch above.

Oyvind sat by himself with the future stretching before him like a long, smooth sheet of ice, across which for the first time he found himself sweeping onward from shore to shore. That poverty hemmed him in on every side, he felt, but for that reason his whole mind was bent on breaking through it. From Marit it had undoubtedly parted him forever; he regarded her as half engaged to Jon Hatlen; but he had determined to vie with him and her through the entire race of life. Never again to be rebuffed as he had been yesterday, and in view of this to keep out of the way until he made something of himself, and then, with the aid of Almighty God, to continue to be something,—occupied all his thoughts, and there arose within his soul not a single doubt of his success. He had a dim idea that through study he would get on best; to what goal it would lead he must consider later.

There was coasting in the evening; the children came to the hill, but Oyvind was not with them. He sat reading by the fire-place, feeling that he had not a moment to lose. The children waited a long time; at length, one and another became impatient, approached the house, and laying their faces against the window-pane shouted in; but Oyvind pretended not to hear them. Others came, and evening after evening they lingered about outside, in great surprise; but Oyvind turned his back to them and went on reading, striving faithfully to gather the meaning of the words. Afterwards he heard that Marit was not there either. He read with a diligence which even his father was forced to say went too far. He became grave; his face, which had been so round and soft, grew thinner and sharper, his eye more stern; he rarely sang, and never played; the right time never seemed to come. When the temptation to do so beset him, he felt as if some one whispered, "later, later!" and always "later!" The children slid, shouted, and laughed a while as of old, but when they failed to entice him out either through his own love of coasting, or by shouting to him with their faces pressed against the window-pane, they gradually fell away, found other playgrounds, and soon the hill was deserted.

But the school-master soon noticed that this was not the old Oyvind who read because it was his turn, and played because it was a necessity. He often talked with him, coaxed and admonished him; but he did not succeed in finding his way to the boy's heart so easily as in days of old. He spoke also with the parents, the result of the conference being that he came down one Sunday evening, late in the winter, and said, after he had sat a while,—

"Come now, Oyvind, let us go out; I want to have a talk with you."

Oyvind put on his things and went with him. They wended their way up toward the Heidegards; a brisk conversation was kept up, but about nothing in particular; when they drew near the gards the school-master turned aside in the direction of one that lay in the centre, and when they had advanced a little farther, shouting and merriment met them.

"What is going on here?" asked Oyvind.

"There is a dance here," said the school-master; "shall we not go in?"

"No."

"Will you not take part in a dance, boy?"

"No; not yet."

"Not yet? When, then?"

Oyvind did not answer.

"What do you mean by *yet*?"

As the youth did not answer, the school-master said,—

"Come, now, no such nonsense."

"No, I will not go."

He was very decided and at the same time agitated.

"The idea of your own school-master standing here and begging you to go to a dance."

There was a long pause.

"Is there any one in there whom you are afraid to see?"

"I am sure I cannot tell who may be in there."

"But is there likely to be any one?"

Oyvind was silent. Then the school-master walked straight up to him, and laying his hand on his shoulder, said,—

"Are you afraid to see Marit?"

Oyvind looked down; his breathing became heavy and quick.

"Tell me, Oyvind, my boy?"

Oyvind made no reply.

"You are perhaps ashamed to confess it since you are not yet confirmed; but tell me, nevertheless, my dear Oyvind, and you shall not regret it."

Oyvind raised his eyes but could not speak the word, and let his gaze wander away.

"You are not happy, either, of late. Does she care more for any one else than for you?"

Oyvind was still silent, and the school-master, feeling slightly hurt, turned away from him. They retraced their steps. After they had walked a long distance, the school-master paused long enough for Oyvind to come up to his side.

"I presume you are very anxious to be confirmed," said he.

"Yes."

"What do you think of doing afterwards?"

"I should like to go to the seminary."

"And then become a school-master?"

"No."

"You do not think that is great enough?"

Oyvind made no reply. Again they walked on for some distance.

"When you have been through the seminary, what will you do?"

"I have not fairly considered that."

"If you had money, I dare say you would like to buy yourself a gard?"

"Yes, but keep the mills."

"Then you had better enter the agricultural school."

"Do pupils learn as much there as at the seminary?"

"Oh, no! but they learn what they can make use of later."

"Do they get numbers there too?"

"Why do you ask?"

"I should like to be a good scholar."

"That you can surely be without a number."

They walked on in silence again until they saw Pladsen; a light shone from the house, the cliff hanging over it was black now in the winter evening; the lake below was covered with smooth, glittering ice, but there was no snow on the forest skirting the silent bay; the moon sailed overhead, mirroring the forest trees in the ice.

"It is beautiful here at Pladsen," said the school-master.

There were times when Oyvind could see these things with the same eyes with which he looked when his mother told him nursery tales, or with the vision he had when he coasted on the hill-side, and this was one of those times,—all lay exalted and purified before him.

"Yes, it is beautiful," said he, but he sighed.

"Your father has found everything he wanted in this home; you, too, might be contented here."

The joyous aspect of the spot suddenly disappeared. The school-master stood as if awaiting an answer; receiving none, he shook his head and entered the house with Oyvind. He sat a while with the family, but was rather silent than talkative, whereupon the others too became silent. When he took his leave, both husband and wife followed him outside of the door; it seemed as if both expected him to say something. Meanwhile, they stood gazing up into the night.

"It has grown so unusually quiet here," finally said the mother, "since the children have gone away with their sports."

"Nor have you a *child* in the house any longer, either," said the school-master.

The mother knew what he meant.

"Oyvind has not been happy of late," said she.

"Ah, no! he who is ambitious never is happy,"—and he gazed up with an old man's calmness into God's peaceful heavens above.

CHAPTER VI.

Half a year later—in the autumn it was (the confirmation had been postponed until then)—the candidates for confirmation of the main parish sat in the parsonage servant's hall, waiting examination, among them was Oyvind Pladsen and Marit Heidegards. Marit had just come down from the priest, from whom she had received a handsome book and much praise; she laughed and chatted with her girl friends on all sides and glanced around among the boys. Marit was a full-grown girl, easy and frank in her whole address, and the boys as well as the girls knew that Jon Hatlen, the best match in the parish, was courting her,—well might she be happy as she sat there. Down by the door stood some girls and boys who had not passed; they were crying, while Marit and her friends were laughing; among them was a little boy in his father's boots and his mother's Sunday kerchief.

"Oh, dear! oh, dear!" sobbed he, "I dare not go home again."

And this overcame those who had not yet been up with the power of sympathy; there was a universal silence. Anxiety filled their throats and eyes; they could not see distinctly, neither could they swallow; and this they felt a continual desire to do.

One sat reckoning over how much he knew; and although but a few hours before he had discovered that he knew everything, now he found out just as confidently that he knew nothing, not even how to read in a book.

Another summed up the list of his sins, from the time he was large enough to remember until now, and he decided that it would not be at all remarkable if the Lord decreed that he should be rejected.

A third sat taking note of all things about him: if the clock which was about to strike did not make its first stroke before he could count twenty, he would pass; if the person he heard in the passage proved to be the gard-boy Lars, he would pass; if the great rain-drop, working its way down over the pane, came as far as the moulding of the window, he would pass. The final and decisive proof was to be if he succeeded in twisting his right foot about the left,—and this it was quite impossible for him to do.

A fourth was convinced in his own mind that if he was only questioned about Joseph in Bible history and about baptism in the Catechism, or about Saul, or about domestic duties, or about Jesus, or about the Commandments, or— he still sat rehearsing when he was called.

A fifth had taken a special fancy to the Sermon on the Mount; he had dreamed about the Sermon on the Mount; he was sure of being questioned on the Sermon on the Mount; he kept repeating the Sermon on the Mount to himself; he had to go out doors and read over the Sermon on the Mount—when he was called up to be examined on the great and the small prophets.

A sixth thought of the priest who was an excellent man and knew his father so well; he thought, too, of the schoolmaster, who had such a kindly face, and of God who was all goodness and mercy, and who had aided so many before both Jacob and Joseph; and then he remembered that his mother and brothers and sisters were at home praying for him, which surely must help.

The seventh renounced all he had meant to become in this world. Once he had thought that he would like to push on as far as being a king, once as far as general or priest; now that time was over. But even to the moment of his coming here he had thought of going to sea and becoming a captain; perhaps a pirate, and acquiring enormous riches; now he gave up first the riches, then the pirate, then the captain, then the mate; he paused at sailor, at the utmost boatswain; indeed, it was possible that he would not go to sea at all, but would take a houseman's place on his father's gard.

The eighth was more hopeful about his case but not certain, for even the aptest scholar was not certain. He thought of the clothes he was to be confirmed in, wondering what they would be used for if he did not pass. But if he passed he was going to town to get a broadcloth suit, and coming home again to dance at Christmas to the envy of all the boys and the astonishment of all the girls.

The ninth reckoned otherwise: he prepared a little account book with the Lord, in which he set down on one side, as it were, "Debit:" he must let me pass, and on the other "Credit:" then I will never tell any more lies, never tittle-tattle any more, always go to church, let the girls alone, and break myself of swearing.

The tenth, however, thought that if Ole Hansen had passed last year it would be more than unjust if he who had always done better at school, and, moreover, came of a better family, did not get through this year.

By his side sat the eleventh, who was wrestling with the most alarming plans of revenge in the event of his not being passed: either to burn down the school-house, or to run away from the parish and come back again as the denouncing judge of the priest and the whole school commission, but magnanimously allow mercy to take the place of justice. To begin with, he would take service at the house of the priest of the neighboring parish, and there stand number one next year, and answer so that the whole church would marvel.

But the twelfth sat alone under the clock, with both hands in his pockets, and looked mournfully out over the assemblage. No one here knew what a burden he bore, what a responsibility he had assumed. At home there was one who knew,—for he was betrothed. A large, long-legged spider was crawling over the floor and drew near his foot; he was in the habit of treading on this loathsome insect, but to-day he tenderly raised his foot that it might go in peace whither it would. His voice was as gentle as a collect, his eyes said incessantly that all men were good, his hands made a humble movement out of his pockets up to his hair to stroke it down more smoothly. If he could only glide gently through this dangerous needle's eye, he would doubtless grow out again on the other side, chew tobacco, and announce his engagement.

And down on a low stool with his legs drawn up under him, sat the anxious thirteenth; his little flashing eyes sped round the room three times each second, and through the passionate, obstinate head stormed in motley confusion the combined thoughts of the other twelve: from the mightiest hope to the most crushing doubt, from the most humble resolves to the most devastating plans of revenge; and, meanwhile, he had eaten up all the loose flesh on his right thumb, and was busied now with his nails, sending large pieces across the floor.

Oyvind sat by the window, he had been upstairs and had answered everything that had been asked him; but the priest had not said anything, neither had the school-master. For more than half a year he had been considering what they both would say when they came to know how hard he had toiled, and he felt now deeply disappointed as well as wounded. There sat Marit, who for far less exertion and knowledge had received both encouragement and reward; it was just in order to stand high in her eyes that he had striven, and now she smilingly won what he had labored with so much self-denial to attain. Her laughter and joking burned into his soul, the freedom with which she moved about pained him. He had carefully avoided speaking with her since that evening, it would take years, he thought; but the sight of her sitting there so happy and superior, weighed him to the ground, and all his proud determinations drooped like leaves after a rain.

He strove gradually to shake off his depression. Everything depended on whether he became number one to-day, and for this he was waiting. It was the school-master's wont to linger a little after the rest with the priest to arrange about the order of the young people, and afterwards to go down and report the result; it was, to be sure, not the final decision, merely what the priest and he had for the present agreed upon. The conversation became livelier after a considerable number had been examined and passed; but now the ambitious ones plainly distinguished themselves from the happy ones; the latter left as soon as they found company, in order to announce their good fortune to their parents, or they waited for the sake of others who were not yet ready; the former, on the contrary, grew more and more silent and their eyes were fixed in suspense on the door.

At length the children were all through, the last had come down, and so the school-master must now be talking with the priest. Oyvind glanced at Marit; she was just as happy as before, but she remained in her seat, whether waiting for her own pleasure or for some one else, he knew not. How pretty Marit had become! He had never seen so dazzlingly lovely a complexion; her nose was slightly turned up, and a dainty smile played about the mouth. She kept her eyes partially closed when not looking directly at any one, but for that reason her gaze always had unsuspected power when it did come; and, as though she wished herself to add that she meant nothing by this, she half smiled at the same moment. Her hair was rather dark than light, but it was wavy and crept far over the brow on either side, so that, together with the half closed eyes, it gave the face a hidden expression that one could never weary of studying. It never seemed quite sure whom it was she was looking for when she was sitting alone and among others, nor what she really had in mind when she turned to speak to any one, for she took back immediately, as it were, what she gave. "Under all this Jon Hatlen is hidden, I suppose," thought Oyvind, but still stared constantly at her.

Now came the school-master. All left their places and stormed about him.

"What number am I?"—"And I?"—"And I—I?"

"Hush! you overgrown young ones! No uproar here! Be quiet and you shall hear about it, children." He looked slowly around. "You are number two," said he to a boy with blue eyes, who was gazing up at him most beseechingly; and the boy danced out of the circle. "You are number three," he tapped a red-haired, active little fellow who stood tugging at his jacket. "You are number five; you number eight," and so on. Here he caught sight of Marit. "You are number one of the girls,"—she blushed crimson over face and neck, but tried to smile. "You are number twelve; you have been lazy, you rogue, and full of mischief; you number eleven, nothing better to be expected, my boy; you, number thirteen, must study hard and come to the next examination, or it will go badly with you!"

Oyvind could bear it no longer; number one, to be sure, had not been mentioned, but he had been standing all the time so that the school-master could see him.

"School-master!" He did not hear. "School-master!" Oyvind had to repeat this three times before it was heard. At last the school-master looked at him.

"Number nine or ten, I do not remember which," said he, and turned to another.

"Who is number one, then?" inquired Hans, who was Oyvind's best friend.

"It is not you, curly-head!" said the school-master, rapping him over the hand with a roll of paper.

"Who is it, then?" asked others. "Who is it? Yes; who is it?"

"He will find that out who has the number," replied the school-master, sternly. He would have no more questions. "Now go home nicely, children. Give thanks to your God and gladden your parents. Thank your old school-master too; you would have been in a pretty fix if it had not been for him."

They thanked him, laughed, and went their way jubilantly, for at this moment when they were about to go home to their parents they all felt happy. Only one remained behind, who could not at once find his books, and who when he had found them sat down as if he must read them over again.

The school-master went up to him.

"Well, Oyvind, are you not going with the rest?"

There was no reply.

"Why do you open your books?"

"I want to find out what I answered wrong to-day."

"You answered nothing wrong."

Then Oyvind looked at him; tears filled his eyes, but he gazed intently at the school-master, while one by one trickled down his cheeks, and not a word did he say. The school-master sat down in front of him.

"Are you not glad that you passed?"

There was a quivering about the lips but no reply.

"Your mother and father will be very glad," said the school-master, and looked at Oyvind.

The boy struggled hard to gain power of utterance, finally he asked in low, broken tones,—

"Is it—because I—am a houseman's son that I only stand number nine or ten?"

"No doubt that was it," replied the school-master.

"Then it is of no use for me to work," said Oyvind, drearily, and all his bright dreams vanished. Suddenly he raised his head, lifted his right hand, and bringing it down on the table with all his might, flung himself forward on his face and burst into passionate tears.

The school-master let him lie and weep,—weep as long as he would. It lasted a long time, but the school-master waited until the weeping grew more childlike. Then taking Oyvind's head in both hands, he raised it and gazed into the tear-stained face.

"Do you believe that it is God who has been with you now," said he, drawing the boy affectionately toward him.

Oyvind was still sobbing, but not so violently as before; his tears flowed more calmly, but he neither dared look at him who questioned nor answer.

"This, Oyvind, has been a well-merited recompense. You have not studied from love of your religion, or of your parents; you have studied from vanity."

There was silence in the room after every sentence the school-master uttered. Oyvind felt his gaze resting on him, and he melted and grew humble under it.

"With such wrath in your heart, you could not have come forward to make a covenant with your God. Do you think you could, Oyvind?"

"No," the boy stammered, as well as he was able.

"And if you stood there with vain joy, over being number one, would you not be coming forward with a sin?"

"Yes, I should," whispered Oyvind, and his lips quivered.

"You still love me, Oyvind?"

"Yes;" here he looked up for the first time.

"Then I will tell you that it was I who had you put down; for I am very fond of you, Oyvind."

The other looked at him, blinked several times, and the tears rolled down in rapid succession.

"You are not displeased with me for that?"

"No;" he looked up full in the school-master's face, although his voice was choked.

"My dear child, I will stand by you as long as I live."

The school-master waited for Oyvind until the latter had gathered together his books, then said that he would accompany him home. They walked slowly along. At first Oyvind was silent and his struggle went on, but gradually he gained his self-control. He was convinced that what had occurred was the best thing that in any way could have happened to him; and before he reached home, his belief in this had become so strong that he gave thanks to his God, and told the school-master so.

"Yes, now we can think of accomplishing something in life," said the school-master, "instead of playing blind-man's buff, and chasing after numbers. What do you say to the seminary?"

"Why, I should like very much to go there."

"Are you thinking of the agricultural school?"

"Yes."

"That is, without doubt, the best; it provides other openings than a school-master's position."

"But how can I go there? I earnestly desire it, but I have not the means."

"Be industrious and good, and I dare say the means will be found."

Oyvind felt completely overwhelmed with gratitude. His eyes sparkled, his breath came lightly, he glowed with that infinite love that bears us along when we experience some unexpected kindness from a fellow-creature. At such a moment, we fancy that our whole future will be like wandering in the fresh mountain air; we are wafted along more than we walk.

When they reached home both parents were within, and had been sitting there in quiet expectation, although it was during working hours of a busy time. The school-master entered first, Oyvind followed; both were smiling.

"Well?" said the father, laying aside a hymn-book, in which he had just been reading a "Prayer for a Confirmation Candidate."

His mother stood by the hearth, not daring to say anything; she was smiling, but her hand was trembling. Evidently she was expecting good news, but did not wish to betray herself.

"I merely had to come to gladden you with the news, that he answered every question put to him; and that the priest said, when Oyvind had left him, that he had never had a more apt scholar."

"Is it possible!" said the mother, much affected.

"Well, that is good," said his father, clearing his throat unsteadily.

After it had been still for some time, the mother asked, softly,—

"What number will he have?"

"Number nine or ten," said the school-master, calmly.

The mother looked at the father; he first at her, then at Oyvind, and said,—

"A houseman's son can expect no more."

Oyvind returned his gaze. Something rose up in his throat once more, but he hastily forced himself to think of things that he loved, one by one, until it was choked down again.

"Now I had better go," said the school-master, and nodding, turned away.

Both parents followed him as usual out on the door-step; here the school-master took a quid of tobacco, and smiling said,—

"He will be number one, after all; but it is not worth while that he should know anything about it until the day comes."

"No, no," said the father, and nodded.

"No, no," said the mother, and she nodded too; after which she grasped the school-master's hand and added: "We thank you for all you do for him."

"Yes, you have our thanks," said the father, and the school-master moved away.

They long stood there gazing after him.

CHAPTER VII.

The school-master had judged the boy correctly when he asked the priest to try whether Oyvind could bear to stand number one. During the three weeks which elapsed before the confirmation, he was with the boy every day. It is one thing for a young, tender soul to yield to an impression; what through faith it shall attain is another thing. Many dark hours fell upon Oyvind before he learned to choose the goal of his future from something better than ambition and defiance. Often in the midst of his work he lost his interest and stopped short: what was it all for, what would he gain by it?—and then presently he would remember the school-master, his words and his kindness; and this human medium forced him to rise up again every time he fell from a comprehension of his higher duty.

In those days while they were preparing at Pladsen for the confirmation, they were also preparing for Oyvind's departure for the agricultural school, for this was to take place the following day. Tailor and shoemaker were sitting in the family-room; the mother was baking in the kitchen, the father working at a chest. There was a great deal said about what Oyvind would cost his parents in the next two years; about his not being able to come home the first Christmas, perhaps not the second either, and how hard it would be to be parted so long. They spoke also of the love Oyvind should bear his parents who were willing to sacrifice themselves for their child's sake. Oyvind sat like one who had tried sailing out into the world on his own responsibility, but had been wrecked and was now picked up by kind people.

Such is the feeling that humility gives, and with it comes much more. As the great day drew near he dared call himself prepared, and also dared look forward with trustful resignation. Whenever Marit's image would present itself, he cautiously thrust it aside, although he felt a pang in so doing. He tried to gain practice in this, but never made any progress in strength; on the contrary, it was the pain that grew. Therefore he was weary the last evening, when, after a long self-examination, he prayed that the Lord would not put him to the test in this matter.

The school-master came as the day was drawing to a close. They all sat down together in the family-room, after washing and dressing themselves neat and clean, as was customary the evening before going to communion, or morning service. The mother was agitated, the father silent; parting was to follow the morrow's ceremony, and it was uncertain when they could all sit down together again. The school-master brought out the hymn-books, read the service, sang with the family, and afterwards said a short prayer, just as the words came into his mind.

These four people now sat together until late in the evening, the thoughts of each centering within; then they parted with the best wishes for the coming day and what it was to consecrate. Oyvind was obliged to admit, as he laid himself down, that he had never gone to bed so happy before; he gave this an interpretation of his own,—he understood it to mean: I have never before gone to bed feeling so resigned to God's will and so happy in it. Marit's face at once rose up before him again, and the last thing he was conscious of was that he lay and examined himself: not quite happy, not quite,—and that he answered: yes, quite; but again: not quite; yes, quite; no, not quite.

When he awoke he at once remembered the day, prayed, and felt strong, as one does in the morning. Since the summer, he had slept alone in the attic; now he rose, and put on his handsome new clothes, very carefully, for he had never owned such before. There was especially a round broadcloth jacket, which he had to examine over and over again before he became accustomed to it. He hung up a little looking-glass when he had adjusted his collar, and for the fourth time drew on his jacket. At sight of his own contented face, with the unusually light hair surrounding it, reflected and smiling in the glass, it occurred to him that this must certainly be vanity again. "Yes, but people must be well-dressed and tidy," he reasoned, drawing his face away from the glass, as if it were a sin to look in it. "To be sure, but not quite so delighted with themselves, for the sake of the matter." "No, certainly not, but the Lord must also like to have one care to look well." "That may be; but He would surely like it better to have you do so without taking so much notice of it yourself." "That is true; but it happens now because everything is so new." "Yes, but you must gradually lay the habit aside."—He caught himself carrying on such a self-examining conversation, now upon one theme, now upon another, so that not a sin should fall on the day and stain it; but at the same time he knew that he had other struggles to meet.

When he came down-stairs, his parents sat all dressed, waiting breakfast for him. He went up to them and taking their hands thanked them for the clothes, and received in return a "wear-them-out-with-good-health." They sat down to table, prayed silently, and ate. The mother cleared the table, and carried in the lunch-box for the journey to church. The father put on his jacket, the mother fastened her kerchief; they took their hymn-books, locked up the house, and started. As soon as they had reached the upper road they met the church-faring people, driving and walking, the confirmation candidates scattered among them, and in one group and another white-haired grand-parents, who had felt moved to come out on this great occasion.

Footnote 1: A common expression among the peasantry of Norway, meaning: "You are welcome."

It was an autumn day without sunshine, as when the weather is about to change. Clouds gathered together and dispersed again; sometimes out of one great mass were formed twenty smaller ones, which sped across the sky with orders for a storm; but below, on the earth, it was still calm, the foliage hung lifeless, not a leaf stirring; the air was a trifle sultry; people carried their outer wraps with them but did not use them. An unusually large multitude had assembled round the church, which stood in an open space; but the confirmation children immediately went into the church in order to be arranged in their places before service began. Then it was that the school-master, in a blue broadcloth suit, frock coat, and knee-breeches, high shoes, stiff cravat, and a pipe protruding from his back coat pocket, came down towards them, nodded and smiled, tapped one on the shoulder, spoke a few words to another about answering loudly and distinctly, and meanwhile worked his way along to the poor-box, where Oyvind stood answering all the questions of his friend Hans in reference to his journey.

"Good-day, Oyvind. How fine you look to-day!" He took him by the jacket collar as if he wished to speak to him. "Listen. I believe everything good of you. I have been talking with the priest; you will be allowed to keep your place; go up to number one and answer distinctly!"

Oyvind looked up at him amazed; the school-master nodded; the boy took a few steps, stopped, a few steps more, stopped again: "Yes, it surely is so; he has spoken to the priest for me,"—and the boy walked swiftly up to his place.

"You are to be number one, after all," some one whispered to him.

"Yes," answered Oyvind, in a low voice, but did not feel quite sure yet whether he dared think so.

The assignment of places was over, the priest had come, the bells were ringing, and the people pouring into church. Then Oyvind saw Marit Heidegards just in front of him; she saw him too; but they were both so awed by the sacredness of the place that they dared not greet each other. He only noticed that she was dazzlingly beautiful and that her hair was uncovered; more he did not see. Oyvind, who for more than half a year had been building such great plans about standing opposite her, forgot, now that it had come to the point, both the place and her, and that he had in any way thought of them.

After all was ended the relatives and acquaintances came up to offer their congratulations; next came Oyvind's comrades to take leave of him, as they had heard that he was to depart the next day; then there came many little ones with whom he had coasted on the hill-sides and whom he had assisted at school, and who now could not help whimpering a little at parting. Last came the school-master, silently took Oyvind and his parents by the hands, and made a sign to start for home; he wanted to accompany them. The four were together once more, and this was to be the last evening. On the way home they met many others who took leave of Oyvind and wished him good luck; but they had no other conversation until they sat down together in the family-room.

The school-master tried to keep them in good spirits; the fact was now that the time had come they all shrank from the two long years of separation, for up to this time they had never been parted a single day; but none of them would acknowledge it. The later it grew the more dejected Oyvind became; he was forced to go out to recover his composure a little.

It was dusk now and there were strange sounds in the air. Oyvind remained standing on the door-step gazing upward. From the brow of the cliff he then heard his own name called, quite softly; it was no delusion, for it was repeated twice. He looked up and faintly distinguished a female form crouching between the trees and looking down.

"Who is it?" asked he.

"I hear you are going away," said a low voice, "so I had to come to you and say good-by, as you would not come to me."

"Dear me! Is that you, Marit? I shall come up to you."

"No, pray do not. I have waited so long, and if you come I should have to wait still longer; no one knows where I am and I must hurry home."

"It was kind of you to come," said he.

"I could not bear to have you leave so, Oyvind; we have known each other since we were children."

"Yes; we have."

"And now we have not spoken to each other for half a year."

"No; we have not."

"We parted so strangely, too, that time."

"We did. I think I must come up to you!"

"Oh, no! do not come! But tell me: you are not angry with me?"

"Goodness! how could you think so?"

"Good-by, then, Oyvind, and my thanks for all the happy times we have had together!"

"Wait, Marit!"

"Indeed I must go; they will miss me."

"Marit! Marit!"

"No, I dare not stay away any longer, Oyvind. Good-by."

"Good-by!"

Afterwards he moved about as in a dream, and answered very absently when he was addressed. This was ascribed to his journey, as was quite natural; and indeed it occupied his whole mind at the moment when the school-master took leave of him in the evening and put something into his hand, which he afterwards found to be a five-dollar bill. But later, when he went to bed, he thought not of the journey, but of the words which had come down from the brow of the cliff, and those that had been sent up again. As a child Marit was not allowed to come on the cliff, because her grandfather feared she might fall down. Perhaps she will come down some day, any way.

CHAPTER VIII.

DEAR PARENTS,—We have to study much more now than at first, but as I am less behind the others than I was, it is not so hard. I shall change many things in father's place when I come home; for there is much that is wrong there, and it is wonderful that it has prospered as well as it has. But I shall make everything right, for I have learned a great deal. I want to go to some place where I can put into practice all I now know, and so I must look for a high position when I get through here. No one here considers Jon Hatlen as clever as he is thought to be at home with us; but as he has a gard of his own, this does not concern any one but himself. Many who go from here get very high salaries, but they are paid so well because ours is the best agricultural school in the country. Some say the one in the next district is better, but this is by no means true. There are two words here: one is called Theory, the other Practice. It is well to have them both, for one is nothing without the other; but still the latter is the better. Now the former means, to understand the cause and principle of a work; the latter, to be able to perform it: as, for instance, in regard to a quagmire; for there are many who know what should be done with a quagmire and yet do it wrong, because they are not able to put their knowledge into practice. Many, on the other hand, are skillful in doing, but do not know what ought to be done; and thus they too may make bad work of it, for there are many kinds of quagmires. But we at the agricultural school learn both words. The superintendent is so skillful that he has no equal. At the last agricultural meeting for the whole country, he led in two discussions, and the other superintendents had only one each, and upon careful consideration his statements were always sustained. At the meeting before the last, where he was not present, there was nothing but idle talk. The lieutenant who teaches surveying was chosen by the superintendent only on account of his ability, for the other schools have no lieutenant. He is so clever that he was the best scholar at the military academy. The school-master asks if I go to church. Yes, of course I go to church, for now the priest has an assistant, and his sermons fill all the congregation with terror, and it is a pleasure to listen to him. He belongs to the new religion they have in Christiania, and people think him too strict, but it is good for them that he is so. Just now we are studying much history, which we have not done before, and it is curious to observe all that has happened in the world, but especially in our country, for we have always won, except when we have lost, and then we always had the smaller number. We now have liberty; and no other nation has so much of it as we, except America; but there they are not happy. Our freedom should be loved by us above everything. Now I will close for this time, for I have written a very long letter. The school-master will read it, I suppose, and when he answers for you, get him to tell me some news about one thing or another, for he never does so of himself. But now accept hearty greetings from your affectionate son, O. THORESEN.

DEAR PARENTS,—Now I must tell you that we have had examinations, and that I stood 'excellent' in many things, and 'very good' in writing and surveying, but 'good' in Norwegian composition. This comes, the superintendent says, from my not having read enough, and he has made me a present of some of Ole Vig's books, which are matchless, for I understand everything in them. The superintendent is very kind to me, and he tells us many things. Everything here is very inferior compared with what they have abroad; we understand almost nothing, but learn everything from the Scotch and Swiss, although horticulture we learn from the Dutch. Many visit these countries. In Sweden, too, they are much more clever than we, and there the superintendent himself has been. I have been here now nearly a year, and I thought that I had learned a great deal; but when I heard what those who passed the examination knew, and considered that they would not amount to anything either when they came into contact with foreigners, I became very despondent. And then the soil here in Norway is so poor compared with what it is abroad; it does not at all repay us for what we do with it. Moreover, people will not learn from the experience of others; and even if they would, and if the soil was much better, they really have not the money to cultivate it. It is remarkable that things have prospered as well as they have. I am now in the highest class, and am to remain there a year before I get through. But most of my companions have left and I long for home. I feel alone, although I am not so by any means, but one has such a strange feeling when one has been long absent. I once thought I should become so much of a scholar here; but I am not making the progress I anticipated. What shall I do with myself when I leave here? First, of course, I will come home; afterwards, I suppose, I will have to seek something to do, but it must not be far away. Farewell, now, dear parents! Give greetings to all who inquire for me, and tell them that I have everything pleasant here but that now I long to be at home again. Your affectionate son, OYVIND THORESEN PLADSEN.

DEAR SCHOOL-MASTER,—With this I ask if you will deliver the inclosed letter and not speak of it to any one. And if you will not, then you must burn it.
OYVIND THORESEN PLADSEN.

TO THE MOST HONORED MAIDEN, MARIT KNUDSDATTER NORDISTUEN AT THE UPPER HEIDEGARDS:—
You will no doubt be much surprised at receiving a letter from me; but you need not be for I only wish to ask how you are. You must send me a few words as soon as possible, giving me all particulars. Regarding myself, I have to say that I shall be through here in a year.
Most respectfully,
OYVIND PLADSEN.

TO OYVIND PLADSEN, AT THE AGRICULTURAL SCHOOL:— Your letter was duly received by me from the school-master, and I will answer since you request it. But I am afraid to do so, now that you are so learned; and I have a letter-writer, but it does not help me. So I will have to try what I can do, and you must take the will for the deed; but do not show this, for if you do you are not the one I think you are. Nor must you keep it, for then some one might see it, but you must burn it, and this you will have to promise me to do. There were so many things I wanted to write about, but I do not quite dare. We have had a good harvest; potatoes bring a high price, and here at the Heidegards we have plenty of them. But the bear has done much mischief among the cattle this summer: he killed two of Ole Nedregard's cattle and injured one belonging to our houseman so badly that it had to be killed for beef. I am weaving a large piece of cloth, something like a Scotch plaid, and it is difficult. And now I will tell you that I am still at home, and that there are those who would like to have it otherwise. Now I have no more to write about for this time, and so I must bid you farewell. MARIT KNUDSDATTER. P.S.—Be sure and burn this letter.

TO THE AGRICULTURIST, OYVIND THORESEN PLADSEN:— As I have told you before, Oyvind, he who walks with God has come into the good inheritance. But now you must listen to my advice, and that is not to take the world with yearning and tribulation, but to trust in God and not allow your heart to consume you, for if you do you will have another god besides Him. Next I must inform you that your father and your mother are well, but I am troubled with one of my hips; for now the war breaks out afresh with all that was suffered in it. What youth sows age must reap; and this is true both in regard to the mind and the body, which now throbs and pains, and tempts one to make any number of lamentations. But old age should not complain; for wisdom flows from wounds, and pain preaches patience, that man may grow strong enough for the last journey. To-day I have taken up my pen for many reasons, and first and above all for the sake of Marit, who has become a God-fearing maiden, but who is as light of foot as a reindeer, and of rather a fickle disposition. She would be glad to abide by one thing, but is prevented from so doing by her nature; but I have often before seen that with hearts of such weak stuff the Lord is indulgent and long-suffering, and does not allow them to be tempted beyond their strength, lest they break to pieces, for she is very fragile. I duly gave her your letter, and she hid it from all save her own heart. If God will lend His aid in this matter, I have nothing against it, for Marit is most charming to young men, as plainly can be seen, and she has abundance of earthly goods, and the heavenly ones she has too, with all her fickleness. For the fear of God in her mind is like water in a shallow pond: it is there when it rains, but it is gone when the sun shines. My eyes can endure no more at present, for they see well at a distance, but pain me and fill with tears when I look at small objects. In conclusion, I will advise you, Oyvind, to have your God with you in all your desires and undertakings, for it is written: "Better is an handful with quietness, than both the hands full with travail and vexation of spirit." Ecclesiastes, iv. 6. Your old school-master, BAARD ANDERSEN OPDAL.

TO THE MOST HONORED MAIDEN, MARIT KNUDSDATTER HEIDEGARDS:— You have my thanks for your letter, which I have read and burned, as you requested. You write of many things, but not at all concerning that of which I wanted you to write. Nor do I dare write anything definite before I know how you are in *every respect*. The school-master's letter says nothing that one can depend on, but he praises you and he says you are fickle. That, indeed, you were before. Now I do not know what to think, and so you must write, for it will not be well with me until you do. Just now I remember best about your coming to the cliff that last evening and what you said then. I will say no more this time, and so farewell. Most respectfully, OYVIND PLADSEN.

TO OYVIND THORESEN PLADSEN:— The school-master has given me another letter from you, and I have just read it, but I do not understand it in the least, and that, I dare say, is because I am not learned. You want to know how it is with me in every respect; and I am healthy and well, and there is nothing at all the matter with me. I eat heartily, especially when I get milk porridge. I sleep at night, and occasionally in the day-time too. I have danced a great deal this winter, for there have been many parties here, and that has been very pleasant. I go to church when the snow is not too deep; but we have had a great deal of snow this winter. Now, I presume, you know everything, and if you do not, I can think of nothing better than for you to write to me once more. MARIT KNUDSDATTER.

TO THE MOST HONORED MAIDEN, MARIT KNUDSDATTER HEIDEGARDS:— I have received your letter, but you seem inclined to leave me no wiser than I was before. Perhaps this may be meant for an answer. I do not know. I dare not write anything that I wish to write, for I do not know you. But possibly you do not know me either. You must not think that I am any longer the soft cheese you squeezed the water away from when I sat watching you dance. I have laid on many shelves to dry since that time. Neither am I like those long-haired dogs who drop their ears at the least provocation and take flight from people, as in former days. I can stand fire now. Your letter was very playful, but it jested where it should not have jested at all, for you understood me very well, and you could see that I did not ask in sport, but because of late I can think of nothing else than the subject I questioned you about. I was waiting in deep anxiety, and there came to me only foolery and laughter. Farewell, Marit Heidegards, I shall not look at you too much, as I did at that dance. May you both eat well, and sleep well, and get your new web finished, and above all, may you be able to shovel away the snow which lies in front of the church-door. Most respectfully, OYVIND THORESEN PLADSEN.

TO THE AGRICULTURIST, OYVIND THORESEN, AT THE AGRICULTURAL SCHOOL:— Notwithstanding my advanced years, and the weakness of my eyes, and the pain in my right hip, I must yield to the importunity of the young, for we old people are needed by them when they have caught themselves in some snare. They entice us and weep until they are set free, but then at once run away from us again, and will take no further advice. Now it is Marit; she coaxes me with many sweet words to write at the same time she does, for she takes comfort in not writing alone. I have read your letter; she thought that she had Jon Hatlen or some other fool to deal with, and not one whom school-master Baard had trained; but now she is in a dilemma. However, you have been too severe, for there are certain women who take to jesting in order to avoid weeping, and who make no difference between the two. But it pleases me to have you take serious things seriously, for otherwise you could not laugh at nonsense. Concerning the feelings of both, it is now apparent from many things that you are bent on having each other. About Marit I have often been in doubt, for she is like the wind's course; but I have now learned that notwithstanding this she has resisted Jon Hatlen's advances, at which her grandfather's wrath is sorely kindled. She was happy when your offer came, and if she jested it was from joy, not from any harm. She has endured much, and has done so in order to wait for him on whom her mind was fixed. And now you will not have her, but cast her away as you would a naughty child. This was what I wanted to tell you. And this counsel I must add, that you should come to an understanding with her, for you can find enough else to be at variance with. I am like the old man who has lived through three generations; I have seen folly and its course. Your mother and father send love by me. They are expecting you home; but I would not write of this before, lest you should become homesick. You do not know your father; he is like a tree which makes no moan until it is hewn down. But if ever any mischance should befall you, then you will learn to know him, and you will wonder at the richness of his nature. He has had heavy burdens to bear, and is silent in worldly matters; but your mother has relieved his mind from earthly anxiety, and now daylight is beginning to break through the gloom. Now my eyes grow dim, my hand refuses to do more. Therefore I commend you to Him whose eye ever watches, and whose hand is never weary. BAARD ANDERSEN OPDAL.

TO OYVIND PLADSEN:— You seem to be displeased with me, and this greatly grieves me. For I did not mean to make you angry. I meant well. I know I have often failed to do rightly by you, and that is why I write to you now; but you must not show the letter to any one. Once I had everything just as I desired, and then I was not kind; but now there is no one who cares for me, and I am very wretched. Jon Hatlen has made a lampoon about me, and all the boys sing it, and I no longer dare go to the dances. Both the old people know about it, and I have to listen to many harsh words. Now I am sitting alone writing, and you must not show my letter. You have learned much and are able to advise me, but you are now far away. I have often been down to see your parents, and have talked with your mother, and we have become good friends; but I did not like to say anything about it, for you wrote so strangely. The schoolmaster only makes fun of me, and he knows nothing about the lampoon, for no one in the parish would presume to sing such a thing to him. I stand alone now, and have no one to speak with. I remember when we were children, and you were so kind to me; and I always sat on your sled, and I could wish that I were a child again. I cannot ask you to answer me, for I dare not do so. But if you will answer just once more I will never forget it in you, Oyvind. MARIT KNUDSDATTER.

Please burn this letter; I scarcely know whether I dare send it.

DEAR MARIT,—Thank you for your letter; you wrote it in a lucky hour. I will tell you now, Marit, that I love you so much that I can scarcely wait here any longer; and if you love me as truly in return all the lampoons of Jon and harsh words of others shall be like leaves which grow too plentifully on the tree. Since I received your letter I feel like a new being, for double my former strength has come to me, and I fear no one in the whole world. After I had sent my last letter I regretted it so that I almost became ill. And now you shall hear what the result of this was. The superintendent took me aside and asked what was the matter with me; he fancied I was studying too hard. Then he told me that when my year was out I might remain here one more, without expense. I could help him with sundry things, and he would teach me more. Then I thought that work was the only thing I had to rely on, and I thanked him very much; and I do not yet repent it, although now I long for you, for the longer I stay here the better right I shall have to ask for you one day. How happy I am now! I work like three people, and never will I be behind-hand in any work! But you must have a book that I am reading, for there is much in it about love. I read in it in the evening when the others are sleeping, and then I read your letter over again. Have you thought about our meeting? I think of it so often, and you, too, must try and find out how delightful it will be. I am truly happy that I have toiled and studied so much, although it was hard before; for now I can say what I please to you, and smile over it in my heart. I shall give you many books to read, that you may see how much tribulation they have borne who have truly loved each other, and that they would rather die of grief than forsake each other. And that is what we would do, and do it with the greatest joy. True, it will be nearly two years before we see each other, and still longer before we get each other; but with every day that passes there is one day less to wait; we must think of this while we are working. My next letter shall be about many things; but this evening I have no more paper, and the others are asleep. Now I will go to bed and think of you, and I will do so until I fall asleep. Your friend, OYVIND PLADSEN.

CHAPTER IX.

One Saturday, in midsummer, Thore Pladsen rowed across the lake to meet his son, who was expected to arrive that afternoon from the agricultural school, where he had finished his course. The mother had hired women several days beforehand, and everything was scoured and clean. The bedroom had been put in order some time before, a stove had been set up, and there Oyvind was to be. To-day the mother carried in fresh greens, laid out clean linen, made up the bed, and all the while kept looking out to see if, perchance, any boat were coming across the lake. A plentiful table was spread in the house, and there was always something wanting, or flies to chase away, and the bedroom was dusty,—continually dusty. Still no boat came. The mother leaned against the window and looked across the waters; then she heard a step near at hand on the road, and turned her head. It was the school-master, who was coming slowly down the hill, supporting himself on a staff, for his hip troubled him. His intelligent eyes looked calm. He paused to rest, and nodded to her:—

"Not come yet?"

"No; I expect them every moment."

"Fine weather for haymaking, to-day."

"But warm for old folks to be walking."

The school-master looked at her, smiling,—

"Have any young folks been out to-day?"

"Yes; but are gone again."

"Yes, yes, to be sure; there will most likely be a meeting somewhere this evening."

"I presume there will be. Thore says they shall not meet in his house until they have the old man's consent."

"Right, quite right."

Presently the mother cried,—

"There! I think they are coming."

The school-master looked long in the distance.

"Yes, indeed! it is they."

The mother left the window, and he went into the house. After he had rested a little and taken something to drink, they proceeded down to the shore, while the boat darted toward them, making rapid headway, for both father and son were rowing. The oarsmen had thrown off their jackets, the waters whitened beneath their strokes; and so the boat soon drew near those who were waiting. Oyvind turned his head and looked up; he saw the two at the landing-place, and resting his oars, he shouted,—

"Good-day, mother! Good-day, school-master!"

"What a manly voice he has," said the mother, her face sparkling. "O dear, O dear! he is as fair as ever," she added.

The school-master drew in the boat. The father laid down his oars, Oyvind sprang past him and out of the boat, shook hands first with his mother, then with the school-master. He laughed and laughed again; and, quite contrary to the custom of peasants, immediately began to pour out a flood of words about the examination, the journey, the superintendent's certificate, and good offers; he inquired about the crops and his acquaintances, all save one. The father had paused to carry things up from the boat, but, wanting to hear, too, thought they might remain there for the present, and joined the others. And so they walked up toward the house, Oyvind laughing and talking, the mother laughing, too, for she was utterly at a loss to know what to say. The school-master moved slowly along at Oyvind's side, watching his old pupil closely; the father walked at a respectful distance. And thus they reached home. Oyvind was delighted with everything he saw: first because the house was painted, then because the mill was enlarged, then because the leaden windows had been taken out in the family-room and in the bed-chamber, and white glass had taken the place of green, and the window frames had been made larger. When he entered everything seemed astonishingly small, and not at all as he remembered it, but very cheerful. The clock cackled like a fat hen, the carved chairs almost seemed as if they would speak; he knew every dish on the table spread before him, the freshly white-washed hearth smiled welcome; the greens, decorating the walls, scattered about them their fragrance, the juniper, strewn over the floor, gave evidence of the festival.

They all sat down to the meal; but there was not much eaten, for Oyvind rattled away without ceasing. The others viewed him now more composedly, and observed in what respect he had altered, in what he remained unchanged; looked at what was entirely new about him, even to the blue broadcloth suit he wore. Once when he had been telling a long story about one of his companions and finally concluded, as there was a little pause, the father said,—

"I scarcely understand a word that you say, boy; you talk so very fast."

They all laughed heartily, and Oyvind not the least. He knew very well this was true, but it was not possible for him to speak more slowly. Everything new he had seen and learned, during his long absence from home, had so affected his imagination and understanding, and had so driven him out of his accustomed demeanor, that faculties which long had lain dormant were roused up, as it were, and his brain was in a state of constant activity. Moreover, they observed that he had a habit of arbitrarily taking up two or three words here and there, and repeating them again and again from sheer haste. He seemed to be stumbling over himself. Sometimes this appeared absurd, but then he laughed and it was forgotten. The school-master and the father sat watching to see if any of the old thoughtfulness was gone; but it did not seem so. Oyvind remembered everything, and was even the one to remind the others that the boat should be unloaded. He unpacked his clothes at once and hung them up, displayed his books, his watch, everything new, and all was well cared for, his mother said. He was exceedingly pleased with his little room. He would remain at home for the present, he said,—help with the hay-making, and study. Where he should go later he did not know; but it made not the least difference to him. He had acquired a briskness and vigor of thought which it did one good to see, and an animation in the expression of his feelings which is so refreshing to a person who the whole year through strives to repress his own. The school-master grew ten years younger.

"Now we have come *so far* with him," said he, beaming with satisfaction as he rose to go.

When the mother returned from waiting on him, as usual, to the door-step, she called Oyvind into the bedroom.

"Some one will be waiting for you at nine o'clock," whispered she.

"Where?"

"On the cliff."

Oyvind glanced at the clock; it was nearly nine. He could not wait in the house, but went out, clambered up the side of the cliff, paused on the top, and looked around. The house lay directly below; the bushes on the roof had grown large, all the young trees round about him had also grown, and he recognized every one of them. His eyes wandered down the road, which ran along the cliff, and was bordered by the forest on the other side. The road lay there, gray and solemn, but the forest was enlivened with varied foliage; the trees were tall and well grown. In the little bay lay a boat with unfurled sail; it was laden with planks and awaiting a breeze. Oyvind gazed across the water which had borne him away and home again. There it stretched before him, calm and smooth; some sea-birds flew over it, but made no noise, for it was late. His father came walking up from the mill, paused on the door-step, took a survey of all about him, as his son had done, then went down to the water to take the boat in for the night. The mother appeared at the side of the house, for she had been in the kitchen. She raised her eyes toward the cliff as she crossed the farm-yard with something for the hens, looked up again and began to hum. Oyvind sat down to wait. The underbrush was so dense that he could not see very far into the forest, but he listened to the slightest sound. For a long time he heard nothing but the birds that flew up and cheated him,—after a while a squirrel that was leaping from tree to tree. But at length there was a rustling farther off; it ceased a moment, and then began again. He rises, his heart throbs, the blood rushes to his head; then something breaks through the brushes close by him; but it is a large, shaggy dog, which, on seeing him, pauses on three legs without stirring. It is the dog from the Upper Heidegards, and close behind him another rustling is heard. The dog turns his head and wags his tail; now Marit appears.

A bush caught her dress; she turned to free it, and so she was standing when Oyvind saw her first. Her head was bare, her hair twisted up as girls usually wear it in every-day attire; she had on a thick plaid dress without sleeves, and nothing about the neck except a turned-down linen collar. She had just stolen away from work in the fields, and had not ventured on any change of dress. Now she looked up askance and smiled; her white teeth shone, her eyes sparkled beneath the half-closed lids. Thus she stood for a moment working with her fingers, and then she came forward, growing rosier and rosier with each step. He advanced to meet her, and took her hand between both of his. Her eyes were fixed on the ground, and so they stood.

"Thank you for all your letters," was the first thing he said; and when she looked up a little and laughed, he felt that she was the most roguish troll he could meet in a wood; but he was captured, and she, too, was evidently caught.

"How tall you have grown," said she, meaning something quite different.

She looked at him more and more, laughed more and more, and he laughed, too; but they said nothing. The dog had seated himself on the slope, and was surveying the gard. Thore observed the dog's head from the water, but could not for his life understand what it could be that was showing itself on the cliff above.

But the two had now let go of each other's hands and were beginning to talk a little. And when Oyvind was once under way he burst into such a rapid stream of words that Marit had to laugh at him.

"Yes, you see, this is the way it is when I am happy—truly happy, you see; and as soon as it was settled between us two, it seemed as if there burst open a lock within me—wide open, you see."

She laughed. Presently she said,—

"I know almost by heart all the letters you sent me."

"And I yours! But you always wrote such short ones."

"Because you always wanted them to be so long."

"And when I desired that we should write more about something, then you changed the subject."

"'I show to the best advantage when you see my tail,' said the hulder."

Footnote 1: The hulder in the Norse folk-lore appears like a beautiful woman, and usually wears a blue petticoat and a white sword; but she unfortunately has a long tail, like a cow's, which she anxiously strives to conceal when she is among people. She is fond of cattle, particularly brindled, of which she possesses a beautiful and thriving stock. They are without horns. She was once at a merry-making, where every one was desirous of dancing with the handsome, strange damsel; but in the midst of the mirth a young man, who had just begun a dance with her, happened to cast his eye on her tail. Immediately guessing whom he had gotten for a partner, he was not a little terrified; but, collecting himself, and unwilling to betray her, he merely said to her when the dance was over: "Fair maid, you will lose your garter." She instantly vanished, but afterwards rewarded the silent and considerate youth with beautiful presents and a good breed of cattle. FAYE'S *Traditions.*—NOTE BY TRANSLATOR.

"Ah! that is so. You have never told me how you got rid of Jon Hatlen."

"I laughed."

"How?"

"Laughed. Do not you know what it is to laugh?"

"Yes; I can laugh."

"Let me see!"

"Whoever heard of such a thing! Surely, I must have something to laugh at."

"I do not need that when I am happy."

"Are you happy now, Marit?"

"Pray, am I laughing now?"

"Yes; you are, indeed."

He took both her hands in his and clapped them together over and over again, gazing into her face. Here the dog began to growl, then his hair bristled and he fell to barking at something below, growing more and more savage, and finally quite furious. Marit sprang back in alarm; but Oyvind went forward and looked down. It was his father the dog was barking at. He was standing at the foot of the cliff with both hands in his pockets, gazing at the dog.

"Are you there, you two? What mad dog is that you have up there?"

"It is the dog from the Heidegards," answered Oyvind, somewhat embarrassed.

"How the deuce did it get up there?"

Now the mother had put her head out of the kitchen door, for she had heard the dreadful noise, and at once knew what it meant; and laughing, she said,—

"That dog is roaming about there every day, so there is nothing remarkable in it."

"Well, I must say it is a fierce dog."

"It will behave better if I stroke it," thought Oyvind, and he did so.

The dog stopped barking, but growled. The father walked away as though he knew nothing, and the two on the cliff were saved from discovery.

"It was all right this time," said Marit, as they drew near to each other again.

"Do you expect it to be worse hereafter?"

"I know one who will keep a close watch on us—that I do."

"Your grandfather?"

"Yes, indeed."

"But he shall do us no harm."

"Not the least."

"And you promise that?"

"Yes, I promise it, Oyvind."

"How beautiful you are, Marit!"

"So the fox said to the raven and got the cheese."

"I mean to have the cheese, too, I can assure you."

"You shall not have it."

"But I will take it."

She turned her head, but he did not take it.

"I can tell you one thing, Oyvind, though." She looked up sideways as she spoke.

"Well?"

"How homely you have grown!"

"Ah! you are going to give me the cheese, anyway; are you?"

"No, I am not," and she turned away again.

"Now I must go, Oyvind."

"I will go with you."

"But not beyond the woods; grandfather might see you."

"No, not beyond the woods. Dear me! are you running?"

"Why, we cannot walk side by side here."

"But this is not going together?"

"Catch me, then!"

She ran; he after her; and soon she was fast in the bushes, so that he overtook her.

"Have I caught you forever, Merit?" His hand was on her waist.

"I think so," said she, and laughed; but she was both flushed and serious.

"Well, now is the time," thought he, and he made a movement to kiss her; but she bent her head down under his arm, laughed, and ran away. She paused, though, by the last trees.

"And when shall we meet again?" whispered she.

"To-morrow, to-morrow!" he whispered in return.

"Yes; to-morrow."

"Good-by," and she ran on.

"Marit!" She stopped. "Say, was it not strange that we met first on the cliff?"

"Yes, it was." She ran on again.

Oyvind gazed long after her. The dog ran on before her, barking; Marit followed, quieting him. Oyvind turned, took off his cap and tossed it into the air, caught it, and threw it up again.

"Now I really think I am beginning to be happy," said the boy, and went singing homeward.

CHAPTER X.

One afternoon later in the summer, as his mother and a girl were raking hay, while Oyvind and his father were carrying it in, there came a little barefooted and bareheaded boy, skipping down the hill-side and across the meadows to Oyvind, and gave him a note.

"You run well, my boy," said Oyvind.

"I am paid for it," answered the boy.

On being asked if he was to have an answer, the reply was No; and the boy took his way home over the cliff, for some one was coming after him up on the road, he said. Oyvind opened the note with some difficulty, for it was folded in a strip, then tied in a knot, then sealed and stamped; and the note ran thus:—

"He is now on the march; but he moves slowly. Run into the woods and hide yourself! THE ONE YOU KNOW."

"I will do no such thing," thought Oyvind; and gazed defiantly up the hills. Nor did he wait long before an old man appeared on the hill-top, paused to rest, walked on a little, rested again. Both Thore and his wife stopped to look. Thore soon smiled, however; his wife, on the other hand, changed color.

"Do you know him?"

"Yes, it is not very easy to make a mistake here."

Father and son again began to carry hay; but the latter took care that they were always together. The old man on the hill slowly drew near, like a heavy western storm. He was very tall and rather corpulent; he was lame and walked with a labored gait, leaning on a staff. Soon he came so near that they could see him distinctly; he paused, removed his cap and wiped away the perspiration with a handkerchief. He was quite bald far back on the head; he had a round, wrinkled face, small, glittering, blinking eyes, bushy eyebrows, and had lost none of his teeth. When he spoke it was in a sharp, shrill voice, that seemed to be hopping over gravel and stones; but it lingered on an "r" here and there with great satisfaction, rolling it over for several yards, and at the same time making a tremendous leap in pitch. He had been known in his younger days as a lively but quick-tempered man; in his old age, through much adversity, he had become irritable and suspicious.

Thore and his son came and went many times before Ole could make his way to them; they both knew that he did not come for any good purpose, therefore it was all the more comical that he never got there. Both had to walk very serious, and talk in a whisper; but as this did not come to an end it became ludicrous. Only half a word that is to the point can kindle laughter under such circumstances, and especially when it is dangerous to laugh. When at last Ole was only a few rods distant, but which seemed never to grow less, Oyvind said, dryly, in a low tone,—

"He must carry a heavy load, that man,"—and more was not required.

"I think you are not very wise," whispered the father, although he was laughing himself.

"Hem, hem!" said Ole, coughing on the hill.

"He is getting his throat ready," whispered Thore.

Oyvind fell on his knees in front of the haycock, buried his head in the hay, and laughed. His father also bowed down.

"Suppose we go into the barn," whispered he, and taking an armful of hay he trotted off. Oyvind picked up a little tuft, rushed after him, bent crooked with laughter, and dropped down as soon as he was inside the barn. His father was a grave man, but if he once got to laughing, there first began within him a low chuckling, with an occasional ha-ha-ha, gradually growing longer and longer, until all blended in a single loud peal, after which came wave after wave with a longer gasp between each. Now he was under way. The son lay on the floor, the father stood beside him, both laughing with all their might. Occasionally they had such fits of laughter.

"But this is inconvenient," said the father.

Finally they were at a loss to know how this would end, for the old man must surely have reached the gard.

"I will not go out," said the father; "I have no business with him."

"Well, then, I will not go out either," replied Oyvind.

"Hem, hem!" was heard just outside of the barn wall.

The father held up a threatening finger to his boy.

"Come, out with you!"

"Yes; you go first!"

"No, you be off at once."

"Well, go you first."

And they brushed the dust off each other, and advanced very seriously. When they came below the barn-bridge they saw Ole standing with his face towards the kitchen door, as if he were reflecting. He held his cap in the same hand as his staff, and with his handkerchief was wiping the sweat from his bald head, at the same time pulling at the bushy tufts behind his ears and about his neck until they stuck out like spikes. Oyvind hung behind his father, so the latter was obliged to stand still, and in order to put an end to this he said with excessive gravity,—

"Is the old gentleman out for a walk?"

Ole turned, looked sharply at him, and put on his cap before he replied,—

"Yes, so it seems."

"Perhaps you are tired; will you not walk in?"

"Oh! I can rest very well here; my errand will not take long."

Some one set the kitchen door ajar and looked out; between it and Thore stood old Ole, with his cap-visor down over his eyes, for the cap was too large now that he had lost his hair. In order to be able to see he threw his head pretty far back; he held his staff in his right hand, while the left was firmly pressed against his side when he was not gesticulating; and this he never did more vigorously than by stretching the hand half way out and holding it passive a moment, as a guard for his dignity.

"Is that your son who is standing behind you?" he began, abruptly.

"So they say."

"Oyvind is his name, is it not?"

"Yes; they call him Oyvind."

"He has been at one of those agricultural schools down south, I believe?"

"There was something of the kind; yes."

"Well, my girl—she—my granddaughter—Marit, you know—she has gone mad of late."

"That is too bad."

"She refuses to marry."

"Well, really?"

"She will not have any of the gard boys who offer themselves."

"Ah, indeed."

"But people say he is to blame; he who is standing there."

"Is that so?"

"He is said to have turned her head—yes; he there, your son Oyvind."

"The deuce he has!"

"See you, I do not like to have any one take my horses when I let them loose on the mountains, neither do I choose to have any one take my daughters when I allow them to go to a dance. I will not have it."

"No, of course not."

"I cannot go with them; I am old, I cannot be forever on the lookout."

"No, no! no, no!"

"Yes, you see, I will have order and propriety; there the block must stand, and there the axe must lie, and there the knife, and there they must sweep, and there throw rubbish out,—not outside the door, but yonder in the corner, just there—yes; and nowhere else. So, when I say to her: 'not this one but that one!' I expect it to be that one, and not this one!"

"Certainly."

"But it is not so. For three years she has persisted in thwarting me, and for three years we have not been happy together. This is bad; and if he is at the bottom of it, I will tell him so that you may hear it, you, his father, that it will not do him any good. He may as well give it up."

"Yes, yes."

Ole looked a moment at Thore, then he said,—

"Your answers are short."

"A sausage is no longer."

Here Oyvind had to laugh, although he was in no mood to do so. But with daring persons fear always borders on laughter, and now it inclined to the latter.

"What are you laughing at?" asked Ole, shortly and sharply.

"I?"

"Are you laughing at me?"

"The Lord forbid!" but his own answer increased his desire to laugh.

Ole saw this, and grew absolutely furious. Both Thore and Oyvind tried to make amends with serious faces and entreaties to walk in; but it was the pent-up wrath of three years that was now seeking vent, and there was no checking it.

"You need not think you can make a fool of me," he began; "I am on a lawful errand: I am protecting my grandchild's happiness, as I understand it, and puppy laughter shall not hinder me. One does not bring up girls to toss them down into the first houseman's place that opens its doors, and one does not manage an estate for forty years only to hand the whole over to the first one who makes a fool of the girl. My daughter made herself ridiculous until she was allowed to marry a vagabond. He drank them both into the grave, and I had to take the child and pay for the fun; but, by my troth! it shall not be the same with my granddaughter, and now you know *that*! I tell you, as sure as my name is Ole Nordistuen of the Heidegards, the priest shall sooner publish the bans of the hulder-folks up in the Nordal forest than give out such names from the pulpit as Marit's and yours, you Christmas clown! Do you think you are going to drive respectable suitors away from the gard, forsooth? Well; you just try to come there, and you shall have such a journey down the hills that your shoes will come after you like smoke. You snickering fox! I suppose you have a notion that I do not know what you are thinking of, both you and she. Yes, you think that old Ole Nordistuen will turn his nose to the skies yonder, in the churchyard, and then you will trip forward to the altar. No; I have lived now sixty-six years, and I will prove to you, boy, that I shall live until you waste away over it, both of you! I can tell you this, too, that you may cling to the house like new-fallen snow, yet not so much as see the soles of her feet; for I mean to send her from the parish. I am going to send her where she will be safe; so you may flutter about here like a chattering jay all you please, and marry the rain and the north wind. This is all I have to say to you; but now you, who are his father, know my sentiments, and if you desire the welfare of him whom this concerns, you had better advise him to lead the stream where it can find its course; across my possessions it is forbidden."

He turned away with short, hasty steps, lifting his right foot rather higher than the left, and grumbling to himself.

Those left behind were completely sobered; a foreboding of evil had become blended with their jesting and laughter, and the house seemed, for a while, as empty as after a great fright. The mother who, from the kitchen door had heard everything, anxiously sought Oyvind's eyes, scarcely able to keep back her tears, but she would not make it harder for him by saying a single word. After they had all silently entered the house, the father sat down by the window, and gazed out after Ole, with much earnestness in his face; Oyvind's eyes hung on the slightest change of countenance; for on his father's first words almost depended the future of the two young people. If Thore united his refusal with Ole's, it could scarcely be overcome. Oyvind's thoughts flew, terrified, from obstacle to obstacle; for a time he saw only poverty, opposition, misunderstanding, and a sense of wounded honor, and every prop he tried to grasp seemed to glide away from him. It increased his uneasiness that his mother was standing with her hand on the latch of the kitchen-door, uncertain whether she had the courage to remain inside and await the issue, and that she at last lost heart entirely and stole out. Oyvind gazed fixedly at his father, who never took his eyes from the window; the son did not dare speak, for the other must have time to think the matter over fully. But at the same moment his soul had fully run its course of anxiety, and regained its poise once more. "No one but God can part us in the end," he thought to himself, as he looked at his father's wrinkled brow. Soon after this something occurred. Thore drew a long sigh, rose, glanced round the room, and met his son's gaze. He paused, and looked long at him.

"It was my will that you should give her up, for one should hesitate about succeeding through entreaties or threats. But if you are determined not to give her up, you may let me know when the opportunity comes, and perhaps I can help you."

He started off to his work, and the son followed.

But that evening Oyvind had his plan formed: he would endeavor to become agriculturist for the district, and ask the inspector and the school-master to aid him. "If she only remains firm, with God's help, I shall win her through my work."

He waited in vain for Marit that evening, but as he walked about he sang his favorite song:—

> "Hold thy head up, thou eager boy!
> Time a hope or two may destroy,
> Soon in thy eye though is beaming,
> Light that above thee is beaming!
> "Hold thy head up, and gaze about!
> Something thou'lt find that "Come!" does shout;

Thousands of tongues it has bringing
Tidings of peace with their singing.
"Hold thy head up; within thee, too,
Rises a mighty vault of blue,
Wherein are harp tones sounding,
Swinging, exulting, rebounding.
"Hold thy head up, and loudly sing!
Keep not back what would sprout in spring;
Powers fermenting, glowing,
Must find a time for growing.
"Hold thy head up; baptism take,
From the hope that on high does break,
Arches of light o'er us throwing,
And in each life-spark glowing."

Footnote 1: Auber Forestier's translation.

CHAPTER XI.

It was during the noonday rest; the people at the great Heidegards were sleeping, the hay was scattered over the meadows, the rakes were staked in the ground. Below the barn-bridge stood the hay sleds, the harness lay, taken off, beside them, and the horses were tethered at a little distance. With the exception of the latter and some hens that had strayed across the fields, not a living creature was visible on the whole plain.

There was a notch in the mountains above the gards, and through it the road led to the Heidegard saeters,—large, fertile mountain plains. A man was standing in this notch, taking a survey of the plain below, just as if he were watching for some one. Behind him lay a little mountain lake, from which flowed the brook which made this mountain pass; on either side of this lake ran cattle-paths, leading to the saeters, which could be seen in the distance. There floated toward him a shouting and a barking, cattle-bells tinkled among the mountain ridges; for the cows had straggled apart in search of water, and the dogs and herd-boys were vainly striving to drive them together. The cows came galloping along with the most absurd antics and involuntary plunges, and with short, mad bellowing, their tails held aloft, they rushed down into the water, where they came to a stand; every time they moved their heads the tinkling of their bells was heard across the lake. The dogs drank a little, but stayed behind on firm land; the herd-boys followed, and seated themselves on the warm, smooth hill-side. Here they drew forth their lunch boxes, exchanged with one another, bragged about their dogs, oxen, and the family they lived with, then undressed, and sprang into the water with the cows. The dogs persisted in not going in; but loitered lazily around, their heads hanging, with hot eyes and lolling tongues. Round about on the slopes not a bird was to be seen, not a sound was heard, save the prattling of children and the tinkling of bells; the heather was parched and dry, the sun blazed on the hill-sides, so that everything was scorched by its heat.

It was Oyvind who was sitting up there in the mid-day sun, waiting. He sat in his shirt-sleeves, close by the brook which flowed from the lake. No one yet appeared on the Heidegard plain, and he was gradually beginning to grow anxious when suddenly a large dog came walking with heavy steps out of a door in Nordistuen, followed by a girl in white sleeves. She tripped across the meadow toward the cliff; he felt a strong desire to shout down to her, but dared not. He took a careful survey of the gard to see if any one might come out and notice her, but there seemed to be no danger of detection, and several times he rose from impatience.

She arrived at last, following a path by the side of the brook, the dog a little in advance of her, snuffing the air, she catching hold of the low shrubs, and walking with more and more weary gait. Oyvind sprang downward; the dog growled and was hushed; but as soon as Marit saw Oyvind coming she sat down on a large stone, as red as blood, tired and overcome by the heat. He flung himself down on the stone by her side.

"Thank you for coming."

"What heat and what a distance! Have you been here long?"

"No. Since we are watched in the evening, we must make use of the noon. But after this I think we will not act so secretly, nor take so much trouble; it was just about this I wanted to speak to you."

"Not so secretly?"

"I know very well that all that is done secretly pleases you best; but to show courage pleases you also. To-day I have come to have a long talk with you, and now you must listen."

"Is it true that you are trying to be agriculturist for the district?"

"Yes, and I expect to succeed. In this I have a double purpose: first, to win a position for myself; but secondly, and chiefly, to accomplish something which your grandfather can see and understand. Luckily it chances that most of the Heidegard freeholders are young people who wish for improvements and desire help; they have money, too. So I shall begin among them. I shall regulate everything from their stables to their water-pipes; I shall give lectures and work; I shall fairly besiege the old man with good deeds."

"Those are brave words. What more, Oyvind?"

"Why, the rest simply concerns us two. You must not go away."

"Not if he orders it?"

"And keep nothing secret that concerns us two."

"Even if he torments me?"

"We gain more and defend ourselves better by allowing everything to be open. We must manage to be so constantly before the eyes of people, that they are constantly forced to talk about how fond we are of each other; so much the sooner will they wish that all may go well with us. You must not leave home. There is danger of gossip forcing its way between those who are parted. We pay no heed to any idle talk the first year, but we begin by degrees to believe in it the second. We two will meet once a week and laugh away the mischief people would like to make between us; we shall be able to meet occasionally at a dance, and keep step together until everything sings about us, while those who backbite us are sitting around. We shall meet at church and greet each other so that it may attract the attention of all those who wish us a hundred miles apart. If any one makes a song about us we will sit down together and try to get up one in answer to it; we must succeed if we assist each other. No one can harm us if we keep together, and thus *show* people that we keep together. All unhappy love belongs either to timid people, or weak people, or sick people, or calculating people, who keep waiting for some special opportunity, or cunning people, who, in the end, smart for their own cunning; or to sensuous people that do not care enough for each other to forget rank and distinction; they go and hide from sight, they send letters, they tremble at a word, and finally they mistake fear, that constant uneasiness and irritation in the blood, for love, become wretched and dissolve like sugar. Oh pshaw! if they truly loved each other they would have no fear; they would laugh, and would openly march to the church door, in the face of every smile and every word. I have read about it in books, and I have seen it for myself. That is a pitiful love which chooses a secret course. Love naturally begins in secresy because it begins in shyness; but it must live openly because it lives in joy. It is as when the leaves are changing; that which is to grow cannot conceal itself, and in every instance you see that all which is dry falls from the tree the moment the new leaves begin to sprout. He who gains love casts off all the old, dead rubbish he formerly clung to, the sap wells up and rushes onward; and should no one notice it then? Hey, my girl! they shall become happy at seeing us happy; two who are betrothed and remain true to each other confer a benefit on people, for they give them a poem which their children learn by heart to the shame of their unbelieving parents. I have read of many such cases; and some still live in the memory of the people of this parish, and those who relate these stories, and are moved by them, are the children of the very persons who once caused all the mischief. Yes, Marit, now we two will join hands, so; yes, and we will promise each other to cling together, so; yes, and now it will all come right. Hurrah!"

He was about to take hold of her head, but she turned it away and glided down off the stone.

He kept his seat; she came back, and leaning her arms on his knee, stood talking with him, looking up into his face.

"Listen, Oyvind; what if he is determined I shall leave home, how then?"

"Then you must say No, right out."

"Oh, dear! how would that be possible?"

"He cannot carry you out to the carriage."

"If he does not quite do that, he can force me in many other ways."

"That I do not believe; you owe obedience, to be sure, as long as it is not a sin; but it is also your duty to let him fully understand how hard it is for you to be obedient this time. I am sure he will change his mind when he sees this; now he thinks, like most people, that it is only childish nonsense. Prove to him that it is something more."

"He is not to be trifled with, I can assure you. He watches me like a tethered goat."

"But you tug at the tether several times a day."

"That is not true."

"Yes, you do; every time you think of me in secret you tug at it."

"Yes, in that way. But are you so very sure that I think often of you?"

"You would not be sitting here if you did not."

"Why, dear me! did you not send word for me to come?"

"But you came because your thoughts drove you here."

"Rather because the weather was so fine."

"You said a while ago that it was too warm."

"To go *up* hill, yes; but *down* again?"

"Why did you come up, then?"
"That I might run down again."
"Why did you not run down before this?"
"Because I had to rest."
"And talk with me about love?"
"It was an easy matter to give you the pleasure of listening."
"While the birds sang."
"And the others were sleeping."
"And the bells rang."
"In the shady grove."

Here they both saw Marit's grandfather come sauntering out into the yard, and go to the bell-rope to ring the farm people up. The people came slowly forth from the barns, sheds, and houses, moved sleepily toward their horses and rakes, scattered themselves over the meadow, and presently all was life and work again. Only the grandfather went in and out of the houses, and finally up on the highest barn-bridge and looked out. There came running up to him a little boy, whom he must have called. The boy, sure enough, started off in the direction of Pladsen. The grandfather, meanwhile, moved about the gard, often looking upward and having a suspicion, at least, that the black spot on the "giant rock" was Marit and Oyvind. Now for the second time Marit's great dog was the cause of trouble. He saw a strange horse drive in to the Heidegards, and believing himself to be only doing his duty, began to bark with all his might. They hushed the dog, but he had grown angry and would not be quiet; the grandfather stood below staring up. But matters grew still worse, for all the herd-boys' dogs heard with surprise the strange voice and came running up. When they saw that it was a large, wolf-like giant, all the stiff-haired Lapp-dogs gathered about him. Marit became so terrified that she ran away without saying farewell. Oyvind rushed into the midst of the fray, kicked and fought; but the dogs merely changed the field of battle, and then flew at one another again, with hideous howls and kicks; Oyvind after them again, and so it kept on until they had rolled over to the edge of the brook, when he once more came running up. The result of this was that they all tumbled together into the water, just at a place where it was quite deep, and there they parted, shame-faced. Thus ended this forest battle. Oyvind walked through the forest until he reached the parish road; but Marit met her grandfather up by the fence. This was the dog's fault.

"Where do you come from?"
"From the wood."
"What were you doing there?"
"Plucking berries."
"That is not true."
"No; neither is it."
"What were you doing, then?"
"I was talking with some one."
"Was it with the Pladsen boy?"
"Yes."
"Hear me now, Marit; to-morrow you leave home."
"No."
"Listen to me, Marit; I have but one single thing to say, only one: you *shall* go."
"You cannot lift me into the carriage."
"Indeed? Can I not?"
"No; because you will not."
"Will I not? Listen now, Marit, just for sport, you see, just for sport. I am going to tell you that I will crush the backbone of that worthless fellow of yours."
"No; you would not dare do so."
"I would not dare? Do you say I would not dare? Who should interfere? Who?"
"The school-master."
"School—school—school-master. Does he trouble his head about that fellow, do you think?"
"Yes; it is he who has kept him at the agricultural school."
"The school-master?"
"The school-master."
"Hearken now, Marit; I will have no more of this nonsense; you shall leave the parish. You only cause me sorrow and trouble; that was the way with your mother, too, only sorrow and trouble. I am an old man. I want to see you well provided for. I will not live in people's talk as a fool just for this matter. I only wish your own good; you should

understand this, Marit. Soon I will be gone, and then you will be left alone. What would have become of your mother if it had not been for me? Listen, Marit; be sensible, pay heed to what I have to say. I only desire your own good."

"No, you do not."

"Indeed? What do I want, then?"

"To carry out your own will, that is what you want; but you do not ask about mine."

"And have you a will, you young sea-gull, you? Do you suppose you know what is for your good, you fool? I will give you a taste of the rod, I will, for all you are so big and tall. Listen now, Marit; let me talk kindly with you. You are not so bad at heart, but you have lost your senses. You must listen to me. I am an old and sensible man. We will talk kindly together a little; I have not done so remarkably well in the world as folks think; a poor bird on the wing could easily fly away with the little I have; your father handled it roughly, indeed he did. Let us care for ourselves in this world, it is the best thing we can do. It is all very well for the school-master to talk, for he has money himself; so has the priest;—let them preach. But with us who must slave for our daily bread, it is quite different. I am old. I know much. I have seen many things; love, you see, may do very well to talk about; yes, but it is not worth much. It may answer for priests and such folks, peasants must look at it in a different light. First food, you see, then God's Word, and then a little writing and arithmetic, and then a little love, if it happens to come in the way; but, by the Eternals! there is no use in beginning with love and ending with food. What can you say, now, Marit?"

"I do not know."

"You do not know what you ought to answer?"

"Yes, indeed, I know that."

"Well, then?"

"May I say it?"

"Yes; of course you may say it."

"I care a great deal for that love of mine."

He stood aghast for a moment, recalling a hundred similar conversations with similar results, then he shook his head, turned his back, and walked away.

He picked a quarrel with the housemen, abused the girls, beat the large dog, and almost frightened the life out of a little hen that had strayed into the field; but to Marit he said nothing.

That evening Marit was so happy when she went up-stairs to bed, that she opened the window, lay in the window-frame, looked out and sang. She had found a pretty little love-song, and it was that she sang.

"Lovest thou but me,
I will e'er love thee,
All my days on earth, so fondly;
Short were summer's days,
Now the flower decays,—
Comes again with spring, so kindly.

"What you said last year
Still rings in my ear,
As I all alone am sitting,
And your thoughts do try
In my heart to fly,—
Picture life in sunshine flitting.

"Litli—litli—loy,
Well I hear the boy,
Sighs behind the birches heaving.
I am in dismay,
Thou must show the way,
For the night her shroud is weaving.

"Flomma, lomma, hys,
Sang I of a kiss,
No, thou surely art mistaken.
Didst thou hear it, say?
Cast the thought away;
Look on me as one forsaken.

"Oh, good-night! good-night!
Dreams of eyes so bright,
Hold me now in soft embraces,
But that wily word,

Which thou thought'st unheard,
Leaves in me of love no traces.
"I my window close,
But in sweet repose
Songs from thee I hear returning;
Calling me they smile,
And my thoughts beguile,—
Must I e'er for thee be yearning?"

CHAPTER XII.

Several years have passed since the last scene.

It is well on in the autumn. The school-master comes walking up to Nordistuen, opens the outer door, finds no one at home, opens another, finds no one at home; and thus he keeps on until he reaches the innermost room in the long building. There Ole Nordistuen is sitting alone, by the side of his bed, his eyes fixed on his hands.

The school-master salutes him, and receives a greeting in return; he finds a stool, and seats himself in front of Ole.

"You have sent for me," he says.

"I have."

The school-master takes a fresh quid of tobacco, glances around the room, picks up a book that is lying on the bench, and turns over the leaves.

"What did you want of me?"

"I was just sitting here thinking it over."

The school-master gives himself plenty of time, searches for his spectacles in order to read the title of the book, wipes them and puts them on.

"You are growing old, now, Ole."

"Yes, it was about that I wanted to talk with you. I am tottering downward; I will soon rest in the grave."

"You must see to it that you rest well there, Ole."

He closes the book and sits looking at the binding.

"That is a good book you are holding in your hands."

"It is not bad. How often have you gone beyond the cover, Ole?"

"Why, of late, I"—

The school-master lays aside the book and puts away his spectacles.

"Things are not going as you wish to have them, Ole?"

"They have not done so as far back as I can remember."

"Ah, so it was with me for a long time. I lived at variance with a good friend, and wanted *him* to come to *me*, and all the while I was unhappy. At last I took it into my head to go to *him*, and since then all has been well with me."

Ole looks up and says nothing.

The school-master: "How do you think the gard is doing, Ole?"

"Failing, like myself."

"Who shall have it when you are gone?"

"That is what I do not know, and it is that, too, which troubles me."

"Your neighbors are doing well now, Ole."

"Yes, they have that agriculturist to help them."

The school-master turned unconcernedly toward the window: "You should have help,—you, too, Ole. You cannot walk much, and you know very little of the new ways of management."

Ole: "I do not suppose there is any one who would help me."

"Have you asked for it?"

Ole is silent.

The school-master: "I myself dealt just so with the Lord for a long time. 'You are not kind to me,' I said to Him. 'Have you prayed me to be so?' asked He. No; I had not done so. Then I prayed, and since then all has been truly well with me."

Ole is silent; but now the school-master, too, is silent.

Finally Ole says:—

"I have a grandchild; she knows what would please me before I am taken away, but she does not do it."

The school-master smiles.

"Possibly it would not please her?"

Ole makes no reply.

The school-master: "There are many things which trouble you; but as far as I can understand they all concern the gard."

Ole says, quietly,—

"It has been handed down for many generations, and the soil is good. All that father after father has toiled for lies in it; but now it does not thrive. Nor do I know who shall drive in when I am driven out. It will not be one of the family."

"Your granddaughter will preserve the family."

"But how can he who takes her take the gard? That is what I want to know before I die. You have no time to lose, Baard, either for me or for the gard."

They were both silent; at last the school-master says,—

"Shall we walk out and take a look at the gard in this fine weather?"

"Yes; let us do so. I have work-people on the slope; they are gathering leaves, but they do not work except when I am watching them."

He totters off after his large cap and staff, and says, meanwhile,—

"They do not seem to like to work for me; I cannot understand it."

When they were once out and turning the corner of the house, he paused.

"Just look here. No order: the wood flung about, the axe not even stuck in the block."

He stooped with difficulty, picked up the axe, and drove it in fast.

"Here you see a skin that has fallen down; but has any one hung it up again?"

He did it himself.

"And the store-house; do you think the ladder is carried away?"

He set it aside. He paused, and looking at the school-master, said,—

"This is the way it is every single day."

As they proceeded upward they heard a merry song from the slopes.

"Why, they are singing over their work," said the school-master.

"That is little Knut Ostistuen who is singing; he is helping his father gather leaves. Over yonder *my* people are working; you will not find them singing."

"That is not one of the parish songs, is it?"

"No, it is not."

"Oyvind Pladsen has been much in Ostistuen; perhaps that is one of the songs he has introduced into the parish, for there is always singing where he is."

There was no reply to this.

The field they were crossing was not in good condition; it required attention. The school-master commented on this, and then Ole stopped.

"It is not in my power to do more," said he, quite pathetically. "Hired work-people without attention cost too much. But it is hard to walk over such a field, I can assure you."

As their conversation now turned on the size of the gard, and what portion of it most needed cultivation, they decided to go up the slope that they might have a view of the whole. When they at length had reached a high elevation, and could take it all in, the old man became moved.

"Indeed, I should not like to leave it so. We have labored hard down there, both I and those who went before me, but there is nothing to show for it."

A song rang out directly over their heads, but with the peculiar shrilling of a boy's voice when it is poured out with all its might. They were not far from the tree in whose top was perched little Knut Ostistuen, gathering leaves for his father, and they were compelled to listen to the boy:—

"When on mountain peaks you hie,
'Mid green slopes to tarry,
In your scrip pray no more tie,
Than you well can carry.
Take no hindrances along
To the crystal fountains;
Drown them in a cheerful song,
Send them down the mountains.

"Birds there greet you from the trees,
Gossip seeks the valley;
Purer, sweeter grows the breeze,
As you upward sally.

> Fill your lungs, and onward rove,
>   Ever gayly singing,
> Childhood's memories, heath and grove,
>   Rosy-hued, are bringing.
> "Pause the shady groves among,
> Hear yon mighty roaring,
> Solitude's majestic song
> Upward far is soaring.
> All the world's distraction comes
>   When there rolls a pebble;
> Each forgotten duty hums
>   In the brooklet's treble.
> "Pray, while overhead, dear heart,
>   Anxious mem'ries hover;
> Then go on: the better part
>   You'll above discover.
> Who hath chosen Christ as guide,
>   Daniel and Moses,
> Finds contentment far and wide,
>   And in peace reposes."

Footnote 1: Auber Forestier's translation.

Ole had sat down and covered his face with his hands.

"Here I will talk with you," said the school-master, and seated himself by his side.

Down at Pladsen, Oyvind had just returned home from a somewhat long journey, the post-boy was still at the door, as the horse was resting. Although Oyvind now had a good income as agriculturist of the district, he still lived in his little room down at Pladsen, and helped his parents every spare moment. Pladsen was cultivated from one end to the other, but it was so small that Oyvind called it "mother's toy-farm," for it was she, in particular, who saw to the farming.

He had changed his clothes, his father had come in from the mill, white with meal, and had also dressed. They just stood talking about taking a short walk before supper, when the mother came in quite pale.

"Here are singular strangers coming up to the house; oh dear! look out!"

Both men turned to the window, and Oyvind was the first to exclaim:—

"It is the school-master, and—yes, I almost believe—why, certainly it is he!"

"Yes, it is old Ole Nordistuen," said Thore, moving away from the window that he might not be seen; for the two were already near the door.

Just as Oyvind was leaving the window he caught the school-master's eye, Baard smiled, and cast a glance back at old Ole, who was laboring along with his staff in small, short steps, one foot being constantly raised higher than the other. Outside the school-master was heard to say, "He has recently returned home, I suppose," and Ole to exclaim twice over, "Well, well!"

They remained a long time quiet in the passage. The mother had crept up to the corner where the milk-shelf was; Oyvind had assumed his favorite position, that is, he leaned with his back against the large table, with his face toward the door; his father was sitting near him. At length there came a knock at the door, and in stepped the school-master, who drew off his hat, afterward Ole, who pulled off his cap, and then turned to shut the door. It took him a long time to do so; he was evidently embarrassed. Thore rising, asked them to be seated; they sat down, side by side, on the bench in front of the window. Thore took his seat again.

And the wooing proceeded as shall now be told.

The school-master: "We are having fine weather this autumn, after all."

Thore: "It has been mending of late."

"It is likely to remain pleasant, now that the wind is over in that quarter."

"Are you through with your harvesting up yonder?"

"Not yet; Ole Nordistuen here, whom, perhaps, you know, would like very much to have help from you, Oyvind, if there is nothing else in the way."

Oyvind: "If help is desired, I shall do what I can."

"Well, there is no great hurry. The gard is not doing well, he thinks, and he believes what is wanting is the right kind of tillage and superintendence."

Oyvind: "I am so little at home."

The school-master looks at Ole. The latter feels that he must now rush into the fire; he clears his throat a couple of times, and begins hastily and shortly,—

"It was—it is—yes. What I meant was that you should be in a certain way established—that you should—yes—be the same as at home up yonder with us,—be there, when you were not away."

"Many thanks for the offer, but I should rather remain where I now live."

Ole looks at the school-master, who says,—

"Ole's brain seems to be in a whirl to-day. The fact is he has been here once before, and the recollection of that makes his words get all confused."

Ole, quickly: "That is it, yes; I ran a madman's race. I strove against the girl until the tree split. But let by-gones be by-gones; the wind, not the snow, beats down the grain; the rain-brook does not tear up large stones; snow does not lie long on the ground in May; it is not the thunder that kills people."

They all four laugh; the school-master says:

"Ole means that he does not want you to remember that time any longer; nor you, either, Thore."

Ole looks at them, uncertain whether he dare begin again.

Then Thore says,—

"The briar takes hold with many teeth, but causes no wound. In me there are certainly no thorns left."

Ole: "I did not know the boy then. Now I see that what he sows thrives; the harvest answers to the promise of the spring; there is money in his finger-tips, and I should like to get hold of him."

Oyvind looks at the father, he at the mother, she from them to the school-master, and then all three at the latter.

"Ole thinks that he has a large gard"—

Ole breaks in: "A large gard, but badly managed. I can do no more. I am old, and my legs refuse to run the errands of my head. But it will pay to take hold up yonder."

"The largest gard in the parish, and that by a great deal," interrupts the school-master.

"The largest gard in the parish; that is just the misfortune; shoes that are too large fall off; it is a fine thing to have a good gun, but one should be able to lift it." Then turning quickly towards Oyvind, "Would you be willing to lend a hand to it?"

"Do you mean for me to be gard overseer?"

"Precisely—yes; you should have the gard."

"I should *have* the gard?"

"Just so—yes: then you could manage it."

"But"—

"You will not?"

"Why, of course, I will."

"Yes, yes, yes, yes; then it is decided, as the hen said when she flew into the water."

"But"—

Ole looks puzzled at the school-master.

"Oyvind is asking, I suppose, whether he shall have Marit, to."

Ole, abruptly: "Marit in the bargain; Marit in the bargain!"

Then Oyvind burst out laughing, and jumped right up; all three laughed with him. Oyvind rubbed his hands, paced the floor, and kept repeating again and again: "Marit in the bargain! Marit in the bargain!" Thore gave a deep chuckle, the mother in the corner kept her eyes fastened on her son until they filled with tears.

Ole, in great excitement: "What do you think of the gard?"

"Magnificent land!"

"Magnificent land; is it not?"

"No pasture equal to it!"

"No pasture equal to it! Something can be done with it?"

"It will become the best gard in the district!"

"It will become the best gard in the district! Do you think so? Do you mean that?"

"As surely as I am standing here!"

"There, is not that just what I have said?"

They both talked equally fast, and fitted together like the cogs of two wheels.

"But money, you see, money? I have no money."

"We will get on slowly without money; but get on we shall!"

"We shall get on! Of course we will! But if we *had* money, it would go faster you say?"

"Many times faster."

"Many times? We ought to have money! Yes, yes; a man can chew who has not all his teeth; he who drives with oxen will get on, too."

The mother stood blinking at Thore, who gave her many quick side glances as he sat swaying his body to and fro, and stroking his knees with his hands. The school-master also winked at him. Thore's lips parted, he coughed a little, and made an effort to speak; but Ole and Oyvind both kept on talking in an uninterrupted stream, laughed and kept up such a clatter that no one else could be heard.

"You must be quiet for a little while, Thore has something he wants to say," puts in the school-master.

They pause and look at Thore, who finally begins, in a low tone:—

"It has so happened that we have had a mill on our place. Of late it has turned out that we have had two. These mills have always brought in a few shillings during the year; but neither my father nor I have used any of these shillings except while Oyvind was away. The school-master has managed them, and he says they have prospered well where they are; but now it is best that Oyvind should take them for Nordistuen."

The mother stood in a corner, shrinking away into almost nothing, as she gazed with sparkling eyes at Thore, who looked very grave, and had an almost stupid expression on his face. Ole Nordistuen sat nearly opposite him, with wide-gaping mouth. Oyvind was the first to rouse from his astonishment, and burst out,—

"Does it not seem as if good luck went with me!"

With this he crossed the floor to his father, and gave him a slap on the shoulder that rang through the room. "You, father!" cried he, and rubbing his hands together he continued his walk.

"How much money might it be?" finally asked Ole, in a low tone, of the school-master.

"It is not so little."

"Some hundreds?"

"Rather more."

"Rather more? Oyvind, rather more! Lord help us, what a gard it will be!"

He got up, laughing aloud.

"I must go with you up to Marit," says Oyvind. "We can use the conveyance that is standing outside, then it will not take long."

"Yes, at once! at once! Do you, too, want everything done with haste?"

"Yes, with haste and wrong."

"With haste and wrong! Just the way it was with me when I was young, precisely."

"Here is your cap and staff; now I am going to drive you away."

"You are going to drive me away, ha—ha—ha! But you are coming with me; are you not? You are coming with me? All the rest of you come along, too; we must sit together this evening as long as the coals are alive. Come along!"

They promised that they would come. Oyvind helped Ole into the conveyance, and they drove off to Nordistuen. The large dog was not the only one up there who was surprised when Ole Nordistuen came driving into the gard with Oyvind Pladsen. While Oyvind was helping Ole out of the conveyance, and servants and laborers were gaping at them, Marit came out in the passage to see what the dog kept barking at; but paused, as if suddenly bewitched, turned fiery red, and ran in. Old Ole, meanwhile, shouted so tremendously for her when he got into the house that she had to come forward again.

"Go and make yourself trim, girl; here is the one who is to have the gard!"

"Is that true?" she cries, involuntarily, and so loud that the words rang through the room.

"Yes; it is true!" replies Oyvind, clapping his hands.

At this she swings round on her toe, flings away what she has in her hand, and runs out; but Oyvind follows her.

Soon came the school-master, and Thore and his wife. The old man had ordered candles put on the table, which he had had spread with a white cloth. Wine and beer were offered, and Ole kept going round himself, lifting his feet even higher than usual; but the right foot always higher than the left.

Before this little tale ends, it may be told that five weeks later Oyvind and Marit were united in the parish church. The school-master himself led the singing on the occasion, for the assistant chorister was ill. His voice was broken now, for he was old; but it seemed to Oyvind that it did the heart good to hear him. When the young man had given Marit his hand, and was leading her to the altar, the school-master nodded at him from the chancel, just as Oyvind had seen him do, in fancy, when sitting sorrowfully at that dance long ago. Oyvind nodded back while tears welled up to his eyes.

These tears at the dance were the forerunners of those at the wedding. Between them lay Oyvind's faith and his work.

Here endeth the story of A HAPPY BOY.

Arne: Early Tales and Sketches

CHAPTER I.

THERE was a deep gorge between two mountains; through this gorge a large, full stream flowed heavily over a rough and stony bottom. Both sides were high and steep, and so one side was bare; but close to its foot, and so near the stream that the latter sprinkled it with moisture every spring and autumn, stood a group of fresh-looking trees, gazing upward and onward, yet unable to advance this way or that.

"What if we should clothe the mountain?" said the juniper one day to the foreign oak, to which it stood nearer than all the others. The oak looked down to find out who it was that spoke, and then it looked up again without deigning a reply. The river rushed along so violently that it worked itself into a white foam; the north wind had forced its way through the gorge and shrieked in the clefts of the rocks; the naked mountain, with its great weight, hung heavily over and felt cold. "What if we should clothe the mountain?" said the juniper to the fir on the other side. "If anybody is to do it, I suppose it must be we," said the fir, taking hold of its beard and glancing toward the birch. "What do you think?" But the birch peered cautiously up at the mountain, which hung over it so threateningly that it seemed as if it could scarcely breathe. "Let us clothe it in God's name!" said the birch. And so, though there were but these three, they undertook to clothe the mountain. The juniper went first.

When they had gone a little way, they met the heather. The juniper seemed as though about to go past it. "Nay, take the heather along," said the fir. And the heather joined them. Soon it began to glide on before the juniper. "Catch hold of me," said the heather. The juniper did so, and where there was only a wee crevice, the heather thrust in a finger, and where it first had placed a finger, the juniper took hold with its whole hand. They crawled and crept along, the fir laboring on behind, the birch also. "This is well worth doing," said the birch.

But the mountain began to ponder on what manner of insignificant objects these might be that were clambering up over it. And after it had been considering the matter a few hundred years it sent a little brook down to inquire. It was yet in the time of the spring freshets, and the brook stole on until it reached the heather. "Dear, dear heather, cannot you let me pass; I am so small." The heather was very busy; only raised itself a little and pressed onward. In, under, and onward went the brook. "Dear, dear juniper, cannot you let me pass; I am so small." The juniper looked sharply at it; but if the heather had let it pass, why, in all reason, it must do so too. Under it and onward went the brook; and now came to the spot where the fir stood puffing on the hill-side. "Dear, dear fir, cannot you let me pass; I am really so small," said the brook,—and it kissed the fir's foot and made itself so very sweet. The fir became bashful at this, and let it pass. But the birch raised itself before the brook asked it. "Hi, hi, hi!" said the brook and grew. "Ha, ha, ha!" said the brook and grew. "Ho, ho, ho!" said the brook, and flung the heather and the juniper and the fir and the birch flat on their faces and backs, up and down these great hills. The mountain sat for many hundred years musing on whether it had not smiled a little that day.

It was plain enough: the mountain did not want to be clad. The heather fretted over this until it grew green again, and then it started forward. "Fresh courage!" said the heather.

The juniper had half raised itself to look at the heather, and continued to keep this position, until at length it stood upright. It scratched its head and set forth again, taking such a vigorous foothold that it seemed as though the mountain must feel it. "If you will not have me, then I will have you." The fir crooked its toes a little to find out whether they were whole, then lifted one foot, found it whole, then the other, which proved also to be whole, then both of them. It first investigated the ground it had been over, next where it had been lying, and finally where it should go. After this it began to wend its way slowly along, and acted just as though it had never fallen. The birch had become most wretchedly soiled, but now rose up and made itself tidy. Then they sped onward, faster and faster, upward and on either side, in sunshine and in rain. "What in the world can this be?" said the mountain, all glittering with dew, as the summer sun shone down on it,—the birds sang, the wood-mouse piped, the hare hopped along, and the ermine hid itself and screamed.

Then the day came when the heather could peep with one eye over the edge of the mountain. "Oh dear, oh dear, oh dear!" said the heather, and away it went. "Dear me! what is it the heather sees?" said the juniper, and moved on until it could peer up. "Oh dear, oh dear!" it shrieked, and was gone. "What is the matter with the juniper to-day?" said the fir, and took long strides onward in the heat of the sun. Soon it could raise itself on its toes and peep up. "Oh dear!" Branches and needles stood on end in wonderment. It worked its way forward, came up, and was gone. "What is it all the others see, and not I?" said the birch; and, lifting well its skirts, it tripped after. It stretched its whole head up at once. "Oh,—oh!—is not here a great forest of fir and heather, of juniper and birch, standing upon the table-land waiting for us?" said the birch; and its leaves quivered in the sunshine so that the dew trembled. "Aye, this is what it is to reach the goal!" said the juniper.

CHAPTER II.

Up on the hill-top it was that Arne was born. His mother's name was Margit, and she was the only child at the houseman's place,—Kampen. Once, in her eighteenth year, she stayed too long at a dance; her companions had left her, and so Margit thought that the way home would be just as long whether she waited until the dancing was over or not. And thus it happened that she kept her seat until the fiddler, known as Nils the tailor, suddenly laid aside his fiddle, as was his wont when drink took possession of him, let others troll the tune, seized the prettiest girl, moved his foot as evenly as the rhythm of a song, and with his boot-heel took the hat from the head of the tallest person present. "Ho!" said he. When Margit went home that evening, the moon-beams played on the snow with most wondrous beauty. After she had reached her bed-chamber she was moved to look out once more. She took off her boddice, but remained standing with it in her hand. Then she felt that she was cold, closed the door hastily, undressed, and nestled in under the robe. That night Margit dreamed about a great red cow that had wandered into the field. She went to drive it out, but though she tried hard, she could not stir from the spot; the cow stood calmly grazing there until it grew plump and well fed, and every now and then it looked at her, with large, heavy eyes.

The next time there was a dance in the parish Margit was present. She cared little for dancing that evening; she kept her seat to listen to the music, and it seemed strange to her that there were not others also who preferred this. But when the evening had worn on, the fiddler arose and wanted to dance. All at once he went directly to Margit Kampen. She scarcely knew what she was about, but she danced with Nils the tailor.

Soon the weather grew warm, and there was no more dancing. That spring Margit took such interest in a little lamb that had fallen ill, that her mother almost thought she was overdoing it.

"It is only a little lamb," said the mother.

"Yes, but it is ill," replied Margit.

It was some time since she had been to church; she wished to have her mother go, she said, and some one must be at home. One Sunday, later in the summer, the weather was so fine that the hay could well be left out for twenty-four hours, and the mother said that now they surely might both go. Margit could not reasonably object to this, and got ready for church; but when they were so far on their way that they could hear the church-bells, she burst into tears. The mother grew deathly pale: but they went on, the mother in advance, Margit following, listened to the sermon, joined in all the hymns to the very last, followed the prayer, and heard the bell ring before they left. But when they were seated in the family-room at home again, the mother took Margit's face between her hands and said:—

"Hide nothing from me, my child."

There came another winter when Margit did not dance. But Nils the tailor fiddled, took more strong drink than ever, and always, toward the close of the evening, swung the prettiest girl at the party. In those days, it was told as a certain fact that he could marry whom he pleased among the daughters of the first gard-owners in the parish; some added that Eli Böen herself had courted him for her daughter Birgit, who was madly in love with him.

But just at that time an infant of the houseman's daughter at Kampen was brought to baptism; it was christened Arne, and tailor Nils was spoken of as its father.

The evening of the same day Nils was at a large wedding; there he got drunk. He would not play, but danced all the time, and scarcely brooked having others on the floor. But when he crossed to Birgit Böen and asked her to dance, she declined. He gave a short laugh, turned on his heel, and caught hold of the first girl he encountered. She resisted. He looked down; it was a little dark maiden who had been sitting gazing fixedly at him, and who was now pale. Bowing lightly over her, he whispered,—

"Will you not dance with *me*, Karen?"

She made no reply. He asked once more. Then she answered in a whisper, as he had asked,—

"*That* dance might go farther than I wished."

He drew slowly back, but once in the middle of the floor, he made a spring and danced the halling alone. No one else was dancing; the others stood looking on in silence.

Afterwards he went out in the barn, and there he lay down and wept. Margit kept at home with the little boy. She heard about Nils, how he went from dance to dance, and she looked at the child and wept,—looked at him again and was happy. The first thing she taught him was to say papa; but this she dared not do when the mother, or the grandmother, as she was henceforth called, chanced to be near. The result of this was that it was the grandmother whom the boy called papa. It cost Margit much to break him of this, and thus she fostered in him an early shrewdness. He was not very large before he knew that Nils the tailor was his father, and when he reached the age in which the romantic acquires a flavor, he became also aware what sort of a man tailor Nils was. The grandmother had strictly forbidden even the mention of his name; what she mainly strove for was to have the houseman's place, Kampen, become an independent gard, so that her daughter and her boy might be free from care. She availed herself of the gard-owner's poverty, effected the purchase of the place, paid off a portion of the money each year, and managed the business like a man, for she had been a widow for fourteen years. Kampen was a large place, and had been extended until now it fed four cows, sixteen sheep, and a horse in which she was half owner.

Nils the tailor meanwhile took to roving about the parish; his business had fallen off, partly because he felt less interest in it, partly also because he was not liked as before. He gave, therefore, more time to fiddling; this led oftener to drinking and thence to fighting and evil days. There were those who had heard him say he was unhappy.

Arne might have been about six years old, when one winter day he was frolicking in the bed, whose coverlet he had up for a sail, while he was steering with a ladle. The grandmother sat spinning in the room, absorbed in her own thoughts, and nodded occasionally as though she would make a fixed fact of something she was thinking about. The boy knew that he was unheeded, and he fell to singing, just as he had learned it, the rough, wild song about tailor Nils:—

> "Unless 'twas only yesterday hither first you came,
> You've surely heard already of Nils the tailor's fame.
> "Unless 'twas but this morning you came among us first,
> You've heard how he knocked over tall Johan Knutson Kirst.
> "How, in his famous barn-fight with Ola Stor-Johann,
> He said, 'Bring down your porridge when we two fight again.'
> "That fighting fellow, Bugge, a famous man was he:
> His name was known all over fjord and fell and sea.
> "'Now, choose the place, you tailor, where I shall knock you down,
> And then I'll spit upon it, and there I'll lay your crown.'
> "'Ah, only come so near, I may catch your scent, my man,
> Your bragging hurts nobody; don't dream it ever can.'
> "The first round was a poor one, and neither man could beat;
> But both kept in their places, and steady on their feet.
> "The second round, poor Bugge was beaten black and blue.
> 'Little Bugge, are you tired? It's going hard with you.'
> "The third round, Bugge tumbled, and bleeding there he lay.
> 'Now, Bugge, where's your bragging?' 'Bad luck to me to-day!'"

More the boy did not sing; but there were two other stanzas which his mother was not likely to have taught him:—

> "Have you seen a tree cast its shadow on yesterday's snow?
> Have you seen how Nils does his smiles on the girls bestow?
> "Have you looked at Nils when to dance he just commences?
> Come, my girl, you must go; it is too late, when you've lost your senses."

These two stanzas the grandmother knew, and they came all the more distinctly into her mind because they were not sung. She said nothing to the boy; but to the mother she said, "Teach the boy well about your own shame; do not forget the last verses."

Nils the tailor was so broken down by drink that he was no longer the man he had been, and some people thought his end could not be far distant.

It so happened that two American gentlemen were visiting in the parish, and having heard that a wedding was going on in the vicinity, wanted to attend it, that they might learn the customs of the country. Nils was playing there. They gave each a dollar to the fiddler, and asked for a halling; but no one would come forward to dance it, however much it was urged. Several begged Nils himself to dance. "He was best, after all," they said. He refused, but the request became still more urgent, and finally unanimous. This was what he wanted. He gave his fiddle to another player, took off his jacket and cap, and stepped smiling into the middle of the room. He was followed by the same eager attention as of old, and this gave him his old strength. The people crowded closely together, those who were farthest back climbing upon tables and benches. Some of the girls were perched up higher than all the rest, and foremost among these—a tall girl with sunny brown hair of a varying tint, with blue eyes deeply set beneath a strong forehead, a large mouth that often smiled, drawing a little to one side as it did so—was Birgit Böen. Nils saw her, as he glanced up at the beam. The music struck up, a deep silence followed, and he began. He dashed forward along the floor, his body inclining to one side, half aslant, keeping time to the fiddle. Crouching down, he balanced himself, now on one foot, now on the other, flung his legs crosswise under him, sprang up again, stood as though about to make a fling, and then moved on aslant as before. The fiddle was handled by skillful fingers, and more and more fire was thrown into the tune. Nils threw his head farther and farther back, and suddenly his boot-heel touched the beam, sending the dust from the ceiling in showers over them all. The people laughed and shouted about him; the girls stood well-nigh breathless. The tune hurrahed with the rest, stimulating him anew with more and more strongly-marked accents, nor did he resist the exciting influences. He bent forward, hopped along in time to the music, made ready apparently for a fling, but only as a hoax, and then moved on, his body aslant as before; and when he seemed the least prepared for it, his boot-heel thundered against the beam again and again, whereupon he turned summersaults forwards and backwards in the air, landing each time erect on his feet. He broke off abruptly, and the tune, running through some wild variations, worked its way down to a deep tone in the bass, where it quivered and vibrated, and died away with a long-drawn stroke of the bow. The crowd dispersed, and loud, eager conversation, mingled with shouts and exclamations, broke the silence. Nils stood leaning against the wall, and the American gentlemen went over to him, with their interpreter, and each gave him five dollars.

The Americans talked a little with the interpreter, whereupon the latter asked Nils if he would go with them as their servant; he should have whatever wages he wanted. "Whither?" asked Nils. The people crowded about them as closely as possible. "Out into the world," was the reply. "When?" asked Nils, and looking around with a shining face, he caught Birgit Böen's eyes, and did not let them go again. "In a week, when we come back here," was the answer. "It is possible I will be ready," replied Nils, weighing his two five-dollar pieces. He had rested one arm on the shoulder of a man standing near him, and it trembled so that the man wanted to help him to the bench.

"It is nothing," replied Nils, made some wavering steps across the floor, then some firm ones, and, turning, asked for a spring-dance.

All the girls had come to the front. Casting a long, lingering look about him, he went straightway to one of them in a dark skirt; it was Birgit Böen. He held out his hand, and she gave him both of hers; then he laughed, drew back, caught hold of the girl beside her, and danced away with perfect abandon. The blood coursed up in Birgit's neck and face. A tall man, with a mild countenance, was standing directly behind her; he took her by the hand and danced off after Nils. The latter saw this, and—it might have been only through heedlessness—he danced so hard against them that the man and Birgit were sent reeling over and fell heavily on the floor. Shouting and laughter arose about them. Birgit got up at last, went aside, and wept bitterly.

The man with the mild face rose more slowly and went straight over to Nils, who was still dancing. "You had better stop a little," said the man. Nils did not hear, and then the man took him by the arm. Nils tore himself away and looked at him. "I do not know you," said he, with a smile. "No; but you shall learn to know me," said the man with the mild face, and with this he struck Nils a blow over one eye. Nils, who was wholly unprepared for this, was plunged heavily across the sharp-edged hearth-stone, and when he promptly tried to rise, he found that he could not; his back was broken.

At Kampen a change had taken place. The grandmother had been growing very feeble of late, and when she realized this she strove harder than ever to save money enough to pay off the last installment on the gard. "Then you and the boy will have all you need," she said to her daughter. "And if you let any one come in and waste it for you, I will turn in my grave." During the autumn, too, she had the pleasure of being able to stroll up to the former head-gard with the last remaining portion of the debt, and happy was she when she had taken her seat again, and could say, "Now that is done!" But at that very time she was attacked by her last illness; she betook herself forthwith to her bed, and never rose again. Her daughter buried her in a vacant spot in the churchyard, and placed over her a handsome cross, whereon was inscribed her name and age, with a verse from one of Kingo's hymns. A fortnight after the grandmother was laid in her grave, her Sunday gown was made over into clothes for the boy, and when he put them on, he became as solemn as though he were his grandmother come back again. Of his own accord, he went to the book with big print and large clasps she had read and sung from every Sunday, opened it, and there inside found her spectacles. These the boy had never been permitted to touch during his grandmother's lifetime; now he timidly took them up, put them on his nose, and looked through them into the book. All was misty. "How strange," thought the boy, "it was through them grandmother could read the word of God." He held them high up toward the light to see what the matter was, and—the spectacles lay on the floor.

He was much alarmed, and when the door at that moment opened, it seemed to him as though his grandmother must be coming in, but it was his mother, and behind her, six men, who, with much tramping and noise, were bearing in a litter, which they placed in the middle of the floor. For a long time the door was left open, so that it grew cold in the room.

On the litter lay a man with dark hair and pale face; the mother moved about weeping. "Lay him carefully on the bed," she begged, herself lending a helping hand. But while the men were moving with him, something made a noise under their feet. "Oh, it is only grandmother's spectacles," thought the boy, but he did not say so.

CHAPTER III.

It was in the autumn, as before stated. A week after Nils the tailor was borne into Margit Kampen's home, there came word to him from the Americans that he must hold himself in readiness to start. He lay just then writhing under a terrible attack of pain, and, gnashing his teeth, he shrieked, "Let them go to hell!" Margit stood motionless, as though he had made no answer. He noticed this, and presently he repeated slowly and feebly, "Let them—go."

As the winter advanced, he improved so much that he was able to sit up, although his health was shattered for life. The first time he actually sat up, he took out his fiddle and tuned it, but became so agitated that he had to go to bed again. He grew very taciturn, but was not hard to get along with; and as time wore on, he taught the boy to read, and began to take work in at home. He never went out, and would not talk with those who dropped in to see him. At first Margit used to bring him the parish news; he was always gloomy afterwards, so she ceased to do so.

When spring had fairly set in, he and Margit would sit longer than usual talking together after the evening meal. The boy was then sent off to bed. Some time later in the spring their bans were published in church, after which they were quietly married.

He did his share of work in the fields now, and managed everything in a sensible, orderly way. Margit said to the boy, "There is both profit and pleasure in him. Now you must be obedient and good, that you may do your best for him."

Margit had remained tolerably stout through all her sorrow; she had a ruddy face and very large eyes, which looked all the larger because there was a ring round them. She had full lips, a round face, and looked healthy and strong, although she was not very strong. At this period of her life, she was looking better than ever; and she always sang when she was at work, as had ever been her wont.

One Sunday afternoon, father and son went out to see how the crops were thriving that year. Arne ran about his father, shooting with a bow and arrow. Nils had himself made them for the boy. Thus they passed on directly up toward the road leading past the church and parsonage, down to what was called the broad valley. Nils seated himself on a stone by the roadside and fell to dreaming; the boy shot into the road and sprang after his arrow,—it was in the direction of the church. "Not too far away!" said the father. While the boy was playing there, he paused, as though listening. "Father, I hear music!" The father listened too; they heard the sounds of fiddling, almost drowned at times by loud shouts and wild uproar; but above all rose the steady rumbling of cart-wheels and the clatter of horses' feet; it was a bridal procession, wending its way home from church. "Come here, boy," shouted the father, and Arne knew by the tones of the voice that he must make haste. The father had hurriedly risen and hidden behind a large tree. The boy hastened after him. "Not here, over there!" cried the father, and the boy stepped behind an alder-copse. Already the carts were winding round the birch-grove; they came at a wild speed, the horses were white with foam, drunken people were crying and shouting; father and son counted cart after cart,—there were in all fourteen. In the first sat two fiddlers, and the wedding march sounded merrily through the clear air,—a boy stood behind and drove. Afterwards came a crowned bride, who sat on a high seat and glittered in the sunshine; she smiled, and her mouth drew to one side; beside her sat a man clad in blue and with a mild face. The bridal train followed, the men sat on the women's laps; small boys were sitting behind, drunken men were driving,—there were six people to one horse; the man who presided at the feast came in the last cart, holding a keg of brandy on his lap. They passed by screaming and singing, and drove recklessly down the hill; the fiddling, the voices, the rattling of wheels, lingered behind them in the dust; the breeze bore up single shrieks, soon only a dull rumbling, and then nothing. Nils stood motionless; there was a rustling behind him, he turned; it was the boy who was creeping forward.

"Who was it, father?" But the boy started, for his father's face was dreadful. Arne stood motionless waiting for an answer; then he remained where he was because he got none. After some time he became impatient and ventured again. "Shall we go?" Nils was still gazing after the bridal train, but he now controlled himself and started on. Arne followed after. He put an arrow into the bow, shot it, and ran. "Do not trample down the grass," said Nils gruffly. The boy let the arrow lie and came back. After a while he had forgotten this, and once when his father paused, he lay down and turned summersaults. "Do not trample down the grass, I say." Here Arne was seized by one arm, and lifted by it with such violence that it was almost put out of joint. Afterward, he walked quietly behind.

At the door Margit awaited them; she had just come in from the stable, where she had evidently had pretty hard work, for her hair was tumbled, her linen soiled, her dress likewise, but she stood in the door smiling. "A couple of the cows got loose and have been into mischief; now they are tied again."

"You might make yourself a little tidy on Sunday," said Nils, as he went past into the house.

"Yes, there is some sense in tidying up now that the work is done," said Margit, and followed him. She began to fix herself at once, and sang while she was doing so. Now Margit sang well, but sometimes there was a little huskiness in her voice.

"Stop that screaming," said Nils; he had thrown himself on his back across the bed. Margit stopped.

Then the boy came storming in. "There has come into the yard a great black dog, a dreadful looking"—

"Hold your tongue, boy," said Nils from the bed, and thrust out one foot to stamp on the floor with it. "A devilish noise that boy is always making," he muttered afterward, and drew his foot up again.

The mother held up a warning finger to the boy. "You surely must see that father is not in a good humor," she meant. "Will you not have some strong coffee with syrup in it?" said she; she wanted to put him in a good humor again. This was a drink the grandmother had liked, and the rest of them too. Nils did not like it at all, but had drunk it because the others did so. "Will you not have some strong coffee with syrup in it?" repeated Margit; for he had made no reply the first time. Nils raised himself up on both elbows and shrieked, "Do you think I will pour down such slops?"

Margit was struck with surprise, and, taking the boy with her, went out.

They had a number of things to attend to outside, and did not come in before supper-time. Then Nils was gone. Arne was sent out into the field to call him, but found him nowhere. They waited until the supper was nearly cold, then ate, and still Nils had not come. Margit became uneasy, sent the boy to bed, and sat down to wait. A little after midnight Nils appeared.

"Where have you been, dear?" asked she.

"That is none of your business," he answered, and slowly sat down on the bench.

He was drunk.

After this, Nils often went out in the parish, and always came home drunk. "I cannot stand it at home here with you," said he once when he came in. She tried gently to defend herself, and then he stamped on the floor and bade her be silent: if he was drunk, it was her fault; if he was wicked, it was her fault too; if he was a cripple and an unfortunate being for his whole life, why, she was to blame too, and that infernal boy of hers.

"Why were you always dangling after me?" said he, and wept. "What harm had I done you that you could not leave me in peace?"

"Lord have mercy on me!" said Margit. "Was it I who went after you?"

"Yes, it was!" he shrieked as he arose, and amid tears he continued: "You have succeeded in getting what you wanted. I drag myself about from tree to tree. I go every day and look at my own grave. But I could have lived in splendor with the finest gard girl in the parish. I might have traveled as far as the sun goes, had not you and your damned boy put yourselves in my way."

She tried again to defend herself. "It was, at all events, not the boy's fault."

"If you do not hold your tongue, I will strike you!"—and he struck her.

After he had slept himself sober the next day, he was ashamed, and was especially kind to the boy. But soon he was drunk again, and then he struck the mother. At last he got to striking her almost every time he was drunk. The boy cried and lamented; then he struck him too. Sometimes his repentance was so deep that he felt compelled to leave the house. About this time his fondness for dancing revived. He began to go about fiddling as in former days, and took the boy with him to carry the fiddle-case. Thus Arne saw a great deal. The mother wept because he had to go along, but dared not say so to the father. "Hold faithfully to God, and learn nothing evil," she begged, and tenderly caressed her boy. But at the dances there was a great deal of diversion; at home with the mother there was none at all. Arne turned more and more from her and to the father; she saw this and was silent. At the dances Arne learned many songs, and he sang them at home to his father; this amused the latter, and now and then the boy could even get him to laugh. This was so flattering to Arne that he exerted himself to learn as many songs as possible; soon he noticed what kind the father liked best, and what it was that made him laugh. When there was not enough of this element in the songs he was singing, the boy added to it himself, and this early gave him practice in adapting words to music. It was chiefly lampoons and odious things about people who had risen to power and prosperity, that the father liked and the boy sang.

The mother finally concluded to take him with her to the stable of evenings; numerous were the pretexts he found to escape going, but when, nevertheless, she managed to take him with her, she talked kindly to him about God and good things, usually ending by taking him in her arms, and, amid blinding tears, begging him, entreating him not to become a bad man.

The mother taught the boy to read, and he was surprisingly quick at learning. The father was proud of this, and, especially when he was drunk, told Arne he had his head.

Soon the father fell into the habit, when drink got the better of him, of calling on Arne at dancing-parties to sing for the people. The boy always obeyed, singing song after song amid laughter and uproar; the applause pleased the son almost more than it did the father, and finally there was no end to the songs Arne could sing. Anxious mothers who heard this, went themselves to his mother and told her of it; their reason for so doing being that the character of these songs was not what it should be. The mother put her arms about her boy and forbade him, in the name of God and all that was sacred, to sing such songs, and now it seemed to Arne that everything he took delight in his mother opposed. For the first time he told his father what his mother had said. She had to suffer for this the next time the father was drunk; he held his peace until then. But no sooner had it become clear to the boy what he had done than in his soul he implored pardon of God and her; he could not bring himself to do so in spoken words. His mother was just as kind as ever to him, and this cut him to the quick.

Once, however, he forgot this. He had a faculty for mimicking people. Above all, he could talk and sing as others did. The mother came in one evening when Arne was entertaining his father with this, and it occurred to the father, after she had gone out, that the boy should imitate his mother's singing. Arne refused at first, but his father, who lay over on the bed and laughed until it shook, insisted finally that he should sing like his mother. She is gone, thought the boy, and cannot hear it, and he mimicked her singing as it sounded sometimes when she was hoarse and choked with tears. The father laughed until it seemed almost hideous to the boy, and he stopped of himself. Just then the mother came in from the kitchen; she looked long and hard at the boy, as she crossed the floor to a shelf after a milk-pan and turned to carry it out.

A burning heat ran through his whole body; she had heard it all. He sprang down from the table where he had been sitting, went out, cast himself on the ground, and it seemed as though he must bury himself out of sight. He could not rest, and got up feeling that he must go farther on. He went past the barn, and behind it sat the mother, sewing on a fine, new shirt, just for him. She had always been in the habit of singing a hymn over her work when she sat sewing, but now she was not singing. She was not weeping, either; she only sat and sewed. Arne could bear it no longer he flung himself down in the grass directly in front of her, looked up at her, and wept and sobbed bitterly. The mother dropped her work and took his head between her hands.

"Poor Arne!" said she, and laid her own beside his. He did not try to say a word, but wept as he had never done before. "I knew you were good at heart," said the mother, and stroked down his hair.

"Mother, you must not say no to what I am going to ask for," was the first thing he could say.

"That you know I cannot do," answered she.

He tried to stop crying, and then stammered out, with his head still in her lap: "Mother, sing something for me."

"My dear, I cannot," said she, softly.

"Mother, sing something for me," begged the boy, "or I believe I will never be able to look at you again."

She stroked his hair, but was silent.

"Mother, sing, sing, I say! Sing," he begged, "or I will go so far away that I will never come home any more."

And while he, now fourteen in his fifteenth year as he was, lay there with his head in his mother's lap, she began to sing over him:—

> "Father, stretch forth Thy mighty hand,
> Thy Holy Spirit send yonder:
> Bless Thou the child on the lonely strand,
> Nor in its sports let it wander.
> Slipp'ry the way, the water deep,—
> Lord, in Thy arm but the darling keep,
> Then through Thy mercy 't will never
> Drown, but with Thee live forever.
>
> "Missing her child, in disquiet sore,
> Much for its safety fearing,
> Often the mother calls from her door,
> Never an answer hearing,—
> Then comes the thought: where'er it be,
> Blessed Lord, it is near to Thee;
> Jesus will guide his brother
> Home to the anxious mother."

She sang several verses. Arne lay still: there descended upon him a blessed peace, and under its influence he felt a refreshing weariness. The last thing he distinctly heard was about Jesus: it bore him into the midst of a great light, and there it seemed as though twelve or thirteen were singing; but the mother's voice rose above them all. A lovelier voice he had never heard; he prayed that he might sing thus. It seemed to him that if he were to sing right softly he might do so; and now he sang softly, tried again softly, and still more softly, and then, rejoiced at the bliss that seemed almost dawning for him, he joined in with full voice, and the spell was broken. He awakened, looked about him, listened, but heard nothing, save the everlasting, mighty roar of the force, and the little creek that flowed past the barn, with its low and incessant murmuring. The mother was gone,—she had laid under his head the half-finished shirt and her jacket.

CHAPTER IV.

WHEN the time came to take the herds up into the woods, Arne wanted to tend them. His father objected; the boy had never tended cattle, and he was now in his fifteenth year. But he was so urgent that it was finally arranged as he wished; and the entire spring, summer, and autumn he was in the woods by himself the livelong day, only going home to sleep.

He took his books up there with him. He read and carved letters in the bark of the trees; he went about thinking, longing, and singing. When he came home in the evening his father was often drunk, and beat the mother, cursed her and the parish, and talked about how he might once have journeyed far away. Then the longing for travel entered the boy's mind too. There was no comfort at home, and the books opened other worlds to him; sometimes it seemed as though the air, too, wafted him far away over the lofty mountains.

So it happened about midsummer that he met Kristian, the captain's eldest son, who came with the servant boy to the woods after the horses, in order to get a ride home. He was a few years older than Arne, light-hearted and gay, unstable in all his thoughts, but nevertheless firm in his resolves. He spoke rapidly and in broken sentences, and usually about two things at once; rode horseback without a saddle, shot birds on the wing, went fly-fishing, and seemed to Arne the goal of his aspirations. He also had his head full of travel, and told Arne about foreign lands until everything about them was radiant. He discovered Arne's fondness for reading, and now carried up to him those books he had read himself. After Arne had finished reading these, Kristian brought him new ones; he sat there himself on Sundays, and taught Arne how to find his way in the geography and the map; and all summer and autumn Arne read until he grew pale and thin.

In the winter he was allowed to read at home; partly because he was to be confirmed the next year, partly because he always knew how to manage his father. He began to go to school; but there he took most comfort when he closed his eyes and fancied himself over his books at home; besides, there were no longer any companions for him among the peasant boys.

His father's ill-treatment of the mother increased with years, as did also his fondness for drink and his bodily suffering. And when Arne, notwithstanding this, had to sit and amuse him, in order to furnish the mother with an hour's peace, and then often talk of things he now, in his heart, despised, he felt growing within him a hatred for his father. This he hid far down in his heart, as he did his love for his mother. When he was with Kristian, their talk ran on great journeys and books; even to him he said nothing about how things were at home. But many times after these wide-ranging talks, when he was walking home alone, wondering what might now meet him there, he wept and prayed to God, in the starry heavens, to grant that he might soon be allowed to go away.

In the summer he and Kristian were confirmed. Directly afterward, the latter carried out his plan. His father had to let him go from home and become a sailor. He presented Arne with his books, promised to write often to him,—and went away.

Now Arne was alone.

About this time he was again filled with a desire to write songs. He no longer patched up old ones; he made new ones, and wove into them all that grieved him most.

But his heart grew too heavy, and his sorrow broke forth in his songs. He now lay through long, sleepless nights, brooding, until he felt sure that he could bear this no longer, but must journey far away, seek Kristian, and not say a word about it to any one. He thought of his mother, and what would become of her,—and he could scarcely look her in the face.

He sat up late one evening reading. When his heart became too gloomy, he took refuge in his books, and did not perceive that they increased the venom. His father was at a wedding, but was expected home that evening; his mother was tired, and dreaded her husband's return; had therefore gone to bed. Arne started up at the sound of a heavy fall in the passage and the rattling of something hard, which struck against the door. It was his father who had come home.

Arne opened the door and looked at him.

"Is that you, my clever boy? Come and help your father up!"

He was raised up and helped in toward the bench. Arne took up the fiddle-case, carried it in, and closed the door.

"Yes, look at me, you clever boy. I am not handsome now; this is no longer tailor Nils. This I say—to you, that you—never shall drink brandy; it is—the world and the flesh and the devil—He resisteth the proud but giveth grace unto the humble.—Ah, woe, woe is me!—How far it has gone with me!"

He sat still a while, then he sang, weeping,—

> "Merciful Lord, I come to Thee;
> Help, if there can be help for me;
> Though by the mire of sin defiled,
> I'm still thine own dear ransomed child."

"Lord, I am not worthy that Thou shouldest come under my roof; but speak the word only"—He flung himself down, hid his face in his hands, and sobbed convulsively. Long he lay thus, and then he repeated word for word from the Bible, as he had learned it probably more than twenty years before: "Then she came and worshiped Him, saying, Lord, help me! But he answered and said, It is not meet to take the children's bread, and to cast it to dogs. And she said, Truth, Lord, yet the dogs eat of the crumbs which fall from their master's table!"

He was silent now, and dissolved in a flood of tears.

The mother had awakened long since, but had not dared raise her eyes, now that her husband was weeping like one who is saved; she leaned on her elbows and looked up.

But scarcely had Nils described her, than he shrieked out: "Are you staring at me; you, too?—you want to see, I suppose, what you have brought me to. Aye, this is the way I look, exactly so!" He rose up, and she hid herself under the robe. "No, do not hide, I will find you easily enough," said he, extending his right hand, and groping his way along with outstretched forefinger. "Tickle, tickle!" said he, as he drew off the covers and placed his finger on her throat.

"Father!" said Arne.

"Oh dear! how shriveled up and thin you have grown. There is not much flesh here. Tickle, tickle."

The mother convulsively seized his hand with both of hers, but could not free herself, and so rolled herself into a ball.

"Father!" said Arne.

"So life has come into you now. How she writhes, the fright! Tickle, tickle!"

"Father!" said Arne. The room seemed to swim about him.

"Tickle, I say!"

She let go his hands and gave up.

"Father!" shouted Arne. He sprang to the corner, where stood an axe.

"It is only from obstinacy that you do not scream. You had better not do so either; I have taken such a frightful fancy. Tickle, tickle!"

"Father!" shrieked Arne, seizing the axe, but remained standing as though nailed to the spot, for at that moment the father drew himself up, gave a piercing cry, clutched at his breast, and fell over. "Jesus Christ!" said he, and lay quite still.

Arne knew not where he stood or what he stood over; he waited, as it were, for the room to burst asunder, and for a strong light to break in somewhere. The mother began to draw her breath heavily, as though she were rolling off some great weight. She finally half rose, and saw the father lying stretched out on the floor, the son standing beside him with an axe.

"Merciful Lord, what have you done?" she shrieked, and started up out of bed, threw her skirt about her, and came nearer; then Arne felt as if his tongue were unloosed.

"He fell down himself," said he.

"Arne, Arne, I do not believe you," cried the mother, in a loud, rebuking tone. "Now Jesus be with you!" and she flung herself over the corpse, with piteous lamentation.

Now the boy came out of his stupor, and dropping down on his knees, exclaimed, "As surely as I look for mercy from God, he fell as he stood there."

"Then our Lord himself has been here," said she, quietly; and, sitting on the floor, she fixed her eyes on the corpse.

Nils lay precisely as he fell, stiff, with open eyes and mouth. His hands had drawn near together, as though he had tried to clasp them, but had been unable to do so.

"Take hold of your father, you are so strong, and help me lay him on the bed."

And they took hold of him and laid him on the bed. Margit closed his eyes and mouth, stretched him out and folded his hands.

Mother and son stood and looked at him. All they had experienced until then neither seemed so long nor contained so much as this moment. If the devil himself had been there, the Lord had been there also; the encounter had been short. All the past was now settled.

It was a little after midnight, and they had to be there with the dead man until day dawned. Arne crossed the floor, and made a great fire on the hearth, the mother sat down by it. And now, as she sat there, it rushed through her mind how many evil days she had had with Nils; and then she thanked God, in a loud, fervent prayer, for what He had done. "But I have truly had some good days also," said she, and wept as though she regretted her recent thankfulness; and it ended in her taking the greatest blame on herself who had acted contrary to God's commandment, out of love for the departed one, had been disobedient to her mother, and therefore had been punished through this sinful love.

Arne sat down directly opposite her. The mother's eyes were fixed on the bed.

"Arne, you must remember that it was for your sake I bore it all," and she wept, yearning for a loving word in order to gain a support against her own self-accusations, and comfort for all coming time. The boy trembled and could not answer. "You must never leave me," sobbed she.

Then it came suddenly to his mind what she had been, in all this time of sorrow, and how boundless would be her desolation should he, as a reward for her great fidelity, forsake her now.

"Never, never!" he whispered, longing to go to her, yet unable to do so.

They kept their seats, but their tears flowed freely together. She prayed aloud, now for the dead man, now for herself and her boy; and thus, amid prayers and tears, the time passed. Finally she said:—

"Arne, you have such a fine voice, you must sit over by the bed and sing for your father."

And it seemed as though strength was forthwith given him to do so. He got up, and went to fetch a hymn-book, then lit a torch, and with the torch in one hand, the hymn-book in the other, he sat down at the head of the bed and, in a clear voice, sang Kingo's one hundred and twenty-seventh hymn:—

> "Turn from us, gracious Lord, thy dire displeasure!
> Let not thy bloody rod, beyond all measure,
> Chasten thy children, laden with sore oppressions,
> For our transgressions."

CHAPTER V.

ARNE became habitually silent and shy. He tended cattle and made songs. He passed his nineteenth birthday, and still he kept on tending cattle. He borrowed books from the priest and read; but he took interest in nothing else.

The priest sent word to him one day that he had better become a school-master, "because the parish ought to derive benefit from your talents and knowledge." Arne made no reply to this; but the next day, while driving the sheep before him, he made the following song:—

> "Oh, my pet lamb, lift your head,
> Though the stoniest path you tread,
> Over the mountains lonely,
> Still your bells follow only.
> "Oh, my pet lamb, walk with care,
> Lest you spoil all your wool beware,
> Mother must soon be sewing
> Skins for the summer's going.
> "Oh, my pet lamb, try to grow
> Fat and fine wheresoe'er you go!
> Know you not, little sweeting,
> A spring lamb is dainty eating!"

One day in his twentieth year Arne chanced to overhear a conversation between his mother and the wife of the former gard owner; they were disputing about the horse they owned in common.

"I must wait to hear what Arne says," remarked the mother.

"That lazy fellow!" was the reply. "He would like, I dare say, to have the horse go ranging about the woods as he does himself."

The mother was now silent, although before she had been arguing her own case well.

Arne turned as red as fire. It had not occurred to him before that his mother might have to listen to taunting words for his sake, and yet perhaps she had often been obliged to do so. Why had she not told him of this?

He considered the matter well, and now it struck him that his mother scarcely ever talked with him. But neither did he talk with her. With whom did he talk, after all?

Often on Sunday, when he sat quietly at home, he felt a desire to read sermons to his mother, whose eyes were poor; she had wept too much in her day. But he did not have the courage to do so. Many times he had wanted to offer to read aloud to her from his own books, when all was still in the house, and he thought the time must hang heavily on her hands. But his courage failed him for this too.

"It cannot matter much. I must give up tending the herds, and move down to mother."

He let several days pass, and became firm in his resolve. Then he drove the cattle far around in the wood, and made the following song:—

> "The vale is full of trouble, but here sweet Peace may reign;
> Within this quiet forest no bailiffs may distrain;
> None fight, as in the vale, in the Blessed Church's name,
> Yet if a church were here, it would no doubt be just the same.
> "How peaceful is the forest:—true, the hawk is far from kind,
> I fear he now is striving the plumpest sparrow to find;
> I fear yon eagle's coming to rob the kid of breath,
> And yet perchance if long it lived, it might be tired to death.
> "The woodman fells one tree, and another rots away,
> The red fox killed the lambkin white at sunset yesterday;
> The wolf, though, killed the fox, and the wolf itself must die,
> For Arne shot him down to-day before the dew was dry.
> "I'll hie me to the valley back—the forest is as bad;
> And I must see to take good heed, lest thinking drive me mad.
> I saw a boy in my dreams, though where I cannot tell—
> But I know he had killed his father—I think it was in Hell."

He came home and told his mother that she might send out in the parish after another herd-boy; he wanted to manage the gard himself. Thus it was arranged; but the mother was always after him with warnings not to overtax himself with work. She used also to prepare such good meals for him at this time that he often felt ashamed; but he said nothing.

He was working at a song, the refrain of which was "Over the lofty mountains." He never succeeded in finishing it, and this was chiefly because he wanted to have the refrain in every other line; finally he gave it up.

But many of the songs he made got out among the people, where they were well liked; there were those who wished very much to talk with him, especially as they had known him from boyhood up. But Arne was shy of all whom he did not know, and thought ill of them, chiefly because he believed they thought ill of him.

His constant companion in the fields was a middle-aged man, called Upland Knut, who had a habit of singing over his work; but he always sang the same song. After listening to this for a few months, Arne was moved to ask him if he did not know any others.

"No," was the man's reply.

Then after the lapse of several days, once when Knut was singing his song, Arne asked:

"How did you chance to learn this *one*?"

"Oh, it just happened so," said the man.

Arne went straight from him into the house; but there sat his mother weeping, a sight he had not seen since his father's death. He pretended not to notice her, and went toward the door again; but he felt his mother looking sorrowfully after him again and he had to stop.

"What are you crying for, mother?"

For a while his words were the only sound in the room, and therefore they came back to him again and again, so often that he felt they had not been said gently enough. He asked once more:—

"What are you crying for?"

"Oh, I am sure I do not know;" but now she wept harder than ever.

He waited a long time, then was forced to say, as courageously as he could:—

"There must be something you are crying about!"

Again there was silence. He felt very guilty, although *she* had said nothing, and *he* knew nothing.

"It just happened so," said the mother. Presently she added, "I am after all most fortunate," and then she wept.

But Arne hastened out, and he felt drawn toward the Kamp gorge. He sat down to look into it, and while he was sitting there, he too wept. "If I only knew what I was crying for," mused Arne.

Above him, in the new-plowed field, Upland Knut was singing his song:—

> "Ingerid Sletten of Willow-pool
> Had no costly trinkets to wear;
> But a cap she had that was far more fair,
> Although it was only of wool.
> "It had no trimming, and now was old,
> But her mother who long had gone
> Had given it her, and so it shone
> To Ingerid more than gold.
> "For twenty years she laid it aside,
> That it might not be worn away;
> 'My cap I'll wear on that blissful day
> When I shall become a bride.'
> "For thirty years she laid it aside
> Lest the colors might fade away.
> 'My cap I'll wear when to God I pray
> A happy and grateful bride.'
> "For forty years she laid it aside,
> Still holding her mother as dear;
> 'My little cap, I certainly fear
> I never shall be a bride.'
> "She went to look for the cap one day
> In the chest where it long had lain;
> But ah! her looking was all in vain,—
> The cap had moldered away."

Arne sat and listened as though the words had been music far away up the slope. He went up to Knut.

"Have you a mother?" asked he.

"No."

"Have you a father?"

"Oh, no; I have no father."

"Is it long since they died?"

"Oh, yes; it is long since."

"You have not many, I dare say, who care for you?"

"Oh, no; not many."

"Have you any one here?"

"No, not here."

"But yonder in your native parish?"

"Oh, no; not there either."

"Have you not any one at all who cares for you?"

"Oh, no; I have not."

But Arne went from him loving his own mother so intensely that it seemed as though his heart would break; and he felt, as it were, a blissful light over him. "Thou Heavenly Father," thought he, "Thou hast given her to me, and such unspeakable love with the gift, and I put this away from me; and one day when I want it, she will be perhaps no more!" He felt a desire to go to her, if for nothing else only to look at her. But on the way, it suddenly occurred to him: "Perhaps because you did not appreciate her you may soon have to endure the grief of losing her!" He stood still at once. "Almighty God! what then would become of me?"

He felt as though some calamity must be happening at home. He hastened toward the house; cold sweat stood on his brow; his feet scarcely touched the ground. He tore open the passage door, but within the whole atmosphere was at once filled with peace. He softly opened the door into the family-room. The mother had gone to bed, the moon shone full in her face, and she lay sleeping calmly as a child.

CHAPTER VI.

SOME days after this, mother and son, who of late had been more together, agreed to be present at the wedding of some relatives at a neighboring gard. The mother had not been to any party since she was a girl.

They knew few people at the wedding, save by name, and Arne thought it especially strange that everybody stared at him wherever he went.

Once some words were spoken behind him in the passage; he was not sure, but he fancied he understood them, and every drop of blood rushed into his face whenever he thought of them.

He could not keep his eyes off the man who had spoken these words; finally, he took a seat beside him. But as he drew up to the table he thought the conversation took another turn.

"Well, now I am going to tell you a story, which proves that nothing can be buried so deep down in night that it will not find its way into daylight," said the man, and Arne was sure he looked at *him*. He was an ill-favored man, with thin, red hair encircling a great, round brow. Beneath were a pair of very small eyes and a little bottle-shaped nose; but the mouth was very large, with very pale, out-turned lips. When he laughed, he showed his gums. His hands lay on the table: they were clumsy and coarse, but the wrists were slender. He looked sharp and talked fast, but with much effort. People nicknamed him the Rattle-tongue, and Arne knew that tailor Nils had dealt roughly with him in the old days.

"Yes, there is a great deal of wickedness in this world; it comes nearer home to us than we think. But no matter; you shall hear now of an ugly deed. Those who are old remember Alf, Scrip Alf. 'Sure to come back!' said Alf; that saying comes from him; for when he had struck a bargain—and he could trade, that fellow!—he flung his scrip on his back. 'Sure to come back,' said Alf. A devilish good fellow, fine fellow, splendid fellow, this Alf, Scrip Alf!

"Well, there was Alf and Big Lazy-bones—aye, you knew Big Lazy-bones?—he was big and he was lazy too. He looked too long at a shining black horse Scrip Alf drove and had trained to spring like a summer frog. And before Big Lazy-bones knew what he was about, he had given fifty dollars for the nag Big Lazy-bones mounted a carriole, as large as life, to drive like a king with his fifty-dollar horse; but now he might lash and swear until the gard was all in a smoke; the horse ran, for all that, against all the doors and walls that were in the way; he was stone blind.

"Afterwards, Alf and Big Lazy-bones fell to quarreling about this horse all through the parish, just like a couple of dogs. Big Lazy-bones wanted his money back; but you may believe he never got so much as two Danish shillings. Scrip Alf thrashed him until the hair flew. 'Sure to come back,' said Alf. Devilish good fellow, fine fellow, splendid fellow, this Alf—Scrip Alf.

"Well, then, some years passed by without his being heard of again.

"It might have been ten years later that he was published on the church hill; there had been left to him a tremendous fortune. Big Lazy-bones was standing by. 'I knew very well,' said he, 'that it was money that was crying for Scrip Alf, and not people.'

"Now there was a great deal of gossip about Alf; and out of it all was gathered that he had been seen last on this side of Rören, and not on the other. Yes, you remember the Rören road—the old road?

"But Big Lazy-bones had succeeded in rising to great power and splendor, owning both farm and complete outfit.

"Moreover, he had professed great piety, and everybody knew he did not become pious for nothing—any more than other folks do. People began to talk about it.

"It was at this time that the Rören road was to be changed, old-time folks wanted to go straight ahead, and so it went directly over Rören; but we like things level, and so the road now runs down by the river. There was a mining and a blasting, until one might have expected Rören to come tumbling down. All sorts of officials came there, but the amtmand oftenest of all, for he was allowed double mileage. And now, one day while they were digging down among the rocks, some one went to pick up a stone, but got hold of a hand that was sticking out of the rocks, and so strong was this hand that it sent the man who took hold of it reeling backwards. Now he who found this hand was Big Lazy-bones. The lensmand was sauntering about there, he was called, and the skeleton of a whole man was dug out. The doctor was sent for too; he put the bones so skillfully together that now only the flesh was wanting. But people claimed that this skeleton was precisely the same size as Scrip Alf. 'Sure to come back!' said Alf.

"Every one thought it most strange that a dead hand could upset a fellow like Big Lazy-bones, even when it did not strike at all. The lensmand talked seriously to him about it,—of course when no one was by to hear. But then Big Lazy-bones swore until everything grew black about the lensmand.

"'Well, well,' said the lensmand, 'if you had nothing to do with this, you are just the fellow to go to bed with the skeleton to-night; hey?' 'To be sure I am,' replied Big Lazy-bones. And now the doctor jointed the bones firmly together, and placed the skeleton in one of the beds of the barracks. In the other Big Lazy-bones was to sleep, but the lensmand laid down in his gown, close up to the wall. When it grew dark and Big Lazy-bones had to go in to his bed-fellow, it just seemed as though the door shut of itself, and he stood in the dark. But Big Lazy-bones fell to singing hymns, for he had a strong voice. 'Why are you singing hymns?' asked the lensmand, outside of the wall. 'No one knows whether he has had the chorister,' answered Big Lazy-bones. Afterward he fell to praying with all his might. 'Why are you praying?' asked the lensmand, outside of the wall. 'He has no doubt been a great sinner,' answered Big Lazy-bones. Then for a long time all was still, and it really seemed as though the lensmand must be sleeping. Then there was a shriek that made the barracks shake. 'Sure to come back!' An infernal noise and uproar arose: 'Hand over those fifty dollars of mine!' bellowed Big Lazy-bones, and there followed a screaming and a wrestling; the lensmand flung open the door, people rushed in with sticks and stones, and there lay Big Lazy-bones in the middle of the floor, and on him was the skeleton."

It was very still around the table. Finally a man who was about to light his clay pipe, said:—

"He surely went mad after that day."

"He did."

Arne felt every one looking at him, and therefore he could not raise his eyes.

"It is, as I have said," put in the first speaker; "nothing can be buried so deep down in night that it will not find its way into daylight!"

"Well, now I will tell about a son who beat his own father," said a fair, heavily-built man, with a round face. Arne knew not where he was sitting.

"It was a bully of a powerful race, over in Hardanger; he was the ruin of many people. His father and he disagreed about the yearly allowance, and the result of this was that the man had no peace at home or in the parish.

"Owing to this he grew more and more wicked, and his father took him to task. 'I will take rebuke from no one,' said the son. 'From me you shall take it as long as I live,' said the father. 'If you do not hold your tongue I will beat you,' said the son, and sprang to his feet. 'Aye, do so if you dare, and you will never prosper in the world,' answered the father, as he too rose. 'Do you think so?'—and the son rushed at him and knocked him down. But the father did not resist; he crossed his arms and let his son do as he chose with him.

"The son beat him, seized hold of him and dragged him to the door. 'I will have peace in the house!' But when they came to the door, the father raised himself up. 'Not farther than to the door,' said he, 'for so far I dragged my own father.' The son paid no heed to this, but dragged his head across the threshold. 'Not farther than to the door, I say!' Here the old man flung his son down at his feet, and chastised him, just as though he were a child."

"That was badly done," said several.

"Did not strike his father, though," Arne thought some one said; but he was not sure of it.

"Now I shall tell *you* something," said Arne, rising up, as pale as death, not knowing what he was going to say. He only saw the words floating about him like great snow-flakes. "I will make a grasp at them hap-hazard!" and he began.

"A troll met a boy who was walking along a road crying. 'Of whom are you most afraid?' said the troll, 'of yourself, or of others?' But the boy was crying, because he had dreamed in the night that he had been forced to kill his wicked father, and so he answered, 'I am most afraid of myself.' 'Then be at peace with yourself, and never cry any more; for hereafter you shall only be at war with others.' And the troll went his way. But the first person the boy met laughed at him, and so the boy had to laugh back again. The next person he met struck him; the boy had to defend himself, and struck back. The third person he met tried to kill him, and so the boy had to take his life. Then everybody said hard things about him, and therefore he knew only hard things to say of everybody. They locked their cupboards and doors against him, so he had to steal his way to what he needed; he even had to steal his night's rest. Since they would not let him do anything good, he had to do something bad. Then the parish said, 'We must get rid of this boy; he is so bad'; and one fine day they put him out of the way. But the boy had not the least idea that he had done anything wicked, and so after death he came strolling right into the presence of the Lord. There on a bench sat the father he had not slain, and right opposite, on another bench, sat all those who had forced him to do wrong.

"'Which bench are you afraid of?' asked the Lord, and the boy pointed to the long one.

"'Sit down there, beside your father,' said the Lord, and the boy turned to do so.

"Then the father fell from the bench, with a great gash in his neck. In his place there came one in the likeness of the boy, with repentant countenance and ghastly features; then another with drunken face and drooping form; still another with the face of a madman, with tattered clothes and with hideous laughter.

"'Thus it might have been with you,' said the Lord.

"'Can that really be?' replied the boy, touching the hem of the Lord's garment.

"Then both benches fell down from heaven, and the boy stood beside the Lord again and laughed.

"'Remember this when you awaken,' said the Lord, and at that moment the boy awoke.

"Now the boy who dreamed thus is I, and they who tempted him by thinking him wicked are you. I no longer fear myself, but I am afraid of you. Do not stir up my evil passions, for it is doubtful whether I may get hold of the Lord's garment."

He rushed out, and the men looked at each other.

CHAPTER VII.

IT was the next day, in the barn of the same gard. Arne had been drunk for the first time in his life, was ill in consequence of it, and had been lying in the barn almost twenty-four hours. Now, turning over, he had propped himself up on his elbows, and thus talked with himself:—

"Everything I look at becomes cowardice. That I did not run away when I was a boy, was cowardice; that I listened to father rather than to mother, was cowardice; that I sang those wicked songs for him was cowardice; I became a herd-boy, that was from cowardice;—I took to reading—oh, yes! that was from cowardice, too; I wanted to hide away from myself. Even after I was grown up, I did not help mother against father—cowardice; that I did not that night—ugh!—cowardice! I should most likely have waited until *she* was killed. I could not stand it at home after that—cowardice; neither did I go my way—cowardice; I did nothing, I tended cattle—cowardice. To be sure, I had promised mother to stay with her; but I should actually have been cowardly enough to break the promise, had I not been afraid to mingle with people. For I am afraid of people chiefly because I believe they see how bad I am. And it is fear of people makes me speak ill of them—cursed cowardice! I make rhymes from cowardice. I dare not think in a straightforward manner about my own affairs, and so I turn to those of others—and that is to be a poet.

"I should have sat down and cried until the hills were turned into water, that is what I should have done; but instead I say: 'Hush, hush!' and set myself to rocking. And even my songs are cowardly; for were they courageous they would be better. I am afraid of strong thoughts; afraid of everything that is strong; if I do rise up to strength, it is in a frenzy, and frenzy is cowardice. I am more clever, more capable, better informed than I seem to be. I am better than my words; but through cowardice I dare not be what I am. Fy! I drank brandy from cowardice; I wanted to deaden the pain! Fy! it hurt. I drank, nevertheless; drank, nevertheless; drank my father's heart's blood, and yet I drank! The fact is, my cowardice is beyond all bounds; but the most cowardly thing of all is that I can sit here and say all this to myself.

"Kill myself? Pooh! For that I am too cowardly. And then I believe in God,—yes, I believe in God. I long to go to Him; but cowardice keeps me from Him. From so great a change a cowardly person winces. But what if I tried as well as I am able? Almighty God! What if I tried? I might find a cure that even my milksop nature could bear; for I have no bone in me any longer, nor gristle; only something fluid, slush.... What if I tried, with good, mild books,—I am afraid of the strong ones,—with pleasant stories and legends, all such as are mild; and then a sermon every Sunday and a prayer every evening, and regular work, that religion may find fruitful soil; it cannot do so amid slothfulness. What if I tried, dear, gentle God of my childhood,—what if I tried?"

But some one opened the barn-door, and hurried across the floor, pale as death, although drops of sweat rolled down the face. It was Arne's mother. It was the second day she had been seeking for her son. She called his name but did not pause to listen; only called and rushed about, till he answered from the hay-mow, where he was lying. She gave a loud shriek, sprang to the mow more lightly than a boy, and threw herself upon him.

"Arne, Arne, are you here? So I have really found you. I have been looking for you since yesterday; I have searched the whole night! Poor, poor Arne! I saw they had wounded you. I wanted so much to talk with you and comfort you; but then I never dare talk with you! Arne, I saw you drink! O God Almighty! let me never see it again!"

It was long before she could say more. "Jesus have mercy on you, my child; I saw you drink! Suddenly you were gone, drunk and crushed with grief as you were, and I ran around to all the houses. I went far out in the field; I did not find you. I searched in every copse; I asked every one. I was *here*, too, but you did not answer me—Arne, Arne! I walked along the river; but it did not seem to be deep enough anywhere"—She pressed up close to him. "Then it came with such relief to my mind that you might have gone home, and I am sure I was not more than a quarter of an hour getting over the road. I opened the door and looked in every room, and then first remembered that I myself had the key; you could not possibly have entered. Arne, last night I searched along the road on both sides; I dared not go to the Kamp gorge. I know not how I came here; no one helped me; but the Lord put it into my heart that you must be here!"

He tried to soothe her.

"Arne, indeed, you must never drink brandy again."

"No, you may be sure of that."

"They must have been very rough with you. Were they rough with you?"

"Oh, no; it was I who was *cowardly*." He laid stress on the word.

"I cannot exactly understand why they should be rough with you. What was it they did to you? You will never tell me anything," and she began to weep again.

"You never tell me anything, either," said Arne, gently.

"But you are most to blame, Arne. I got so into the habit of being silent in your father's day that you ought to have helped me a little on the way! My God! there are only two of us, and we have suffered so much together!"

"Let us see if we cannot do better," whispered Arne. "Next Sunday I will read the sermon to you."

"God bless you for that! Arne?"

"Yes?"

"I have something I ought to say to you."

"Say it, mother."

"I have sinned greatly against you; I have done something wrong."

"You, mother?" And it touched him so deeply that his own good, infinitely patient mother should accuse herself of having sinned against him, who had never been really good to her, that he put his arm round her, patted her, and burst into tears.

"Yes, I have; and yet I could not help it."

"Oh, you have never wronged me in any way."

"Yes, I have,—God knows it; it was only because I was so fond of you. But you must forgive me; do you hear?"

"Yes, I will forgive you."

"Well, then, I will tell you about it another time; but you will forgive me?"

"Oh, yes, mother!"

"You see, it is perhaps because of this that it has been so hard to talk with you; I have sinned against you."

"I beg of you not to talk so, mother."

"I am happy now, having been able to say so much."

"We must talk more together, we two, mother."

"Yes, that we must; and then you will really read the sermon for me?"

"Yes, I will do so."

"Poor Arne! God bless you!"

"I think it is best for us to go home."

"Yes, we will go home."

"Why are you looking round so, mother?"

"Your father lay in this barn, and wept."

"Father?" said Arne, and grew very pale.

"Poor Nils! It was the day you were christened. Why are you looking round, Arne?"

CHAPTER VIII.

FROM the day that Arne tried with his whole heart to live closer to his mother his relations with other people were entirely changed. He looked on them more with the mother's mild eyes. But he often found it hard to keep true to his resolve; for what he thought most deeply about his mother did not always understand. Here is a song from those days:—

"It was such a pleasant, sunny day,
In-doors I could not think of staying:
I strolled to the wood, on my back I lay,
And rocked what my mind was saying;
But there crawled emmets, and gnats stung there,
The wasps and the clegs brought dire despair.

"'My dear, will you not go out in this pleasant weather?' said mother. She sat singing on the porch.

"It was such a pleasant, sunny day,
In-doors I could not think of staying:
I strayed to a field, on my back I lay,
And sang what my mind was saying;
But snakes came out to enjoy the sun,
Three ells were they long, and away I run.

"'In such pleasant weather we can go barefoot,' said mother, and she pulled off her stockings.

"It was such a pleasant, sunny day,
In-doors I could no longer tarry:
I stepped in a boat, on my back I lay,
The tide did me onward carry;
The sun, though, scorched till my nose was burned;
There's limit to all, so to shore I turned.

"'What fine days these are for drying the hay!' said mother, as she shook it with a rake.

"It was such a pleasant, sunny day,
In-doors I could not think of staying:
I climbed up a tree, and thought there I'd stay,
For there were cool breezes playing.
A grub to fall on my neck then there chanced;
I sprang down and screamed, and how madly I danced.

"'Well, if the cow does not thrive such a day as this, she never will,' said mother, as she gazed up the slope.

"It was such a pleasant, sunny day,
In-doors I could no peace discover:
I made for the force that did loudly play,
For *there* it must surely hover;
But there I drowned while the sun still shone.
If you made this song, it is surely not my own.

"'It would take only about three such sunny days to get everything under cover,' said mother; and off she started to make my bed."

Nevertheless, this companionship with his mother brought every day more and more comfort to Arne. What she did not understand formed quite as much of a tie between them as what she did understand. For the fact of her not comprehending a thing made him think it over oftener, and she grew only the dearer to him because he found her limits on every side. Yes, she became infinitely dear to him.

As a child, Arne had not cared much for nursery stories. Now, as a grown person, he longed for them, and they led to traditions and ancient ballads. His mind was filled with a wonderful yearning; he walked much alone, and many of the places round about, which formerly he had not noticed, seemed strangely beautiful. In the days when he had gone with those of his own age to the priest's to prepare for confirmation, he had often played with them by a large lake below the parsonage, called Black Water, because it was deep and black. He began to think of this lake now, and one evening he wended his way thither.

He sat down behind a copse, just at the foot of the parsonage. This lay on the side of a very steep hill, which towered up beyond until it became a high mountain; the opposite bank was similar, and therefore huge shadows were cast over the lake from both sides, but in its centre was a stripe of beautiful silvery water. All was at rest; the sun was just setting; a faint sound of tinkling bells floated over from the opposite shore; otherwise profound silence reigned. Arne did not look right across the lake, but first turned his eyes toward its lower end, for there the sun was shedding a sprinkling of burning red, ere it departed. Down there the mountains had parted to make room between them for a long, low valley, and against this the waves dashed; and it seemed as though the mountains had gradually sloped together to form a swing in which to rock this valley, which was dotted with its many gards. The curling smoke rose upward, and passed from sight; the fields were green and reeking; boats laden with hay were approaching the landings. Arne saw many people passing to and fro, but could hear no noise. Thence the eye wandered beyond the shore, where God's dark forest alone loomed up. Through the forest and along the lake men had drawn a road, as it were, with a finger, for a winding streak of dust plainly marked its course. This Arne's eye followed until it came directly opposite to where he was sitting; there the forest ended; the mountains made a little more room, and straightways gard after gard lay spread about. The houses were still larger than those at the lower end, were painted red, and had higher windows, which now were in a blaze of light. The hills sparkled in dazzling sunshine; the smallest child playing about could be plainly seen; glittering white sand lay dry on the shore, and upon this little children bounded with their dogs. But suddenly the whole scene became desolate and gloomy; the houses dark red, the meadows dingy green, the sand grayish-white, and the children small clumps: a mass of mist had risen above the mountains, and had shut out the sun. Arne kept his eye fixed on the lake; there he found everything again. The fields were rocking there, and the forest silently joined them; the houses stood looking down, doors open, and children going out and in. Nursery tales and childish things came thronging into his mind, as little fish come after a bait, swim away, come back again, but do not nibble.

"Let us sit down here until your mother comes; the priest's lady will surely get through some time."

Arne was startled; some one had sat down just behind him.

"But I might be allowed to stay just this one night," said a beseeching voice, choked with tears; it seemed to be that of a young girl, not quite grown up.

"Do not cry any more; it is shocking to cry because you must go home to your mother." This last came in a mild voice that spoke slowly and belonged to a man.

"That is not the reason I am crying."

"Why are you crying, then?"

"Because I shall no longer be with Mathilde."

This was the name of the priest's only daughter, and reminded Arne that a peasant girl had been brought up with her.

"That could not last forever, any way."

"Yes, but just one day longer, dear!" and she sobbed violently.

"It is best you should go home at once; perhaps it is already too late."

"Too late? Why so? Who ever heard of such a thing?"

"You are peasant-born, and a peasant you shall remain: we cannot afford to keep a fine lady."

"I should still be a peasant, even if I remained here."

"You are no judge of that."

"I have always worn peasant's clothes."

"It is not that which makes the difference."

"I have been spinning and weaving and cooking."

"It is not *that*, either."

"I can talk just as you and mother do."

"Not that, either."

"Then I do not know what it can be," said the girl, and laughed.

"Time will show. Besides, I am afraid you already have too many ideas."

"Ideas, ideas! You are always saying that. I have no ideas." She wept again.

"Oh, you are a weathercock,—that you are!"

"The priest never said so."

"No, but now *I* say so."

"A weathercock? Who ever heard of such a thing? I will not be a weathercock."

"Come, then, what will you be?"

"What will I be? Did you ever hear the like? I will be nothing."

"Very good, then; be nothing."

Now the girl laughed. Presently she said, gravely, "It is unkind of you to say I am nothing."

"Dear me, when that was what you wanted to be yourself!"

"No, I do not want to be nothing."

"Very good, then; be everything."

The girl laughed. Presently, with a sorrowful voice, "The priest never fooled with me in this way."

"No, he only made a fool of you."

"The priest? You have never been so kind to me as the priest has."

"No, for that would have spoiled you."

"Sour milk can never become sweet."

"Oh, yes, when it is boiled to whey."

Here the girl burst out laughing.

"There comes your mother."

Then she grew sober again.

"Such a long-winded woman as the priest's lady I have never met in all the days of my life," here interposed a shrill, rattling voice. "Make haste, now, Baard. Get up and push the boat out. We will not get home to-night. The lady wished me to see that Eli kept her feet dry. Dear me, you will have to see to that yourself. Every morning she must take a walk, for the sake of her health. It is health, health, from morning till night. Get up, now, Baard, and push out the boat. Just think, I have to set sponge this evening!"

"The chest has not come yet," said he, and lay still.

"But the chest is not to come, either; it is to remain until the first Sunday there is service. Do you hear, Eli? Pick yourself up; take your bundle, and come. Get up, now, Baard!"

She led the way, and the girl followed.

"Come, now, I say,—come now!" resounded from below.

"Have you looked after the plug in the boat?" asked Baard, still without rising.

"Yes, it is there;" and Arne heard her just then hammering it in with the scoop. "But get up, I say, Baard! Surely we are not to stay here all night?"

"I am waiting for the chest."

"But, my dear, bless you, I have told you it is to wait until the first Sunday there is service."

"There it comes," said Baard, and they heard the rattling of a cart.

"Why, I said it was to wait until the first Sunday there is service."

"I said we were to take it along."

Without anything further, the wife hastened up to the cart, and carried the bundle, the lunch-box, and other small things down to the boat. Then Baard arose, went up, and took the chest himself.

But behind the cart there came rushing along a girl in a straw hat, with floating hair; it was the priest's daughter.

"Eli! Eli!" she called, as she ran.

"Mathilde! Mathilde!" Eli answered, and ran toward her.

They met on the hill, put their arms about each other, and wept. Then Mathilde took up something she had set down on the grass: it was a bird-cage.

"You shall have Narrifas; yes, you shall. Mother wishes it, too. You shall, after all, have Narrifas,—indeed, you shall; and then you will think of me. And very often row—row—row over to me," and the tears of both flowed freely.

"Eli! Come, now, Eli! Do not stand there!" was heard from below.

"But I want to go along," said Mathilde. "I want to go and sleep with you to-night!"

"Yes, yes, yes!" and with arms twined about each other's necks they moved down toward the landing.

Presently Arne saw the boat out on the water. Eli stood high on the stern, with the bird-cage, and waved her hand; Mathilde was left behind, and sat on the stone landing weeping.

She remained sitting there as long as the boat was on the water; it was but a short distance across to the red house, as said before; and Arne kept his seat, too. He watched the boat, as she did. It soon passed into the darkness, and he waited until it drew up to the shore: then he saw Eli and her parents in the water; in it he followed them up toward the houses, until they came to the prettiest one of them all. He saw the mother go in first, then the father with the chest, and last of all the daughter, so far as he could judge from their size. Soon after the daughter came out again, and sat down in front of the store-house door, probably that she might gaze over at the other side, where at that moment the sun was shedding its parting rays. But the young lady from the parsonage had already gone, and Arne alone sat watching Eli in the water.

"I wonder if she sees me!"

He got up and moved away. The sun had set, but the sky was bright and clear blue, as it often is of a summer night. Mist from land and water rose and floated over the mountains on both sides; but the peaks held themselves above it, and stood peering at one another. He went higher up. The lake grew blacker and deeper, and seemed, as it were, to contract. The upper valley shortened, and drew closer to the lake. The mountains were nearer to the eye, but looked more like a shapeless mass, for the light of the sun defines. The sky itself appeared nearer, and all surrounding objects became friendly and familiar.

CHAPTER IX.

LOVE and woman were beginning to play a prominent part in his thoughts; in the ancient ballads and stories of the olden times such themes were reflected as in a magic mirror, just as the girl had been in the lake. He constantly brooded over them, and after that evening he found pleasure in singing about them; for they seemed, as it were, to have come nearer home to him. But the thought glided away, and floated back again with a song that was unknown to him; he felt as though another had made it for him,—

"Fair Venevill bounded on lithesome feet
Her lover to meet.
He sang till it sounded afar away,
'Good-day, good-day,'
While blithesome birds were singing on every blooming spray
'On Midsummer Day
There is dancing and play;
But now I know not whether she weaves her wreath or nay.'
"She wove him a wreath of corn-flowers blue:
'Mine eyes so true.'
He took it, but soon away it was flung:
'Farewell!' he sung;
And still with merry singing across the fields he sprung
'On Midsummer Day,' etc.
"She wove him a chain. 'Oh, keep it with care!
'T is made of my hair.'
She yielded him then, in an hour of bliss,
Her pure first kiss;
But he blushed as deeply as she the while her lips met his.
'On Midsummer Day,' etc.
"She wove him a wreath with a lily-band:
'My true right hand.'
She wove him another with roses aglow:
'My left hand, now.'
He took them gently from her, but blushes dyed his brow
'On Midsummer Day,' etc.
"She wove him a wreath of all flowers round:
'All I have found.'
She wept, but she gathered and wove on still:
'Take all you will.'
Without a word he took it, and fled across the hill.
'On Midsummer Day,' etc.
"She wove on, bewildered and out of breath:
'My bridal wreath.'
She wove till her fingers aweary had grown:
'Now put it on.'
But when she turned to see him, she found that he had gone.
'On Midsummer Day,' etc.
"She wove on in haste, as for life and death,
Her bridal wreath;
But the Midsummer sun no longer shone,
And the flowers were gone;
But though she had no flowers, wild fancy still wove on.
'On Midsummer-Day

> There is dancing and play;
> But now I know not whether she weaves her wreath or nay."

It was his own intense melancholy that called forth the first image of love that glided so gloomily through his soul. A twofold longing,—to have some one to love and to become something great,—blended together and became one. At this time he was working again at the song, "Over the lofty mountains," altering it, and all the while singing and thinking quietly to himself, "Surely I will get 'over' some day; I will sing until I gain courage." He did not forget his mother in these his thoughts of roving; indeed, he took comfort in the thought that as soon as he got firm foothold in the strange land, he would come back after her, and offer her conditions which he never could be able to provide for her at home. But in the midst of all these mighty yearnings there played something calm, cheering, refined, that darted away and came again, took hold and fled, and, dreamer that he had become, he was more in the power of these spontaneous thoughts than he himself was aware.

There lived in the parish a jovial man whose name was Ejnar Aasen. When he was twenty years old he had broken his leg; since then he had walked with a cane; but wherever he came hobbling along, there was always mirth afoot. The man was rich. On his property there was a large nut-wood, and there was sure to be assembled, on one of the brightest, pleasantest days in autumn, a group of merry girls gathering nuts. At these nutting-parties he had plenty of feasting for his guests all day, and dancing in the evening. For most of these girls he had been godfather; indeed, he was the godfather of half the parish; all the children called him godfather, and from them every one else, both old and young, learned to do so.

Godfather and Arne were well acquainted, and he liked the young man because of the verses he made. Now godfather asked Arne to come to the nutting-party. Arne blushed and declined; he was not used to being with girls, he said.

"Then you must get used to it," replied godfather.

Arne could not sleep at night because of this; fear and yearning were at war within him; but whatever the result might be, he went along, and was about the only youth among all these girls. He could not deny that he felt disappointed; they were neither those he had sung about, nor those he had feared to meet. There was an excitement and merriment, the like of which he had never known before, and the first thing that struck him was that they could laugh over nothing in the world; and if three laughed, why, then, five laughed, simply because those three laughed. They all acted as though they were members of the same household; and yet many of them had not met before that day. If they caught the bough they were jumping after, they laughed at that, and if they did not catch it, they laughed at that, too. They fought for the hook to draw it down with; those who got it laughed, and those who did not get it, laughed also. Godfather hobbled after them with his cane, and offered all the hindrance in his power. Those whom he caught laughed because he caught them, and those whom he did not catch laughed because he did not catch them. But they all laughed at Arne for being sober, and when he tried to laugh, they laughed, because he was laughing at last.

They seated themselves finally on a large hill, godfather in the centre, and all the girls around him. The hill commanded a fine outlook; the sun scorched; but the girls heeded it not, they sat, casting nut-husks and shells at one another, giving the kernels to godfather. He tried to quiet them at last, striking at them with his cane, as far as he could reach; for now he wanted them to tell stories, above all, something amusing. But to get them started seemed more difficult than to stop a carriage on a hill-side. Godfather began himself. There were many who did not want to listen; for they knew already everything he had to tell; but they all ended by listening attentively. Before they knew what they were about, they sat in the centre, and each took her turn in following his example as best she could. Now Arne was much astonished to find that just in proportion to the noise the girls had made before was the gravity of the stories they now told. Love was the chief theme of these.

"But you, Aasa, have a good one; I remember that from last year," said godfather, turning to a plump girl with a round, pleasant face, who sat braiding the hair of a younger sister, whose head was in her lap.

"Several that are here may know that," said she.

"Well, give it to us anyway," they begged.

"I will not have to be urged long," said she, and, still braiding, she told and sang, as follows:—

"There was a grown-up youth who tended cattle, and he was in the habit of driving his herds upward, along the banks of a broad stream. High up on his way, there was a crag which hung out so far over the stream, that when he stood on it he could call out to any one on the other side. For on the other side of the stream there was a herd-girl whom he could see all day long, but he could not come over to her.

> 'Now, tell me thy name, thou girl that art sitting,
> Up there with thy sheep, so busily knitting?'

he asked, over and over again, for many days, until at last one day there came the answer,—

> 'My name floats about like a duck in wet weather;—
> Come over, thou boy in the cap of brown leather.'

"But this made the youth no wiser than before, and he thought he would pay no further heed to the girl. This was not so easy, though, for, let him drive the cattle where he would, he was always drawn back to the crag. Then the youth grew alarmed, and called over:—

> 'Well, who is your father, and where are you biding?
> On the road to the church I have ne'er seen you riding.'

"The youth more than half believed her, in fact, to be a hulder.

> 'My house is burned down, and my father is drowned,
> And the road to the church-hill I never have found.'

"Now this also made the youth no wiser than before. By day he lingered on the crag, and by night he dreamed that she was dancing around him, and gave him a lash with a great cow's-tail each time he tried to take hold of her. Soon he could not sleep at all, neither could he work, and the poor youth was in a wretched state. Again he called aloud,—

> 'If thou art a hulder, then pray do not spell me,—
> If thou art a maiden, then hasten to tell me?'

"But there came no answer, and then he was sure that this was a hulder. He gave up tending cattle, but it was just as bad, for wherever he went, or whatever he did, he thought of the fair hulder who blew on the horn.

"Then one day, as he stood chopping wood, there came a girl through the yard who actually looked like the hulder. But when she came nearer, it was not she. He thought much about this; then the girl came back, and in the distance it was the hulder, and he ran directly toward her. But the moment he came near her it was not she.

"After this, let the youth be at church, at a dance, at other social gatherings, or where he would, the girl was there too; when he was far from her, she seemed to be the hulder; near to her, she seemed to be another; he asked her then whether it were she or not; but she laughed at him. It is just as well to spring into it as to creep into it, thought the youth, and so he married the girl.

"No sooner was this done than the youth ceased to like the girl. Away from her, he longed for her; but when with her, he longed for one he did not see; therefore he was harsh toward his wife; she bore this and was silent.

"But one day, when he was searching for the horses, he found his way to the crag, and sitting down, he called out,—

> 'Like fairy moonlight to me thou seemest,
> Like midsummer fires from afar thou gleamest.'

"He thought it did him good to sit there, and he fell into the way of going thither whenever anything went amiss at home. The wife wept when she was left alone.

"But one day, while the youth was sitting on the crag, the hulder, her living self, appeared on the opposite side, and blew her horn. He eagerly cried,—

> 'Ah, dear, art thou come! all around thee is shining!
> Ah, blow now again! I am sitting here pining.'

"Then she answered,—

> 'Away from thy mind the dreams I am blowing,—
> The rye is all rotting for want of mowing.'

"But the youth was frightened, and went home again. Before long, though, he was so tired of his wife that he felt compelled to wander off to the wood and take his seat on the crag. Then a voice sang,—

> 'I dreamed thou wast here; ho, hasten to bind me!
> No, not over there, but behind you will find me.'

"The youth started up, looked about him, and espied a green skirt disappearing through the woods. He pursued. Now there was a chase through the woods. As fleet of foot as the hulder was, no mortal could be; he cast steel over her again and again; she ran on the same as before. By and by she began to grow tired. The youth knew this from her foot-fall, though her form convinced him that it was the hulder herself, and none other. 'You shall surely be mine now,' thought the youth, and suddenly flung his arms about her with such force that both he and she rolled far down the hill before they could stop. Then the hulder laughed until the youth thought the mountains fairly rang; he took her on his knee, and she looked so fair, just as he had once thought his wife would look.

"'Oh, dear, who are you that are so fair?' asked the youth, and as he caressed her, he felt that her cheeks were warm and glowing.

"'Why, good gracious, I am your wife,' said she."

The girls laughed, and thought the youth was very foolish. But godfather asked Arne if he had been listening.

"Well, now, I will tell you something," said a little girl, with a little round face, and such a very little nose.

"There was a little youth who wanted very much to woo a little maiden; they were both grown up, yet were both very small indeed. But the youth could not muster up courage enough to begin his wooing. He always joined her after church, but they did not then get beyond the weather in their talk; he sought her at the dances, and he danced her almost to death, but talk with her he could not. 'You must learn to write, and then you will not have to,' said he to himself, and so the youth took to writing; but he never thought he could do well enough, and so he wrote a whole year before he dared think of a letter. Then the trouble was how to deliver it so that no one should see, and he waited until once they chanced to meet alone behind the church.

"'I have a letter for you,' said the youth.

"'But I cannot read writing,' answered the maiden.

"And the youth got no further.

"Then he took service at her father's house, and hung round her the whole day long. Once he came very near speaking to her; he had already opened his mouth, when there flew into it a large fly. 'If only no one comes and takes her from me,' thought the youth. But there came no one to take her from him, because she was so small.

"Some one did come along, though, at last, for he was small too. The youth well knew what he was after, and when he and the girl went up-stairs together, the youth made his way to the key-hole. Now he who was within offered himself. 'Alas, dunce that I am, not to have made more haste!' thought the youth. He who was inside kissed the girl right on the lips. 'That must have tasted good,' thought the youth. But he who was inside had drawn the girl down on his knee. 'What a world we live in!' said the youth, and wept. This the girl heard, and went to the door.

"'What do you want of me, you ugly boy, that you never give me any peace?'

"'I?—I only wanted to ask you if I might be your groomsman.'

"'No; my brothers are to be the groomsmen,' answered the girl,—and slammed the door in his face.

"And the youth got no further."

The girls laughed a great deal at this story, and sent a shower of husks flying round after it.

Godfather now wanted Eli Böen to tell something.

What should it be?

Why, she might tell what she had told over on the hill, when he was with them, the time she gave him the new garters. It was a good while before Eli was ready, for she laughed so hard, but at last she told:—

"A girl and a boy were walking together on the same road. 'Why, see the thrush that is following us,' said the girl. 'It is I whom it is following,' said the boy. 'It is just as likely to be me,' answered the girl. 'That we can soon see,' remarked the boy; 'now you take the lower road, and I will take the upper one, and we will meet at the top of the hill.' They did so. 'Was it not following me?' asked the boy, when they met. 'No, it was following me,' answered the girl. 'Then there must be two.' They walked together again a little way, but then there was only one thrush; the boy thought it flew on his side; but the girl thought it flew on hers. 'The deuce! I'll not bother my head any more about that thrush,' said the boy. 'Nor I either,' replied the girl.

"But no sooner had they said this than the thrush was gone. 'It was on *your* side,' said the boy. 'No, I thank you; I saw plainly it was on *yours*. But there! There it comes again!' called out the girl. 'Yes, it is on *my* side!' cried the boy. But now the girl became angry. 'May all the plagues take me if I walk with you any longer!' and she went her own way. Then the thrush left the boy, and the way became so tedious that he began to call out. She answered. 'Is the thrush with you?' shouted the boy. 'No, it is with you.' 'Oh, dear! You must come here again, then perhaps it will come too.' And the girl came again; they took each other by the hand and walked together. 'Kvit, kvit, kvit, kvit!' was heard on the girl's side. 'Kvit, kvit, kvit, kvit!' was heard on the boy's side. 'Kvit, kvit, kvit, kvit, kvit, kvit, kvit, kvit!' was heard on both sides, and when they came to look, there were a thousand million thrushes round about them. 'Why, how strange!' said the girl, and looked up at the boy. 'Bless you!' said the boy, and caressed the girl."

This story all the girls thought fine.

Then godfather suggested that they should tell what they had dreamed the night before, and he would decide who had had the finest dream.

What! tell their dreams? No, indeed! And there was no end to the laughing and whispering. But then one after another began to remark that she had had such a fine dream last night; others, again, that, fine as the ones they had had, it could not by any means be. And finally, they all were seized with a desire to tell their dreams. But it must not be out loud, it must only be to *one*, and that must by no means be godfather. Arne was sitting quietly on the hill, and so he was the one to whom they dared tell their dreams.

Arne took a seat beneath a hazel, and then she who had told the first story came to him. She thought a long time, and then told as follows:—

"I dreamed I stood by a great lake. Then I saw some one go on the water, and it was one whom I will not name. He climbed up in a large pond-lily, and sat and sang. But I went out on one of those large leaves that the pond-lily has, and which lie and float; on it I wanted to row over to him. But no sooner had I stepped on the leaf than it began to sink with me, and I grew much alarmed and cried. Then he came rowing over to me in the pond-lily, lifted me up to where he sat, and we rowed all over the lake. Was not that a nice dream?"

The little maiden who had told the little story now came.

"I dreamed I had caught a little bird, and I was so happy that I did not want to let it go until I got home. But there I did not dare let go of it, lest father and mother should tell me I must let it out again. So I went up in the garret with it, but there the cat was lurking, and so I could not let go of it there either. Then I did not know what to do, so I took it up in the hay-loft; but, good gracious! there were so many cracks there that it could easily fly away! Well, then I went out in the yard again, and there I thought stood one whom I will not name. He was playing with a large, black dog. 'I would rather play with that bird of yours,' said he, and came close up to me. But I thought I started to run, and he and the large dog after me, and thus I ran all round the yard; but then mother opened the front door, drew me quickly in, and slammed the door. Outside, the boy stood laughing, with his face against the window-pane. 'See, here is the bird!' said he,—and, just think, he really had the bird! Was not that a funny dream?"

Then she came who had told about all the thrushes,—Eli they had called her. It was the Eli he had seen that evening in the boat and in the water. She was the same and yet not the same, so grown-up and pretty she looked as she sat there, with her delicately cut face and slender form. She laughed immoderately, and therefore it was long before she could control herself; but then she told as follows:—

"I had been feeling so glad that I was coming to the nutting-party to-day that I dreamed last night I was sitting here on the hill. The sun shone brightly, and I had a whole lapful of nuts. But then there came a little squirrel, right in among the nuts, and it sat on its hind legs in my lap and ate them all up. Was not that a funny dream?"

Yet other dreams were told Arne, and then he was to decide which was the finest. He had to take a long time to consider, and meanwhile godfather started off with the whole crowd for the gard, and Arne was to follow. They sprang down the hill, formed in a row when they had reached the plain, and sang all the way to the house.

Arne still sat there listening to the singing. The sun fell directly on the group, it shone on their white sleeves; soon they twined their arms about each other's waists; they went dancing across the meadow, godfather after them with his cane, because they were treading down his grass. Arne thought no more about the dreams. Soon he even left off watching the girls; his thoughts wandered far beyond the valley, as did the fine sunbeams, and he sat alone there on the hill and spun. Before he was aware of it, he was entangled in a close web of melancholy; he yearned to break away, and never in the world before so ardently as now. He faithfully promised himself that when he got home he would talk with his mother, come of it what would.

His thoughts grew stronger, and drifted into the song,—

"Over the lofty mountains."

Words had never flowed so readily as now, nor had they ever blended so surely into verse,—they almost seemed like girls sitting around on a hill. He had a scrap of paper about him and placing it on his knee, he wrote. When the song was complete, he arose, like one who was released, felt that he could not see people, and took the forest road home, although he knew that the night, too, would be needed for this. The first time he sat down to rest on the way, he felt for the song, that he might sing it aloud as he went along, and let it be borne all over the parish; but he found he had left it in the place where it was written.

One of the girls went up the hill to look for him, did not find him, but found his song.

CHAPTER X.

To talk with the mother was more easily thought than done. Arne alluded to Kristian and the letter that never came; but the mother went away from him, and for whole days after he thought her eyes looked red. He had also another indication of her feelings, and that was that she prepared unusually good meals for him.

He had to go up in the woods to fetch an armful of fuel one day; the road led through the forest, and just where he was to do his chopping was the place where people went to pick whortleberries in the autumn. He had put down his axe in order to take off his jacket, and was just about beginning, when two girls came walking along with berry pails. It was his wont to hide himself rather than meet girls, and so he did now.

"O dear, O dear! What a lot of berries! Eli, Eli!"

"Yes, dear, I see them."

"Well, then, do not go any farther; here are many pailfuls!"

"I thought there was a rustling in that bush over there!"

"Oh, you must be mad!" and the girls rushed at each other, and put their arms about each other's waists. They stood for a long while so still, that they scarcely breathed.

"It is surely nothing; let us go on picking!"

"Yes, I really think we will."

And so they began to gather berries.

"It was very kind of you, Eli, to come over to the parsonage to-day. Have you anything to tell me?"

"I have been at godfather's."

"Yes, you told me that; but have you nothing about *him*,—you know who?"

"Oh, yes!"

"Oh, oh! Eli, is that so? Make haste; tell me!"

"He has been there again!"

"Oh, nonsense!"

"Yes, indeed; both father and mother pretended they did not see it, but I went up in the garret and hid."

"More, more! Did he follow you there?"

"I think father told him where I was; he is always so provoking."

"And so he came? Sit down, sit down here beside me. Well, so he came?"

"Yes; but he did not say much, for he was so bashful."

"Every word! Do you hear? every word!"

"'Are you afraid of me?' said he. 'Why should I be afraid?' said I. 'You know what it is I want of you,' said he, and sat down on the chest beside me."

"Beside you!"

"And then he put his arm round my waist."

"His arm round your waist? Are you wild?"

"I wanted to get away from him, but he would not let me go. 'Dear Eli,' said he,"—she laughed, and the other girl laughed too.

"Well? well?"

"'Will you be my wife?'"

"Ha, ha, ha!"

"Ha, ha, ha!"

And then both—"Ha, ha, ha, ha, ha, ha!"

Finally, the laughter, too, had to come to an end, and then a long silence ensued. After a while, the first one asked, but softly, "Say,—was it not too bad that he put his arm round your waist?"

Either the other one made no reply to this, or else she spoke in such a low tone that it could not be heard; perhaps, too, she answered only with a smile. Presently the first one asked:—

"Have neither your father nor your mother said anything since?"

"Father came up and looked at me, but I kept hiding; for he laughed every time he saw me."

"But your mother?"

"Why, she said nothing; but she was less harsh than usual."

"Well, you certainly refused him?"

"Of course."

Then there was a long silence again.

"Eli!"

"Well?"

"Do you think any one will ever come that way to me?"

"Yes, to be sure."

"How you talk! O—h! say, Eli? What if he should put his arm round my waist?" She covered her face.

There was much laughter, afterwards whispering and tittering.

The girls soon went away. They had neither seen Arne, nor the axe and the jacket, and he was glad.

Some days later he put Upland Knut in the houseman's place under Kampen.

"You shall no longer be lonely," said Arne.

Arne himself took to steady work. He had early learned to cut with the hand-saw, for he had himself added much to the house at home. Now he wanted to work at his trade, for he knew it was well to have some definite occupation; it was also good for him to get out among people; and so changed had he gradually become, that he longed for this whenever he had kept to himself for a while. Thus it came to pass that he was at the parsonage for a time that winter doing carpentering, and the two girls were often together there. Arne wondered, when he saw them, who it could be that was now courting Eli Böen.

It so happened one day, when they went out for a ride, that Arne had to drive for the young lady of the parsonage and Eli; he had good ears, yet could not hear what they were talking about; sometimes Mathilde spoke to him, at which Eli laughed and hid her face. Once Mathilde asked if it was true he could make verses. "No!" he said promptly: then they both laughed, chattered, and laughed. This made him indignant, and he pretended not to see them.

Once he was sitting in the servants' hall, when there was dancing there. Mathilde and Eli both came in to look on. They were disputing about something in the corner where they stood. Eli would not, but Mathilde would, and she won. Then they both crossed the floor to him, courtesied, and asked whether he could dance. He answered "No," and then they both turned, laughed, and ran away. "They keep up a perpetual laughter," thought Arne, and became sober. But the priest had a little adopted son, about ten or twelve years old, of whom Arne thought a good deal; from this boy Arne learned to dance when no one else was present.

Eli had a little brother about the same age as the priest's adopted son. These two were playmates, and Arne made sleds, skees, and snares for them; and he often talked with them about their sisters, especially about Eli. One day Eli's brother brought word that Arne should not be so careless with his hair.

"Who said so?"

"Eli said so; but I was not to tell that she said so."

Some days after, Arne sent a message to Eli that she should laugh a little less. The boy came back with the reply that Arne should laugh a little more.

Once the boy asked for something he had written. Arne let him have it, and thought no more of it. After a while the boy thought he would please Arne with the tidings that both the girls liked his writing very much.

"Why, have they seen it?"

"Yes, it was for them I wanted it."

Arne asked the boys to bring him something their sisters had written; they did so. Arne corrected the mistakes with a carpenter's pencil. He asked the boys to place the paper where it could easily be found. Afterwards he found it again in his jacket pocket, but at the bottom was written, "Corrected by a conceited fellow!"

The next day Arne finished his work at the parsonage, and set out for home. So gentle as he was this winter, his mother had never seen him since those sorrowful days after his father's death. He read the sermon for her, went with her to church, and was very kind to her. But she well knew it was all to get her consent to journey away from her when spring came. Then one day he had a message from Böen to know if he would come there and do some carpentering.

Arne was quite startled, and answered "Yes," as though he scarcely knew what he was saying. No sooner had the messenger gone than the mother said,

"You may well be astonished! From Böen?"

"Is that so strange?" asked Arne, but did not look at her as he spoke.

"From Böen?" cried the mother, once more.

"Well, why not as well from there as from another gard?" Arne now looked up a little.

"From Böen and Birgit Böen! Baard, who gave your father the blow that was his ruin, and that for Birgit Böen's sake!"

"What do you say?" now cried the youth. "Was that Baard Böen?"

Son and mother stood and looked at each other. Between the two a whole life was unfolded, and this was a moment wherein they could see the black thread which all along had been woven through it. They fell later to talking about the father's proud days, when old Eli Böen herself had courted him for her daughter Birgit, and got a refusal. They went through his whole life just as far as where he was knocked down, and both found out that Baard's fault had been the least. Nevertheless, it was he who had given the father that fatal blow,—he it was.

"Am I not yet done with father?" then thought Arne, and decided at the same moment to go.

When Arne came walking, with the hand-saw on his shoulder, over the ice and up toward Böen, it seemed to him a pretty gard. The house always looked as though it were newly painted; he was a little chilled, and that was perhaps why it seemed so cozy to him. He did not go directly in, but went beyond toward the stable, where a flock of shaggy goats were standing in the snow, gnawing at the bark of some fir branches. A shepherd dog walked to and fro on the barn-bridge, and barked as though the devil himself was coming to the gard; but the moment Arne stood still, he wagged his tail and let him pat him. The kitchen door on the farther side of the house was often opened, and Arne looked down there each time; but it was either the dairy-maid, with tubs and pails, or the cook, who was throwing something out to the goats. Inside the barn they were threshing with frequent strokes, and to the left, in front of the wood-shed, stood a boy chopping wood; behind him there were many layers of wood piled up.

Arne put down his saw and went into the kitchen; there white sand was spread on the floor, and finely cut juniper leaves strewed over it; on the walls glittered copper kettles, and crockery stood in rows. They were cooking dinner. Arne asked to speak with Baard. "Go into the sitting-room," some one said, pointing to the door. He went; there was no latch to the door, but a brass handle; it was cheerful in there, and brightly painted, the ceiling was decorated with many roses, the cupboards were red, with the owner's name in black, the bed-stead was also red, but bordered with blue stripes. By the stove sat a broad-shouldered man, with a mild face, and long, yellow hair; he was putting hoops about some pails; by the long table sat a tall, slender woman, with a high linen cap on her head, and dressed in tight-fitting clothes; she was sorting corn into two heaps. Besides these there were no others in the room.

"Good day, and bless the work!" said Arne, drawing off his hat. Both looked up; the man smiled, and asked who it was.

"It is he who is to do carpentering."

The man smiled more, and said, as he nodded his head and began his work again,—

"Well, then, it is Arne Kampen!"

"Arne Kampen?" cried the wife, and stared fixedly before her.

The man looked up hastily, and smiled again. "The son of tailor Nils," he said, and went on once more with his work.

After a while, the wife got up, crossed the floor to the shelf, turned, went to the cupboard, turned again, and as she at last was rummaging in a table drawer, she asked, without looking up,—

"Is *he* to work *here*?"

"Yes, that he is," said the man, also without looking up. "It seems no one has asked you to sit down," he observed, addressing himself to Arne.

The latter took a seat; the wife left the room, the man continued to work; and so Arne asked if he too should begin.

"Let us first have dinner."

The wife did not come in again; but the next time the kitchen-door opened it was Eli who came. She appeared at first not to notice Arne; when he rose to go to her, she stood still, and half turned to give him her hand, but she did not look at him. They exchanged a few words; the father worked on. Eli had her hair braided, wore a tight-sleeved dress, was slender and straight, had round wrists and small hands. She laid the table; the working-people dined in the next room, but Arne with the family in this one; it so happened that they had their meals separately to-day; usually they all ate at the same table in the large, light kitchen.

"Is not mother coming?" asked the man.

"No, she is up-stairs weighing wool."

"Have you asked her?"

"Yes; but she says she does not want anything."

There was silence for a while.

"But it is cold up-stairs."

"She did not want me to make a fire."

After dinner Arne began work; in the evening he was again with the family in the sitting-room. Then the wife, too, was there. The women were sewing. The husband was busy with some trifles, and Arne helped him; there was a prolonged silence, for Eli, who usually led in conversation, was also silent. Arne thought with dismay that it probably was often thus at his own home; but he realized it now for the first time. Eli drew a long breath at last, as though she had restrained herself long enough, and then she fell to laughing. Then the father also laughed, and Arne, too, thought it was laughable, and joined in. From this time forth they talked of various things; but it ended in Arne and Eli doing most of the talking, the father putting in an occasional word. But once, when Arne had been speaking for some time and happened to look up, he met the eyes of the mother, Birgit; she had dropped her sewing, and sat staring fixedly at him. Now she picked up her work again, but at the first word he spoke she raised her eyes.

Bed-time came, and each one went his way. Arne thought he would notice the dream he had the first night in a new place; but there seemed to be no sense in it. The whole day long he had talked little or none with the master of the gard, but at night it was of him he dreamed. The last thing was that Baard sat playing cards with tailor Nils. The latter was very angry and pale in the face; but Baard smiled and won the game.

Arne remained several days, during which time there was scarcely any talking, but a great deal of work. Not only those in the family room were silent, but the servants, the tenants, even the women. There was an old dog on the gard that barked every time strangers came; but the gard people never heard the dog without saying "hush!" and then he went growling off and laid down again. At home at Kampen there was a large weather-vane on the house, which turned with the wind; there was a still larger vane here, to which Arne's attention was attracted because it did not turn. When there was a strong current of wind, the vane struggled to get loose, and Arne looked at it until he felt compelled to go up on the roof and set the vane free. It was not frozen fast, as he had supposed, but a pin was stuck through it that it might be kept still. This Arne took out and threw down; the pin struck Baard, who came walking along. He glanced up.

"What are you doing there?"

"I am letting loose the vane."

"Do not do so; it makes such a wailing noise when it is in motion."

Arne sat astride the gable.

"That is better than always being quiet."

Baard looked up at Arne, and Arne looked down on Baard; then Baard smiled.

"He who has to howl when he talks had much better keep silent, I am sure."

Now it often happens that words haunt us long after they were uttered, especially when they were the last ones heard. So these words haunted Arne when he crept down in the cold from the roof, and were still with him in the evening when he entered the family room. Eli was standing, in the twilight, by a window, gazing out over the ice which lay glittering beneath the moon's beams. Arne went to the other window and looked out as she was doing. Within all was cozy and quiet, without it was cold; a sharp wind swept across the valley, so shaking the trees that the shadows they cast in the moonlight did not lie still, but went groping about in the snow. From the parsonage there glimmered a light, opening out and closing in, assuming many shapes and colors, as light is apt to do when one gazes at it too long. The mountain loomed up beyond, dark and gloomy, with romance in its depths and moonshine on its upper banks of snow. The sky was aglow with stars, and a little flickering northern light appeared in one quarter of the horizon, but did not spread. A short distance from the window, down toward the lake, there were some trees whose shadows kept prowling from one to the other, but the great ash stood alone, writing on the snow.

The night was very still,—only now and then something shrieked and howled with a long, wailing cry.

"What is that?" asked Arne.

"It is the weather-vane," said Eli; and afterwards she continued more softly, as though to herself: "It must have been let loose."

But Arne had been feeling like one who wanted to speak and could not. Now he said:—

"Do you remember the story about the thrushes that sang?"

"Yes."

"Why, to be sure, it was you who told that one! It was a pretty story."

She said, in so gentle a voice that it seemed as though it were the first time he heard it,—

"I often think there is something that sings when it is quite still."

"That is the good within ourselves."

She looked at him as though there were something too much in that answer; they were both quiet afterward. Then she asked, as she traced figures with one finger on the window-pane,—

"Have you made any songs lately?"

He blushed; but this she did not see. Therefore she asked again,—

"How do you manage when you make songs?"

"Would you really like to know?"

"Oh, yes."

"I hoard up the thoughts that others are in the habit of letting go," he answered evasively.

She was long silent, for she had doubtless been making an attempt at a song or two. What if she had had those thoughts and let them go.

"That is strange," said she, as though to herself, and fell to tracing figures on the pane again.

"I made a song after I had seen you the first time."

"Where was that?"

"Over by the parsonage, the evening you left there. I saw you in the lake."

She laughed, then was still a while.

"Let me hear that song."

Arne had never before done such a thing, but now he sang for her the song,—

"Fair Venevill bounded on lithesome feet, Her lover to meet," etc.

Eli stood there very attentive; she stood there long after he was through. At last she burst out,—

"Oh, how I pity her!"

"It seems as though I had not made it myself," said Arne, for he felt ashamed at having produced it. Nor did he understand how he had come to do so. He remained standing there as if looking after the song.

Then she said: "But I hope it will not be that way with me!"

"No, no, no! I was only thinking of myself."

"Is that to be your fate, then?"

"I do not know; but I felt so at that time—indeed, I do not understand it now, but I once had such a heavy heart."

"That was strange." She began to write on the window-pane again.

The next day, when Arne came in to dinner he went over to the window. Outside it was gray and foggy, within warm and pleasant; but on the window-pane a finger had traced "Arne, Arne, Arne!" and over again "Arne." It was the window where Eli had stood the preceding evening.

But Eli did not come down-stairs that day; she was feeling ill. She had not been well at all of late; she had said so herself, and it was plainly to be seen.

CHAPTER XI.

A DAY later Arne came in and announced that he had just heard on the gard that the priest's daughter Mathilde had that very moment started for the town, as she thought, for a few days, but, as had been decided, to stay there for a year or two. Eli had heard nothing of this before, and fell fainting.

It was the first time Arne had seen any one faint, and he was much alarmed; he ran for the maid-servants, they went for the parents, who started at once; there was confusion all over the gard, even the shepherd-dog barked on the barn-bridge. When Arne came in again, later, the mother was on her knees by the bedside, the father stood holding the sick girl's head. The maid-servants were running, one for water, another for medicine, which was kept in a cupboard, a third was unfastening Eli's jacket at the throat.

"The Lord help and bless us!" cried the mother. "It was certainly wrong that we said nothing to her; it was you, Baard, who would have it so. The Lord help and bless us!"

Baard made no reply.

"I said we had better tell her; but nothing is ever done as I wish. The Lord help and bless us! You are always so underhand with her, Baard; you do not understand her; you do not know what it is to care for any one."

Baard still made no reply.

"She is not like others; they can bear sorrow, but it completely upsets her, poor thing, she is so slight. And especially now when she is not well at all. Wake up again, my dear child, and we will be kind to you! Wake up again, Eli, my own dear child, and do not grieve us so!"

Then Baard said,—

"You are either too silent, or you talk too much;" and he looked over at Arne, as though he did not wish him to hear all this, but to go away. As the maid-servants remained in the room, however, Arne thought that he might stay, too, but he walked to the window. Now the patient rallied so far that she could look about her and recognize people; but at the same moment her memory returned; she shrieked "Mathilde," burst into hysterical weeping, and sobbed until it was painful to be in the room with her. The mother tried to comfort her; the father had placed himself where he might be seen; but the sick girl waved her hand to them. "Go away!" she cried, "I do not love you!"

"Good gracious! You do not love your parents?" said the mother.

"No! You are cruel to me, and take from me the only joy I have!"

"Eli, Eli! Do not speak such dreadful words!" begged the mother.

"Yes, mother," she shrieked; "now I must say it! Yes, mother! You want me to marry that hateful man, and I will not. You shut me up here, where I am never happy, except when I am to go out! You take Mathilde from me, the only person I love and long for in the world! O God, what will become of me when Mathilde is no longer here—especially now that I have so much, so much I cannot manage when I have no one to talk with?"

"But you really have so seldom been with her lately," said Baard.

"What did that matter when I had her over at the window yonder!" answered the sick girl, and she cried in such a child-like way, that it seemed to Arne as though he had never before seen anything like it.

"But you could not see her there," said Baard.

"I could see the gard," answered she; and the mother added, hotly,—

"You do not understand such things at all."

Then Baard said no more.

"Now I can never go to the window!" said Eli. "I went there in the morning when I got up; in the evening I sat there in the moonlight: and I went there when I had no one else to go to. Mathilde, Mathilde!"

She writhed in the bed, and again gave way to hysterical weeping. Baard sat down on a stool near by and watched her.

But Eli did not get over this as soon as her parents may have expected. Toward evening they first saw that she was likely to have a protracted illness, the seeds of which had doubtless been gathering for some time; and Arne was called in to assist in carrying her up to her own room. She was unconscious, and lay very pale and still; the mother sat down beside her; the father stood at the foot of the bed and looked on; afterwards he went down to his work. Arne did the same; but that night when he went to bed he prayed for her, prayed that she, young and fair as she was, might have a happy life, and that no one might shut out joy from her.

The following day the father and mother sat talking together when Arne came in; the mother had been shedding tears. Arne asked how things were going; each waited for the other to speak, and therefore it was long before he got a reply; but finally the father said, "It looks pretty bad."

Later, Arne heard that Eli had been delirious the whole night; or, as the father said, had been raving. Now she lay violently ill, knew no one, would not take any food, and the parents were just sitting there, deliberating whether they should call in the doctor. When, later, they went up-stairs to the sick girl, and Arne was left alone again, he felt as though life and death were both up there, but he sat outside.

In a few days, though, she was better. Once when the father was keeping watch, she took a fancy to have Narrifas, the bird which Mathilde had given her, standing beside the bed. Then Baard told her the truth, that in all this confusion the bird had been forgotten, and that it was dead. The mother came just while Baard was telling this, and she burst out in the door,—"Good gracious me! how heedless you are, Baard, to tell such things to that sick child! See, now she is fainting away again; Heaven forgive you for what you have done!"

Every time the patient revived she screamed for the bird, said that it would never go well with Mathilde since Narrifas was dead, wanted to go to her, and fell into a swoon again. Baard stood there and looked on until he could bear it no longer; then he wanted to help wait on her too; but the mother pushed him away, saying that she would take care of the sick girl alone. Then Baard gazed at both of them a long while, after which he put on his cap with both hands, turned, and went out.

The priest and his wife came over later; for the illness had taken fresh hold on Eli, and had become so bad that they knew not whether it was tending to life or death.

Both the priest and the priest's wife reasoned with Baard, and urged that he was too harsh with Eli; they had heard about the bird, and the priest told him bluntly that such conduct was rough; he would take the child home to the parsonage, he said, as soon as she had improved enough to be moved. The priest's wife finally would not even see Baard; she wept and sat with the sick girl, sent for the doctor, took his orders herself, and came over several times each day to carry them out. Baard went wandering about from place to place in the yard, going chiefly where he could be alone; he would often stand still for a long time, then straighten his cap with both hands, and find something to do.

The mother did not speak to him any more; they scarcely looked at each other. Baard went up to the sick girl's room several times each day; he took off his shoes at the bottom of the stairs, laid down his hat outside of the door, which he opened cautiously. The moment he came in, Birgit would turn as though she had not seen him, and then sit as before, with her head in her hand, looking straight before her and at the sick girl. The latter lay still and pale, unconscious of anything about her. Baard would stand a while at the foot of the bed, look at them both, and say nothing. Once, when Eli moved as though about to awaken, he stole away directly as softly as he had come.

Arne often thought that words had now been exchanged between husband and wife and parents and child, which had been long brewing, and which would not soon be forgotten. He longed to get away, although he would have liked first to know how Eli's illness would end. But this he could learn even if he left, he thought; he went, therefore, to Baard, and said that he wished to go home; the work for which he had come was done. Baard sat outside on the chopping-block when Arne came to tell him this. He sat digging in the snow with a pin. Arne knew the pin; for it was the same that had fastened the weather vane. Without looking up Baard said,—

"I suppose it is not pleasant to be here now, but I feel as if I did not want you to leave."

Baard said no more; nor did Arne speak. He stood a while, then went away and busied himself with some work, as though it were decided that he should remain.

Later, when Arne was called in to dinner, Baard still sat on the chopping-block. Arne went over to him and asked how Eli was getting on.

"I think she must be pretty bad to-day," said Baard; "I see that mother is crying."

Arne felt as though some one had bidden him to sit down, and he sat down directly opposite Baard on the end of a fallen tree.

"I have been thinking of your father these days," said Baard, so unexpectedly, that Arne could make no reply. "You know, I dare say, what there was between us two?"

"Yes, I know."

"Ah, well, you only know half, as might have been expected, and naturally lay the greatest blame on me."

Arne answered presently: "You have doubtless settled that matter with your God, as my father has surely done."

"Ah, well, that may be as one takes it," answered Baard. "When I found this pin again, it seemed so strange to me that you should come here and loosen the vane. Just as well first as last, thought I." He had taken off his cap and sat looking into it.

Arne did not yet understand that by this Baard meant that he now wanted to talk with him about his father. Indeed, he still did not understand it, even after Baard was well under way, so little was this like the man. But what had been working before in his mind, he gradually comprehended as the story advanced, and if he had hitherto had respect for this blundering but thoroughly good man, it was not lessened now.

"I might have been about fourteen years old," said Baard, then paused, as he did from time to time throughout his whole story, said a few words more, and paused again in such a manner that his story bore the strong impress of having every word weighed. "I might have been about fourteen years old when I became acquainted with your father, who was of the same age. He was very wild, and could not bear to have any one above him. And what he never could forgive me was, that I was the head of the class when we were confirmed, and he was number two. He often offered to wrestle with me, but nothing ever came of it; I suppose because we were neither of us sure of ourselves. But it is strange that he fought every day, and no misfortune befell him; the one time I tried my hand it turned out as badly as could be; but, to be sure, I had waited a long time too.

"Nils fluttered about all the girls and they about him. There was only one I wanted, but he took her from me at every dance, at every wedding, at every party; it was the one to whom I am now married.... I often had a desire, as I sat looking on, to make a trial of strength with him, just because of this matter; but I was afraid I might lose, and I knew that if I did so I should lose her too. When the others had gone, I would lift the weights he had lifted, kick the beam he had kicked, but the next time he danced away from me with the girl, I did not dare tackle him, although it chanced once, as Nils stood joking with her right before my face, that I laid hold of a good sized fellow who stood by and tossed him against the beam, as though for sport. Nils grew pale, too, that time.

"If he had only been kind to the girl; but he was false to her, and that evening after evening. I almost think she cared more for him each time. Then it was that the last thing happened. I thought now it must either break or bear. Nor did the Lord want him to go about any longer; and therefore he fell a little more heavily than I had intended. I never saw him after that."

They sat for a long time silent. Finally Baard continued:—

"I offered myself again. She answered neither yes nor no; and so I thought she would like me better afterwards. We were married; the wedding took place down in the valley, at the house of her father's sister, who left her property to her; we began with plenty, and what we then had has increased. Our gards lay alongside of each other, and they have since been thrown into one, as had been my idea from boyhood up. But many other things did not turn out as I had planned."

He was long silent; Arne thought, for a while, he was weeping; it was not so. But he spoke in a still gentler tone than usual when he began again,—

"At first she was quiet and very sorrowful. I had nothing to say for her comfort, and so I was silent. Later, she fell at times into that commanding way that you have perhaps noticed in her; yet it was after all a change, and so I was silent then, too. But a truly happy day I have not had since I was married, and that has been now for twenty years."

He broke the pin in two; then he sat a while looking at the pieces.

"When Eli grew to be a large girl, I thought she would find more happiness among strangers than here. It is seldom that I have insisted on anything; it usually has been wrong, too, when I have; and so it was with this. The mother yearned for her child, although only the lake parted them; and at last I found out that Eli was not under the best influences over at the parsonage, for there is really much good-natured nonsense about the priest's family; but I found it out too late. Now she seems to care for neither father nor mother."

He had taken his cap off again; now his long hair fell over his eyes; he stroked it aside, and put on his cap with both hands, as though about to go; but as in getting up he turned toward the house, he stopped and added, with a glance at the chamber window,—

"I thought it was best she and Mathilde should not bid each other good-by; but that proved to be wrong. I told her the little bird was dead, for it was my fault, you know, and it seemed to me right to confess; but that was wrong too. And so it is with everything. I have always meant to do the best, but it has turned out to be the worst; and now it has gone so far that they speak ill of me, both wife and daughter, and I am alone here."

A girl now called out to them that dinner was getting cold. Baard got up. "I hear the horses neighing," said he, "somebody must have forgotten them;" and with this he went over to the stable to give them hay.

CHAPTER XII.

ELI was very weak after her illness; the mother sat over her night and day, and was never down-stairs; the father made his usual visits up to the sick-room in his stocking feet, and leaving his cap outside of the door. Arne was still at the gard; he and the father sat together of evenings; he had come to think a good deal of Baard, who was a well-educated man, a deep thinker, but seemed to be afraid of what he knew. Arne helped him to get things right in his mind and told him much that he did not know before, and Baard was very grateful.

Eli could now sit up at intervals; and as she began to improve she took many fancies into her head. Thus it was that one evening as Arne sat in the room below Eli's chamber singing songs in a loud voice, the mother came down and brought word that Eli wanted to know if he would not come up-stairs and sing that she might hear the words. Arne had undoubtedly been singing for Eli all along; for when her mother gave him the message he grew red, and rose as though he would deny what he had been doing, although no one had charged him with it. He soon recovered his composure, and said evasively that there was very little he could sing. But the mother remarked that it did not seem so when he was alone.

Arne yielded and went. He had not seen Eli since the day he had helped carry her up-stairs; he felt that she must now be greatly changed, and was almost afraid to see her. But when he softly opened the door and entered, it was so dark in the room that he saw no one. He paused on the threshold.

"Who is it?" asked Eli, in a clear, low voice.

"It is Arne Kampen," he answered, in a guarded tone, that the words might fall softly.

"It was kind of you to come."

"How are you now, Eli?"

"Thank you, I am better."

"Please sit down, Arne," said she, presently, and Arne felt his way to a chair that stood by the foot of the bed. "It was so nice to hear you singing, you must sing a little for me up here."

"If I only knew anything that was suitable."

There was silence for a moment; then she said, "Sing a hymn," and he did so; it was a part of one of the confirmation hymns. When he had finished, he heard that she was weeping, and so he dared not sing any more; but presently she said, "Sing another one like that," and he sang another, choosing the one usually sung when the candidates for confirmation are standing in the church aisle.

"How many things I have thought of while I have been lying here," said Eli. He did not know what to answer, and he heard her weeping quietly in the dark. A clock was ticking on the wall, it gave warning that it was about to strike, and then struck; Eli drew a long breath several times as though she would ease her breast, and then she said, "One knows so little. I have known neither father nor mother. I have not been kind to them,—and that is why it gives me such strange feelings to hear that confirmation hymn."

When people talk in the dark, they are always more truthful than when they see each other face to face; they can say more, too.

"It is good to hear your words," replied Arne; he was thinking of what she had said when she was taken ill.

She knew what he meant; and so she remarked, "Had not this happened to me, God only knows how long it might have been before I had found my mother."

"She has been talking with you now?"

"Every day; she has done nothing else."

"Then, I dare say, you have heard many things."
"You may well say so."
"I suppose she talked about my father?"
"Yes."
"Does she still think of him?"
"She does."
"He was not kind to her."
"Poor mother!"
"He was worst of all, though, to himself."
Thoughts now arose that neither liked to express to the other. Eli was the first to break the silence.
"They say you are like your father."
"So I have heard," he answered, evasively.
She paid no heed to the tone of his voice; and so, after a while, she continued, "Could he, too, make songs?"
"No."
"Sing a song for me,—one you have made yourself."
But Arne was not in the habit of confessing that the songs he sang were his own. "I have none," said he.
"Indeed you have, and I am sure you will sing them for me if I ask it."
What he had never done for others, he now did for her. He sang the following song:—

> "The tree's early leaf-buds were bursting their brown:
> 'Shall I take them away?' said the frost, sweeping down.
> 'No, dear; leave them alone
> Till blossoms here have grown,'
> Prayed the tree, while it trembled from rootlet to crown.
> "The tree bore its blossoms, and all the birds sung:
> 'Shall I take them away?' said the wind, as it swung.
> 'No, dear; leave them alone
> Till berries here have grown,'
> Said the tree, while its leaflets all quivering hung.
> "The tree bore its fruit in the midsummer glow:
> Said the girl, 'May I gather thy berries or no?'
> 'Yes, dear, all thou canst see;
> Take them; all are for thee,'
> Said the tree, while it bent down its laden boughs low."

This song almost took her breath away. He, too, sat there silent, after he was through, as though he had sung more than he cared to say to her.

Darkness has great power over those who are sitting in it and dare not speak; they are never so near each other as then. If Eli only turned, only moved her hand on the bed-cover, only breathed a little more heavily than usual, Arne heard it. "Arne, could not you teach me to make songs?"
"Have you never tried?"
"Yes, these last few days I have; but I have not succeeded."
"Why, what did you want to have in them?"
"Something about my mother, who cared so much for your father."
"That is a sad theme."
"I have cried over it, too."
"You must not think of what you are going to put in your songs; it comes of itself."
"How does it come?"
"As other precious things, when you least expect it."
They were both silent.
"I wonder, Arne, that you are longing to go away when you have so much that is beautiful within yourself."
"Do *you* know that I am longing?"
She made no reply to this, but lay still a few moments, as though in thought.
"Arne, you must not go away!" said she, and this sent a glow through him.
"Well, sometimes I have less desire to go."
"Your mother must be very fond of you. I should like to see your mother."
"Come over to Kampen when you are well."

And now all at once he pictured her sitting in the cheerful room at Kampen, looking out on the mountains; his chest began to heave, the blood rushed to his head. "It is warm in here," said he, getting up.

She heard this. "Are you going, Arne?" asked she, and he sat down again.

"You must come over to us often; mother likes you so much."

"I should be glad to come myself; but I must have some errand, though."

Eli was silent for a while, as if she were considering something. "I believe," said she, "that mother has something she wants to ask of you."

He heard her turn in bed. There was no sound to be heard, either in the room or outside, save the ticking of the clock on the wall. At last she burst out,—

"How I wish it were summer!"

"That it were summer?" and there rose up in his mind, blended with fragrant foliage and the tinkling of cattle bells, shouts from the mountains, singing from the valleys, Black Water glittering in the sunshine, the gards rocking in it, and Eli coming out and sitting down, as she had done that evening long ago.

"If it were summer," said she, "and I were sitting on the hill, I really believe I could sing a song."

He laughed and asked: "What would it be about?"

"Oh, something easy, about—I do not know myself—"

"Tell me, Eli!" and he sprang up in delight; then, recollecting himself, he sat down again.

"No; not for all the world!" She laughed.

"I sang for you when you asked me."

"Yes, you did; but—no! no!"

"Eli, do you think I would make sport of your little verse?"

"No; I do not think so, Arne; but it is not anything I have made myself."

"It is by some one else, then."

"Yes, it just came floating of itself."

"Then you can surely repeat it to me."

"No, no; it is not altogether that either, Arne. Do not ask me any more." She must have hid her face in the bedclothes, for the last words seemed to come out of them.

"You are not as kind to me now, Eli, as I was to you!" he said, and rose.

"Arne, there is a difference—you do not understand me—but it was—I do not know myself—another time—do not be angry with me, Arne! Do not go away from me!" She began to weep.

"Eli, what is the matter?" He listened. "Are you feeling ill?" He did not think she was. She still wept; he thought that he must either go forward or backward.

"Eli!"

"Yes!"

They both spoke in whispers.

"Give me your hand!"

She did not answer; he listened intently, eagerly, felt about on the coverlid, and clasped a warm little hand that lay outside.

They heard steps on the stairs, and let go of each other's hands. It was Eli's mother, who was bringing in a light. "You are sitting quite too long in the dark," said she, and put the candlestick on the table. But neither Eli nor Arne could bear the light; she turned toward the pillow, he held his hand up before his eyes. "Oh, yes; it hurts the eyes a little at first," said her mother; "but that will soon pass off."

Arne searched on the floor for the cap he did not have with him, and then he left the room.

The next day he heard that Eli was coming down-stairs for a little while after dinner. He gathered together his tools, and said good-by. When she came down he was gone.

CHAPTER XIII.

SPRING comes late in the mountains. The mail that passed along the highway during the winter three times a week, in April only passes once, and the inhabitants know then that in the outside world the snow is thawed, the ice broken; that the steamers are running, and the plow put into the earth. Here, the snow still lies three ells deep; the cattle low in the stalls, and the birds come, but hide themselves, shivering with the cold. Occasionally some traveler arrives, saying he has left his cart down in the valley, and he has flowers with him, which he shows,—he has gathered them by the wayside. Then the people become restless, go about talking together, look at the sky and down in the valley, wondering how much the sun gains each day. They strew ashes on the snow, and think of those who are now gathering flowers.

It was at such a time that old Margit Kampen came walking up to the parsonage and asked to speak with "father." She was invited into the study, where the priest, a slender, fair-haired, gentle-looking man with large eyes and spectacles, received her kindly, knew who she was, and asked her to sit down.

"Is it now something about Arne again?" he inquired, as though they had often talked together about him.

"Heaven help me!" said Margit; "it is never anything but good I have to say of him, and yet my heart is so heavy." She looked very sad as she spoke.

"Has that longing come back again?" asked the priest.

"Worse than ever," said the mother. "I do not even believe he will stay with me until spring comes to us here."

"And yet he has promised never to leave you."

"True enough; but, dear me, he must manage for himself now; when the mind is set upon going, go one must, I suppose. But what will become of me?"

"Still I will believe, as long as possible, that he will not leave you," said the priest.

"Certainly not; but what if he should never be content at home? I would then have it on my conscience that I stood in his way. There are times when I think I ought to ask him myself to go away."

"How do you know that he is longing now more than ever?"

"Oh, from many things. Since midwinter he has not worked out in the parish a single day. On the other hand, he has made three trips to town, and has stayed away a long while each time. He scarcely ever talks now when he is working, as he often used to do. He sits for hours by the little window up-stairs, and looks out over the mountains in the direction of the Kamp gorge; he sometimes stays there a whole Sunday afternoon, and often when it is moonlight, he sits there far into the night."

"Does he never read to you?"

"Of course he reads and sings to me every Sunday; but he always seems in a hurry, except now and then, when he overdoes it."

"Does he never come and talk with you?"

"He often lets so long a time pass without saying a word, that I cannot help crying when I sit alone. Then, I suppose, he sees this, for he begins to talk with me, but it is always about trifles, never about anything serious."

The priest was walking up and down; now he stopped and asked, "Why do you not speak with him about it?"

It was some time before she made any reply to this; she sighed several times, she looked first downward, then on either side,—she folded the handkerchief she carried.

"I came here to-day to have a talk with father about something that lies heavily on my heart."

"Speak freely, it will lighten the burden."

"I know that; for I have now dragged it along alone these many years, and it grows heavier each year."

"What is it, my good woman?"

There was a brief pause; then she said, "I have sinned greatly against my son,"—and she began to cry.

The priest came close up to her. "Confess it to me," said he, "then we will together pray God that you may be forgiven."

Margit sobbed and dried her eyes, but began to weep afresh as soon as she tried to speak, and this was repeated several times. The priest comforted her, and said she surely could not have been guilty of anything very sinful, that she was no doubt too strict with herself, and so on. Margit wept, however, and could not muster the courage to begin until the priest had seated himself by her side and spoken kindly words to her. Then, in broken sentences, she faltered forth her confession:—

"He had a hard time of it when he was a boy, and so his mind became bent on travel. Then he met Kristian, he who has grown so very rich over there where they dig for gold. Kristian gave Arne so many books that he ceased to be like the rest of us; they sat together in the long evenings, and when Kristian went away, my boy longed to follow him. Just at that time, though, his father fell down dead, and Arne promised never to leave me. Yet I was like a hen that had brooded a duck's egg, when the young duckling had burst the shell, he wanted to go out on the great water, and I remained on the bank screaming. If he did not actually go away himself, his heart went in his songs, and every morning I thought I would find his bed empty.

"Then there came a letter for him from a far-off country, and I knew it must be from Kristian. God forgive me, I hid it! I thought that would be the end of the matter, but still another one came, and as I had kept the first from him, I had to keep the second one too. But, indeed, it seemed as though they would burn a hole in the chest where they lay, for my thoughts would go there from the time I opened my eyes in the morning until I closed them at night. And you never have known anything so bad as this, for there came a third! I stood holding it in my hand for a quarter of an hour; I carried it in my bosom for three days, weighing within me whether I should give it to him or lay it away with the others, but perhaps it would have power to lure the boy away from me, and I could not help it, I put the letter away with the others. Now I went about in sorrow every day, both because of those that were in the chest and because of the new ones that might come. I was afraid of every person who came to our house. When we were in the house together, and there came a knock at the door, I trembled, for it might be a letter, and then *he* would get it. When he was out in the parish, I kept thinking at home that now perhaps he would get a letter while he was away, and that it might have something in it about those that had come before. When he was coming home, I watched his face in the distance, and, dear me! how happy I was when I saw him smiling, for then I knew he had no letter! He had grown so handsome, too, just like his father, but much fairer and more gentle-looking. And then he had such a voice for singing: when he sat outside of the door at sunset, singing toward the mountain ridge and listening for the echo, I felt in my heart that I never could live without him! If I only saw him, or if I knew he was anywhere around, and he looked tolerably happy, and would only give me a word now and then, I wished for nothing more on earth, and would not have had a single tear unshed.

"But just as he seemed to be getting on better, and to be feeling more at ease among people, there came word from the parish post-office that a fourth letter had now come, and that in it there were two hundred dollars! I thought I should drop right down on the spot where I stood. What should I do now? The letter, of course, I could get out of the way; but the money? I could not sleep for several nights on account of this money. I kept it up in the garret for a while, then left it in the cellar behind a barrel, and once I was so beside myself that I laid it in the window so that he might find it. When I heard him coming, I took it away again. At last I found a way, though. I gave him the money and said it had been out at interest since mother's lifetime. He spent it in improving the gard, as had been in my own mind, and there it was not lost. But then it happened that same autumn that he sat one evening wondering why Kristian had so entirely forgotten him.

"Now the wound opened afresh, and the money burned. What I had done as a sin, and the sin had been of no use to me!

"The mother who has sinned against her own child is the most unhappy of all mothers,—and yet I only did it out of love. So I shall be punished, I dare say, by losing what is dearest to me. For since midwinter he has taken up again the tune he sings when he is longing; he has sung it from boyhood up, and I never hear it without growing pale. Then I feel I could give up all for him, and now you shall see for yourself,"—she took a scrap of paper out of her bosom, unfolded it, and gave it to the priest,—"here is something he is writing at from time to time; it certainly belongs to that song. I brought it with me, for I cannot read such fine writing; please see if there is anything in it about his going away."

There was only one stanza on this paper. For the second one there were half and whole lines here and there, as if it were a song he had forgotten, and was now calling to mind again, verse by verse. The first stanza ran,—

> "Oh, how I wonder what I should see
> Over the lofty mountains!
> Snow here shuts out the view from me,
> Round about stands the green pine-tree.
> Longing to hasten over—
> Dare it become a rover?"

"Is it about his going away?" asked Margit, her eyes fixed eagerly on the priest's face.

"Yes, it is," answered he, and let the paper drop.

"Was I not sure of it! Ah, me! I know that tune so well!" She looked at the priest, her hands folded, anxious, intent, while tear after tear trickled down her cheek.

But the priest knew as little how to advise as she. "The boy must be left to himself in this matter," said he. "Life cannot be altered for his sake, but it depends on himself whether he shall one day find out its meaning. Now it seems he wants to go away to do so."

"But was it not just so with the old woman?" said Margit.

"With the old woman?" repeated the priest.

"Yes; she who went out to fetch the sunshine into her house, instead of cutting windows in the walls."

The priest was astonished at her shrewdness; but it was not the first time she had surprised him when she was on this theme; for Margit, indeed, had not thought of anything else for seven or eight years.

"Do you think he will leave me? What shall I do? And the money? And the letters?" All this crowded upon her at once.

"Well, it was not right about the letters. You can hardly be justified in withholding from your son what belonged to him. It was still worse, however, to place a fellow Christian in a bad light when it was not deserved, and the worst of all was that it was one whom Arne loved and who was very fond of him in return. But we will pray God to forgive you, we will both pray."

Margit bowed her head; she still sat with her hands folded.

"How earnestly I would pray him for forgiveness, if I only knew he would stay!" She was probably confounding in her mind the Lord and Arne.

The priest pretended he had not noticed this. "Do you mean to confess this to him at once?" he asked.

She looked down and said in a low tone, "If I dared wait a little while I should like to do so."

The priest turned aside to hide a smile, as he asked, "Do you not think your sin becomes greater the longer you delay the confession?"

Both hands were busied with her handkerchief: she folded it into a very small square, and tried to get it into a still smaller one, but that was not possible.

"If I confess about the letters, I am afraid he will leave me."

"You dare not place your reliance on the Lord, then?"

"Why, to be sure I do!" she said hurriedly; then she added softly, "But what if he should go anyway?"

"So, then, you are more afraid of Arne's leaving you than of continuing in sin?"

Margit had unfolded her handkerchief again; she put it now to her eyes, for she was beginning to weep.

The priest watched her for a while, then he continued: "Why did you tell me all this when you did not mean it to lead to anything?" He waited a long time, but she did not answer. "You thought, perhaps, your sin would become less when you had confessed it?"

"I thought that it would," said she, softly, with her head bowed still farther down on her breast.

The priest smiled and got up. "Well, well, my dear Margit, you must act so that you will have joy in your old age."

"If I could only keep what I have!" said she; and the priest thought she dared not imagine any greater happiness than living in her constant state of anxiety. He smiled as he lit his pipe.

"If we only had a little girl who could get hold of him, then you should see that he would stay!"

She looked up quickly, and her eyes followed the priest until he paused in front of her.

"Eli Böen? What"—

She colored and looked down again; but she made no reply.

The priest, who had stood still, waiting, said finally, but this time in quite a low tone "What if we should arrange it so that they should meet oftener at the parsonage?"

She glanced up at the priest to find out whether he was really in earnest. But she did not quite dare believe him.

The priest had begun to walk up and down again, but now he paused. "See here, Margit! When it comes to the point, perhaps this was your whole errand here to-day, hey?"

She bowed her head far down, she thrust two fingers into the folded handkerchief, and brought out a corner of it. "Well, yes, God help me; that was exactly what I wanted."

The priest burst out laughing, and rubbed his hands. "Perhaps that was what you wanted the last time you were here, too?"

She drew the corner of the handkerchief farther out; she stretched it and stretched it. "Since you ask me, yes, it was just that."

"Ha, ha, ha, ha! Ah, Margit! Margit! We shall see what we can do; for, to tell the truth, my wife and daughter have for a long time had the same thoughts as you."

"Is it possible?" She looked up, at once so happy and so bashful, that the priest had his own delight in her open, pretty face, in which the childlike expression had been preserved through all sorrow and anxiety.

"Ah, well, Margit, you, whose love is so great, will, I have no doubt, obtain forgiveness, for love's sake, both from your God and from your son, for the wrong you have done. You have probably been punished enough already in the continual, wearing anxiety you have lived in; we shall, if God is willing, bring this to a speedy end, for, if He *wishes* this, He will help us a little now."

She drew a long sigh, which she repeated again and again; then she arose, gave her thanks, dropped a courtesy, and courtesied again at the door. But she was scarcely well outside before a change came over her. She cast upward a look beaming with gratitude, and she hurried more and more the farther she got away from people, and lightly as she tripped down toward Kampen that day, she had not done for many, many years. When she got so far on her way that she could see the thick smoke curling gayly up from the chimney, she blessed the house, the whole gard, the priest, and Arne,—and then remembered that they were going to have smoked beef for dinner,—her favorite dish!

CHAPTER XIV.

KAMPEN was a beautiful gard. It lay in the midst of a plain, bordered below by the Kamp gorge, and above by the parish road; on the opposite side of the road was a thick wood, a little farther beyond, a rising mountain ridge, and behind this the blue, snow-capped mountains. On the other side of the gorge there was also a broad mountain range, which first entirely surrounded Black Water on the side where Böen lay, then grew higher toward Kampen, but at the same time turned aside to make way for the broad basin called the lower parish, and which began just below, for Kampen was the last gard in the upper parish.

The front door of the dwelling-house was turned toward the road; it was probably about two thousand paces off; a path with leafy birch-trees on either side led thither. The wood lay on both sides of the clearing; the fields and meadows could, therefore, extend as far as the owners themselves wished; it was in all respects a most excellent gard. A little garden lay in front of the house. Arne managed it as his books directed. To the left were the stables and other out-houses. They were nearly all new built, and formed a square opposite the dwelling-house. The latter was painted red, with white window-frames and doors, was two stories high, thatched with turf, and small shrubs grew on the roof; the one gable had a vane staff, on which turned an iron cock, with high, spread tail.

Spring had come to the mountain districts. It was a Sunday morning; there was a little heaviness in the air, but it was calm and without frost; mist hung over the wood, but Margit thought it would lift during the day. Arne had read the sermon for his mother and sung the hymns, which had done him good; now he was in full trim, ready to go up to the parsonage. He opened the door, the fresh perfume of the leaves was wafted toward him, the garden lay dew-covered and bowed by the morning mist, and from the Kamp gorge there came a roaring, mingled at intervals with mighty booms, making everything tremble to the ear and the eye.

Arne walked upward. The farther he got from the force the less awe-inspiring became its roar, which finally spread itself like the deep tones of an organ over the whole landscape.

"The Lord be with him on his way!" said the mother, opening the window and looking after him until the shrubbery closed about him. The fog lifted more and more, the sun cut through it; there was life now about the fields and in the garden; all Arne's work sprouted out in fresh growth, sending fragrance and joy up to the mother. Spring is lovely to those who long have been surrounded by winter.

Arne had no fixed errand at the parsonage, but still he wanted to learn about the papers he and the priest took together. Recently he had seen the names of several Norsemen who had done remarkably well digging gold in America, and among them was Kristian. Now Arne had heard a rumor that Kristian was expected home. He could, no doubt, get information about this at the parsonage,—and if Kristian had really returned, then Arne would go to him in the interval between spring and haying time. This was working in his mind until he had advanced so far that he could see Black Water, and Böen on the other side. The fog had lifted there, too; the sun was playing on the green, the mountain loomed up with shining peak, but the fog was still lying in its lap; the wood darkened the water on the right side, but in front of the house the ground was more flat, and its white sand glittered in the sunshine. Suddenly his thoughts sped to the red-painted building with white doors and window-frames, that he had had in mind when he painted his own. He did not remember those first gloomy days he had passed there; he only thought of that bright summer they had both seen, he and Eli, up beside her sick-bed. Since then he had not been to Böen, nor would he go there, not for the whole world. If only his thoughts barely touched on it, he grew crimson and abashed; and yet this happened again every day, and many times a day. If there was anything which could drive him out of the parish, it was just this!

Onward he went, as though he would flee from his thoughts, but the farther he walked the nearer opposite Böen he came, and the more he gazed upon it. The fog was entirely gone, the sky clear from one mountain outline to the other, the birds sailed along and called aloud to one another in the glad sunny air, the fields responded with millions of flowers; the Kamp force did not here compel gladness to bow the knee in submission and awe, but buoyant and frolicsome it tumbled over, singing, twinkling, rejoicing without end!

Arne had walked till he was in a glowing heat; he flung himself down in the grass at the foot of a hill, looked over towards Böen, then turned away to avoid seeing it. Presently he heard singing above him, pure and clear, as song had never sounded to him before; it floated out over the meadow, mingled with the chattering of the birds, and he was scarcely sure of the tune before he recognized the words too,—for the tune was his favorite one, and the words were those that had been working in his mind from the time he was a boy, and forgotten the same day he had brought them forth! He sprang up as though he would catch them, then paused and listened; here came the first stanza, here came the second, here came the third and the fourth of his own forgotten song streaming down to him:—

> "Oh, how I wonder what I should see
> Over the lofty mountains!
> Snow here shuts out the view from me,
> Round about stands the green pine-tree,
> Longing to hasten over—
> Dare it become a rover?
>
> "Soars the eagle with strong wing play,
> Over the lofty mountains;
> Rows through the young and vigorous day
> Sating his courage in quest of prey;
> When he will swooping downward,
> Tow'rd far-off lands gazing onward.
>
> "Leaf-heavy apple, wilt thou not go
> Over the lofty mountains?
> Forth putting buds 'mid summer's glow,
> Thou wilt till next time wait, I know;
> All of these birds art swinging,
> Knowing not what they're singing.
>
> "He who for twenty years longed to flee
> Over the lofty mountains,
> Nor beyond them can hope to see,
> Smaller each year feels himself to be;
> Hears what the birds are singing,
> Thou art with confidence swinging.
>
> "Bird, with thy chatt'ring, what wouldst thou here
> Over the lofty mountains?
> Fairer the lands beyond must appear,
> Higher the trees and the skies far more clear.
> Wouldst thou but longing be bringing,
> Bird, but no wings with thy singing?
>
> "Shall I the journey never take
> Over the lofty mountains?
> Must my poor thoughts on this rock-wall break?
> Must it a dread, ice-bound prison make,
> Shutting at last in around me,
> Till for my tomb it surround me?
>
> "Forth will I! forth! Oh, far, far away,
> Over the lofty mountains!
> I will be crushed and consumed if I stay;
> Courage tow'rs up and seeks the way,
> Let it its flight now be taking,
> Not on this rock-wall be breaking!
>
> "One day I know I shall wander afar
> Over the lofty mountains!
> Lord, my God, is thy door ajar?
> Good is thy home where the blessed are;
> Keep it though closed a while longer,
> Till my deep longing grow stronger."

Arne stood still until the last verse, the last word, had died away. Again he heard the birds sporting and twittering, but he knew not whether he himself dared stir. Find out who had been singing, though, he must; he raised his foot and trod so carefully that he could not hear the grass rustle. A little butterfly alighted on a flower, directly at his feet, had to start up again, flew only a little piece farther, had to start up again, and so on all over the hill as he crept cautiously up. Soon he came to a leafy bush, and cared to go no farther, for now he could see. A bird flew up from the bush, gave a startled cry and darted over the sloping hill-side, and then she who was sitting within view looked up. Arne stooped far down, holding his breath, his heart throbbing so wildly that he heard its every beat, listening, not daring to move a leaf, for it was, indeed, she,—it was Eli whom he saw!

After a long, long while, he looked up just a little, and would gladly have drawn a step nearer but he thought the bird might perhaps have its nest under the bush, and was afraid he would tread on it. He peered out between the leaves as they blew aside and closed together again. The sun shone directly on her. She wore a black dress without sleeves, and had a boy's straw hat perched lightly on her head, and slanting a little to one side. In her lap lay a book, and on it a profusion of wild flowers; her right hand was dreamily toying with them; in her left, which rested on her knee, her head was bowed. She was gazing in the direction of the bird's flight, and it really seemed as though she had been weeping.

Anything more lovely Arne had neither seen nor dreamed of in his whole life; the sun, too, had scattered all its gold over her and the spot where she was sitting, and the song still floated about her, although its last notes had long since been sung, so that he thought, breathed—aye, even his heart beat in time to it.

She took up the book and opened it, but soon closed it again and sat as before, beginning to hum something else. It was, "The tree's early leaf-buds were bursting their brown." He knew it at once, although she did not quite remember either the words or the tune, and made many mistakes. The stanza she knew best was the last one, therefore she often repeated it; but she sang it thus:—

> "The tree bore its berries, so mellow and red:
> 'May I gather thy berries?' a sweet maiden said.
> 'Yes, dear; all thou canst see;
> Take them; all are for thee;'
> Said the tree—trala-lala, trala, lala—said."

Then suddenly she sprang up, scattering the flowers all around her, and sang aloud, so that the tune, as it quivered through the air, could easily be heard all the way over to Böen. And then she ran away. Should he call after her? No! There she went skipping over the hills, singing, trolling; her hat fell off, she picked it up again; and then she stood still in the midst of the tallest grass.

"Shall I call after her? She is looking round!"

He quickly stooped down. It was a long while before he dared peep forth again; at first he only raised his head; he could not see her: then he drew himself up on his knees, and still could not see her; finally, he got all the way up. No, she was gone! He no longer wanted to go to the parsonage. He wanted nothing!

Later he sat where she had been sitting, still sat there until the sun drew near the meridian. The lake was not ruffled by a single ripple; the smoke from the gards began to curl upward; the land-rails, one after another, had ceased their call; the small birds, though, continued their sportive gambols, but withdrew to the wood; the dew was gone and the grass looked sober; not a breath of wind stirred the leaves; it was about an hour from noon. Arne scarcely knew how it was that he found himself seated there, weaving together a little song; a sweet melody offered itself for it, and into a heart curiously full of all that was gentle, the tune came and went until the picture was complete. He sang the song calmly as he had made it:—

> "He went in the forest the whole day long,
> The whole day long;
> For there he had heard such a wonderful song,
> A wonderful song.
> "He fashioned a flute from a willow spray,
> A willow spray,
> To see if within it the sweet tune lay,
> The sweet tune lay.
> "It whispered and told him its name at last,
> Its name at last;
> But then, while he listened, away it passed,
> Away it passed.
> "But oft when he slumbered, again it stole,
> Again it stole,
> With touches of love upon his soul,
> Upon his soul.
> "Then he tried to catch it, and keep it fast,
> And keep it fast;
> But he woke, and away in the night it passed,
> In the night it passed.

"'My Lord, let me pass in the night, I pray,
In the night, I pray;
For the tune has taken my heart away,
My heart away.'
"Then answered the Lord, 'It is thy friend
It is thy friend,
Though not for an hour shall thy longing end,
Thy longing end;
"'And all the others are nothing to thee,
Nothing to thee,
To this that thou seekest and never shalt see,
Never shalt see.'"

CHAPTER XV.

IT was a Sunday evening in midsummer; the priest had returned from church, and Margit had been sitting with him until it was nearly seven o'clock. Now she took her leave, and hastened down the steps and out into the yard, for there she had just caught sight of Eli Böen, who had been playing for some time with the priest's son and her own brother.

"Good evening!" said Margit, standing still, "and God bless you all!"

"Good evening!" replied Eli, blushing crimson, and showing a desire to stop playing, although the boys urged her to continue; but she begged to be excused, and they had to let her go for that evening.

"It seems to me I ought to know you," said Margit.

"That is quite likely," was the reply.

"This surely never can be Eli Böen?"

Yes, it was she.

"Oh, dear me! So you are Eli Böen! Yes, now I see you are like your mother."

Eli's auburn hair had become unfastened, so that it floated carelessly about her; her face was as hot and as red as a berry, her bosom heaved, she could not speak, and laughed because she was so out of breath.

"Yes, that is the way with young people."

Margit looked at Eli with satisfaction as she spoke.

"I suppose you do not know me?"

Eli had no doubt wanted to ask who she was, but could not command the courage to do so, because the other was so much older than she; now she said that she did not remember having seen her before.

"Well, to be sure, that is scarcely to be expected; old folks seldom get out. You may perhaps know my son, Arne Kampen. I am his mother." She stole a sly glance, as she spoke, at Eli, on whom these words wrought a considerable change. "I am inclined to think he worked over at Böen once, did he not?"

Yes, it was Eli's impression, too, that he had done so.

"The weather is fine this evening. We turned our hay to-day, and got it in before I left home; it is really blessed weather."

"There will surely be a good hay-harvest this year," Eli observed.

"Yes, you may well say so. I suppose everything looks splendidly over at Böen."

"They are through harvesting there."

"Oh, of course; plenty of help, stirring people. Are you going home this evening?"

No, she did not intend to do so. They talked together about one thing and another and gradually became so well acquainted that Margit felt at liberty to ask Eli to walk a short distance with her.

"Could you not keep me company a few steps?" said she. "I so seldom find any one to talk with, and I dare say it will make no difference to you."

Eli excused herself because she had not her jacket on.

"Well, I know, it is really a shame to ask such a thing the first time I meet a person; but then one has to bear with old folks."

Eli said she was quite willing to go, she only wanted to fetch her jacket.

It was a close-fitting jacket; when it was hooked, she looked as if she wore a complete dress; but now she only fastened the two lowest hooks, she was so warm. Her fine linen had a small turned down collar, and was fastened at the throat with a silver button, in the form of a bird with outspread wings. Such a one tailor Nils had worn the first time Margit Kampen had danced with him.

"What a handsome button," she remarked, looking at it.

"My mother gave it to me," said Eli.

"Yes, so I thought," and Margit helped the girl adjust it as she spoke.

Now they walked on along the road. The new-mown hay was lying about in heaps. Margit took up a handful, smelled it, and thought it was good. She asked about the live stock at the parsonage, was led thereby to inquire about that at Böen, and then told how much they had at Kampen.

"The gard has prospered finely of late years, and it can be made as much larger as we ourselves wish. It feeds twelve milch cows now, and could feed more; but Arne reads a great many books, and manages according to them, and so he must have his cows fed in a first-rate way."

Eli made no reply to all this, as was quite natural; but Margit asked her how old she was. She was nineteen.

"Have you taken any part in the house-work? You look so dainty, I suppose it has not been much."

Oh, yes, she had helped in various ways, especially of late.

"Well, it is a good thing to become accustomed to a little of everything; if one should get a large house of one's own, there might be many things to be done. But, to be sure, when one finds good help already in the house, it does not matter so very much."

Eli now thought she ought to turn back, for they had gone far beyond the parsonage lands.

"It will be some time yet before the sun sets; it would be kind if you would chat with me a little longer." And Eli went on.

Then Margit began to talk about Arne. "I do not know if you are very well acquainted with him. He can teach you something about everything. Bless me! how much that boy has read!"

Eli confessed that she was aware he had read a great deal.

"Oh, yes; that is really the least that can be said of him. Why, his conduct to his mother all his days is something far beyond that. If the old saying is true, that one who is good to his mother is sure to be good to his wife, the girl Arne chooses will not have very much to grumble about. What is it you are looking for, child?"

"I only lost a little twig I had in my hand."

They were both silent after this, and walked on without looking at each other.

"He has such strange ways," began the mother, presently; "he was so often frightened when he was a child that he got into the habit of thinking everything over to himself, and such folks never know how to put themselves forward."

Now Eli insisted on turning back, but Margit assured her that it was only a short distance now to Kampen, and see Kampen she must, as she was so near. But Eli thought it was too late that day.

"There is always some one who can go home with you," said Margit.

"No, no," promptly replied Eli, and was about to leave.

"To be sure, Arne is not at home," said Margit; "so it will not be he; but there will be sure to be some one else."

Now Eli had less objection to going; besides, she wanted very much to see Kampen. "If only it does not grow too late," said she.

"Well, if we stand here much longer talking about it, I suppose it may grow too late," and they went on.

"You have read a great deal, I dare say; you who were brought up at the priest's?"

Yes, Eli had read a good deal.

"That will be useful," Margit suggested, "when you are married to one who knows less than you."

Eli thought she would never be married to such a person.

"Ah, well, it would perhaps not be best either; but in this parish there is so little learning."

Eli asked where the smoke rising yonder in the wood came from.

"It comes from the new houseman's place belonging to Kampen. A man called Upland Knut lives there. He was alone in the world, and so Arne gave him that place to clear. He knows what it is to be lonely, my poor Arne."

Soon they reached an ascent whence the gard could be seen. The sun shone full in their faces; they held up their hands to shade their eyes and gazed down at Kampen. It lay in the midst of a plain, the houses red painted and with white window-frames; the grass in the surrounding meadows had been mown, the hay might still be seen in heaps here and there, the grain-fields lay green and rich among the pale meadows; over by the cow-house all was stir and bustle: the cows, sheep, and goats were just coming home, their bells were tinkling the dogs were barking, the milk-maids shouting, while above all rose with awful din the roar of the force in the Kamp gorge. The longer Eli looked, the more completely this grand tune filled her ears, and at last it seemed so appalling to her that her heart throbbed wildly; it roared and thundered through her head until she grew bewildered, and at the same time felt so warm and tender that involuntarily she took such short, hesitating steps, that Margit begged her to walk a little faster.

She started. "I never heard anything like that waterfall," said she; "I am almost afraid of it."

"You will soon get used to it," said the mother; "at last you would even miss it if you could not hear it."

"Dear me! do you think so?" cried Eli.

"Well, you will see," said Margit, smiling.

"Come now, let us first look at the cattle," she continued, turning off from the main road. "These trees on each side Nils planted. He wanted to have everything nice, Nils did, that is what Arne likes too; look! there you can see the garden my boy has laid out."

"Oh, how pretty!" cried Eli, running over to the garden fence. She had often seen Kampen, but only from a distance, where the garden was not visible.

"We will look at that after a while," said Margit.

Eli hastily glanced through the windows, as she went past the house; there was no one inside.

They stationed themselves on the barn-bridge and watched the cows as they passed lowing into the stable. Margit named them to Eli, told how much milk each one gave, and which of them calved in the summer, which did not. The sheep were counted and let into the fold; they were of a large, foreign breed; Arne had raised them from two lambs he got from the south. "He gives much attention to all such things, although you would not think it of him."

They now went into the barn, and examined the hay that had been housed, and Eli had to smell it—"for such hay is not to be found everywhere." Margit pointed through the barn-hatch over the fields, and told what each one yielded and how much was sown of each kind of seed.

They went out toward the house; but Eli, who had not spoken a word in reply to all that had been said, as they passed by the garden, asked if she might go into it. And when leave had been given her to go, she begged to be allowed to pluck a flower or two. There was a little bench away in one corner; she went and sat down on it, only to try it, apparently, for she rose at once.

"We must hurry now, if we would not be too late," said Margit, standing in the door. And now they went in. Margit asked Eli if she should offer her some refreshments on this her first visit; but Eli blushed and hastily declined. Then the girl's eyes wandered all around the room they had entered; it was where the family sat in the day-time, and the windows opened on the road; the room was not large but it was cozy, and there was a clock and a stove in it. On the wall hung Nils's fiddle, dingy and old, but with new strings. Near it also hung a couple of guns belonging to Arne, an English angling-rod and other rare things which the mother took down and showed to Eli, who looked at them and handled them. The room was without paint, for Arne disliked it; nor was there any painting in the room looking toward the Kamp gorge, with the fresh green mountains directly opposite and the blue ones in the background; this latter room,—which was in the new part of the building, as was the entire half of the house it was in,—was larger and prettier than the first. The two smaller rooms in the wing were painted, for there the mother was to live when she was old, and Arne had brought a wife into the house. They went into the kitchen, the store-house, the bake-house, Eli spoke not a single word; indeed, she viewed everything about her as though from afar off; only when anything was held out for her inspection she touched it, but very daintily. Margit, who had kept up an unbroken stream of chatter the whole way, now led her into the passage again; they must go and take a look up-stairs.

There also were well-arranged rooms, corresponding with those below; but they were new and had scarcely yet been occupied, except one, which looked toward the gorge. In these rooms were kept all sorts of articles which were not in daily household use. Here hung a whole lot of robes, together with other bedclothes; the mother took hold of them, lifted them up, and now and then insisted on having Eli do the same. Meanwhile, it actually seemed as though the young girl were gaining a little courage, or else her pleasure in these things increased; for to some of them she went back a second time, asked questions about them, and became more and more interested.

Finally the mother said, "Now at last we will go into Arne's own room;" and then they went into the room overlooking the Kamp gorge. Once more the awful din of the force smote upon their ears, for the window was open. They were up so high that they could see the spray rising between the mountains, but not the force itself, save in one spot farther on, where a fragment had fallen from the cliff, just where the torrent, with all its might, took its final leap into the depths below. Fresh turf covered the upward turned side of this fallen piece of rock, a few fir cones had buried themselves in it, and sent forth a growth of trees with their roots in the crevices. The wind had tugged at and shaken the trees, the force had washed them so completely that there was not a branch four ells from the roots; they were crooked in the knees, their boughs knotted and gnarled, yet they kept their footing, and shot far up between the rocky walls. This was the first thing Eli noticed from the window; the next, the dazzling white snow-capped peaks rising above the green mountains. She turned her eyes away, let them wander over the peaceful, fruitful fields, and finally about the room where she stood; the roar of the force had hitherto prevented this.

How calm and cheerful it was within, compared with the scene without. She did not look at any single article, because one blended into the other, and most of them were new to her, for Arne had centred his affections in this room, and, simple as it was, it was artistic in almost every particular. It seemed as though the sound of his songs came floating toward her, while she stood there, or as though he himself smiled at her from every object. The first thing her eyes singled out in the room, was a broad, handsomely carved book-shelf. There were so many books on it that she did not believe the priest had more. A pretty cabinet was the next thing she noticed. Here he kept many rare things, his mother said. Here, too, he had his money, she added, in a whisper. They had twice had property left to them, she told afterwards; they would have one more inheritance besides, if things went as they should. "But money is not the best thing in the world, after all. Arne may get what is far better."

There were many little trinkets in the room which were interesting to examine, and Eli looked at them all, as happy as a child.

Margit patted her on the shoulder, saying, as she looked brightly into her eyes, "I have never seen you before to-day, my child, but I am already very fond of you." Before Eli had time to feel embarrassed, Margit pulled at her dress, and said, quite softly, "You see that little red chest; there is something nice in that, I can tell you."

Eli looked at the chest: it was a small, square one, which she at once longed to call her own.

"Arne does not want me to know what is in that chest," whispered the mother, "and he always keeps the key hid." She walked up to some clothes hanging on the wall, took down a velvet waistcoat, felt in the watch-pocket, and there found the key. "Come, now, you shall see," she whispered.

Eli did not think the mother was doing quite right, but women are women,—and these two now crossed softly over to the chest and knelt in front of it. As the mother raised the lid, so pleasant a perfume rose toward them that Eli clapped her hands even before she had seen anything. Spread over the top was a kerchief which the mother took away. "Now you shall see," she whispered, as she took up a fine, black silk neckerchief, such a one as men do not wear. "It looks just as if it were for a girl," said the mother. "Here is another," she added.

Eli could not help taking hold of this; but when the mother insisted upon trying it on her, she declined, and hung her head. The mother carefully folded them up again.

"See!" she then said, taking up some pretty silk ribbons; "everything here looks as if it were meant for a girl."

Eli grew red as fire, but not a sound escaped her; her bosom heaved, her eyes had a shy look, otherwise she stood immovable.

"Here are more things still!" The mother took hold of a beautiful black dress pattern, as she spoke. "This is fine goods, I dare say," said she, as she held it up to the light.

Eli's hands trembled, when the mother asked her to take hold of the cloth, she felt the blood rushing to her head; she would gladly have turned away, but this was not easy to do.

"He has bought something every time he has been to town," said the mother.

Eli could scarcely control herself any longer; her eyes roamed about the chest from one article to another, and back again to the dress goods; she, in fact, saw nothing else. But the mother persisted, and the last thing she took up was wrapped in paper; they slowly unwrapped it; this became attractive again. Eli grew eager; it proved to be a pair of small shoes. They had never seen anything like these, either one of them; the mother wondered how they could be made. Eli said nothing, but when she went to touch the shoes, all her fingers made marks on them; she felt so ashamed that she came very near bursting into tears. She longed most of all to take her leave, but she dared not speak, nor dare she do anything to make the mother look up.

Margit was wholly occupied with her own thoughts. "Does it not look just as if he had bought them one by one for some one he had not the courage to give them to?" said she, as she put each article back in the place where she had found it; she must have had practice in so doing. "Now let us see what there is in this little box," she added, softly opening it, as though now they were going to find something really choice.

There lay a buckle, broad enough for a belt; that was the first thing she showed Eli; the next was two gold rings, tied together, and then the girl caught sight of a velvet hymn-book with silver clasps; further she could not look, for on the silver of the book was engraved, in small letters, "Eli, Baardsdatter Böen."

Margit called her attention to something, got no reply, but saw that tear after tear was trickling down on the silk kerchief, and spreading over it. Then the mother laid down the brooch she held in her hand, closed the little box, turned round and clasped Eli in her arms. The daughter wept on her shoulder, and the mother wept over her, but neither of them spoke a word.

A little while later, Eli was walking alone in the garden: the mother had gone into the kitchen to prepare something good for supper, for now Arne would soon be home. By and by, Margit came out into the garden to look for her young friend, and found her sitting writing in the sand. As the mother joined her, Eli quickly smoothed the sand over what she had written,—looked up and smiled; she had been weeping.

"There is nothing to cry about, my child," said Margit, and gave her a pat.

They saw a black object moving between the bushes on the road. Eli stole into the house, the mother followed her. Here a bounteous repast was awaiting them: cream pudding, smoked meat, and cakes; but Eli had no eyes for these things; she crossed the floor to the corner where the clock stood, sat down on a chair close to the wall, and trembled if she only heard a cat stir. The mother stood by the table. Firm steps were heard on the flag-stones, a short, light step in the passage, the door was gently opened, and Arne came in.

The first object his eyes lighted on was Eli in the clock corner; he let go of the door and stood still. This made Eli yet more embarrassed; she got up, regretted at once having done so, and turned towards the wall.

"Are *you* here?" said Arne, softly, blushing crimson.

Eli shaded her eyes with one hand, as one does when the sun shines too full in the face.

"How—?" He could get no farther, but he advanced a step or two.

She put her hand down again, turned toward him, then, bowing her head, she burst into tears.

"God bless you, Eli!" said he, and drew his arm around her; she nestled close up to him. He whispered something in her ear; she made no reply, but clasped her hands about his neck.

They stood thus for a long time, and not a sound was heard save the roar of the force, sending forth its eternal song. By and by some one was heard weeping near the table. Arne looked up: it was the mother.

"Now I am sure you will not leave me, Arne," said she, approaching him. She wept freely, but it did her good, she said.

When Arne and Eli walked home together in the bright summer evening, they did not talk much about their new-born happiness. They let Nature herself take the lead in the conversation,—so quiet, bright, and grand, she seemed, as she accompanied them. But it was on his way back to Kampen from this their first summer-night's walk, with his face turned toward the rising sun, that he laid the foundations of a poem, which he was then in no frame of mind to construct, but which, later, when it was finished, became for a while his daily song. It ran thus:—

> "I hoped to become something great one day;
> I thought it would be when I got away.
> Each thought that my bosom entered
> On far-off journeys was centred.
> A maiden then into my eyes did look;
> My rovings soon lost their pleasure.
> The loftiest aim my heart can brook
> Is her to proclaim my treasure.
> "I hoped to become something great one day;
> I thought it would be when I got away.
> To meet with the great in learning
> Intensely my heart was yearning.
> She taught me, she did, for she spoke a word:
> 'The best gift of God's bestowing
> Is not to be called a distinguished lord,
> But ever a *man* to be growing.
> "I hoped to become something great one day;
> I thought it would be when I got away.
> My home seemed so cold, neglected,
> I felt like a stranger suspected.
> When her I discovered, then love I did see
> In every glance that found me;
> Wherever I turned friends waited for me,
> And life became new around me."

There came afterwards many a summer evening walk, followed by many a song. One of these must be recorded:—

> "The cause of this all is beyond my knowing;
> No storm there has been and no floods have been flowing.
> A sparkling and glittering brook, it would seem,
> Has poured itself into the broader stream
> Which constantly growing seeks the ocean.

"There is something we can from our lives not sever;
In need it is near and forsakes us never,—
A power that draws, a loving breast,
Which sadness, shyness, and all unrest
Can gather in peace in a bridal present.
"Could I but by spirits through life be attended,
As pure as the thought which has now me befriended!
The ordering spirit of God it was.
He ruleth the world with sacred laws.
Toward goodness eternal I am progressing."

But perhaps none of them better expressed his fervent gratitude than the following:—

"The power that gave me my little song
Has caused that as rain has been my sadness,
And that as sunshine has been my gladness,
The spring-time wants of my soul along.
Whate'er betided
It did no harm;
My song all guided
To love so warm.
"The power that gave me my little song
Has given me friendship for all that's yearning.
For freedom's blessings my blood is burning;
The foe I am of every wrong.
I sought my station,
Spite every storm,
And found salvation
In love so warm.
"The power that gave me my little song
Must make me able to sing the others,
And now and then to make glad my brothers
Whom I may meet in the worldly throng,—
For there was never
A sweeter charm
Than singing ever
In love so warm."

CHAPTER XVI.

It was late in the autumn; the harvesters were at work housing the grain. The day was clear, it had rained during the night; and in the morning, therefore, the air was as mild as in summer-time. It was a Saturday, and yet many boats were making their way across Black Water toward the church; the men, in their shirt sleeves, were rowing; the women sat in the stern, with light-colored kerchiefs on their heads. A still greater number of boats were steering over to Böen, in order to move away from there later in grand procession, for on this day Baard Böen gave a wedding for his daughter Eli and Arne Nils' son Kampen.

All the doors were open; people were going in and out; children, with pieces of cake in their hands, stood about the yard, afraid of their new clothes, and looking shyly at one another; an old woman sat upon the store-house steps alone,—it was Margit Kampen. She wore a large silver ring, with several small rings fastened to the upper silver plate; now and then she looked at it; Nils had given it to her the day of their wedding and she had never worn it since.

The man who presided at the feast, and the two young groomsmen, the priest's son and Eli's brother, went about in the two or three rooms, offering refreshments to the wedding guests as they arrived to be present on this great occasion. Up-stairs in Eli's room were the bride, the priest's wife, and Mathilde,—the last-named had come from town for the sole purpose of decking the bride; this the girls had promised each other from their childhood. Arne—wearing a broadcloth suit, with close-fitting roundabout and with a collar that Eli had made—stood in one of the down-stairs rooms by the window on which Eli had written "Arne."

Outside in the passage two persons met as they came each from some duty of the day. One of them was on his way from the landing-place, where he had been helping to put the church boats in order; he wore a black broadcloth roundabout, with blue wadmal trousers, whose dye rubbed off, so that his hands were blue; his white collar looked well with his fair face and long light hair; his high forehead was calm; about the mouth played a smile. It was Baard. She whom he met in the passage was just coming from the kitchen. She was dressed for church, was tall and slender, and walked with a firm though hurried step through the door. When she met Baard she paused, and her mouth drew up to one side. It was Birgit, his wife. Each had something to say, but it only found expression through both standing still. Baard was the most embarrassed of the two; he smiled more and more, but it was his embarrassment that came to his aid, forcing him to start up-stairs without further delay. "Perhaps you will come too," he said, as he passed, and Birgit followed him. Up-stairs in the garret they were entirely alone; yet Baard locked the door after them, and he was a long time about it. When finally he turned, Birgit stood by the window gazing out; it was in order to avoid looking into the room. Baard brought forth a small flask from his breast pocket and a little silver cup. He wanted to pour out some wine for his wife, but she would not have any, although he assured her that it was wine that had been sent from the parsonage. Then he drank himself, but paused several times to offer the cup to her. He corked the flask, put both it and the cup away in his breast-pocket again, and sat down on a chest. It very evidently pained him that his wife would not drink with him.

He breathed heavily several times. Birgit stood leaning with one hand against the window frame. Baard had something to say, but now it seemed even harder to speak than before.

"Birgit!" said he, "I dare say you are thinking of the same to-day that I am."

Then he heard her move from one side of the window to the other, and again she leaned her head on her arm.

"Oh, yes; you know who I mean. He it was who parted us two. I thought it would not go beyond the wedding, but it has lasted much longer."

He heard her sigh, he saw her again change her place; but he did not see her face. He himself was struggling so hard that he had to wipe his face with his jacket sleeve. After a long conflict he began again: "To-day a son of his, well-educated and handsome, becomes one of us, and to him we have given our only daughter. Now, how would it be, Birgit, if we two were to have our wedding to-day?"

His voice trembled, and he cleared his throat. Birgit, who had raised her head, now leaned it on her arm again, but said nothing. Baard waited for some time; he heard her breathe, but he got no answer,—and he had nothing further to say himself either. He looked up and grew very pale; for she did not even turn her head. Then he rose.

At the same moment there was a gentle knock at the door, and a soft voice asked, "Are you coming, mother?" It was Eli. There was something in the tone that made Baard involuntarily pause and glance at Birgit. Birgit also raised her head; she looked towards the door, and her eyes fell on Baard's pale face. "Are you coming, mother?" was once more asked from without.

"Yes, I am coming now!" said Birgit, in a broken voice, as she firmly crossed the floor to where Baard stood, gave him her hand, and burst into the most passionate weeping. The two hands met, they were both toil-worn now, but they clasped as firmly as though they had been seeking each other for twenty years. They still clung together as they went toward the door, and when a while later the bridal procession was passing down to the landing-place, and Arne gave his hand to Eli to take the lead, Baard, seeing it, took his wife by the hand, contrary to all custom, and followed them, smiling contentedly.

Behind them, Margit Kampen walked alone, as was her wont.

Baard was in high spirits that day; he sat talking with the rowers. One of these who kept looking up at the mountains remarked, that it was strange that even such a steep rock could be clad.

"It must, whether it would or no," said Baard, and his eyes wandered all along the procession until they rested on the bridal pair and his wife. "Who could have foretold this twenty years ago?" said he.

Early tales and sketches
THE RAILROAD AND THE CHURCHYARD.

CHAPTER I.

Knud Aakre belonged to an old family in the parish, where it had always been renowned for its intelligence and its devotion to the public welfare. His father had worked his way up to the priesthood, but had died early, and as the widow came from a peasant stock, the children were brought up as peasants. Knud had, therefore, received only the education afforded by the public schools of his day; but his father's library had early inspired him with a love of knowledge. This was further stimulated by his friend Henrik Wergeland, who frequently visited him, sent him books, seeds, and much valuable counsel. Following some of the latter, Knud early founded a club, which in the beginning had a very miscellaneous object, for instance: "to give the members practice in debating and to study the constitution," but which later was turned into a practical agricultural society for the entire bailiwick. According to Wergeland's advice, he also founded a parish library, giving his father's books as its first endowment. A suggestion from the same quarter led him to start a Sunday-school on his gard, for those who might wish to learn writing, arithmetic, and history. All this drew attention to him, so that he was elected member of the parish board of supervisors, of which he soon became chairman. In this capacity, he took a deep interest in the schools, which he brought into a remarkably good condition.

Knud Aakre was a short man, brisk in his movements, with small, restless eyes and very disorderly hair. He had large lips, which were in constant motion, and a row of splendid teeth which always seemed to be working with them, for they glistened while his words were snapped out, crisp and clear, crackling like sparks from a great fire.

Foremost among the many he had helped to gain an education was his neighbor Lars Högstad. Lars was not much younger than Knud, but he had developed more slowly. Knud liked to talk about what he read and thought, and he found in Lars, whose manner was quiet and grave, a good listener, who by degrees grew to be a man of excellent judgment. The relations between them soon became such that Knud was never willing to take any important step without first consulting Lars Högstad, and the matter on hand was thus likely to gain some practical amendment. So Knud drew his neighbor into the board of supervisors, and gradually into everything in which he himself took part. They always drove together to the meetings of the board, where Lars never spoke; but on the way back and forth Knud learned his opinions. The two were looked upon as inseparable.

One fine autumn day the board of supervisors convened to consider, among other things, a proposal from the bailiff to sell the parish grain magazine and with the proceeds establish a small savings-bank. Knud Aakre, the chairman, would undoubtedly have approved this measure had he relied on his unbiased judgment. But he was prejudiced, partly because the proposal came from the bailiff, whom Wergeland did not like, and who was consequently no favorite of Knud's either, and partly because the grain magazine had been built by his influential paternal grandfather and by him presented to the parish. Indeed, Knud was rather inclined to view the proposition as a personal insult, therefore he had not spoken of it to any one, not even to Lars, and the latter never entered on a topic that had not first been set afloat by some one else.

As chairman, Knud Aakre read the proposal without adding any comments; but, as was his wont, his eyes sought Lars, who usually sat or stood a little aside, holding a straw between his teeth,—he always had one when he took part in a conversation; he either used it as a tooth-pick, or he let it hang loosely in one corner of his mouth, turning it more rapidly or more slowly, according to the mood he was in. To his surprise Knud saw that the straw was moving very fast.

"Do you think we should agree to this?" he asked, quickly.

Lars answered, dryly,—

"Yes, I do."

The whole board, feeling that Knud held quite a different opinion, looked in astonishment at Lars, but the latter said no more, nor was he further questioned. Knud turned to another matter, as though nothing had transpired. Not until the close of the meeting did he resume the subject, and then asked, with apparent indifference, if it would not be well to send the proposal back to the bailiff for further consideration, as it certainly did not meet the views of the people, for the parish valued the grain magazine. No one replied. Knud asked whether he should enter the resolution in the register, the measure did not seem to be a wise one.

"Against one vote," added Lars.

"Against two," cried another, promptly.

"Against three," came from a third; and before the chairman could realize what was taking place, a majority had voted in favor of the proposal.

Knud was so surprised that he forgot to offer any opposition. He recorded the proceedings and read, in a low voice: "The measure is recommended,—adjourned."

His face was fiery red as he rose and put up the minute-book; but he determined to bring forward the question once more at the meeting of the representatives. Out in the yard, he put his horse to the wagon, and Lars came and took his seat at his side. They discussed various topics on their way home, but not the one they had nearest at heart.

The next day Knud's wife sought Lars's wife to inquire if there was anything wrong between the two men, for Knud had acted so strangely when he came home. A short distance above the gard buildings she met Lars's wife, who was on her way to ask the same question, for her husband, too, had been out of sorts the day before. Lars's wife was a quiet, bashful person, somewhat cowed, not by harsh words, but by silence, for Lars never spoke to her unless she had done something amiss, or he feared that she might do wrong. Knud Aakre's wife, on the other hand, talked more with her husband, and particularly about the board, for lately it had taken his thoughts, work, and affection away from her and the children. She was as jealous of it as of a woman; she wept at night over the board and quarreled with her husband about it during the day. But for that very reason she could say nothing about it now when for once he had returned home unhappy; for she immediately became more wretched than he, and for her life she could not rest until she had discovered what was the matter. Consequently, when Lars's wife could not give her the desired information, she had to go out in the parish to seek it. Here she obtained it, and of course was at once of her husband's opinion; she found Lars incomprehensible, not to say wicked. When, however, she let her husband perceive this, she felt that as yet there was no breach between Lars and him; that, on the contrary, he clung warmly to him.

The representatives met. Lars Högstad drove over to Aakre in the morning; Knud came out of the house and took his seat beside him. They exchanged the usual greetings, spoke perhaps rather less than was their wont on the way, and not of the proposal. All the members of the board were present; some, too, had found their way in as spectators, which Knud did not like, for it showed that there was a stir in town about the matter. Lars was armed with his straw, and he stood by the stove warming himself, for the autumn was beginning to be cold. The chairman read the proposal, in a subdued, cautious manner, remarking when he was through, that it must be remembered this came from the bailiff, who was not apt to be very felicitous in his propositions. The building, it was well known, was a gift, and it is not customary to part with gifts, least of all when there is no need of doing so.

Lars, who never before had spoken at the meetings, now took the floor, to the astonishment of all. His voice trembled, but whether it did so out of regard for Knud, or from anxiety lest his own cause should be lost, shall remain unsaid. But his arguments were good and clear, and full of a logic and confidence which had scarcely been heard at these meetings before. And when he had gone over all the ground, he added, in conclusion:—

"What does it matter if the proposal does come from the bailiff? This affects the question as little as who erected the building, or in what way it came into the public possession."

Knud Aakre had grown very red in the face (he blushed easily), and he shifted uneasily from side to side, as was his wont when he was impatient, but none the less did he exert himself to be circumspect and to speak in a low voice. There were savings-banks enough in the country, he thought, and quite near at hand, he might almost say *too* near. But if, after all, it was deemed expedient to have one, there were surely other ways of reaching it than those leading over the gifts of the dead and the love of the living. His voice was a little unsteady when he said this, but quickly recovered as he proceeded to speak of the grain magazine in itself, and to show what its advantages were.

Lars answered him thoroughly on the last point, and then added,—

"However, one thing and another lead me to doubt whether this parish is managed for the sake of the living or the dead; furthermore, whether it is the love and hatred of a single family which controls matters here, or the good of the whole."

Knud answered quickly,—

"I do not know whether he who has just spoken has been least benefited by this family,—both by the dead and by him who now lives."

The first shot was aimed at the fact that Knud's powerful grandfather had saved the gard for Lars's paternal grandfather, when the latter, on his part, was absent on a little excursion to the penitentiary.

The straw which long had been in brisk motion, suddenly became still.

"It is not my way to keep talking everywhere about myself and my family," said Lars, then turned again with calm superiority to the subject under discussion, briefly reviewing all the points with one definite object. Knud had to admit to himself that he had never viewed the matter from such a broad standpoint; involuntarily he raised his eyes and looked at Lars, who stood before him, tall, heavily built, with clearness on the vigorous brow and in the deep eyes. The lips were tightly compressed, the straw still played in the corner of his mouth; all the surrounding lines indicated vigor. He kept his hands behind him, and stood rigidly erect, while his voice was as deep and as hollow as if it proceeded from the depths of the earth. For the first time in his life Knud saw him as he was, and in his inmost soul he was afraid of him; for this man must always have been his superior. He had taken all Knud himself knew and could impart; he had rejected the tares and retained what had produced this strong, hidden growth.

He had been fostered and loved by Knud, but had now become a giant who hated Knud deeply, terribly. Knud could not explain to himself why, but as he looked at Lars he instinctively felt this to be so, and all else becoming swallowed up in this thought he started up, exclaiming,—

"But Lars! Lars! what in Heaven's name is the matter with you?" His agitation overcame him,—"you, whom I have—you who have"—

Powerless to utter another word, he sat down; but in his effort to gain the mastery over the emotion he deemed Lars unworthy of seeing, he brought his fist down with violence on the table, while his eyes flashed beneath his stiff, disorderly hair, which always hung over them. Lars acted as if he had not been interrupted, and turning toward the others he asked if this was to be the decisive blow; for if such were the case there was no need for further remarks.

This calmness was more than Knud could endure.

"What is it that has come among us?" cried he. "We who have, until to-day, been actuated by love and zeal alone, are now stirred up against each other, as though goaded on by some evil spirit," and he cast a fiery glance at Lars, who replied,—

"It must be you yourself who bring in this spirit, Knud; for I have kept strictly to the matter before us. But you never can see the advantage of anything you do not want yourself; now we shall learn what becomes of the love and the zeal when once this matter is decided as we wish."

"Have I then illy served the interests of the parish?"

There was no reply. This grieved Knud, and he continued,—

"I really did persuade myself that I had accomplished various things—various things which have been of advantage to the parish; but perhaps I have deceived myself."

He was again overcome by his feelings; for his was a fiery nature, ever variable in its moods, and the breach with Lars pained him so deeply that he could scarcely control himself. Lars answered,—

"Yes, I know you appropriate the credit for all that is done here, and if one should judge by the amount of speaking at these meetings, you certainly have accomplished the most."

"Is that the way of it?" shouted Knud, looking sharply at Lars. "It is you who deserve the entire honor?"

"Since we must finally talk about ourselves," said Lars, "I am free to admit that every question has been carefully considered by both of us before it was introduced here."

Here little Knud Aakre regained his ready speech:—

"Take the honor, in God's name; I am quite able to live without it; there are other things that are harder to lose!"

Involuntarily Lars evaded his gaze, but said, as he set the straw in very rapid motion,—

"If I were to express *my* opinion, I should say that there is not very much to take credit for. No doubt the priest and the school-masters are content with what has been done; but certainly the common people say that up to the present time the taxes of this parish have grown heavier and heavier."

Here arose a murmur in the crowd, and the people grew very restless. Lars continued,—

"Finally, to-day we have a matter brought before us that might make the parish some little amends for all it has paid out; this is perhaps the reason why it encounters such opposition. This is a question which concerns the parish; it is for the welfare of all; it is our duty to protect it from becoming a mere family matter."

People exchanged glances, and spoke in half-audible tones; one of them remarked, as he rose to go for his dinner-pail, that these were the truest words he had heard in these meetings for many years. Now all rose from their seats, the conversation became general, and Knud Aakre, who alone remained sitting, felt that all was lost, fearfully lost, and made no further effort to save it. The truth was, he possessed something of the temperament attributed to Frenchmen: he was very good at a first, second, or even third attack, but poor at self-defense, for his sensibilities overwhelmed his thoughts.

He was unable to comprehend this, nor could he sit still any longer, and so resigning his place to the vice-chairman, he left. The others could not refrain from a smile.

He had come to the meeting in company with Lars, but went home alone, although the way was long. It was a cold autumn day, the forest was jagged and bare, the meadow gray-yellow, frost was beginning here and there to remain on the road-side. Disappointment is a terrible companion. Knud felt so small, so desolate, as he walked along; but Lars appeared everywhere before him, towering up to the sky, in the dusk of the evening, like a giant. It vexed him to think it was his own fault that this had been the decisive battle; he had staked too much on one single little issue. But surprise, pain, anger, had mastered him; they still burned, tingled, moaned, and stormed within him. He heard the rumbling of cart-wheels behind him; it was Lars driving his superb horse past him, in a brisk trot, making the hard road resound like distant thunder. Knud watched the broad-shouldered form that sat erect in the cart, while the horse, eager for home, sped onward, without any effort on the part of Lars, who merely gave him a loose rein. It was but a picture of this man's power: he was driving onward to the goal! Knud felt himself cast out of his cart, to stagger on alone in the chill autumn air.

In his home at Aakre Knud's wife was waiting for him. She knew that a battle was inevitable; she had never in her life trusted Lars, and now she was positively afraid of him. It had been no comfort to her that he and her husband had driven away together; it would not have consoled her had they returned in the same way. But darkness had fallen and they had not come. She stood in the doorway, gazing out on the road in front of the house; she walked down the hill and back again, but no cart appeared.

Finally she hears a rattling on the hard road, her heart throbs as the wheels go round, she clings to the casement, peering out into the night; the cart draws near; only one is in it; she recognizes Lars, who sees and recognizes her, but drives past without stopping. Now she became thoroughly alarmed. Her limbs gave way under her, she tottered in and sank down on the bench by the window. The children gathered anxiously about her, the youngest one asked for papa; she never spoke with them but of him. He had such a noble disposition, and this was what made her love him; but now his heart was not with his family, it was engrossed in all sorts of business which brought him only unhappiness, and consequently they were all unhappy.

If only no misfortune had befallen him! Knud was so hot-tempered. Why had Lars come home alone? Why did he not stop? Should she run after him, or down the road after her husband? She was in an agony of distress, and the children pressed around her, asking what was the matter. But this she would not tell them, so rising she said they must eat supper alone, then got everything ready and helped them. All the while she kept glancing out on the road. He did not come. She undressed the children and put them to bed, and the youngest repeated the evening prayer while she bowed over him. She herself prayed with such fervor in the words which the infant lips so soothingly uttered that she did not heed the steps outside.

Knud stood upon the threshold, gazing at his little company at prayer. The mother drew herself up; all the children shouted: "Papa!" but he seated himself at once, and said, softly:

"Oh, let him say it once more!"

The mother turned again to the bedside, that he, meanwhile, should not see her face, for it would have seemed like intruding on his grief before he felt the need of revealing it. The little one folded its hands over its breast, all the rest did likewise, and it repeated,—

"I, a little child, pray Heaven
That my sins may be forgiven,
With time I'll larger, wiser grow,
And my father and mother joy shall know,
If only Thou, dearest, dearest Lord,
Will help me to keep Thy precious word!
And now to our Heavenly Father's merciful keeping
Our souls let us trust while we're sleeping."

What peace now fell upon the room! Not a minute had elapsed ere all the children were sleeping as in the arms of God; but the mother moved softly away and placed supper before the father, who was, however, unable to eat. But after he had gone to bed, he said,—

"Henceforth I shall be at home."

And his wife lay at his side trembling with joy which she dared not betray; and she thanked God for all that had happened, for whatever it might be it had resulted in good!

CHAPTER II.

IN the course of a year Lars had become chairman of the parish board of supervisors, president of the savings-bank, and leading commissioner in the court of reconciliation; in short, he held every office to which his election had been possible. In the board of supervisors for the amt (county) he was silent during the first year, but the second year he created the same sensation when he spoke as in the parish board; for here, too, coming forward in opposition to him who had previously been the guiding power, he became victorious over the entire rank and file and was from that time himself the leader. From this his path led him to the storthing (parliament), where his fame had preceded him, and where consequently there was no lack of challenges. But here, although steady and firm, he always remained retiring. He did not care for power except where he was well known, nor would he endanger his leadership at home by a possible defeat abroad.

For he had a pleasant life at home. When he stood by the church wall on Sundays, and the congregation walked slowly past, saluting him and stealing side glances at him, and one after another paused in order to exchange a few words with him,—then truly it might be said that he controlled the entire parish with a straw, for of course this hung in the corner of his mouth.

He deserved his honors. The road leading to the church, he had opened; the new church they were standing beside, he had built; this and much more was the fruit of the savings-bank which he had founded and now managed himself. For its resources were further made fruitful, and the parish was constantly held up as an example to all others of self-management and good order.

Knud Aakre had entirely withdrawn from the field, although at first he attended a few of the meetings of the board, because he had promised himself that he would continue to offer his services, even if it were not altogether pleasing to his pride. In the first proposal he had made, he became so greatly perplexed by Lars, who insisted upon having it represented in all its details, that, somewhat hurt, he said: "When Columbus discovered America he did not have it divided into parishes and deaneries; this came gradually;" whereupon Lars, in his reply, compared the discovery of America with Knud's proposal,—it so happened that this treated of stable improvements,—and afterwards Knud was known by no other name in the board than "Discovery of America." So Knud thought that as his usefulness had ceased, so too had his obligations to work, and he refused to accept further reëlections.

But he continued to be industrious; and in order that he might still have a field for usefulness, he enlarged his Sunday-school, and placed it, by means of small contributions from the attendants, in communication with the mission cause, of which he soon became the centre and leader in his own and the surrounding counties. Thereupon Lars Högstad remarked, that if ever Knud undertook to collect money for any purpose, he must know beforehand that it was to do good thousands of miles from home.

There was, be it observed, no more strife between them. To be sure, they no longer associated with each other, but they bowed and spoke when they met. Knud always felt a little pain at the mere thought of Lars, but strove to suppress it, and persuade himself that matters could not have been otherwise. At a large wedding-party, many years afterward, where both were present and both were in good spirits, Knud mounted a chair and proposed a toast for the chairman of the parish board, and the first representative their amt had sent to the storthing! He spoke until he became deeply moved, and, as usual, expressed himself in an exceedingly handsome way. Every one thought it was honorably done, and Lars came up to him, and his gaze was unsteady as he said that for much of what he knew and was he was indebted to him.

At the next election of the board of supervisors Knud was again made chairman!

But had Lars Högstad foreseen what now followed, he would certainly not have used his influence for this. "Every event happens in its own time," says an old proverb, and just as Knud Aakre again entered the board, the best men of the parish were threatened with ruin, as the result of a speculation craze which had long been raging, but which now first began to demand its victims. It was said that Lars Högstad was the cause of this great disaster, for he had taught the parish to speculate. This penny fever had originated in the parish board of supervisors, for the board itself was the greatest speculator of all. Every one down to the laboring youth of twenty years desired in his transactions to make ten dollars out of one; a beginning of extreme avarice in the efforts to hoard, was followed by an excessive extravagance, and as all minds were bent only on money, there had at the same time developed a spirit of suspicion, of intolerance, of caviling, which resulted in lawsuits and hatred. This also was due to the example of the board, it was said, for among the first things Lars had done as chairman was to sue the venerable old priest for holding doubtful titles. The priest had lost, but had also immediately resigned. At that time some had praised, some censured this suit; but it had proved a bad example. Now came the consequences of Lars's management, in the form of loss to every single man of property in the parish, consequently public opinion underwent a sharp change! The opposing force, too, soon found a leader, for Knud Aakre had come into the board, introduced there by Lars himself!

The struggle began forthwith. All those youths to whom Knud in his time had given instructions, were now grown up and were the most enlightened men in the parish, thoroughly at home in all its transactions and public affairs. It was against these men that Lars now had to contend, and they had borne him a grudge from their childhood up. When of an evening after one of these stormy proceedings he stood on the steps in front of his house, gazing over the parish, he could hear a sound as of distant rumbling thunder rising toward him from the large gards, now lying in the storm.

He knew that the day they met their ruin, the savings-bank and himself would be overthrown, and all his long efforts would culminate in imprecations heaped on his head.

In these days of conflict and despair, a party of railroad commissioners, who were to survey the route for a new road, made their appearance one evening at Högstad, the first gard at the entrance to the parish. In the course of conversation during the evening, Lars learned that there was a question whether the road should run through this valley or another parallel to it.

Like a flash of lightning it darted through his mind that if he could succeed in having it laid here, all property would rise in value, and not only would he himself be saved but his fame would be transmitted to the latest posterity! He could not sleep that night, for his eyes were dazzled by a glowing light, and sometimes he could even hear the sound of the cars. The next day he went himself with the commissioners while they examined the locality; his horse took them, and to his gard they returned. The next day they drove through the other valley; he was still with them, and he drove them back again to his house. They found a brilliant illumination at Högstad; the first men of the parish had been invited to be present at a magnificent party given in honor of the commissioners; it lasted until morning. But to no avail, for the nearer they came to a final issue, the more plainly it appeared that the road could not pass through this locality without undue expense. The entrance to the valley lay through a narrow gorge, and just as it swung into the parish, the swollen river swung in also, so that the railroad would either have to take the same curve along the mountain that the highway now made, thus running at a needlessly high altitude and crossing the river twice, or it would have to run straight forward, and thus through the old, now unused churchyard. Now the church had but recently been removed, and it was not long since the last burial had taken place there.

If it only depended on a bit of old churchyard, thought Lars, whether or not this great blessing came into the parish, then he must use his name and his energy for the removal of this obstacle! He at once set forth on a visit to the priest and the dean, and furthermore to the diocese council; he talked and he negotiated, for he was armed with all possible facts concerning the immense advantage of the railroad on one hand, and the sentiments of the parish on the other, and actually succeeded in winning all parties. It was promised him that by a removal of part of the bodies to the new churchyard the objections might be considered set aside, and the royal permission obtained for the churchyard to be taken for the line of railroad. It was told him that nothing was now needed but for him to set the question afloat in the board of supervisors.

The parish had grown as excited as himself: the spirit of speculation which for many years had been the only one prevailing in the parish, now became madly jubilant. There was nothing spoken or thought of but Lars's journey and its possible results. When he returned with the most magnificent promises, they made much of him; songs were sung in his praise; indeed, if at that time the largest gards had gone to destruction, one after another, no one would have paid the slightest attention to it: the speculation craze had given way to the railroad craze.

The board of supervisors assembled: there was presented for approval a respectful petition, that the old churchyard might be appropriated as the route of the railroad. This was unanimously adopted; there was even mention of giving Lars a vote of thanks and a coffee-pot in the form of a locomotive. But it was finally thought best to wait until the whole plan was carried into execution. The petition came back from the diocese council, with a demand for a list of all bodies that would have to be removed. The priest made out such a list, but instead of sending it direct, he had his own reasons for sending it through the parish board. One of the members carried it to the next meeting. Here it fell to the lot of Lars, as chairman, to open the envelope and read the list.

Now it chanced that the first body to be disinterred was that of Lars's own grandfather! A little shudder ran through the assembly! Lars himself was startled, but nevertheless continued to read. Then it furthermore chanced that the second body was that of Knud Aakre's grandfather, for these two men had died within a short time of each other. Knud Aakre sprang from his seat; Lars paused; every one looked up in consternation, for old Knud Aakre had been the benefactor of the parish and its best beloved man, time out of mind. There was a dead silence, which lasted for some minutes. At last Lars cleared his throat and went on reading. But the further he proceeded the worse the matter grew; for the nearer they came to their own time, the dearer were the dead. When he had finished, Knud Aakre asked quietly whether the others did not agree with him in thinking that the air about them was filled with spirits. It was just beginning to grow dark in the room, and although they were mature men and were sitting in numbers together, they could not refrain from feeling alarmed. Lars produced a bundle of matches from his pocket and struck a light, dryly remarking, that this was no more than they knew beforehand.

"Yes, it is," said Knud pacing the floor, "it is more than I knew before. Now I begin to think that even railroads can be purchased too dearly."

These words sent a quiver through the audience, and observing that they had better further consider the matter, Knud made a motion to that effect.

"In the excitement which had prevailed," he said, "the benefit likely to be derived from the road had been overestimated. Even if the railroad did not pass through this parish, there would have to be stations at both ends of the valley; true, it would always be a little more troublesome to drive to them than to a station right in our midst; yet the difficulty would not be so very great that it would be necessary because of it to violate the repose of the dead."

Knud was one of those who when his thoughts were once in rapid motion could present the most convincing arguments; a moment before what he now said had not occurred to his mind, nevertheless it struck home to all. Lars felt the danger of his position, and concluding that it was best to be cautious, apparently acquiesced in Knud's proposition to reconsider. Such emotions are always worse in the beginning, he thought; it is wisest to temporize with them.

But he had miscalculated. In ever increasing waves the dread of touching the dead of their own families swept over the inhabitants of the parish; what none of them had thought of as long as the matter existed merely in the abstract, now became a serious question when it was brought home to themselves. The women especially were excited, and the road near the court-house was black with people the day of the next meeting. It was a warm summer day, the windows were removed, and there were as many without the house as within. All felt that a great battle was about to be fought.

Lars came driving up with his handsome horse, and was greeted by all; he looked calmly and confidently around, not seeming to be surprised at anything. He took a seat near the window, found his straw, and a suspicion of a smile played over his keen face as he saw Knud Aakre rise to his feet to act as spokesman for all the dead in the old Högstad churchyard.

But Knud Aakre did not begin with the churchyard. He began with an accurate exposition of how greatly the profits likely to accrue from having the railroad run through the parish had been overestimated in all this turmoil. He had positive proofs for every statement he made, for he had calculated the distance of each gard from the nearest station, and finally he asked,—

"Why has there been so much ado about this railroad, if not in behalf of the parish?"

This he could easily explain to them. There were those who had occasioned so great a disturbance that a still greater one was required to conceal it. Moreover, there were those who in the first outburst of excitement could sell their gards and belongings to strangers who were foolish enough to purchase. It was a shameful speculation which not only the living but the dead must serve to promote!

The effect of his address was very considerable. But Lars had once for all resolved to preserve his composure let come what would. He replied, therefore, with a smile, that he had been under the impression that Knud himself was eager for the railroad, and certainly no one would accuse him of having any knowledge of speculation. (Here followed a little laugh.) Knud had not evinced the slightest objection to the removal of the bodies of common people for the sake of the railroad; but when his own grandfather's body was in question then it suddenly affected the welfare of the whole community! He said no more, but looked with a faint smile at Knud, as did also several others. Meanwhile, Knud Aakre surprised both him and them by replying:—

"I confess it; I did not comprehend the matter until it touched my own family feelings; it is possible that this may be a shame, but it would have been a far greater one not to have realized it at last—as is the case with Lars! Never," he concluded, "could this raillery have been more out of place; for to people with common decency the whole affair is absolutely revolting."

"This feeling is something that has come up quite recently," replied Lars, "we may therefore hope that it will soon pass over again. May it not perhaps help the matter a little to think what the priest, dean, diocese council, engineers, and government will all say if we first unanimously set the ball in motion, then come and beg to have it stopped? If we first are jubilant and sing songs, then weep and deliver funeral orations? If they do not say that we have gone mad in this parish, they must at all events say that we have acted rather strangely of late."

"Yes, God knows, they may well think so!" replied Knud. "We have, indeed, acted very strangely of late, and it is high time for us to mend our ways. Things have come to a serious pass when we can each disinter his own grandfather to make way for a railroad; when we can disturb the resting-place of the dead in order that our own burdens may the more easily be carried. For is not this rooting in our churchyard in order to make it yield us food the same thing? What is buried there in the name of Jesus, we take up in Moloch's name—this is but little better than eating the bones of our ancestors."

"Such is the course of nature," said Lars, dryly.

"Yes, of plants and of animals."

"And are not we animals?"

"We are, but also the children of the living God, who have buried our dead in faith in Him: it is He who shall rouse them and not we."

"Oh, you are talking idly! Are we not obliged to have the graves dug up at any rate, when their turn comes? What harm is there in having it happen a few years earlier?"

"I will tell you. What was born of them still draws the breath of life; what they built up yet remains; what they loved, taught, and suffered for, lives about us and within us; and should we not allow them to rest in peace?"

"Your warmth shows me that you are thinking of your own grandfather again," replied Lars, "and I must say it seems to me high time the parish should be rid of *him*. He monopolized too much space while he lived; and so it is scarcely worth while to have him lie in the way now that he is dead. Should his corpse prevent a blessing to this parish that would extend through a hundred generations, we may truly say that of all who have been born here, *he* has done us the greatest harm."

Knud Aakre tossed back his disorderly hair, his eyes flashed, his whole person looked like a bent steel spring.

"How much of a blessing what you are speaking about may be, I have already shown. It has the same character as all the other blessings with which you have supplied the parish, namely, a doubtful one. It is true, you have provided us with a new church, but you have also filled it with a new spirit,—and it is not that of love. True, you have furnished us with new roads, but also with new roads to destruction, as is now plainly manifest in the misfortunes of many. True, you have diminished our public taxes, but you have increased our private ones; lawsuits, promissory notes, and bankruptcies are no fruitful gifts to a community. And *you* dare dishonor in his grave the man whom the whole parish blesses? You dare assert that he lies in our way; aye, no doubt he does lie in your way, this is plain enough now, for his grave will be the cause of your downfall! The spirit which has reigned over you, and until to-day over us all, was not born to rule but to enter into servitude. The churchyard will surely be allowed to remain in peace; but to-day it shall have one grave added to it, namely, that of your popularity which is now to be buried there."

Lars Högstad rose, white as a sheet; his lips parted, but he was unable to utter a word, and the straw fell. After three or four vain efforts to find it again and recover his powers of speech, he burst forth like a volcano with,—

"And so these are the thanks I get for all my toil and drudgery! If such a woman-preacher is to be allowed to rule—why, then, may the devil be your chairman if ever I set my foot here again! I have kept things together until this day, and after me your trash will fall into a thousand pieces, but let it tumble down now—here is the register!" And he flung it on the table. "Shame on such an assembly of old women and brats!" Here he struck the table with great violence. "Shame on the whole parish that it can see a man rewarded as I am now."

He brought down his fist once more with such force that the great court-house table shook, and the inkstand with its entire contents tumbled to the floor, marking for all future generations the spot where Lars Högstad fell in spite of all his prudence, his long rule, and his patience.

He rushed to the door and in a few moments had left the place. The entire assembly remained motionless; for the might of his voice and of his wrath had frightened them, until Knud Aakre, remembering the taunt he had received at the time of *his* fall, with beaming countenance and imitating Lars's voice, exclaimed:—

"Is *this* to be the decisive blow in the matter?"

The whole assembly burst into peals of merriment at these words! The solemn meeting ended in laughter, talk, and high glee; only a few left the place, those remaining behind called for drink to add to their food, and a night of thunder succeeded a day of lightning. Every one felt as happy and independent as of yore, ere the commanding spirit of Lars had cowed their souls into dumb obedience. They drank toasts to their freedom; they sang, indeed, finally they danced, Knud Aakre and the vice-chairman taking the lead and all the rest following, while boys and girls joined in, and the young folks outside shouted "Hurrah!" for such a jollification they had never before seen!

CHAPTER III.

Lars moved about in the large rooms at Högstad, without speaking a word. His wife, who loved him, but always in fear and trembling, dared not come into his presence. The management of the gard and of the house might be carried on as best it could, while on the other hand there kept growing a multitude of letters, which passed back and forth between Högstad and the parish, and Högstad and the post-office; for Lars had claims against the parish board, and these not being satisfied he prosecuted; against the savings-bank, which were also unsatisfied, and so resulted in another suit. He took offense at expressions in the letters he received and went to law again, now against the chairman of the parish board, now against the president of the savings-bank. At the same time there were dreadful articles in the newspapers, which report attributed to him, and which were the cause of great dissension in the parish, inciting neighbor against neighbor. Sometimes he was absent whole weeks, no one knew where, and when he returned he lived as secluded as before. At church he had not been seen after the great scene at the representatives' meeting.

Then one Saturday evening the priest brought tidings that the railroad was to run through the parish after all, and across the old churchyard! It struck like lightning into every home. The unanimous opposition of the parish board had been in vain, Lars Högstad's influence had been stronger. This was the meaning of his journeys, this was his work! Involuntary admiration of the man and his stubborn persistence tended to suppress the dissatisfaction of the people at their own defeat, and the more they discussed the matter the more reconciled they became; for a fact accomplished always contains within itself reasons why it is so, which gradually force themselves upon us after there is no longer possibility of change. The people assembled about the church the next day, and they could not help laughing as they met one another. And just as the whole congregation, young and old, men and women, aye, even children, were all talking about Lars Högstad, his ability, his rigorous will, his immense influence, he himself with his whole household came driving up in four conveyances, one after the other. It was two years since his last visit there! He alighted and passed through the crowd, while all, as by one impulse, unhesitatingly greeted him, but he did not deign to bestow a glance on either side, nor to return a single salutation. His little wife, pale as death, followed him. Inside of the church, the astonishment grew to such a pitch that as one after another caught sight of him they stopped singing and only stared at him. Knud Aakre, who sat in his pew in front of Lars, noticed that there was something the matter, and as he perceived nothing remarkable in front of him, he turned round. He saw Lars bowed over his hymn-book, searching for the place.

He had not seen him since that evening at the meeting, and such a complete change he had not believed possible. For this was no victor! The thin, soft hair was thinner than ever, the face was haggard and emaciated, the eyes hollow and bloodshot, the giant neck had dwindled into wrinkles and cords. Knud comprehended at a glance what this man had gone through; he was seized with a feeling of strong sympathy, indeed, he felt something of the old love stirring within his breast. He prayed for Lars to his God, and made a resolute vow that he would seek him after service; but Lars had started on ahead. Knud resolved to call on him that evening. His wife, however, held him back.

"Lars is one of those," said she, "who can scarcely bear a debt of gratitude: keep away from him until he has an opportunity to do you some favor, and then perhaps he will come to you!"

But he did not come. He appeared now and then at church, but nowhere else, and he associated with no one. On the other hand, he now devoted himself to his gard and other business with the passionate zeal of one who had determined to make amends in one year for the neglect of many; and, indeed, there were those who said that this was imperative.

Railroad operations in the valley began very soon. As the line was to go directly past Lars's gard, he tore down the portion of his house that faced the road, in order to build a large and handsome balcony, for he was determined that his gard should attract attention. This work was just being done when the temporary rails for the conveyance of gravel and timber to the road were laid and a small locomotive was sent to the spot. It was a beautiful autumn evening that the first gravel car was to pass over the road. Lars stood on his front steps, to hear the first signal and to see the first column of smoke; all the people of the gard were gathered about him. He gazed over the parish, illumined by the setting sun, and he felt that he would be remembered as long as a train should come roaring through this fertile valley. A sense of forgiveness glided into his soul. He looked toward the churchyard, a part of which still remained, with crosses bowed down to the ground, but a part of it was now the railroad. He was just endeavoring to define his own feeling when the first signal whistled, and presently the train came slowly working its way along, attended by a cloud of smoke, mingled with sparks, for the locomotive was fed with pine wood. The wind blew toward the house so that those standing without were soon enveloped in a dense smoke, but as this cleared away Lars saw the train working its way down through the valley like a strong will.

He was content, and entered his house like one who has come from a long day's work. The image of his grandfather stood before him at this moment. This grandfather had raised the family from poverty to prosperity; true, a portion of his honor as a citizen was consumed in the act, but he had advanced nevertheless! His faults were the prevailing ones of his time: they were based on the uncertain boundary lines of the moral conceptions of his day. Every age has its uncertain moral distinctions and its victims to the endeavor to define them properly.

Honor be to him in his grave, for he had suffered and toiled! Peace be with him! It must be good to rest in the end. But he was not allowed to rest because of his grandson's vast ambition; his ashes were thrown up with the stones and the gravel. Nonsense! he would only smile that his grandson's work passed over his head.

Amid thoughts like these Lars had undressed and gone to bed. Once more his grandfather's image glided before him. It was sterner now than the first time. Weariness enfeebles us, and Lars began to reproach himself. But he defended himself also. What did his grandfather want? Surely he ought to be satisfied now, for the family honor was proclaimed in loud tones above his grave. Who else had such a monument? And yet what is this? These two monstrous eyes of fire and this hissing, roaring sound belong no longer to the locomotive, for they turn away from the railroad track. And from the churchyard straight toward the house comes an immense procession. The eyes of fire are his grandfather's, and the long line of followers are all the dead. The train advances steadily toward the gard, roaring, crackling, flashing. The windows blaze in the reflection of the dead men's eyes. Lars made a mighty effort to control himself, for this was a dream, unquestionably but a dream. Only wait until I am awake! There, now I am awake. Come on, poor ghosts!

And lo! they really did come from the churchyard, overthrowing road, rails, locomotive and train, so that these fell with a mighty crash to the ground, and the green sod appeared in their stead, dotted with graves and crosses as before. Like mighty champions they advanced, and the hymn, "Let the dead repose in peace!" preceded them. Lars knew it; for through all these years it had been sighing within his soul, and now it had become his requiem; for this was death and death's visions. The cold sweat started out over his whole body, for nearer and nearer—and behold, on the window pane! there they are now, and he heard some one speak his name. Overpowered with dread he struggled to scream; for he was being strangled, a cold hand was clinching his throat and he regained his voice in an agonized: "Help me!" and awoke. The window had been broken in from the outside; the pieces flew all about his head. He sprang up. A man stood at the window, surrounded by smoke and flames.

"The gard is on fire, Lars! We will help you out!"

It was Knud Aakre.

When Lars regained his consciousness, he was lying outside in a bleak wind, which chilled his limbs. There was not a soul with him; he saw the flaming gard to the left; around him his cattle were grazing and making their voices heard; the sheep were huddled together in a frightened flock; the household goods were scattered about, and when he looked again he saw some one sitting on a knoll close by, weeping. It was his wife. He called her by name. She started.

"The Lord Jesus be praised that you are alive!" cried she, coming forward and seating herself, or rather throwing herself down in front of him. "O God! O God! We surely have had enough of this railroad now!"

"The railroad?" asked he, but ere the words had escaped his lips, a clear comprehension of the case passed like a shudder over him; for, of course, sparks from the locomotive that had fallen among the shavings of the new side wall had been the cause of the fire. Lars sat there brooding in silence; his wife, not daring to utter another word, began to search for his clothes; for what she had spread over him, as he lay senseless, had fallen off. He accepted her attentions in silence, but as she knelt before him to cover his feet, he laid his hand on her head. Falling forward she buried her face in his lap and wept aloud. There were many who eyed her curiously. But Lars understood her and said,—

"You are the only friend I have."

Even though it had cost the gard to hear these words, it mattered not to her; she felt so happy that she gained courage, and rising up and looking humbly into her husband's face, she said,—

"Because there is no one else who understands you."

Then a hard heart melted, and tears rolled down the man's cheeks as he clung to his wife's hand.

Now he talked to her as to his own soul. Now too she opened to him her mind. They also talked about how all this had happened, or rather he listened while she told about it. Knud Aakre had been the first to see the fire, had roused his people, sent the girls out over his parish, while he had hastened himself with men and horses to the scene of the conflagration, where all were sleeping. He had engineered the extinguishing of the flames and the rescuing of the household goods, and had himself dragged Lars from the burning room, and carried him to the left side of the house from where the wind was blowing and had laid him out here in the churchyard.

And while they were talking of this, some one came driving rapidly up the road and turned into the churchyard, where he alighted. It was Knud, who had been home after his church-cart,—the one in which they had so many times ridden together to and from the meetings of the parish board. Now he requested Lars to get in and ride home with him. They grasped each other by the hand, the one sitting, the other standing.

"Come with me now," said Knud.

Without a word of reply, Lars rose. Side by side they walked to the cart. Lars was helped in; Knud sat down beside him. What they talked about as they drove along, or afterwards in the little chamber at Aakre, where they remained together until late in the morning, has never been known. But from that day they were inseparable as before.

As soon as misfortune overtakes a man, every one learns what he is worth. And so the parish undertook to rebuild Lars Högstad's houses, and to make them larger and handsomer than any others in the valley. He was reëlected chairman, but with Knud Aakre at his side; he never again failed to take counsel of Knud's intelligence and heart—and from that day forth nothing went to ruin.

THROND.

THERE was once a man named Alf, who had raised great expectations among his fellow-parishioners because he excelled most of them both in the work he accomplished and in the advice he gave. Now when this man was thirty years old, he went to live up the mountain and cleared a piece of land for farming, about fourteen miles from any settlement. Many people wondered how he could endure thus depending on himself for companionship, but they were still more astonished when, a few years later, a young girl from the valley, and one, too, who had been the gayest of the gay at all the social gatherings and dances of the parish, was willing to share his solitude.

This couple were called "the people in the wood," and the man was known by the name "Alf in the wood." People viewed him with inquisitive eyes when they met him at church or at work, because they did not understand him; but neither did he take the trouble to give them any explanation of his conduct. His wife was only seen in the parish twice, and on one of these occasions it was to present a child for baptism.

This child was a son, and he was called Thrond. When he grew larger his parents often talked about needing help, and as they could not afford to take a full-grown servant, they hired what they called "a half:" they brought into their house a girl of fourteen, who took care of the boy while the father and mother were busy in the field.

This girl was not the brightest person in the world, and the boy soon observed that his mother's words were easy to comprehend, but that it was hard to get at the meaning of what Ragnhild said. He never talked much with his father, and he was rather afraid of him, for the house had to be kept very quiet when he was at home.

One Christmas Eve—they were burning two candles on the table, and the father was drinking from a white flask—the father took the boy up in his arms and set him on his lap, looked him sternly in the eyes and exclaimed,—

"Ugh, boy!" Then he added more gently: "Why, you are not so much afraid. Would you have the courage to listen to a story?"

The boy made no reply, but he looked full in his father's face. His father then told him about a man from Vaage, whose name was Blessom. This man was in Copenhagen for the purpose of getting the king's verdict in a law-suit he was engaged in, and he was detained so long that Christmas Eve overtook him there. Blessom was greatly annoyed at this, and as he was sauntering about the streets fancying himself at home, he saw a very large man, in a white, short coat, walking in front of him.

"How fast you are walking!" said Blessom.

"I have a long distance to go in order to get home this evening," replied the man.

"Where are you going?"

"To Vaage," answered the man, and walked on.

"Why, that is very nice," said Blessom, "for that is where I was going, too."

"Well, then, you may ride with me, if you will stand on the runners of my sledge," answered the man, and turned into a side street where his horse was standing.

He mounted his seat and looked over his shoulder at Blessom, who was just getting on the runners.

"You had better hold fast," said the stranger.

Blessom did as he was told, and it was well he did, for their journey was evidently not by land.

"It seems to me that you are driving on the water," cried Blessom.

"I am," said the man, and the spray whirled about them.

But after a while it seemed to Blessom their course no longer lay on the water.

"It seems to me we are moving through the air," said he.

"Yes, so we are," replied the stranger.

But when they had gone still farther, Blessom thought he recognized the parish they were driving through.

"Is not this Vaage?" cried he.

"Yes, now we are there," replied the stranger, and it seemed to Blessom that they had gone pretty fast.

"Thank you for the good ride," said he.

"Thanks to yourself," replied the man, and added, as he whipped up his horse, "Now you had better not look after me."

"No, indeed," thought Blessom, and started over the hills for home.

But just then so loud and terrible a crash was heard behind him that it seemed as if the whole mountain must be tumbling down, and a bright light was shed over the surrounding landscape; he looked round and beheld the stranger in the white coat driving through the crackling flames into the open mountain, which was yawning wide to receive him, like some huge gate. Blessom felt somewhat strange in regard to his traveling companion; and thought he would look in another direction; but as he had turned his head so it remained, and never more could Blessom get it straight again.

The boy had never heard anything to equal this in all his life. He dared not ask his father for more, but early the next morning he asked his mother if she knew any stories. Yes, of course she did; but hers were chiefly about princesses who were in captivity for seven years, until the right prince came along. The boy believed that everything he heard or read about took place close around him.

He was about eight years old when the first stranger entered their door one winter evening. He had black hair, and this was something Thrond had never seen before. The stranger saluted them with a short "Good-evening!" and came forward. Thrond grew frightened and sat down on a cricket by the hearth. The mother asked the man to take a seat on the bench along the wall; he did so, and then the mother could examine his face more closely.

"Dear me! is not this Knud the fiddler?" cried she.

"Yes, to be sure it is. It has been a long time since I played at your wedding."

"Oh, yes; it is quite a while now. Have you been on a long journey?"

"I have been playing for Christmas, on the other side of the mountain. But half way down the slope I began to feel very badly, and I was obliged to come in here to rest."

The mother brought forward food for him; he sat down to the table, but did not say "in the name of Jesus," as the boy had been accustomed to hear. When he had finished eating, he got up from the table, and said,—

"Now I feel very comfortable; let me rest a little while."

And he was allowed to rest on Thrond's bed.

For Thrond a bed was made on the floor. As the boy lay there, he felt cold on the side that was turned away from the fire, and that was the left side. He discovered that it was because this side was exposed to the chill night air; for he was lying out in the wood. How came he in the wood? He got up and looked about him, and saw that there was fire burning a long distance off, and that he was actually alone in the wood. He longed to go home to the fire; but could not stir from the spot. Then a great fear overcame him; for wild beasts might be roaming about, trolls and ghosts might appear to him; he must get home to the fire; but he could not stir from the spot. Then his terror grew, he strove with all his might to gain self-control, and was at last able to cry, "Mother," and then he awoke.

"Dear child, you have had bad dreams," said she, and took him up.

A shudder ran through him, and he glanced round. The stranger was gone, and he dared not inquire after him.

His mother appeared in her black dress, and started for the parish. She came home with two new strangers, who also had black hair and who wore flat caps. They did not say "in the name of Jesus," when they ate, and they talked in low tones with the father. Afterward the latter and they went into the barn, and came out again with a large box, which the men carried between them. They placed it on a sled, and said farewell. Then the mother said:—

"Wait a little, and take with you the smaller box he brought here with him."

And she went in to get it. But one of the men said,—

"*He* can have that," and he pointed at Thrond.

"Use it as well as *he* who is now lying *here*," added the other stranger, pointing at the large box.

Then they both laughed and went on. Thrond looked at the little box which thus came into his possession.

"What is there in it?" asked he.

"Carry it in and find out," said the mother.

He did as he was told, but his mother helped him open it. Then a great joy lighted up his face; for he saw something very light and fine lying there.

"Take it up," said his mother.

He put just one finger down on it, but quickly drew it back again, in great alarm.

"It cries," said he.

"Have courage," said his mother, and he grasped it with his whole hand and drew it forth from the box.

He weighed it and turned it round, he laughed and felt of it.

"Dear me! what is it?" asked he, for it was as light as a toy.

"It is a fiddle."

This was the way that Thrond Alfson got his first violin.

The father could play a little, and he taught the boy how to handle the instrument; the mother could sing the tunes she remembered from her dancing days, and these the boy learned, but soon began to make new ones for himself. He played all the time he was not at his books; he played until his father once told him he was fading away before his eyes. All the boy had read and heard until that time was put into the fiddle. The tender, delicate string was his mother; the one that lay close beside it, and always accompanied his mother, was Ragnhild. The coarse string, which he seldom ventured to play on, was his father. But of the last solemn string he was half afraid, and he gave no name to it. When he played a wrong note on the E string, it was the cat; but when he took a wrong note on his father's string, it was the ox. The bow was Blessom, who drove from Copenhagen to Vaage in one night. And every tune he played represented something. The one containing the long solemn tones was his mother in her black dress. The one that jerked and skipped was like Moses, who stuttered and smote the rock with his staff. The one that had to be played quietly, with the bow moving lightly over the strings, was the hulder in yonder fog, calling together her cattle, where no one but herself could see.

But the music wafted him onward over the mountains, and a great yearning took possession of his soul. One day when his father told about a little boy who had been playing at the fair and who had earned a great deal of money, Thrond waited for his mother in the kitchen and asked her softly if he could not go to the fair and play for people.

"Who ever heard of such a thing!" said his mother; but she immediately spoke to his father about it.

"He will get out into the world soon enough," answered the father; and he spoke in such a way that the mother did not ask again.

Shortly after this, the father and mother were talking at table about some new settlers who had recently moved up on the mountain and were about to be married. They had no fiddler for the wedding, the father said.

"Could not I be the fiddler?" whispered the boy, when he was alone in the kitchen once more with his mother.

"What, a little boy like you?" said she; but she went out to the barn where his father was and told him about it.

"He has never been in the parish," she added, "he has never seen a church."

"I should not think you would ask about such things," said Alf; but neither did he say anything more, and so the mother thought she had permission. Consequently she went over to the new settlers and offered the boy's services.

"The way he plays," said she, "no little boy has ever played before;" and the boy was to be allowed to come.

What joy there was at home! Thrond played from morning until evening and practiced new tunes; at night he dreamed about them: they bore him far over the hills, away to foreign lands, as though he were afloat on sailing clouds. His mother made a new suit of clothes for him; but his father would not take part in what was going on.

The last night he did not sleep, but thought out a new tune about the church which he had never seen. He was up early in the morning, and so was his mother, in order to get him his breakfast, but he could not eat. He put on his new clothes and took his fiddle in his hand, and it seemed to him as though a bright light were glowing before his eyes. His mother accompanied him out on the flag-stone, and stood watching him as he ascended the slopes;—it was the first time he had left home.

His father got quietly out of bed and walked to the window; he stood there following the boy with his eyes until he heard the mother out on the flag-stone, then he went back to bed and was lying down when she came in.

She kept stirring about him, as if she wanted to relieve her mind of something. And finally it came out:—

"I really think I must walk down to the church and see how things are going."

He made no reply, and therefore she considered the matter settled, dressed herself and started.

It was a glorious, sunny day, the boy walked rapidly onward; he listened to the song of the birds and saw the sun glittering among the foliage, while he proceeded on his way, with his fiddle under his arm. And when he reached the bride's house, he was still so occupied with his own thoughts, that he observed neither the bridal splendor nor the procession; he merely asked if they were about to start, and learned that they were. He walked on in advance with his fiddle, and he played the whole morning into it, and the tones he produced resounded through the trees.

"Will we soon see the church?" he asked over his shoulder.

For a long time he received only "No" for an answer, but at last some one said:

"As soon as you reach that crag yonder, you will see it."

He threw his newest tune into the fiddle, the bow danced on the strings, and he kept his eyes fixed intently before him. There lay the parish right in front of him!

The first thing he saw was a little light mist, curling like smoke on the opposite mountain side. His eyes wandered over the green meadow and the large houses, with windows which glistened beneath the scorching rays of the sun, like the glacier on a winter's day. The houses kept increasing in size, the windows in number, and here on one side of him lay the enormous red house, in front of which horses were tied; little children were playing on a hill, dogs were sitting watching them. But everywhere there penetrated a long, heavy tone, that shook him from head to foot, and everything he saw seemed to vibrate with that tone. Then suddenly he saw a large, straight house, with a tall, glittering staff reaching up to the skies. And below, a hundred windows blazed, so that the house seemed to be enveloped in flames. This must be the church, the boy thought, and the music must come from it! Round about stood a vast multitude of people, and they all looked alike! He put them forthwith into relations with the church, and thus acquired a respect mingled with awe for the smallest child he saw.

"Now I must play," thought Thrond, and tried to do so.

But what was this? The fiddle had no longer any sound in it. There must be some defect in the strings; he examined, but could find none.

"Then it must be because I do not press on hard enough," and he drew his bow with a firmer hand; but the fiddle seemed as if it were cracked.

He changed the tune that was meant to represent the church into another, but with equally bad results; no music was produced, only squeaking and wailing. He felt the cold sweat start out over his face, he thought of all these wise people who were standing here and perhaps laughing him to scorn, this boy who at home could play so beautifully but who here failed to bring out a single tone!

"Thank God that mother is not here to see my shame!" said he softly to himself, as he played among the people; but lo! there she stood, in her black dress, and she shrank farther and farther away.

At that moment he beheld far up on the spire, the black-haired man who had given him the fiddle. "Give it back to me," he now shouted, laughing and stretching out his arms, and the spire went up and down with him, up and down. But the boy took the fiddle under one arm, screaming, "You shall not have it!" and turning, ran away from the people, beyond the houses, onward through meadow and field, until his strength forsook him, and then sank to the ground.

There he lay for a long time, with his face toward the earth, and when finally he looked round he saw and heard only God's infinite blue sky that floated above him, with its everlasting sough. This was so terrible to him that he had to turn his face to the ground again. When he raised his head once more his eyes fell on his fiddle, which lay at his side.

"This is all your fault!" shouted the boy, and seized the instrument with the intention of dashing it to pieces, but hesitated as he looked at it.

"We have had many a happy hour together," said he, then paused. Presently he said: "The strings must be severed, for they are worthless." And he took out a knife and cut. "Oh!" cried the E string, in a short, pained tone. The boy cut. "Oh!" wailed the next; but the boy cut. "Oh!" said the third, mournfully; and he paused at the fourth. A sharp pain seized him; that fourth string, to which he never dared give a name, he did not cut. Now a feeling came over him that it was not the fault of the strings that he was unable to play, and just then he saw his mother walking slowly up the slope toward where he was lying, that she might take him home with her. A greater fright than ever overcame him; he held the fiddle by the severed strings, sprang to his feet, and shouted down to her,—

"No, mother! I will not go home again until I can play what I have seen to-day."

A DANGEROUS WOOING.

WHEN Aslaug had become a grown-up girl, there was not much peace to be had at Huseby; for there the finest boys in the parish quarreled and fought night after night. It was worst of all on Saturday nights; but then old Knud Huseby never went to bed without keeping his leather breeches on, nor without having a birch stick by his bedside.

"If I have a daughter, I shall look after her, too," said old Huseby.

Thore Næset was only a houseman's son; nevertheless there were those who said that he was the one who came oftenest to see the gardman's daughter at Huseby. Old Knud did not like this, and declared also that it was not true, "for he had never seen him there." But people smiled slyly among themselves, and thought that had he searched in the corners of the room instead of fighting with all those who were making a noise and uproar in the middle of the floor, he would have found Thore.

Spring came and Aslaug went to the sæter with the cattle. Then, when the day was warm down in the valley, and the mountain rose cool above the haze, and when the bells tinkled, the shepherd dog barked, and Aslaug sang and blew the loor on the mountain side, then the hearts of the young fellows who were at work down on the meadow would ache, and the first Saturday night they all started up to the mountain sæter, one faster than the other. But still more rapidly did they come down again, for behind the door at the sæter there stood one who received each of them as he came, and gave him so sound a whipping that he forever afterward remembered the threat that followed it,—

"Come again another time and you shall have some more."

According to what these young fellows knew, there was only one in the parish who could use his fists in this way, and that was Thore Næset. And these rich gardmen's sons thought it was a shame that this houseman's son should cut them all out at the Huseby sæter.

So thought, also, old Knud, when the matter reached his ears, and said, moreover, that if there was nobody else who could tackle Thore, then he and his sons would try it. Knud, it is true, was growing old, but although he was nearly sixty, he would at times have a wrestle or two with his eldest son, when it was too dull for him at some party or other.

Up to the Huseby sæter there was but one road, and that led straight through the gard. The next Saturday evening, as Thore was going to the sæter, and was stealing on his tiptoes across the yard, a man rushed right at his breast as he came near the barn.

"What do you want of me?" said Thore, and knocked his assailant flat on the ground.

"That you shall soon find out," said another fellow from behind, giving Thore a blow on the back of the head. This was the brother of the former assailant.

"Here comes the third," said old Knud, rushing forward to join the fray.

The danger made Thore stronger. He was as limber as a willow and his blows left their marks. He dodged from one side to the other. Where the blows fell he was not, and where his opponents least expected blows from him, they got them. He was, however, at last completely beaten; but old Knud frequently said afterwards that a stouter fellow he had scarcely ever tackled. The fight was continued until blood flowed, but then Huseby cried,—

"Stop!" and added, "If you can manage to get by the Huseby wolf and his cubs next Saturday night, the girl shall be yours."

Thore dragged himself homeward as best he could; and as soon as he got home he went to bed.

At Huseby there was much talk about the fight; but everybody said,—

"What did he want there?"

There was one, however, who did not say so, and that was Aslaug. She had expected Thore that Saturday night, and when she heard what had taken place between him and her father, she sat down and had a good cry, saying to herself,—

"If I cannot have Thore, there will never be another happy day for me in this world."

Thore had to keep his bed all day Sunday; and Monday, too, he felt that he must do the same. Tuesday came, and it was such a beautiful day. It had rained during the night. The mountain was wet and green. The fragrance of the leaves was wafted in through the open window; down the mountain sides came the sound of the cow-bells, and some one was heard singing up in the glen. Had it not been for his mother, who was sitting in the room, Thore would have wept from impatient vexation.

Wednesday came and still Thore was in bed; but on Thursday he began to wonder whether he could not get well by Saturday; and on Friday he rose. He remembered well the words Aslaug's father had spoken: "If you can manage to get by the Huseby wolf and his cubs next Saturday, the girl shall be yours." He looked over toward the Huseby sæter again and again. "I cannot get more than another thrashing," thought Thore.

Up to the Huseby sæter there was but one road, as before stated; but a clever fellow might manage to get there, even if he did not take the beaten track. If he rowed out on the fjord below, and past the little tongue of land yonder, and thus reached the other side of the mountain, he might contrive to climb it, though it was so steep that a goat could scarcely venture there—and a goat is not very apt to be timid in climbing the mountains, you know.

Saturday came, and Thore stayed without doors all day long. The sunlight played upon the foliage, and every now and then an alluring song was heard from the mountains. As evening drew near, and the mist was stealing up the slope, he was still sitting outside of the door. He looked up the mountain, and all was still. He looked over toward the Huseby gard. Then he pushed out his boat and rowed round the point of land.

Up at the sæter sat Aslaug, through with her day's work. She was thinking that Thore would not come this evening, but that there would come all the more in his stead. Presently she let loose the dog, but told no one whither she was going. She seated herself where she could look down into the valley; but a dense fog was rising, and, moreover, she felt little disposed to look down that way, for everything reminded her of what had occurred. So she moved, and without thinking what she was doing, she happened to go over to the other side of the mountain, and there she sat down and gazed out over the sea. There was so much peace in this far-reaching sea-view!

Then she felt like singing. She chose a song with long notes, and the music sounded far into the still night. She felt gladdened by it, and so she sang another verse. But then it seemed to her as if some one answered her from the glen far below. "Dear me, what can that be?" thought Aslaug. She went forward to the brink of the precipice, and threw her arms around a slender birch, which hung trembling over the steep. She looked down but saw nothing. The fjord lay silent and calm. Not even a bird ruffled its smooth surface. Aslaug sat down and began singing again. Then she was sure that some one responded with the same tune and nearer than the first time. "It must be somebody, after all." Aslaug sprang up and bent out over the brink of the steep; and there, down at the foot of a rocky wall, she saw a boat moored, and it was so far down that it appeared like a tiny shell. She looked a little farther up, and her eyes fell on a red cap, and under the cap she saw a young man, who was working his way up the almost perpendicular side of the mountain. "Dear me, who can that be?" asked Aslaug, as she let go of the birch and sprang far back.

She dared not answer her own question, for she knew very well who it was. She threw herself down on the greensward and took hold of the grass with both hands, as though it were *she* who must not let go her hold. But the grass came up by the roots.

She cried aloud and prayed God to help Thore. But then it struck her that this conduct of Thore's was really tempting God, and therefore no help could be expected.

"Just this once!" she implored.

And she threw her arms around the dog, as if it were Thore she were keeping from loosing his hold. She rolled over the grass with him, and the moments seemed years. But then the dog tore himself away. "Bow-bow," he barked over the brink of the steep and wagged his tail. "Bow-wow," he barked at Aslaug, and threw his forepaws up on her. "Bow-wow," over the precipice again; and a red cap appeared over the brow of the mountain and Thore lay in her arms.

Now when old Knud Huseby heard of this, he made a very sensible remark, for he said,—

"That boy is worth having; the girl shall be his."

THE BEAR HUNTER.

A WORSE boy to tell lies than the priest's oldest son could scarcely be found in the whole parish; he was also a very good reader; there was no lack on that score, and what he read the peasants were glad to hear, but when it was something they were well pleased with, he would make up more of the same kind, as much as he thought they wanted. His own stories were mostly about strong men and about love.

Soon the priest noticed that the threshing up in the barn was being done in a more and more lazy manner; he went to see what the matter was, and behold it was Thorvald, who stood there telling stories. Soon the quantity of wood brought home from the forest became wonderfully small; he went to see what the trouble was, and there stood Thorvald again, telling stories. There must be an end to this, thought the priest; and he sent the boy to the nearest school.

Only peasant children attended this school, but the priest thought it would be too expensive to keep a private tutor for this one boy. But Thorvald had not been a week among the scholars, before one of his schoolmates came in pale as a corpse, and said he had met some of the underground folk coming along the road. Another boy, still paler, followed, and said that he had actually seen a man without a head walking about and moving the boats down by the landing-place. And what was worst of all, little Knud Pladsen and his young sister, one evening, as they were returning home from school, came running back, almost out of their senses, crying, and declaring that they had heard the bear up near the parsonage; nay, little Marit had even seen his gray eyes sparkle. But now the school-master got terribly angry, struck the table with his ferule, and asked what the deuce—God pardon me my wicked sin—had gotten into the school-children.

"One is growing more crazy than the other," said he. "There lurks a hulder in every bush; there sits a merman under every boat; the bear is out in midwinter! Have you no more faith in your God or in your catechism," quoth he, "or do you believe in all kinds of deviltry, and in all the terrible powers of darkness, and in bears roaming about in the middle of winter?"

But then he calmed down somewhat after a while, and asked little Marit whether she really did not dare to go home. The child sobbed and cried, and declared that it was utterly impossible. The school-master then said that Thorvald, who was the eldest of those remaining, should go with her through the wood.

"No, he has seen the bear himself," cried Marit; "it was he who told us about it."

Thorvald shrank within himself, where he was sitting, especially when the school-master looked at him and drew the ferule affectionately through his left hand.

"Have you seen the bear?" he asked, quietly.

"Well, at any rate, I know," said Thorvald, "that our overseer found a bear's den up in the priest's wood, the day he was out ptarmigan shooting."

"But have you seen the bear yourself?"

"It was not one, it was two large ones, and perhaps there were two smaller ones besides, as the old ones generally have their last year's cubs and this year's, too, with them."

"But have *you* seen them?" reiterated the school-master, still more mildly, as he kept drawing the ferule between his fingers.

Thorvald was silent for a moment.

"I saw the bear that Lars, the hunter, felled last year, at any rate."

Then the school-master came a step nearer, and asked, so pleasantly that the boy became frightened,—

"Have you seen the bears up in the parsonage wood, I ask?"

Thorvald did not say another word.

"Perhaps your memory did not serve you quite right this time?" said the school-master, taking the boy by the jacket collar and striking his own side with the ferule.

Thorvald did not say a word; the other children dared not look that way. Then the school-master said earnestly,—

"It is wicked for a priest's son to tell lies, and still more wicked to teach the poor peasant children to do such things."

And so the boy escaped for that time.

But the next day at school (the teacher had been called up to the priest's and the children were left to themselves) Marit was the first one to ask Thorvald to tell her something about the bear again.

"But you get so frightened," said he.

"Oh, I think I will have to stand it," said she, and moved closer to her brother.

"Ah, now you had better believe it will be shot!" said Thorvald, and nodded his head. "There has come a fellow to the parish who is able to shoot it. No sooner had Lars, the hunter, heard about the bear's den up in the parsonage wood, than he came running through seven whole parishes with a rifle as heavy as the upper mill-stone, and as long as from here to Hans Volden, who sits yonder."

"Mercy!" cried all the children.

"As long?" repeated Thorvald; "yes, it is certainly as long as from here to yonder bench."

"Have you seen it?" asked Ole Böen.

"Have I seen it, do you say? Why, I have been helping to clean it, and that is what Lars will not allow everybody to do, let me tell you. Of course *I* could not lift it, but that made no difference; I only cleaned the lock, and that is not the easiest work, I can tell you."

"People say that gun of Lars's has taken to missing its mark of late," said Hans Volden, leaning back, with both his feet on the desk. "Ever since that time when Lars shot, up at Osmark, at a bear that was asleep, it misses fire twice and misses the mark the third time."

"Yes, ever since he shot at a bear that was asleep," chimed in the girls.

"The fool!" added the boys.

"There is only one way in which this difficulty with the rifle can be remedied," said Ole Böen, "and that is to thrust a living snake down its barrel."

"Yes, we all know that," said the girls. They wanted to hear something new.

"It is now winter, and snakes are not to be found, and so Lars cannot depend very much upon his rifle," said Hans Volden, thoughtfully.

"He wants Niels Böen along with him, does he not?" asked Thorvald.

"Yes," said the boy from Böen's, who was, of course, best posted in regard to this; "but Niels will get permission neither from his mother nor from his sister. His father certainly died from the wrestle he had with the bear up at the sæter last year, and now they have no one but Niels."

"Is it so dangerous, then?" asked a little boy.

"Dangerous?" cried Thorvald. "The bear has as much sense as ten men, and as much strength as twelve."

"Yes, we know that," said the girls once more. They were bent on hearing something new.

"But Niels is like his father; I dare say he will go along," continued Thorvald.

"Of course he will go along," said Ole Böen; "this morning early, before any one was stirring over yonder at our gard, I saw Niels Böen, Lars the hunter, and one man more, going up the mountain with their rifles. I should not be surprised if they were going to the parsonage wood."

"Was it early?" asked the children, in concert.

"Very early! I was up before mother, and started the fire."

"Did Lars have the long rifle?" asked Hans.

"That I do not know, but the one he had was as long as from here to the chair."

"Oh, what a story!" said Thorvald.

"Why, you said so yourself," answered Ole.

"No, the long rifle which I saw, he will scarcely use any more."

"Well, this one was, at all events, as long—as long—as from here, nearly over to the chair."

"Ah! perhaps he had it with him then after all."

"Just think," said Marit, "now they are up among the bears."

"And at this very moment they may be in a fight," said Thorvald.

Then followed a deep, nay, almost solemn silence.

"I think I will go," said Thorvald, taking his cap.

"Yes! yes! then you will find out something," shouted all the rest, and they became full of life again.

"But the school-master?" said he, and stopped.

"Nonsense! you are the priest's son," said Ole Böen.

"Yes, if the school-master touches me with a finger!" said Thorvald, with a significant nod, in the midst of the deep silence of the rest.

"Will you hit him back?" asked they, eagerly.

"Who knows?" said Thorvald, nodding, and went away.

They thought it best to study while he was gone, but none of them were able to do so,—they had to keep talking about the bear. They began guessing how the affair would turn out. Hans bet with Ole that Lars's rifle had missed fire, and that the bear had sprung at him. Little Knud Pladsen thought they had all fared badly, and the girls took his side. But there came Thorvald.

"Let us go," said he, as he pulled open the door, so excited that he could scarcely speak.

"But the school-master?" asked some of the children.

"The deuce take the school-master! The bear! The bear!" cried Thorvald, and could say no more.

"Is it shot?" asked one, very softly, and the others dared not draw their breath.

Thorvald sat panting for a while, finally he got up, mounted one of the benches, swung his cap, and shouted,—

"Let us go, I say. I will take all the responsibility."

"But where shall we go?" asked Hans.

"The largest bear has been borne down, the others still remain. Niels Böen has been badly hurt, because Lars's rifle missed its mark, and the bears rushed straight at them. The boy who went with them saved himself only by throwing himself flat on the ground, and pretending to be dead, and the bear did not touch him. As soon as Lars and Niels had killed their bear, they shot his also. Hurrah!"

"Hurrah!" shouted all, both girls and boys, and up from their seats, and out through the door, they sprang, and off they ran over field and wood to Böen, as though there was no such thing as a school-master in the whole world.

The girls soon complained that they were not able to keep up, but the boys took them by the hand and away they all rushed.

"Take care not to touch it!" said Thorvald; "it sometimes happens that the bears become alive again."

"Is that so?" asked Marit.

"Yes, and they appear in a new form, so have a care!"

And they kept running.

"Lars shot the largest one ten times before it fell," he began again.

"Just think! ten times!"

And they kept running.

"And Niels stabbed it eighteen times with his knife before it fell!"

"Mercy! what a bear!"

And the children ran so that the sweat poured down from their faces.

Finally they reached the place. Ole Böen pushed the door open and got in first.

"Have a care!" cried Hans after him.

Marit and a little girl that Thorvald and Hans had led between them, were the next ones, and then came Thorvald, who did not go far forward, but remained standing where he could observe the whole scene.

"See the blood!" said he to Hans.

The others hardly knew whether they should venture in just yet.

"Do you see it?" asked a girl of a boy, who stood by her side in the door.

"Yes, it is as large as the captain's large horse," answered he, and went on talking to her. It was bound with iron chains, he said, and had even broken the one that had been put about its fore-legs. He could see distinctly that it was alive, and the blood was flowing from it like a waterfall.

Of course, this was not true; but they forgot that when they caught sight of the bear, the rifle, and Niels, who sat there with bandaged wounds after the fight with the bear, and when they heard old Lars the hunter tell how all had happened. So eagerly, and with so much interest did they look and listen, that they did not observe that some one came behind them who also began to tell his story, and that in the following manner:—

"I will teach you to leave the school without my permission, that I will!"

A cry of fright arose from the whole crowd, and out through the door, through the veranda, and out into the yard they ran. Soon they appeared like a lot of black balls, rolling one by one, over the snow-white field, and when the school-master on his old legs followed them to the school-house, he could hear the children reading from afar off; they read until the walls fairly rattled.

Aye, that was a glorious day, the day when the bear-hunter came home! It began in sunshine and ended in rain, but such days are usually the best growing days.

THE FATHER.

THE man whose story is here to be told was the wealthiest and most influential person in his parish; his name was Thord Överaas. He appeared in the priest's study one day, tall and earnest.

"I have gotten a son," said he, "and I wish to present him for baptism."

"What shall his name be?"

"Finn,—after my father."

"And the sponsors?"

They were mentioned, and proved to be the best men and women of Thord's relations in the parish.

"Is there anything else?" inquired the priest, and looked up.

The peasant hesitated a little.

"I should like very much to have him baptized by himself," said he, finally.

"That is to say on a week-day?"

"Next Saturday, at twelve o'clock noon."

"Is there anything else?" inquired the priest.

"There is nothing else;" and the peasant twirled his cap, as though he were about to go.

Then the priest rose. "There is yet this, however," said he, and walking toward Thord, he took him by the hand and looked gravely into his eyes: "God grant that the child may become a blessing to you!"

One day sixteen years later, Thord stood once more in the priest's study.

"Really, you carry your age astonishingly well, Thord," said the priest; for he saw no change whatever in the man.

"That is because I have no troubles," replied Thord.

To this the priest said nothing, but after a while he asked: "What is your pleasure this evening?"

"I have come this evening about that son of mine who is to be confirmed to-morrow."

"He is a bright boy."

"I did not wish to pay the priest until I heard what number the boy would have when he takes his place in church to-morrow."

"He will stand number one."

"So I have heard; and here are ten dollars for the priest."

"Is there anything else I can do for you?" inquired the priest, fixing his eyes on Thord.

"There is nothing else."

Thord went out.

Eight years more rolled by, and then one day a noise was heard outside of the priest's study, for many men were approaching, and at their head was Thord, who entered first.

The priest looked up and recognized him.

"You come well attended this evening, Thord," said he.

"I am here to request that the bans may be published for my son: he is about to marry Karen Storliden, daughter of Gudmund, who stands here beside me."

"Why, that is the richest girl in the parish."

"So they say," replied the peasant, stroking back his hair with one hand.

The priest sat a while as if in deep thought, then entered the names in his book, without making any comments, and the men wrote their signatures underneath. Thord laid three dollars on the table.

"One is all I am to have," said the priest.

"I know that very well; but he is my only child, I want to do it handsomely."

The priest took the money.

"This is now the third time, Thord, that you have come here on your son's account."

"But now I am through with him," said Thord, and folding up his pocket-book he said farewell and walked away.

The men slowly followed him.

A fortnight later, the father and son were rowing across the lake, one calm, still day, to Storliden to make arrangements for the wedding.

"This thwart is not secure," said the son, and stood up to straighten the seat on which he was sitting.

At the same moment the board he was standing on slipped from under him; he threw out his arms, uttered a shriek, and fell overboard.

"Take hold of the oar!" shouted the father, springing to his feet and holding out the oar.

But when the son had made a couple of efforts he grew stiff.

"Wait a moment!" cried the father, and began to row toward his son.

Then the son rolled over on his back, gave his father one long look, and sank.

Thord could scarcely believe it; he held the boat still, and stared at the spot where his son had gone down, as though he must surely come to the surface again. There rose some bubbles, then some more, and finally one large one that burst; and the lake lay there as smooth and bright as a mirror again.

For three days and three nights people saw the father rowing round and round the spot, without taking either food or sleep; he was dragging the lake for the body of his son. And toward morning of the third day he found it, and carried it in his arms up over the hills to his gard.

It might have been about a year from that day, when the priest, late one autumn evening, heard some one in the passage outside of the door, carefully trying to find the latch. The priest opened the door, and in walked a tall, thin man, with bowed form and white hair. The priest looked long at him before he recognized him. It was Thord.

"Are you out walking so late?" said the priest, and stood still in front of him.

"Ah, yes! it is late," said Thord, and took a seat.

The priest sat down also, as though waiting. A long, long silence followed. At last Thord said,—

"I have something with me that I should like to give to the poor; I want it to be invested as a legacy in my son's name."

He rose, laid some money on the table, and sat down again. The priest counted it.

"It is a great deal of money," said he.

"It is half the price of my gard. I sold it to-day."

The priest sat long in silence. At last he asked, but gently,—

"What do you propose to do now, Thord?"

"Something better."

They sat there for a while, Thord with downcast eyes, the priest with his eyes fixed on Thord. Presently the priest said, slowly and softly,—

"I think your son has at last brought you a true blessing."

"Yes, I think so myself," said Thord, looking up, while two big tears coursed slowly down his cheeks.

THE EAGLE'S NEST.

THE Endregards was the name of a small solitary parish, surrounded by lofty mountains. It lay in a flat and fertile valley, and was intersected by a broad river that flowed down from the mountains. This river emptied into a lake, which was situated close by the parish, and presented a fine view of the surrounding country.

Up the Endre-Lake the man had come rowing, who had first cleared this valley; his name was Endre, and it was his descendants who dwelt here. Some said he had fled hither on account of a murder he had committed, and that was why his family were so dark; others said this was on account of the mountains, which shut out the sun at five o'clock of a midsummer afternoon.

Over this parish there hung an eagle's nest. It was built on a cliff far up the mountains; all could see the mother eagle alight in her nest, but no one could reach it. The male eagle went sailing over the parish, now swooping down after a lamb, now after a kid; once he had also taken a little child and borne it away; therefore there was no safety in the parish as long as the eagle had a nest in this mountain. There was a tradition among the people, that in old times there were two brothers who had climbed up to the nest and torn it down; but nowadays there was no one who was able to reach it.

Whenever two met at the Endregards, they talked about the eagle's nest, and looked up. Every one knew, when the eagles reappeared in the new year, where they had swooped down and done mischief, and who had last endeavored to reach the nest. The youth of the place, from early boyhood, practiced climbing mountains and trees, wrestling and scuffling, in order that one day they might reach the cliff and demolish the nest, as those two brothers had done.

At the time of which this story tells, the best boy at the Endregards was named Leif, and he was not of the Endre family. He had curly hair and small eyes, was clever in all play, and was fond of the fair sex. He early said of himself, that one day he would reach the eagle's nest; but old people remarked that he should not have said so aloud.

This annoyed him, and even before he had reached his prime he made the ascent. It was one bright Sunday forenoon, early in the summer; the young eagles must be just about hatched. A vast multitude of people had gathered together at the foot of the mountain to behold the feat; the old people advising him against attempting it, the young ones urging him on.

But he hearkened only to his own desires, and waiting until the mother eagle left her nest, he gave one spring into the air, and hung in a tree several yards from the ground. The tree grew in a cleft in the rock, and from this cleft he began to climb upward. Small stones loosened under his feet, earth and gravel came rolling down, otherwise all was still, save for the stream flowing behind, with its suppressed, ceaseless murmur. Soon he had reached a point where the mountain began to project; here he hung long by one hand, while his foot groped for a sure resting-place, for he could not see. Many, especially women, turned away, saying he would never have done this had he had parents living. He found footing at last, however sought again, now with the hand, now with the foot, failed, slipped, then hung fast again. They who stood below could hear one another breathing.

Suddenly there rose to her feet, a tall, young girl, who had been sitting on a stone apart from the rest; it was said that she had been betrothed to Leif from early childhood, although he was not of her kindred. Stretching out her arms she called aloud: "Leif, Leif, why do you do this?" Every eye was turned on her. Her father, who was standing close by, gave her a stern look, but she heeded him not. "Come down again, Leif," she cried; "I love you, and there is nothing to be gained up there!"

They could see that he was considering; he hesitated a moment or two, and then started onward. For a long time all went well, for he was sure-footed and had a strong grip; but after a while it seemed as if he were growing weary, for he often paused. Presently a little stone came rolling down as a harbinger, and every one who stood there had to watch its course to the bottom. Some could endure it no longer, and went away. The girl alone still stood on the stone, and wringing her hands continued to gaze upward.

Once more Leif took hold with one hand but it slipped; she saw this distinctly; then he tried the other; it slipped also. "Leif!" she shouted, so loud that her voice rang through the mountains, and all the others chimed in with her. "He is slipping!" they cried, and stretched up their hands to him, both men and women. He was indeed slipping, carrying with him sand, stones, and earth; slipping, continually slipping, ever faster and faster. The people turned away, and then they heard a rustling and scraping in the mountain behind them, after which, something fell with a heavy thud, like a great piece of wet earth.

When they could look round again, he was lying there crushed and mutilated beyond recognition. The girl had fallen down on the stone, and her father took her up in his arms and bore her away.

The youths who had taken the most pains to incite Leif to the perilous ascent now dared not lend a hand to pick him up; some were even unable to look at him. So the old people had to go forward. The eldest of them, as he took hold of the body, said: "It is very sad, but," he added, casting a look upward, "it is, after all, well that something hangs so high that it cannot be reached by every one."

Three Comedies

THE NEWLY-MARRIED COUPLE
DRAMATIS PERSONAE

The FATHER.
The MOTHER.
LAURA, their daughter.
AXEL, her husband.
MATHILDE, her friend.

ACT I

(SCENE.—A handsomely furnished, carpeted room, with a door at the back leading to a lobby. The FATHER is sitting on a couch on the left-hand side, in the foreground, reading a newspaper. Other papers are lying on a small table in front of him. AXEL is on another couch drawn up in a similar position on the right-hand side. A newspaper, which he is not reading, is lying on his knee. The MOTHER is sitting, sewing, in an easy-chair drawn up beside a table in the middle of the room.)

LAURA enters.

Laura. Good morning, mother! (Kisses her.)

Mother. Good morning, dear. Have you slept well?

Laura. Very well, thanks. Good morning, dad! (Kisses him.)

Father. Good morning, little one, good morning. Happy and in good spirits?

Laura. Very. (Passes in front of AXEL.) Good morning, Axel! (Sits down at the table, opposite her mother.)

Axel. Good morning.

Mother. I am very sorry to say, my child, that I must give up going to the ball with you to-night. It is such a long way to go, in this cold spring weather.

Father (without looking up from his paper). Your mother is not well. She was coughing in the night.

Laura. Coughing again?

Father. Twice. (The MOTHER coughs, and he looks up.) There, do you hear that? Your mother must not go out, on any account.

Laura. Then I won't go, either.

Father. That will be just as well; it is such raw weather. (To the MOTHER.) But you have no shawl on, my love; where is your shawl?

Laura. Axel, fetch mother's shawl; it is hanging in the lobby. (AXEL goes out into the lobby.)

Mother. We are not really into spring yet. I am surprised the stove is not lit in here.

Laura (to AXEL, who is arranging the shawl over the MOTHER'S shoulders). Axel, ring the bell and let us have a fire. (He does so, and gives the necessary instructions to the Servant.)

Mother. If none of us are going to the ball, we ought to send them a note. Perhaps you would see to that, Axel?

Axel. Certainly—but will it do for us to stay away from this ball?

Laura. Surely you heard father say that mother has been coughing in the night.

Axel. Yes, I heard; but the ball is being given by the only friend I have in these parts, in your honour and mine. We are the reason of the whole entertainment—surely we cannot stay away from it?

Laura. But it wouldn't be any pleasure to us to go without mother.

Axel. One often has to do what is not any pleasure.

Laura. When it is a matter of duty, certainly. But our first duty is to mother, and we cannot possibly leave her alone at home when she is ill.

Axel. I had no idea she was ill.

Father (as he reads). She coughed twice in the night. She coughed only a moment ago.

Mother. Axel means that a cough or two isn't illness, and he is quite right.

Father (still reading). A cough may be a sign of something very serious. (Clears his throat.) The chest—or the lungs. (Clears his throat again.) I don't think I feel quite the thing myself, either.

Laura. Daddy dear, you are too lightly clothed.

Mother. You dress as if it were summer—and it certainly isn't that.

Father. The fire will burn up directly. (Clears his throat again.) No, not quite the thing at all.

Laura. Axel! (He goes up to her.) You might read the paper to us till breakfast is ready.

Axel. Certainly. But first of all I want to know if we really are not to go to the ball?

Laura. You can go, if you like, and take our excuses.

Mother. That wouldn't do. Remember you are married now.

Axel. That is exactly why it seems to me that Laura cannot stay at home. The fact that she is my wife ought to have most weight with her now; and this ball is being given for us two, who have nothing the matter with us, besides being mainly a dance for young people—

Mother. And not for old folk.

Laura. Thank you; mother has taken to dancing again since I have grown up. I have never been to a ball without mother's leading off the dances.

Mother. Axel apparently thinks it would have been much better if I had not done so.

Father (as he reads). Mother dances most elegantly.

Axel. Surely I should know that, seeing how often I have had the honour of leading off with mother. But on this occasion forty or fifty people have been invited, a lot of trouble and expense incurred and a lot of pleasure arranged, solely for our sakes. It would be simply wicked to disappoint them.

Father (still reading). We can give a ball for them, in return.

Mother. All the more as we owe heaps of people an invitation.

Laura. Yes, that will be better; we have more room here, too. (A pause.)

Axel (leaning over LAURA'S chair). Think of your new ball dress—my first present to you. Won't that tempt you? Blue muslin, with silver stars all over it? Shall they not shine for the first time to-night?

Laura (smiling). No, there would be no shine in the stars if mother were not at the dance.

Axel. Very well—I will send our excuses. (Turns to go out.)

Father (still reading). Perhaps it will be better for me to write. (AXEL stops.)

Mother. Yes, you will do it best.

MATHILDE comes in, followed by a Servant, who throws the doors open.

Mathilde. Breakfast is ready.

Father (taking his wife's arm). Keep your shawl on, my dear; it is cold in the hall. (They go out.)

Axel (as he offers LAURA his arm and leads her towards the door). Let me have a word with you, before we follow them!

Laura. But it is breakfast time.

Axel (to MATHILDE, who is standing behind them waiting). Do you mind going on? (MATHILDE goes out, followed by the Servant. AXEL turns to LAURA.) Will nothing move you? Go with me to this dance!

Laura. I thought that was what you were going to say.

Axel. For *my* sake!

Laura. But you saw for yourself that mother and father do not wish it?

Axel. *I* wish it.

Laura. When mother and father do not?

Axel. Then I suppose you are their daughter in the first place, and my wife only in the second?

Laura (with a laugh). Well, that is only natural.

Axel. No, it is not natural; because two days ago you promised to forsake your father and your mother and follow me.

Laura (laughing). To the ball? I certainly never promised that.

Axel. Wherever I wish.

Laura. But you mustn't wish that, Axel darling—because it is quite impossible.

Axel. It is quite possible, if you like to do it.

Laura. Yes, but I don't like.

Axel. That same day you also heard that a man is his wife's lord and master. You must be willing to leave them, if I wish it; it was on those terms that you gave me your hand, you obstinate little woman.

Laura. It was just so as to be able to be always with father and mother, that I did it.

Axel. So that was it. Then you have no wish to be always with me?

Laura. Yes—but not to forsake them.

Axel. Never?

Laura. Never? (Softly.) Yes, some day—when I must.

Axel. When must you?

Laura. When? When mother and father—are gone. But why think about such things?

Axel. Don't cry, darling! Listen to me. Would you never be willing to follow me—until they have left us?

Laura. No!—how can you think so?

Axel. Ah, Laura, you don't love me.

Laura. Why do you say such a thing? You only want to make me unhappy.

Axel. You don't even know what love is.

Laura. I don't?—That is not kind of you.

Axel. Tell me what it is then, sweetheart!

Laura (kissing him). Now you mustn't talk about it any more; because you know, if you do, I shall have red eyes, and then father and mother will want to know why they are red, and I shall not be able to tell them, and it will be very embarrassing.

Axel. Better a few tears now than many later on.

Laura. But what have I done to cry about?

Axel. You have given your hand without giving your heart with it; your tongue said "yes," but not your will; you have given yourself without realising what it means. And so, what ought to be the greatest and purest happiness in my life begins to turn to sorrow, and the future looks dark.

Laura. Oh, dear!—and is all this my fault?

Axel. No, it is my own fault. I have been deluding myself with flattering hopes. I thought it would be so easy a matter for my love to awaken yours; but I cannot make you understand me. Every way I have tried has failed. So I must call up my courage, and try the last chance.

Laura. The last chance? What do you mean?

Axel. Laura, I can't tell you how dearly I love you!

Laura. If you did, you wouldn't hurt me. I never hurt you.

Axel. Well, give in to me in just this one thing, and I shall believe it is the promise of more. Go with me to the ball!

Laura. You know I cannot do that!

Axel. Ah! then I dare not delay any longer!

Laura. You frighten me! You look so angry.

Axel. No, no. But things cannot go on like this any longer. I can't stand it!

Laura. Am I so bad, then? No one ever told me so before.

Axel. Don't cry, my dainty little fairy. You have nothing to blame yourself for—except for being so bewitchingly sweet whether you are laughing or crying. You exhale sweetness like a flower. I want your influence to pervade every place where I am, to distract me when I am moody and laugh away my longings. Hush, hush—no red eyes. Let no one see that. Here is your mother coming—no, it is Mathilde.

Enter MATHILDE.

Mathilde. Your coffee is getting cold.

Axel. We are just coming. At least, Laura is. I want to speak to you for a moment, if I may.

Mathilde. To me?

Axel. If you will allow me.

Mathilde. By all means.

Laura. But you are coming in to breakfast?

Axel. In a moment, darling.

Laura. And you are not angry with me any longer?

Axel (following her). I never was that. I never could be!

Laura. I am so glad! (Runs out.)

Mathilde. What is it you want?

Axel. Can you keep a secret?

Mathilde. No.

Axel. You won't?

Mathilde. No.

Axel. You won't share any more confidences with me? (Takes her hand.) You used to—

Mathilde (drawing back her hand and moving away from him). Yes, I used to.

Axel. Why won't you any longer? (Goes up to her.) What is changed?

Mathilde. You. You are married now.

Axel. No, that is just what I am not.

Mathilde. Indeed.

Axel. You have sharp eyes. You must have seen that.

Mathilde. I thought it was all just as you wished.

Axel. You are giving me very abrupt answers. Have I offended you?

Mathilde. What makes you ask that?

Axel. Because lately you have avoided me. Remember how kind you were to me once—indeed, that I owe you everything. It was through you, you know, that I got at her. I had to make assignations with you, in order to meet her. I had to offer you my arm so as to be able to give her the other, and to talk to you so that she might hear my voice. The little darling thought she was doing you a service—

Mathilde. When as a matter of fact it was I that was doing her one—

Axel. Yes, and without suspecting it! That was the amusing part of it.

Mathilde. Yes, that was the amusing part of it.

Axel. But soon people began to say that you and I were secretly engaged, and that we were making a stalking-horse of Laura; so for her sake I had to bring matters to a head rather quickly.

Mathilde. Yes, you took a good many people by surprise.

Axel. Including even yourself, I believe—not to mention the old folk and Laura. But the worst of it is that I took my own happiness by surprise, too.

Mathilde. What do you mean?

Axel. Of course I knew Laura was only a child; but I thought she would grow up when she felt the approach of love. But she has never felt its approach; she is like a bud that will not open, and I cannot warm the atmosphere. But you could do that—you, in whom she has confided all her first longings—you, whose kind heart knows so well how to sacrifice its happiness for others. You know you are to some extent responsible, too, for the fact that the most important event in her life came upon her a little unpreparedly; so you ought to take her by the hand and guide her first steps away from her parents and towards me—direct her affections towards me—

Mathilde. I? (A pause.)

Axel. Won't you?

Mathilde. No—

Axel. But why not? You love her, don't you?

Mathilde. I do; but this is a thing—

Axel.—that you can do quite well! For you are better off than the rest of us—you have many more ways of reaching a person's soul than we have. Sometimes when we have been discussing something, and then you have given your opinion, it has reminded me of the refrains to the old ballads, which sum up the essence of the whole poem in two lines.

Mathilde. Yes, I have heard you flatter before.

Axel. I flatter? Why, what I have just asked you to do is a clearer proof than anything else how great my—

Mathilde. Stop, stop! I won't do it!

Axel. Why not? At least be frank with me!

Mathilde. Because—oh, because—(Turns away.)

Axel. But what has made you so unkind? (MATHILDE stops for a moment, as though she were going to answer; then goes hurriedly out.) What on earth is the matter with her? Has anything gone wrong between her and Laura? Or is it something about the house that is worrying her? She is too level-headed to be disturbed by trifles.—Well, whatever it is, it must look after itself; I have something else to think about. If the one of them *can't* understand me, and the other *won't*, and the old couple neither can nor will, I must act on my own account—and the sooner the better! Later on, it would look to other people like a rupture. It must be done now, before we settle down to this state of things; for if we were to do that, it would be all up with us. To acquiesce in such an unnatural state of affairs would be like crippling one's self on purpose. I am entangled hand and foot here in the meshes of a net of circumspection. I shall have to sail along at "dead slow" all my life—creep about among their furniture and their flowers as warily as among their habits. You might just as well try to stand the house on its head as to alter the slightest thing in it. I daren't move!—and it is becoming unbearable. Would it be a breach of a law of nature to move this couch a little closer to the wall, or this chair further away from it? And has it been ordained from all eternity that this table must stand just where it does? *Can* it be shifted? (Moves it.) It actually can! And the couch, too. Why does it stand so far forward? (Pushes it back.) And why are these chairs everlastingly in the way? This one shall stand there—and this one there. (Moves them.) I will have room for my legs; I positively believe I have forgotten how to walk. For a whole year I have hardly heard the sound of my own footstep—or of my own voice; they do nothing but whisper and cough here. I wonder if I have any voice left? (Sings.)

> *"Bursting every bar and band,*
> *My fetters will I shatter;*
> *Striding out, with sword in hand,*
> *Where the fight"*—

(He stops abruptly, at the entrance of the FATHER, the MOTHER, LAURA and MATHILDE, who have come hurriedly from the breakfast table. A long pause.)

Laura. Axel, dear!

Mathilde. What, all by himself?

Mother. Do you think you are at a ball?

Father. And playing the part of musician as well as dancer?

Axel. I am amusing myself.

Father. With our furniture?

Axel. I only wanted to see if it was possible to move it.

Mother. If it was possible to move it?

Laura. But what were you shouting about?

Axel. I only wanted to try if I had any voice left.

Laura. If you had any voice left?

Mother. There is a big wood near the house, where you can practise that.

Father. And a waterfall—if you are anxious to emulate Demosthenes.

Laura. Axel, dear—are you out of your mind?

Axel. No, but I think I soon shall be.

Mother. Is there anything wrong?

Axel. Yes, a great deal.

Mother. What is it? Some unpleasant news by post?

Axel. No, not that—but I am unhappy.

Mother. Two days after your wedding?

Father. You have a very odd way of showing it.

Axel. I am taken like that sometimes.

Mother. But what is it? Evidently you are not as happy as we hoped you would be. Confide in us, Axel; we are your parents now, you know.

Axel. It is something I have been thinking about for a long time, but have not had the courage to mention.

Mother. Why? Aren't we good to you?

Axel. You are much too good to me.

Father. What do you mean by that?

Axel. That everything is made far too smooth for me here; my faculties get no exercise; I cannot satisfy my longing for activity and conflict—nor my ambition.

Father. Dear me! What do you want, if you please?

Axel. I want to work for myself, to owe my position in life to my own efforts—to become something.

Father. Really.—What a foolish idea! (Moves towards the door.)

Mother. But an idea we must take an interest in. He is our child's husband now, remember. What do you want to be, my boy? Member of Parliament?

Axel. No; but my uncle, who has about the largest legal practice in these parts, offered long ago to hand it over to me.

Mother. But you wouldn't be able to look after it from here, would you, Axel?

Father (at the door). A ridiculous idea!—Come back to breakfast. (Turns to go.)

Mother. That is true, isn't it? You couldn't look after it from here?

Axel. No; but I can move into town.

All. Move into town? (A pause. The FATHER turns back from the door.)

Father. That is still more impossible, of course.

Mother. There must be something at the bottom of this. Is anything worrying you? (Lowering her voice.) Are you in debt?

Axel. No, thanks to the kindness of you two. You have freed me from that.

Mother. Then what is it, Axel? You have been so, strange lately—what is it, my dear boy?

Father. Nonsensical ideas—probably his stomach is disordered. Remember the last time I ate lobster!—Come along in and have a glass of sherry, and you will forget all about it.

Axel. No, it isn't a thing one can forget. It is always in my thoughts—more and more insistently. I must have work for my mind—some outlet for my ambition. I am bored here.

Mother. Two days after your wedding!

Father. Set to work then, for heaven's sake! What is there to hinder you? Would you like to take charge of one of my farms? Or to start some improvements on the estate?—or anything you please! I have no doubt you have ideas, and I will provide the money—only do not let us have any of this fuss!

Axel. But then I shall be indebted to you for everything, and shall feel dependent.

Father. So you would rather feel indebted to your uncle?

Axel. He will give me nothing. I must buy it from him.

Father. Really!—How?

Axel. With my work and my——. Oh well, I suppose you would lend me a little capital?

Father. Not a penny.

Axel. But why?

Father. I will tell you why. Because my son in law must be my son-in-law, and not a speculating lawyer who sits with his door open and a sign hung out to beg for custom.

Axel. Is a lawyer's profession a dishonourable one, then?

Father. No, it is not. But you have been received into one of the oldest and richest families in the country, and you owe some respect to its traditions. Generation after generation, from time immemorial, the heads of our family have been lords of the manor—not office seekers or fortune hunters. The honourable offices I have held have all been offered to me and not sought by me; and I am not going to have you chattering about your university degree or your talents. You shall stay quietly here, and you will be offered more than you want.

Mother. Come, come, my dear, don't get heated over it; that always makes you so unwell. Let us arrive at some arrangement without wrangling. Axel, you must be reasonable; you know he cannot stand any over-exertion. Laura, get your father a glass of water. Come, my dear, let us go back to the dining-room.

Father. Thanks, I have no appetite left now.

Mother. There, you see!—Axel, Axel!

Laura. For shame, Axel!

Mother. Sit down, dear, sit down! My goodness, how hot you are!

Father. It is so warm in here.

Mother. That is the stove. Shut it down, Mathilde!

Laura (to AXEL). You are a nice one, I must say!

Father. The chairs—put them straight! (They do so.) And the table! (They do so.) That is better.

Mother. That is the worst of a stranger in the house—something of this sort may so easily happen.

Father. But a thing like this!—I have never in my life been contradicted before.

Mother. It is for the first and last time! He will soon learn who you are and what is due to you.

Father. And to think that, the first time, it should be my son-in-law that—

Mother. He will regret it for the rest of your life, you may be sure, and when you are gone he will have no peace of mind. We can only hope that the atmosphere of affection in this house will improve him. Really, lately, Axel has behaved as if he were bewitched.

Laura. Yes, hasn't he?

Mother. Good gracious, Laura, do you mean that you—

Laura. No, I didn't mean anything.

Mother. Laura, are you trying to conceal something?

Father. And from us? (Gets up.) Are things as bad as that?

Laura. I assure you, dear people, it is nothing; it is only—

Father and Mother (together). Only—?

Laura. No, no, it is nothing—only you frighten me so.

Father and Mother (together). She is crying!

Mathilde. She is crying!

Father. Now, sir—why is she crying?

Laura. But, father, father—look, I am not crying the least bit.

Mother and Mathilde. Yes, she is crying!

Axel. Yes—and will cry every day until we make a change here! (A pause, while they all look at him.) Well, as so much has been said, it may as well all come out. Our marriage is not a happy one, because it lacks the most essential thing of all.

Mother. Merciful heavens, what are you saying!

Father. Compose yourself; let me talk to him. What do you mean, sir?

Axel. Laura does not love me—

Laura. Yes, that is what he says!

Axel. She hasn't the least idea what love means, and will never learn as long as she is in her father's house.

Mother and Father. Why?

Axel. Because she lives only for her parents; me, she looks upon merely as an elder brother who is to assist her in loving them.

Mother. Is that so distasteful to you, then?

Axel. No, no. I am devoted to you and grateful to you, and I am proud of being your son; but it is only through her that I am that—and she has never yet really taken me to her heart. I am quite at liberty to go away or to stay, as I please; *she* is a fixture here. There is never one of her requests to me, scarcely a single wish she expresses—indeed, scarcely a sign of endearment she shows me, that she has not first of all divided up into three portions; and I get my one-third of it, and get it last or not at all.

Mother. He is jealous—and of us!

Father. Jealous of us!

Laura. Yes, indeed he is, mother.

Father. This is mere fancy, Axel—a ridiculous idea. Do not let any one else hear you saying that.

Axel. No, it is neither mere fancy nor is it ridiculous. It colours the whole of our relations to one another; it gnaws at my feelings, and then I torment her, make you angry, and lead an idle, empty, ill-tempered existence—

Father. You are ill, there is no doubt about it.

Axel. I am, and you have made me ill.

Father and Mother (together). We have?

Father. Please be a little—

Axel. You allow her to treat me simply as the largest sized of all the dolls you have given her to play with. You cannot bear to see her give away any more of her affection than she might give to one of her dolls.

Father. Please talk in a more seemly manner! Please show us a proper respect—

Axel. Forgive me, my dear parents, if I don't. What I mean is that a child cannot be a wife, and as long as she remains with you she will always be a child.

Mother. But, Axel, did we not tell you she was only a child—

Father. We warned you, we asked you to wait a year or two—

Mother. Because we could not see that she loved you sufficiently.

Father. But your answer was that it was just the child in her that you loved.

Mother. Just the child's innocence and simplicity. You said you felt purer in her presence; indeed, that she sometimes made you feel as if you were in church. And we, her father and mother, understood that, for we had felt it ourselves.

Father. We felt that just as much as you, my son.

Mother. Do you remember one morning, when she was asleep, that you said her life was a dream which it would be a sin to disturb?

Father. And said that the mere thought of her made you tread more softly for fear of waking her.

Axel. That is quite true. Her childlike nature shed happiness upon me, her gentle innocence stilled me. It is quite true that I felt her influence upon my senses like that of a beautiful morning.

Father. And now you are impatient with her for being a child!

Axel. Exactly! At the time when I was longing to lead her to the altar, I daresay I only thought of her as an inspiration to my better self and my best impulses. She was to me what the Madonna is to a good Catholic; but now she has become something more than that. The distance between us no longer exists; I cannot be satisfied with mere adoration, I must love; I cannot be satisfied with kneeling to her, I need my arms around her. Her glance has the same delicacy it always had, the same innocence; but I can no longer sit and gaze at her by the hour. Her glance must lose itself in mine in complete surrender. Her hand, her arm, her mouth are the same as they were; but I need to feel her hand stroking my hair, her arm round my neck, her mouth on mine; her thoughts must embrace mine and be like sunshine in my heart. She was a symbol to me, but the symbol has become flesh and blood. When first she came into my thoughts it was as a child; but I have watched her day by day grow into a woman, whose shyness and ignorance make her turn away from me, but whom I must possess. (LAURA moves quickly towards him.)

Mother. He loves our child!

Father. He loves her! (Embraces his wife.) What more is there to say, then? Everything is as it should be. Come along and have a glass of sherry!

Axel. No, everything is not as it should be. I can get her gratitude sometimes in a lucky moment, but not her heart. If I am fond of a certain thing, she is not. If I wish a thing, she wishes the opposite—for instance, if it's only a question of going to a ball, she won't take any pleasure in it unless her mother can go too.

Mother. Good heavens, is it nothing but that!

Laura. No, mother, it is nothing else; it is this ball.

Father. Then for any sake go to the ball! You are a couple of noodles. Come along, now.

Axel. The ball? It is not the ball. I don't care a bit about the ball.

Laura. No, that is just it, mother. When he gets what he wants, it turns out that it wasn't what he wanted at all, but something quite different. I don't understand what it is.

Axel. No, because it is not a question of any one thing, but of our whole relations to one another. Love is what I miss; she does not know what it means, and never will know—as long as she remains at home here. (A pause.)

Mother (slowly). As long as she remains at home?

Father (coming nearer to him, and trembling slightly). What do you mean by that?

Axel. It will be only when Laura finds she can no longer lean upon her parents, that she may possibly come to lean upon me.

Mother. What does he mean?

Father. I don't understand—

Axel. If she is to be something more than a good daughter—if she is to be a good wife—Laura must go away from here.

Mother. Laura go away?

Father. Our child?

Laura (to her MOTHER). Mother!

Axel. It would be wronging her whom I love so deeply, it would be wronging myself, and wronging you who mean so well, if now, when the power is in my hands, I had not the spirit to make use of it. Here, Laura lives only for you; when you die, life will be over for her. But that is not what marriage means, that is not what she promised at the altar, and that is what I cannot submit to. To go on like this will only make us all unhappy; and that is why Laura must go with me! (The MOTHER starts forward; LAURA goes to MATHILDE.)

Father. You cannot mean what you say.

Axel. I am in deadly earnest, and no one can shake my resolution.

Mother. Then Heaven have mercy on us! (A pause.)

Father. You know, Axel, that God gave us five children; and you know, too, that He took four away from us again. Laura is now our only child, our only joy.

Mother. We can't bear to lose her, Axel! She has never been away from us a single day since she was born. She is the spoilt child of our sorrow; if death itself claimed her, we should have to hold fast on to her.

Father. Axel, you are not a wicked man; you have not come amongst us to make us all unhappy?

Axel. If I were to give in now, this state of things would occur again every week or so, and none of us could stand that. For that reason, my dear parents, prove yourselves capable of a sacrifice. Let us put an end to it once for all—and let Laura move into town with me next week.

Father. Good heavens—it is impossible!

Mother. You won't have the heart to do that. Look at her, and then say that again! (AXEL turns away.) No, I knew you could not. (To the FATHER.) You talk to him! Tell him the truth, set him right, since he has broken in upon a good and loving family only to bring misfortune to it.

Father. In this house, as far back as I can remember, no hard words have ever been used. It seems to me like some evil dream, that I am struggling to wake out of and cannot! (A pause.) Mr. Hargaut, when we gave our daughter to you, we made no conditions. We admitted you into a happy family, to a position of wealth, to a promising future; and we expected, in return, some little affection, some little appreciation—at least some little respect. But you behave like—like a stranger, who is admitted to one's intimacy and good offices, and then one morning goes off with the most valuable possessions in the house—like an ungrateful, cruel—! We have confided our child, the dearest, sweetest child, our only child, to—a man without a heart! We were two happy parents, rich in her love—parents whom every one envied and we now are two poor bereaved wretches, who must creep away together into a corner in their unhappy disillusionment. (Sits down.)

Mother. And this is the way you can treat the man who has given you everything! What answer have you to give him?

Axel. It makes my heart bleed. If I had thought it would be as hard as this, indeed I would never have begun it; but if we leave the matter unsettled, now that it has been broached, we shall never be on proper terms with one another again. Of that I am certain. If it is a matter that pains us all, for that very reason let us go through with it and get it settled.

Father. Poor confiding fools that we have been!

Mother. Can't you give us some respite, so that we may think things over quietly? This is simply tearing us apart.

Axel. It would only prolong your pain, and it would end in your hating me. No, it must be done now—at once; otherwise it will never be done.

Mother. Oh dear, oh dear! (Sits down.)

Father. Axel! Listen to us for a moment! It is quite possible you may be in the right; but for that very reason I beg you—I, who have never yet begged anything of any one—I beg you, be merciful! I am an old man, and cannot stand it—and she (looking at his wife) still less.

Axel. Ah, I am not hard-hearted—but I must try to be resolute. If I lose now, I shall be losing her for life, I know. Therefore she *shall* go with me!

Mother (springing up). No, she shall not! If you loved her, as you say you do, you hypocrite, you would remain where she is—and here she shall stay!

Laura (who has been standing beside MATHILDE, goes to her MOTHER). Yes, to my dying day.

Father (getting up). No! We must not alter God's law. It is written: "A man shall forsake his father and his mother, and cleave only unto his wife"—and in the same way she must cleave only to him. Laura shall go when he wishes.

Laura. Father, can you—have you the heart to—?

Father. No, I haven't the heart to, my child. But I shall do it nevertheless, because it is right. Oh, Laura!—(Embraces her. The MOTHER joins her embrace to his.)

Mathilde (to AXEL). You Jesuit!—You have no consideration, no mercy; you trample upon hearts as you would upon the grass that grows in your path. But you shall not find this so easy as you think. It is true she is a child—but I shall go with her! I don't know you, and I don't trust you. (Clenches her fist.) But I shall watch over her!

Curtain.

ACT II

(SCENE.—AXEL's house, a year later. The room is arranged almost identically like that in the first act. Two large portraits of LAURA'S parents, very well executed, hang in full view. LAURA is sitting at the table, MATHILDE on the couch on the right.)

Mathilde (reading aloud from a book). "'No,' was the decided answer. Originally it was he that was to blame, but now it is she. He tore her from her parents, her home and her familiar surroundings; but since then he has sought her forgiveness so perseveringly, and her love so humbly, that it would take all the obstinacy of a spoilt child to withstand him. Just as formerly he could think of nothing but his love, so now she will consider nothing except her self-love; but she is so much the more to blame than he, as her motives are less good than his. She is like a child that has woke up too early in the morning; it strikes and kicks at any one that comes to pet it."

Laura. Mathilde—does it really say that?

Mathilde. Indeed it does.

Laura. Just as you read it?

Mathilde. Look for yourself.

Laura (takes the book and looks at it, then lays it down). It is almost our own story, word for word. I would give anything to know who has written it.

Mathilde. It is a mere coincidence—

Laura. No, some wicked wretch has seen something like this—some creature that is heartless enough to be able to mock at a parent's love; it must be some one who either is worthless himself or has had worthless parents!

Mathilde. Why, Laura, how seriously you take it!

Laura. Yes, it irritates me, this libelling of all fidelity. What is fidelity, if it does not mean that a child should be true to its parents?

Mathilde. But I was just reading to you about that. (Reads.) "The object of fidelity changes, as we ourselves change. The child's duty is to be true to its parents; the married, to one another; the aged, to their children—"

Laura. Don't read any more! I won't hear any more! Its whole train of thought offends me. (After a pause.) What a horrid book! (Indifferently.) What happens to them in the end?

Mathilde (in the same tone). To whom?

Laura. That couple—in the book.

Mathilde (still in an indifferent tone). It doesn't end happily. (A pause.)

Laura (looking up). Which of them suffers?

Mathilde. Which do you think?

Laura (beginning to sew again). She, I should think—because she is unhappy already.

Mathilde. You have guessed right. She falls in love.

Laura (astonished). Falls in love?

Mathilde. Yes. Sometime or other, love is awakened in the heart of every woman; and then, if she cannot love her husband, in the course of time she will love some one else.

Laura (dismayed). Some one else!

Mathilde. Yes. (A pause.)

Laura. That is horrible! (Begins to sew, then lays her hand down on the table, then begins to sew again.) And what happens to him?

Mathilde. He falls ill, very ill. And then some one finds him out and comforts him—a woman.

Laura (looking up). How does that happen?

Mathilde. His heart is like an empty house, in an atmosphere of sadness and longing. Little by little she—the woman who comforts him—creeps into it; and so in time there comes the day when he can say he is happy. (A pause.)

Laura (quietly). Who is she?

Mathilde. One of those poor-spirited creatures that can be content with the aftermath of love.

Laura (after a pause, during which she has been looking fixedly at MATHILDE). Could you be that?

Mathilde. No!—I must be first or nothing!

Laura. But about her?

Mathilde. The wife?

Laura. Yes. What happens to her?

Mathilde. Directly she realises that love for another has taken possession of her husband, she turns towards him with all her heart; but it is too late then. (LAURA sits absorbed for a few moments; then gets up hurriedly and goes to a little work-table that is standing at the end of the couch on the left, opens it, looks for something in it, stops to think, then looks in it again.) What are you looking for?

Laura. A photograph.

Mathilde. Axel's?

Laura. No—but what has become of it?

Mathilde. Don't you remember that one day you took it up and said you would not have it? So I hid it.

Laura. You?

Mathilde. Yes—till you should ask about it. (Gets up, opens her work-table that stands by the right-hand couch.) Here it is. (Gives it to her.)

Laura. So you have got it! (Lays it in her table drawer without looking at it, shuts the drawer, goes a few paces away, then comes back, turns the key in the drawer and takes it out.) Has Axel read the new book?

Mathilde. I don't know. Shall I give it to him?

Laura. Just as you like. Perhaps you would like to read it aloud to him. (A Maid comes in with a letter; LAURA takes it, and the Maid goes out again.) From my parents! (Kisses the letter with emotion.) The only ones who love me! (Goes out hurriedly. At the same moment AXEL comes in from the outer door.)

Axel. She always goes when I come in!

Mathilde (getting up). This time it was an accident, though. (Looks at him.) How pale you are!

Axel (seriously). I am rather worried.—Have you read the new novel?

Mathilde (putting the book in her pocket). What novel?

Axel. "The Newly-Married Couple"—quite a small book.

Mathilde. Oh, that one—I have just been reading it.

Axel (eagerly). And Laura too? Has Laura read it?

Mathilde. She thinks it is a poor story.

Axel. It isn't that, but it is an extraordinary one. It quite startles me—it is like coming into one's own room and seeing one's self sitting there. It has caught hold of unformed thoughts that lie hidden deep in my soul.

Mathilde. Every good book does that.

Axel. Everything will happen to me just as it does in that book; the premises are all here, only I had not recognised them.

Mathilde. I have heard of very young doctors feeling the symptoms of all the diseases they read about.

Axel. Oh, but this is more than mere imagination. My temptations come bodily before me. My thoughts are the result of what happens, just as naturally as smoke is the result of fire—and these thoughts (lancing at MATHILDE) lead me far.

Mathilde. As far as I can see, the book only teaches consideration for a woman, especially if she is young.

Axel. That is true. But, look here—a young man, brought up among students, cannot possibly possess, ready-made, all this consideration that a woman's nature requires. He doesn't become a married man in one day, but by degrees. He cannot make a clean sweep of his habits and take up the silken bonds of duty, all in a moment. The inspiration of a first love gives him the capacity, but he has to learn how to use it. I never saw what I had neglected till I had frightened her away from me. But what is there that I have not done, since then, to win her? I have gone very gently to work and tried from every side to get at her—I have tempted her with gifts and with penitence—but you can see for yourself she shrinks from me more and more. My thoughts, wearied with longings and with the strain of inventing new devices, follow her, and my love for her only grows—but there are times when such thoughts are succeeded by a void so great that my whole life seems slipping away into it. It is then I need some one to cling to—. Oh, Mathilde, you have meant very much to me at times like that. (Goes up to her.)

Mathilde (getting up). Yes, all sorts of things happen in a year that one never thought of at the beginning of it.

Axel (sitting down). Good God, what a year! I haven't the courage to face another like it. This book has frightened me.

Mathilde (aside). That's a good thing, anyway.

Axel (getting up). Besides—the amount of work I have to do, to keep up everything here just as she was accustomed to have it, is getting to be too much for me, Mathilde. It won't answer in the long run. If only I had the reward of thanks that the humblest working-man gets-if it were only a smile; but when I have been travelling about for a week at a time, exposed to all sorts of weather in these open boats in winter, do I get any welcome on my home-coming? When I sit up late, night after night, does she ever realise whom I am doing it for? Has she as much as noticed that I have done so—or that I have, at great expense, furnished this house like her parents'? No, she takes everything as a matter of course; and if any one were to say to her, "He has done all this for your sake," she would merely answer, "He need not have done so, I had it all in my own home."

Mathilde. Yes, you have come to a turning-point now.

Axel. What do you mean?

Mathilde. Nothing particular—here she comes!

Axel. Has anything happened? She is in such a hurry!

LAURA comes in with an open letter in her hand.

Laura (in a low voice, to MATHILDE). Mother and father are so lonely at home that they are going abroad, to Italy; but they are coming here, Mathilde, before they leave the country.

Mathilde. Coming here? When?

Laura. Directly. I hadn't noticed—the letter is written from the nearest posting station; they want to take us by surprise—they will be here in a few minutes. Good heavens, what are we to do?

Mathilde (quickly). Tell Axel that!

Laura. I tell him?

Mathilde. Yes, you must.

Laura (in a frightened voice). I?

Mathilde (to AXEL). Laura has something she wants to tell you.

Laura. Mathilde!

Axel. This is something new.

Laura. Oh, do tell him, Mathilde. (MATHILDE says nothing, but goes to the back of the room.)

Axel (coming up to her). What is it?

Laura (timidly). My parents are coming.

Axel. Here?

Laura. Yes.

Axel. When? To-day?

Laura. Yes. Almost directly.

Axel. And no one has told me! (Takes up his hat to go.)

Laura (frightened). Axel!

Axel. It is certainly not for the pleasure of finding me here that they are coming.

Laura. But you mustn't go!

Mathilde. No, you mustn't do that.

Axel. Are they not going to put up here?

Laura. Yes, I thought—if you are willing—in your room.

Axel. So that is what it is to be—I am to go away and they are to take my place.

Mathilde. Take my room, and I will move into Laura's. I will easily arrange that. (Goes out.)

Axel. Why all this beating about the bush? It is quite natural that you should want to see them, and equally natural that I should remove myself when they come; only you should have broken it to me—a little more considerately. Because I suppose they are coming now to take you with them—and, even if it means nothing to you to put an end to everything like this, at all events you ought to know what it means to me!

Laura. I did not know till this moment that they were coming.

Axel. But it must be your letters that have brought them here—your complaints—

Laura. I have made no complaints.

Axel. You have only told them how matters stand here.

Laura. Never. (A pause.)

Axel (in astonishment). What have you been writing to them all this year, then—a letter every day?

Laura. I have told them everything was going well here.

Axel. Is it possible? All this time? Laura! Dare I believe it? Such consideration—(Comes nearer to her.) Ah, at last, then—?

Laura (frightened). I did it out of consideration for them.

Axel (coldly). For them? Well, I am sorry for them, then. They will soon see how things stand between us.

Laura. They are only to be here a day or two. Then they go abroad.

Axel. Abroad? But I suppose some one is going with them?—you, perhaps?

Laura. You can't, can you?

Axel. No.—So you are going away from me, Laura!—I am to remain here with Mathilde—it is just like that book.

Laura. With Mathilde? Well—perhaps Mathilde could go with them?

Axel. You know we can't do without her here—as things are at present.

Laura. Perhaps you would rather I—?

Axel. There is no need for you to ask my leave. You go if you wish.

Laura. Yes, you can do without *me*.—All the same, I think I shall stay!

Axel. You will stay—with me?

Laura. Yes.

Axel (in a happier voice, coming up to her). *That* is not out of consideration for your parents?

Laura. No, that it isn't! (He draws back in astonishment. MATHILDE comes in.)

Mathilde. It is all arranged. (To AXEL.) You will stay, then?

Axel (looking at LAURA). I don't know.—If I go away for these few days, perhaps it will be better.

Mathilde (coming forward). Very well, then I shall go away too!

Laura. You?

Axel. You?

Mathilde. Yes, I don't want to have anything to do with what happens. (A pause.)

Axel. What do you think will happen?

Mathilde. That is best left unsaid—till anything does happen. (A pause.)

Axel. You are thinking too hardly of your friend now.

Laura (quietly). Mathilde is not my friend.

Axel. Mathilde not your—

Laura (as before). A person who is always deceiving one is no friend.

Axel. Has Mathilde deceived anybody? You are unjust.

Laura (as before). Am I? It is Mathilde's fault that I am unhappy now.

Axel. Laura!

Laura. My dear, you may defend her, if you choose; but you must allow me to tell you plainly that it is Mathilde's advice that has guided me from the days of my innocent childhood, and has led me into all the misery I am suffering now! If it were not for her I should not be married to-day and separated from my parents. She came here with me—not to help me, as she pretended—but to be able still to spy on me, quietly and secretly, in her usual way, and afterwards to make use of what she had discovered. But she devotes herself to you; because she—no, I won't say it! (With growing vehemence.) Well, just you conspire against me, you two—and see whether I am a child any longer! The tree that you have torn up by the roots and transplanted will yield you no fruit for the first year, however much you shake its branches! I don't care if things do happen as they do in that story she has taken such pleasure in reading to me; but I shall never live to see the day when I shall beg for any one's love! And now my parents are coming to see everything, everything—and that is just what I want them to do! Because I won't be led like a child, and I won't be deceived! I won't! (Stands quite still for a moment, then bursts into a violent fit of crying and runs out.)

Axel (after a pause). What is the meaning of that?

Mathilde. She hates me.

Axel (astonished). When did it come to that?

Mathilde. Little by little. Is it the first time you have noticed it?

Axel (still more astonished). Have you no longer her confidence, then?

Mathilde. No more than you.

Axel. She, who once believed every one—!

Mathilde. Now she believes no one. (A pause.)

Axel. And what is still more amazing—only there is no mistaking it—is that she is jealous!

Mathilde. Yes.

Axel. And of you?—When there is not the slightest foundation—. (Stops involuntarily and looks at her; she crosses the room.)

Mathilde. You should only be glad that this has happened.

Axel. That she is jealous?—or what do you mean?

Mathilde. It has helped her. She is on the high road to loving you now.

Axel. Now?

Mathilde. Love often comes in that way—especially to the one who has been made uneasy.

Axel. And you are to be the scapegoat?

Mathilde. I am accustomed to that.

Axel (quickly, as he comes nearer to her). You must have known love yourself, Mathilde?

Mathilde (starts, then says). Yes, I have loved too.

Axel. Unhappily?

Mathilde. Not happily. But why do you ask?

Axel. Those who have been through such an experience are less selfish than the rest of us and are capable of more.

Mathilde. Yes. Love is always a consecration, but not always for the same kind of service.

Axel. Sometimes it only brings unhappiness.

Mathilde. Yes, when people have nothing in them, and no pride.

Axel. The more I get to know of you, the less I seem really to know you. What sort of a man can this fellow be, that you have loved without return?

Mathilde (in a subdued voice). A man to whom I am now very grateful; because marriage is not my vocation.

Axel. What is your vocation, then?

Mathilde. One that one is unwilling to speak about, until one knows that it has been successful.—And I don't believe I should have discovered it, but for him.

Axel. And is your mind quite at peace now? Have you no longings?

Mathilde (speaking here, and in what follows, with some vehemence). Yes, a longing to travel—a long, long way! To fill my soul with splendid pictures!—Oh, if you have any regard for me—

Axel. I have more than that, Mathilde—the warmest gratitude—and more than that, I—

Mathilde (interrupting him). Well, then, make it up with Laura! Then I shall be able to go abroad with her parents. Oh, if I don't get away—far away—there is something within me that will die!

Axel. Go away then, Mathilde—you say so, and therefore I believe you.

Mathilde. But I am not going till you two are reconciled! I don't want all three of us to be unhappy. No, I am not unhappy; but I shall be if you are—and if I don't get abroad now!

Axel. What can I do in the matter?

Mathilde (quickly). Stay here and give the old folk a welcome! Behave to Laura as if there were nothing the matter, and she will say nothing!

Axel. Why do you think she will say nothing?

Mathilde. Because of all I have done to make that likely!

Axel. You?

Mathilde. Yes—no—yes; at least, not as you wanted me to, but indirectly—

Axel. Even at the beginning of all this?

Mathilde. No, not then, it is true. But forget that, because now I have made it good! I did not know you then—and there were reasons—

Axel (going nearer to her). Mathilde, you have filled me with an extraordinary regard for you—as if everything that I have been denied in another quarter was to be found in you, and as if now for the first time I—

Mathilde. There is the carriage!

Axel. What shall I do?

Mathilde. Go down and welcome the old folk! Be quick! Look, Laura is down there already—oh, don't let her miss you just at this moment! There, that is right. (He goes.) Yes, that was right; this is my first real victory! (Goes out. Voices are heard without, and soon afterwards the MOTHER comes in with LAURA, and after her the FATHER with AXEL and MATHILDE.)

Mother. So here I am in your home, my darling child! (Kisses her.) It is really worth being separated, for the pleasure of meeting again! (Kisses her.) And such nice letters from you, every single day—thank you, darling! (Kisses her again.) And you look just the same—just the same! Perhaps a trifle paler, but that is natural. (Kisses her.)

Axel (to the FATHER, who is taking off a coat and several comforters). May I?

Father (bowing). Thank you, I can manage quite well myself.

Axel. But let me hang them up for you?

Father. Much obliged—I will do it myself! (Takes them out into the hall.)

Mother (to LAURA, in a low voice). It was hard work to get your father to come, I can tell you. He still cannot forget—. But we had to see our little girl before we set off on our travels; and we had to travel, because it was getting so lonely at home.

Laura. Dear mother! (She and MATHILDE help her to take her things off.)

Axel (to the FATHER, who has come in again). I hope you had a pleasant journey, sir?

Father. Remarkably pleasant.

Axel. Caught no cold, I hope?

Father. Nothing to speak of—just a trifle—a slightly relaxed throat; out late—and heavy dews. You are well?

Axel. Very well, thank you.

Father. I am extremely pleased to hear it.

Mother (to the FATHER). But, do you see—?

Father. What, my love?

Mother. Do you mean to say you don't see?

Father. No, what is it?

Mother. We are at home again! This is our own room over again!

Father (in astonishment). Upon my word—!

Mother. The carpet, the curtains, the furniture, everything—even down to their arrangement in the room! (Goes across to AXEL and takes his hand.) A more touching proof of your love for her we could never have had! (To the FATHER.) Isn't that so?

Father (struggling with his astonishment). Yes, I must say—

Mother. And you never wrote us a single word about this, Laura?

Mathilde. It is not only this room, but the whole house is arranged like yours as far as possible.

Mother. The whole house! Is it possible!

Father. It is the most charming way of giving pleasure to a young wife that I ever heard of!

Mother. I am so astonished, Laura, at your never having mentioned a word of all this in your letters.

Father. Never a word of it!

Mother. Hadn't you noticed it?

Father. Ah, well—what one sees every day, one is apt to think every one knows all about—isn't that it, little girl? That is the explanation, isn't it?

Mother. And Axel has given you all this by his own exertions! Aren't you proud of that?

Father (clapping her on the back). Of course she is, but it was never Laura's way to say much about her feelings; although this is really something so—

Mother (laughing). Her letters lately have been nothing but dissertations upon love.

Laura. Mother—!

Mother. Oh, I am going to tell! But you have a good husband, Laura.

Laura. Mother—!

Mother (in a lower voice). You have paid him some little attentions in return, of course?—given him something, or—

Father (pushing in between them). Worked something for him, eh?

(MATHILDE, in the meantime, has brought in wine and filled some glasses.)

Axel. Now, a glass of wine to welcome you—sherry, your favourite wine, sir.

Mother. He remembers that! (They each take a glass in their hands.)

Axel. Laura and I bid you heartily welcome here in our house! And we hope you will find everything here—(with emotion) just as you would wish it. I will do my best that you shall, and I am sure Laura will too.

Mother. Of course she will!—Drink his health! (AXEL touches her glass with his; her hand trembles, and she spills come wine.) You have filled the glasses too full, my dear! (They all clink glasses and drink.)

Father (when the glasses have been filled again). My wife and I—thank you very much for your welcome. We could not set out on our journey without first seeing our child—our two children. A good friend of ours (looking at MATHILDE) advised us to come unexpectedly. At first we did not want to but now we are glad we did; because now we can see for ourselves that Laura told the truth in her letters. You are happy—and therefore we old folk must be happy too, and bury all recollection of what—what evidently happened for the best. Hm, hm!—At one time we could not think it was so—and that was why we did not wish to be parted from our child; but now we can make our minds quite easy about it—because now we can trust you. I have complete trust in you, Axel, my dear son—God bless you! (They grasp hands, and drink to each other again.)

Mother. Do you know what I should like?

All. No!

Mother. I should like Axel to tell us how your reconciliation came about.

Laura. Mother!

Mother. Why should you be shy about it? Why have you never told us about it? Good gracious, didn't you think your parents would be only too glad to hear how lucky their little girl was?

Father. I think it is a very good idea of your mother's. Now let us sit down and hear all about it. (They sit down; LAURA turns away.) No, come and sit down beside your mother, Laura! We are going to have a good look at you while he tells us about it. (Pulls her to him.)

Mother. And don't forget anything, Axel! Tell us of the very first sign of love, the first little kindness, Laura showed you.

Axel. Yes, I will tell you how it came about.

Laura (getting up). But, Axel—!

Axel. I shall only be supplementing what you told in your letters, Laura.

Mother. It is all to your credit, my child! Now be quiet and listen to him, and correct him if he forgets anything. (Pulls her down to her seat again.)

Axel. Yes, my dear parents. You know, of course, that we did not begin very well—

Father. Quite so—but you can pass over that.

Axel. As soon as she was left to depend on herself alone, I realised the great wrong I had done to Laura. She used to tremble when I came near her, and before long she used to tremble just as much before any one. At first I felt the humility of a strong man who has triumphed; but after a time I became anxious, for I had acted too strongly. Then I dedicated my love to the task of winning back, in a Jacob's seven years of service, what I had lost in one moment. You see this house—I made everything smooth in it for her feet. You see what we have round us—I set that before her eyes. By means of nights of work, by exerting myself to the uttermost, I got it all together, bit by bit—in order that she should never feel anything strange or inhospitable in her home, but only what she was accustomed to and fond of. She understood; and soon the birds of spring began to flutter about our home. And, though she always ran away when I came, I was conscious of her presence in a hundred little loving touches in my room—at my desk—

Laura (ashamed). Oh, it isn't true!

Axel. Don't believe her! Laura is so kind-hearted—her fear of me made her shy, but she could not withstand her own kind impulses and my humble faithfulness. When I was sitting late in my room, working for her, she was sitting up in hers—at any rate I often thought I heard her footstep; and when I came home late after a wearisome journey, if she did not run to welcome me, it was not because she was wanting in wifely gratitude—Laura has no lack of that—but because she did not wish to betray her happiness till the great day of our reconciliation should come. (LAURA gets up.)

Father. Then you were not reconciled immediately?

Axel. Not immediately.

Mother (anxiously, in a subdued voice). My goodness, Laura did not say a word about that!

Axel. Because she loved you, and did not want to distress you unnecessarily. But does not her very silence about it show that she was waiting for me? That was her love's first gift to me. (LAURA sits down again.) After a while she gave me others. She saw that I was not angry; on the contrary, she saw that where I had erred, I had erred through my love for her; and she is so loving herself, that little by little she schooled herself to meet me in gentle silence—she longed to be a good wife. And then, one lovely morning—just like to-day—we both had been reading a book which was like a voice from afar, threatening our happiness, and we were driven together by fear. Then, all at once, all the doors and windows flew wide open! It was your letter! The room seemed to glow with warmth—just as it does now with you sitting there; summer went singing through the house—and then I saw in her eyes that all the blossoms were going to unfold their petals! Then I knelt down before her, as I do now, and said: For your parents' sake, that they may be happy about us—for my sake, that I may not be punished any longer—for your own sake, that you may be able again to live as the fulness of your kind heart prompts—let us find one another now! And then Laura answered— (LAURA throws herself into his arms, in a burst of tears. All get up.)

Mother. That was beautiful, children!

Father. As beautiful as if we were young again ourselves, and had found one another!—How well he told it, too!

Mother. Yes, it was just as if it was all happening before our eyes!

Father. Wasn't it?—He's a very gifted man.

Mother (in a low voice). He will do something big!

Father (in the same tones). Ay, a big man—and one of our family!

Axel (who has advanced towards the foreground with LAURA). So that was your answer, Laura?

Laura. You haven't remembered everything.

Mother. Is there something more? Let us hear some more!

Axel. What did you say, then?

Laura. You know I said that something had held me back a long, long time! I saw well enough that you were fond of me, but I was afraid it was only as you would be fond of a child.

Axel. Laura!

Laura. I am not so clever as—as some others, you know; but I am not a child any longer, because now I love you!

Axel. You are a child, all the same!

Father (to the MOTHER). But what about our arrangements? We were to have gone on our travels at once.

Axel. No, stay with us a few days now! (LAURA makes a sign to him.) Not?

Laura (softly). I would rather be alone with you, now.

Mother. What are you saying, Laura?

Laura. I?—I was saying that I should like to ask you, if you are going abroad now, to take Mathilde with you.

Mother. That is very nice of you, Laura, to remember Mathilde. People generally say that newly-married couples think of no one but themselves.

Father. No, Laura is not like that!

All. No, Laura is not like that!

Laura (gently). Mathilde, forgive me! (They embrace, and LAURA says softly:) I understand you now for the first time!

Mathilde. Not quite.

Laura. I know that I should never have got Axel, but for you.

Mathilde. That is true.

Laura. Oh, Mathilde, I am so happy now!

Mathilde. And I wish you every happiness.

Axel (taking LAURA'S arm). Now you may go and travel abroad, Mathilde!

Mathilde. Yes!—and my next book shall be a better one.

Axel. Your next—?

Curtain.

LEONARDA
A PLAY IN FOUR ACTS

DRAMATIS PERSONAE

The BISHOP.
CORNELIA, his sister.
HAGBART, his nephew.
The GRANDMOTHER.
LEONARDA FALK.
AAGOT, her niece.
GENERAL ROSEN.
CHIEF JUSTICE RÖST.
MRS. RÖST.
PEDERSEN, agent to Mrs. Falk.
HANS.
A Maid.

ACT I

(SCENE.—A large room in LEONARDA FALK's house. At the back, folding doors which are standing open. Antique furniture. LEONARDA, dressed in a riding-habit, is standing beside a writing-desk on the left, talking to her agent PEDERSEN.)

Leonarda. It is a complete loss.

Pedersen. But, Mrs. Falk—

Leonarda. A loss, every scrap of it. I can't sell burnt bricks. How much is there of it? Two kilns' full, that is 24,000 bricks—at their present price about thirty pounds' worth. What am I to do with you?—send you about your business?

Pedersen. Madam, it is the first time—

Leonarda. No, indeed it is not; that is to say, it is certainly the first time the bricks have been burnt, but your accounts have been wrong over and over again, so that I have been led into sending out faulty invoices. What is the matter with you?

Pedersen. Madam, I beg—.

Enter HANS.

Hans. Your horse is saddled, madam, and the General is coming up the avenue.

Leonarda. Very well. (HANS goes out.) Have you taken to drink, Pedersen?

Pedersen. No, madam.

Leonarda. That wouldn't be like you. But what is it? You look quite changed.—Pedersen! I believe I know! I saw you rowing back across the river last night, from the summer-house in the wood. Are you in love? (PEDERSEN turns away.) So that is it. And crossed in love? (She goes up to him, puts her hand on his shoulder and stands with her back turned to the audience, as he does.) Are you engaged to her?

Pedersen. Yes.

Leonarda. Then she is not treating you well? She is not true to you? (Stoops and looks into his face.) And you love her in spite of it? (Moves away from him.) Then you are a weak man, Pedersen. We cannot possibly love those who are false to us. (Draws on one of her gloves.) We may suffer horribly for a while; but love them—no!

Pedersen (still turning away from her). It is easy for those to talk who have not experienced it.

Leonarda. Experienced it?—You never can tell that. Come to me this evening at seven o'clock.

Pedersen. Yes, madam.

Leonarda. I will talk things over with you then. We will go for a stroll together.

Pedersen. Thank you, madam.

Leonarda. I believe I may be able to help you in your trouble, Pedersen. That is all right—don't think any more about the bricks, or of what I said. Forgive me! (Holds out her hand to him.)

Pedersen (grasping her hand). Oh, madam!

Enter GENERAL ROSEN.

Rosen. Good morning! (PEDERSEN crosses the room.) Bless my soul, Pedersen, you look like a pat of melting butter! (PEDERSEN goes out. ROSEN turns to LEONARDA.) Have you been playing father confessor so early in the morning, and on such a fine day too? That is too bad.—By the way, have you heard from Aagot?

Leonarda (putting on her hat). No, I don't know what has come over the child. It is close on a fortnight since—

Rosen. She is enjoying herself. I remember when I was enjoying myself I never used to write letters.

Leonarda (looking at him). You were enjoying yourself last night, I rather think?

Rosen. Do I show it? Dear, dear! I thought that after a bath and a ride—

Leonarda. This sort of thing cannot go on!

Rosen. You know quite well that if I can't be here I have to go to my club.

Leonarda. But can't you go to your club without—? (Stops, with a gesture of disgust.)

Rosen. I know what you mean, worse luck. But they always give one a glass too much.

Leonarda. One glass? Say three!

Rosen. Three, if you like. You know I never was good at counting.

Leonarda. Well, now you can go for your ride alone.

Rosen. Oh, but—

Leonarda. Yes, I am not going for a ride to-day with a man who was tipsy last night. (Takes off her hat.) Hans! (HANS is heard answering her from without.) Put my horse up for the present!

Rosen. You are punishing yourself as well as me, you know. You ought to be out on a day like this—and it is a sin to deprive the countryside of the pleasure of seeing you!

Leonarda. Will nothing ever make you take things seriously?

Rosen. Yes. When the day comes that you are in need of anything, I will be serious.

Leonarda. And you propose to hang about here waiting, till I have some ill luck? You will have to wait a long time, I hope. (Goes to her desk.)

Rosen. I hope so too!—because meanwhile I shall be able to continue coming here.

Leonarda. Till you get your orders from America.

Rosen. Of course—till I get my orders from Sherman.

Leonarda. You have not had any orders, then?

Rosen. No.

Leonarda. It is beginning to look very suspicious. How long is it since I made you write to him?

Rosen. Oh, I am sure I forget.

Leonarda. It has just struck me—. I suppose you did write?

Rosen. Of course I did. I always do what you tell me.

Leonarda. You stand there twirling your moustache—and when you do that I always know there is some nonsense going on—.

Rosen. How can you suppose such a thing?

Leonarda. You have never written! Why on earth did that never strike me before?

Rosen. I have written repeatedly, I assure you!

Leonarda. But not to Sherman? You have not reported yourself for service again?

Rosen. Do you remember the Russian cigarettes I have so often spoken of? I have got some now. I brought a few with me to try; may I offer you one?

Leonarda. Are you not ashamed to look me in the face?

Rosen. I do everything you tell me—

Leonarda. You have been putting me off with evasions for more than two months—playing a perfect comedy with me! To think that an officer, who has been through the American war and won honours, rank, and a definite position, could throw away his time in this way—and in other ways too—for a whole year now—

Rosen. Excuse me—only eight months.

Leonarda. And isn't that long enough?

Rosen. Too long. But you know, better than any one, why I have done it!

Leonarda. Did I ask you to come here? Do you think you can tire me out?

Rosen. Leonarda! (She looks at him; he bows formally.) I beg your pardon. Mrs. Falk.

Leonarda. You shall write the letter here, now, and report yourself for immediate service.

Rosen. If you order me to.

Leonarda. I shall post it.

Rosen. Many thanks.

Leonarda. You are twirling your moustache again. What are you planning in your mind?

Rosen. I?—Shall I write here? (Goes to the desk.)

Leonarda. Yes. (He takes up a pen.) Ah, I know what it is! As soon as you get home, you will write another letter recalling this one.

Rosen. Yes, naturally.

Leonarda. Ha, ha, ha! (Sits down.) Well, I give you up!

Rosen. Thank you!—Then will you try one of my cigarettes?

Leonarda. No.

Rosen. Nor come for a ride?

Leonarda. No.

Rosen. Am I to come here this evening?

Leonarda. I shall be engaged.

Rosen. But you will be riding to-morrow morning?

Leonarda. I don't know.

Rosen. Then I shall take the liberty of coming to ask I wish you a very good day.

Leonarda. Look, there is a strange man at the door (Gets up.)

Rosen. What? (Turns round.) He? Has he the face to come here? (Looks out of the open window.) Pst! Pst!—Hans!—Don't you see my horse has got loose? (Goes hurriedly out past the stranger, who bows to him.) Pst! Pst!

Enter HAGBART.

Hagbart. Madam! (Stops short.)

Leonarda. May I ask—?

Hagbart. You do not know me, then?

Leonarda. No.

Hagbart. I am Hagbart Tallhaug.

Leonarda. And you dare to tell me so—with a smile on your lips?

Hagbart. If you will only allow me to—

Leonarda. How is it you dare to come here?

Hagbart. If you will only allow me to—

Leonarda. Not a word! Or can there be two men of that name?

Hagbart. No.

Leonarda. So it was you who came forward at the Philharmonic concert, when I was seeking admittance for myself and my adopted daughter, and spoke of me as "a woman of doubtful reputation"? Is that so?

Hagbart. Yes, madam; and I must—

Leonarda (interrupting him impetuously). Then get out of here!—Hans! (HANS is heard answering her from without.)

Hagbart. Mrs. Falk, first allow me to—.
Enter HANS.
Leonarda. Hans, will you see this gentleman off my premises.
Hans. Certainly, ma'am.
Hagbart. Wait a moment, Hans!
Hans. Shall I, ma'am? (Looks at LEONARDA.)
Hagbart. It concerns your niece, Mrs. Falk.
Leonarda. Aagot! Has anything happened to her? I have had no letter from her!
Hagbart. Wait outside, Hans!
Hans (to LEONARDA). Shall I, ma'am?
Leonarda. Yes, yes! (HANS goes out.) What is it?
Hagbart. No bad news.
Leonarda. But how is it you are here on her behalf?
Hagbart. It is difficult to avoid people at a watering-place, you know—although I must admit your niece did her best. She treated me as contemptuously as possible even went farther than that; but she could not prevent my talking to people she used to talk to, or my happening to be where she was; so that—well—she heard them talk about me, and heard me talk to them—and in the end she talked to me herself.
Leonarda. Talked to you?
Hagbart. Yes, it is no good denying it—she actually talked to me, and that more than once.
Leonarda. But what is the meaning of this visit to me?
Hagbart. If you will only allow me to—
Leonarda. I want you to deliver your message briefly and concisely—and not a word more than that.
Hagbart. But I cannot do that until you have allowed me to—
Leonarda. Whether you can or not, I shall allow nothing else. I am not going to give you an excuse for saying that you have been holding conversations with me too.
Hagbart. If you have no objection, I am in love with your niece, Mrs. Falk.
Leonarda. You? With Aagot?—It serves you right!
Hagbart. I know.
Leonarda. Ha, ha! That is how the land lies.
HANS appears at the open door.
Hans. Can I go now, ma'am?
Leonarda. Ha, ha!—Yes, you can go. (Exit HANS) Well, what more have you to tell me? Have you given Aagot any hint of this?
Hagbart. Yes.
Leonarda. And what answer did you get?—You are silent. Do you find it difficult to tell me?
Hagbart. I am very glad you take it so well, Mrs. Falk.
Leonarda. Yes, it's funny, isn't it?—Well, what did Aagot say? She generally has plenty to say.
Hagbart. Indeed she has. We came here to-day by the same boat—
Leonarda. By the same boat? Aagot and you? Have you been persecuting her?
Hagbart. Mrs. Falk, you cannot possibly understand if you will not allow me to—
Leonarda. I wish to hear the rest of it from my niece, as I suppose she will be here directly.
Hagbart. Of course, but still—
Leonarda. There will be no more of that sort of thing here! If you intend to persecute my niece with your attentions in the same way as you have persecuted me with your malice, you are at liberty to try. But you shall not come here! I can forbid it here.
Hagbart. But, my dear Mrs. Falk—
Leonarda. I am really beginning to lose my patience, or rather I have lost it already. What have you come here for?
Hagbart. As there is no help for it—well, I will tell you straight out, although it may be a shock to you—I am here to ask for your niece's hand.
Leonarda (taking up her gloves). If I were a man, so that there should be nothing "doubtful" about my reply, I would strike you across the face with my gloves.
Hagbart. But you are a woman, so you will not.
Enter HANS.
Hans. Here is Miss Aagot, ma'am.
Aagot (from without). Aunt!
Leonarda. Aagot!
Enter AAGOT. HANS goes out.

Aagot. Aunt!—That wretched Hans! I was signalling to him—I wanted to surprise you. (Throws herself into LEONARDA'S arms.)

Leonarda. Child, have you deceived me?

Aagot. Deceived you? I?

Leonarda. I knew it! (Embraces her.) Forgive me! I had a moment's horrible doubt—but as soon as I looked at you it was gone!—Welcome, welcome! How pretty you look! Welcome!

Aagot. Oh, aunt!

Leonarda. What is it?

Aagot. You know.

Leonarda. His shameless persecution of you? Yes! (Meanwhile HAGBART has slipped out.)

Aagot. Hush!—Oh, he has gone!—Have you been cross with him?

Leonarda. Not as cross as he deserved—

Aagot. Didn't I tell him so?

Leonarda (laughing). What did you tell him?

Aagot. How hasty you could be!—Were you really cruel to him?

Leonarda. Do you mean to say you have any sympathy—with him?

Aagot. Have I any—? But, good heavens, hasn't he told you?

Leonarda. What?

Aagot. That he—that I—that we—oh, aunt, don't look so dreadfully at me!—You don't know, then?

Leonarda. No!

Aagot. Heaven help me! Aunt—!

Leonarda. You don't mean to say that you—?

Aagot. Yes, aunt.

Leonarda. With him, who—. In spite of that, you—Get away from me!

Aagot. Dear, darling aunt, listen to me!

Leonarda. Go away to him! Away with you!

Aagot. Have you looked at him, aunt? Have you seen how handsome he is?

Leonarda. Handsome? He!

Aagot. No, not a bit handsome, of course! Really, you are going too far!

Leonarda. To me he is the man who made a laughingstock of me in a censorious little town by calling me "a woman of doubtful reputation." And one day he presents himself here as my adopted daughter's lover, and you expect me to think him handsome! You ungrateful child!

Aagot. Aunt!

Leonarda. I have sacrificed eight years of my life—eight years—in this little hole, stinting myself in every possible way; and you, for whom I have done this, are hardly grown up before you fly into the arms of a man who has covered me with shame. And I am supposed to put up with it as something quite natural!—and to say nothing except that I think he is handsome! I—I won't look at you! Go away!

Aagot (in tears). Don't you suppose I have said all that to myself, a thousand times? That was why I didn't write. I have been most dreadfully distressed to know what to do.

Leonarda. At the very first hint of such a thing you might to have taken refuge here—with me—if you had had a scrap of loyalty in you.

Aagot. Aunt! (Goes on her knees.) Oh, aunt!

Leonarda. To think you could behave so contemptibly!

Aagot. Aunt!—It was just because he was so sorry for the way he had behaved to you, that I first—

Leonarda. Sorry? He came here with a smile on his lips!

Aagot. That was because he was in such a fright, aunt.

Leonarda. Do people smile because they are in a fright?

Aagot. Others don't, but he does. Do you know, dear, he was just the same with me at first—he smiled and looked so silly; and afterwards he told me that it was simply from fright.

Leonarda. If he had felt any qualms of conscience at all, as you pretend he did, he would at least have taken the very first opportunity to apologise.

Aagot. Didn't he do that?

Leonarda. No; he stood here beating about the bush and smiling—

Aagot. Then you must have frightened the sense out of him, aunt. He is shy, you know.—Aunt, let me tell you he is studying for the church.

Leonarda. Oh, he is that too, is he!

Aagot. Of course he is. You know he is the bishop's nephew, and is studying for the church, and of course that is what made him so prejudiced. But his behaviour that day was just what opened his eyes—because he is very kind-hearted. Dear, darling aunt—

Leonarda. Get up! It is silly to lie there like that. Where did you learn that trick?

Aagot (getting up). I am sure I don't know. But you frighten me so. (Cries.)

Leonarda. I can't help that. You frightened me first, you know, child.

Aagot. Yes, but it is all quite different from what you think, aunt. He is no longer our enemy. He has reproached himself so genuinely for treating you as he did—it is perfectly true, aunt. We all heard him say so. He said so first to other people, so that it should come round to me; and then I heard him saying so to them; and eventually he told me so, in so many words.

Leonarda. Why did you not write and tell me?

Aagot. Because you are not like other people, aunt! If I had as much as mentioned he was there, you would have told me to come home again at once. You aren't like others, you know.

Leonarda. But how in the world did it come about that you—?

Aagot. You know, dear, that if any one sings *your* praises, that is enough to make me their friend at once. And when, to crown all, this man did it who had behaved so unjustly to you, you can well believe that I went about singing for joy all day. That was the beginning of it—

Leonarda. Yes, tell me the whole story.

Aagot. That would be simply impossible, aunt! It would take me days!—But I can tell you this, that I had no idea what it was that was upsetting my nerves in such a manner.

Leonarda. If you felt like that, why did you not come away?

Aagot. That was just what I did! But that was also just what made the whole thing happen!

Leonarda. How? Try and tell me a little more calmly and consecutively!

Aagot. Thank you, aunt! It is good of you to listen to me! Good heavens, how I—. (Bursts into tears.)

Leonarda. There—there! Tell me all about it from beginning to end.

Aagot. Yes—I was quite feverish for about a week—I thought I was ill—and the others kept asking what was the matter with me. And really I didn't know. There is a whole heap of things I could tell you about those few days—but you wouldn't be able to understand.

Leonarda. Yes, I should.

Aagot. No, you couldn't possibly! I can't, either. I was so wretched then—and now I am so happy—

Leonarda. Well, tell me about it another time. But how did things come to a head?

Aagot. He spoke to me—straight out!

Leonarda. Proposed to you?

Aagot. Yes.—Oh, I feel I am blushing again at the very thought of it.

Leonarda. And you looked foolish?

Aagot. I don't know what I looked like!

Leonarda. What did you do?

Aagot. I gave one scream—a real good scream—and ran; ran home, packed my trunk, and got on board the boat as quick as I could.

Leonarda. And was that all?

Aagot. All? It happened out of doors amongst all the people.

Leonarda. Aagot!

Aagot. It happened so frightfully unexpectedly. I never was so frightened in my life—and so ashamed of myself afterwards. I did nothing but cry on the boat, all the way.

Leonarda. But he must have come by the same boat.

Aagot. Just fancy, he had travelled overland across the promontory and caught the boat on the other side. And I knew nothing about it till I saw him before my eyes! I thought I should sink through the deck. I wanted to run away then, but—oh, aunt, I couldn't! He looked at me with such a wonderful look in his eyes, and took hold of my hands. He spoke to me, but I don't know what he said; everything seemed to be going round and round. And his eyes, aunt! Ah, you haven't looked at them, and that is why you took it so—so—

Leonarda. No, dear.

Aagot. There is something about his mere presence—something so true. And when he looks at me and says—not in words, you know, but still says all the same "I love you so much," I tremble all over. Oh, aunt, kiss me!—There! Thank heaven!—Do you know what he said to-day?

Leonarda. No.

Aagot. That the woman who had fostered—that was the word he used—such a solemn word, but then he is studying for the church—well, that the woman who had fostered such a girl—he meant me, you know—I thought of all my faults, but he will get to know them soon enough—

Leonarda. Well? That the woman who had fostered such a girl as you—

Aagot. —as me, could not have her equal anywhere!

Leonarda. You must have been praising me up nicely?

Aagot. On the contrary. It was afterwards when he said he would come here first, before me—it was his duty, he said, to stand the first shock. "For heaven's sake don't," I said; "you don't know her, she will crush you!"

Leonarda. Oh, Aagot!

Aagot. It was then that he said, "No, the woman who has fostered such a girl," etcetera, etcetera. Ah, now I see you have been horrid to him.

Leonarda. I had been worried all the morning—and I misunderstood—

Aagot. You shall have no more worries after this. Because people are so kind, you know, and you are going to move about among them again. You, who are so good yourself—

Leonarda. No, that is just what I am not.

Aagot. You? You are only so very difficult to understand, aunt!—Oh, what is it, dear?

Leonarda. I am unhappy, Aagot!

Aagot. Why, aunt? About me?

Leonarda. You are the sunshine of my life; you have brought light and warmth and gentleness into it—but it is just because of that—

Aagot. Because of that? Aunt, I don't understand you.

Leonarda. I am clumsy, I am hard, I am suspicious—wicked. I am a savage, with no more self-restraint than I ever had. What sort of a figure must I cut in his eyes—and in yours? Tell me! Am I not a clumsy, ugly—

Aagot. You are the sweetest woman in the whole work! It is only your indomitable strength and courage and youthfulness—

Leonarda. No, no—tell me the truth! I deserve it! Because, you know, it has been for your sake that for eight years I have only associated with work-people. All that I have will be yours. So have some respect for me, Aagot—tell me the truth! Am I not—what shall I say? Tell me what I am!

Aagot. Adorable!

Leonarda. No, no! I have never realised as strongly as I do now how I have buried myself all these eight years. All the books I have read about the great movements going on in the world outside have not really enlightened me. All that I have read and thought fades away before the first gleam of life that reaches me from the real world of men and women. I see new beauty merely in your new clothes, your fashionable hat—the colours you are wearing—the way they are blended. They mean something that I know nothing of. You bring a fragrance in with you—a breath of freshness; you are so dainty and full of life; whereas everything here has become so old, so heavy, so disjointed—and my life most of all.

Aagot. Well, I must tell you what he said, since you won't believe what I say.

Leonarda. But he knew nothing about me?

Aagot. No—it only indirectly referred to you. He said he had never wanted so much to get to know any one, as he wanted to get to know you, because seeing much of me had made him discover you—that was the very expression he used! And it was an extraordinary chance that—

Leonarda. Stop! I can't bear to think of it!—To think it should be the very man whom we—we—

Aagot. Hated so!—yes, isn't it extraordinary?

Leonarda. The very first time you have been away from me!

Aagot. Yes!

Leonarda. And you come back in a halo of reconciliation and affection for him!

Aagot. But who is responsible for that, I should like to know! And you talk about your life here having made you clumsy and ugly—you, who can manufacture a goddess of victory like me!

Leonarda. No, I don't complain when I see you and hear you—when I have you with me! That is worth paying a price for. It was selfish of me to think for a moment that the price was too high. You are in the springtime of your life—while I—

Aagot. You? What is wrong with your life?

Leonarda. I am beginning to think my life is over.

Aagot. Yours? Your life over? Oh, you pain me by saying such a thing.

Leonarda. I am very happy—very happy about all this! Believe me that is so. But you know—

Aagot. I know how tremendously and incomprehensibly you have changed!

Leonarda. Go, my child—and bring him back!

Aagot. How delicious that sounds! Bring him back! (Gets up, then stops.) Thank you, my dear, sweet, darling aunt! (She runs out. LEONARDA falls into a chair by the table and buries her head in her hands. AAGOT'S voice is heard without: "Yes, come along!" and HAGBART'S, answering: "Is it true?")

Aagot (coming in with HAGBART). Come along! (LEONARDA gets up, dries her eyes, and meets them with a smile.) Aunt, here he is!

Hagbart. Mrs. Falk!

Leonarda. Forgive me!

Hagbart. What?—No, you must forgive me! I haven t been able to ask you to! I—

Aagot. We can talk about that another time! Let aunt look at you now!

Leonarda. You two won't disappoint one another. I can see that.

Aagot. It is wonderfully sweet of you, aunt!

Leonarda. Yes, love one another! Bring some beauty, some warmth, some colour into this cold house!

Aagot. Oh, aunt—!

Leonarda. Have you kissed her yet? (AAGOT moves a little away from HAGBART.) Go on! (They embrace.)

Aagot (running from him to LEONARDA). But, dearest aunt, are you crying?

Leonarda. Don't bother about me!—Have you told your uncle, the bishop, about it?

Hagbart. Not yet.

Leonarda. You haven't?—Well, you have the worst of it before you yet, I am afraid.

Hagbart. No; now that I have got as far as this, nothing shall stand in my way!

Aagot. Do you hear that, aunt?

Curtain.

ACT II

(SCENE.—A room in the BISHOP's house, some weeks later. A door at the back of the room leads to another large room. Another door in the right-hand wall; windows in the left. Well forward, by one of the windows, a large easy-chair. Farther back, a writing-desk and chair. On the right, near the door, a couch, and chairs ranged along the wall. Chairs also alongside the door at the back. The Bishop is sitting on the couch, talking to HAGBART.)

Bishop. My dear Hagbart, you keep on telling me that you have acted up to your convictions. Very well, do you want to forbid my acting up to mine?

Hagbart. You know that all I ask, uncle, is that you will see her and talk to her first.

Bishop. But if that is exactly what I don't wish to do? You have made things difficult for us, you know, by choosing a wife out of your own class—although at the same time we have grown fonder of her every day, and are ready to do anything for *her*. But farther than that we cannot go. Do you want to read my letter?

Hagbart. No.

Bishop. I think you should. It is quite a polite letter.

Hagbart. I know you can put things politely enough. But it is the fact, uncle—the fact of your doing it!

Bishop. Yes—I cannot alter that.

Hagbart. Could you not at all events postpone sending the letter?

Bishop. It is sent.

Hagbart. Sent?

Bishop. This morning. Yes. So there is nothing more to be done.

Hagbart. Uncle, you are cruel!

Bishop. How can you say that, Hagbart? I have acquiesced in your giving up your clerical career—and Heaven alone knows what a grief that is to me. (Gets up.) But I will not acquiesce in your bringing into my house a woman who does not even bear her husband's name. Do we as much as know who her husband was? She was both married and divorced abroad. And we don't know anything more about her life since then; it is scarcely likely it has been blameless. Since she came here she has never once been to church. She has led a most eccentric life, and lately has been allowing a man of very evil reputation to visit her.

Hagbart. General Rosen?

Bishop. Yes, General Rosen. He is next door to a drunkard. And he is a dissolute fellow in other ways, too.

Hagbart. He goes everywhere, all the same. He even comes here.

Bishop. Well, you see, he distinguished himself on military service; he has many sociable qualities, and he is well connected. It is the way of the world.

Hagbart. But Mrs. Falk is not to be received?

Bishop. She is a woman.

Hagbart. How long will this sort of thing be endured?

Bishop. Come, come—are you getting those ideas into your head too? You seem to have imbibed a lot of new doctrines lately!

Hagbart. You should have seen her and talked to her once at least, before making up your mind.

Bishop. I will tell you something in confidence, Hagbart. Justice Röst, who lives out there in the country, has often seen General Rosen coming away from her house at most unseemly hours. I will have nothing to do with women of that sort.

Hagbart. What about men of that sort?

Bishop. Well, as I said, that is quite another matter.

Hagbart. Quite so.—Mrs. Falk takes compassion on the General; she interests herself in him. That is all.

Bishop. Did she know him previously, then?

Hagbart. Very likely.

Bishop. Then she has her own private reasons for acting as she does.

Hagbart. Shall I tell you what it is? She has a kinder heart than any of us, and can make a sacrifice more willingly.

Bishop. So you know that?

Hagbart. Yes. Hers is a finer nature than any of ours; it is more completely developed, intellectually and morally.

Bishop. I am listening to you with the profoundest amazement!

Hagbart. Oh, don't misunderstand me! She has her faults.

Bishop. Really, you admit that!—I want to beg something of you earnestly, Hagbart. Go away for a little while.

Hagbart. Go away!

Bishop. Yes, to your uncle's, for instance. Only for a week or a fortnight. You need to clear your thoughts, badly—about all sorts of things. Your brain is in a whirl.

Hagbart. That is true; but—

Bishop. Speak out!

Hagbart. My brain has been in a whirl much longer than you have had any idea of. It has been so ever since that day in winter when I did Mrs. Falk such a horrible injustice.

Bishop. Not exactly an injustice, but—

Hagbart. Yes, an injustice! It was a turning point in my life. To think that I should have given way to such a fanatical outburst! It ended in my being terrified at myself—well, I won't bore you with the whole story of my long fight with myself. You saw nothing of it, because I was not here. But at last, when I got ill and had to go away and take the waters, and then happened to see Aagot—the effect on me was more than anything I could have imagined. I seemed to see the truth; mankind seemed different, and I seemed to hear the voice of life itself at last. You cannot imagine the upheaval it caused in me. It must be that she had something within her that I lacked, and had always lacked! It was her wonderful naturalness; everything she did was done with more charm and gaiety than I found in any one else, and she was quite unconscious of it herself. I used to ask myself what was the reason of it—how it could be that it had been her lot to grow up so free and wholesome. I realised that it was because I had been oblivious to what I lacked myself, that I had been so fanatically severe upon others. I knew it is humiliating to confess it, but it is true. I have always been blundering and impetuous.—But what was I going to say?

Bishop. You were going to speak about Mrs. Falk, I presume.

Hagbart. Yes!—My dear uncle, don't take it amiss. But all this time I have never been able to keep away from her.

Bishop. Then it is she you have been talking to?

Hagbart. Of course!—and of course, that is to say, to Aagot too. You propose my going away. I cannot! If I could multiply myself by two, or if I could double the length of the days, I should never have enough of being with her! No, I have seen daylight now. On no account can I go away.

Bishop. And you call that seeing daylight! Poor boy!

Hagbart. I cannot discuss it with you. You would no more understand than you did that day when you took away those books of grandmother's from me and put them in the lumber-room.

Bishop. Oh, you are bringing that up again? Well, you are at liberty to do as you please. You shall not have the right to say I have exercised any compulsion.

Hagbart. No, uncle, you are very good—to me.

Bishop. But there is a new fact to be taken into consideration. I have noticed it for some days.

Hagbart. What do you mean?

Bishop. In all this conversation we have just had, you have only mentioned Aagot's name twice, at most.

Hagbart. But we were not talking about Aagot.

Bishop. Are you not in love with her any longer?

Hagbart. Not in love with Aagot? (Laughs.) Can you ask that? Do you mean to say—?

Bishop. Yes, I mean to say—

Hagbart (laughing again). No, that is quite a misunderstanding on your part, uncle.

Bishop. Well, I say it again: go away for a week or a fortnight, Hagbart! Consider the situation from a distance—both your own position and that of others!

Hagbart. It is impossible, absolutely impossible, uncle. It would be just as useful to say to me: "Lie down and go to sleep for a week or a fortnight, Hagbart; it will do you good"! No. All my faculties are awake at last—yes, at last—so much so, that sometimes I can scarcely control myself.

Bishop. That is the very reason.

Hagbart. The very reason why I must go straight ahead, for once in my life! No, I must stay here now.—Well, good morning, uncle! I must go out for a turn.

Bishop. Go to call on Mrs. Falk, you mean.

Hagbart (laughing). Unfortunately I haven't the face to do that till this afternoon; I was there the whole day yesterday. But our conversation has set all my thoughts agog again, and when I have no means of appeasing them I have to go out and walk. Thank you, uncle, for being so indulgent to me!

Bishop. Then you don't wish to read my letter?

Hagbart. Ah, that is true—the letter! That upsets the whole thing again. I don't know how I came to forget that.

Bishop. You see for yourself how confused and distracted you are. You need to pull yourself together. Go away for a little!

Hagbart. It is impossible!—Good-bye, uncle!

Bishop. Here is grandmother!

Enter the GRANDMOTHER and CORNELIA.

Hagbart. Good morning, grandmother! Have you slept well?

Grandmother (coming forward on CORNELIA's arm). Excellently!

Cornelia. She slept well into the morning.

Bishop. I am delighted, grandmother. (Takes her other arm.)

Grandmother. You needn't shout so loud. It is a fine day to-day and I can hear very well. (To HAGBART.) You didn't come in to see me last night.

Hagbart. I came in too late, grandmother.

Grandmother. I tell you, you needn't talk so loud.

Cornelia. She always wants to make out that she can hear.

Grandmother (as they settle her in the big chair by the window). This is a nice seat—

Bishop. And I am always delighted to see you sitting there.

Grandmother. The window—and the mirror over there.

Cornelia. Yes, it enables you to see everything.

Grandmother. How you do shout, all you good people!

Bishop. I must go and change my things, if you will excuse me. (Goes out to the right.)

Cornelia. Do you want anything more?

Grandmother. No, thank you. (CORNELIA goes out at the back.)

Hagbart. Dear, good grandmother! You are the only one here who understands me!

Grandmother (trying to look round the room). Are we alone?

Hagbart. Yes.

Grandmother. Has your uncle called on Mrs. Falk?

Hagbart. No, worse luck; he has written her a letter.

Grandmother. I thought as much.

Hagbart. Isn't it shameful, grandmother! He won't see her once, or talk to her, before judging her.

Grandmother. They are all alike, these—. Are we alone?

Hagbart. Yes, grandmother.

Grandmother. You must have patience, Hagbart! You used to be patient.

Hagbart. Yes, grandmother.

Grandmother. I have seen so many generations—so many different ways of behaving. In my day we were tolerant.

Hagbart. I enjoyed reading your books so much, grandmother!

Grandmother. Of course you did.—Are we alone?

Hagbart. Yes, grandmother.

Grandmother. I am quite in love with your fiancée, Hagbart. She is like what girls were in my day.

Hagbart. Courageous, weren't they?

Grandmother. Yes, and independent. They seem quite different nowadays.—Are we alone?

Hagbart. Yes.

Grandmother. You get married—and I will come and live with you and her. Hush!

Hagbart. Do you mean it?

Grandmother. Hush! (Looks out of the window.) There is Justice Röst coming, with his wife. Go and tell your uncle!

Hagbart. Yes.

Grandmother. I might have expected it. They came up from the country yesterday.

Hagbart. Good-bye, then, grandmother!

Grandmother. Good-bye, my boy! (HAGBART goes out to the right. The door at the back is opened. CORNELIA ushers in RÖST and MRS. RÖST.)

Cornelia. Please walk in!

Mrs. Röst. Thank you! You must excuse us for calling so early. We came up from the country yesterday, and my husband has to go to the courts for a little while!

Röst. I have to go to the courts to-day. (The BISHOP conies in from the right.)

Bishop. Welcome!

Röst and Mrs. Röst. Thank you!

Mrs. Röst. You must excuse our calling so early; but we came up from the country yesterday, and my husband has to go to the courts to-day.

Röst. I have to go to the courts for a little while.

Bishop. I know.

Mrs. Röst. And there is the old lady in her chair already!

Röst. Good morning, my dear madam!

Mrs. Röst. Good morning!—No, please don't get up!

Grandmother. Oh, I can get up still.

Röst. Ah, I wish I were as active as you!

Mrs. Röst. My husband was saying to Miss Cornelia only last night—

Grandmother. You need not strain yourself so. I can hear perfectly well. (The others exchange glances.)

Röst. I was saying to Miss Cornelia only last night—we met for a few moments after the service—

Grandmother. I know, I know.

Röst. I said I had never known any one of over ninety have all their faculties so remarkably clear—

Mrs. Röst.—so remarkably clear as yours! And such good health, too! My husband has suffered a great deal from asthma lately.

Röst. I have suffered a great deal from asthma lately.

Mrs. Röst. And I from a heart trouble, which—

Grandmother. We did not know anything about such ailments in my day.

Mrs. Röst. Isn't she sweet! She doesn't remember that people were sometimes ill in her day.

Bishop. Lovely weather we are having!

Röst. Delightful weather! I cannot in the least understand how it is that I—. (The BISHOP brings a chair forward for him.) Oh, please don't trouble, my lord! Allow me.

Mrs. Röst. My husband must have caught cold. (RÖST sits down.)

Cornelia. It certainly was draughty in church last night.

Röst. But we sat in the corner farthest from the door.

Mrs. Röst. We sat in the corner farthest from the door. That was why we were not able to bid your lordship good evening afterwards.

Bishop. There was such a crowd.

Röst, Mrs. Röst, and Cornelia. Such a crowd!

Mrs. Röst. These services must be a great help in your lordship's labours.

Röst. Yes, every one says that.

Bishop. Yes, if only the result were something a little more practical. We live in sad times.

All three (as before). Sad times!

Mrs. Röst. We only just heard yesterday and we met so many friends that I was prevented from asking your sister about it—we have only just heard—

Röst. And that is why we have come here to-day. We believe in being straightforward!

Mrs. Röst. Straightforward! That is my husband's motto.

Bishop. Probably you mean about Hagbart's engagement?

Röst and Mrs. Röst. To Miss Falk?

Cornelia. Yes, it is quite true.

Mrs. Röst. Really?

Cornelia. My brother came to the conclusion that he had no right to oppose it.

Röst. Quite so. It must have been a difficult matter for your lordship to decide.

Bishop. I cannot deny that it was.

Mrs. Röst. How Mr. Tallhaug has changed!

Röst. Yes, it seems only the other day he—

Bishop. We must not be too severe on young people in that respect nowadays, Mrs. Röst.

Röst. It is the spirit of the time!

Bishop. Besides, I must say that the young lady is by no means displeasing to me.

Cornelia. My brother has a very good opinion of her—although he finds her manner perhaps a little free, a little too impetuous.

Mrs. Röst. But her adoptive mother?

Röst. Yes, her adoptive mother!

Cornelia. My brother has decided not to call on her.

Röst and Mrs. Röst. Really!

Mrs. Röst. We are extremely glad to hear that!

Röst. It was what we wanted to know! Everybody we met yesterday was anxious to know.

Mrs. Röst. Everybody! We were so concerned about it.

Cornelia. My brother has written to her, to make it quite clear to her.

Röst. Naturally!

Mrs. Röst. We are very glad to hear it!

Grandmother (looking out of the window). There is a carriage stopping at the door.

Cornelia. I thought I heard a carriage, too. (Gets up.)

Grandmother. There is a lady getting out of it.

Mrs. Röst. A lady?—Good heavens, surely it is not—? (Gets up.)

Röst. What do you say? (Gets up.)

Cornelia. She has a veil on.

Mrs. Röst. I really believe—! (To her husband.) You look, my dear—you know her.

Röst. It is she; I recognise her coachman Hans.

Bishop (who has got up). But perhaps it is Miss Aagot?

Cornelia. No, it is not Miss Aagot.—She is in the house by this time. What are we to do?

Mrs. Röst. Has she not had your lordship's letter?

Bishop. Yes, this morning.

Röst. And in spite of that—?

Bishop. Perhaps for that very reason. Ahem!—Cornelia, you must go down and—

Cornelia. Not on any account! I refuse!

Mrs. Röst (to her husband). Come, dear! Be quick, let us get away. (Looks for her parasol.) Where is my parasol?

Bishop (in a low voice). Won't you wait a little while Mr. Röst?

Röst. Oho!

Mrs. Röst. My parasol! I can't find my parasol.

Röst. Because you have got it in your hand, my love!

Mrs. Röst. So I have! You see how upset I am. Make haste—come along! Can we get out this way?

Röst. Through the Bishop's bedroom!

Mrs. Röst. Oh!—But if you come with me, my dear!—Are we to meet this woman? Why do you stand still? Surely you don't want to—?

Röst. Let us wait a little.

Mrs. Röst. Wait? So that you may talk to her? Oh, you men—you are all alike!

Bishop. But, you know, some one must—. Cornelia!

Cornelia. Not for worlds! I am not going to stir an inch.

Grandmother. Gracchus!

Bishop. Yes, grandmother?

Mrs. Röst. Now the old lady is going to interfere. I thought as much!

Grandmother. Courtesy is a duty that every one must recognise.

Bishop. You are quite right. (Goes towards the back of the room; at the same time a knock is heard on the door). Come in! (The door opens, and LEONARDA enters.)

Mrs. Röst. It is she!

Röst. Be quiet!

Mrs. Röst. But wouldn't you rather—?

Leonarda. Excuse me, am I speaking to the Bishop?

Bishop. Yes, madam. Whom have I the honour to—?

Leonarda. Mrs. Falk.

Bishop. Allow me to introduce my sister—and Mr. Justice Röst and Mrs. Röst—and this is—

Leonarda. "Grandmamma" of whom I have heard, I think!

Bishop. Yes. Let me present Mrs. Falk to you, grandmother.

Grandmother (getting up). I am very glad to see you, ma'am.

Mrs. Röst and Cornelia. What does she say?

Grandmother. As the oldest of the family—which is the only merit I possess—let me bid you welcome. (LEONARDA gives a start, then kneels down and kisses her hand.)

Mrs. Röst. Good gracious!

Cornelia. Well!

Mrs. Röst. Let us go away!

Röst (in a low voice). Does your lordship wish—?

Bishop (in the same tone). No, thank you—I must go through with it now.

Röst. Good morning, then!

Bishop. Many thanks for your visit and for being so frank with me.

Mrs. Röst. That is always our way, your lordship. Good morning!

Cornelia (as they advance to take leave of her). I will see you out.

Röst (to the GRANDMOTHER). I hope I shall always see you looking as well, madam!

Mrs. Röst. Good-bye, madam! No, please don't disturb yourself. You have over-exerted yourself just now you know.

Grandmother. The same to you.

Röst and Mrs. Röst. I beg your pardon?

Bishop. She thought you were wishing her good day—or something of that sort.

Röst and Mrs. Röst. Oh, I see! (They laugh. They both ceremoniously in silence to LEONARDA as they pass her; CORNELIA and the BISHOP go with them to see them out, the BISHOP turning at the door and coming back into the room.)

Bishop (to LEONARDA). Won't you sit down?

Leonarda. Your lordship sent me a letter to-day. (She pauses for an answer, but without effect.) In it you give me to understand, as politely as possible, that your family does not wish to have any intercourse with me.

Bishop. I imagined, Mrs. Falk, that you had no such desire, either previously or now.

Leonarda. What it rally means is that you want me to make over my property to the two young people, and disappear.

Bishop. If you choose to interpret it in that way, Mrs. Falk.

Leonarda. I presume your nephew has told you that my means are not such as to allow of my providing for one establishment here and another for myself elsewhere.

Bishop. Quite so. But could you not sell your property?

Leonarda. And all three of us leave here, your lordship means? Of course that would be possible; but the property is just now becoming of some value, because of the projected railway—and, besides, it has been so long in our family.

Bishop. It is a very fine property.

Leonarda. And very dear to us.

Bishop. It pains me deeply that things should have taken this turn.

Leonarda. Then may I not hope that the fact may influence your lordship's decision in some degree?

Bishop. My decision, madam, has nothing to do with your property.

Leonarda. During all these eight years have I offended you in any way—or any one here?

Bishop. Mrs. Falk, you know quite well that you have not.

Leonarda. Or is it on account of the way I have brought up my niece—?

Bishop. Your niece does you the greatest credit, madam.

Leonarda. Then perhaps some of my people have been laying complaints about me?—or some one has been complaining of them?

Bishop. Not even the most censorious person, my dear madam, could pretend that you have been anything but exemplary in that respect.

Leonarda. Then what is it?

Bishop. You can scarcely expect me to tell a lady—

Leonarda. I will help you out. It is my past life.

Bishop. Since you say it yourself—yes.

Leonarda. Do you consider that nothing can expiate a past—about which, moreover, you know nothing?

Bishop. I have not seen in you any signs of a desire to expiate it, Mrs. Falk.

Leonarda. You mean that you have not seen me at confession or in church?

Bishop. Yes.

Leonarda. Do you want me to seek expiation by being untrue to myself?

Bishop. No; but the way I refer to is the only sure one.

Leonarda. There are others. I have chosen the way hard work and duty.

Bishop. I said the only sure way, Mrs. Falk. Your way does not protect against temptation.

Leonarda. You have something definite in your mind when you say that, have you not?—Shall I help you out again? It is General Rosen.

Bishop. Precisely.

Leonarda. You think I ought to send him away?

Bishop. Yes.

Leonarda. But it would be all up with him if I did. And there is a good deal of ability in him.

Bishop. I have neither the right nor the desire to meddle in affairs I know nothing of; but I must say that only a person of unimpeachable reputation should attempt the rescue of such a man as General Rosen.

Leonarda. You are quite right.

Bishop. You are paying too high a price for it, Mrs. Falk, and without any certainty of achieving anything.

Leonarda. Maybe. But there is one aspect of the matter that you have forgotten.

Bishop. And that is?

Leonarda. Compassion.

Bishop. Quite so.—Yes.—Of course, if you approach the matter from that point of view, I have nothing to say.

Leonarda. You don't believe it?

Bishop. I only wish the matter depended upon what I myself believe. But it does not, Mrs. Falk.

Leonarda. But surely you will admit that one ought to do good even at the risk of one's reputation?

Bishop. Undoubtedly.

Leonarda. Well, will your lordship not apply that maxim to yourself? It is quite possible that for a while your congregation's faith in you might be a little disturbed if you were to call upon me; but you know now, from my own lips, that the rumours you have heard are false, and that you ought rather to be all the more anxious to support me in what I am trying to do. And in that way you will do a good turn to these two young people, and to me, without driving me away. For some years now I have lived only for others. One does not do that without making some sacrifices, my lord—especially when, as in my case, one does not feel that one's life is quite over.

Bishop. You look the picture of youth, Mrs. Falk!

Leonarda. Oh, no—still I have not done it without a struggle. And now I want a little reward for it. Who would not? I want to spend my life with those for whom I have sacrificed myself; I want to see their happiness and make it mine. Do not rob me of that, my lord! It depends upon you!

Bishop. I do not quite see how it depends upon me.

Leonarda. It depends upon you for this reason; if my exile is to be the price paid for her marriage, my niece will never consent to wed your nephew.

Bishop. That would be very distressing to me, Mrs. Falk.

Leonarda. I made haste to come to you, before she should know anything about it. I have brought your letter with me. Take it back, my lord! (Searches in her pocket for the letter.)

Bishop (noticing her growing anxiety). What is wrong?

Leonarda. The letter!—I laid it on my desk while I dressed to come out, meaning to bring it with me—but in my hurry and anxiety I have forgotten it! And now Aagot is making out accounts at that very desk. If she sees your handwriting she will suspect something at once, because of course we have been expecting you every day.

Bishop. Well, I suppose there is nothing to be done?

Leonarda. Indeed there is. When she comes here—for she will understand everything and come straight here—could not your lordship meet her yourself, and say to her—. (Stops short.)

Bishop. Say what?

Leonarda. "I have been mistaken. People should be judged, not by their mistakes, but by what they have achieved; not by their beliefs, but by their efforts towards goodness and truth. I mean to teach my congregation that lesson by calling upon your aunt next Sunday." (The GRANDMOTHER nods at her approvingly. LEONARDA sees this, takes her hand, and turns again towards the BISHOP.) This venerable lady pleads for me too. She belongs to a day that was more tolerant than ours—at all events than ours is in this little out-of-the-way place. All the wisdom of her long life is summed up in these two words: Have forbearance!

Bishop. There is one kind of forbearance, Mrs. Falk, that is forbidden us—the forbearance that would efface the distinction between good and evil. That is what the "toleration" of my grandmother's day meant; but it is not an example to be followed.

Leonarda (leaving the GRANDMOTHER's side). If I have erred—if I seem of no account, from the lofty standpoint from which you look upon life—remember that you serve One who was the friend of sinners.

Bishop. I will be your friend when I see you seeking your soul's salvation. I will do all I can then.

Leonarda. Help me to expiate my past! That means everything to me—and is not much for you to do. I only ask for a little show of courtesy, instead of indignities! I will contrive that we shall seldom meet. Only don't drive me away—because that means exposing me to contempt. Believe me, I will give you no cause for shame; and your good deed will be rewarded by the gratitude of the young people.

Bishop. I am deeply distressed at having to take up this attitude towards you. You are bound to think me hardhearted; but that is not the case. I have to consider that I am the guardian of thousands of anxious consciences. I dare not for my nephew's sake offend the respect they feel for me, the trust they put in me; nor dare I disregard the law we all must follow. For a bishop to do as I have done in opening my doors to your niece, is in itself no small thing, when you consider the dissensions that are going on in the Church nowadays. I cannot, I dare not, go farther and open my doors to a woman whom my whole congregation—albeit unjustly—well, I won't wound your feelings by going on.

Leonarda. Really?

Bishop. Believe me, it gives me great pain. You have made a remarkable impression upon me personally. (Meanwhile the GRANDMOTHER has got up to go out of the room.)

Leonarda. Are you going away? (The BISHOP goes to the wall and rings a bell.)

Grandmother. Yes—I am too old for these scenes. And, after what I have just heard, I am sure I have no right to sit here either. (CORNELIA comes in, takes her arm, and assists her out.)

Leonarda (coming forward). Now I can say this to your lordship: you have no courage. Standing face to face with me here, you know what you ought to do, but dare not do it.

Bishop. You are a woman—so I will not answer.

Leonarda. It is because I am a woman that you have said things to me to-day that you would not have said to—to General Rosen, for instance—a man who is allowed to come to your lordship's house in spite of his past life, and his present life too.

Bishop. He shall come here no more in future. Beside, you cannot deny that there is a difference between your two cases.

Leonarda. There is indeed a difference: but I did not expect the distinction to be made on these lines. Nor did I imagine, my lord, that your duty was to protect, not the weaker vessel, but the stronger—to countenance open vice, and refuse help to those who are unjustly accused!

Bishop. Do you think there is any use in our prolonging this conversation?

AAGOT opens the door at the back and calls from the doorway.

Aagot. Aunt!

Leonarda. Aagot! Good heavens!

Aagot (coming forward). Aunt!

Leonarda. Then you know? (AAGOT throws herself into her arms.) My child!

Aagot. I felt sure you would be here, heaven help me!

Leonarda. Control yourself, my child!

Aagot. No, I cannot. This is too much.

Bishop. Would you ladies rather be alone?

Aagot. Where is Hagbart?

Bishop. He has gone out for a walk.

Aagot. It makes me boil with rage! So this was to be the price of my being received into your family—that I was to sell the one who has been a mother to me! Sell her, whom I love and honour more than all the world!

Bishop. Mrs. Falk, do you wish to continue?—or—

Aagot. Continue what? Your negotiations for the sale of my dear one? No. And if it were a question of being admitted to heaven without her, I should refuse!

Bishop. Child! Child!

Aagot. You must let me speak! I must say what is in my heart. And this, at any rate, is in it—that I hold fast to those I love, with all the strength that is in my being!

Bishop. You are young, and speak with the exaggeration of youth. But I think we should do better to put an end to this interview; it can lead to nothing.

Leonarda. Let us go.

HAGBART appears at the door.

Aagot (seeing him before the others). Hagbart!

Hagbart. I heard your voice from outside. Mrs. Falk—

Aagot. Hagbart! (She goes towards him, but as he hastens to her side she draws back.) No—don't touch me!

Hagbart. But, Aagot—?

Aagot. Why did you not manage to prevent this? You never said a word to me about it!

Hagbart. Because really I knew nothing about it.

Aagot. One becomes conscious of such things as that without needing to be told. It hasn't weighed much on your mind!—Did you not know of it just now?

Hagbart. Yes, but—

Aagot. And you didn't fly to tell us?

Hagbart. It is true I—

Aagot. Your mind was taken up with something else altogether. And my only aim in life has been that everything should be made right for her! I thought you were going to do that.

Hagbart. You are unjust, Aagot. What can I do—?

Aagot. No, you are too much of a dreamer. But this you must realise—that I am not going to buy an honoured position at the price of insults to my aunt; that is the very last thing possible.

Hagbart. Of course! But need there be any question of that? I will come and live with you two, and—

Aagot. You talk like a fool!

Leonarda. Aagot! Aagot!

Aagot. Oh, I feel so hurt, so deceived, so mortified—I must say it out. Because to-day is not the first of it—nor is this the only thing.

Leonarda. No, I can understand that. But what is it? You are wounding his love for you.

Aagot (bitterly). His love for me!

Leonarda. Are you out of your mind? You are talking wildly!

Aagot. No, I am only telling the truth!

Leonarda (earnestly, and lowering her voice). Angry words, Aagot? You, who have seen into the bottom of his heart in quiet sacred moments! You who know how true, how steadfast he is! He is different from other men, Aagot—

Aagot (drawing away from her). Stop! stop! You don't see!

Leonarda. You are out of your senses, my child! Your behaviour is disgracing us.

Aagot. The greatest disgrace is his, then—because it is not me he loves! (Bursts into tears and rushes to the back of the room.)

Bishop (to HAGBART, in a low voice). I hope now you will go away for a little while.

Hagbart. Yes.

Bishop. Come away, then. (Goes out to the left, HAGBART follows him.)

Aagot (coming forward to LEONARDA). Can you forgive me?

Leonarda. Let us go home.

Aagot. But say something kind to me.

Leonarda. No.

Aagot. I won't let you go away till you do.

Leonarda. I cannot.

Aagot. Aunt, I am not jealous of you.

Leonarda. Be quiet!

Aagot. Only you must let me go away for a few days—I must get things straight in my mind. (Bursts into tears.) Oh, aunt—for pity's sake—do you love him? (LEONARDA tries to get away from her.) I don't love him any longer! If you love him, aunt, I will give him up!

Leonarda. At least hold your tongue about it, here in another person's house!—If you are not coming with me, I am going home by myself.

Aagot. Then I shall never follow you.

Leonarda. You are completely out of your senses!

Aagot. Yes; I cannot live, unless you speak to me gently and look at me kindly.—God keep you, aunt, now and always!

Leonarda (turning to her). My child!

Aagot. Ah! (Throws herself into her arms.)

Leonarda. Let us go home!
Aagot. Yes.
Curtain.

ACT III

(SCENE—The garden at LEONARDA FALK'S house some days later. On the left, a summer-house with table and chairs. A large basket, half full of apples, is on the table. LEONARDA is standing talking to PEDERSEN.)

Leonarda. Very well, Pedersen; if the horses are not needed here, we may as well send to fetch Miss Aagot home. Can we send to-day?

Pedersen. Certainly, ma'am.

Leonarda. Then please send Hans as soon as possible with a pair of horses to the hill farm for her. It is too cold for her to be up there now, anyway.

Pedersen. I will do so. (Turns to go.)

Leonarda. By the way, Pedersen, how has that little affair of yours been going?

Pedersen. Oh—

Leonarda. Come to me this evening. We will see if we can continue our little talk about it.

Pedersen. I have been wishing for that for a long time, ma'am.

Leonarda. Yes, for the last eight or ten days I have not been able to think of anything properly.

Pedersen. We have all noticed that there has been something wrong with you, ma'am.

Leonarda. We all have our troubles. (PEDERSEN waits; but as LEONARDA begins to pick apples carefully from a young tree and put them in a small basket that is on her arm, he goes out to the left. HAGBART appears from the right, and stands for a minute without her seeing him.)

Hagbart. Mrs. Falk! (LEONARDA gives a. little scream.) I beg your pardon, but I have been looking for you everywhere. How are you? I have only just this moment got back.

Leonarda. Aagot is not at home.

Hagbart. I know. Has she been away the whole time?

Leonarda. Yes.

Hagbart. Will she be away long?

Leonarda. I am sending the horses up to-day, so she should be here by the day after to-morrow.

Hagbart. It was you I wanted to speak to, Mrs. Falk.

Leonarda. About Aagot?

Hagbart. Yes, about Aagot—amongst other things.

Leonarda. But couldn't you wait—till some other time?

Hagbart. Mrs. Falk, I came straight here from the steamer; so you can see for yourself—

Leonarda. But if it concerns Aagot, and she is not here?

Hagbart. The part of it that concerns Aagot is soon said. She was perfectly right—only I did not know it at the time.

Leonarda. Good God!

Hagbart. I do not love Aagot.

Leonarda. But if Aagot loves you?

Hagbart. She has showed me lately that she does not. Did she not tell you so, plainly?

Leonarda. She was—how shall I put it?—too excited for me to attach much importance to what she said.

Hagbart. Then she did tell you so. I thought she had—indeed I was sure of it. Aagot does not love me, but she loves you. She wants you to be happy.

Leonarda. If you do not love Aagot, it seems to me you ought not to have come here.

Hagbart. Perhaps you are right. But I am not the same man as I was when I used to come here before; nor do I come for the same reason.

Leonarda. If you do not love Aagot, I must repeat that you have no right to be here. You owe that much consideration both to her and to me.

Hagbart. I assure you that it is from nothing but the sincerest consideration for you that I am here now.

Leonarda (who up to this point has been standing by the tree). Then I must go!

Hagbart. You won't do that!

Leonarda. You seem to me completely changed.

Hagbart. Thank goodness for that!—because I don't feel any great respect for the man I was before. Many people can decide such things in a moment, but it has taken me time to see my course clearly.

Leonarda. I don't understand you.

Hagbart (almost before the words are out of her mouth, coming close to her). You do understand me!

Leonarda. It would be wicked! Take care!

Hagbart. Your hand is trembling—

Leonarda. That is not true!

Hagbart. They say there is a devil in every one that should not be waked. It is a foolish saying, because these devils are our vital forces.

Leonarda. But we ought to have them under control. That is the lesson my life has taught me; it has cost me dear, and I mean to profit by it.

Hagbart. If I did not believe that it was the impulse of truth itself that guided me to you, I should not be standing here. I have had a long struggle. I have had to give up one prejudice after another, to enable my soul to find itself fully and go forward confidently. It has brought me to you—and now we will go forward together.

Leonarda. That might have been, without this.

Hagbart. I love you! It is you I have loved in her—since the very first day. I love you!

Leonarda. Then have respect for me—and go!

Hagbart. Leonarda!

Leonarda. No, no! (Shrinks away from him.) Oh, why did this happen?

Hagbart. It has come upon us step by step. The cruel obstacles in our way have only proved friends to us, in bringing us together. Give yourself up to happiness, as I do now!

Leonarda. I do not deserve happiness. I have never expected that.

Hagbart. I don't know what you have gone through to make you what you are now—so beautiful, so good, so true; but this I do know, that if the others had not judged you by your failures, I should not have loved you for what you have achieved. And I thought that might give me some value in your eyes.

Leonarda. Thank you for that, from my heart!—But the world disapproves of such things. It disapproves of a young man's making love to an older woman, and if—

Hagbart. I have never cared much about the world's opinion, even in the days when I was most hidebound in prejudice. It is your opinion I want—yours only!

Leonarda. And my answer is that one who is alone can get along without the world's sympathy—but it is different with a couple. They will soon feel the cold wind of the world's displeasure blowing between them.

Hagbart. When you answer me, it makes what I have said seem so formal and ceremonious—so clumsy. But I must just be as I am; I cannot alter myself. Dearest, from the moment I felt certain that it was you I loved, only one thing seemed of any importance to me—everything else was blotted out. And that is why I do not understand what you say. Do you suppose they will try to make me tire of you? Do you suppose that is possible?

Leonarda. Not now, but later on. There will come a time—

Hagbart. Yes, a time of work—self-development! It has come now. That is why I, am here! Perhaps a time of conflict may come too—heaven send that it may! Are we to pay any heed to that? No! You are free, and I am free; and our future is in our own hands.

Leonarda. Besides, I have grown old—

Hagbart. You!

Leonarda.—and jealous, and troublesome; while you are the incarnation of youth and joy.

Hagbart. You have more youth in you than I. You are an enchantress! All your life you will be showing me new aspects of yourself—as you are doing now. Each year will invest you with a new beauty, new spiritual power. Do you think I only half understand you, or only half love you? I want to sit close in your heart, warmed by its glow. It is the irresistible power of truth that has drawn me to you. My whole life will not be long enough for me to sound the unfathomable depths of your soul.

Leonarda. Your words are like the spring breezes, alluring and intoxicating, but full of deadly peril too.

Hagbart. You love me! I knew it before I came here to-day. I saw it the moment I stood here. Love is the very breath of life to you, surpassingly more than to any one else I have ever seen; and that is why you have suffered so terribly from the disappointments and emptiness of life. And now, when love is calling to you—love that is true and sincere—you are trembling!

Leonarda. You understand me in a way I thought impossible! It takes away all my resolution; it—

Hagbart. Surely you saw it in all the many talks we love had?

Leonarda. Yes.

Hagbart. Then is that not a proof that we two—?

Leonarda. Yes, it is true! I can hide nothing from you. (Bursts into tears.)

Hagbart. But why this unhappiness?

Leonarda. I don't know! It pursues me all day, and all through the sleepless night. (Weeps helplessly.)

Hagbart. But it has no real existence. It might, in the case of others; but not in our case—not for us.

Leonarda. I spoke in my distress, without thinking. I threw out the first thing that came into my head, to try and stop you. But it is not that—oh, God! (Sways as if half swooning.)

Hagbart (rushing to her side). Leonarda!

Leonarda. No, no! Let me be!

Hagbart. You know your love is too strong for you—will you not give way to it?

Leonarda. Hagbart, there is something about it that is not right—

Hagbart. Do you mean in the way it has come about? In Aagot's having been the means of leading me to you? Think of it, and you will see that it could not have happened otherwise.

Leonarda. Talking about it will not help me. I must see Aagot; I must speak to Aagot.

Hagbart. But you have done that! You know it is you that love me, and not she. You know it is you that I love, and not her. What more do you need?

Leonarda. I want time. I want not to lose the self-control I have won for myself by years of renunciation and self-sacrifice, and was so proud of. But it won't obey me when you speak to me. Your words possess me in spite of myself. If there is any happiness on earth, it is to find one's every thought faultlessly understood. But that happiness brings a pain with it—for me, at any rate. No, don't answer! You are too strong for me; because I love you—love you as only one can who has never believed such joy could exist or could possibly come to her—and now the depths of my peace are troubled with the thought that it is treachery to my child.

Hagbart. But you know that it is not!

Leonarda. I don't know. Let me have time to think! I am afraid, and my fear revives forgotten memories. More than that—I am afraid of the immensity of my love for you, afraid of dragging you with me into a whirlpool of disaster!—No, don't answer! Don't touch me!—Hagbart, do you love me?

Hagbart. Can you ask that?

Leonarda. Then help me! Go away!—Be generous. Let my heart know this triumph and see you in its glorious rays! Other women do not need that, perhaps—but I need it—go!

Hagbart. Leonarda!

Leonarda. Wait till you hear from me. It will not be long. Whatever happens, be patient—and remember, I love you!—No, don't say anything! I have neither courage nor strength for anything more. (Her voice sinks to a whisper.) Go! (He turns to go.) Hagbart! (He stops.) What you have said to me to-day has given me the greatest happiness of my life. But your going away now without a word will be more to me than all you have said. (He goes out.)

Leonarda (stands for some moments in a kind of ecstasy, moves, and stands still again. Suddenly she calls out): Aagot!

Aagot (from without). Are you there?

Leonarda. My dear child! (Goes out, and comes in again with AAGOT in her arms.) Did you walk?

Aagot. The whole way! (She is carrying her hat in her hand, appears hot and sunburnt, and bears evident signs of having made a long journey on foot. She takes off a knapsack which she has been carrying on her back.) I washed in a brook to-day and used it as a looking-glass as well!

Leonarda. Have you been walking all night?

Aagot. No; I slept for a little while at Opsal, but I was out by sunrise. It was lovely!

Leonarda. And I have just been arranging to send and fetch you.

Aagot. Really? Well, they can fetch my things. I could not wait any longer.

Leonarda. You look so well.

Aagot. Oh, that is because I am so sunburnt.

Leonarda. You are feeling all right again, then—now?

Aagot. Splendid, aunt! All that is over, now.—I have had a letter from grandmother.

Leonarda. Was that letter from her that I sent on to you? I could not make out whom it was from.

Aagot. Yes, it was from her. Here it is. You must hear it.

Leonarda. Yes.

Aagot (reads). "My dear child. I have not written a letter for many years, so I do not know what this will be like. But Hagbart is away, so I must tell you myself. Do not be distressed any longer. As soon as you are married, I will come and live with you." Isn't that glorious, aunt? (She is trembling with happiness, and throws her arms round LEONARDA'S neck.)

Leonarda. But—

Aagot. But what? There is no more "but" about it, don't you see! It is on your account.

Leonarda. On my account? Yes, but—what about you? How do you stand—with Hagbart?

Aagot. Oh, that?—Well, I will tell you the whole story! I can do that now.—Oh, don't take it all so seriously, aunt! It really is nothing. But let us sit down. (Brings forward a seat, as she speaks.) I really feel as if I wanted to sit down for a little while, too!—Well, you see, it came upon me like an unexpected attack—a blow from behind, as it were. Now, my dear aunt, don't look so troubled. It is all over now. As a matter of fact, the beginning of it all was a play I saw.

Leonarda. A play?

Aagot. We saw it together once, you and I, do you remember? Scribe's Bataille de Dames.

Leonarda. Yes.

Aagot. And I remember thinking and saying to you: That fellow Henri, in the play, was a stupid fellow. He had the choice between a strong-natured, handsome, spirited woman, who was ready to give her life for him, and a child who was really a stupid little thing—for she was, it is no use denying it, aunt—and he chose the insignificant little person. No, I would rather sit down here; I can rest better so. Ah, that is good! And now you mustn't look me in the face oftener than I want to let you, because you take it too dreadfully solemnly, and I am going to tell you something foolish now.—All of a sudden it flashed across my mind: Good heavens! the woman was—, and the little hussy with the curly hair was—, and he? But Hagbart is a man of some sense: he had chosen otherwise! And I did not know; but I realised at the same time that almost from the first day Hagbart used always to talk to you, and only to you, and hardly at all to me except to talk about you. I got so miserable about it that I felt as if some one had put a knife into my heart; and from that moment—I am so ashamed of it now—I had no more peace. I carried an aching pain in my heart night and day, and I thought my heart itself would break merely to see him speak to you or you to him. I am ashamed of myself; because what was more natural than that he should never be tired of talking to you? I never should, myself!

Leonarda. But still I don't see—I don't understand yet—

Aagot. Wait a bit! Oh, don't look so anxiously at me! It is all over now, you know.

Leonarda. What is all over?

Aagot. Bless my soul, wait! Aunt, dear, you are more impatient than I am myself! I do not want you to think me worse than I am, so I must first tell you how I fought with myself. I lay and cried all night, because I could not talk to you about it, and in the daytime I forced myself to seem merry and lively and happy. And then, aunt, one day I said to myself quite honestly: Why should you feel aggrieved at his loving her more than you? What are you, compared with her? And how splendid it would be, I thought, for my dear aunt to find some one she could truly love, and that it should be I that had brought them together!

Leonarda. That was splendid of you, Aagot!

Aagot. Yes, but now I mustn't make myself out better than I am, either. Because I did not always manage to look at it that way; very often something very like a sob kept rising in my throat. But then I used to talk to myself seriously, and say: Even supposing it is your own happiness you are giving up for her sake, is that too much for you to do for her? No, a thousand times no! And even supposing he does not love you any more, ought you not to be able to conquer your own feelings? Surely it would be cowardly not to be able to do that! Think no more of him, if he does not love you!

Leonarda. Aagot, I cannot tell you how I admire you, and love you, and how proud I am of you!

Aagot. Oh, aunt, I never realised as I did then what you have been to me! I knew that if I were capable of any great deed, anything really good or really fine, it was you that had planted the impulse in me. And then I sought every opportunity to bring this about; I wanted to take ever so humble a part in it, but without your hearing a word or a sigh from me. Besides, I had you always before me as an example; because I knew that you would have done it for me—indeed that you had already done as much. Your example was like a shining beacon to me, aunt!

Leonarda. Aagot!

Aagot. But you don't seem to be as happy about it as I am! Don't you understand yet how it all happened?

Leonarda. Yes, but—about the result of it?

Aagot. Dearest, you know all about that!—No, it is true, you don't! I must not forget to tell you that; otherwise you won't be able to understand why I behaved so stupidly at the Bishop's.

Leonarda. No.

Aagot. Well, you see, when I was full of this splendid determination to sacrifice myself so as to make you happy, I used to feel a regular fury come over me because Hagbart noticed no change in me—or, to be more correct, did not understand it in the least. He used to go about as if he were in a dream. Isn't it extraordinary how one thing leads to another? My feeling was stronger than I had any idea of; because when the Bishop wanted to slight you—and that was like a stab from behind, too!—I absolutely lost my head with Hagbart because of his not having prevented that, instead of going about dreaming. I don't know—but—well, you saw yourself what happened. I blurted out the first thing that came into my head and was abominably rude; you were angry; then we made friends again and I went away—and then, aunt—

Leonarda. And then—?

Aagot. Then I thought it all over! All the beautiful things you said to me about him, as we were going home, came back to me more and more forcibly. I saw you as I had always known you, noble and gentle.—It was so wonderful up there, too! The air, the clearness, the sense of space! And the lake, almost always calm, because it was so sheltered! And the wonderful stillness, especially in the evening!—And so it healed, just as a wound heals.

Leonarda. What healed?

Aagot. The pain in my heart, aunt. All the difficulties vanished. I know Hagbart to be what you said—noble and true. And you too, aunt! You would neither of you have wished to give me a moment's pain, even unconsciously, I knew. It was so good to realise that! It was so restful, that often while I was thinking of it, I went to sleep where I sat—I was so happy!—Ah, how I love him! And then came grandmother's letter—.

HANS comes in, but does not see AAGOT at first.

Hans. Then I am to fetch Miss Aagot—why, there she is!

Aagot (getting up). You quite frightened me, Hans!

Hans. Welcome back, miss!

Aagot. Thank you.

Hans. Well, you have saved me a journey, miss, I suppose?

Aagot. Yes. But someone must go and fetch my things.

Hans. Of course, miss.—But what is the matter with the mistress?

Aagot. Aunt!—Heavens, what is the matter?

Hans. The mistress has not looked well lately.

Aagot. Hasn't she? Aunt, dear! Shall I—? Would you like to—? Aunt!

Hans. Shall I fetch some one to—

Leonarda. No, no!—But you, Aagot—will you-. Oh, my God!—Will you run in—and get—

Aagot. Your bottle of drops?

Leonarda. Yes. (AAGOT runs out.) Hans, go as quickly as you can to the General's—ask him to come here! At once!

Hans. Yes, ma'am.

Leonarda. Hans!

Hans. Yes, ma'am.

Leonarda. Go on horseback. You may not find the General at home—and have to go elsewhere after him.

Hans. Yes, ma'am. (Goes out. AAGOT re-enters.)

Aagot. Here it is, aunt!

Leonarda. Thank you. It is over now.

Aagot. But what was it, aunt?

Leonarda. It was something, dear—something that comes over one sometimes at the change of the year.

Curtain.

(The interval between this act and the next should be very short.)

ACT IV

(SCENE.—A room in the BISHOP'S house, the same evening. The lights are lit. The BISHOP comes in with LEONARDA, who is in travelling dress, with a shawl over her arm and a bag in her hand. The BISHOP makes a movement as though to relieve her of them, but she puts them down herself.)

Leonarda. Your lordship must excuse me for troubling you so late as this; but the reason of it is something over which I have no control.——Is your nephew here?

Bishop. No, but I expect him. He has been here twice this afternoon already to see me, but I was out.

Leonarda. I will make haste then, and do what I have to do before he comes.

Bishop. Shall I give instructions that we are to be told when he comes in?

Leonarda. If you please.

Bishop (ringing the bell). Grandmother says that as soon as he came back to-day, he went at once to see you.

Leonarda. Yes.

Enter a Maid.

Bishop (to the Maid). Be so good as to let me know when Mr. Hagbart comes in. (Exit Maid.)

Leonarda. Has he had a talk with his grandmother?

Bishop. Yes.

Leonarda. After he—? (Checks herself.)

Bishop. After he had been to see you.

Leonarda. Did he tell her anything?

Bishop. He was very much agitated, apparently. I did not ask grandmother any further questions; I can imagine what passed between them.—Has he spoken to you?

Leonarda. Yes.

Bishop. And you, Mrs. Falk?

Leonarda. I—? Well, I am here.

Bishop. Going on a journey, if I am not mistaken?

Leonarda. Going on a journey. Things are turning out as you wished after all, my lord.

Bishop. And he is to know nothing about it?

Leonarda. No one—except the person who will accompany me. I am sailing for England by to-night's boat.

Bishop (looking at his watch). You haven't much time, then.

Leonarda. I only want to entrust to your lordship a deed of gift of my property here.

Bishop. In favour of your niece?

Leonarda. Yes, for Aagot. She shall have everything.

Bishop. But last time, Mrs. Falk, you said—

Leonarda. Oh, I have enough for my journey. Later on I shall want nothing; I can provide for myself.

Bishop. But what about Aagot? Will you not wait until she comes home?

Leonarda. She came home to-day. She is resting now. But I have sent back my carriage to bring her here immediately. I want to ask you to take her in—I know no one else—and to comfort her—

Bishop. Indeed I will, Mrs. Falk. I understand what this must cost you.

Leonarda. And will you try—to—to bring those two together again?

Bishop. But they don't love each other!

Leonarda. Aagot loves him. And—as they both love me—my idea was that when I am gone, and they know that it was my wish, the love they both have for me may bring them together again. I hope so—they are both so young.

Bishop. I will do all I can.

Leonarda. Thank you. And I want to make bold to beg you to let grandmother go and live in the country with Aagot—or let Aagot come and live here, whichever they prefer. It would divert Aagot's mind if she had the care of grandmother; and she is very fond of her.

Bishop. And grandmother of her.

Leonarda. And wherever the grandmother is, Hagbart will be too. Very likely the old lady would help them.

Bishop. I think your idea is an excellent one; and I am amazed that you have had time and strength to think it all out in this manner.

Leonarda. Is grandmother still up?

Bishop. Yes; I have just come from her room. Hagbart has excited her; she can stand so little.

Leonarda. Then I expect I had better not go and bid her good-bye. I should have liked to, otherwise.

Bishop. I don't think I ought to allow it.

Leonarda. Then please say good-bye to her from me—and thank her.

Bishop. I will.

Leonarda. And ask her—to help—

Bishop. I will do everything I possibly can.

Leonarda. And your lordship must forgive me for all the upset I have caused here. I did not intend it.

Bishop. I am only sorry that I did not know you sooner. Many things might have been different.

Leonarda. We won't talk about that now.

Enter Maid.

Maid. I was asked to bring you this card, ma'am.

Leonarda. Thank you. Is the General in the hall?

Maid. Yes.

Bishop. General Rosen—here?

Leonarda. I took the liberty of asking him to call for me here when the boat was signalled.

Bishop. Ask the General to come in. (Exit Maid.) Then it is General Rosen that is to—. (Checks himself.)

Leonarda (searching in her bag).—that is to accompany me? He is my husband.

Bishop. The husband you divorced.

Leonarda. Yes.

Bishop. I see I have done you a great injustice, Mrs. Falk.

Leonarda. Yes. (GENERAL ROSEN comes in, dressed in a smart travelling suit and looking very spruce.)

General Rosen. I beg your lordship's pardon—but, time is up.—Mrs. Falk, is this yours? (Gives her a letter.)

Leonarda. Yes.—When Aagot comes, will your lordship give her this?—and help her?

Bishop. I will, Mrs. Falk. God bless you!

Enter Maid.

Maid. Mr. Hagbart has just come in.

Leonarda. Good-bye!—Say good-bye to—

Bishop (taking her hand). What you are doing is more than any one of us could have done.

Leonarda. It all depends on how deeply one loves.—Thank you, and good-bye!

Bishop. Good-bye! (GENERAL ROSEN offers LEONARDA his arm. She takes it, and they go out. The BISHOP follows them. HAGBART comes in from the right, looks round in astonishment, then goes towards the back of the room and meets the BISHOP in the doorway.)

Bishop. Is that you? (Both come forward without speaking.)

Hagbart (in a low voice, but evidently under the influence of great emotion). I can tell by your voice—and your face—that you know about it.

Bishop. You mean that you think I have had a talk with grandmother?

Hagbart. Yes.

Bishop. Well, I have. She told me nothing definite, but I see how things stand. I saw that sooner than you did yourself, you know.

Hagbart. That is true. The fight is over now, as far as I am concerned.

Bishop. Scarcely that, Hagbart.

Hagbart. Oh, you won't admit it, I know. But I call it the most decisive victory of my life. I love Mrs. Falk—and she loves me.

Bishop. If you were not in such an excited condition—

Hagbart. It is not excitement, it is happiness. But here, with you—oh, I have not come to ask for your blessing; we must do without that! But I have come to tell you the fact, because it was my duty to do so.—Does it grieve you so much?

Bishop. Yes.

Hagbart. Uncle, I feel hurt at that.

Bishop. My boy—!

Hagbart. I feel hurt both on her account and on my own. It shows that you know neither of us.

Bishop. Let us sit down and talk quietly, Hagbart.

Hagbart. I must ask you to make no attempt to persuade me to alter my decision.

Bishop. Make your mind easy on that score. Your feelings do you honour—and I know now that she is worthy of them.

Hagbart. What—do you say that? (They sit down.)

Bishop. My dear Hagbart, let me tell you this at once. I have gone through an experience, too, since the last time we met. And it has taught me that I had no right to treat Mrs. Falk as I did.

Hagbart. Is it possible?

Bishop. I judged her both too quickly and too harshly. That is one of our besetting sins. And I have paid too much heed to the opinion of others, and too little to the charity that should give us courage to do good. She, whom I despised, has taught me that.

Hagbart. You do not know how grateful and how happy you have made me by saying that!

Bishop. I have something more to say. At the time we held that unjust opinion of her, we misled you—for you relied on our opinion then—until you ended by sharing our views and being even more vehement in the matter than we, as young people will. That created a reaction in you, which in the end led to love. If that love had been a sin, we should have been to blame for it.

Hagbart. Is it a sin, then?

Bishop. No. But when you felt that we were inclined to look upon it in that light, that very fact stirred up your sense of justice and increased your love. You have a noble heart.

Hagbart. Ah, how I shall love you after this, uncle!

Bishop. And that is why I wanted you to sit down here just now, Hagbart—to beg your pardon—and hers. And my congregation's, too. It is my duty to guide them, but I was not willing to trust them enough. By far the greater number among them are good people; they would have followed me if I had had the courage to go forward.

Hagbart. Uncle, I admire and revere you more than I have ever done before—more than any one has ever done!

Bishop (getting up). My dear boy!

Hagbart (throwing himself into his arms). Uncle!

Bishop. Is your love strong enough to bear—

Hagbart. Anything!

Bishop. Because sometimes love is given to us to teach us self-sacrifice.

The GRANDMOTHER comes in.

Grandmother. I heard Hagbart's voice.

Hagbart. Grandmother! (He and the BISHOP go to help her.) Grandmother! You don't know how happy I am! (Takes her by the arm.)

Grandmother. Is that true?

Bishop (taking her other arm). You should not walk about without help.

Grandmother. I heard Hagbart's voice. He was talking so loud, that I thought something had happened.

Hagbart. So it has—something good! Uncle consents! He is splendid! He has made everything all right again, and better than ever! Oh, grandmother, I wish you were not so old! I feel as if I should like to take you up in my arms and dance you round the room.

Grandmother. You mustn't do that, my dear. (They put her into her chair.) Now! What is your last bit of news?

Hagbart. My last bit of news? I have no fresh news! There is nothing more to tell!

Bishop. Yes, Hagbart, there is.

Hagbart. Why do you say that so seriously?—You look so serious—and seem agitated! Uncle! (The noise of wheels is heard outside.)

Bishop. Wait a little, my dear boy. Wait a little! (Goes out by the door at the back.)

Hagbart. Grandmother, what can it be?

Grandmother. I don't know.—But happiness is often so brief.

Hagbart. Happiness so brief? What do you mean?—Good God, grandmother, don't torture me!

Grandmother. I assure you, I know nothing about it—only—

Hagbart. Only—what?

Grandmother. While your uncle was with me, Mrs. Falk was announced.

Hagbart. Mrs. Falk? Has she been here? Just now?

Grandmother. Yes, just now.

Hagbart. Then something must have happened! Perhaps it was she that uncle—. (Rushes to the door, which opens, and the BISHOP comes in with AAGOT on his arm, followed by CORNELIA.) Aagot!

Aagot. Hagbart!—(Anxiously.) Is aunt not here!

Cornelia. What, grandmother here! (Goes to her.)

Bishop. My dear Aagot, your aunt entrusted this letter to me to give to you.

Hagbart. A letter—?

Grandmother. What is the matter? Let me see! (CORNELIA moves her chair nearer to the others.)

Hagbart. Read it aloud, Aagot!

Aagot (reads). "My darling. When you receive this letter I shall have—gone away. I love the man you—." (With a cry, she falls swooning. The BISHOP catches her in his arms.)

Grandmother. She has gone away?

Cornelia. She loves the man you—? Good God, look at Hagbart!

Bishop. Cornelia! (She goes to him, and they lay AAGOT on the couch. CORNELIA stays beside her. The BISHOP turns to HAGBART.) Hagbart! (HAGBART throws himself into his arms.) Courage! Courage, my boy!

Grandmother (getting up). It is like going back to the days of great emotions!

The Curtain falls slowly.

A GAUNTLET

A PLAY IN THREE ACTS

DRAMATIS PERSONAE
RIIS.
MRS. RIIS.
SVAVA, their daughter.
MARGIT, their maid.

CHRISTENSEN.
MRS. CHRISTENSEN.
ALFRED, *their son, betrothed to Svava.*
DR. NORDAN.
THOMAS, *his servant.*
HOFF.

The action of the play passes in Christiania.

ACT I

(SCENE.—A room in RIIS' house. An open door at the back leads into a park and gives a glimpse of the sea beyond. Windows on each side of the door. Doors also in the right and left walls. Beyond the door on the right is a piano; opposite to the piano a cupboard. In the foreground, to the right and left, two couches with small tables in front of them. Easy-chairs and smaller hairs scattered about. MRS. RIIS is sitting on the couch to the left, and DR. NORDAN in a chair in the centre of the room. He is wearing a straw hat pushed on to the back of his head, and has a large handkerchief spread over his knees. He is sitting with his arms folded, leaning upon his stick.)

Mrs. Riis. A penny for your thoughts!

Nordan. What was it you were asking me about?

Mrs. Riis. About that matter of Mrs. North, of course.

Nordan. That matter of Mrs. North? Well, I was talking to Christensen about it just now. He has advanced the money and is going to try and get the bank to suspend proceedings. I have told you that already. What else do you want to know?

Mrs. Riis. I want to know how much gossip there is about it, my dear friend.

Nordan. Oh, men don't gossip about each other's affairs.—By the way, isn't our friend in there (nodding towards the door on the right) going to be told about it? This seem, a good opportunity.

Mrs. Riis. Let us wait.

Nordan. Because Christensen will have to be repaid, you know. I told him he would be.

Mrs. Riis. Naturally. What else would you suppose?

Nordan (getting up). Well, I am going away for my holidays, so Christensen must look after it now.—Was it a very grand party yesterday?

Mrs. Riis. There was not much display.

Nordan. No, the Christensens' parties are never very luxurious. But I suppose there were a lot of people?

Mrs. Riis. I have never seen so many at a private entertainment.

Nordan. Is Svava up?

Mrs. Riis. She is out bathing.

Nordan. Already? Did you come home early, then?

Mrs. Riis. At about twelve, I think. Svava wanted to come home. My husband was late, I think.

Nordan. The card tables. She looked radiant, I suppose, eh?

Mrs. Riis. Why didn't you come?

Nordan. I never go to betrothal parties, and I never go to Weddings—never! I can't bear the sight of the poor victims in their veils and wreaths.

Mrs. Riis. But, my dear doctor, you surely think—as we all do—that this will be a happy marriage?

Nordan. He is a fine lad. But, all the same—I have been taken in so often.—Oh, well!

Mrs. Riis. She was so happy, and is just as happy to-day.

Nordan. It is a pity I shall not see her. Good-bye, Mrs. Riis.

Mrs. Riis. Good-bye, doctor. Then you are off to-day?

Nordan. Yes, I need a change of air.

Mrs. Riis. Quite so. Well, I hope you will enjoy yourself—and, many thanks for what you have done!

Nordan. It is I ought to thank you, my dear lady! I aim vexed not to be able to say good-bye to Svava. (Goes out. MRS. RIIS takes up a magazine from the table on the left and settles herself comfortably on a couch from which she can see into the park. During what follows she reads whenever opportunity allows. RIIS comes in through the door to the right, in his shirt sleeves and struggling with his collar.)

Riis. Good morning! Was that Nordan that went out just now?

Mrs. Riis. Yes. (RIIS crosses the room, then turns back and disappears through the door on the right. He comes back again immediately and goes through the same proceeding, all the tine busy with his collar.) Can I help you at all?

Riis. No—thanks all the same! These new-fangled shirts are troublesome things. I bought some in Paris.

Mrs. Riis. Yes, I believe you have bought a whole dozen.

Riis. A dozen and a half. (Goes into his room, comes out again in apparently the same difficulties, and walks about as before.) As a matter of fact I am wondering about something.

Mrs. Riis. It must be something complicated.

Riis. It is—it is. No doubt of it!—This collar is the very—Ah, at last! (Goes into his room and comes out again, this time with his necktie in his hand.) I have been wondering—wondering—what our dear girl's character is made up of?

Mrs. Riis. What it is made up of?

Riis. Yes—what characteristics she gets from you and what from me, and so forth. In what respects, that is to say, she takes after your family, and in what respect after mine, and so forth. Svava is a remarkable girl.

Mrs. Riis. She is that.

Riis. She is neither altogether you nor altogether me nor is she exactly a compound of us both.

Mrs. Riis. Svava is something more than that.

Riis. A considerable deal more than that, too. (Disappears again; then comes out with his coat on, brushing himself.) What did you say?

Mrs. Riis. I did not speak.—I rather think it is my mother that Svava is most like.

Riis. I should think so! Svava, with her quiet pleasant ways! What a thing to say!

Mrs. Riis. Svava can be passionate enough.

Riis. Svava never forgets her manners as your mother did.

Mrs. Riis. You never understood mother. Still, no doubt they are unlike in a great many things.

Riis. Absolutely!—Can you see now how right I was in chattering to her in various languages from the beginning, even when she was quite tiny? Can you see that now? You were opposed to my doing it.

Mrs. Riis. I was opposed to your perpetually plaguing the child, and also to the endless jumping from one thing to another.

Riis. But look at the result, my dear! Look at the result! (Begins to hum a tune.)

Mrs. Riis. You are surely never going to pretend that it is the languages that have made her what she is?

Riis (as he disappears). No, not the languages; but—(His voice is heard from within his room)—the language have done a wonderful lot! She has savoir vivre—what? (Comes out again.)

Mrs. Riis. I am sure that is not what Svava is most admired for.

Riis. No, no. On the boat, a man asked me if I were related to the Miss Riis who had founded the Kindergartens in the town. I said I had the honour to be her father. You should have seen his face! I nearly had a fit.

Mrs. Riis. Yes, the Kindergartens have been a great success from the very first.

Riis. And they are responsible for her getting engaged, too—aren't they? What?

Mrs. Riis. You must ask her.

Riis. You have never even noticed my new suit.

Mrs. Riis. Indeed I have.

Riis. I didn't hear as much as the tiniest cry of admiration from you. Look at the harmony of it all!—the scheme of colour, even down to the shoes!—what? And the handkerchief, too!

Mrs. Riis. How old are you, dear?

Riis. Hold your tongue!—Anyway, how old do you think people take me to be?

Mrs. Riis. Forty, of course.

Riis. "Of course"? I don't see that it is so obvious. This suit is a kind of Bridal Symphony, composed at Cologne when I got the telegram telling me of Svava's engagement. Just think of it! At Cologne—not ten hours' journey from Paris! But I could not wait ten hours; I had risen too much in my own estimation in view of my approaching relationship with the richest family in the country.

Mrs. Riis. Is that suit all you have to show for it, then?

Riis. What a question! Just you wait till I have got my luggage through the custom-house!

Mrs. Riis. We shall be quite out of it, I suppose?

Riis. You out of it! When a very lucky daddy finds himself in Paris at a most tremendous moment—

Mrs. Riis. And what did you think of the party yesterday?

Riis. I was quite delighted with the boat for being late so that I was landed in the middle of a fête champêtre as by magic. And Naturally one had a tremendous welcome as the party was in honour of one's own only daughter!

Mrs. Riis. What time did you come in last night?

Riis. Don't you understand that we had to play cards yesterday, too? I could not get out of it; I had to make a fourth with Abraham, Isaac, and Jacob—that is to say, with our host, a cabinet minister, and old Holk. It was a tremendous honour to lose one's money to grand folk like that. Because I always lose, you know.—I came home about three o'clock, I should think.—What is that you are reading?

Mrs. Riis. The Fortnightly.

Riis. Has there been anything good in it while I have been away? (Begins to hum a tune.)

Mrs. Riis. Yes—there is an article here on heredity that you must read. It has some reference to what we began to talk about.

Riis. Do you know this tune? (Goes over to the piano.) It is all the rage now. I heard it all over Germany. (Begins to play and sing, but breaks off suddenly.) I will go and fetch the music, while I think of it! (Goes into his room and comes out again with the music. Sits down and begins to play and sing again. SVAVA comes in by it, door on the left. RIIS stops when he sees her, and jumps up.) Good morning, my child! Good morning! I have hardly had a chance to say a word to you yet. At the party everyone took you away from me! (Kisses her, and comes forward with her.)

Svava. Why were you so long of coming back from abroad?

Riis. Why don't people give one some warning when they are going to get engaged?

Svava. Because people don't know anything about it themselves, till it happens! Good morning again, mother. (Kneels down beside her.)

Mrs. Riis. There is a delicious freshness about you, dear! Did you have a walk in the wood after your swim?

Svava (getting up). Yes, and just as I got home a few minutes ago Alfred passed the house and called up to me. He is coming in directly.

Riis. To tell you the truth—and one ought always to tell the truth—I had quite given up the hope of such happiness coming to our dear girl.

Svava. I know you had. I had quite given it up myself.

Riis. Until your fairy prince came?

Svava. Until my fairy prince came. And he took his time about it, too!

Riis. You had been waiting for him a long time, though—hadn't you?

Svava. Not a bit of it! I never once thought of him.

Riis. Now you are talking in riddles.

Svava. Yes, it is a riddle to understand how two people, who have seen each other from childhood without even giving each other a thought, suddenly—! Because that was really how it happened. It all dates from a certain moment—and then, all at once, he became quite another man in my eyes.

Riis. But in every one else's, I suppose, he is the same us before?

Svava. I hope so!

Riis. He is more lively than he was, at any rate—in my eyes.

Svava. Yes, I saw you laughing together last night. What was it?

Riis. We were discussing the best way of getting through the world. I gave him my three famous rules of life.

Mrs. Riis and Svava (together). Already!

Riis. They were a great success. Do you remember them, you bad girl?

Svava. Rule number one: Never make a fool of yourself.

Riis. Rule number two: Never be a burden to any one.

Svava. Rule number three: Always be in the fashion. They are not very hard to remember, because they art neither obscure nor profound.

Riis. But all the harder to put into practice! And thus is a great virtue in all rules of life.—I congratulate you on your new morning frock. Under the circumstances it is really charming.

Svava. "Under the circumstances" means, I suppose, considering that you have had no hand in it.

Riis. Yes, because I should never have chosen that trimming. However, the "under the circumstances" is not so bad. A good cut, too—yes. Aha! Just you wail till my portmanteau comes!

Svava. Some surprises for us?

Riis. Big ones!—By the way, I have something here. (Goes into his room.)

Svava. Do you know, mother, he seems to me more restless than ever.

Mrs. Riis. That is happiness, dear.

Svava. And yet father's restlessness has always something a little sad about it. He is—. (RIIS comes out of his room again.) Do you know what I heard a cabinet minister say about you yesterday?

Riis. A man of that stamp is sure to say something worth hearing.

Svava. "We all always look upon your father, Miss Riis, as our Well-dressed man par excellence."

Riis. Ah, a bien dit son excellence! But I can tell you something better than that. You are getting your father a knighthood.

Svava. I am?

Riis. Yes, who else? Of course the Government has once or twice made use of me to some small degree in connection with various commercial treaties; but now, as our great man's brother-in-law, I am going to be made a Knight of St. Olaf!

Svava. I congratulate you.

Riis. Well, when it rains on the parson it drips on the clerk, you know.

Svava. You are really most unexpectedly modest in your new position.

Riis. Am I not!—And now you shall see me as a modest showman of beautiful dresses—that is to say, of drawings of dresses—still more modest than the showman, from the latest play at the Français.

Svava. Oh no, dad—not now!

Mrs. Riis. We won't start on that till the afternoon.

Riis. One would really think I were the only woman of the lot! However, as you please. You rule the world! Well, then, I have another proposition to make, in two parts. Part one, that we sit down!

Svava. We sit down! (She and her father sit.)

Riis. And next, that you tell your newly-returned parent exactly how it all happened. All about that "riddle," you know!

Svava. Oh, that!—You must excuse me; I cannot t you about that.

Riis. Not in all its sweet details, of course! Good heavens, who would be so barbarous as to ask such a thing in the first delicious month of an engagement! No, I of only I want you to tell us what was the primum mobile in the matter.

Svava. Oh, I understand. Yes, I will tell you that because that really means teaching you to know Alfred's true character.

Riis. For instance—how did you come to speak to him?

Svava. Well, that was those darling Kindergartens of ours—

Riis. Oho!—Your darling Kindergartens, you mean?

Svava. What, when there are over a hundred girls there—?

Riis. Never mind about that! I suppose he came to bring a donation?

Svava. Yes, he came several times with a donation—

Riis. Aha!

Svava. And one day we were talking about luxury saying that it was better to use one's time and money in our way, than to use them in luxurious living.

Riis. But how do you define luxury?

Svava. We did not discuss that at all. But I saw that he considered luxury to be immoral.

Riis. Luxury immoral!

Svava. Yes, I know that is not your opinion. But it is mine.

Riis. Your mother's, you mean, and your grand mother's.

Svava. Exactly; but mine too, if you don't object?

Riis. Not I!

Svava. I mentioned that little incident that happened to us when we were in America—do you remember? We had gone to a temperance meeting, and saw women drive up who were going to support the cause of abstinence, and yet were—well, of course we did not know their circumstances—but to judge from their appearance, with their carriages and horses, their jewellery and dresses—especially their jewellery—they must have been worth, say—

Riis. Say many thousands of dollars! No doubt about it.

Svava. There is no doubt about it. And don't you think that is really just as disgraceful debauchery, in its town way, as drink is in its?

Riis. Oh, well—!

Svava. Yes, you shrug your shoulders. Alfred did not do that. He told me of his own experiences—in great cities. It was horrible!

Riis. What was horrible?

Svava. The contrast between poverty and wealth—between the bitterest want and the most reckless luxury.

Riis. Oh—that! I thought, perhaps—. However, go on!

Svava. He did not sit looking quite indifferent and clean his nails.

Riis. I beg your pardon.

Svava. Oh, please go on, dear!—No, he prophesied a great social revolution, and spoke so fervently about it—and it was then that he told me what his ideas about wealth were. It was the greatest possible surprise to me—and a new idea to me, too, to some extent. You should have seen how handsome he looked!

Riis. Handsome, did you say?

Svava. Isn't he handsome? I think so, at all events. And so does mother, I think?

Mrs. Riis (without looking up from her book). And so does mother.

Riis. Mothers always fall in love with their daughters' young men—but they fall out again when they become their mothers-in-law!

Svava. Is that your experience?

Riis. That is my experience. So Alfred Christensen has blossomed into a beauty? Well, we must consider that settled.

Svava. He stood there so sure of himself, and looking so honest and clean—for that is an essential thing, you know.

Riis. What exactly do you mean by "clean," my dear?

Svava. I mean just what the word means.

Riis. Exactly—but I want to know what meaning attach to the word.

Svava. Well—the meaning that I hope any one would attach to it if they used the word of me.

Riis. Do you attach the same meaning to it if it is used' of a man, as you would if it were used of a girl?

Svava. Yes, of course.

Riis. And do you suppose that Christensen's son—

Svava (getting up). Father, you are insulting me!

Riis. How can the fact of his being his father's son I an insult to you?

Svava. In that respect he is not his father's son! I am not likely to make any mistake in a thing of that sort!

Mrs. Riis. I am just reading about inherited tendencies. It is Not necessary to suppose that he has inherited all his father's.

Riis. Oh, well—have it as you please! I am afraid all these superhuman theories of yours. You will never get through the world with them.

Svava. What do you mean?—Mother, what does father mean?

Mrs. Riis. I suppose he means that all men are alike. And one must allow that it is true.

Svava. You do not really mean that?

Riis. But why get so excited about it?—Come and sit down! And, besides, how can you possibly tell?

Svava. Tell? What?

Riis. Well, in each individual case—

Svava.—whether the man I see standing before me or walking past me is an unclean, disgusting beast—or a man?

Riis. Etcetera, etcetera!—You may make mistakes, my dear Svava?

Svava. No—not any more than I should make a mistake about you, father, when you begin to tease me with your horrid principles! Because, in spite of them, you are the chastest and most refined man I know.

Mrs. Riis (laying down her book). Are you going to keep that morning frock on, dear child? Won't you change your dress before Alfred comes?

Svava. No, mother, I am not going to be put off like that.—By this time I have seen so many of my girl friends giving themselves trustfully to their "fairy prince," as they think, and waking in the arms of a beast. I shall not risk that! I shall not make that mistake!

Mrs. Riis. Well, as it is, there is no occasion for you to get heated about it. Alfred is a man of honour.

Svava. He is. But I have heard of one shocking experience after another. There was poor Helga, only a month ago! And I myself—I can speak about it now, for I am happy now and feel secure—I can tell you now why I have been so long about it. For a long time I did nut dare to trust myself; because I too have been on the brink of being deceived.

Riis and Mrs. Riis (together, starting up from their chairs). You, Svava?

Svava. I was quite young at the time. Like most young girls, I was looking for my ideal, and found it in a young, vivacious man—I won't describe him more accurately. He had—oh, the noblest principles and the highest aims—the most complete contrast to you in that respect father! To say I loved him, is much too mild; I worshipped him. But I never can tell you what I discovered or how I discovered it. It was the time when you all thought I had—

Mrs. Riis.—something wrong with your lungs? Is it possible, child? Was it then?

Svava. Yes, it was then.—No one could endure or forgive being deceived like that!

Mrs. Riis. And you never said a word to me?

Svava. Only those who have made such a mistake as I did can understand the shame one feels.—Well, it is all over now. But this much is certain, that no one who has had such an experience once will make the same mistake again. (Meanwhile RIIS has gone into his room.)

Mrs. Riis. Perhaps it was a good thing for you, after all?

Svava. I am sure it was.—Well, it is all done with now. But it was not quite done with till I found Alfred. Where is father?

Mrs. Riis. Your father? Here he comes.

Riis (coming out of his room, with his hat on, and drawing on his gloves). Look here, little girl! I must go and see what has happened to my luggage at the Customs. I will go to the station and telegraph. You must have all your things looking very nice, you know, because the King is coming here in a day or two—and so it is worth it! Good-bye, then, my dear girl! (Kisses her.) You have made us very happy—so very happy. It is true you have certain ideas that are not—. Well, never mind! Goodbye! (Goes out.)

Mrs. Riis. Good-bye!

Riis (drawing off his gloves). Did you notice the tune I was playing when you came in? (Sits down at the piano.) I heard it everywhere in Germany. (Begins to play and sing, but stops short.) But, bless my soul, here is the music! You can play it and sing it for yourself. (Goes out, humming the air.)

Svava. He is delightful! There is really something so innocent about him. Did you notice him yesterday? He was simply coruscating.

Mrs. Riis. You did not see yourself, my dear!

Svava. Why? Was I sparkling, too?

Mrs. Riis. Your father's daughter—absolutely!

Svava. Yes, it is no use denying, mother, that however great one's happiness is, the friendliness of others increases it. I was thinking to-day over all the things that gave me so much happiness yesterday, and felt—oh, I can't tell you what I felt! (Nestles in her mother's arms.)

Mrs. Riis. You are a very lucky girl!—Now I must go and do my housekeeping.

Svava. Shall I help you?

Mrs. Riis. No, thank you, dear. (They cross the room together.)

Svava. Well, then, I will run through father's song once or twice—and Alfred should be here directly. (MRS. RIIS goes out by the door on the left. SVAVA sits down at the piano. ALFRED comes in softly from the left, and bends over her shoulder so that his face comes close to hers.)

Alfred. Good morning, darling!

Svava (jumping up). Alfred! I did not hear the door!

Alfred. Because you were playing. Something very pretty, too!

Svava. I enjoyed myself so much yesterday!

Alfred. I do not believe you have any idea what an impression you made!

Svava. Just a suspicion. But you must not talk about that, because it would be most improper for me to confess it!

Alfred. Every one was singing your praises to me, and a mother and father too. We are all very happy at how, to-day.

Svava. So we are here!—What is that you have got in your hand? A letter?

Alfred. Yes, a letter. Your maid who opened the door gave it to me. Someone has been clever enough to count upon my coming here some time this morning.

Svava. You don't think that was difficult to guess?

Alfred. Not particularly. It is from Edward Hansen.

Svava. But you can take a short cut to his house through our park. (Points to the right.)

Alfred. Yes, I know. And as he says it is urgent, and underlines the word—

Svava.—you can have my key. Here it is. (Gives it to him.)

Alfred. Thank you, dear, very much.

Svava. Oh, it is only selfishness; we shall have you back again all the sooner.

Alfred. I will stay here till lunch time.

Svava. You will stay here a great deal longer than that. We have a frightful lot to talk about—all about yesterday, and—

Alfred. Of course we have!

Svava. And lots of other things as well.

Alfred. I have a most important question to ask you.

Svava. Have you?

Alfred. Perhaps you will find the answer by the time I come back.

Svava. It can't be so very difficult, then!

Alfred. Indeed it is. But sometimes you have inspirations.

Svava. What is it?

Alfred. Why did we two not find each other many years ago?

Svava. Because we were not ready for it, of course!

Alfred. How do you know that?

Svava. Because I know that at that time I was quite another girl from what I am now.

Alfred. But there is a natural affinity between those that love one another. I am sure of it. And it was just as much the case at that time, surely?

Svava. We do not feel the natural affinity as long as we are developing on different lines.

Alfred. Have we been doing that? And nevertheless we—

Svava. Nevertheless we love one another. Our paths may be as unlike as they please, if only they lead together in the end.

Alfred. To the same way of thinking, you mean?

Svava. Yes, to our being such comrades as we are now.

Alfred. Such true comrades?

Svava. Such true comrades!

Alfred. Still, it is just at moments like this, when I hold you in my arms as I do now, that I ask myself over and over again why I did not do this long ago.

Svava. Oh, I don't think about that—not the least bit! It is the safest place in the world—that is what I think!

Alfred. Perhaps before this year it would not have been so.

Svava. What do you mean?

Alfred. I mean—well, I mean practically the same as you; that I have not always been the man I am now.—But I must hurry away. The letter says it is something urgent. (They cross the room together.)

Svava. One minute won't make any difference, will it?—because there is something I must say to you first.

Alfred (standing still). What is it?

Svava. When I saw you standing amongst all the others yesterday, I felt for the first moment as if I did not know you. Some change seemed to have come over you—the effect of the others, perhaps—anyway you really *were* actually different.

Alfred. Of course. People always are that, among strangers. When you came in with the ladies, it just seemed to me as if I had never observed you carefully before. Besides, there are certain things one cannot know till one sees a person amongst others. It was the first time I realised how tall you are—and your way of bending just a tiny bit to one side when you bow to any one. And your colouring! I had never properly seen—

Svava. Do be quiet, and let me get a word in!

Alfred. No, no! Here we are, back in the room—and I *must* be off now!

Svava. Only just a moment. You interrupted me, you know! When I saw you standing there among the men for the first moment I felt just as if I did not know you. But at the same moment you caught sight of me and nodded. I don't know what sort of a transformation came over us both; but I felt myself blushing as red as fire. And it was some time before I had the courage to look at you again.

Alfred. Well, do you know what happened to me? Every time any one came to dance with you, didn't I envy him! Oh, not at all!—To tell you the truth, I cannot bear any one else to touch you. (Clasps her in his arms.) And I have not told you the best part of it yet.

Svava. What is that?

Alfred. That when I see you amongst other people, and catch—say—a glimpse of your arm, I think to myself: That arm has been round my neck and round no one else's in the whole world! She is mine, mine, mine—and no one else's!—There, that is the best part of it all!—Look here, here we are back again in the room! It is witchcraft! Now I must go. (Crosses the room.) Good-bye! (Lets her go, then catches hold of her again.) Why didn't I find my happiness many years ago?—Good-bye!

Svava. I think I will come with you.

Alfred. Yes, do!

Svava. No, I forgot—I must learn this song before father comes back. If I don't learn it now, I expect you will take care I don't do so to-day. (A ring is heard at the front door.)

Alfred. Here is some one coming! Let me get away first. (Hurries out to the right. SVAVA stands waving her hand to him, then turns to the piano. The maid MARGIT enters.)

Margit. A gentleman has called, miss, who wants to know if—

Svava. A gentleman? Don't you know who he is?

Margit. No, miss.

Svava. What is he like?

Margit. He looks rather—

Svava. Rather suspicious?

Margit. No, far from it, miss—a very nice gentleman.

Svava. Tell him my father is not at home; he has gone down to the station.

Margit. I told him so, miss, but it is you he wants to see.

Svava. Ask my mother to come in here!—Oh, no, why should she! Let him come in. (MARGIT shows in HOFF, and goes out.)

Hoff. Is it Miss Riis I have the honour to—? Yes, I see it is. My name is Hoff—Karl Hoff. I am a commercial traveller—travel in iron.

Svava. But what has that to do with me?

Hoff. Just this much, that if I had been an ordinary stay-at-home man, a great many things would not have happened.

Svava. What would not have happened?

Hoff (taking a large pocket-book out of his docket, and extracting a letter from it). Will you condescend to read this? Or perhaps you would rather not?

Svava. How can I tell?

Hoff. Of course, you must first—Allow me. (Gives her the letter.)

Svava (reading). "To-night between ten and eleven that is to say, if the booby has not come home. I love you so dearly! Put a light in the hall window."

Hoff. "The booby" is me.

Svava. But I don't understand—?

Hoff. Here is another.

Svava. "I am full of remorse. Your cough frightens me; and now, when you are expecting—" But what in the world has this to do with me?

Hoff (after a moment's thought). What do you suppose?

Svava. Is it some one you want me to help?

Hoff. No, poor soul, she doesn't need help any more. She is dead.

Svava. Dead? Was she your wife?

Hoff. That's it. She was my wife. I found these and come other things in a little box. At the bottom were these notes—there are more of them—and some cotton wool on the top of them. On the top of that lay some earrings and things that had been her mother's. And also (producing some bracelets) these bracelets. They are certainly much too costly to have been her mother's.

Svava. I suppose she died suddenly, as she did not—

Hoff. I cannot say. Consumptives never think they are going to die. Anyway she was very delicate and weak.—May I sit down?

Svava. Please do. Are there any children?

Hoff (after a moment's thought). I believe not.

Svava. You believe not? I asked because I thought you wanted our Society to help you. This really is all very distressful to me.

Hoff. I thought it would be—I thought as much. Besides, I am not really sure if I—. You cannot understand this, then?

Svava. No, I cannot.

Hoff. No, you cannot.-I have heard so much good spoken of you for many years. My wife used to sing your praises, too.

Svava. Did she know me?

Hoff. She was Maren Tang—who used to be companion to—

Svava.—to Mrs. Christensen, my future mother-in-law? Was it she? She was such a well-bred, quiet woman. Are you sure you are not mistaken? One or two notes, unsigned and undated—what?

Hoff. Did you not recognise the handwriting?

Svava. I? No. Besides, isn't it a disguised hand?

Hoff. Yes, but not much disguised.

Svava. I presume you had some more definite errand with me?

Hoff. Yes, I had—but I think I will let it alone. You do not understand anything about this, I can see Perhaps you think I am a little crazy? I am not so sure you would not be right.

Svava. But there was something you wanted to say to me?

Hoff. Yes, there was. You see, these Kindergartens—

Svava. Oh, so it was them, all the time?

Hoff. No, it was not them. But they are responsible for my having for a long time thought very highly of you, Miss Riis. If you will excuse my saying so, I had never before seen fashionable young ladies trying to do anything useful—never. I am only a little broken-down tradesman travelling for a firm—a worthless sort of chap in many ways, and one that very likely deserves what he has got—but anyway I wanted you to be spared. Indeed thought it was my duty—absolutely my duty. But now when I see you sitting there before me—well, now I only I feel miserably unhappy. So I won't trouble you at all (Gets up.) Not at all.

Svava. I really cannot understand—

Hoff. Please don't bother about me! And please forgive my disturbing you.—No, you really must not give me another thought! Just imagine that I have not been here—that is all. (As he reaches the door, he meets ALFRED coming in. As soon as he sees that SVAVA is watching them, he goes hurriedly out. SVAVA sees the meeting between the two and gives a little scream, then rushes to meet ALFRED. But as soon as she is face to face with him, she seems terrified. As he comes nearer to take her in his arms she cries out: "Don't touch me!" and hurries out by the door on the left. She is heard locking and bolting it on the inside. Then a violent outburst of weeping is heard, the sound being somewhat deadened by the distance, but only for a few moments. Then the sound of singing is heard outside, and a few seconds later RIIS comes into the room. The curtain falls as he enters.)

ACT II

(SCENE.—The same as in Act I. SVAVA is lying on the couch to the right, resting her head on one hand, looking out towards the park. Her mother is sitting beside her.)

Mrs. Riis. Decisions as hasty as yours, Svava, are not really decisions at all. There is always a great deal more to be taken into consideration than one realises at first. Take time to think it over! I believe he is a fine fellow. Give him time to show it; don't break it off immediately!

Svava. Why do you keep on saying that to me?

Mrs. Riis. Well, dear, you know I have never had the chance of saying anything to you till to-day.

Svava. But you keep harping on that one string.

Mrs. Riis. What note do you want me to strike, then?

Svava. The note your dear good mother would have struck—quite a different one altogether.

Mrs. Riis. It is one thing to teach your child how to make a proper choice in life, but—

Svava. But quite another thing to put into practice what you teach?

Mrs. Riis. No; I was going to say that life itself is quite another thing. In daily life, and especially in married life, it is sometimes advisable to make allowances.

Svava. Yes, on points that do not really matter.

Mrs. Riis. Only on points that do not matter?

Svava. Yes—personal peculiarities, and things like that, which after all are only excrescences; but not on points that concern one's moral growth.

Mrs. Riis. Yes, on those points too.

Svava. On those points too?—But isn't it just for the sake of our own self-development that we marry? What else should we marry for?

Mrs. Riis. Oh, you will see!

Svava. No, indeed I shall not; because I do not intend to marry on such conditions.

Mrs. Riis. You should have said that sooner. It is too late now.

Svava (sitting upright). Too late? If I had been married twenty years, I would have done just the same! (Lies down again.)

Mrs. Riis. Heaven help you, then!—You haven't an idea, not the smallest idea, what a net you are entangled in! But you will find it out, as soon as you begin to struggle in earnest. Or do you really want your father and me to throw away all that we have worked for here?—to begin all over again in a foreign country? Because he has repeatedly said, during the last day or two, that he will not be mixed up in the scandal that would be the result of your breaking this off. He would go abroad, and I should have to go with him. Ah, you wince at the thought of that!—Think of all your friends, too. It is a serious matter to have been set on such an eminence as you were at your betrothal party. It is like being lifted up high on a platform that others are carrying on their shoulders; take care you do not fall down from it! That is what you will do, if you offend their principles of right behaviour.

Svava. Is that sort of thing a principle of right behaviour?

Mrs. Riis. I do not say that. But undoubtedly, one their principles of right behaviour—and perhaps the most important—is that all scandal must be avoided. No one relishes being disgraced, Svava—particularly the most influential people in a place. And least of all, by a long way, do people relish their own child being disgraced.

Svava (half raising herself). Good Lord! is it *I* that am disgracing him?

Mrs. Riis. No, of course, it is he himself—

Svava. Very well, then! (Sinks down upon the couch again.)

Mrs. Riis. But you will never get them to understand that. I assure you, you won't. As long as what he has done is only whispered about in his family and amongst his intimate friends, they don't consider him disgraced at all. There are too many that do just the same. It is only when the knowledge of it becomes common property, that they consider it a disgrace. And if it became known that there was a formal breach between you—the Christensens' eldest son ignominiously refused because of his past life—they would consider it the most shocking scandal that could possibly overtake them! And we should feel the effect of it, in particular. And so would those that are dependent on us—and they are not so few in number, as you know, because you have interested yourself in them, particularly in the children. You would have t. give up all the interests you have made for Yourself here—because you would have to go with us. I am certain your father is in earnest about that.

Svava. Oh! Oh!

Mrs. Riis. I almost wish I could tell you why I am so certain of that. But I cannot—at all events not now. No, you must not tempt me to.—Here comes your father. Only take time to reflect, Svava! No breaking of it off, no scandal! (RIIS comes in from outside, with an opened letter in his hand.)

Riis. Oh, there you are! (Goes into his room, lays down his hat and stick, and comes out again.) You have taken no serious step yet, I hope—eh?

Mrs. Riis. No, but—

Riis. Very well. Now here is a letter from the Christensens. If you won't receive either your dance or his letters, you will have to put up with his family's interference in the matter. Everything must come to an end sooner or later. (Reads.) "My wife, my son and I will do ourselves the honour of paying you a visit between eleven and twelve o'clock." The only wonder is, that I have not had some such letter before this! I am sure they have been patient enough.

Mrs. Riis. Well, we have got no farther to-day, either.

Riis. What are you thinking of, child? Can't you see what it must all lead to? You are a good-hearted girl, I know—I am sure you don't want to ruin us all absolutely? I certainly consider, Svava, that you have acted quite severely enough now in this matter. They have suffered a nasty shock to their self-confidence, both of them; you may be quite sure of that. What more do you want? If you are really determined to carry the matter farther—well—make your conditions! There is no doubt they will be agreed to.

Svava. For shame! For shame!

Riis (despairingly). What is the use of taking it in this way!

Mrs. Riis. What, indeed! You ought rather to try and make things a bit easier, Svava.

Riis. And you really might condescend, too, to consider who it is that you are throwing over—a member of one of the richest families in the country, and, I venture to say, one of the most honourable too. I have never heard of anything so idiotic! Yes, I repeat—idiotic, idiotic! What if he have made a false step—or two—well, good heavens—

Svava. Yes, bring heaven into it, too!

Riis. Indeed I well may! There is good need. As I was saying, if he have made a false step, surely the poor fellow has been sufficiently punished for it now. Beside it is certainly our duty to be a little reasonable with one another—it is a commandment, you know, that we are to be reasonable and forgiving. We must be forgiving! And more than that, we must help the erring—we must raise up the fallen and set them in the right way. Yes, set them in the right way. You could do that so splendidly! It is exactly in your line. You know very well, my dear child, it is very seldom I talk about morals and that sort of thing. It doesn't sit well on me at all; I know that only too well. But on this occasion I cannot help it. Begin with forgiveness, my child; begin with that! After all, can you contemplate living together with anyone for any length of time without—without—well, without *that*?

Svava. But there is no question of living with anyone, for any length of time, or of forgiveness—because I do not mean to have anything more to do with him.

Riis. Really, this is beyond all bounds! Because he has dared to fall in love with some one before you—?

Svava. Some one?

Riis. Well, if there was more than one, I am sure I know nothing about it. No, indeed I do not! Besides, the way people gossip and backbite is the very devil! But, as I was saying, because he dared to look at some one before he looked at you—before he ever *thought* of you—is that a reason for throwing him over for good and all? How many would ever get married under those circumstances, I should like to know? Everybody confirms the opinion that he is an honourable, fine young fellow, to whom the proudest girl might confidently entrust herself—you said so yourself, only a day or two ago! Do not deny it! And now he is suddenly to be thrown over, because you are not the first girl he has ever met! Pride should have some limits, remember! I have never heard of anything more preposterous, if you ask me.

Mrs. Riis. Men are not like that.

Riis. And what about girls? Are they like that? I am quite sure they do not ask whether their fiancés have been married before—observe, I said "married." You can imagine he has been married. Well, why not? That is what other girls do—you cannot deny it. I know you know it. You have been to dances; who are most in request there? Precisely those who have the reputation of being something of a Don Juan. They take the wind out of all the other fellows' sails.

You have seen it yourself a hundred times. And it is not only at dances that this applied. Don't you suppose they get married—and as a rule make the very best matches?

Mrs. Riis. That is true.

Riis. Of course it is true. And as a rule they make the very best husbands, too!

Mrs. Riis. Hm!

Riis. Oh, indeed they do!—with some exceptions, of course, naturally. The fact is, that marriage has an ennobling influence, and provides a beautiful vocation for a woman—the most beautiful vocation possible!

Svava (who has got up). I can just manage to listen to such things from you—because I expected no better from you.

Riis. Thank you very much!

Svava (who has come forward). One would really think that marriage were a sort of superior wash-house for men—

Riis. Ha, ha!

Svava.—and that men could come there and take a dip when they please—and in what state they please!

Riis. Oh, really—!

Svava. I mean it! And it is flattering—very flattering—for me, as your daughter, to feel that you look upon me as so peculiarly suited for the washerwoman's post! None of that for me, thank you!

Riis. But this is—

Svava. No, just listen to me for a little! I don't think I have said too much, the last day or two.

Riis. No, we have not been allowed to say a word to you.

Svava. Look here, father. You have a fine supply of principles, for show purposes.

Riis. For—?

Svava. I do not mean by that, that they are not your own. But you are so good and so honourable, your whole life is so refined, that I do not attach the least importance to your principles. But to mother's I do attach importance, for hers are what have formed mine. And now just when I want to act up to them, she deserts me.

Riis and Mrs. Riis (together). Svava!

Svava. It is mother I am angry with! It is mother I cannot have patience with!

Riis. Really, Svava—!

Svava. Because if there has been one point on which mother and I have been agreed, it has been on the subject of the unprincipled way men prepare themselves for marriage, and the sort of marriages that are the result. We have watched the course of it, mother and I, for many years; and we had come to one and the same conclusion, that it is *before* marriage that a marriage is marred. But when, the other day, mother began to turn round—

Mrs. Riis. No, you have no right to say that! I am convinced that Alfred is as honourable—

Svava. But when, the other day, mother began to turn round—well, I could not have been more amazed if some one had come in and told me they had met her out in the street when she was actually sitting here talking to me.

Mrs. Riis. I only ask you to take time to consider! I am not contradicting you!

Svava. Oh, let me speak now! Let me give you just one instance. One day, before I was really grown up, I came running into this room from the park. We had just bought the property, and I was so happy. Mother was standing over there leaning against the door and crying. It was a lovely summer's day. "Why are you crying, mother?" I said. For some time she seemed as if she did not see me. "Why are you crying, mother?" I repeated, and went nearer to her, but did not like to touch her. She turned away from me, and walked up and down once or twice. Then she came to me. "My child," she said, drawing me to her, "never give in to what is not good and pure, on any account whatever! It is so cowardly, and one repents it so bitterly; it means perpetually giving in, more and more and more." I do not know what she referred to, and I have never asked. But no one can imagine what an effect it all had on me—the beautiful summer day, and mother crying, and the heartfelt tones of her voice! I cannot give in; do not ask me to. Everything that made marriage seem beautiful to me is gone—my faith, my feeling of security—all gone! No, no, no! I can never begin with that, and it is wicked of you to want to make me believe I can. After such a disillusionment and such a humiliation? No! I would rather never be married—even it I have to go away from here. I daresay I shall find something to fill my life; it is only for the moment that I am so helpless. And anything is better than to fill it with what is unclean. If I did not refuse that without hesitation, I should be an accomplice to it. Perhaps some people could put up with that. I cannot—no, I cannot. Do you think it is arrogance on my part? Or because I am angry? If you knew what we two had planned and schemed, you would understand me. And if you knew what I have thought of him, how I have admired him—you did the same yourselves—and how wretched I feel now, how utterly robbed of everything!—Who is it that is crying? Is it you, mother? (She runs to her mother, kneels down and buries her head in her lap. A pause. RIIS goes into his room.) Why cannot we three hold together? If we do, what have we to be afraid of? What is it that stands in the way? Father, what is it that stands in the way?—But where is father? (Sees NORDAN outside the window.) Uncle Nordan! This is a surprise! (Hurries across the room, throws herself into NORDAN's arms as he enters, and bursts into tears.)

Nordan. Oh, you goose! You great goose!

Svava. You must come and talk to me!

Nordan. Isn't that what I am here for?

Svava. And I thought you were up in the mountains and could not hear from us.

Nordan. So I was. But when I got telegram after telegram, as long as they could reach me, and then one express letter after another—and now the end of it all is—well, I don't suppose I dare even mention his name here now? (RIIS comes in from his room.)

Riis. At last! We have been so anxious for you to come!

Mrs. Riis (who has at last risen and come forward). Thank you for coming, dear doctor!

Nordan (looking at her). There is something serious up, then?

Mrs. Riis. I have something I want to say to you.

Nordan. Yes, but just now away you go, you two! Let me talk to this booby. (MRS. RIIS goes out to the left. SVAVA follows her for a minute.)

Riis. I just want to tell you that in a little while—

Nordan.—the whole pack of Christensens will be here? I know that. Go away now.

Riis. Nordan! (Whispers to him.)

Nordan. Yes, yes!—Quite so!—No, of course not! (Tries to stop his whispering.) Do you suppose I don't know what I am about? Be off with you! (SVAVA comes in, as her father goes out.)

Svava. Dear Uncle Nordan! At last, somebody that will agree with me!

Nordan. Am I?

Svava. Oh, Uncle Nordan, you don't know what these days have been like!

Nordan. And the nights too, I expect?—although, with all that, you don't look so bad.

Svava. The last night or two I have slept.

Nordan. Really? Then I see how things stand. You are a tough customer, you are!

Svava. Oh, don't begin saying a lot of things you don't mean, uncle.

Nordan. Things I don't mean!

Svava. You always do, you know. But we haven't time for that now. I am all on fire!

Nordan. Well, what is this you have been doing?

Svava. Ah, you see, you are beginning again!

Nordan. Beginning again? Who the devil has put the idea into your head that I ever say anything but what I mean? Come and let us sit down. (Brings a chair forward.)

Svava (bringing her chair close to his). There now!

Nordan. Since I was here last, I believe you have promulgated a brand-new law on the subject of love? I congratulate you.

Svava. Have I?

Nordan. A superhuman, Svava-woven one—derived from seraphic heights, I should imagine! "There shall be only one love in a man's life, and it shall be directed only to one object." Full stop!

Svava. Have I said anything like that?

Nordan. Is it not you that have thrown over a young man because he has had the audacity to fall in love before he saw you?

Svava. Do you take it in that way, too?

Nordan. In that way? Is there any other way for a sensible man to take it? A fine young fellow honesty, adores you; a distinguished family throw their doors wide open to you, as if you were a princess; and then you turn round and say: "You have not waited for me ever since you were a child! Away with you!"

Svava (springing up). What, you too! You too! And the same talk! The same stupid talk!

Nordan. I can tell you what it is; if you do not give consideration to everything that can be said on the other side, you are stupid.—No, it is no use going away from me and marching up and down! I shall begin and march up and down too, if you do! Come here and sit. Or *daren't* you go thoroughly into the question with me?

Svava. Yes, I dare. (Sits down again.)

Nordan. Well, to begin with, do you not think there must certainly be two sides to a question that is discussed by serious men and women all over the world?

Svava. This only concerns me! And as far as I am concerned there is only one side to it.

Nordan. You do not understand me, child! You shall settle your own affairs ultimately, and nobody else—of course. But suppose what you have to settle is not quite so simple as you think it? Suppose it is a problem that at the present moment is exercising the minds of thousands and thousands of people? Do you not think it is your duty to give some consideration to the usual attitude towards it, and to what is generally thought and said about it? Do you think it is conscientious to condemn in a single instance without doing that?

Svava. I understand! I think I have done what you are urging me to do. Ask mother!

Nordan. Oh, I daresay you and your mother have chattered and read a lot about marriage and the woman question, and about abolishing distinctions of class—now you want to abolish distinctions of sex too. But as regards this special question?

Svava. What do you consider I have overlooked?

Nordan. Just this. Are you right in being equally as strict with men as with women? Eh?

Svava. Yes, of course.

Nordan. Is it so much a matter of course? Go out and ask any one you meet. Out of every hundred you ask, ninety will say "no"—even out of a hundred women!

Svava. Do you think so? I think people are beginning to think otherwise.

Nordan. Possibly. But experience is necessary if one is to answer a question like that.

Svava. Do you mean what you say?

Nordan. That is none of your business. Besides, I always mean what I say.—A woman can marry when is sixteen; a man must wait till he is five-and-twenty, or thirty. There is a difference.

Svava. There *is* a difference! There are many, many times more unmarried women than men, and they exhibit self-control. Men find it more convenient to make a law of their want of self-control!

Nordan. An answer like that only displays ignorance. Man is a polygamous animal, like many other animals—a theory that is very strongly supported by the fact that women so outnumber men in the world. I daresay that is something you have never heard before?

Svava. Yes, I have heard it!

Nordan. Don't you laugh at science! What else we to put faith in, I should like to know?

Svava. I should just like men to have the same trouble over their children that women do! Just let them have that, Uncle Nordan, and I fancy they would soon change their principles! Just let them experience it!

Nordan. They have no time for that; they have to govern the world.

Svava. Yes, they have allotted the parts themselves!—Now, tell me this, Dr. Nordan. Is it cowardly not to practise what you preach?

Nordan. Of course it is.

Svava. Then why do you not do it?

Nordan. I? I have always been a regular monster. Don't you know that, dear child?

Svava. Dear Uncle Nordan—you have such long white locks; why do you wear them like that?

Nordan. Oh, well—I have my reasons.

Svava. What are they?

Nordan. We won't go into that now.

Svava. You told me the reason once.

Nordan. Did I?

Svava. I wanted, one day, to take hold of your hair, but you would not let me. You said: "Do you know why you must not do that?"—"No," I said.—"Because no one has done that for more than thirty years."—"Who was it that did it last?" I asked.—"It was a little girl, that you are very like," you answered.

Nordan. So I told you that, did I?

Svava. "And she was one of your grandmother's younger sisters," you said to me.

Nordan. She was. It was quite true. And you are like her, my child.

Svava. And then you told me that the year you went to college she was standing beside you one day and caught up some locks of your hair in her fingers. "You must never wear your hair shorter than this," she said. She went away, and you went away; and when, one day, you wrote and asked her whether you two did not belong to one another, her answer was "yes." And a month later she was dead.

Nordan. She was dead.

Svava. And ever since then—you dear, queer old uncle—you have considered yourself as married to her. (He nods.) And ever since the evening you told me that—and I lay awake a long time, thinking over it—I wanted, even when I was quite a young girl, to choose some one I could have perfect confidence in. And then I chose wrong.

Nordan. Did you, Svava?

Svava. Do not ask me any more about that.—Then I chose once again, and this time I was certain! For never had truer eyes looked in mine. And how happy we were together! Day after day it always seemed new, and the days were always too short. I dare not think about now. Oh, it is sinful to deceive us so!—not deceit in words, it is true, but in letting us give them our admiration and our most intimate confidences. Not in words, no—and yet, it is in words; because they accept all we say, and are silent themselves, and by that very fact make our words their own. Our simple-mindedness pleases them as a bit of unspoilt nature, and it is just by means of that that they deceive us. It creates an intimacy between us and an atmosphere of happy give-and-take of jests, which we think can exist only on one presupposition—and really it is all a sham. I cannot understand how any one can so treat the one he loves—for he did love me!

Nordan. He does love you.

Svava (getting up). But not as I loved him! All these years I have not been frittering away my love. Besides, I have had too high an ideal of what loving and being loved should be; and just for that reason I felt a deep desire to be loved—I can say so to you. And when love came, seemed to take all my strength from me; but I felt I should always be safe with him, and so I let him see it and gloried in his seeing it. That is the bitterest part of it to me now—because he was unworthy of it. He has said to me: "I cannot bear to see any one else touch you!" and "When I catch a glimpse of your arm, I think to myself that it has been round my neck—mine, and no one else's in the world." And I felt proud and happy when he said so, because I thought it was true. Hundreds of times I had imagined some one's saying that to me some day. But I never imagined that the one who would say it would be a man who—oh, it is disgusting! When I think what it means, it makes me ready to hate him. The mere thought that he has had his arms round me—has touched me—makes me shudder! I am not laying down rules for any one else, but what I am doing seems to me a matter of course. Every fibre of my being tells me that. I must be left in peace!

Nordan. I see that this is more serious, and goes deeper, than I had any suspicion of. None of them understand it that way, Alfred least of all. He is only hurt—distressed and hurt at the thought that you could distrust him.

Svava. I know that.

Nordan. Yes—well—don't take up such a high and mighty attitude! I assure you that is how it will appear to most people.

Svava. Do you think so? I think people are beginning to think otherwise.

Nordan. Most people will think: "Other girls forgive things like that, especially when they love a man."

Svava. There are some that will answer: "If she had not loved him, she might have forgiven him."

Nordan. And yet, Svava?—and yet?

Svava. But, uncle, do you not understand? I do not know that I can explain it, either; because, to do that, I should have to explain what it is that we read into the face, the character, the manner of the man we love—his voice, his smile. That is what I have lost. Its meaning is gone.

Nordan. For a while, yes—till you have had a breathing space.

Svava. No, no, no! Do you remember that song of mine, about the beloved one's image? that one always sees it as if it were framed in happiness? Do you remember it?

Nordan. Yes.

Svava. Very well—I cannot see it like that any longer. I see it, of course—but always with pain. Always! Am I to forgive that, because other girls forgive it? What is that they have loved, these other girls? Can you tell me that? Because what I loved is gone. I am not going to sit down and try to conjure it up in my imagination again. I shall find something else to do.

Nordan. You are embittered now. You have had your ideal thoroughly shattered, and as long as you are smarting from that it is no use reasoning with you. So I will only beg one thing of you—one single little thing. But you must promise me to do it?

Svava. If I can.

Nordan. You can. There are things to take into consideration. Ask for time to think it all over!

Svava. Ah!—mother has been writing to you!

Nordan. And if she has? Your mother knows what depends upon it.

Svava. What depends upon it? Why do you speak so mysteriously, as if we were not on secure ground? Aren't we? Father talks about giving up this place. Why?

Nordan. I suppose he thinks it will be necessary.

Svava. Father? On grounds of economy?

Nordan. Not in the least! No, but all the gossips in the place will be at you. What you propose to do is a regular challenge, you know.

Svava. Oh, we can stand criticism! Father has some queer principles, you know; but his own life—. Surely no one has any doubt about that?

Nordan. Listen to me, my child. You cannot prevent people inventing things. So be careful!

Svava. What do you mean?

Nordan. I mean that you ought to go for a stroll in the park and pull yourself together a little, before the Christensens come. Try to be calm; come in calmly, and request time to think it over. That is all you have to do! They will make no difficulty about that, because they must agree. Nothing has happened yet, and all ways are still open. Do as I ask!

Svava. I *have* thought it over—and you will never get me to do anything else.

Nordan. No, no. It is only a matter of form.

Svava. What? You mean something more than that, I know.

Nordan. What an obstinate girl you are!—Can you not do it then, let me say, for your mother's sake? Your mother is a good woman.

Svava. What will they think, if I come in and say: "Will you not give me time to consider the matter?" No, I cannot do that.

Nordan. What will you say, then?

Svava. I would rather say nothing at all. But if I absolutely must say something—

Nordan. Of course you must!

Svava. Well, I will go out now and think it over. (Turns to go, but stops.) But what you want can never be.

Nordan. It must be!

Svava (standing by the door). You said just now: "Your mother is a good woman." It sounded almost as if you laid stress on the word "mother"?

Nordan. Suppose I did?

Svava. Is father not that, too?

Nordan. Your father a good woman?

Svava. Why do you try to turn it off with a joke?

Nordan. Because it is serious, confound it all!

Svava. Can I not believe father—?

Nordan. Hush!

Svava. Father?—Is it possible that he too—? Do people say that? (NORDAN does not answer, and does not move.) Shameful! Impossible! I say it is impossible! (Rushes out. RIIS comes in from the right.)

Riis. What is the matter with Svava?

Nordan (coming forward). There was nothing else for it.

Riis. Nothing else for it? What do you mean?

Nordan. No, devil take it!—there was nothing else for it.

Riis. Quite so—but what?

Nordan. What do you say?

Riis. No, what were you saying—?

Nordan. What was I saying?

Riis. You said there was nothing else for it. You alarm me.

Nordan. Do I? Then you did not hear right. (Moves away from him.)

Riis. Didn't hear right? You were swearing about it too!

Nordan. That I certainly did not.

Riis. Very well then, you didn't. But how did you get on with Svava? Won't you answer me?

Nordan. How did I get on with Svava?

Riis. Why are you so preoccupied? Are things so bad, then?

Nordan. Preoccupied? Why should I be that?

Riis. You ought to know best. I was asking about Svava—how you got on with Svava—and I think I have the right to know.

Nordan. Look here, Riis.

Riis. Yes? (NORDAN takes him by the arm.) What is it?

Nordan. Did you see Svava?

Riis. Hurrying away out through the park? Yes. My dear chap, what was it?

Nordan. It was the Greek tragedy.

Riis. The Greek—?

Nordan. Only the name—only the name! Well, you know what the word means, don't you?

Riis. The Greek—?

Nordan. No, no—not "Greek," but "tragedy"?

Riis. Something mournful—?

Nordan. Far from it! Something amusing! It came to Greece with the worship of Dionysus, in whose train there was a goat—

Riis (draws his arm away). A goat? What on earth—?

Nordan. Yes, you may well be surprised—because it sang!

Riis. Sang?

Nordan. Yes—and is still singing, of course! And paints! There are pictures by him in every exhibition. And works in bronze and marble! Wonderful! And such a courtier as he is, too! It is he that designs ball-dresses and arranges entertainments—

Riis. Have you gone raving mad?

Nordan. Why do you ask that?

Riis. I am waiting patiently here till you have done talking such damned nonsense! We are accustomed to something of the sort when you are in one of those humours, but to-day I can't understand a blessed word of what you are saying.

Nordan. Don't you, my dear fellow?

Riis. Can you not tell me what my daughter said? Isn't it ridiculous that I cannot get that out of you! Now, briefly and intelligibly, what did she say?

Nordan. Do you want to know?

Riis. He asks that!

Nordan. She said she pitied all the innocent young girls that, generation after generation, disappear—

Riis. Where to?

Nordan. That is just it—where to? She said: "They are brought up in pious ignorance, and finally the unsuspecting creatures are wrapped up in a long white veil that they shall not be able to see distinctly where they are being taken to."

Riis. Now you are talking your mythology again. Am I not to—

Nordan. Be quiet! It is your daughter that is speaking. "But I will not do that," she said. "I will enter confidently into the holy estate of matrimony, and sit down by the hearth in the land of my fathers, and bring up children in the sight of my husband. But he shall be as chaste as I; for otherwise he stains my child's head, when he kisses it, and dishonours me."—There, that is what she said, and she looked so splendid as she said it. (A ring is heard at the bell.)

Riis. They are upon us! They are upon us! What in the world is going to happen? We are in a muddle of the most preposterous theories! The whole heathen mythology is buzzing round in my head! (Hurries to the door to meet MR. and MRS. CHRISTENSEN, whom MARGIT is showing in.) I am so happy to see you!—so very happy! But your son?

Christensen. We could not get him to come with us.

Riis. I am very sorry!—At the same time, I quite understand.

Christensen. I admire the beauty of this place afresh every time I see it, my dear sir!

Mrs. Christensen. This beautiful old park! I wanted once—. Oh, good morning, doctor! How are you?

Nordan. So, so!

Riis (to MARGIT). Please tell Mrs. Riis. And—oh, there she is. (MRS. RIIS comes in by the door at the left.) And tell Miss Svava.

Nordan. She is out in the park (pointing)—out that way. (Exit MARGIT.)

Riis. No, this way!—That's right! Go straight on till you find her.

Mrs. Christensen (who meantime has come forward with MRS. RIIS). I have been thinking so much about you the last day or two, my dear! What a tiresome business this is!

Mrs. Riis. Do you mind my asking if you knew anything about it before?

Mrs. Christensen. What is there that a mother—and a wife—escapes the knowledge of nowadays, my dear! She was in my service, you know. Come here! (Tells MRS. RIIS something in a whisper, ending with something about "discovery" and "dismissal.")

Riis (offering the ladies chairs). Won't you sit down?—Oh, I beg your pardon! I did not see—. (Hurries to CHRISTENSEN.) Excuse me, but are you really comfortable in that chair?

Christensen. Thank you, I am just as uncomfortable here as anywhere else. It is the sitting down and getting up again that bothers me more than anything else. (Looks round.) I have just been to see him.

Riis. Hoff?

Christensen. Honest fellow. Stupid.

Riis. So long as he holds his tongue—

Christensen. He'll do that.

Riis. Thank heaven for that! Then we have only ourselves to consider. I suppose it cost you a bit?

Christensen. Not a penny!

Riis. You got out of it cheap, then.

Christensen. Yes, didn't I? Still, as a matter of fact, he has cost me quite enough already—although he knows nothing about that.

Riis. Indeed? When he failed, I suppose.

Christensen. No, when he married.

Riis. Oh, I understand.

Christensen. And I didn't think I should hear any more about it after that.—You ladies seem to be having a fine game of whispering! (MRS. CHRISTENSEN comes forward. RIIS places chairs for her and his wife.)

Mrs. Christensen. I was telling Mrs. Riis about the Miss Tang affair. She really seems to have risen from her grave!

Christensen. Is your daughter at home, may I ask?

Riis. I have sent to fetch her.

Mrs. Christensen. I hope the last few days have taught her a lesson too, poor girl! She suffers from a fault that unusually clever people are very liable to—I mean self-righteousness.

Riis. Exactly! You are perfectly right! But I should call it arrogance!

Mrs. Christensen. I should not like to say that—but presumption, perhaps.

Mrs. Riis. Why do you say that, Mrs. Christensen?

Mrs. Christensen. Because of various conversations I have had with her. I was speaking to her once about a man's being his wife's master. In these days it is a good thing to impress that on young girls.

Christensen. Yes, indeed!

Mrs. Christensen. And when I reminded her of certain words of St. Paul's, she said: "Yes, it is behind those bars that we women are still shut up." Then I knew that something would happen. Pride goes before a fall, you know.

Christensen. Oh, come, come! That won't do at all! Your chain of reasoning isn't sound!

Mrs. Christensen. How?

Christensen. It is not. Because in the first place it was not Miss Riis that fell, but your precious son. And in the second place his fall was not a consequence of Miss Riis's pride, because of course it happened many years before Miss Riis showed any of her pride. So that if you knew that his fall would happen as a consequence of Miss Riis's pride, you knew something that you certainly did not know.

Mrs. Christensen. Oh, you are making fun of me!

Christensen. I ought to be at a committee meeting punctually at one.—May I ask what has become of your daughter?

Riis. Indeed I am really beginning to wonder—(During the foregoing, NORDAN has remained in the background, sometimes in the room and sometimes outside in the park. MARGIT now goes fast the window outside, and NORDAN is heard speaking to her.)

Nordan. Have you only just found her?

Margit. No, sir—I have been down once already to take Miss Riis her hat, gloves and parasol.

Nordan. Is she going out?

Margit. I don't know, sir. (Goes out.)

Christensen. Dear me!

Riis. What does it mean? (Turns to go and fetch her.)

Nordan. No, no! Do not you go!

Mrs. Riis. I expect I had better go—

Riis. Yes, you go!

Nordan. No, I will go. I am afraid I am responsible for—. (As he goes) I'll answer for it I will bring her back!

Christensen. Dear me!

Mrs. Christensen (getting up). I am afraid, my dear Mrs. Riis, we have come at an inconvenient time for your daughter?

Riis. Ah, you must be lenient with her! I assure you it is these high-flown ideas—this reading, that her mother has not been nearly firm enough in keeping her from.

Mrs. Riis. I? What are you talking about?

Riis. I say that this is a very important moment! And at moments like this one sees very clearly, very—well, that is what happens!

Christensen. Your husband, Mrs. Riis, has suddenly had the same sort of revelation as our parson had lately—I should say, my wife's parson. It was one day just after dinner—after an extremely good dinner, by the way—a moment when a man often has very bright ideas. We were talking about all the things a woman has to learn now, as compared with the old days, and how some people say it is mere waste of time because she will forget it all again when she marries. "Yes," said parson, looking very pleased, "my wife has completely forgotten how to spell; I hope she will soon forget how to write, too!"

Mrs. Christensen. You imitate people so well, that one cannot help laughing—although it isn't right. (CHRISTENSEN looks at his watch.)

Riis. It doesn't look as if they were coming back?—Will you go, or shall I?

Mrs. Riis (getting up). I will go. But you could not expect them already—

Riis (coming close up to her and speaking in an undertone). This is your doing! I see it clearly!

Mrs. Riis. I do not think you know what you are saying. (Goes out.)

Riis (coming forward). I really must apologise most humbly! It is the last thing I should ever have expected of Svava—because I pride myself that the obligations of courtesy have never been disregarded in my house before.

Mrs. Christensen. Perhaps something has happened?

Riis. I beg your pardon?—Good heavens!

Mrs. Christensen. Oh, do not misunderstand me! I only mean that young girls are so easily agitated, and then they do not like to show themselves.

Riis. All the same, Mrs. Christensen, all the same! At such a moment as this, too!—You really must excuse me, I shall have no peace till I find out for myself what has happened! (Hurries out.)

Christensen. If Alfred had been here, I suppose he would have been running about all over the park after these females, too.

Mrs. Christensen. Really, my dear!

Christensen. Aren't we alone?

Mrs. Christensen. Yes, but still—!

Christensen. Well, I say, as a certain famous man said before me: "What the devil was he doing in that galley?"

Mrs. Christensen. Do have a moment's patience! It is really necessary.

Christensen. Bah! Necessary! Riis is more afraid of a rupture than any of us. Did you see him just now?

Mrs. Christensen. Yes, of course I did, but—

Christensen. She has already gone much farther than she has any right to.

Mrs. Christensen. So Alfred thinks, too.

Christensen. Then he should have been here now, to say so. I asked him to come.

Mrs. Christensen. He is in love, and that makes a man a little timid.

Christensen. Nonsense!

Mrs. Christensen. Oh, that passes off when one is in love as often as you are. (Gets up.) Here they come!—No, not Svava.

Christensen. Is she not with them?

Mrs. Christensen. I don't see her.

Riis (appearing at the door). Here they are!

Mrs. Christensen. And your daughter too?

Riis. Yes, Svava too. She asked the others to go on ahead of her. I expect she wanted to collect herself a little.

Mrs. Christensen (sitting down again). Ah, you see, it was just what I thought, poor child!

Mrs. Riis (coming in). She will be here in a moment! (Goes up to MRS. CHRISTENSEN.) You must forgive her, Mrs. Christensen; she has had a bad time of it.

Mrs. Christensen. Bless my soul, of course I understand that! The first time one has an experience of this kind, it tells on one.

Christensen. This is positively beginning to get amusing!

Enter NORDAN.

Nordan. Here we are! She asked me to come on little ahead of her.

Riis. She is not going to keep us waiting any longer, I hope?

Nordan. She was just behind me.

Riis. Here she is! (Goes to the door to meet her; NORDAN and MRS. RIIS do the same from the other side of the room.)

Christensen. One would think she were the Queen of Sheba.

(SVAVA comes in, wearing her hat, and with her gloves and parasol in her hand. CHRISTENSEN and MRS. CHRISTENSEN get up from their seats. She bows slightly to them, and comes to the front of the stage on the right-hand side. All sit down in silence. NORDAN is at the extreme left, then MRS. RIIS, MRS. CHRISTENSEN and CHRISTENSEN. At the extreme right, but a little behind the others, is RIIS, who is sitting down one minute and standing the next.)

Mrs. Christensen. My dear Svava, we have come here to—well, you know what we have come for. What has happened has distressed us very much; but what is done cannot be undone. None of us can excuse Alfred. But all the same we think that he might be granted forgiveness, especially at the hands of one who must know that he loves her, and loves her sincerely. That makes it a different matter altogether, of course.

Christensen. Of course!

Riis. Of course!

Nordan. Of course!

Mrs. Christensen. And, even if you don't quite agree with me about that, I hope you will agree with me about Alfred himself. I mean to say, that we consider his character, my dear Svava, should vouch to you for his fidelity. I know that, if you require it, he will give you his word of honour that—

Mrs. Riis (getting up). No! No!

Mrs. Christensen. What is the matter, my dear Mrs. Riis?

Mrs. Riis. No words of honour! He has to take an oath when he marries, anyway.

Nordan. But surely two make it all the safer, Mrs. Riis?

Mrs. Riis. No, no! No oath! (Sits down again.)

Christensen. I was struck with our friend Dr. Nordan's remark. Tell me, my dear sir, do you also take it for granted that the sort of thing my son has done ought to be an absolute bar to marriage with an honourable woman?

Nordan. Quite the contrary! I am quite sure it never prevents any one getting married—and remarkably well married. It is only Svava that is behaving in an extraordinary manner in every respect.

Mrs. Christensen. I would not go so far as to say that; but there is one thing that Svava has overlooked. She is acting as if she were free. But she is not by any means free. A betrothal is equivalent to a marriage; at any rate, I am old-fashioned enough to consider it so, And the man to whom I have given my hand is thereby made my master and given authority over me, and I owe to him—as to a superior authority—my respect, whether he act well or ill. I cannot give him notice, or run away from him.

Riis. That is old-fashioned and sensible. I thank you heartily, Mrs. Christensen!

Nordan. And I too!

Mrs. Riis. But if it is too late after the betrothal—. (Checks herself.)

Mrs. Christensen. What do you mean, dear Mrs. Riis?

Mrs. Riis. Oh, nothing nothing at all.

Nordan. Mrs. Riis means that if it is too late after the betrothal, why do people not speak out before they are betrothed?

Riis. What a thing to say!

Christensen. Well, it wouldn't be such a bad thing, would it? I imagine proposals in future being worded somewhat in this way: "My dear Miss So-and-So, up to date I have had such and such a number of love affairs—that is to say, so many big ones and so many little ones." Don't you think it would be a capital way to lead the conversation on to—

Nordan.—to assuring her that she is the only one you have ever loved?

Christensen. Well, not exactly that, but—

Riis. Here comes Alfred!

Mrs. Riis. Alfred?

Mrs. Christensen. Yes, it really is he!

Riis (who has gone to the door to meet ALFRED). Ah, that is right! We are so glad you have come!

Christensen. Well, my boy?

Alfred. When it came to the point, I could not do anything else—I had to come here.

Christensen. I quite agree with you.

Riis. Yes, it was only the natural thing to do. (ALFRED comes forward and bows respectfully to SVAVA. She bows slightly, but without looking at him. He steps back again.)

Nordan. Good morning, my boy!

Alfred. Perhaps I have come at an inconvenient moment.

Riis. Not a bit of it! Quite the contrary!

Alfred. At the same time, it seems evident to me that my presence is not welcome to Miss Riis. (No one answers him.)

Mrs. Christensen. But it is a family council we are holding—isn't it, my dear girl?

Riis. I assure you, you *are* welcome! And we are all particularly anxious to hear what you have to say!

Christensen. That is so.

Alfred. I have not succeeded in getting a hearing yet, you know. I have been refused admittance repeatedly—both in person and when I wrote. So I thought that if I came now, perhaps I should get a hearing.

Riis. Of course. Who can object to that?

Nordan. You shall have your hearing.

Alfred. Perhaps I may take Miss Riis's silence to mean permission? In that case—well—it is nothing so very much that I have to say, either. It is merely to remind you that, when I asked for Miss Riis's hand, it was because I loved her with all my heart—her and no one else. I could not imagine any greater happiness, and any greater honour, than to be loved by her in return. And so I think still. (He pauses, as if he expected an answer. They all look at SVAVA.) What explanation I could have given of my own free will—indeed what explanation, under other circumstances, I should have felt impelled to give—I shall say nothing about now. But I *owe* no explanation! My honour demands that I should make point of that. It is my future that I owe to her. And with regard to that I must confess I have been hurt—deeply hurt—by the fact that Miss Riis could doubt me for a moment. Never in my life has any one doubted me before. With all respect, I must insist that my word shall be taken. (They are all silent.) That is all I have to say.

Mrs. Riis (getting up unwillingly). But, Alfred, suppose a woman, under the same circumstances, had come and said the same thing—who would believe her? (They are all silent. SVAVA bursts into tears.)

Mrs. Christensen. Poor child!

Riis. Believe her?

Mrs. Riis. Yes, believe her. Believe her if, after past like that, she came and assured us that she would make an honest wife?

Christensen. After a past like that?

Mrs. Riis. Perhaps that is putting it too harshly. But why should you require her to believe a man any more readily than a man would believe her? Because he would not believe her for a moment.

Riis (coming up behind her). Are you absolutely mad?

Christensen (half rising). Excuse me, ladies and gentlemen; the two young people must settle the affair now! (Sits down again.)

Alfred. I must confess I have never thought of what Mrs. Riis has just said, because such a thing never could happen. No man of honour would choose a woman of whose past he was not certain. Never!

Mrs. Riis. But what about a woman of honour, Alfred?

Alfred. Ah, that is quite different.

Nordan. To put it precisely: a woman owes a man both her past and her future; a man owes a woman only his future.

Alfred. Well, if you like to put it that way—yes.

Nordan (to SVAVA, as he gets up). I wanted you to postpone your answer, my child. But now I think you ought to answer at once. (SVAVA goes up to ALFRED, flings her glove in his face, and goes straight into her room. ALFRED turns and looks after her. RIIS disappears into his room on the right. Every one has risen from their seats. MRS. CHRISTENSEN takes ALFRED by the arm and goes nut with him; CHRISTENSEN follows them. MRS. RIIS is standing at the door of the room which SVAVA has locked after her.)

Nordan. That was throwing down a gauntlet, if you like!

Mrs. Riis (calling through the door). Svava!

Christensen (coming in and speaking to NORDAN, who has taken no notice of him and has not turned round). Then it is to be war?—Well, I fancy I know a thing or two about war. (Goes out. NORDAN turns round and stands looking after him.)

Mrs. Riis (still at the door). Svava! (RIIS comes rushing out of his room, with his hat on and his gloves and stick in his hand, and follows the CHRISTENSENS.) Svava!

ACT III

SCENE I

(SCENE.—DR. NORDAN'S garden, behind his neat one-storied house. He is sitting on a chair in the foreground reading. His old servant, THOMAS, opens the how door and looks out.)

Thomas. Doctor!

Nordan. What is it? (ALFRED comes into sight in the doorway.) Oh, it is you! (Gets up.) Well, my boy! You don't look up to much!

Alfred. No, but never mind that. Can you give me a bit of breakfast?

Nordan. Have you had no breakfast yet? Have you not been home then?—not been home all night?—not since yesterday? (Calls) Thomas!

Alfred. And when I have had something to eat, may I have a talk with you?

Nordan. Of course, my dear boy. (To THOMAS, who has come out of the house) Get some breakfast laid in that room, please (pointing to a window on the left).

Alfred. And may I have a wash too?

Nordan. Go with Thomas. I will be with you directly. (ALFRED and THOMAS go into the house. Then a carriage is heard stopping outside.) There is a carriage. Go and see who it is, Thomas. I won't see any patients! I am going away to-morrow.

Thomas. It is Mr. Christensen. (Goes into the house again.)

Nordan. Oho! (Goes to the window on the left.) Alfred!

Alfred (coming to the window). Yes?

Nordan. It is your father! If you do not want to be seen, pull down the blind. (The blind is dulled dawn.)

Thomas (showing in CHRISTENSEN). Will you come this way please, sir. (CHRISTENSEN is in court dress protected by a dustcoat, and wears the cross of a Knight Commander of the Order of St. Olaf.)

Christensen. I hope I do not disturb you, doctor?

Nordan. Not at all!—In full dress! I congratulate you.

Christensen. Yes, we newly-fledged knights have to go to Court to-day. But do you mind if I spend a minute or two here with you before I go on to the palace?—Any news from over there? From the Riis's?

Nordan. No. They are sitting waiting for the "war" to begin, I expect.

Christensen. They shall not have to wait long, then! I have made up my mind to begin it to-day. Has she come to her senses, by any chance? Women usually feel things like that very acutely. But they usually get over it, too.

Nordan. I do not think so. But I bow before your experience.

Christensen. Thank you! I should think that, as an old hand at playing the buffer in family jars, you had a much greater experience. Yesterday she was like an electric eel! And she gave her shock, too! The boy has not been home since. I am almost glad of that; it shows he has some sense of shame. I was beginning to doubt it.

Nordan. It is the coming "war" that interests me.

Christensen. Oh, you are anxious to see that, are you? Very well. As a matter of fact there is no need to draw up a plan of campaign. That affair of Mrs. North's can be taken up again any day, my dear fellow! It is in the hands of the bank, you know.

Nordan. But what has that to do with your son engagement?

Christensen. What has it to do with it? Miss Riis gives my son his dismissal because she cannot tolerate his conduct before marriage. Her own father indulges in the same sort of conduct when he is well on in married life! Tableau vivant très curieux!—to use a language Mr. Riis is very fond of.

Nordan. It is a shame to talk like that—because your son is the only one to blame in this matter.

Christensen. My son is not in the least to blame in the matter! He has not done the slightest thing that could harm or discredit the Riis's—not the slightest thing! He is a man of honour, who has given Miss Riis his promise and has kept it. Will any one dare to contradict that? Or to suggest that he will not keep his promise? If any one doubts him, it is an insult. Dr. Nordan! In this matter the alternatives are either an apology and peace—or war. For I am not going to put up with this sort of thing; and if my son puts up with it, I shall despise him.

Nordan. Oh, I quite believe your son had every honourable intention when he gave his promise. And very likely he would have kept it, too; I cannot say for certain, because I have learnt to doubt. I am a doctor—I have seen too much—and he did not appear to great advantage yesterday. You really must forgive my saying so—but after the liveliness of his young days, coupled with the tendencies he has inherited, do you think he really had any right to be surprised if people doubted him?—if his fiancée doubted him? Had he really any right to feel insulted, or to demand apologies? Apologies for what? For having doubted his virtue?—Just consider that!

Christensen. Why, what—?

Nordan. One moment! I was only half done. You said something about a reconciliation, you know; of course by that you meant a marriage. If your son is willing to marry a woman who distrusts him, then I shall despise him.

Christensen. Really—!

Nordan. Yes, indeed I shall. Our opinions are as different as all that. To my way of thinking, your son's only course is to submit—and wait; to keep silence, and wait—always supposing, of course, that he still loves her. That is my view of it.

Christensen. Well, I imagine that there are very few candidates for matrimony who have not been guilty of what my son has been guilty of; indeed, I am sure of it. And I imagine, too, that they have the same unfortunate "hereditary tendencies"—an expression on which you laid stress out of special friendship for me. But is that any reason why girls who are betrothed should behave as Miss Riis has been doing?—scream, and run away, and create a scandal? We should not be able to hear ourselves speak! It would be the queerest sort of anarchy the world has ever seen! Why, such doctrines as that are contrary to the very nature and order of things! They are mad! And when, into the bargain, they are thrown at our heads as if they were decisions of a High Court of Morality—well, then I strike! Good-bye! (Starts to go, but turns back.) And who is it that these High Court of Morality's decisions would for the most part affect, do you suppose? Just the ablest and most vigorous of our young men. Are we going to turn them out and make a separate despised caste of them? And what things would be affected, do you suppose? A great part of the world's literature and art; a great part of all that is loveliest and most captivating in the life of to-day; the world's greatest cities, most particularly—those wonders of the world—teeming with their millions of people! Let me tell you this: the life that disregards marriage or loosens the bonds of marriage, or transforms the whole institution—you know very well what I mean—the life that is accused of using the "weapons of seduction" in its fashions, its luxury, its entertainments, its art, its theatre—that life is one of the most potent factors in these teeming cities, one of the most fruitful sources of their existence! No one who has seen it can have any doubt about it, however ingenuous he may pretend to be. Are we to wish to play havoc with all that too?—to disown the flower of the world's youth, and ruin the world's finest cities? It seems to me that people wish to do so much in the name of morality, that they end by wishing to do what would be subversive of all morality.

Nordan. You are certainly embarking on your little war in the true statesmanlike spirit!

Christensen. It is nothing but sound common-sense, my dear sir; that is all that is necessary, I am sure. I shall have the whole town on my side, you may be certain of that!

Thomas (appearing at the house door). Doctor!

Nordan (turning round). Is it possible! (Hurries to the doorway, in which MRS. RIIS appears.)

Mrs. Riis. May I—?

Nordan. Of course! Will you come out here?

Mrs. Riis (to CHRISTENSEN, who bows to her). My visit is really to you, Mr. Christensen.

Christensen. I am honoured.

Mrs. Riis. I happened to look out into the street just as your carriage stopped and you got out. So I thought I would seize the opportunity—because you threatened us yesterday, you know. Is that not so? You declared war against us?

Christensen. My recollection of it is that war was declared, Mrs. Riis, but that I merely accepted the challenge.

Mrs. Riis. And what line is your campaign going to take, if I may ask the question?

Christensen. I have just had the honour of explaining my position to the doctor. I do not know whether it would be gallant to do as much to you.

Nordan. I will do it, then. The campaign will be directed against your husband. Mr. Christensen takes the offensive.

Mrs. Riis. Naturally!—because you know you can strike at him. But I have come to ask you to think better of it.

Christensen (with a laugh). Really?

Mrs. Riis. Once—many years ago now—I took my child in my arms and threatened to leave my husband. Thereupon he mentioned the name of another man, and shielded himself behind that—for it was a distinguished name. "See how lenient that man's wife is," he said. "And, because she is so, all her friends are lenient, and that will be all the better for their child." Those were his words.

Christensen. Well, as far as the advice they implied was concerned, it was good advice—and no doubt you followed it.

Mrs. Riis. The position of a divorced woman is a very humiliating one in the eyes of the world, and the daughter of such a woman fares very little better. The rich and distinguished folk who lead the fashion take care of that.

Christensen. But what—?

Mrs. Riis. That is my excuse for not having the courage to leave him. I was thinking of my child's future. But it is my husband's excuse, too; because he is one of those who follows the example of others.

Christensen. We all do that, Mrs. Riis.

Mrs. Riis. But it is the leaders of society that set the example, for the most part; and in this matter they set a tempting one. I suppose I can hardly be mistaken in thinking that I have heard your view of this matter, all along, through my husband's mouth? Or, if I am mistaken in that, I at all events surely heard it more accurately yesterday, when I heard your voice in everything that your son said?

Christensen. I stand by every word of what my son said.

Mrs. Riis. I thought so. This campaign of yours will really be a remarkable one! I see your influence in everything that has happened, from first to last. You are the moving spirit of the whole campaign—on both sides!

Nordan. Before you answer, Christensen—may I ask you, Mrs. Riis, to consider whether you want to make the breach hopelessly irreparable? Do you mean to make a reconciliation between the young people quite impossible?

Mrs. Riis. It is impossible, as it is.

Nordan. Why?

Mrs. Riis. Because all confidence is destroyed.

Nordan. More so now than before?

Mrs. Riis. Yes. I will confess that up to the moment. When Alfred's word of honour was offered yesterday—up to the moment when he demanded that his word of honour should be believed—I did not recognise the fact that it was my own story over again. But it was—word for word my own story! That was just the way we began; who will vouch for it that the sequel would not be the same as in our case?

Christensen. My son's character will vouch for that, Mrs. Riis!

Mrs. Riis. Character? A nice sort of character a man is likely to develop who indulges in secret and illicit courses from his boyhood! That is the very way faithlessness is bred. If any one wants to know the reason why character is such a rare thing, I think they will find the answer in that.

Christensen. A man's youth is by no means the test of his life. That depends on his marriage.

Mrs. Riis. And why should a man's faithlessness disappear when he is married? Can you tell me that?

Christensen. Because then he loves, of course.

Mrs. Riis. Because he loves? But do you mean that he has not loved before then? How absolutely you men have blinded yourselves!—No, love is not the least likely to be lasting when the will is vitiated. And that is what it is—vitiated by the life a bachelor leads.

Christensen. And yet I know plenty of sensual men who have strong wills.

Mrs. Riis. I am not speaking of strength of will, but of purity, faithfulness, nobility of will.

Christensen. Well, if my son is to be judged by any such nonsensical standard as that, I am devoutly thankful he has got out of the whole thing before it became serious—indeed I am! Now we have had enough of this. (Prepares to go.)

Mrs. Riis. As far as your son is concerned—. (Turns to NORDAN.) Doctor, answer me this, so that his father may hear it before he goes. When you refused to go with us to the betrothal party, had you already heard some thing about Alfred Christensen? Was what you had heard of such a nature that you felt you could not trust him?

Nordan (after a moment's thought). Not altogether, certainly.

Mrs. Riis (to CHRISTENSEN). There, you hear!—But will you let me ask you this, doctor: why did you not say so? Good God, why did you not speak?

Nordan. Listen to me, Mrs. Riis. When two young people, who after all are suited to one another—for they are that, are they not?

Christensen. They are that, I admit.

Nordan. When all of a sudden they fall madly in love with one another, what are you to do?

Christensen. Oh, rake up all sorts of stories and exaggerations—create a scandal!

Nordan. Indeed, I must confess—what as a matter of fact I have said—that I have become accustomed to things not being exactly as they should be in that respect. I looked upon these young people's engagement in the same light as I have looked on others—on most others—that is cruel to say, as a lottery. It might turn out well; on the other hand it might turn out very badly.

Mrs. Riis. And you were willing to risk my daughter, whom you are so fond of—for I know you are fond of her—in a lottery? Could one possibly have a clearer proof of the real state of things?

Nordan. Yes, certainly! You yourself, Mrs. Riis—what did you do?

Mrs. Riis. I—?

Christensen. Bravo!

Nordan. You knew what Hoff had said—and more too. (CHRISTENSEN laughs quietly.) Nevertheless you helped your husband, if not actually to try and get her to overlook it, at all events to smooth things over.

Christensen. Bravo!

Nordan. And you called in my help to induce her to take time to think it over.

Christensen. Mothers observe a considerable difference between theory and practice in these matters, I notice.

Nordan. It was only when I saw how deeply it affected Svava—what a horror she had of it—that my eyes were opened. And the longer I listened to her, the more sympathy I felt for her; for I was young myself once—and loved. But that was such a long time ago—and I have grown tired—

Mrs. Riis (who has sat down at the little table). My God!

Nordan. Yes, Mrs. Riis. Let me tell you candidly—it is the mothers, and no one else, that by degrees have made me callous. Mothers look upon the whole thing so callously. The fact is that as a rule they know what is what.

Christensen. That they do, the dear creatures! And Mrs. Riis is no exception to the rule. You must admit, my dear madam, that you did all you could to hold on to a young man who had had a lively past? Not to mention the fact that this same young man had an extremely good social position—a thing I only allude to incidentally.

Nordan. Exactly. Rather than not give their daughters a prospect of what they call "a good marriage" they straightway forget all that they have suffered themselves.

Mrs. Riis. You see, we do not know that it will turn out the same in their case.

Nordan. You don't know it?

Mrs. Riis. No, I tell you that I did not think so! We believe that the man our daughter is going to marry is so much better. We believe that in their case there are stronger guarantees—that the circumstances are altogether different. It is so! It is a kind of illusion that takes hold of us.

Christensen. When there is a prospect of a good marriage, yes! I entirely agree with you, Mrs. Riis—for the first time. Moreover, I think there is another side to it. Isn't it possible that women have not suffered so much after all from the fact that men are men? What? I fancy the suffering has been more acute than serious—something like sea-sickness; when it is over—well, it is over. And so when it is the daughters' turn to go on board, the dear mothers think: "Oh, they will be able to get over it too! Only let us get them off!" For they are so anxious to get them off, that is the truth!

Mrs. Riis (getting up and coming forward). Well, if it is so, surely it is nothing to make fun of! It only shows what a woman can sink to, from living with a man.

Christensen Indeed!

Mrs. Riis. Yes—because each generation of women is endowed with a stronger and stronger aspiration for a pure life. It results unconsciously from the maternal instinct, and is intended as a protection for the defenceless. Even worthless mothers feel that. But if they succumb in spite of it, and each generation of married women in its turn sinks as deep as you say, the reason of it can only be the privilege that men enjoy as part of their education.

Christensen. What privilege?

Mrs. Riis. That of living as they please when they are bachelors, and then having their word of honour believed in when they choose to enter the married state. As long as women are powerless to put an end to that horrible privilege or to make themselves independent of it, so long will one half of the world continue to be sacrificed on account of the other half—on account of the other half's lack of self-control. That one privilege turns out to be more powerful than all the striving for liberty in the world. And that is not a laughing matter.

Christensen. You are picturing to yourself a different world from this, and different natures from ours, Mrs. Riis. And that—if you will excuse my saying so—is obviously all the answer that is necessary to what you say.

Mrs. Riis. Well, then, give that answer openly! Why do you not openly acknowledge that as your standpoint?

Christensen. But don't we?

Mrs. Riis. No—not here, at all events. On the contrary, you range yourselves ostensibly under our banner, while all the time you are secretly betraying it. Why have you not the courage to unfurl your own? Let these bachelor customs of yours be sanctioned as entirely suitable—then we should be able to join issue with you. And then every innocent bride would be able to know what it is she is entering upon—and in what capacity.

Nordan. That would be simply nothing more or less than abolishing marriage.

Mrs. Riis. Would not that be more honest, too? Because now it is only being corrupted, long before it begins.

Christensen. Oh, of course it is all the men's fault! It is the fashion to say that now—it is part of the "struggle for freedom." Down with man's authority, of course!

Mrs. Riis. The authority his bachelor life has won for him!

Nordan. Ha, ha!

Mrs. Riis. Do not let us cover up the real issue with phrases! Let us rather speak of the "desolate hearth" that the poet writes of. Marriage laid in ruins is what he means by that; and what is the cause of it? What is the cause of the chilly, horrible commonplace of every-day life—sensual, idle, brutish? I could paint it even more vividly, but I will not. I will refrain, for instance, from bringing up the subject of hereditary disease. Let the question be thrashed out openly! Then perhaps a fire will be kindled—and our consciences stirred! It must become the most momentous question in every home. That is what is needed!

Christensen. Our conversation has soared to such heights that it really seems quite an anti-climax for me to say that I must go to a "higher place"!—but you must excuse me all the same.

Mrs. Riis. I hope I have not delayed you?

Christensen. No, there is plenty of time. I am only longing fervently—you really must not be offended—to get away from here.

Mrs. Riis. To your—equals?

Christensen. What a remarkable thing that you should remind me of them! And, by the way, that reminds me that I am scarcely likely to meet you or your family in future.

Mrs. Riis. No. Our acquaintance with you is at an end.

Christensen. Thank God for that!—All I hope now is that I shall succeed in apportioning the ridicule with some degree of justice.

Mrs. Riis. You need only publish your autobiography!

Christensen. No—I think it should rather be your family principles, madam! They are really very quaint. And when I relate the manner in which they are put into practice by yourselves, I rather think that people will be quite sufficiently amused. To speak seriously for a moment—I mean to attack your husband's reputation in private and in public, until he quits the town. I am not the sort of man to accept a humiliation like this without returning the compliment. (Turns to go.)

Nordan. This is shocking!

Alfred (appearing in the doorway of the house). Father!

Christensen. You here?—How ill you look, my boy! Where have you been?

Alfred. I came here at the same time as you did, and have heard everything. Let me tell you this at once, that if you take another step against the Riis's, I shall go round and tell every one the reason why Miss Riis threw me over. I shall tell them exactly what it was. Oh, it is no use looking at me with that mocking expression! I shall do it—and at once, too.

Christensen. I think you may spare yourself the trouble. The gossip about a broken engagement will get all over the town quicker than you could spread it.

Nordan (going up to ALFRED). One word, my boy—do you still love her?

Alfred. Do you ask that because she has been unjust to me? Well, now I know quite well what led to it—and inevitably led to it. I understand now!

Christensen. And forgive her? Without anything more?

Alfred. I love her more than ever—whatever she thinks of me!

Christensen. Well, upon my word! What next, I should like to know? You claim your right to resume the rôle of lover, and leave us and other honest folk to put the best face we can on the muddle you have made! I suppose you are going across the road now to tell her how much you enjoyed yourself yesterday?—or to ask for a respite till to-morrow, to give you time to pass decently through a process of purification? May I ask where you are going to find it and what it is going to consist of? Oh, don't look so melodramatic! If you can put up with what you got from Riis's girl yesterday and her mother to-day, surely you can put up with a little angry talk or a little chaff from your father. I have had to put up with the whole affair—the betrothal and the breaking it off as well! And then to be sprinkled with essence of morality into the bargain! Good Lord! I hope at least I shall not smell of it still when I get to the palace. (Goes towards the house, but turns back at the door.) You will find same money in the office to pay for a trip abroad. (Exit.)

Nordan. Does that mean banishment?
Alfred. Of course it does. (Appears very much agitated.)
Mrs. Riis. Doctor, you must come over to our house with me—and at once!
Nordan. How is she?
Mrs. Riis. I don't know.
Nordan. You don't know?
Mrs. Riis. She wanted to be alone yesterday. And to-day she went out early.
Nordan. Has anything happened, then?
Mrs. Riis. Yes. You told me yesterday that you had given her a hint about—her father.
Nordan. Well?
Mrs. Riis. And so I felt that it could not be concealed any longer.
Nordan. And you have—?
Mrs. Riis. I have written to her.
Nordan. Written?
Mrs. Riis. It seemed the easiest way—and we should escape talking about it. All yesterday afternoon and last night I was writing, and tearing it up, and writing again—writing—writing! It was not a long letter, when all was done, but it took it out of me.
Nordan. And has she had the letter?
Mrs. Riis. When she had had her breakfast this morning and gone out, I sent it after her. And now, my dear friend, I want to beg you to go and have a talk with her—then you can let me know when I may go to her. Because I am frightened! (Hides her face in her hands.)
Nordan. The moment you came I saw something serious had happened. You argued so vehemently, too. Well, matters have developed, and no mistake!
Mrs. Riis. You mustn't go away, doctor! Don't go away from her now!
Nordan. Oh, that is it, is it?—Thomas!
Enter THOMAS.
Thomas. Yes, sir.
Nordan. You need not pack my things.
Thomas. Not pack, sir?—Very good, sir. (Gives the doctor his stick and goes to open the house door for them.)
Nordan. Allow me, Mrs. Riis. (Offers her his arm.)
Alfred (coming forward). Mrs. Riis! May I speak to her?
Mrs. Riis. Speak to her? No, that is impossible.
Nordan. You heard, my boy, what she has to think about to-day.
Mrs. Riis. And if she would not speak to you before, it is not likely she will now.
Alfred. If she should ask to speak to me, will you tell her I am here? I shall stay here till she does.
Mrs. Riis. But what is the use of that?
Alfred. Well, that will be our affair. I know she wants to speak to me, just as much as I do to her. Only tell her I am here! That is all I ask. (Goes away into the farther part of the garden.)
Nordan. He does not know what he is talking about.
Mrs. Riis. Dear Dr. Nordan, let us go! I am so frightened.
Nordan. Not more than I am, I think.—So she knows it now, does she! (They go out.)

SCENE II

(SCENE.—The same as in Acts I. and II. SVAVA comes into the room slowly and looks round; then goes to the door and looks round outside the house, then comes in again. As she turns back, she sees NORDAN standing in the doorway.)

Svava. You!—Oh, Uncle Nordan! (Sobs.)

Nordan. My child! My dear child! Calm yourself!

Svava. But haven't you seen mother? She said she had gone across to see you.

Nordan. Yes, she is coming directly. But look here—suppose you and I go for a good long walk together, instead of talking to your mother or anyone? A long quiet walk? Eh?

Svava. I can't.

Nordan. Why?

Svava. Because I must make an end of all this.

Nordan. What do you mean?

Svava (without answering his question). Uncle—?

Nordan. Yes?

Svava. Does Alfred know this?—Did he know it before?

Nordan. Yes.

Svava. Of course every one knew it except me. Oh, how I wish I could hide myself away from every one! I will, too. I see the real state of things now for the first time. I have been like a child trying to push a mountain away with its two hands—and they have all been standing round, laughing at me, of course. But let me speak to Alfred!

Nordan. To Alfred?

Svava. I behaved so wrongly yesterday. I ought never to have gone into the room—but you gave me no choice when you came to me. I went with you almost unconsciously.

Nordan. I suppose it was thinking of your father—of what I told you about him—that made you—

Svava. I did not understand all at once. But, when I was by myself, it all flashed across me—mother's strange uneasiness—father's threats about leaving the country—all sorts of expressions, and signs—lots and lots of things I had never understood and never even thought twice about! I chased them out of my mind, but back they came!—back and back again! It seemed to paralyse me. And when you took me by the arm and said: "Now you must go in!"—I hardly had strength to think. Everything seemed to be going round and round.

Nordan. Yes, I made a regular mess of it—both on that occasion and the time before.

Svava. No, it was all quite right—quite right! We certainly went a little off the lines, it is true. I must speak to Alfred; the matter must not rest as it is. But, except for that, it was all quite right. And now I have got to make an end of it all.

Nordan. What do you mean?

Svava. Where is mother?

Nordan. My dear girl, you ought not to try and do anything to-day. I should advise you not to speak to anybody. If you do—well, I don't know what may happen.

Svava. But I know.—Oh, it is no use talking to me like that! You think I am simply a bundle of nerves to-day. And it is quite true—I am. But if you try to thwart me it will only make me worse.

Nordan. I am not trying to thwart you at all. I only—

Svava. Yes, yes, I know.—Where is mother, then? And you must bring Alfred here. I cannot go to him, can I? Or do you think he has too much pride to come, after what happened yesterday? Oh, no, he is not like that! Tell him he must not be proud with one who is so humiliated. (Bursts into tears.)

Nordan. But do you think you are able for it?

Svava. You don't know how much I can stand! Anyway, I must get done with it all, quickly. It has lasted long enough.

Nordan. Then shall I ask your mother—?

Svava. Yes!—and will you ask Alfred?

Nordan. Presently, yes. And if you should—

Svava. No, there is no "if" about it!

Nordan.—if you should want me, I won't go away till you are "done with it all," as you say. (SVAVA goes up to him and embraces him. He goes out. After a short pause MRS. RIIS comes in.)

Mrs. Riis (going to SVAVA). My child! (Stops.)

Svava. No, mother, I cannot come near you. Besides, I am trembling all over. And you don't understand what it is? It has not dawned upon you that you cannot treat me like this?

Mrs. Riis. Treat you like this, Svava? What do you mean?

Svava. Good heavens, mother!—letting me live here day after day, year after year, without letting me know what I was living with? Allowing me to preach the strictest principles, from a house like ours? What will people say of us, now that everything will be known!

Mrs. Riis. Surely you would not have wished me to tell my child that—

Svava. Not while I was a child. But when I had grown up, yes—under any circumstances! I ought to have been allowed the choice whether I would live at home under such conditions or not! I ought to have been allowed to know what every one else knew—or what they may get to know at any moment.

Mrs. Riis. I have never looked at it in that light.

Svava. Never looked at it in that light? Mother!

Mrs. Riis. Never!—To shield you and have peace in our home while you were a child, and peace afterwards in your studies, your interests and your pleasures—for you are not like other girls, you know, Svava—to ensure this, I have been almost incredibly careful that no hint of this should come to your ears. I believed that to be my duty. You have no conception what I have stooped to—for your sake, my child.

Svava. But you had no right to do it, mother!

Mrs. Riis. No right?—

Svava. No! To degrade yourself for my sake was to degrade me too.

Mrs. Riis (with emotion). Oh, my God—!

Svava. I do not reproach you for anything, mother! I would not do that for the world—my dear mother! I am only so infinitely distressed and appalled at the thought of your having to go about carrying such a secret with you! Never able to be your real self with me for a moment! Always hiding something! And to have to listen to my praises of what so little deserved praise—to see me putting my faith in him, caressing him—oh, mother, mother!

Mrs. Riis. Yes, dear, I felt that myself—many and many a time. But I felt that I dared not tell you. It was wrong—so very wrong! I understand that now! But would you have had me leave him at once, as soon as I knew of it myself?

Svava. I cannot take upon myself to say. You decided that for yourself. Each one must decide that for herself—according to the measure of her love and her strength. But when the thing went on after I was grown up—! Naturally that was why I made a second mistake. I had been brought up to make mistakes, you see. (RIIS is heard outside the window, humming a tune.)

Mrs. Riis. Good heavens, there he is! (RIIS is seen passing the left-hand window. When he reaches the door, however, he stops and, with the words, "Oh, by the bye!" turns back and goes hurriedly out.)

Mrs. Riis. You look quite changed, my child! Svava, you frighten me! Surely you are not going to—?

Svava. What is it that is in your mind, mother?

Mrs. Riis. The thought that, as I have endured so much for your sake, you might make up your mind to endure a little for mine.

Svava. A little of this? No, not for a moment!

Mrs. Riis. But what are you going to do?

Svava. Go away from here at once, of course.

Mrs. Riis (with a cry). Then I shall go with you!

Svava. You? Away from father?

Mrs. Riis. It has been for your sake that I have stayed with him. I won't stay here a day without you!—Ah, you don't want me with you!

Svava. Mother, dear—I must have time to accustom myself to the changed state of things. You have quite changed in my eyes too, you see. I have been mistaken in you, and I must get accustomed to that idea. I must be alone!—Oh, don't look so unhappy, dear!

Mrs. Riis. And this is the end of it all—this is the end of it!

Svava. I cannot act otherwise, dear. I must go away now to my Kindergartens and give up my life entirely to that work. I must, I must! If I cannot be alone there, I must go farther afield.

Mrs. Riis. This is the cruellest part of it all—the cruellest part! Listen, is that—? Yes, it is he. Do not say anything now! For my sake say nothing now; I cannot bear anything more on the top of this!—Try to be friendly to him! Svava—do you hear me! (RIIS comes back, still humming a tune; this time he has his overcoat over his arm. SVAVA comes hurriedly forward, and after a moment's hesitation sits down with her back half turned to him, and tries to busy herself with something. RIIS puts down his overcoat. He is in court dress and wears the Order of St. Olaf.)

Riis. Good morning, ladies! Good morning!

Mrs. Riis. Good morning!

Riis. Here is the latest great piece of news for you: Who do you think drove me from the palace? Christensen!

Mrs. Riis. Really?

Riis. Yes! Our wrathful friend of yesterday! Yes! He and one of my fellow-directors. I was one of the first persons he greeted when he got to the palace. He introduced me to people, chatted with me—paid me the most marked attention!

Mrs. Riis. You don't mean it?

Riis. Consequently nothing really happened here yesterday! No gloves were thrown about at all, least of all in his eldest son's face! Christensen, the worthy knight of to-day's making, feels the necessity for peace! We ended by drinking a bottle of champagne at my brother's.

Mrs. Riis. How amusing!

Riis. Therefore, ladies—smiles, if you please! Nothing has happened here, absolutely nothing! We begin again with an absolutely clean slate, without a smear upon it!

Mrs. Riis. What a piece of luck!

Riis. Yes, isn't it! That rather violent outburst of our daughter's has unburdened her mind and cleared the ideas in other people's heads. The general atmosphere is agreeably clear, not to say favourable.

Mrs. Riis. And what was it like at the palace?

Riis. Well, I can tell you this—when I looked round at our batch of new-fledged knights, it did not exactly impress me that it is virtue that is rewarded in this world of ours. However, we were all confronted with an alarmingly solemn document. It was about something we swore to preserve—I fancy it was the State—or perhaps the Church—I am really not sure, because I didn't read it. They all signed it!

Mrs. Riis. You, as well?

Riis. I, as well. Do you suppose I was going to be left out of such good company? Up at those exalted heights one obtains a happier and freer outlook upon life. We were all friends up there. People came up and congratulated me—and after a bit I wasn't sure whether it was on my daughter's account or on my own; and, what is more, I never knew I had so many friends in the town, let alone at Court! But in such brilliant company and such an atmosphere of praises and compliments and general amiability, one was not inclined to be particular! And there were only men present! You know—you ladies must excuse me—there is sometimes a peculiar charm in being only with men, especially on great occasions like that. Conversation becomes more pointed, more actual, more robust—and laughter more full of zest. Men seem to understand one another almost without the need of words.

Mrs. Riis. I suppose you are feeling very happy to-day, then?

Riis. I should think I am!—and I only wish every one were the same! I daresay life might be better than it is; but, as I saw it under those circumstances from those exalted heights, it might also be much worse. And, as for us men—oh, well, we have our faults, no doubt, but we are very good company for all that. It would be a dull world without us, I am sure. Let us take life as it comes, my dear Svava! (Comes nearer to her. She gets up.) What is the matter? Are you still in a bad temper?—when you have had the pleasure of boxing his ears with your own gloves, before the whole family circle? What more can you reasonably ask of life? I should say you ought to have a good laugh over it!—Or is there something up? What? Come, what is the matter now?

Mrs. Riis. The fact is—

Riis. Well, the fact is—?

Mrs. Riis. The fact is that Alfred will be here in a moment.

Riis. Alfred here? In a moment? Hurrah! I quite understand! But why didn't you tell me so at once?

Mrs. Riis. You have talked the whole time since you came in.

Riis. I do believe I have!—Well, if you are going to take it seriously, my dear Svava, perhaps you will allow your "knightly" father to take it lightly? The whole thing amuses me so tremendously. I was put into good spirits to-day the moment I saw, from Christensen's face, that there was nothing in the wind. And so Alfred is coming here directly! Then I understand everything. Hurrah, once more! I assure you that is the best of all the good things that have happened to-day. I really think I must play a festal overture till he comes! (Goes towards the piano, singing.)

Mrs. Riis. No, no, dear! Do you hear? No, no! (RIIS plays on, without listening to hey, till she goes up to him, and stops him, pointing to SVAVA.)

Svava. Oh, let him play, mother—let him play! It is the innocent gaiety that I have admired since I was a child! (Bursts into tears, but collects herself.) How hateful! How horrible!

Riis. My dear child, you look as if you wanted to be throwing down gauntlets to-day too! Isn't that all done with?

Svava. No, indeed it is not!

Riis. You shall have the loan of my gloves, if you haven't—

Mrs. Riis. Oh, don't say those things to her!

Svava. Oh, yes, let him! Let him mock at us, mother dear! A man of his moral earnestness has the right to mock at us!

Riis. What are you talking about? Does it show a lack of moral earnestness not to be in love with old maids and sour-faced virtue?

Svava. Father, you are—

Mrs. Riis. No, Svava!

Riis. Oh, let her say what she wants! It is something quite new to see a well-brought-up girl throw her gloves in her fiancé's face and accusations in her father's! Especially when it is all done in the name of morality!

Svava. Don't talk about morality! Or go and talk to Mrs. North about it!

Riis. Mrs.—Mrs.—? What has she to do with—?

Svava. Be quiet! I know everything! You have—

Mrs. Riis. Svava!

Svava. Ah, yes-for mother's sake I won't go on. But, when I threw down my much discussed gauntlet yesterday, I knew about it then. That was why I did it! It was a protest against everything of the kind, against its beginning and its continuation, against him and against you! I understood—then—your pious zeal in the matter, and the show of scandalised morality you allowed mother to be a witness of!

Mrs. Riis. Svava!

Svava. I understand now, for the first time, what your consideration, your politeness to mother—which I have so often admired—all meant! Your fun, your good temper, your care of your appearance!—Oh, I never can believe in anything any more! It is horrible, horrible!

Mrs. Riis. Svava, dear!

Svava. All life seems to have become unclean for me! My nearest and dearest all soiled and smirched! That is why, ever since yesterday, I have had the feeling of being an outcast; and that is what I am—an outcast from all that I prized and reverenced—and that without my having done the slightest thing to deserve it. Even so, it is not the pain of it that I feel most deeply; it is the humiliation, the shame. All that I have so often said must seem now to be nothing but empty words—all that I have done myself must seem of no account—and this without its being my fault! For it is your fault! I thought, too, that I knew something about life; but there was more for me to learn! I see that you wanted me to give way to such an extent that I should end by acquiescing in it. I understand now, for the first time, what your teaching meant—and the things that you invoked mother and heaven to witness. But it is of no use! I can tell you that it is about as much as one can stand, to have the thoughts I have had yesterday—last night—to-day. However, it is once and for all; after this, nothing can ever take me by surprise again. To think that any man could have the heart to let his child have such an experience!

Mrs. Riis. Svava—look at your father!

Svava. Yes—but if you think what I am saying now is hard, remember what I said to you before I knew this—no longer ago than yesterday morning. That will give you some idea of how I believed in you, father—and some idea of what I am feeling now! Oh—!

Riis. Svava!

Svava. You have ruined my home for me! Almost every other hour in it has been corrupted—and I cannot face a future like that.

Riis and Mrs. Riis (together). But, Svava—!

Svava. No, I cannot! My faith in you is destroyed—so that I can never think of this as a home again. It makes me feel as if I were merely living with you as a lodger—from yesterday onwards, merely a lodger in the house.

Riis. Don't say that! My child!

Svava. Yes, I am your child. It only needed you to say it like that, for me to feel it deeply. To think of all the experiences we two have had together—all the happy times we have had on our travels, in our amusements—and then to think that I can never look back on them again, never take them up again! That is why I cannot stay here.

Riis. You cannot stay here!

Svava. It would remind me of everything too painfully. I should see everything in a distorted light.

Mrs. Riis. But you will see that you cannot bear to go away, either!

Riis. But—I can go!

Mrs Riis. You?

Riis. Yes, and your mother and you stay here?—Oh, Svava—!

Svava. No, I cannot accept that—come what may!

Riis. Do not say any more! Svava, I entreat you! Do not make me too utterly miserable! Remember that never, until to-day—I never thought to make you—. If you cannot bear to be with me any more—if you cannot—then let me go away! It is I that am to blame, I know. Listen, Svava! It must be I, not you! You must stay here!

Mrs. Riis (listening). Good heavens, there is Alfred!

Riis. Alfred! (A pause. ALFRED appears in the doorway.)

Alfred (after a moment). Perhaps I had better go away again?

Riis (to ALFRED). Go away again?—Go away again, did you say?—No, not on any account! No!—No, you could not have come at a more fortunate moment! My boy, my dear boy! Thank you!

Mrs. Riis (to SVAVA). Would you rather be alone—?

Svava. No, no, no!

Riis. You want to speak to Svava, don't you? I think it will be best for me to leave you together. You need to talk things over frankly with her—to be alone—naturally! You will excuse me, then, if I leave you, won't you? I have something very important to do in town, so you will excuse me! I must hurry and change my clothes—so please excuse me! (Goes into his room.)

Alfred. Oh, but I can come some other time.

Mrs. Riis. But I expect you would like to talk to her now?

Alfred. It is no question of what I would like. I see—and I heard Dr. Nordan say—that Miss Riis is quite worn out. But I felt it my duty, all the same, to call.

Svava. And I thank you for doing so! It is more—far more—than I have deserved. But I want to tell you at once that what happened yesterday—I mean, the form my behaviour took yesterday—was due to the fact that, only an hour before then, something had come to my knowledge that I had never known before. And that was mixed up with it. (She can scarcely conceal her emotion.)

Alfred. I knew that to-day you would be regretting what happened yesterday—you are so good. And that was my only hope of seeing you again.

Riis (coming out of his room partly dressed to go out). Does any one want anything done in town? If so, I shall be happy to see to it! It has occurred to me that perhaps these ladies would like to go away for a little trip somewhere—what do you two say to that? When one's thoughts are beginning to get a little—what shall I call it?—a little too much for one, or perhaps I should rather say a trifle too serious, it is often a wonderful diversion to go away for a little change. I have often found it so myself—often, I assure you! Just think it over, won't you? I could see about making plans for you at once, if you think so—eh? Well, then, good-bye for the present! And—think it over! I think myself it is such an excellent plan! (Goes out. SVAVA looks at her mother with a smile, and hides her face in her hands.)

Mrs. Riis. I must go away for a few minutes and—

Svava. Mother!

Mrs. Riis. I really must, dear! I must collect my thoughts. This has been too much for me. I shall not go farther away than into my room there (pointing to the room on the left). And I will come back directly. (SVAVA throws herself into a chair by the table, overcome by her emotion.)

Alfred. It looks as if we two were to have to settle this matter, after all.

Svava. Yes.

Alfred. I daresay that you will understand that since yesterday I have done nothing else but invent speeches to make to you—but now I do not feel as if it had been of much use.

Svava. It was good of you to come.

Alfred. But you must let me make one request of you, and that from my heart: Wait for me! Because I know now what will show me the way to your heart. We had planned out our life together, you and I; and, although I shall do it alone, I shall carry out our plans unfalteringly. And then perhaps, some day, when you see how faithful I have been——. I know I ought not to worry you, least of all to-day. But give me an answer! You need scarcely say anything—but just give me an answer!

Svava. But what for?

Alfred. I must have it to live on—and the more difficult the prize is to attain, the better worth living will life be to me. Give me an answer!

Svava (tries to speak, but bursts into tears). Ah, you see how everything upsets me to-day. I cannot. Besides, what do you want me to do? To wait? What would that mean? It would mean being ready and yet not ready; trying to forget and yet always having it before my mind. (Is overcome again by her emotion.) No!

Alfred. I see you need to be alone. But I cannot bring myself to go away. (SVAVA gets up, and tries to regain control over herself. ALFRED goes to her and throws himself on his knees beside her.) Give me just one word.

Svava. But do you not understand that if you could give me back once more the happiness that complete trust gives—do you think I should wait for you to ask anything of me then? No, I should go to you and thank you on my knees. Can you doubt that for a moment?

Alfred. No, no!

Svava. But I have not got it.

Alfred. Svava!

Svava. Oh, please—!

Alfred. Good-bye—good-bye! But I shall see you again some day? I shall see you again? (Turns to go, but stops at the door.) I must have a sign—something definite to take with me! Stretch out a hand to me! (At these words SVAVA turns to him and stretches out both her hands to him. He goes out. MRS. RIIS comes in from her room.)

Mrs. Riis. Did you promise him anything?

Svava. I think so. (Throws herself into her mother's arms.)

Mary

THE HOMESTEAD AND THE RACE

THE coast line of the south of Norway is very irregular. This is the work of the mountains and rivers. The former end in hillocks and headlands, off which often lie islands; the latter have dug out valleys and end in fjords or smaller inlets.

In one of these inlets, known as "Kroken" (the nook), lies the homestead. The original name of the place was Krokskogen. In the documents of the Danish government officials this was transformed into Krogskoven; now it is Krogskogen. The owners originally called themselves Kroken; Anders and Hans Kroken were the regularly recurring names. In course of time they came to call themselves Krogh; the general in the Danish army subscribed himself *Von* Krogh. Now they are Krog, plain and simple.

The passengers on the small steamers which, on their way to and from the neighbouring town, touch at the landing-place below the little chapel, never fail to remark on the beautifully sheltered, snug situation of Krogskogen.

The mountains rise high on the horizon, but here they have dwindled down. The families between two long wooded ridges which project into the sea—its buildings so close to the right-hand ridge that to the steamer-passengers it seems as if a man might easily jump from their roofs on to the steep hill-side. The west wind cannot find its way in here. The place seems, after the manner of children playing at hide-and-seek, to have the right to cry: *Pax!* to it. And it is almost in a position to say the same to the north and east winds. Only a gale from the south can make its entrance, and that in humble fashion. Islands, one large and two small, detain and chasten it before they allow it to pass. The tall trees in front of the houses merely bow their topmost branches rhythmically; they abate none of their dignity.

In this sheltered bay is the best bathing-place of the whole neighbourhood. In summer the youth of the town used to come out here on the Saturday evenings and Sundays to disport themselves in the sandy shallows or to swim out to the large island and back. It was at the left side of the bay, reckoning from Krogskogen, that this went on, the side where the river falls into the sea, where the landing-place lies, and, a little above it and nearer the ridge, the chapel, with the graves of the Krog family clustered round it. The distance from here to the houses on the right is considerable. Up there the noise made by the merry bathers was seldom heard. But Anders Krog often came down to watch them, when they had lighted fires on the beach or in the wood on the point. He doubtless came to keep an eye on the fires; but nothing was ever said of this. Anders was known as the politest man, "the most thorough gentleman," in the town. His large, peculiarly bright eyes beamed a gentle welcome into the faces of all; the few words which fell from him expressed only kindly interest. He soon passed on, to climb the ridge and take his usual slow walk round. As long as his tall, slightly stooping form was visible in the wood above, there was silence. But what a good time the bathers had here! They were for the most part working men from the town, members of gymnastic societies or choral unions, troops of boys. Their gathering-place was beside the landing-stage and the chapel. There they undressed. The main road which follows the coast passes the spot; but it was little frequented in summer; people came to the place by boat or in the small steamers. So long as the bathers kept a watchman on the ridge, they were certain of not being surprised.

Up at the house it was quiet, always quiet. The front of the main building does not even face the bay; it looks on the fields. The building is of two high storeys, with the roof flattened over the gables—a long, broad house.

The foundation wall rises very high in front; a flight of easy steps leads up to the door. The whole building is painted white, except the foundation wall and the windows, which are black. The outhouses lie nearer the ridge; they cannot be seen from the steamer. At one side of the main building an orchard slopes towards the sea; at the other is a large flower and kitchen garden.

The level land, a long, narrow strip, lies between the ridges. It is carefully and skilfully cultivated. The big Dutch cows thrive here.

The history of the property and that of its owners was predetermined by the woods. These were large and valuable, and fortunately came in good time under careful Dutch management. This happened in the days when the small Dutch merchant-vessels traded directly with the owners of the woods in Norway. The Dutchmen were supplied with timber, and in turn supplied the Norwegians with their civilisation and its products. Krogskogen was specially fortunate, for, some three hundred years ago, the owner of one of the "koffs" which lay loading in the bay, fell in love with the peasant's fair-haired daughter. He ended by buying the whole place. A beautifully painted portrait of him and her still hangs in the best room of the house, in the corner nearest the bay. It represents a tall, thin man, with peculiarly bright eyes. He is dark-haired, and has a slight stoop of the neck. The race must have been a vigorous one, for the Krogs are like this to-day.

The first Dutch owner was not called Krog, nor did he live at Krogskogen; but the son who inherited the place was baptised Anders Krog, after his mother's father; he called his son Hans, after his own father; and since then these two names have alternated. If there were several sons, one was always named Klas and another Jürges, which names in the course of time became Klaus and Jörgen. The family continued to intermarry with its Dutch kinsfolk, so that the race was as much Dutch as Norwegian; for long all the domestic arrangements at Krogskogen were Dutch. In a manner, the nationalities did not seem really to mix. The reason of this probably was that the Dutch element was not pure Dutch—if it had been, it would have intermingled more easily with the Norwegian; it was a mixture of Dutch and Spanish. The black hair, the bright eyes, the lean body, were inherited by the men from generation to generation; the women inherited the fairness and the strong build; in them Norwegian blood flowed along with Dutch. Rarely indeed did the one sex make over any of its family characteristics to the other; occasionally fair and dark hair met in red, and once in a way the bright eyes would make their appearance in a woman's face.

It was a peculiarity of the race that in all its families more daughters than sons were born. The Krogs were fine-looking men and women, and, as a rule, were well off; consequently, the family made good connections and held a good position. They had the character of being clannish and able to hold their own.

One quality which marked them all was that of prudent moderation. In Norway a fortune rarely descends to the third generation. If it is not squandered in the second, it is certain to be in the third. Not so in this case. To the main branch of the Krog family the woods were now the same source of wealth that they had been three hundred years before.

A desire which was transmitted from generation to generation was the desire to travel. In the book-cases at Krogskogen books of travel predominated, and additions were constantly made to their number. Even as children the Krogs travelled. They planned tours with the help of books, pictures, and maps. They sat at the table and played at travelling. They voyaged from one town built of coloured card-board houses to another of the same description. They navigated cardboard ships, loaded with beans, coffee, salt, and wooden pegs. In the bay they rowed and sailed and swam from the pier to the island. One day it was from Europe to America, another, from Japan to Ceylon. Or they crossed the ridge, that is the Andes, to the most wonderful Indian villages.

No sooner were they grown up than they insisted on seeing something of the world. They generally began with a voyage to Holland and a visit to their kinsfolk there. Some two hundred years ago a youth of the family, after a very short stay in Holland, went off in a Dutch East Indiaman. He, however, returned to Amsterdam, resolved to become an architect and engineer—the professions were at that time combined. He made himself a name, and in course of time was called to Copenhagen to teach. He entered the military service and rose to the rank of general in the engineer corps. At the time of his retirement his earnings, added to his patrimony, constituted a considerable fortune. He settled at Krogskogen, which he bought after the death of a childless brother. He called himself Hans *von* Krogh. It was he who erected the present house, which is of stone, a very unusual building material in a Norwegian forest district. The old engineer-architect wanted occupation and amusement. Though he was not married, he made the house large, "for those to come." He rebuilt the farm-steading; he drained and he planted; he sent to Holland for a gardener—old Siemens, of whose strictness and angry insistence upon cleanliness and order stories are still told. For him the General put up hot-houses and built a cottage.

The General lived to be a very old man. After his day nothing special happened until the younger of two brothers emigrated to America and settled on the shores of Lake Michigan—at that time virgin soil. This was regarded as a great event. The man's name was Anders Krog. He prospered over there, and people wondered that he did not marry. He invited one of his brother's sons to come out to him, promising to make him his heir. And thus it came about that Hans, the elder brother of the Anders Krog of our story, went to America.

At exactly the same time, however, arrived a young Norwegian girl, also a Krog; and with her the elderly uncle fell in love. He proposed to Hans to pay his journey home. But the young man felt that he would disgrace himself by returning. He stayed on and set up in business for himself—in the timber trade, which he understood. The undertaking prospered. By rights Hans should have gone home and taken possession of Krogskogen at the time of his father's death; but he refused to do so. The younger brother, Anders, who in the meantime had also taken to trade, and acquired the largest grocery business in the neighbouring town, was obliged to take over the property as well.

Young Anders Krog was not really a good business man. But his extraordinary conscientiousness and considerateness soon gained him the custom of the whole town. Another man in his place might have made a fortune; he did not. When he entered on possession of Krogskogen he had not yet paid up the price of his business in town, and in taking over the property he incurred a still larger debt. For both he had been made to pay well. Travel he must, but he had to content himself with going off for a month each year—one year to England, another to France, and so on. His greatest desire was a visit to America, but on this he dared not venture yet. He contented himself with reading of the new wonderland. Reading was his chief pleasure; next to it came gardening, in which he possessed more skill than most trained gardeners.

This quiet man with the bright eyes was shyer than a girl of fourteen. Every week-day morning he chose, if possible, a seat by himself on the little steamer which took him to town as long as the bay was not frozen over. In going on shore he showed extreme consideration for others; then he hurried off, bowing respectfully to his acquaintances, to his house on the market-place, where he was to be found until evening, when he returned as he had come. At times he cycled. In winter he drove; and at this season he sometimes stayed over night in town, where he occupied two modest attic rooms in his own house.

The town knew of no other man possessing in such a degree all the qualities of a perfect husband. But his invincible modesty made all overtures impossible until ... the right woman came. But then he was already over forty. The same fate befell him as had befallen his uncle and namesake at Lake Michigan; a young girl of his own family came and took possession of him. And she was this very uncle's only child.

He was working one Sunday morning, in his shirt-sleeves, in the kitchen and flower garden on the northern side of the house, when a young girl, wearing a broad-brimmed straw hat, laid her ungloved hands on the white fence and looked in between its round tops.

Anders, bending over a flower-bed, heard a playful: "Good morning!" and started up. Speechless and motionless he stood, with earth-soiled hands, his eyes drinking her in like a revelation.

She laughed and said: "Who am I?" Then his thinking power returned. "You are—you must be——"; he got no further, but smiled a welcome.

"Who am I?"

"Marit Krog from Michigan."

He had heard from his sister, who lived on the farther side of the left ridge, that Marit Krog was on her way to Norway. But he had no idea that she had arrived.

"And you are my father's nephew," said she with an English accent. "How like him you are! How very like!"

She stood looking at him for a moment. Then—"May I come in?"

"Of course you may—but first"——looking at his hands and shirt-sleeves, "first I must——."

"I can go in alone," said she frankly.

"Of course—please do! Go in by the front-door. I'll send the maid—" and he hurried towards the kitchen.

She ran round to the front of the house and up the steps. Turning an enormous key, an old work of art (as was also the iron-work on the door), she stepped into the hall or entrance room. Here there was plenty of light. Marit drew a little. She had learned to use her eyes. She saw at once that all these cupboards, large and small, were of excellent Dutch workmanship, and that the room was larger than it seemed; the furniture took up so much space. On her left an old-fashioned carved staircase led up to the second storey. The door straight in front of her led to the kitchen, she concluded, assisted by her sense of smell; and when the maid-servant issued from it she knew that she had guessed rightly. Through the open door she saw a floor flagged with marble, walls covered with china tiles decorated in blue, and, upon the shelf which extended round the walls, brightly polished copper vessels of many different sizes—a Dutch kitchen.

In the hall she stood upon carpets thicker than any her feet had ever trodden. And quite as thick were those on the stairs, secured with the hugest of brass rods. "The people in this house walk on cushions," she thought to herself; and the idea immediately occurred to her that the house was an enormous bed. Afterwards she always called it "the bed." "Shall we go back to bed now?" she would say, laughing. On both sides of the hall she saw doors and pictured to herself the rooms within. To her left, that is, on the right side of the house, she imagined first a smaller room, and beyond it, nearest the sea, a large room, the whole breadth of the building. And she was correct. To her right she imagined the house divided lengthwise into two rooms. And in this also she was correct. Nor was it surprising that she should be, for her father's house on the shores of Lake Michigan was planned in imitation of this. Upstairs she pictured to herself a broad passage the whole length of the house, with moderate-sized rooms on both sides of it. The carpets were extraordinarily thick down here, but she was certain that they were at least as thick upstairs, real cushion carpets. In this house there were no noises. Its inmates were quiet people.

The servant had opened the door to the left. Marit went into the great room and examined all its pictures and ornaments. It was terribly overcrowded, but all the things in themselves had been well chosen, many of them by connoisseurs—that she saw at once. Some of the paintings were, she felt certain, of great value. But what occupied her most was the thought that not until now had she understood her own old father, although she had lived with him all her life—alone with him; she had lost her mother early. Of just such a quantity of rare and precious things was he composed—in a somewhat confused fashion, which prevented his being appreciated. She felt as if he were standing by her, smiling his gentle, kindly smile, happy because he was understood.

And there he was, sure enough! Through the open door she saw him on the stair. Younger, yes! But that was of no consequence; the eyes were only the brighter and warmer for that. He came towards her with the same walk, the same movement of the arms, the same slight stoop and circumspect carriage. And when he looked at her, and spoke to her, and bade her welcome in her father's gentle, subdued manner, she was conscious in him of the profound respect for the individual human being which, in her estimation, characterised her father beyond any one she had ever known. Her father's hair was thinner, his face was deeply lined, he had lost some of his teeth, his skin was shrivelled. The thought filled her eyes with tears. She looked up into the younger eyes, heard the fresher voice, felt the grasp of the warmer hand. She could not help it—she threw her arms round Anders Krog's neck, laid her head on his breast, and wept.

This settled the matter. There was no resisting this.

Soon afterwards they both got into the boat in which she had come. It was Marit who rowed round the point. Both for his own sake, and because of the bathers, who saw them, he had made some feeble attempts to take the oars. But from the moment when she threw her arms round his neck, he was powerless. He knew that he would henceforth do the will of this girl with the glory of red hair. He sat gazing at her freckled face and freckled hands, at her superb figure, her fresh lips. At the edge of her collar he caught a glimpse of the purest of white skin; there was something in the eyes which corresponded exactly with this. He had not seen his fill when they landed. Nor could he get enough on the way up to his sister's farm—not enough of her soft voice, of her gait, of her dress, of the smile which disclosed her teeth, nor, above all else, of her frank, impetuous talk; all these things were alike bewildering.

Next morning he stayed at home. No sooner had the steamer with which he should have gone to town turned the point, than Marit's white boat came in sight. She had a maid-servant with her who was to keep watch, for to-day she too meant to bathe.

Afterwards she went up to the house. She had planned to stay there to dinner. In the afternoon they walked back together, across the ridge; the boat had been sent home.

Next day she went with him to town. The day after they were in town again, but this time she chose to drive, and made Anders' sister come with them. There was something new every day. The brother and sister simply lived for her, and she accepted the situation as if it were quite natural.

When she had been with them for about three weeks, a cablegram came to Krogskogen from brother Hans, telling that their uncle, Anders, had died suddenly; the news must be broken to Marit.

Never had Anders Krog taken a walk with heavier feet and heart than on the day when he crossed the hill to his sister's with this telegram in his pocket. As he came in sight of the home-like yellow house and steading amongst the trees on the plain below, he heard the dinner-bell ring out cheerily into the bright sunshine. The spread table was waiting. He sat down; he felt as if he could go no farther. Was he not on his way to kill the glad day?

When at length he reached the house, he went in by the kitchen door, along with some labourers who had come from a distance for their dinner. In the kitchen he found his sister, who took him into a back room. She was as much shocked and grieved as he; but she was of a more courageous nature; and she undertook to break the news to Marit, who had not come in yet, but was expected every moment.

Anders Krog in his back room ere long heard a scream which he never forgot. He sprang to his feet with the agony of it, but could not bring himself to leave the room; the sound of bitter sobbing in the next held him fast. It grew louder and louder, interrupted by short cries. The same impetuous strength in her grief as in her joy! It set him pacing the room wildly until his sister opened the door.

"She wants to see you."

Then he was obliged to go in. Exerting all the strength of his will, he entered. Marit was lying on the sofa, but the moment she saw him she sat up and stretched out her arms.

"Come, come! *You* are my father now!"

He crossed the room quickly and bent over her; she put her arm round his neck and drew him down; he was obliged to kneel.

"You must never leave me again! Never, never!"

"Never!" he answered solemnly. She pressed him closer to her; her breast throbbed against his; her head lay against his—wet, burning.

"You must never leave me!"

"Never!" he said once more with all his heart, and folded her in his arms.

She lay down again as if comforted, took hold of his hand, and became quieter. Every time the sobbing began afresh he bent over her with caressing words, and soothed her.

He dared not go home; he stayed there all night. Marit could not sleep, and he had to sit beside her.

By the following day she had made up her mind what was to be done. She must go to America, and he must accompany her. This prompt decision rather disconcerted him. But neither he nor his sister dared oppose her. The sister, however, managed to give another direction to the girl's thoughts. She said: "You ought to be married to each other first." Marit looked at her and replied: "Yes, you are right. Of course we must be." And this thought began to occupy her mind so much that her grief became less acute. Anders had not been asked; but there was no necessity that he should be.

Then came the first letter from Hans. After telling about his uncle's funeral—how he had made all the arrangements, and what they were—he offered to take over his uncle's business and property.

Anders placed unlimited confidence in his brother; the offer was accepted; hence the journey was given up as needless. As soon as the necessary investigations and valuations had been made, Hans named his figure, and asked his brother if he would not invest this sum in the business. The bank deposits and other securities were sent over at once. These alone produced a sum sufficient not only to pay Anders' debts, but also to allow Marit to make all the improvements at Krogskogen which she fancied. Anders wished her to keep the whole fortune in her own hands, but she ridiculed the idea. So he went into partnership with his brother, and was thenceforth, according to Norwegian ideas, a very wealthy man.

Some months after their marriage a change came over Marit. She gave way to strange impulses, seemed unable to distinguish clearly between dream and reality, and was possessed by a desire to make changes in everything that was under her care, both at home and in their house in town. The people who rented part of the latter had to move. She wished to have the house to herself.

Much of her husband's time was occupied in carrying out her plans, more in watching over herself. His gratitude did not find much expression in words; it was to be read in his eyes, in his increased reverence of manner, and above all in his tender care. He was afraid of losing what had come to him so unexpectedly, or of something giving way. His humility led him to feel that his happiness was undeserved.

Marit clung to him closer than ever. Two expressions she never tired of repeating: "You are my father—and more!" and: "You have the most beautiful eyes in the world; and they are mine." Gradually she gave up many of her wonted occupations. In place of them she took to reading aloud to him. From her childhood she had been accustomed to read to her father; this practice was to be begun again. She read American literature, chiefly poetry—read it in the chanting style in which English verse is recited, and carried conviction by her own sincerity. Her voice was soft; it took hold of the words gently, repeated them quietly, as if from memory.

Then came the time when they went every day together to the hot-house. The flowers there were the harbingers of what was growing within her; she wished to see them every day. "I wonder if they are talking about it," she said.

And one day, when winter had given the first sign of departure from the coast, when they two had gathered the first green leaves in the border beneath the sunny wall, she fell ill and knew that the great hour had come. Without excessive previous suffering, and with her hand in his, she bore a daughter. This had been her wish. But it was not her lot to bring up her child; for three days later she herself was dead.

THE NEW MARIT

THE doctor long feared that Krog, too, would die—of pure over-exertion. During his long solitude he had been unaccustomed to give as much of himself, or to receive as much, as life with Marit demanded and gave. Not until she died did it become apparent how weak he was, how little power of resistance was left him. It took months to restore the feeble remnant so far that he could again bear to have people about him. They told him that the child had been taken to his sister's. They asked him if he would like to see it. He turned away almost angrily. The first thing that seriously occupied his thoughts when he grew stronger was the disposal of his business. About this he consulted with a relation, a cross-grained bachelor, generally known as "Uncle Klaus." Through him the business was sold; but not the house in which it was carried on; this was to remain exactly as it was, in remembrance of Marit.

Anders Krog's first walk was down to the chapel and the grave; and this told upon him so terribly that he became ill again. As soon as he recovered, he announced that it was his intention to go abroad and to remain abroad. His sister came to him in alarm: "This cannot be true. You surely do not mean to leave us and your child?"

"Yes," answered he, bursting into tears; "I cannot bear to live in these rooms."

"But you will at least see the child before you go!"

"No! no! Anything rather than that!"

And he left without seeing her.

But it was, naturally, the child that drew him home again. When she was about three years old she was photographed, and that photograph was irresistible. Such a likeness to her mother, such childlike charm, he could not stay away from. From Constantinople, where he received it, he wrote: "It has taken me nearly three years to go through again the experiences of one. I cannot say that I am in complete possession of them all yet. Many more are certain to recur to me when I see the places again where we were together. But the deeper life and thoughts of these three years have at least taught me no longer to dread these places. On the contrary, I am longing to see them."

The meeting with the new Marit was a joy. Not at once, for she naturally began by being afraid of the strange man with the large eyes. But this made the joy all the greater when she gradually, cautiously, approached him. And when she at last sat upon his knee with her two new dolls, a Turkish man and woman, and shoved them up against his nose to make him sneeze, because "auntie" had sneezed, he said, with tears in his eyes: "I have had only one meeting that was sweeter."

She came, with her nurse, to live with him. Their first walk together was to her mother's grave, on which he wished her to lay flowers. She did it, but was determined to take them away with her again. All their efforts were in vain. The nurse at last picked others for her; but these she would not have; she wanted her own. They were obliged to let her take them and to make her lay the new ones on the grave. Anders thought: This is not like her mother.

The attempt was repeated. Mother's grave was to have fresh flowers every day, and Marit was to lay them there. Anders divided the flowers into two bunches; he carried the one and she the other. She was to leave hers and have his to take home again. But this plan succeeded no better; indeed, worse; for when they were ready to leave the churchyard, she insisted that he, too, should take his flowers back with him. He was obliged to give in to her. Next day he tried something different. She carried flowers to her mother's grave, and he gave her sweets to induce her to let them lie there. Yes, she would give up the flowers in exchange for the sweets, which she put into her mouth. But when they were ready to go, she was determined to have the flowers too. He was quite cast down.

It then occurred to him to tell her that Mother was cold; Marit must cover her up. She thereupon proposed that Mother should come home to her own bed. Her father had told her that the empty bed beside his was Mother's; now she constantly asked if Mother were not coming soon. She could not come, he said; she must lie out there in the cold. This produced the desired effect. Marit herself spread the flowers over the grave and let them lie. On the way home she repeated several times: "Mother is not cold now."

Anders wondered what she understood by "Mother." He wished her to be able to recognise her mother's portraits, but before showing her them, exercised her eye with pictures of animals and things. From these he proceeded to photographs of his sister, of himself, and of others whom she knew. When she was quite familiar with them, he produced the earliest photograph of her mother. There was no difficulty; she was shown several, and quickly learned to distinguish them from all others. In the afternoon, when she had been laid down to sleep, she asked to have "Mother" in her arms. Anders did not understand immediately, and she became impatient. Then he brought the first photograph of her mother. She took it at once, clasped it in her arms, and fell asleep. Not until she was four years old, and saw a mother in the kitchen tending her sick child, was he sure that she understood what a mother is; for then she said: "Why doesn't my mother come and undress me and dress me?"

In the end father and daughter became fast friends. But the greatest pleasure of all came when she was old enough for him to tell her about Mother. About Mother, who had come across the sea to Father, bringing little Marit with her. The walks which he had taken with Mother, the two took together—every one of them. He rowed her as Mother had rowed him; they went to town together as Mother and Father had done. There she sat in the chairs which Mother had bought and sat in. At table she sat in Mother's place; in conservatory and garden among the flowers she was Mother, and helped as Mother had done.

What a clever, beautiful child she was! She had her mother's red hair and brilliantly white skin, her large eyes, and the same delicate, long line of eyebrow. Possibly she would also have the same aquiline nose. The hands with the long fingers were not her mother's, nor was the figure. That very slight forward bend at the joining of head and neck was like her father's. She had not her mother's prettily squared shoulders; Marit's sloped, and the arms descended from them in a more even line. Anders could not resist going up every evening to look at her when she was being undressed. The mixture of the masculine and feminine Krog types, which had hitherto been so uncommon, but which her mother had to a certain extent represented, was complete in her. She grew tall, her eyes large, her head shapely. Her father could not get her to associate with other children; it bored her. They did not transport themselves quickly enough into her imaginary world, which was certainly a curious one. The fields were a circus—her father had told her about Buffalo Bill's. The Indians galloped across the plain; she herself, on a white horse, leading. The ridges were boxes, and they were full of people. This the other children could not see. Nor could they understand the travel-game on the table, which her father had taught her to play.

When she was nearly seven, she compelled her father, who was a good cyclist, to buy her a bicycle and teach her to ride it. But this was the drop which caused the cup to overflow. He decided to call in help.

In Paris he had made the acquaintance of a distant relation, Mrs. Dawes by name. This lady had married in England, but after the death of her only child she left her husband, and supported herself by keeping a boarding-house in Paris. In this boarding-house Krog had admired her extremely. He had seldom met a cleverer woman. Now he asked her if she would come and keep his house and educate his child. She promptly telegraphed "Yes," and within a month had sold her business, travelled to Norway, and entered upon all her duties. A disease of the hip-joint from which she had long suffered had become worse, so that she had difficulty in walking. But from the wheeled arm-chair which she brought with her, and which her stout person completely filled, she managed the whole household, including Anders himself. He was quite alarmed by her cleverness. She seldom left her chair, and yet she knew of everything that happened. Walls did not conceal from her eyes; distance did not exist for her. Much of this power of hers was explained by the acuteness of her senses, by her cleverness in interpreting words and signs, reading looks and expressions and drawing inferences from them, and by her skill in the art of questioning. But there was something that defied explanation. When danger threatened any one she loved, she was aware of it—sitting in her chair. With a loud exclamation—always in English on such occasions—she sprang up, and actually ran. This happened, for instance, on the memorable day when Marit, on her bicycle, fell into the river and was fished out again by two men from the steamer; for it was close to the landing-place that the accident occurred; she was on her way there. On the way home she and Mrs. Dawes met—the one dripping with sea-water and screaming, the other dripping with perspiration and screaming.

Mrs. Dawes went the round of the house every day—outside, if necessary, as well as inside—but she seldom went farther. On this round she saw everything—including what was about to happen, the servants declared.

There was a suggestion of floating about her. She sat floating in paper. She carried on, at least according to Anders Krog, a constant correspondence with every one who had ever lived in her house. It was carried on in all languages and upon all subjects; a considerable part of her time was spent in introducing what she read—and she read far into the night—into her letters. She moved her chair to the table on which lay her desk; then she turned away from the table to read. Fastened to the arm of the chair was a reading-desk, on which she laid the book; she seldom held it in her hand. Memoirs were her favourite reading; gossip from them she at once transferred to her letters. Next came art magazines and books of travel. She had a little money of her own, and bought what she wanted.

Along with all this she taught the child. The two sat at the big table in the drawing-room, "Aunt Eva" in her chair of state, the little girl opposite her. But whenever it was necessary, Marit had to come round and stand beside Aunt Eva's desk. The hours of instruction passed so pleasantly that the little one often forgot that she was at lessons. Her father, whose library opened out of the drawing-room, often forgot it too, when he came in and listened to the conversations or to what Mrs. Dawes was telling.

Lessons might be easy, but something else was difficult and led to conflict. Mrs. Dawes wished to bring about a general alteration in the child's habits, and here she had the father against her. But he was, of course, worsted, and that before he understood what she was about. Marit had to learn to obey; she had to learn the meaning of punctuality, of order, of politeness, of tact. She had to practise every day, to hold herself straight at table, to wash her hands an unlimited number of times, always to tell where she was going—and all this against her own will, and really against her father's, too.

Mrs. Dawes had one sure base from which to operate. This was the child's unbounded faith in her mother's perfection. She convinced Marit that her mother had never gone to bed later than eight o'clock. Before getting into bed, too, Mother had always arranged her clothes upon a chair and set her shoes outside the door.

From what Mother had done, and done to perfection, Mrs. Dawes went on to what Mother would have done if she had been in Marit's place, and, also, to what she would not have done if she had been Marit. This proved harder. When Mrs. Dawes, for instance, assured her that her mother had never ridden out of sight on her bicycle, Marit asked: "How do you know that?" "I know it because I know that your father and mother were never away from each other." "That is true, Marit," said her father, glad to be able for once to confirm one of Mrs. Dawes's assertions; most of them were not true.

The farther the work of education progressed, the more interested in it did Mrs. Dawes become, and the stronger did her hold on the child grow. She set herself the task of eradicating Marit's dream-life, an inheritance from her mother, which flourished exuberantly as long as her father encouraged it and took pleasure in it.

One spring Marit rushed in and told her father that in a hollow in the old tree between Mother's and Grandmother's graves there was a little nest, and in the nest were tiny, tiny little eggs. "It's a message from Mother, isn't it?" He nodded, and went with her to look at it. But when they came near, the bird flew out piping lamentably. "Mother says we are not to go nearer?" questioned Marit. To this her father answered: "Yes." "It would be the same as disturbing Mother if we did?" continued she. He nodded.—They walked back to the house, perfectly happy, talking of Mother all the way. When Marit told Mrs. Dawes about this afterwards, Mrs. Dawes said to her: "Your father answers 'Yes' to such questions because he does not want to grieve you, child. If your Mother could send you a message, she would come herself." There was no end to the revolution which those few cruel words wrought. They altered even the relation between the child and her father.

The lessons went on steadily, and so did the training, until Marit was nearly thirteen—tall, very thin, large-eyed, with luxuriant red hair and a pure white skin guiltless of freckles, which was Mrs. Dawes's pride.

About this time Krog came in one day from the library to stop the lessons. This had not happened during all the years they had gone on. Marit was allowed to go. Mrs. Dawes accompanied Anders into the library.

"Be kind enough to read this letter."

She read, and learned what she had had no idea of—that the man who was standing before her, watching her face whilst she read, was a millionaire—and that not in kroner, but in dollars. Since receiving the bank deposits and shares at the time of his uncle's death, he had drawn nothing from America—and this was the result.

"I congratulate you," said Mrs. Dawes, and seized his right hand in both of hers. Her eyes filled with tears: "And I understand you, dear Mr. Krog; it is your wish that we should travel now."

He looked at her, a glad smile in his bright eyes. "Have you any objection, Mrs. Dawes?"

"Not if we take servants with us. You know how lame I am."

"Servants you shall have, and we shall keep a carriage wherever we are. Lessons can go on, can't they?"

"Of course they can. Better than ever!" She beamed and wept. She said to herself that she had never felt so happy.

A fortnight later the three, with maid and manservant, had left Krogskogen.

THE SCEPTRE CHANGES HANDS

TWO years and a half passed, during the course of which Krog was at home several times, unaccompanied by the others. Then it was determined that they should all spend a summer at Krogskogen. With this project in view the three were in a draper's shop in Vienna. Mrs. Dawes and Marit were to have new clothes, Marit especially being in need of them, as she had grown out of hers. It was the first week of May; summer dresses were to be chosen.

"We think, both your father and I, that you must have long dresses now. You are so tall."

Marit looked at her father, but the materials which lay spread out in front of him engaged his attention. Mrs. Dawes spoke for him.

"Your father says that when you are walking with him, gentlemen look at your legs."

Krog began to fidget. Even the lady behind the counter felt that there was thunder in the air. She did not understand the language, but she saw the three faces. At last Anders heard Marit answering in a curious, but quite pleasant voice:

"Is it because Mother had long dresses when she was my age that I am to have them?"

Mrs. Dawes looked with dismay at Anders Krog; but he turned away.

"Aunt Eva," began Marit again; "of course you were with Mother then? at the time she got long dresses? Or was it Father?"

No more was said about long dresses. No more was said at all. They left the shop.

Nothing else happened. As if it had been a matter of course, next day, instead of coming to lessons, she drove with her father, first to arrange about the dresses, and then to the picture-galleries. They went sight-seeing every day until they left. There were no more lessons. In the evenings the three went, as if nothing had occurred, to concert, opera, or theatre. They wished to make good use of the remaining time.

At the beginning of June they were in Copenhagen. There a letter awaited them from "Uncle Klaus." Jörgen Thiis, his adopted son, had received his commission as lieutenant; Klaus meant to give a summer ball at his country-house, but was waiting until they came home. When were they coming?

Marit was delighted at the prospect. She remembered handsome, tall Jörgen. He was a son of the Amtmand[A]; his mother was Klaus Krog's sister.

[A] Chief magistrate of the district.

A ball-dress had now to be thought out; but the deliberations were short, nothing being said on the subject until they were on their way to order it. The one really exciting question: Ought not this dress to be long? they did not discuss. When the decisive moment arrived, and the length of the skirt was to be taken, the dressmaker who was measuring said: "I suppose the young lady's dress is to be long?" Marit looked at Mrs. Dawes, who turned red. What was worse, the dressmaker herself blushed. Then she hastily took the length of the short dress which Marit was wearing.

The ball was given on the 20th of June, a sultry day, without sun. The guests were assembled in the garden in front of the large country-house, when the sailing-boat came in which brought Marit and her father; they were the last to arrive. Old Klaus—tall, thin, wearing remarkably wide white trousers—stalked down to receive her. Standing hatless, with shining bald head and perspiring face, he stopped her with a motion of his hand whilst he looked down at Anders in the boat.

"Are you not coming?"

"No, no! Thanks all the same!"

Off went the boat. Not till now did Klaus look at Marit, whom Mrs. Dawes in her long letters had described as the most beautiful girl she had ever seen. He stared, he bowed, and approached her, reeking of tobacco, his big, smiling, open mouth disclosing unclean teeth. He offered his arm. But Marit, who was wearing a long sleeveless cloak which reached to the ground, pretended not to see this. Klaus was offended, but escorted her up to the others, saying as they arrived: "Here I come with the queen of the ball." This displeased her, and every one else, so the beginning was unfortunate. Jörgen, whose place it was to do so, hastened forward to take her cloak and hat; but she bowed slightly and passed on. There was style in this! As soon as she was out of hearing, comment began. Her bearing in passing them, her face, carriage, gait, the dazzlingly white skin, the sparkling eyes, the arch above them, the shape of the nose—everything was perfect, and made a perfect whole. It was all over with Jörgen Thiis. He himself was a tall, slender man of the Krog type, but with eyes peculiar to himself. At present these were fixed on the door through which Marit had disappeared. He was waiting on the steps.

And when she came out again and stepped forward to take his arm and be conducted down to the others, she was a sight to see—in a short dress of light sea-blue silky material, with transparent silk stockings of the same colour, and silvery shoes with antique buckles. The company were unanimous in admiration, and were still expressing it as they trooped in to take their places at the tables. Nor was the subject dropped there; Marit's beauty became the talk of the town. To think that these regular features and bright eyes, and that white, white skin should be framed in such a glory of red hair! And the whole was in perfect keeping with the tall figure, the slight forward inclination of the shoulders, and a bosom which, though not fully developed yet, nevertheless stood out distinct and free.

The arms, the wrists, the hips, the legs!—it became positively comical when a group of young men were heard maintaining with the utmost eagerness that the ankles were more superb than anything else. Such ankles had never been seen—so slender and so beautifully shaped—no, never!

Jörgen Thiis forgot to speak; he even for a considerable time forgot to eat, though, as a rule, he liked nothing better. He followed Marit about like a sleep-walker. She was never to be seen without him behind her or at her side.

Her father and Mrs. Dawes had, on account of the ball, come in to the town house. They were awakened at dawn of day by loud talking and laughter outside, ending with cheers; the whole company had seen Marit home.

Next day the relations and friends of the Krog family came to call. The elder people who had been at the ball considered Marit to be the most beautiful creature they had ever seen. At nine o'clock in the evening old Klaus had rowed into town and trudged round for the express purpose of getting some of his friends to come out and see her.

In the afternoon Jörgen presented himself in uniform, with new gloves. He had taken the liberty of calling to ask how Miss Krog was. But nothing had as yet been heard of that young lady.

When she did make her appearance, her mind was not occupied with yesterday, but with something quite different. This Mrs. Dawes felt at once. The queen of the ball told nothing about the ball. She contented herself with asking if they had been awakened. Then she went and had something to eat. When she came back, her father told her that Jörgen had called to ask how she was. Marit smiled.

"Do you not like Jörgen?" asked Mrs. Dawes.

"Yes."

"Why did you smile, then?"

"He ate so much."

"His father, the Amtmand, does the same," remarked Krog, laughing. "And he always picks out the daintiest morsels."

"Yes, exactly."

Mrs. Dawes sat waiting for what was to come next; for something was coming. Marit left the room; in a short time she appeared again with her hat on and a parasol in her hand.

"Are you going out?" asked Mrs. Dawes.

Marit was standing pulling on her gloves.

"I am going to order visiting-cards."

"Have you no cards?"

"Yes, but they are not suitable now."

"Why not?" said Mrs. Dawes, much surprised. "You thought them so pretty when we bought them, in Italy."

"Yes—but what I don't think suits me any longer is the name."

"The name?"

Both looked up.

"I feel exactly as if it were no longer mine."

"Marit does not suit you?" said Mrs. Dawes.

Her father added gently: "It was your mother's name."

Marit did not answer at once; she felt the dismay in her father's eyes.

"What do you wish to be called, then, child?" It was again Mrs. Dawes who spoke.

"Mary."

"Mary?"

"Yes. That suits better, it seems to me."

The silent astonishment of her companions evidently troubled her. She added:

"Besides, we are going to America now. There they say Mary."

"But you were baptised Marit," put in her father at last.

"What does that matter?"

"It stands in your certificate of baptism, child," added Mrs. Dawes; "it is your name."

"Yes, it is in the certificate, no doubt—but not in me."

The others stared.

"This grieves your father, child."

"Father is welcome to go on calling me Marit."

Mrs. Dawes looked at her sorrowfully, but said no more. Marit had finished putting on her gloves.

"In America I am called Mary. I know that. Here is a specimen card. It looks nice; doesn't it?"

She drew a very small card from her card-case. Mrs. Dawes looked at it, then handed it to Anders. Upon it was inscribed in minute Italian characters:

Mary Krog.

Anders looked at it, looked long; then laid it on the table, took up his newspaper, and sat as if he were reading.

"I am sorry, Father, that you take it in this way."

Anders Krog said once more, gently, without looking up from his newspaper: "Marit is your mother's name."

"I, too, am fond of Mother's name. But it does not suit me."

She quietly left the room. Mrs. Dawes, who was sitting at the window, watched her going along the street. Anders Krog laid down the newspaper; he could not read. Mrs. Dawes made an attempt to comfort him. "There is something in what she says; Marit no longer suits her."

"Her mother's name," repeated Anders Krog; and the tears fell.

THREE YEARS LATER

THREE years later, in Paris, on a beautiful spring day after rain, Mary and her relation, Alice Clerc, drove down the Avenue du Bois de Boulogne towards the gilded entrance gate. The two had made each other's acquaintance in America, and had met again a year ago in Paris. Alice Clerc lived in Paris now with her father. Mr. Clerc had been the principal dealer in works of art in New York. His wife was a Norwegian lady of the Krog family. After her death he sold his enormous business. The daughter had been brought up in art surroundings, and her art training had been thorough. She had seen the picture-galleries and museums of all countries—had dragged her father as far as Japan. Their house in the Champs Elysées was full of works of art. And she had her own studio there; she modelled. Alice was no longer young; she was a stout, strong person, good-natured and lively.

Anders Krog and his companions had this year come from Spain. The two friends were talking of a portrait of Mary which had been sent from Spain to Alice, and afterwards to Norway. Alice maintained that the artist had plainly intended to produce a resemblance to Donatello's St. Cecilia—in the position of the head, in the shape of the eye, in the line of the neck, and the half-open mouth. But, interesting as this experiment might be, it took away from the likeness. It was, for instance, a loss to the portrait that the eyes were not seen; they were cast down, as in Donatello's work. Mary laughed. It was on purpose to have this resemblance brought out that she had sat for it.

Alice now began to talk about a Norwegian engineer officer whom she had known since the days when she went to Norway in summer with her mother. He had seen Mary's portrait at the Clercs' house, and had fallen in love with it.

"Really?" answered Mary absently.

"He is not the ordinary man, I assure you, nor is it the ordinary falling in love."

"Indeed?"

"I am preparing you. You will of course meet at our house."

"Is that necessary?"

"Very. At least I shall be made to pay for it if you don't."

"Dear me! is he dangerous?"

Alice laughed: "I find him so, at any rate."

"O ho! that alters the situation."

"Now you are misunderstanding me. Wait till you see him."

"Is he so very good-looking?"

Alice laughed. "No, he is positively ugly. Just wait."

As they drove on, the Avenue became more crowded; it was one of the great days.

"What is his name?"

"Frans Röy."

"Röy? That is our lady doctor's name—Miss Röy."

"Yes, she is his sister, he often talks of her."

"She is a fine-looking woman."

Alice drew herself up. "You should see *him*. When I walk with him in the street, people turn round to take another look at him. He is a giant! But not of the kind that run to muscle and flesh. No, very tall, agile."

"A trained athlete, I suppose?"

"Magnificent! His strength is what he is proudest of and delights most in displaying."

"Is he stupid, then?"

"Stupid? Frans Röy?——" She leaned back again, and Mary asked no more.

They had been late in setting out. Endless rows of returning carriages passed them. The three broad driving-roads of the Avenue were crowded. The nearer they came to the iron gate where these three meet in one, the more compact did the rows become. The display of light, many-coloured spring costumes on this first day of sunshine after rain was a unique sight. Amongst the fresh foliage the carriages looked like baskets of flowers among green leaves—one behind the other, one alongside of the other, without beginning, without end.

At the iron gate they came close to the undulating crowd of pedestrians. No sooner were they inside than a disturbance communicated itself from right to left. The people on the right must see something invisible to the others. Some of them were screaming and pointing in the direction of the lakes; the carriages were ordered to drive either to the side or into the cross-roads; the agitation increased; it was soon universal. Gendarmes and park-keepers rushed hither and thither; the carriages were packed so closely together that none of them could move on. A broad space in the centre was soon clear for a considerable distance. All gazed, all questioned ... there it came! A pair of frantic horses with a heavy carriage behind them. On the box both coachman and groom were to be seen. There must have been a struggle, since there had been time to clear the way; or else the horses must have bolted a long way off. Up here, inside the gate, all the carriages had disappeared from the central passage. Alice's stood blocked nearest the gate, against the left footpath. They hear shouts behind them; probably the whole Avenue is being cleared. But no one looks that way, all gaze straight ahead, at the magnificent animals that are tearing frantically towards them. Driven by curiosity, the crowds on both sides swayed back and forwards. Terrified voices outside the gate cried: "Shut the gates!" A furious protest, a thousand-voiced jeer, answered them from within. In the carriages every one was standing; many had mounted the seats, Mary and Alice among the number. It seemed as if the horses' pace increased the nearer they came; both coachman and groom were tugging at the reins with might and main, but this only excited them the more. A man wearing a tall hat was leaning his whole body out of the carriage, probably to discover where he was going to break his neck. Some dogs were following, with strenuous protest. Up here they allured others on to the road, but these did not venture far out. Two or three that did, knocked up against each other with such violence that one fell and was run over; the carriage bounded, the dog howled; his comrades stopped for a moment.

Now a man, disengaging himself from the crowd at the iron gate, ran into the middle of the road. People shouted to him; they waved with sticks and umbrellas; they threatened. Two gendarmes ventured out a few steps after him and gesticulated and shouted; a single park-keeper inside the gate did the same, but ran back terrified. Instead of attending to these shouts and threats, the man measured the horses with his eye, moved to the left, to the right, back again to the left ... evidently preparing to throw himself on them.

The moment the crowd comprehended this, it became silent, so silent that the birds could be heard singing in the trees. And heard, too, the dull, distant sound from the giant town, which never ceases, borne hither by the breeze. Its monotonous tone underlay the twitter of the birds. Strange it was, but the horses of the carriages drawn up by the roadside stood as intent as the human beings; they did not stir a foot.

The frantic pair reach the man in the middle of the avenue. He turns with the speed of an arrow in the direction they are going, and runs along with them, flinging himself against the side of the horse next him....

"It is he!" cried Alice, deathly pale, and gripping Mary so violently that they were both on the point of toppling over. Women's screams resounded wild and shrill, the deeper roars of the men following. He was now hanging on to the horse. Alice closed her eyes. Mary turned away. Was he running, or was he being dragged? Stop them he could not!

Again a few seconds of terrible silence; only the dogs and the horses' hoofs were heard. Then a short cry, then thousands, then jubilation, wild, endless jubilation—handkerchiefs waving, and hats and parasols. The crowd burst into the Avenue again from both sides like a flood. The space by the gate was filled in an instant. The frenzied animals stood trembling, in a lather of foam, close to Alice's carriage. Mary saw a grey-clad Englishman, an erect old man with a white beard and a tall hat; she saw a young lady hanging on his arm, and she heard him say: "Well done, young man!" A roar of laughter followed. And not till now did she see him who had evoked it—still gripping the horse's nostrils, hatless, waistcoat torn, hand bleeding, his perspiring, excited face at this moment turned laughingly towards the Englishman. At exactly the same time the man caught sight of Alice, who was still standing on the seat of her carriage. He instantly deserted horses, carriage, Englishman, and forced his way through the crowd towards her.

"Dear people, get me out of this!" he said quickly, in the broadest of "Eastern" Norwegian. Before Alice had time to answer, or even to step down from the seat, and long before the groom could swing himself down from the box, he had opened the carriage door and was standing beside them. He handed first Alice and then her friend down from the seat. Then he said to the coachman in French:

"Drive me home as soon as you can move. You remember the address?"

"Yes, Monsieur le Capitaine," replied the coachman, touching his hat respectfully, with a look of admiration.

As Frans Röy turned to sit down, his face contracted, and he exclaimed, catching hold of his foot: "Oh!——the devil! that brute must have trodden on me. I never felt it till now."

As he spoke, he met Mary's large, astonished eyes; he had not looked at her before, not even when he was assisting her down from the seat. The change in his expression was so sudden and so extremely comical that both ladies burst out laughing. Frans raised his bleeding hand to his hat—and discovered that he had no hat. Then he laughed too.

The coachman had in the meantime manœuvred them a few yards forwards, and they were beginning to turn.

"I don't suppose I need tell you who she is?" laughed Alice.

"No," answered Röy, looking so hard at Mary that she blushed.

"Good heavens! Think of your daring to do that!" It was Alice who spoke.

"Oh! It's not so dangerous as it looks," he replied, without taking his eyes off Mary. "There's a trick in it. I've done it twice before." He was speaking to Mary alone. "I saw at once that only one horse had lost its head; the other was being dragged along. So I went for the mad one.—Goodness! what a sight I am!" He had not discovered till now that his waistcoat was in rags, that his watch was gone, and that blood was dripping from his hand. Mary offered him her handkerchief. He looked at the delicate square of embroidery and then at her again: "No, Miss Krog; that would be like stitching birch-bark with silk."

Röy lived quite near the iron gate, to the right, so they arrived in a few moments. Thanking them heartily, and without offering his bleeding hand, he jumped out. Whilst he limped across the pavement, erect, huge, and the carriage was turning, Alice whispered in English: "If one could only have a model like that, Mary!"

Mary looked at her in surprise: "Well—is it not possible?"

Alice looked back at Mary, still more surprised: "Nude, I mean."

Mary almost started from her seat, then bent forward and looked straight into Alice's face. Alice met her eyes with a teasing laugh.

Mary leaned back and gazed straight in front of her.

On account of the injury to his foot, Frans Röy had to keep quiet for some days. The first time he called on Alice, Mary, according to agreement, was sent for. But she felt so strangely agitated that she dared not go. Next time curiosity, or whatever the feeling was, brought her. But she came late, and hardly had she looked him in the face again before she wished that she had not come. There was an intensity about him which the fine lady felt to be intrusive, almost insulting. Her whole being was like a surging sea; she followed him with her eyes and with her ears; her thoughts were in a whirl, and so was her blood. This must pass over soon, she thought. But it did not. Alice's entrancement—love, to call it by the right name—audible and visible in every word, every look, added to her confusion. Was he really so ugly? That broad, upright forehead, these small, sparkling eyes, the compressed lips and projecting chin, produced in conjunction an impression of unusual strength; but the face was made comical by there being no nose to speak of. Very comical, too, was most of his conversation. He was in such high spirits and so full of fun and fancies that the rattle never ceased. His manners were not overbearing; on the contrary, he was politeness itself, attentive, at times quite the gallant. What overpowered was his forcefulness. Force spoke in his voice and glanced from his eyes. But the body, too, played its part—the strong hand, the small foot, compact, the shoulders, the neck, the chest—these spoke too, they insisted, they demonstrated. One could not escape from them for a moment. And the talk never ceased.

Mary was unaccustomed to any style of conversation except that of international society—light talk of wind and weather, of the events of the day, of literature and art, of incidents of travel—the whole at arm's length. Here everything was personal and almost intimate. She felt that she herself acted upon Frans like wine. His intoxication increased; he let himself go more and more. This excited her too much; it gave her a feeling of insecurity. As soon as politeness allowed of it, she took leave, nervous, confused, as a matter of fact in wild retreat. She promised herself solemnly that she would never go back again.

Not until later in the day did she join her father and Mrs. Dawes. She did not say a word about her meeting with Frans Röy. Nor had she done so on the previous occasion. Mrs. Dawes told her to look at a visiting-card which was lying on the table.

"Jörgen Thiis? Is he here?"

"He has been here all winter. But he had only just heard of our arrival."

"He asked to be remembered to you," put in Anders, who was, as usual, sitting reading.

It was a rest even to think of Jörgen Thiis. Last winter he and she had seen a good deal of each other in Paris. Both at private houses and at official balls at the Elysées and the Hôtel de Ville he had been of their party. He was a squire to be proud of, good-looking, gentlemanly, courteous.

Her father mentioned that Jörgen was intending to exchange into the diplomatic service.

"Surely money is required for that?" said Mary.

"He is Uncle Klaus's heir," replied Mrs. Dawes.

"Are you certain of this?"

"No, not certain."

"And has not Uncle Klaus lost a good deal of money lately?"

Mrs. Dawes did not answer. Krog said:

"We have heard something to that effect."

"In that case will he be able to help him?"

No one replied.

"Then it does not seem to me that Jörgen's prospects are particularly good," concluded Mary.

Röy was in France on special Government business, which often took him away from Paris. He had to go just at this time, so Mary felt safe. But one morning when she made an early call on Alice—the two had arranged to go into town together—there he sat! He jumped up and came towards her, his eyes beaming admiration and delight upon her. He seized her hand in both of his. She had never beheld such radiant happiness. She felt herself turn scarlet. Alice laughed, which made things worse. But Frans Röy's loquacity came to their assistance. It was excessive to-day even for him. He plunged at once into a description of a gigantic foundry from which he had just come, and drew them along with him. They saw the half-naked men standing with their hooks on the edge of the stream of boiling, bubbling, fiery-red metal; they felt the power of the machinery, and saw the human beings creeping among it like cautious ants in a giant forest. He tried, too, to explain this machinery to them in detail. And he made them understand perfectly; but time wore on, and the two friends had to go.

Alice was in the best of spirits during their drive. It was so evident that Frans had made a strong impression to-day.

On the following morning Mary went off on a motor excursion with some American friends. She was away for several days. And the first thing she did on her return was to call on Alice. There, sure enough, sat Frans Röy! Both he and Alice jumped up, delighted. Alice embraced and kissed her. "Runaway, runaway!" she exclaimed. It is not enough to say that Frans Röy's eyes sparkled; they fired a royal salute. From the moment Mary shook hands with him, he talked incessantly. He was so foolishly in love that Alice began to feel alarmed. Fortunately he had to go soon, to keep a business appointment. Mary was left in a stormy swell; the sea would not go down. Alice saw this and tried to calm her by eager, anxious attempts to explain him. But this only further confused her; she left.

As she came downstairs to join her father and Mrs. Dawes in the afternoon—she had felt it necessary to take a rest—she heard piano-playing. She knew at once that it was Jörgen Thiis who was entertaining the old people. He was a first-rate musician, and he loved their piano. It was to go with them to Norway. She went straight up to him, and thanked him for being so attentive to her father and Aunt Eva; unfortunately they were left much alone. He replied that their appreciation of his music gratified him exceedingly, and that the piano was a great attraction, being a particularly fine instrument.

The conversation during and after dinner showed Mary how accustomed these three were to be together; they could do without her. She felt really grateful, and they had a pleasant evening. There was much talk of home, for which the old people were longing.

Jörgen was hardly gone before Mrs. Dawes said: "What a pleasant, well-bred man Jörgen is, child!"

Anders looked at Mary and smiled.

"At what are you smiling, Father?"

"Nothing"—his smile growing broader.

"You want to know my opinion of him?"

"Yes, what do you think of him?"

Mrs. Dawes was all ear.

"Well...."

"You have not made up your mind?"

"Yes ... yes."

"Speak out, then."

"I do really like him."

"But there is a something?"

Now it was she who smiled. "I don't like the way his eyes seem to draw me in."

Her father laughed:

"To gloat over you like food. Eh?"

"Yes, exactly."

"He's a bon-viveur, you see—like his father."

"But, like his father, he has so many good qualities," put in Mrs. Dawes.

"He has," said Anders Krog seriously.

Mary said no more. She bade them good-night, and offered him her forehead to kiss.

A few days later Mary went to Alice's house at an early hour. Anders Krog had seen some old Chinese porcelain which he thought of buying; but Alice's advice was indispensable. At this time of day and in the studio Mary could be certain of finding her alone—at least alone with her model.

She went straight in without speaking to the porter. Alice opened the door herself. She had on her studio-dress and her hand was dirty, so that she could not take Mary's.

"You are busy with a model," whispered Mary.

"I shall be presently," answered Alice with a curious smile. "The model is waiting in the next room. But come in."

When Mary passed beyond the curtain she saw the reason why the model was waiting in the next room. In the studio sat Frans Röy. Thus early in the day and rapt in thought! He did not even notice them entering. This was the first time Mary had seen him serious; and seriousness became the manly figure and the strong face much better than wanton hilarity.

"Do you not see who has come?" asked Alice.

He sprang up....

The conversation that day was serious. Frans was in a dejected mood; it was easy for Mary to divine that they had been talking about her.

They all consequently felt a little awkward at first, until Alice turned the conversation on a topic from that morning's newspapers. Two murders, instigated by jealousy—one of them of the most terrible description—had horrified them all, but especially Frans. He maintained that the idea of the marriage relation peculiar to the Romance nations is still that of the age when the wife was the husband's property, and when, in consequence of this, unfaithfulness was punished by death. Christianity, he allowed, in course of time, also made the husband the wife's property, especially in Roman Catholic countries. In these the spouses rivalled each other in killing—the wife the husband, the husband the wife. This assertion gave rise to an argument. Mary agreed that neither of the contracting parties owned the other. After marriage, as before, they were free individuals, with a right to dispose of themselves. Love alone decided. If love ceased, because development made of one or other a different being from what he or she was at the time of marriage; or if one of them met another human being who took possession of his or her soul and thoughts and changed the whole tenor of life, then the deserted spouse must submit—neither condemn nor kill. But Frans Röy and she disagreed when they discussed what ought to separate husband and wife—and still more when they came to what ought to keep them together. She was much more exacting than he. He suggested jokingly that her theory was: Married people have full liberty to separate, but this liberty they must not use. She declared his to be: Married people ought as a rule to separate; if they have no real reason, they can borrow one.

This conversation meant more to them than the words implied. It impressed him as a new beauty in her that she was queenly. This cast a new glory over all the rest.

The queenliness did not consist in desire to rule. It was purely self-defence; but the loftiest. Her whole nature was concentrated in it, luminously. "Touch me not!" said eyes, voice, bearing. There was preparedness, undoubtedly, if need were, for the martyr's crown. She became much greater—but also more helpless. Such as she look too high and fall the first step they take. And great is generally their fall.

Frans gazed at her; he forgot to answer, forgot what she had said. He seemed to hear a voice calling: "Protect her!" Chivalry entered into his love, and issued its high behests.

Mary saw him withdraw himself from their conversation; but this did not stop her; the subject was too absorbing. When he came back to it again he heard her divulging her inmost thoughts, undoubtedly with no idea that she was doing so. She told what she had thought ever since she could think on such subjects at all. It came as naturally to her to do so as to lift her dress where the road was dirty, or to swim when she could no longer keep her footing.—Individuality must be preserved, must grow, be neither curbed nor soiled. With this she began, with this she ended. But she was all the time conscious of a curious attraction towards Frans which led her to speak out. It was so long since they had been together. She did not know that the person who can draw forth our thoughts is, in the nature of things, a person who has power over us. She only felt that she was obliged to speak—and to keep control over herself. A sweet feeling, which she experienced for the first time.

The conversation changed into talk which became ever more intimate, and lost itself at last in a silence of looks and long-drawn breaths. Alice had gone to her model. They became confused when they discovered that they were alone. They stopped talking and looked away from each other.

After short visits to one and another of the many works of art in the studio, their attention concentrated itself on a faun without arms. It stood laughing at them. They talked about this fragment of antique sculpture merely that there might not be silence. Where had it been found? To what age did it belong? It must surely have been an animal. They spoke in subdued tones, with caressing voices, and unsteady eyes. Nor were their feet steadier. They felt themselves lighter than before, as if they were in higher air. And it seemed to them as if their thoughts lay bare, and they themselves were transparent.

Presently Alice joined them again. She looked at them with eyes that awoke both. "Have you done with marriage now?" she asked. It was about marriage they had been talking when she left them.

Mary remembered that she had an errand, and that her carriage was waiting. Frans Röy also remembered what he ought to be doing. They went off together, across the court and through the outer gate, to her carriage. But they could not strike the same tone as before, so they did not speak.

Hat in hand, Frans opened the carriage-door. Mary got in without raising her eyes. When, after seating herself, she turned to bow, the strongest eyes she had ever looked into were waiting for her—full of passion and reverence.

Two hours later Frans was with Alice again. He could not remain longer alone with his heaven-storming hopes.

Where had he been in the interval? In town, buying a cast of Donatello's St. Cecilia. He had been obliged to compare. But Alice of course knew, he said, how wretchedly inferior Donatello's Cecilia was.

Alice began to be seriously alarmed. "My dear friend, you will spoil everything for yourself. It is in your nature."

He answered proudly: "Never yet have I seriously set myself an aim which I have not accomplished."

"I quite believe that. You can work, you can overcome difficulties, and you can also wait."

"I can."

"But you cannot suppress yourself; you cannot allow her to come to you."

Frans was hurt. "What do you mean, Alice?"

"I want to remind you, dear friend, that you don't know Mary; you don't know the world she lives in. You are a bear from the backwoods."

"It may be that I am a bear. I don't deny that. But what if she should have become fond of a bear? One is not easily mistaken in such matters."

He would not allow his high hopes to be cast down. He came beseechingly towards her—even tried to embrace her; he was given to hugging.

"Come now, Frans; behave yourself. And remember, this is the second time you have disturbed me."

"You shall be disturbed. You shall not go on modelling your prisoner in there. Dear Alice, my own friend—you shall model my happiness."

"What more can I do for you than I have done?"

"You can procure me admission to the house."

"That is not such an easy matter."

"Bah! You can manage it quite well. You must! you must!"

He talked, coaxed, caressed, until she gave in and promised.

Whatever the reason, her attempt was a failure.

"If I asked my father to receive a young man who has not been introduced to him, he would misunderstand me," said Mary. Alice admitted this at once. She was angry with herself for not having thought of it. Instead of consulting with Mary as to whether the thing might not be managed in another way, she gave up the project altogether. She was still annoyed when she communicated the result to Frans Röy; she had the feeling, she said, that Mary objected to the interference of any third person. She impressed on him again that he must be careful. Frans was miserable. Alice made no attempt to comfort him.

He came back next day. "I cannot give it up," said he. "And I cannot think of anything else."

So long did he sit there, so often did he repeat exactly the same thing in different words, and so unhappy was he, that good-natured Alice became sorry for him.

"Listen!" she said. "I'll invite you and the Krogs here together. Then perhaps the invitation to their house will come of itself."

He jumped up. "That is a splendid idea! Please do, dear Alice!"

"I can't do it immediately. Mr. Krog is ill. We must wait."

He stood looking at her, much disappointed. "But can you not arrange a meeting between us two again?"

"Yes, that I might do."

"Do it then—as soon as possible! dear, dear Alice—as soon as possible!"

This time Alice was successful. Mary was quite ready to meet him again.

They met at Alice's house, to drive together to the exhibition in the Champs Elysées.

To stand together before works of art is the real conversation without words. The few words that are spoken awake hundreds. But these remain unspoken. The one friend feels through the other, or at least they both believe that they do so. They meet in one picture, to separate in another. An hour thus spent teaches them more of each other than weeks of ordinary intercourse. Alice led the two from picture to picture, but was absorbed in her own thoughts—the more completely the farther they went. She saw as an artist sees. The others, who began with the pictures, gradually passed on to discovery of each other through these. With them it was soon a play of undertones, rapid glances, short ejaculations, pointing fingers. But those who feel their way to each other by secret paths enjoy the process exceedingly, and generally allow it to be perceived that they do so. They play a game like that of a pair of sea-birds that dive and come up again far away from each other—to find their way back to each other. The happiness of the moment was increased by the number of eyes which were turned on them.

Downstairs amongst the statuary, Alice led them straight to the centre room. She stopped in front of an empty pedestal and turned to the official in charge. "Is the acrobat not ready yet?" "No, Mademoiselle," he answered; "unfortunately not."

"There must have been another accident?"

"I do not know, Mademoiselle."

Alice explained to Mary that the statue of an acrobat had been broken in the process of setting it up.

"An acrobat?" called Frans Röy. He was standing a short way off; now he hastened up to them. "An acrobat? Did I hear you speaking about an acrobat?"

"Yes," said they, and laughed.

"Is that anything to laugh at?" said he. "I have a cousin who is an acrobat."

The ladies laughed more heartily. Frans was greatly astonished.

"I assure you he is one of the best fellows I know. And marvellously clever. The talent runs in our family. As a boy I was two whole summers in the circus with him."

The others laughed.

"What the deuce can you be laughing at? I never had a better time in my life than in the circus."

The two ladies, unable to control their merriment, hurried towards the door. Röy was obliged to follow, but was offended.

"I have not the faintest idea what is amusing you," he said, when they were all seated in the carriage. Nevertheless he laughed himself.

The little misunderstanding resulted in all three being in the best of humours when they stopped in front of Mary's house. Alice and Frans Röy drove on without her. Frans turned blissfully to Alice and asked if he had not been a good boy to-day? if he had not kept himself well in hand? if his "affair" were not progressing splendidly? He did not wait for her answer; he laughed and chattered; and he was determined to go in with her. But this Alice had no intention of allowing. Then he demanded, as his reward for not persisting, that she should take them both for a drive in the Bois de Boulogne, in the direction of La Bagatelle. It was to be in the morning, about nine o'clock; then the scent of the trees would be strongest, the song of the birds fullest; and then they would still have the place to themselves. This she promised.

On the following Friday she called for Mary before nine in the morning, and they drove on to pick up Frans Röy.

From a long way off Alice saw him marching up and down on the pavement. His face and bearing filled her with a presentiment of mischief. Mary could not see him until they stopped. But then a flame rushed into her face, kindled by the fire in his. He boarded the carriage like a captured vessel. Alice hastened to attract his attention in order to avoid an immediate outburst.

"How lovely the morning is," she said; "just because the sun is not shining in its full strength! Nothing can be more beautiful than this subdued tone over a scene as full of colour as that towards which we are driving."

But Frans did not hear; he understood nothing but Mary. The white veil thrown back over her red hair, the fresh, half open mouth, deprived him of his senses. Alice remarked that the woods had become more fragrant since the Japanese trees had grown up. Each time these flung a wanton puff in among the sober European wood scents, it was as if foreign birds with foreign screams were flying among the trees. Frans Röy at once affirmed that the native birds were thereby inspired with new song. Never had they sung so gloriously as they were singing that morning.

Alice's fear of an explosion increased. She tried to avoid it by drawing his attention to the contrasts of colour in wood and meadow and distance. The drive out to La Bagatelle is peculiarly rich in these. But Frans was sitting with his back to the horses; he had to turn away from Mary and Alice every time to see what Alice wanted him to look at. This made him impatient, the more so as Mary and he were each time interrupted in their conversation.

"Shall we not rather get out and walk a little?" said he.

But Alice was more afraid of this than anything. What might he not take into his head next?

"Do look about you!" she exclaimed. "Is it not as if the colours here were singing in chorus?"

"Where?" said Frans crossly.

"Goodness! Don't you see all the varieties of green in the wood itself? Just look! And then the green of the meadow against these?"

"I have no desire to see it! Not an atom!" He turned towards the ladies again and laughed. "Would it not really be better to get down?" he insisted again. "It's ever so much pleasanter to walk in the wood than to look at it. The same with the meadows."

"It is forbidden to walk on the grass."

"Confound it! Then let us walk on the road, and look at it all. That is surely better than being cooped up in a carriage."

Mary agreed with him.

"Do you suppose that it was to walk I drove you out here? It was to see that historic house, La Bagatelle, and the wood surrounding it. There is nothing like it anywhere. And then I meant to go as far into the country as possible. We can't do all this if we are to walk."

This appeal kept them quiet for a time. The owner of the carriage must be allowed to decide. But now Mary, too, was in wild spirits. Her eyes, usually thoughtful, shone with happiness. To-day she laughed at all Frans's jokes; she laughed at nothing at all. She was perpetually coveting flowers which she saw; and each time they had to stop, to gather both flowers and leaves. She filled the carriage with them, until Alice at last protested. Then she flung them all out, and insisted on being allowed to get out herself.

They stopped and alighted.

They had long ago passed La Bagatelle. The carriage was ordered to turn and drive slowly back; they followed.

They had not taken many steps before Frans Röy began to turn cart-wheels, that is to say, to throw himself forward side-ways upon his hands, turn in the air, and fall again upon his feet—then to go off again sideways upon his hands, ever onwards, ever faster. Presently he turned and came back in the same way. "That is one of my circus tricks," he said, beaming. "Here is another!" He jumped up where he stood, turned round in the air, and came down again on his feet on the exact spot from which he had jumped—then did the same thing again. "Look. Exactly where I jumped from!" he exclaimed triumphantly, and did it two, three, four, five times more.

They admired. And it was a sight worthy of admiration; for the ease with which the tall, strong man performed the feat made it beautiful. Inspired by their praise, he began to spin round at such a rate that they could not bear to look. Nor was it beautiful. They turned away and screamed. This delighted him tremendously. Annoyed by the fact, Alice called out:

"You are a perfect boy; any one would take you for seventeen!"

"How old are you?" asked Mary.

"Over thirty."

They shouted with laughter.

This they should not have done. This he must punish. Before Alice divined his intention, he seized her round the waist, turned, and was off with her in the most frantic gallop up the road, raising clouds of dust. Stout Alice struggled with all her might and screamed. But this was of no avail; it only delighted him. Her hat and her shawl fell off. Mary ran and picked them up, helpless with laughter; for these ungainly and perfectly useless attempts at resistance were irresistibly comic. At last Frans turned, and they came back again at the same wild pace and stopped where Mary stood—Alice's face distorted, perspiring, and red. Her breathless rage, incapable of utterance, made Mary explode. Frans sang: Hop sa-sa! hop-sa-sa! in front of the angry lady, until she could speak and abuse him. Then he laughed.

"And you—?" said Mary, now turning to Frans. "Has it not tired you at all?"

"Not much. I'm quite prepared to take the same trip with you."

Mary was horrified. She had just given Alice her hat, and was standing holding the shawl and her own hat, which she had taken off. With a cry she threw both from her and set off in the homeward direction, towards the waiting carriage.

Not for an instant had Frans Röy thought of doing what he threatened. He had spoken in jest. But when he saw her run, and with a speed for which he would have given neither her nor any other woman credit, his soldier's blood took it as a challenge. Alice saw this and said hurriedly: "Don't do it." The words flung themselves in his way so insistently that he stood doubtful. But Mary yonder on the road in the white dress with the red hair above it, running with a step so swift and light that the very rhythm of it allured him, nay, bereft him of his senses ... he was off before he knew what he was about, just as Alice called for the second time, in an agonised tone: "Don't do it!"

The strip of light above the dust of the road in front of him shone into his eyes and his imagination like the sun. It blinded him. He ran without consciousness of what he was doing. He ran as if: "Catch me! Catch me!" were being shouted in front the whole time. He ran as if the winning of life's highest prize depended on his reaching Mary.

She had a long start of him. Precisely this incited to the uttermost exertion of all his powers. A race for happiness with one who desired to be beaten! Blood at the boiling point surged in his ears; desire burned in it. The longings of all these days and nights were tumultuously urging him on to victory. Speak they would at last. No, speech would be uncalled for; he would have her in his arms.

Now Mary turned her head—saw him, gave a cry, gathered up her dress. She actually owned a still swifter pace, did she! Madness seized Frans. He believed that the cry was a lure. He saw Mary make a forward sign with her hand; he believed that she was showing where she would stop and consider herself safe. He must reach her before she got there. He, too, had a last spurt in reserve; it brought him with a rush close in upon her. He seemed to perceive the fragrance exhaling from her; next moment he must hear her breathing. He was so excited that he did not know he had touched her until she looked round. She let her dress fall at once, and after one or two more swift steps, stood still. His arm went round her waist; he was on fire; he drew her tightly to him—to hear the angriest: "Let me go!" Want of breath gave it its excessive sharpness. Frans was appalled, but felt that he must support her until she recovered breath, and therefore retained his hold. Again came with the same compressed sharpness of breathlessness: "You are no gentleman!" He let go.

The clatter of horses' hoofs was heard; the carriage was approaching rapidly. The servants on the box must have witnessed the whole occurrence; it was to them she had waved. During his wild chase he had seen her alone.

Now she walked towards the carriage. She held her handkerchief to her face; she was crying. The servant jumped down and opened the carriage door.

Frans turned away, desperate, his mind paralysed. Alice came up. She was carrying her own shawl and Mary's hat, and went straight towards the carriage without taking notice of him. When he attempted to join her, she waved him off.

The third day after the occurrence Frans called upon Alice. He was told that she was not at home. The following day he received the same answer. After this he was absent from Paris for some days; but immediately on his return he called again. "She has just gone out," answered the servant. But this time he simply pushed the man aside and went in.

Alice stood eagerly examining a collection of objects of art; table and chairs were covered with them, they stood about everywhere. "Alice—!" said Frans, gently and reproachfully. She started, and at that moment he caught sight of her father behind her. He at once came forward as if he had said nothing.

The art treasures were collected and laid aside, Frans assisting. Mr. Clerc left the room.

"Alice!" now repeated Frans Röy in the same reproachful tone. "You surely do not mean to close your door to me? And just when I am so unhappy?"

She did not answer.

"We who have always been such good friends and had such good times together?"

Alice looked away from him and gave no answer.

"Even if I have behaved foolishly, we two surely know each other too well for that to separate us?"

"There are limits to everything," he heard her say.

He was silent for a moment. "Limits? limits? Come now, Alice. Between us there is surely no—"

Before he could say more she broke out: "It is inexcusable to behave in such a way before other people!" She was scarlet.

"Yes. You mean?" He did not understand.

She turned away. "To treat me in such a manner before Mary——what must Mary think?"

Never until now had it occurred to him that he had behaved badly to her, to Alice, too; all this time he had thought only of Mary. Now, ashamed of himself, dreadfully ashamed of himself, he came forward.

"Will you pardon me, Alice? I was so happy that I did not think. I didn't understand till this moment. Forgive a poor sinner! Won't you look at me?"

She turned her head towards him; her eyes were unhappy and full of tears; they met his, which were also unhappy, but beseeching. It was not long before his and hers melted into each other. He stretched out his arms, embraced her, tried to kiss her; but this he was not allowed to do.

"Alice, dear, sweet Alice, you will help me again!"

"It is of no use. You spoil everything."

"After this, I will do every single thing you ask me."

"You promised the same before."

"But now I have learned a lesson. Now I shall keep my promise. On my honour!"

"Your promises are not to be relied on. For you do not understand."

"I don't understand?"

"No, you don't understand in the least who she is!"

"I confess that I must have been mistaken, for even now I fail to comprehend what made her so angry."

"That I can quite believe."

"Yes. When she threw everything away and ran, I felt certain that it was to get me to run after her."

"Did you not hear me call twice: 'Don't do it!'?"

"Yes, but I did not understand that either."

Alice sat down with a hopeless feeling. She said no more; she thought it useless to do so. He seated himself opposite to her.

"Explain it to me, Alice! Did you not see how she laughed when I danced off with you?"

"Has it not dawned upon you yet that there is a difference between us and her?"

"Mary Krog is most unassuming; she makes no pretensions whatever."

"Quite so. But now you are misunderstanding me again. Whereas we are ordinary beings, whom other people may touch with impunity, she dwells in a remoteness which no one as yet has diminished by one foot. It is not from pride or vanity that she does so."

"No, no!"

"She *is* like that. If she were not, she would have been captured and married long ago. You surely don't imagine that proposals have been wanting?"

"Everyone knows they have not."

"Ask Mrs. Dawes! She keeps a diary of them in her thousand letters. She writes about nothing else now."

"But what, then, is the explanation of it, dear Alice?"

"It is quite simple. She is gentle, sweet-tempered, obliging—all this and more. But she dwells in an enchanted land, into which none may intrude. She preserves it inviolate with extraordinary vigilance and tact."

"To touch her is forbidden, you mean?"

"Absolutely! Fancy your not understanding that yet!"

"I did understand; but I forgot."

Frans Röy sat silent as if he were listening to something far away. Again he heard the sharp cries of fear which thrilled through the air as he drew near, saw the terrified sign to the carriage, felt Mary's trembling body, heard the ejaculation uttered with all her remaining strength, saw her walk on, weeping. All at once he understood! What a stupid, coarse criminal he was!

He sat there dumb, miserable.

But it was not in his nature to give up. His face soon brightened.

"After all, dear Alice, it was only a game."

"To her it was more. You are surely not still in doubt as to that?"

"She has been pursued before, you mean?"

"In many different ways."

"Consequently she imagined——?"

"Of course. You saw that she did."

He did not reply.

"But now tell me, my dear Frans—was it not more than a game to you, too? Was it not all-decisive?"

He bowed his head, ashamed. Then he walked across the room and came back.

"She is a queen. She will not be captured. I should have stopped——?"

"You should never have gone after her. And she would have been yours now."

Frans seated himself again as if a heavy weight were pressing on his shoulders.

"Did she say anything?" asked Alice with a searching look.

He would have preferred not to tell, but the question was repeated.

"She said that I was no gentleman."

Alice declared this to be too bad. Frans then asked if Mary had said anything to her in the carriage.

"Not a word. But I spoke. I abused you—well."

"She has not referred to the matter since?"

Alice shook her head. "Your name is erased from her dictionary, my friend."

Some days after this Frans received by tube-post a hurried note which informed him that at eleven that morning the two ladies would again be at the exhibition in the Champs Elysées. It was eleven when the note came.

Mary had called to ask Alice to go with her to look at a Dutch coast landscape which her father wished to buy. They considered the price rather high; possibly Alice would be able to make better terms. Mary's carriage was waiting at the door. Alice left her, wrote hastily to Frans Röy, and then went to dress, which to-day, contrary to custom, took her a long time. They drove to the exhibition, found the picture, and went to the office, where they had to wait. After making their offer and giving the address, they returned to the ground-floor of the exhibition in search of the acrobat. He stood there now in all his manly strength. Alice reached him first, and exclaimed "Why! it is——," then stopped short and walked away from Mary. She examined the statue from every side, over and over again, without saying a word. Precisely that which distinguished Frans Röy—that his strength did not announce itself in distended muscle, but in the elasticity of a beautifully formed, lithe body—was to be observed here. Frans Röy's toss of the head, his broad forehead aslant in the air, his hand, his short, strong foot—everything was here! The statue affected the beholder like a war-song. For the first time Alice found the word for the effect which Frans produced. She was carried away by the statue as by the rhythm of a march. Exactly what she had often felt when she saw Frans walk! Was this likeness a curious accident, or had he really ... she turned quite hot and had to walk away from the statue and look at something else.

Mary had all the time kept behind Alice, who had quite forgotten her. The question now involuntarily occurred to Alice: Does Mary understand what she sees?

She waited a little before she began to observe. Mary, who was now standing in front of the statue, with her back towards Alice, remained so long motionless that the latter's curiosity increased. She went round and stationed herself among the statues opposite, put on her eye-glass, and looked across. Mary's eyes were half closed; her bosom was heaving. She walked slowly round the statue, then retired to a distance, came back, and stood still again midway between front and side.

Then she looked round for Alice and caught sight of the eye-glasses turned in her direction; Alice was actually holding them on, to see clearer. There could be no mistake—her face was one mischievous smile.

There are things which one woman objects to another understanding. Mary's blood surged; angry and hurt, she took Alice's look as an insult. She turned her back quickly on the acrobat and walked towards the door. But she stopped once or twice, pretending to look at other pieces of sculpture, really to obtain mastery over the uproar in her breast. At last she reached the door. She did not look round to see if Alice were following; she passed through the entrance hall and left the building.

But just as she did so, Frans Röy hurried up—as quickly as if he had been sent for and were arriving too late. He tore off his hat without getting even a nod in answer. He saw nothing but a pair of vacant eyes.

"Oh, please don't be angry any longer!" he said with his broadest east-country accent, good-humouredly and boyishly. Mary's face cleared; she could not help herself; she smiled, and was actually going to take his outstretched hand—when she saw his eyes travel with the speed of lightning to a point behind her and come back with the least little particle of triumph in them. She turned her head and met Alice's eyes. In them there was any amount both of mischief and rejoicing. There had been a plot then! Mary was transformed. As if from the highest church steeple she looked down upon them both—and left them. Her carriage was waiting a short way off; she motioned, and it came in a wide sweep to where she stood. There was no footman; she opened the door before Frans Röy could come to her assistance, and got in as if no one were there. When seated she looked—past Frans—to see if Alice were coming. Fat Alice was waddling slowly along. It was plain, even from a distance, that a wild struggle with suppressed laughter was going on within her. And when she arrived and saw Mary sitting in state looking to the one side, and Frans Röy, the giant, standing on the other like a frightened recruit, she could resist no longer; she gave way to a fit of laughter which shook her heavy body from head to foot. She laughed until the tears rolled down her cheeks, laughed so that it was with difficulty and not without assistance she found the carriage-step and hauled herself up. She sank on the seat beside Mary, convulsed with laughter; the carriage shook, as she sat with her handkerchief to her face, suppressing screams. She caught a glimpse of Mary's scarlet anger and Frans Röy's pale dismay—and laughed the louder. The very coachman was obliged to laugh too, though what the devil it was about he did not know. And thus they drove off.

Another unsuccessful expedition, another defeat of the highest hopes! It was a long time before Alice could say anything. Then she began by pitying Frans Röy.

"You are too severe with him, Mary. Goodness! how miserable he looked!" And the laughter began again.

But Mary, who had been sitting waiting for an opportunity, now broke out:

"What have I to do with your protégé?"

And as if this were not enough, she bent forward to face Alice's laughing eyes:

"You are confusing me with yourself. It is you who are in love with him. Do you imagine that I have not seen that for ever so long? You know best yourselves in what relation you stand to each other. That is no affair of mine. But the 'De'[B] which you both keep up—is it for the purpose of concealment?"

[B] *You* as distinguished from the familiar *thou*.

Alice's laughter ceased. She turned pale, so pale that Mary was alarmed. Mary tried to withdraw her eyes, but could not; Alice's held them fast through painful changes until they lost all expression. Then Alice's head sank back, whilst a long, heavy sigh resembling the groan of a wounded animal escaped her.

Mary sat motionless, aghast at her own speech.

But it was irrevocable.

Alice suddenly raised her head again and told the coachman to stop. "I have a call to make at this house." The carriage stopped; she opened the door, stepped out, and shut it after her.

With a long look at Mary, she said:

"Good-bye!"

"Good-bye!" was answered in a low tone.

Both felt that it was for ever.

Mary drove on. As soon as she reached home, she went straight to the private drawing-room; she had something to say to her father. Before she opened the door, she heard piano-playing, and understood that Jörgen Thiis was there. But this did not stop her. With her hat and spring cloak still on, she unexpectedly appeared in the room. Jörgen Thiis jumped up from the piano and came towards her, his eyes filling with admiration; her face was all aglow from the tumult within. But something proud and repellent in its sparkle caused him to give up his intention of closer approach.

Then his eyes assumed the gloating, greedy expression which Mary so detested. With a slight bow she passed him and went up to her father, who was sitting as usual in the big chair with a book upon his knee.

"Father, what do you say to our going home now?"

Every face brightened. Mrs. Dawes exclaimed: "Jörgen Thiis has just been asking when we intend to go; he wants to travel with us."

Mary did not turn towards Jörgen but continued: "I think the steamer sails from Havre to-morrow?"

"It does," answered her father; "but we can't possibly be ready by that time?"

"Yes, we can!" said Mrs. Dawes. "We have this whole afternoon."

"I shall be delighted to help," said Jörgen Thiis.

Now Mary bestowed a friendly look on him, before mentioning the price which Alice had advised her to offer for the Dutch coast landscape her father wished to buy. She then went off to begin her own packing.

The four met again before the hotel dinner at half-past seven. Mary came into the room looking tired. Jörgen Thiis went up to her and said:

"I hear that you have made Frans Röy's acquaintance, Miss Krog?"

Her father and Mrs. Dawes were listening attentively. This showed that Jörgen must have been talking with them on the subject before she entered. Every new male acquaintance she made was a source of anxiety to them. Mary coloured; she felt herself doing so, and the red deepened. The two were watching.

"I have met him at Miss Clerc's," replied Mary. "She and her mother spent several summers in Norway, and were intimate with his family there; they belong to the same town. Is there anything more you wish to know?"

Jörgen Thiis stood dismayed. The others stared. He said hastily: "I have just been telling your father and Mrs. Dawes that we younger officers consider Frans Röy the best man we have. So I spoke with no unfriendly intention."

"Nor did I suspect you of any. But as I myself have not mentioned the acquaintance here, I do not think that the subject ought to be introduced by strangers."

In utter consternation Jörgen stammered that, that, that he had had no other intention in doing so than to, to, to....

"I know that," Mary replied, cutting short the conversation.

They went down to dinner. At table Jörgen as a matter of course returned to the subject. It could not be allowed to drop thus. All Frans Röy's brother officers, he said, regretted that he had exchanged into the engineers. He was a particularly able strategist. Their military exercises, both theoretical and practical, had provided him with opportunities to distinguish himself. Jörgen gave instances, but the others did not understand them. So he went on to tell anecdotes of Frans Röy as a comrade, as an officer. These were supposed to show how popular and how ready-witted he was. Mary declared that they chiefly showed how boyish he was. Thereupon Jörgen said that he had only heard the stories from others; Frans Röy was older than he.

"What do *you* think of him?" he suddenly asked in a very innocent manner.

Mary did not answer immediately. Her father and Mrs. Dawes looked up.

"He talks a great deal too much."

Jörgen laughed. "Yes; but how can he help that—he who has so much strength?"

"Must it be exercised upon us?"

They all laughed, and the strain which had been making them uncomfortable relaxed. Krog and Mrs. Dawes felt safe, as far as Frans Röy was concerned. So did Jörgen Thiis.

At half-past eight they went upstairs again. Mary at once retired to her room, pleading fatigue. She lay and listened to Jörgen playing. Then she lay and wept.

Next evening, on the sea, wide and motionless, the faint twilight ushered in the summer night. Two pillars of smoke rose in the distance. Except for these, the dull grey above and beneath was unbroken. Mary leaned against the rail. No one was in sight, and the thud of the engine was the only sound.

She had been listening to music downstairs, and had left the others there. An unspeakable feeling of loneliness had driven her up to this barren outlook—clouds as far as the eye could reach.

Nothing but clouds; not even the reflection of the sun which had gone down.

And was there anything more than this left of the brightness of the world from which she came? Was there not the very same emptiness in and around herself? The life of travel was now at an end; neither her father nor Mrs. Dawes could or would continue to lead it; this she understood. At Krogskogen there was not one neighbour she cared for. In the town, half an hour's journey off, there was not a human being to whom she was bound by any tie of intimacy. She had never given herself time to make such ties. She was at home nowhere. The life which springs from the soil of a place and unites us to everything that grows there was not hers. Wherever she made her appearance, the conversation seemed to stop, in order that another subject, suited to her, might be introduced. The globe-trotters who wandered about with her talked of incidents of travel, of the art-galleries and the music of the towns which they were visiting—occasionally, too, of problems which pursued them, let them go where they would. But of these not one affected her personally. The conventional utterances on such subjects she knew by heart. Indeed, the whole was either a kind of practice in language, or else aimless chat to pass the time.

The homage paid her, which at times verged on worship, had begun when she was still a child and took it as fun. In course of time it had become as familiar to her as the figures of a quadrille. One incident which alarmed the whole family, a couple of incidents which were painful, had been long forgotten; the admiration she received meant nothing to her—she remained unsatisfied and lonely.

A convulsive start—and Frans Röy's giant form suddenly appeared before her—so plain, so exact in the smallest detail, that she felt as if she could not stir because of him.

He was not like the rest. Was it this that had frightened her?

The very thought of him made her tremble. Without her willing it, Alice stood beside him, fat and sensual, with desire in her eyes.... What was the relation between these two?... A moment of darkness, one of pain, one of fury. Then Mary wept.

She heard a loud, dull roar, and turned in its direction. An ocean-steamer was bearing down on them—an apparition so unexpected and so gigantic that it took away her breath. It rose out of the sea without warning, and rushed towards them at tremendous speed, becoming larger and larger, a fire-mountain of great and small lights. With a roar it came and it went. One moment, and it was seen in the far distance.

What an impression it made on her, this life rushing past on its way from continent to continent, with its suggestion of constant, fruitful exchange of thoughts and labour! whilst she herself lay drifting in a little tub, which was rocked so violently by the waves from the world-colossus that she had to cling to the first support that offered.

She was alone again in the great void. Deserted. For was it not desertion that everything she had seen and heard in three continents—of the life of the nations, their toil and their pleasure, their art, their music—should have to be left behind? She had seen and heard; and now she was alone, in a dreary, stagnant waste.

AT HOME

THE reality was something quite different.

She saw, the moment she set foot on land, that both old and young were unfeignedly happy to see her again. Every face brightened. Every one whom they met on the way up to the market-place recognised and greeted her with pleasure. She had not thought of them, but they had thought of her.

From the house on the market-place they were to go on later in the day to Krogskogen, with the coasting-steamer. In the interval many of their relations called, who all expressed great pleasure at seeing them home again at last. They told what a success Mary's Spanish portrait had been—in their own town, in Christiania, and then on its tour with other pictures through the country. The notices—but these she had of course read? No, she had read no newspapers, except occasionally one published at the place where they were living. "Do you read no home newspapers?" "Yes, when Father shows me them." Had not her father, had not Mrs. Dawes, told her anything? "No." Why, she was famous now throughout the whole of Norway. For this was the third portrait of her—or was it the fourth? Anyhow it was the finest. It had been reproduced in the illustrated newspapers; and also in an English art-magazine, the *Studio*. Did she not know that? "No." The young people here were very proud of her. They had put off their spring picnic and dance until she came home.

"You are to be fêted!"

"I?"

"The picnic is to be at Marielyst. One steamer goes from here, and another comes from the places on the opposite side. Jörgen Thiis planned it all in Paris."

"Jörgen Thiis?"

"Yes. Did he not tell you about it?"

"No."

As soon as the callers left, Mary went to her father, who was unpacking some of the art treasures which were to remain in town.

"Father, is it the case that you sent my portraits to exhibitions?"

He smiled, and said: "Yes, my child, I did. And they have given pleasure to many. I was asked to send them. They wrote and asked me each time."

He spoke in such a gentle voice, and Mary thought it so considerate of him that he had not told her, and had forbidden Mrs. Dawes to tell—probably Jörgen Thiis too—that she did what she very seldom did, went up to him and kissed him.

So this was what her father, Mrs. Dawes, and Jörgen Thiis had so often sat whispering about. This was why the home newspapers had been kept from her. Everything had been planned—even to the proposal to travel home at this particular moment! She almost began to like Jörgen Thiis.

When they left for Krogskogen in the afternoon, a crowd of young people assembled on the pier called: "Au revoir on Sunday!"

Mary was charmed with the view as they sailed along. The short half hour was spent, as it were, in recognising one old acquaintance after another. The new, or at least much altered, high road along the coast was now finished. It looked remarkably well, especially where it cut across the headlands, often through the rock. At Krogskogen it led, as before, from the one point across the level to the other, passing close to the landing-place and directly below the chapel and the churchyard.

And Krogskogen itself—how snugly it lay! She had remembered its loneliness, but had forgotten how beautiful it was. This calm, glittering bay with the sea-birds! The ripple yonder where the river flows in, the level land stretching back between the heights, and these in their robes of green! Were the trees round the house really no higher? How nice it looked, the house—long and white, with black window frames and black foundation wall. From one chimney thick smoke was rising, in cheerful welcome. She jumped on shore before the others and ran on in front. A little girl, between eight and ten, who was running down from the house, stopped when she saw Mary, and rushed back as hard as she could. But Mary overtook her at the steps. "I've caught you!" she cried, turning her round. "Who are you?" The fair-haired, smiling creature was unable to answer. On the steps stood the maids, and one of them said that the child's name was Nanna, and that she was there to run errands. "You shall be my little maid!" said Mary, and led her up the steps. She nodded to each of the women, and felt that they were disappointed because she hurried on without speaking to them. She was longing to set foot on the thick carpets, to feel the peculiar light of the hall about her, to see the huge cupboards and all the pictures and curios of the Dutch days. And she was longing even more to reach her own room. The silence of the stairs and of the long, rather dark passage—never had it played such a game of whispers with her as it did to-day. She felt it like something soft, half-hidden, confidential and close. It was still speaking when she reached the door of her room; it actually kept her from opening the door for a moment.

Ah!—the room lay steeped in sunshine from the open window which looked over the outbuildings to the ridge. Paler light entered from that looking on the orchard and the bay below, the water of which glittered between the trees. Beyond the trees were seen the islands and the open sea, at this moment pale grey. But from the hill, now in fairest leaf and flower, the fragrance of spring poured in. The room itself, in its white purity, lay like a receptacle for it. There everything arranged itself reverently round the bed, which stood in the middle of the floor. It was more than a bed for a princess; it was the princess herself; everything else seemed to do homage to it.

The excursion to Marielyst was in every way a success. But during the course of it a coolness arose between Mary and Jörgen Thiis.

It happened thus. Jörgen came on board with a tall, strongly-built lady, the sight of whose broad forehead, kindly eyes, small nose, and projecting chin brought a slight blush to Mary's cheeks, which she concealed by rising and asking: "Are you not a sister of Captain Frans Röy?"

"She is," answered Jörgen Thiis. "For safety's sake we are taking a doctor with us."

"I am glad to meet you," said Mary. "Of course I have heard your brother speak of you; he has a great admiration for you."

"So we all have," Jörgen Thiis declared as he left them.

Miss Röy herself had not spoken yet. But her scrutinising eyes expressed admiration of Mary. Now she seated herself beside her.

"Are you to be at home long?"

"I can't say. Possibly we shall not travel any more; my father is not strong enough now."

Miss Röy did not speak again for some time; she sat observing. Mary thought to herself: It is tactful of her not to begin a conversation about her brother.

The two ladies kept together during the sail. And they also sat beside each other when dessert was served out of doors at Marielyst and speeches were made. The success of the entertainment went to Jörgen Thiis's head. One after another came round to him and drank his health; he became sentimental, and made a speech. His toast was "the ideal, the eternal ideal." Fortunate the man to whom it was revealed in his youth! He bore it in his breast as his inextinguishable guiding lamp on the path of life! Pale and excited, Jörgen emptied his glass and flung it away.

This sudden earnestness came so unexpectedly upon the merry company that they laughed—one and all.

Miss Röy said to Mary: "You met Lieutenant Thiis abroad?"

"Both this winter and last," answered Mary carelessly; she was eating ice.

A young girl was standing beside them. "He is a curious man, Jörgen Thiis," said she. "He is so amiable with us; but he is said to be a perfect tyrant with the soldiers."

Mary turned towards her in surprise. "A tyrant—in what way?"

"They say that he irritates them dreadfully—is exacting and ill-tempered, and punishes for nothing."

Mary turned her largest eyes upon Margrete Röy.

"Yes, it is true," said the latter indifferently; she, too, was eating ice.

When, late in the evening, after the dance, they were all trooping down to the steamer, Mary and Jörgen arm in arm, she said to him: "Is it true that the soldiers under your command complain of you?"

"It is quite likely that they do, Miss Krog." He laughed.

"Is there anything to laugh about in that?"

"There is certainly nothing to cry about."

He was in a very jovial mood, and would fain have put his arm round her and danced down to the pier, as many of the others were doing. But Mary warded him off.

"I was very sorry to hear it," she said.

Then he understood that she was in earnest.

"The fact is, Miss Krog, that Norwegians, generally speaking, don't know what obedience and discipline are. During the short time we have them under command, we must teach them."

"Teach them in what way?"

"In small things, of course."

"By plaguing them about small things?"

"Exactly."

"Giving orders for which they see no necessity?"

"Precisely. They must learn to give up reasoning. They must obey. And what they do, they must do properly; exactly as it should be done."

Mary did not answer. She addressed another couple who now made up to them, and continued doing so till they all reached the pier.

On board the steamer she noticed that Jörgen Thiis was out of humour. When they landed, he was not standing at the gangway. Without any previous arrangement, the whole party accompanied her home to the house on the marketplace. They sang and shouted under the windows until she came out on the balcony and threw flowers down on them—those she had brought home with her and any more she could find. Then they dispersed, laughing and joking.

As they were going off, she looked for Jörgen; he was not there. This vexed her; she felt that she had rewarded him ill for one of the most delightful days in her life.

Entertainments, large and small, followed one on the other. But Jörgen Thiis was absent from them all. He had first gone home to see his parents, then to Christiania. Mary had never devoted much thought to Jörgen Thiis, but now that he kept away, she could not help remembering that she had chiefly him to thank for the happy meeting with the young people of her own age. And that remarkable toast of his—"fidelity to the ideal"—at the time he proposed it she had merely thought: How sentimental Jörgen Thiis can be! Now she thought: Perhaps it was an allusion to me? She was accustomed to such exaggerations; and she did not care in the least for Jörgen Thiis. But when she remembered how deeply in love he had fallen at their first meeting, and how all these years he had been exactly the same whenever and wherever they met, the matter assumed a more serious aspect. The gloating, greedy eyes acquired something almost touching. The fact that he could not bear to be with her when she was the least displeased with him was another proof of the strength of his attachment. His saying nothing, but simply staying away, appealed to her.

One day Mille Falke, the consumptive head-schoolmaster's pretty, gentle wife, came out to see Mary. She had had a letter from Jörgen Thiis. A party of ten Christiania people had arranged a trip to the North Cape. They had taken their berths two months ago; now circumstances prevented their going. Jörgen Thiis had been asked if he could not take the tickets and find nine people to accompany him on the glorious excursion. In the small towns there was more neighbourliness; it was easier there to make up such a party. Jörgen Thiis declared himself willing if Mary Krog would agree to go; he knew that in this case he would have no trouble in finding others.

Mrs. Falke laid the matter before Mary with the soft, feline persuasiveness which few could resist. Mary had, however, not the slightest desire either to sit on the deck of a steamer in the midsummer heat, or to interrupt all that was going on at home—it was much too pleasant. At the same time she was unwilling to offend Jörgen Thiis again. She consulted with her father and Mrs. Dawes; she listened once again to Mrs. Falke—and consented.

Early in July the party assembled at night on board the coasting-steamer which was to take them to Bergen, the starting-point of the excursion proper. They were six ladies and four gentlemen. The eldest lady was the respected principal of the chief girls' school in the town—mother of one of the gentlemen and former instructress of three of the other ladies. She was the moral support of the party. Two of its members were on their honeymoon, and they were teased by the others the whole time. It was worth doing, for they were quick-witted, both of them, and gave as good as they got. Then there was a young merchant, who paid attention to two of the ladies, unable—so it was averred—to make up his mind which he liked best. The whole party, including the ladies in question, did their best to assist him in coming to a decision. The very first night on the coasting-steamer, a schoolmaster was christened "the forsaken one." All the others, with the exception of the old lady kept up a constant racket; no one slept. He alone could neither dance nor sing, and he was incapable of flirting; he could not even be flirted with, it put him out so terribly. The consequence was that all the ladies, even Mary, made love to "the forsaken one," simply to enjoy his misery.

The originator of most of the mischief that went on was Jörgen Thiis; teasing was his passion. His inventiveness in this domain was not always free from malice.

At first he himself was unmolested. But in course of time even "the forsaken one" ventured to attack him. His appetite, his inclination to tyrannise, and especially his role as Mary's humble servant, were made subjects of jest. Mary had the Krogs' keen eye for exaggeration in every shape, so she laughed along with the rest, even when it was at his submissiveness to her they were laughing. Jörgen was not in the least disturbed. He ate as much as ever, was as strict as ever in his capacity of leader, and continued, unmoved, to play the part of Mary's inventive, ever-ready squire.

The ship had its full complement of passengers, amongst them a number of foreigners; but Jörgen Thiis's merry party was the centre of attraction. Nature made such perpetual calls on the passengers' admiration that they were not in too close and constant contact with each other. It was as if they were attending some grand performance. One marvel followed the other. The length of the days, too, had its influence. Each night was shorter than the last, until there was none at all. They sailed on into unquenchable, inextinguishable light, and this produced a kind of intoxication. They drank, they danced, they sang; they were all equally highly strung. They proposed things which under other circumstances would have seemed impossible; here they were in keeping with the wildness of the landscape, the intoxication of the light. One day in a strong wind Mary lost her hat; two cavaliers jumped overboard after it. One of them was, of course, Jörgen Thiis. The minds of all were working at higher pressure than that of every day. Some of them became exhausted and slept whole days and nights. But most of them held out—at least as long as they were northward bound—Mary amongst the number.

Jörgen Thiis, with his persistent deference, in the end obliged all of them to treat Mary more or less as he did himself. Nor did anything occur the whole time to disturb this position of hers—thanks principally to her own carefully cultivated reserve of manner.

When they returned to the coasting-steamer, genuine gratitude prompted her to invite Jörgen Thiis to go home with her to Krogskogen. "I can't stand such a sudden break-up," she said.

He stayed for some days, delighted with the beauty and comfort of everything. Such art taste as he possessed lay chiefly in the direction of knick-knacks; he was devoted to foreign curios, and of these there was abundance. The rooms and their furniture and decorations were exactly to his taste. To Mrs. Dawes, who encouraged him to speak freely, he confided that the comfort and quiet disposed him amorously. He sat often and long at the piano extemporising; and it was always in an erotic strain.

He treated Mary with the same deference when they were alone as when they were in company with others. All the time she had known him he had not let fall a single word which could be interpreted as a preface to love-making, no, not even as the preface to a preface. And this she appreciated.

They wandered together through the woods and the fields. They rowed together to relations' houses to pay calls. Jörgen had the key to the bathing-house, where he went before any one else was up, and often again after their excursions.

Mary herself had become more sociable. Jörgen told her so.

"Yes," answered she. "The Norwegian young people associate with each other more like brothers and sisters than those of other countries, and are consequently different—freer, franker. They have infected me."

One morning Jörgen had to go to town, and Mary accompanied him. She wished to call on Uncle Klaus, his foster-father, whom she had not seen since she came home.

Klaus was sitting behind a cloud of smoke, like a spider behind its grey web. He jumped up when he saw Mary enter, declared he was ashamed of himself, and led her into the big drawing-room. Jörgen had warned her that he was not likely to be in a good humour; he had been losing money again. And they had not sat long in the empty, stiff drawing-room before he began to complain of the times. As was his habit, he rounded his back and sprawled out his legs, supporting his elbows on them and pressing the points of his long fingers together.

"Yes, you two are well off, who do nothing but amuse yourselves!"

He possibly thought that this remark demanded some reparation, for his next was: "I have never seen a handsomer pair!"

Jörgen laughed, but coloured to the roots of his hair. Mary sat unmoved.

Jörgen accompanied her to the house on the market-place; it was quite near. He did not say a word on the way, and took leave immediately. Afterwards he sent to let her know that he would be obliged to stay in town till the evening; then he would cycle out. Mary herself left at the previously appointed hour.

On her way home in the steamer she revolved the idea: Jörgen Thiis and herself a pair. No! This she had never contemplated. He was a handsome, well-bred man, a courteous, pleasant companion, a really gifted musician. His ability, his tact, were unanimously acknowledged. Even that which at one time had repelled her so strongly, the sensuality, which would suddenly leap into his eyes and produce that insufferable gloating expression—perhaps it was of this underlying quality that all the rest were cultivated developments? Might it not account for his appreciation of the perfect in art, in discipline, in language? Still there remained something unexplained. But it was a matter of indifference to her what it was. She cast all these reflections aside; it was no concern of hers.

As she came on board she had noticed a peasant-woman who had once been their servant; now she went and sat down beside her. The woman was gratified.

"And how is your father, Miss? I am old now, and I have known many people in my day, but never a kinder man than Mr. Krog. There's no one like him."

The affectionate warmth of these words touched Mary. The woman mentioned one instance after the other of her father's considerateness and generosity; she was still talking of it when they arrived. At first Mary felt as if nothing so pleasant as this had happened to her for a long time. Then she felt afraid. She had actually forgotten how dearly she herself loved her father, and had left off giving expression to her affection. Why? Why did she give her time and thoughts to so much else and not to him, the best and dearest of all?

She hurried up to the house. Although her father was very much of an invalid now, she had latterly spent hardly any of her time with him.

As she approached she saw Jörgen's bicycle propped against the steps; she heard him playing. But she hurried past the drawing-room, and went straight to her father, who was sitting in the office at his desk, writing. She put her arms round him and kissed him, looked into his kind eyes and kissed him again. His bewilderment was so comic that she could not help laughing.

"Yes, you may well look at me, for it is certainly not often I do this. But all the same you are dearer to me than I can tell." And she kissed him again.

"My dear child!" he said, and smiled at her assault. He was happy, that she saw. Into his eyes there gradually crept that curious brightness which none ever forgot. She thought to herself: I'll do this every day now, every day!

Jörgen and she had planned a cycling excursion back into the country. They set off next day. The relation at whose house they stopped that evening, a military man, was delighted to have a visit from them. They were persuaded to stay for several days. The young people of the neighbourhood were summoned; an excursion to a sæter was arranged—again something quite new to Mary. "I know every country except my own," said she. She was determined to travel the next year in Norway; there not much chaperonage would be necessary. With this prospect in view Jörgen and she rode home, enjoying themselves royally.

As they were propping their bicycles against the house, little Nanna came rushing out at the door and down the steps. She was crying and did not see them, as she was looking in the other direction. When Mary called: "What is the matter?" she stopped and burst out: "Oh, come, come! I was to go and call people." Up she rushed again to tell that they were coming, Jörgen after her, Mary behind him—across the hall, up the stairs, along the passage to the last door on the right. Within, on the floor, lay Anders Krog, Mrs. Dawes on her knees beside him, weeping loudly. He was in an apoplectic fit. Jörgen lifted him up, carried him to his bed, and laid him carefully down. Mary had rushed to telephone for the doctor.

The doctor was not at home; she tried place after place to find him, a voice within her all the time crying despairingly: Why had she not been beside her father when this happened? Immediately after vowing to herself that she would show him every day how much she loved him, she had left him! And this very day she had looked forward with pleasure to being able to travel without him! How had she come to be like this? What was the matter with her?

As soon as she had found the doctor, she hurried back to her father. He was now undressed and Jörgen had gone. But Mrs. Dawes sat on a chair beside the pillow, with a letter in her hand, in the deepest distress. The moment she saw Mary, she handed her the letter without taking her eyes from the sick man's face.

It was from a correspondent in America of whom Mary had never heard. It told that her uncle Hans had lost their money and his own. His mind was deranged, and probably had been so for a long time. Mary knew that on the male side of the Krog family it was not uncommon for the old people to become weak-minded. But she was horrified that her father should not have exercised any control over affairs. This, too, was a suspicious sign.

He must have been on his way to Mrs. Dawes with this letter when the seizure occurred, for the door had been opened and he lay close to it.

Mary read the letter twice, then turned towards Mrs. Dawes, who sat crying.

"Well, well, Aunt Eva—it has to be borne."

"Borne? borne? What do you mean? The money loss? Who cares for that? But your father! That man of men—my best friend!"

She watched his closed eyes, weeping all the time, and heaping the best of names and the highest of praise on him—in English. The words in the foreign language seemed to belong to an earlier time; Mary knelt by her father, taking them all in. They told of the days which the two old people had spent together. Each a lament, each an expression of gratitude, they recalled his friendly words, his kind looks, his gifts, his forbearance. They flowed abundant and warm, uttered with the fearlessness of a good conscience; for Mrs. Dawes had tried, as far as it lay in her power, to be to him what he was to her. The more precious the words poured forth in her father's honour over Mary's head, the poorer did they make her feel. For she had been so little to him. Oh, how she repented! oh, how she despaired!

Jörgen Thiis appeared outside the door just as she was rising to her feet. She stooped again, picked up the letter, and was about to give it to him, when Mrs. Dawes, who had also seen him, asked him to help her to her room; she must go to bed. "God only knows if I shall ever get up again! If this is the end with him, it is the end with me too."

Jörgen at once raised the heavy body from the chair and staggered slowly off, supporting it. In Mrs. Dawes's room he rang for a maid; then he went back to Mary. She was standing motionless, holding the letter, which she now handed to him.

He read it carefully and turned pale; for a time he was quite overcome; Mary went a few steps towards him, but this he did not see.

"This has been the cause of the shock," she said.

"Of course," whispered Jörgen, without looking at her. Presently he left the room.

Mary remained alone with her father. His sweet, gentle face called to her; she threw herself down beside him again and sobbed. For him whom she loved best she had done least. Perhaps only because he never drew attention to himself?

She did not leave him until the doctor came, and with him the nurse. Then she went to Mrs. Dawes.

Mrs. Dawes was ill and in despair. Mary tried to comfort her, but she interrupted passionately: "I have been too well off. I have felt too secure. Now misfortune is at hand."

Mary started, for the thought had been in her own heart all the time.

"You are losing us both, poor child! And the money too!"

Mary did not like her mentioning the money. Mrs. Dawes felt this and said:

"You don't understand me, my poor child! It is not your fault, it is ours. We gave in to you too much. But you behaved so badly if we did not."

Mary looked up, startled: "I behaved badly?"

"I spoke to your father, child; I spoke to him on the subject often. But he was so tender-hearted; he always found some excuse."

Jörgen entered with the doctor.

"If any complication arises, Miss Krog, the worst may happen."

"Will he be paralysed?" asked Mrs. Dawes.

The doctor evaded the question; he merely said: "Quiet is all important."

Silence followed this utterance.

"Miss Krog, I cannot allow you to nurse your father. There ought to be two trained nurses."

Mary said nothing. Mrs. Dawes began to cry again. "This is a sad change of days."

The doctor took leave, and was escorted downstairs by Jörgen Thiis. When Jörgen returned, he asked softly: "Shall I go too—or can I be of any use?"

"Oh, do not leave us!" wailed Mrs. Dawes.

Jörgen looked at Mary, who said nothing; nor did she look up. She was weeping silently.

"You know, Miss Krog," said he respectfully, "that there is no one to whom I would so willingly be of service."

"We know that, we know that!" sobbed Mrs. Dawes.

Mary had raised her head, but, Mrs. Dawes having spoken, she said nothing.

When she left the room soon afterwards, Jörgen was just opening his door, which was next to Mary's. He stood for a moment with the door wide open, so that she saw the packed portmanteau behind him. She stopped.

"You are going?" she said.

"Yes," answered he.

"It will be very quiet here now."

Jörgen expected more, but no more came. Then he said:

"The shooting season begins immediately. I had intended to ask your father's permission to shoot in his woods."

"If you consider mine sufficient, you have it."

"Thank you, Miss Krog! You will allow me, too, to look in upon you sometimes, I hope?" He took her hand and bowed deeply over it.

Then he went in to take leave of Mrs. Dawes. With her he stayed ten minutes at least, coming out just as Mary was crossing the passage to her father's room.

As she stood by the bed Anders began to move, and opened his eyes. She knelt down. "Father!"

He seemed to be collecting his thoughts; then he tried to speak, but could not. She said quickly: "We know, Father; we know everything. Don't trouble about it! We'll get on beautifully all the same."

Her father's eyes showed that he took in what she said, though slowly. He tried to lift his hand, and, finding that he could not, looked at her with an expression of painful surprise; she lay down close to him, kissed him and wept.

Anders improved, however, with astonishing rapidity. Was it Mary's presence and untiring attention which helped him? The nurse said that it was.

Then came a time when, though still indefatigable in her attention to the two invalids, she learned to manage both house and farm. She took the accounts and the superintendence into her own hands. It was a task she enjoyed, for she had the gift of order and management. Mrs. Dawes was astonished.

No anxiety for the future did Mary display, no regret for the pleasures of the past. To those who pitied her she said that it was indeed sad that her father and Mrs. Dawes were ill, but that except for this she was perfectly contented.

One unusually warm day in the middle of August she had been very busy since early morning, looking forward all the time to a plunge in the sea as soon as her work was done.

Between five and six they ran down, Mary and little Nanna. They both went into the bathing-house, for it was one of Nanna's greatest pleasures to attend to Mary's beautiful hair; to-day it was to hang loose. After taking it down, Nanna ran up to the big stone on the ridge, to keep a look-out on both sides. Mary meant to go into the water with nothing on, that she might enjoy her bath thoroughly.

She swam out at once to the island. From there she could herself see the inlet on both sides and the roads. No one anywhere, no danger—therefore back again!

The sea caressed and upheld her; upon the arms that clove it the sun played; the land in front lay in the repleteness of a rich aftermath; sea-birds rocked on the waves, others screamed in the air above Mary's head. "Imagine that I was afraid of being alone—!" thought she.

When she approached the shore she did not leave the water, but lay on her back and rested; then took a few strokes and rested again. The beach looked inviting; she lay down on it in the blazing sun, her head supported on a stone, her hair floating. Oh, how delicious! But something suddenly warned her to look up. She could not be troubled. Yes, she ought to look up to where Nanna was sitting. No, she would not; Nanna was on the look-out. Yet the suggestion had put an end to her enjoyment. When she rose to walk along to the bathing-house steps, she saw behind the big stone—Jörgen Thiis with his gun over his shoulder! The little girl was standing on the top of the stone motionless, staring at him as if she were spell-bound.

The blood rushed through Mary's veins in hot waves of fury and loathing. Is he utterly shameless? Or has he gone out of his mind? To outward appearance she behaved as if she saw nothing; she plunged into the sea and swam to the steps, walked calmly up them, and disappeared.

But her breath was coming hard and short, and she was so hot that she forgot to dry herself, forgot to dress. Hotter and hotter she grew, until she was positively boiling with rage and desire for vengeance. The polite Jörgen Thiis had dared to insult her as she had never in her life been insulted!

Her mind wrestled with the thought of this senseless, dishonourable surprisal until she became involved in a train of ideas which carried her away. She was standing again in front of the acrobat's powerful body; Alice's knowing eyes were upon her. She trembled—then screams from the child reached her ear. In her excitement she almost screamed back. What could it mean? There was no window on that side. She dared not look out at the door, for she was naked. Never had she dressed in such haste, but for this very reason everything went wrong, and time passed. She would not appear before Jörgen Thiis half dressed.

Just as she was ready to open, she heard the pitapat of little Nanna's steps on the bridge from the bank. Mary tore the door open; the child came rushing in, hid her head in her mistress's dress, and cried and sobbed so that she could not utter a word.

Mary managed to soothe her, principally by promising that she should be allowed to dress her hair. Then Nanna told that before she had noticed anything, Mr. Thiis was standing behind the stone. She had been sitting singing and had not heard him. He made threatening signs to her. Oh, how frightened she had been—for he looked so dreadful! oh, so dreadful! The moment Mary went into the house, he had rushed straight towards it.

"Jörgen Thiis?"

"Then I screamed as loud as I could scream! *That* stopped him. He turned and was coming back to me, but I jumped off the stone and ran into the wood——" Here words failed her; she hid her face in Mary's skirts again and sobbed.

This was worse than ever! Mary at first felt totally unable to comprehend.

Then it gradually dawned upon her that Jörgen must be another man than she took him for—that he had violent passions—that he had the daring to act with utter recklessness. What if he had come...?

Conscious of her pride and strength, she knew that it would have meant banishment for ever—impossibly anything else.

On the way home she had to send Nanna on in front, because she herself felt hardly able to set one foot before the other, so overpowering were her thoughts.

How could a man control himself in daily intercourse when he was possessed by such passionate desire? It must have been accumulating for ages, or he would never have succumbed to this assault upon himself, or made this assault upon her.

Had he been burning with desire all these years? His homage, his respect, his unwearying attention—was it all smoke from the subterranean crater, which had now suddenly ejected red-hot stones and ashes?

So Jörgen Thiis was dangerous? He did not lose by this in Mary's estimation; he gained! It was praiseworthy, the compulsion which he had exercised over himself—from reverence for her. Ought she to be so angry with him because temptation had set loose the rebellious powers which he had chained?

All the rest of the day, and even when she was undressing, her mind was busy with these thoughts. Next morning she determined that a stop must be put to this. It was a stirring of something which she had suppressed once before, and which must not be allowed to disturb the new order of her life. Therefore she applied herself more diligently than ever to her tasks, and added to their number. She undertook a thorough examination of her father's books and loose memoranda—of the latter there were far too many—in order to find out the general state of his affairs. He must have Norwegian investments, and he could not possibly have spent all the money that had been sent from America. She was, however, unable to find what she was looking for. She could not trouble her father, and Mrs. Dawes knew nothing.

But, close as Mary's application to business was, thoughts of yesterday managed to insinuate themselves. Jörgen's intention had, of course, been to bathe, and to come up and call afterwards. After what had happened he could not do so. Would he ever come again? Would he do so without being invited? He had effectually damaged his own cause. She heard shots in the woods near at hand on the following days; and other people mentioned having heard shooting farther off. But he did not come on the second day, nor yet on the third, nor on the fourth. Of this she approved.

Her thoughts running much on the woods and the heights, her steps also took that direction one day before dinner. The sudden change of weather which is usual in Norway in the second half of August had taken place. It was cold now; she felt the climb with the north wind playing round her very refreshing. She chose the ascent a little below the houses; it was the easiest. She went up quickly, for she was accustomed to the climb and was longing to be at the top, standing in the wind and looking out over the stormy sea. Even from the first knoll she had an enjoyable view of the meadows, where the farm-servants were spreading out the second crop of hay to dry, of the bay, of the islands, of the sea, black to-day, and bearing on its breast numbers of sailing vessels and one or two steamers. Overhead the crows were making a terrible clamour; a trial was unmistakably going on. She saw one after the other cleave the air and disappear farther along the ridge, towards the north. The noise became louder the higher she climbed. She hurried; it might be possible to save the criminal. A cold shiver of agitation ran through her. She thought that when she reached the next height she would be certain to see the birds. Instead she saw, as soon as her head cleared the ridge, a man lying flat on the ground some distance off to the north, directly above the house.

It was Jörgen Thiis! Mary promptly lowered her head again; then the joy of revenge took possession of her, and she mounted quickly, determinedly. Jörgen saw her, jumped up, looking agitated and ashamed, pulled off his cap, put it on again, seemed not to know where to look or to turn. Mary approached slowly, thoroughly enjoying his embarrassment. While still some distance off she called: "So this is your idea of sport! Are you shooting our hens to-day?" Then, as she came nearer: "You have no dog with you? No, of course not; you can shoot hens without a dog. Or perhaps you have none?"

"Yes; but I am not shooting to-day. I have finished."

This quiet, inoffensive answer, which he gave without daring to look at her, produced a revulsion of feeling in Mary. No, she would not be unkind to him! She had heard enough of his uncle's tyranny.

The crows were clamouring louder than ever.

"Listen! They are condemning some poor wretch! I wonder you don't go and help him."

"Indeed I ought to!" cried Jörgen, happy to escape. He picked up his gun and ran, she following, up a short ascent and then along a path on the level. Upon and around two old trees the grey administrators of justice were raving; there were hundreds of them. But the moment they saw a man with a gun, they scattered, cawing, in every direction. Their task was accomplished.

Between two large trees lay an unusually large crow, featherless and bleeding, in its death struggle. Jörgen was going to take hold of it.

"No, don't touch it!" called Mary, and turned away.

She went straight down again as she had come. Hearing Jörgen follow, she stopped.

"You will come with me, won't you, and dine?"

He thanked her. They walked on together silently until they came to where he had been lying. Then he hastily asked:

"How are things going at home?"

She smiled. "Thank you, really well, considering everything."

The smoke from the chimney curled into the air. The roofs with their glazed blue tiles looked affluently comfortable. The large gardens on both sides with their gravel walks lay like striped wings outstretched from the houses. The whole had an air of life, as if it might rise into the air at any moment.

"Had you been lying long here?" Mary asked unmercifully; she regarded Jörgen's mood as a species of possession.

He did not answer. She set off on the last, very steep part of the descent.

"Shall I help you?"

"No, thank you; I have come down here oftener than you."

It was a silent repast. Jörgen always ate slowly, but never had he eaten so slowly as to-day. Mary despatched each course quickly, and then sat and watched him, making an occasional remark, which was politely answered. His eyes, which generally swept over her like waves, ready to draw her in, had difficulty to-day in rising higher than the plate before them. Stopping suddenly, he said: "Are you not well?"

"Yes, thank you; but I have had enough."

A quarter of an hour later Jörgen came out of Anders Krog's room. Mary had just left Mrs. Dawes's, and was opening the door of her own. Jörgen said:

"It seems to me that your father is much better, Miss Krog."

"Yes, he can speak a little now, and also move his arm a little."

Jörgen evidently did not hear.

"Is this your room?—I have never seen it."

She moved out of the way; he looked, and looked again.

"Won't you go in?"

"May I?"

"Certainly."

He approached the threshold and crossed it slowly, she following. Then he stood perfectly still, breathing deeply, she at his side. Was the room hung with lace? He could not collect his impressions ... the bed and the furniture, white with blue, or blue with white; Cupids on the ceiling; paintings, amongst them one of her beautiful mother, with flowers in front of it ... and a fragrance—exhaled not by the flowers alone, but by Mary herself and her belongings. She was there, beside him, in her blue dress with the elbow-sleeves. In the midst of this purity of fragrance and colour he felt ashamed of himself—so ashamed that he could have rushed out. He could not control his feeling; his breast heaved; he trembled, and was on the point of bursting into tears. Then two white arms gleamed, and he heard something said—blue and white and white and blue, the words also. The door was closed behind him—it must have been done to conceal his weakness. The two white arms gleamed again, and he heard distinctly: "Why, Jörgen! Jörgen!" He felt a hand on his arm, and sank on to a chair. She had really said "Jörgen"—said it twice. Now she stroked his forehead and smoothed the hair back from it, with a touch soft as a flower-petal. It loosed something; everything hard and painful melted under her hand and flowed away, leaving an indescribable feeling of warmth. She who now bent over him was, in truth, the first who had helped him since he was a child. He had been so lonely! There was confidence in him in the touch of her hand. How undeserved! But how it comforted him! He dreamed that he, too, was good, was under the control of beneficent powers. The white and the blue spread a canopy over him. Underneath it these large, sympathetic eyes drew his soul into theirs. He said apologetically and very low: "I could not bear it any longer." What it was he had not been able to bear, she understood, for she immediately moved away.

"Mary!" he whispered. The word fell involuntarily from his lips; he was thinking aloud. It alarmed him, it alarmed her. She moved farther away; a confused look came into her eyes; something as it were failed her. He saw this—and before she could foresee, before he himself knew what he was doing, he was beside her, embracing her, pressing her close to him. Excited by the feeling of her body against his, he kissed, kissed, wherever his lips reached. She bent away from him, now to this side, now to that, upon which he kissed her neck, round and round. She felt that she was in danger. She had only one arm free, but with it she pushed him from her, at the same time bending her body so far back that she was on the point of falling. This brought him above her; desire awoke, he would take advantage of the situation. But he had to loosen his right arm to grasp her with. In doing so he released her left arm; she set it against his breast with all her strength, and was now able to turn sidewards and rise to her feet. Their eyes met, fierce and flaming. Neither spoke. They were breathing short and hard.

"Mary!" screamed some one outside. It was Mrs. Dawes. Mrs. Dawes, who was supposed to be unable to leave her bed, stood in the passage. "Mary!" she screamed once again, as if she were about to faint. Both rushed out. Mrs. Dawes was standing in her night-dress outside her open door, leaning against the wall. She was in the act of falling when Jörgen Thiis sprang forward and caught her. One servant after the other rushed upstairs—even little Nanna came. Jörgen stood supporting Mrs. Dawes until, with their united strength, they lifted her and carried her in. She was incapable of setting her foot to the ground again. Her eyes were closed; whether she was in a faint or not they did not know. She was a terrible weight. It was all they could do to get her across the threshold. Then they proceeded slowly towards the bed; but the worst was to come, the lifting her in. Every time the heavy body reached the edge of the bed, the legs refused to follow, and down the unfortunate lady slipped again. She did not help herself in the least, she only groaned; and before they could get a proper grip, she was on the floor. When they had once again raised the weighty mass, but not far enough for it to hold itself in position unsupported, they stood helpless, for they had no idea how to manœuvre it farther. Nanna burst out laughing and ran out of the room. Jörgen shot a furious glance after her. This was too much even for Mary. Three minutes ago she had been engaged in a desperate struggle—now she was seized with such an inclination to laugh that she, too, had to run away. She was standing outside with her handkerchief to her mouth, doubled up with laughter, when the nurse came out of her father's room; he wished to know what was going on. Mary went to him. She could hardly tell him for laughing—tell him, that is, about Mrs. Dawes's position, and Jörgen's and the servants' struggles. Her father tried to ask why Mrs. Dawes had been in the passage. This stopped Mary's laughter. One of the maids came from the other room and said that Mrs. Dawes was now in bed, and that she wished to speak to Miss Krog.

Jörgen was standing at the foot of the bed. Mrs. Dawes lay groaning and weeping and calling for Mary. No sooner did Mary appear at the door than she began:

"What was happening to you, child? Sudden terror seized me. What was going on?"

Mary went up to the bed without looking at Jörgen. She knelt down and put her arm round her old friend's neck.

"Oh, Aunt Eva!" she said, and laid her head on the old lady's breast. Presently she began to cry.

"What is it? What is it? What is making you so unhappy?" moaned Mrs. Dawes, stroking the beautiful hair.

At last Mary looked up. Jörgen Thiis had gone; but she still kept silence.

"I have never felt like that," began Mrs. Dawes again, "except when something dreadful was happening."

Mary kept silence.

"Had Jörgen Thiis anything to do with it?"

Mary gave her a look.

"Ah! that is what I feared. But remember, my child, that he has loved you since the first time he saw you—you, and no one else. That means a great deal. And never once so much as hinted it to you—has he?"

Mary shook her head.

"It's no small thing, that either. It shows strength of character. He has served you and he has honoured you—don't be too hard on him. Not till now, when you are poor, does he dare—but what was it?"

Mary waited a little; then she said:

"First I thought he was ill. Then he suddenly lost his senses."

"Oh, I could tell you something. I too.... Yes, yes, yes!" She seemed lost in thought. Then she murmured: "Those who go for years...."

But Mary cut her short. "Don't let us talk any more about it," she said, rising.

"No. Only it is...."

"No more on that subject, please!" repeated Mary, walking to the window. Standing there she heard Mrs. Dawes say: "You must let me tell you that he has spoken to me—asked me if he dared offer himself to you. He can imagine no greater happiness than to help you when we are no longer able. But he thinks that you are too unapproachable."

Mary made an involuntary movement. Mrs. Dawes saw it.

"Don't be too hard on him, Mary. Do you know, child, that your father and I think ..."

"Now, Aunt Eva!" Mary turned sharply towards her—not as if she were angry, but yet in such a manner as to check the words on the old lady's lips.

Mary remained in the room. She would not risk meeting Jörgen Thiis. When she was doing some small service for Mrs. Dawes, the latter said: "You know, child, that Jörgen is to have Uncle Klaus's money?" As Mary did not answer, she ventured to go on. "And he believes that Uncle Klaus will help him if he marries." This, too, Mary allowed to pass unnoticed.

When there was no longer any danger, she went to her own room. There she recalled the scene from beginning to end. Her cheeks burned, but she was astonished that, dreadful though it had been, she was not really angry.

Just as she was thinking: What will happen next? there was a gentle knock at the door. Now she felt angry, and inclined to jump up and turn the key. Presently, however, she said: "Come in!" The door was opened and closed, but she did not look round from where she sat in her big chair. Gently, humbly, Jörgen came forward and knelt down on one knee in front of her, hiding his face with his hands. There was nothing in the action that offended her. He was strongly agitated. She looked down upon the handsome head with the soft hair, and her eyes fell on the long, true musician's fingers. Something refined about him conciliated her. But a mournful: "Shall I go!" was all that came from him. She waited a little, then in a low voice answered: "Yes." He let his hands drop, seized one of hers and pressed his lips to it—long, but reverently; then rose and left the room.

During the kiss, reverential as it was, a feeling of excitement passed through Mary, of the same nature as that which, when he kissed and kissed again, had made her almost faint away. She sat still, long after he had gone, wondering at this. She once more recalled every particular of their struggle, and shuddered. "Why am I not angry with him?"

Another knock was heard. It was the maid with a request from Mrs. Dawes that Mary would come to her.

"You have let him go, child?"

Mrs. Dawes was in real distress. In her agitation she sat up, supporting herself on one arm. Her cap was awry upon her grey, short hair; the fat neck was redder than usual, as if she were too hot.

"Why did you let him go?" she repeated.

"It was his own wish."

"How can you say such a thing, child? He has been here complaining. He would give his life to stay! You don't understand in the least. You do nothing but reject his advances, and torture him."

She lay down again, in exhaustion and despair. The word "torture" produced a momentary comic impression on Mary; but she herself had the feeling that she ought to have spoken to Jörgen before she let him go. That he was to go, she was quite determined.

On these events followed rather a hard time for them all. A change in the weather affected Anders Krog unfavourably; he was unable to take sufficient nourishment, and had more difficulty in speaking. Mary was much with him; and at these times his eyes rested on her and followed her so persistently that she almost felt afraid.

Mrs. Dawes sent small notes in to him. She could not give up her writing, even in bed. He looked long at Mary each time one of these notes came; so she guessed what they were about.

Mrs. Dawes said to her one day: "You over-estimate your own powers when you believe that you can live here alone with us."

"What do you mean?"

"I mean that, tired as you may be of society in spring, when winter comes it will exercise its attraction again. You are too much accustomed to it."

Mary made no answer at the time, but some days later—the weather had long been bad, and she had not been out—she said to Mrs. Dawes: "You may be right in believing that the life we have lived all these years has taken strong hold of me."

"Stronger than you have any idea of, child."

"But what would you have me do? I cannot leave here. Nor do I wish to."

"No. But you could have a change sometimes."

"How?"

"You know quite well what I mean, child. If you married Jörgen, he would live sometimes here with you, and you sometimes at Stockholm with him."

"A curious married life!"

"I don't believe you can combine the two things in any better way."

"Which two things?"

"What life demands of you and what you are accustomed to."

Mary felt that what Mrs. Dawes had just said expressed her father's wish. She knew that what gave him most anxiety was her future, and that a marriage with Jörgen which ensured Uncle Klaus's protection would give him a feeling of security. It oppressed her to think how little regard to her father's wishes she had hitherto shown.

These days, with their deliberations, struck her as resembling the recitative in an opera, the part which connects two important actions. Now that the season was advancing, she felt like a captive when she looked out across the bay. When she stood on the hill, watching autumn's stern entrance in foaming breakers, she knew that it was bringing imprisonment for the winter. Her spirit stirred in rebellion; she was accustomed to something so different.

Something in her blood stirred too. Her tranquillity was gone. As a memory, Jörgen was not repellent. The atmosphere which he brought with him was actually sympathetic.

That her father had been incapacitated by an apoplectic shock, that Jörgen had been on the spot when this occurred, that he was her father's choice—was there not something in this that linked them together? Was there not fate in it?

To make her appearance at Jörgen's side in Stockholm,^C and afterwards to be sent farther afield—could there be a more fitting conclusion to her life of travel, a better opportunity of turning to advantage all that she had learned during the course of it?

^C The Foreign Office of Sweden was at that time the Foreign Office of Norway also.

Uncle Klaus should help them—help them generously. She knew her power over Uncle Klaus.

"After all, Aunt Eva dear," she said one day when she sat chatting beside Mrs. Dawes's bed; "I think you may write to Jörgen."

Mary herself was standing on the pier when the steamer came in. It was Saturday afternoon; all that could do so were leaving town to enjoy the last days of autumn in the country. The weather was beautiful; in the south of Norway it can be so till far on in September. Mary was dressed in blue and carried a blue parasol, which she waved to Jörgen and some of her girl friends who were standing beside him. All on board moved towards the gangway to watch the meeting.

Jörgen felt, as soon as he reached her side, that he must be cautious. He divined that she had come to meet him here in order that their meeting might not be private.

On the way up to the house they talked of the swallows, which were now assembling for their departure—of the farm-overseer, who had just shot a huge eagle—of the writing-board which Mrs. Dawes had had constructed—of the good aftermath, of the price of fruit and turnips. In the hall she left him with a short "Excuse me!" and hurried upstairs. The boy who was carrying Jörgen's portmanteau had followed them in; Jörgen and he stood still, not knowing where to go. Then Mary called from above: "This way, please!" Opening the door of the visitors' room next her own, she told the boy to take the portmanteau in there. To Jörgen she said: "Shall we go and see Father?" She led the way. The nurse was not in the room. Probably it was to send her away that Mary had run up first.

A light kindled in the sick man's eyes as he saw Jörgen enter. As soon as the door was closed, Mary went up to her father, bent over him, and said: "Jörgen and I are engaged now, Father."

All the affection and happiness that a human face can express beamed from Anders Krog's. Smiling, Mary turned towards Jörgen, who, pale and agitated, was prepared to rush forward and embrace her. But he felt that though his astonishment, his gratitude, and his adoration were quite acceptable to her, she desired no such manifestation of them. This did not detract from his happiness. He met her smiling eyes with an expression of intense, perfect delight. He pressed the hand which Anders Krog could move; he looked into his tearful eyes, his own filling. But no word was spoken until Mary said: "Now we must go to Aunt Eva."

With a feeling of triumph she led the way. He followed, admiring. His heart was full of many feelings, not least among them admiration of the magnanimity with which she had forgiven. He thought: Out in the passage she will turn round, and then ... But she went straight to Mrs. Dawes's door and knocked.

When Mrs. Dawes saw Jörgen, she clapped her fat hands, tugged at her cap, and tried to sit up, but could not for excitement. She fell back again, wept, blessed them, and stretched out her arms. Jörgen allowed himself to be embraced, but would not kiss her.

As soon as sensible conversation became possible, Mary said: "Don't you think too, Aunt Eva, that we ought to go and call on Uncle Klaus to-morrow?"

"Most certainly I do, my child! most certainly! Why should there be any delay?"

Jörgen was radiant. Mary retired, that the two might have a confidential talk.

When Jörgen and she met again, he understood that the watchword was: "Look, but do not touch!" This was hard; but he acknowledged it to be only just that one who had presumed as he had should be compelled to control himself. Mary intended to be her own mistress.

In her triumphant mood she was more beautiful than ever. It seemed to Jörgen an act of grace when she addressed him as "thou." And she condescended no further. He went on hoping, but she gave no more—not the whole of that day. He betook himself to the piano and there poured forth his lament. Mary opened the doors, so that Mrs. Dawes might hear the music. "Poor boy!" said Mrs. Dawes.

Next day Mary did not come downstairs until it was time to set off on their expedition to Uncle Klaus's.

"You are *la grande dame* to-day, and no mistake!" said Jörgen, inspecting her admiringly. She was in her most elegant Parisian walking costume. "Is it to make an impression on Uncle Klaus?"

"Partly. But it is Sunday, you know.—Tell me," and she suddenly became serious; "does Uncle Klaus know about father's misfortune?"

"He knows about his illness, if you mean that."

"No; I mean the cause of it?"

"That I can't say. I came straight from home. I have told nothing—even at home."

Of this Mary approved. Consequently they were on the pleasantest, most confidential terms, both during the walk down to the steamer and on board. There they sat talking in whispers of their wedding, of furlough for the first month after it, of life in Stockholm, of her visits to him there, of his visit to Krogskogen at Christmas, of a trip to Christiania now—in short, there was not a cloud in their sky.

They found Uncle Klaus in his smoke-filled den, where they rather imagined than saw him. He himself was quite startled when Mary in all her glory appeared before him. He led them hurriedly into the large, stiff drawing-room. Even before they were seated, Jörgen said: "We have come, Uncle, to tell you—"

He got no farther, for Uncle Klaus saw in their radiant faces the news which they brought.

"My heartiest congratulations!" The tall man bowed, offering a hand to each. "Yes—every one says that you are the handsomest couple ever seen in this town. For," he added, "we engaged you to each other long ago."

Hardly were they seated before his face became gloomy. He looked compassionately at Mary. "But your father, my poor child!"

"Father is much better now," she answered evasively. Uncle Klaus looked searchingly at her. "But he can never...." He stopped; he was not capable of putting his thought into words; neither was Mary. They sat silent.

When they began to speak again, it was of the unusually bad times. It seemed as if there were to be no end to them. Investments were yielding no interest, the shipping trade was in a bad way, there were no new undertakings, money was not forthcoming. Whilst they were talking, Uncle Klaus looked several times at Jörgen as if he would put more questions but for his presence. Mary understood, and made a sign to Jörgen, who rose and asked permission to go, as he had an appointment with some friends in town. It was, thus, tacitly agreed upon between Mary and him that she should have a private interview with Uncle Klaus. But what was it Uncle Klaus wished to speak to her about? She was most curious.

As soon as the door closed behind Jörgen, the old man, with an anxious look, began: "Is it true, my poor child, that your father has had great losses in America?"

"He has lost everything," Mary replied.

Klaus jumped up, pale with the shock.

"Lost everything?"

He stared at her, open-mouthed and turning purple. Then exclaiming: "Good Lord! This is a simple enough explanation of the shock!" began to march up and down the room as if no one else were present. The wide trousers twisted themselves round his legs; he waved his long arms.

"He has always been a confiding simpleton! an absolute fool! Fancy having a fortune like that invested in another man's business and never looking after it! What a damned—" Here he stopped suddenly and asked in astonishment: "What do you mean to marry upon—?"

Mary had felt herself mortally insulted long before this question came. To behave thus in her presence—to speak thus of her father in her hearing! Nevertheless she answered archly and with her sweetest smile: "On our expectations from you, Uncle Klaus!"

Klaus's astonishment was beyond all measure. She tried to moderate it before it found vent; she joked—said in English that she felt dreadfully sorry for him, as she knew what a poor man he was! But he paid no more attention to her than a bear to the twitter of birds.

Out it came at last. "It is like that scoundrel Jörgen to speculate upon me!" Marching up and down again, faster than before, he continued: "Ha, ha! I might have known it! Whenever anything goes wrong, it is I who must come to the rescue—and at this moment, too, when I am hardly earning my bread! I never knew anything so impudent in my life!" He did not see her, he did not see anything. The rich man was accustomed to give free vent to his petulance, anger, insolence. "Jörgen deserves—confound him!—that I should stop the allowance I give him! He does nothing but ask for more. And now I am to——ha, ha! It's just like him!"

Mary listened, pale as death. Never before had she been so humiliated; never had any human being treated her otherwise than with the deference paid to a privileged person.

But she did not lose her head. "I keep Father's accounts now," she said coldly; "and I see from them that there is money of his in your hands."

"Yes," said Klaus, without stopping and without looking at Mary; "oh, yes—two hundred thousand kroner or so. But if you keep the accounts, you also see that at present these investments hardly yield anything."

"It is not so bad as that," she replied.

"Well—what about them?" asked he, standing still. An idea suddenly occurred to him: "Has Jörgen asked you to sell out?"

"Jörgen has asked nothing of me," Mary said, and rose to her feet.

As she stood there tall, pale, stately, facing him so bravely, Klaus felt himself worsted. He could do nothing but stare. When she said: "I am sorry that I did not know before what kind of man you are!" all his superiority vanished. He felt stupid and helpless, unable to answer, unable even to move. He allowed her to go—the very last thing he intended!

He looked out at the window and saw her sweep past towards the market-place. What a vision of proud beauty she was!

When, in course of time, Jörgen came to fetch Mary, or rather to stay to dinner there with her—for he was certain that they would be invited—an even more violent explosion of wrath awaited him; because now Uncle Klaus was extremely dissatisfied with himself too.

"Why the devil did you not come alone? You were afraid!—And you wanted her to sell shares now, when they are worth nothing—like the cursedly extravagant, reckless fellow you always have been!"

Uncle Klaus was wrong; but Jörgen knew him—knew that he must not answer. He slunk away and joined Mary at the house in the market-place, even more wretched than the day when she found him on the ridge, gazing down into the lost paradise. She herself had been weeping with anger and disappointment; but there was abundance of elasticity in her; now came the rebound. Their fall from the triumphant elevation of half-an-hour ago had been so precipitous that when Jörgen's misery was added as a finishing touch, the whole became ridiculous. She laughed so heartily, so exhilaratingly, that even Jörgen was cured. A quarter of an hour later the two went out to order a good dinner, with champagne. They had agreed to take a walk whilst it was being prepared. But no sooner did they feel the delicious fresh air, than Jörgen rushed upstairs again and telephoned to Krogskogen that they were coming out to dine there. It was a good two hours' walk by the new coast-road—how they would enjoy it!

They set off at a rapid pace. It was the very weather for walking, this bright, cool autumn day with the fresh breeze.

The road followed the coast line, rounding all the rocky headlands; they looked forward to the constant changes—from shore to height, from height to shore. On the sea, dark blue to-day, sailing ships and columns of smoke were to be seen, far as the eye could reach. It being Sunday, there were also pleasure-boats out, some gliding about among the islands, others venturing out to the open sea.

At their quick pace, the two young people were soon in the outskirts of the town. They passed a pretty little house in a garden.

"Who lives there?" asked Mary, admiring it.

"Miss Röy, the doctor," answered Jörgen, immediately adding: "Our annoyance and disappointment made me forget to tell you that I met Frans Röy in town."

Unconsciously Mary stood still; involuntarily she blushed. "Frans Röy?" she repeated, looking hard at him—then walked on without waiting for an answer.

"He is here to inspect the operations at the harbour. You know that Irgens is dead."

"The engineer? is he dead?"

"They say now that Captain Röy will probably take his place."

"Is it work for a man like him?"

"Many are no doubt asking the same question—asking what brings him here," laughed Jörgen.

Mary looked at him and he at Mary. Then he went nearer to her. "But now he comes too late."

He had expected an understanding glance in answer—possibly with a little happiness in it. She walked on without looking at him, and without speaking.

They were silent for a long time, walking fast in the refreshing autumn breeze. At last she turned towards him, with the intention of giving him a pleasant surprise.

"Do you know, Jörgen, that Father has two hundred thousand kroner invested in Uncle Klaus's business?"

"He has two hundred and fifty thousand," Jörgen answered.

She was much surprised—in the first place by Jörgen's knowing, in the second, by the fifty thousand.

"Uncle Klaus himself said two hundred thousand."

"Yes, your father has that sum invested in Uncle's ships and commercial enterprises. But lately, before he was taken ill, he sent Uncle fifty thousand more, which he had lying idle."

"How do you know?"

"Uncle told me."

"There is no note of this last sum in father's books."

"No; your father probably did not take the trouble to enter it; he was not in the habit of doing so. Besides"—here Jörgen paused—"are you in possession of all your father's business papers?"

Into this subject Mary would not enter; she knew that the question was a natural one; but how in the world did Jörgen——? Perhaps through Mrs. Dawes. What he had told her, however, rejoiced her. She stood still; there was something she wanted to say. But the wind caught up her skirts, unloosed some of her hair, and blew about her scarf.

"How perfectly lovely you look!" Jörgen exclaimed.

"But Jörgen—then there is nothing in the way!"

"We can marry, you mean?"

"Yes!" and off she started.

"No, dear. The shares are yielding almost nothing just now."

"What does that matter? We'll risk it, Jörgen!" she cried, radiant with health and courage.

"Without Uncle's consent?" asked Jörgen in a despondent tone.

Mary stood still again. "He would disinherit you?"

Instead of answering directly, Jörgen began mournfully: "I wish you knew, Mary, what I have had to bear from Uncle, from the day he adopted me—the things he has demanded of me, the things he has persecuted me for. To this very day he treats me like a naughty schoolboy. The worst of his bad temper is vented upon me."

The mixture of unhappiness and bitterness depicted on his face led Mary involuntarily to exclaim: "Poor Jörgen—now I begin to understand!"

They walked on. She reflected that Jörgen's power of self-control had been acquired in a hard school; there he had also learned the art of concealment. She could not but admire his tenacity of purpose. What had it not accomplished! Think of his music alone! It, however, had been a great consolation to him. Now she understood his extreme politeness; now she understood his sentimentality; she understood what had made him so exacting and severe with those under his command.

She saw that she herself had probably added to his unhappiness. His long, silent love for her had only been an additional burden; for she had not given him one encouraging word—very much the reverse! What wonder that at last it should have become a kind of possession!

"Poor Jörgen!" she said again, and took his hand.

It was the first token of affection she had bestowed upon him. She had to draw her hand away again immediately to hold down her dress, for a strong wind was blowing at the point, and a sailing-boat was tacking just below them. The people in it waved up to them, and they waved back. How fresh the air was! How brilliantly blue the fjord!

As they were descending towards the bay, Mary asked: "Do you really believe that Uncle Klaus will disinherit you if we marry?"

"My dear girl, we have nothing to marry on!"

"We can sell these shares," she said undauntedly.

"If we were to sell them at their present price, in order to be able to marry at once, he would be absolutely certain to cut me off."

But Mary would not give in. "There are our woods."

"It will be several years before there is any timber to fell."

How well informed Jörgen was! How carefully he had thought the whole thing out!

They had now reached the stretch of level road which led along the shore to the last headland before Krogskogen. At a farm here there was a surly old Lapland dog. Mary and he were good friends. He always barked a little as people came up; probably he did not see well; but as soon as he scented an acquaintance his tail began to wag.

To-day he was furious.

"Dear me!" exclaimed Mary, "is it you who are making him so angry, Jörgen?"

Jörgen did not answer, but stooped to pick up a small stone. When the dog saw this, he scurried off with his tail between his legs to the shelter of a heap of sticks, and there continued to bark.

"Don't do it!" said Mary, as she saw Jörgen taking aim.

"It will be interesting to see whether or not he retreats in the exact direction of my aim—if he does, the stone will hit him on the back." As Jörgen spoke, he pretended to throw. Off rushed the dog. Then he threw, and the stone landed exactly where he had said. The dog howled.

"You see!" said Jörgen exultingly. "There are not many who can throw like that, I can tell you."

"Do you shoot equally well?"

"Certainly. What I do, Mary—it isn't much, I know—but I do it fairly well."

This she was obliged to admit. The dog's distant fury also confirmed the statement.

As they were taking the short cut up to the house, Jörgen began: "Do you think we should say anything to Mrs. Dawes or to your father about this?"

"About Uncle Klaus?"

"Yes. It will only distress them. Can't we say that Uncle Klaus asked us to wait till spring?"

Mary stood still. Such a line of action was not to her mind. But Jörgen continued:

"I know Uncle Klaus better than you do. He will repent soon. He will certainly not give in to us; but he will make a proposal of his own—probably what I am asking you to say—that we should wait till spring."

Mary had already discovered how well informed Jörgen was; so she could not but allow that he was probably better able to judge than she. But she was unaccustomed to roundabout methods.

"Let me manage it," Jörgen said. "I'll spare the old people a disappointment."

"But what am *I* to say, then?" asked Mary.

"What is perfectly true. That Uncle Klaus was delighted to hear of our engagement; but that as times are so bad just now, we shall be obliged to wait. And this is really the case."

Mary agreed, the more willingly because she thought it considerate of Jörgen to wish to spare the old people. For this he received her best thanks—and her hand again. He kept hold of it until they reached the house, and even whilst they mounted the steps. He thought to himself: "This is the pledge of a kiss in the hall. But I'll take ten!"

He opened the door and let Mary pass in first. Nodding brightly to him as she passed, she made quickly for the stairs and disappeared up them. He heard her go into her own room.

Carefully as Jörgen chose his words in communicating the result of their expedition, it was a sad disappointment to the old people. It was inexplicable to them both, but especially to Mrs. Dawes, who thought the decision arrived at cruel. Mary was to spend the long winter alone here, and Jörgen in Stockholm. They might possibly see each other for a few days at Christmas, but that would be all. Curiously enough, the old people's disappointment reacted upon Jörgen. He sat moping like a sick bird, had nothing to say, hardly answered Mrs. Dawes when she spoke to him, and presently went off to prepare for his departure next morning. His leave had expired, and he was going direct to Stockholm.

Mary alone was in good spirits. One would have supposed that she had no concern whatever in the matter. To her the day had, to all appearance, brought no disappointment. The triumphant mood in which she had been ever since she graciously proclaimed their engagement in her father's room, far from having abated, was more pronounced than ever. She went humming about the rooms and passages, and seemed to have no end of arrangements to make, as if it were she who was about to take an important and long journey. At supper she joked and teased until Jörgen began to have an uncomfortable suspicion that she was making fun of him. At last he said plainly that he could not understand her. He thought she ought rather to be sorry for him. She was to remain here in her own comfortable home, working for those whom she loved, whilst he———. Now he *hated* what he was going back to, because it took him away from her! He repented his exchange into the diplomatic service. He loathed Stockholm. He knew what an inferior position a young man occupied there who had no good introductions, and who, in addition to this, was Norwegian. He was, in short, unhappy, and grumbled freely.

"You who distinguished yourself in the confirmation class, Jörgen, don't you know that Jacob had to work seven whole years for Rachel?"

"And how many have I not worked for you, Mary?"

"Ah! the reason of that is that you began far too early. It's a bad habit you have acquired—that of beginning too early."

"Was it possible to see you without...? You are unjust to yourself."

"You had other aims, Jörgen, besides winning me."

"So had that business-man, Jacob. And he had the advantage over me, that whilst working and waiting he could see Rachel as often as he liked."

"Well, well—he who has waited so many years, Jörgen, can surely wait half a year longer."

"It is easy for you to talk, you who have never waited—never for anything!"

Mary was silent.

"But that you should tease me into the bargain, Mary—I who, even when I am beside you, must exist on such meagre fare!"

"You think you have cause of complaint, Jörgen?"

"Yes, I do."

"You began far too early, remember!" And Mary laughed.

This put Jörgen out, but presently he repeated: "You don't understand what it means to wait."

"So much I do understand, that it comes easier to those who live on meagre fare." And she laughed again.

Jörgen was both offended and perplexed. A woman who really cared for him would hardly have behaved thus on the eve of parting from him for several months, and with such poor prospects as they had of being able to marry.

They sat for a short time beside her father, and longer beside Mrs. Dawes. Jörgen was quiet—hardly spoke. But Mary was gay. Mrs. Dawes watched them in surprise. Turning to Jörgen, she said: "Poor boy, you must come here at Christmas!" Mary answered for him: "Aunt Eva, it is just at Christmas that Stockholm is pleasantest."

Suddenly Mary rose and very unexpectedly said good-night, first to Jörgen, then to Mrs. Dawes.

"I am tired after the walk, and I must be up early to-morrow to see Jörgen off."

Jörgen felt that this sudden departure was a piece of deliberate mischief. She wished to escape saying good-night to him in the passage. He vowed to revenge himself. He was skilled in the art.

Mrs. Dawes asked if there were any misunderstanding between them. He said there was none. She did not believe it; he had to assure her again solemnly that he knew of none. But he could not conceal that he was out of temper; he could not even bear to sit there any longer. When he left he found the passage, contrary to custom, dark, and had to grope his way to his own door. Not till he had lit his lamp and listened involuntarily for any sound from Mary's room, did it occur to him that the door-handle had been made noiseless. In the morning it had creaked—very little; but it certainly had creaked. Never had he been in such a well-ordered house as this, where the very slightest thing amiss was instantly put right—even on a Sunday. He could not imagine greater happiness than to return here when everything should be satisfactorily arranged, to rest, and to live as long as he chose in the manner which his ardent desire for the pleasures of the senses pictured.

Therefore patience! He would submit to Mary's caprices now, as he had submitted to his uncle's before—until his time came!

He was undressing, when the door opened noiselessly, and Mary entered, in her night-dress—dazzlingly beautiful. She closed the door behind her and went forward to the lamp. "You shall not wait, Jörgen," said she, as she extinguished the light.

ALONE

NEXT morning she slept too long. She was awakened by singing and playing. First as in a dream and then consciously, through a rushing stream of memories, she heard Jörgen Thiis. He was at the piano, singing in the freshness of the early morning, the windows flung open, his clear, jubilant tenor wafting festal tones up to her.

In a moment she was up and dressing, afraid lest she might be too late to go down with him to the steamer. The wider awake she became with the rapid motion, the more impetuously did her thoughts rush towards him and his joyful agitation. That heartfelt, soul and sense pervading gratitude and praise—she would fain enjoy it in his immediate neighbourhood. She longed to be uplifted and borne in triumph as his life's queen! Of her sovereign grace she had bestowed on him life's highest prize. He was rewarded now for his long sufferings!—without bargaining, without regard for established prejudices. She knew him now; she knew exactly how he would look, exactly in what manner he would make her the partaker of his happiness. Therefore her breast heaved high in expectation of the meeting—expectation of his gratitude and homage.

In her blue morning dress she passed through the little Dutch ante-room and stretched out her hand to open the door of the big drawing-room with the windows to the sea; but so excited was she that she had to pause to take breath—enjoying Jörgen's triumph the while. He was so carried away with his own music that she was quite close to him before he noticed her. He looked up, radiant—rose slowly, silently, as to a festal rite. This impression he would do nothing to destroy. He opened his arms, drew her into his embrace, kissed her hair gently, stroked the cheek that lay bare—slowly, protectingly. He was trying to shield, to hide, to help her with manly tenderness to overcome the feeling of shame from which she must be suffering. His whole attitude was tender and reassuring.

"But we must hurry in to breakfast now," he whispered affectionately, kissing her beautiful hair again, and inhaling its fragrance. Then he passed his arm gently, yet in a controlling manner, round her waist. Near the door he said in a low tone: "You have slept well, since you come so late?" He opened the door with his disengaged hand, and, receiving no answer, looked sympathisingly at her. She was pale and confused. "My sweet one!" he whispered soothingly.

At breakfast there was no end to his consideration for her, especially when it became evident that she could not eat. But time was short; he had to attend to himself; so he could not talk much. Mary did not say a word. But it struck her that Jörgen handled his knife and fork in a new, masterful manner, of a piece with that in which he now spoke to her and looked at her. He evidently desired to inspire her with courage—after what had happened last night. She could have taken her plate with what was on it and flung it in his face!

His triumphal song had been in his own honour! He had been hymning his own worthiness!

A decanter with wine stood on the table. Jörgen poured out a large glass, drank it slowly, and rose with a dignified: "Excuse me!" adding in the doorway: "I must look if the boy has taken my portmanteau."

In a moment he was back again. "Time is almost up." He closed the door, and hurried across the room to Mary, who was now standing at the window. This time he drew her quickly into his arms and began to kiss.

"No more of that, please!" she said with all her old queenliness, and turned away from him. She walked proudly into the hall, put on her coat with the assistance of the maid who hastened to help, chose a hat, looked out to see the state of the weather, and then took her parasol. The maid opened the front door. Mary passed out quickly, Jörgen following, mortally offended. He was unconscious of any transgression.

They walked on for a time silent. But Mary was in such a state of suppressed rage that when she at last remembered to put up her parasol, she almost broke it. Jörgen saw this.

"Remember," she said—and it sounded as if she had suddenly acquired a new voice—"I don't care about letters. And I can't write letters."

"You don't wish me to write to you?" He had also a new voice.

She did not answer, nor did she look at him.

"But if anything should happen——?" said he.

"Well, of course then—! But you forget that you have Mrs. Dawes."

And as if this were not enough, she added: "I don't imagine that you, either, are a good letter-writer, Jörgen. So there will be nothing lost."

He could have struck her.

As ill luck would have it, the surly old Lapland dog was at the landing-place with his master. No sooner did he catch sight of Jörgen than he began to bark. All his master's attempts to silence him were in vain.

Every one turned to look at the new-comers. Jörgen had at once picked up a small stone, and Mary had asked him in a low voice not to throw it. The steamer was now lying to; it diverted the attention of all, including the dog. For this moment Jörgen had been waiting; he flung the stone with all his might, and a loud howl arose. He immediately turned to Mary, swept off his hat with his best smile, and thanked her for the hospitality shown him.

For the sake of appearances she could not but remain on the pier until the steamer went; she was even obliged to wave her parasol once or twice. Smiling and triumphant, Jörgen returned sweeping bows from the steamer's deck.

How furious she was! But he was hardly less so.

"He, who should have thrown himself in the dust before me, and kissed the hem of my dress!" This was Mary's feeling.

She had had a dawning suspicion last night of a want of delicacy in her lover. He would not let her go. She had had to resort to artifice, and had been obliged to lock her door. But she had explained his behaviour to herself as an unfortunate result of those years of longing which had turned his passion into a morbid possession.

Now uncertainty was no longer possible! Only an "experienced hand" could behave like this. She had been deceived! The very best that was in her, fostered and guarded by her noblest instincts, had been led loathsomely astray.

With this thought she wrestled and strove all day long. She called herself betrayed, dishonoured. At first she thrust the blame away from herself. Then she took it all upon herself, and pronounced herself unworthy to live. She did nothing but make mistakes; she was her own betrayer! One hour she said to herself: "Violence was done me, although I gave myself to him voluntarily!" The next she said: "All this has its beginning farther back, and I cannot unravel it."

What a blessing that her own room remained undefiled! The one next it she would never enter again.

With Jörgen she would have nothing more to do! But would he in these circumstances keep silence? She felt certain that he would. His faults did not lie in this direction—otherwise she, too, must have heard something. But that even one human being should exist who——! She wept with anger and impotence. It would break her spirit. It would weigh on her like an incubus—heaviest when she rose highest.

She would meet him! She would tell him what she had taken him for, and what he was—to whom she thought she was going that night and whom she found. He should not be able to boast! But to carry out this intention she must know something about his life. Whom dared she ask? who knew?

When she awoke next morning, her mind was clearer—clearer in the first place as to how she must proceed in acquiring information regarding Jörgen. It must be gathered as opportunity offered, so that no one's attention should be attracted. It was also clear to her that the breach with him, and the meeting which was to prepare it, must be postponed—chiefly for the sake of the old people. But her second and much more important resolve was to restore the equilibrium of her own life, to escape from the unhealthy atmosphere which had been her undoing. This could be done in only one way; she must take up her work again, fit herself to do it better, and gain new courage by success.

Work and duty! She raised herself on her elbow, as if imitating the corresponding uplifting of her mind. The next moment she was out of bed, preparing to begin.

The 50,000 kroner which her father had given to Uncle Klaus, and of which she had found no record in his books—did they not indicate that he probably had money in America over and above that which had been in his brother's business? that the interest which he had not spent had been invested there? that 50,000 kroner of capital had lately been paid up and sent home?

Ever since Jörgen had told her about these 50,000 kroner, the thought of them had been haunting her. Now she must examine her father's American correspondence; they must be mentioned in it. But no American letters could she find, until she opened a small box which was shoved under a book-shelf, and the key of which she found in her father's purse. She remembered that this box had accompanied them on their travels, but she had never known what it contained. In it lay the American correspondence and accounts. It seemed as if, ever since her mother's days, he had kept this American part of his fortune, and everything relating to it, separate from the rest. And a very considerable sum he must still own over there, even although the principal part, the million, was lost. Mary became quite excited. Her father had undoubtedly understood from the fatal letter that everything he possessed in America was lost; and she and the others had received the same impression.

She now went to her father's room, explained things carefully to him, and said that she intended to go to America at once to investigate the matter. He was startled, but soon recognised the necessity of the step, and agreed to it.

Mrs. Dawes was not so confiding. She felt that there was something wrong, and that Mary was seeking distraction. But Mary's manner in telling of her discovery and intention was quite determined. Therefore the old lady confined herself to a gentle reminder of the gales likely to be encountered at this season.

Three days later Mary, with an English-speaking maid, was on her way to America, confident, as she had assured her father, of finding some one among her many acquaintances capable of giving her the assistance she required.

Everything happened as she had hoped, and in six weeks she was home again. It was fortunate that she had gone out when she did, for proceedings were on the point of being taken on the assumption that Anders Krog had been his brother's full partner, whereas his partnership was limited to the amount which he had invested in the business. This Mary was in a position to prove.

Her business success inspired her with courage. Why not go on? She had capital at her disposal now with which to commence operations. She felt very much inclined to try. And the timber trade too! Was she not as capable as any one of learning it? Was book-keeping by double-entry so very difficult? She set to work at once.

Anders Krog seemed to revive after his daughter's return. The certainty that the money which had not been in his brother's business was saved gave him the greatest satisfaction. Mary's future was his one thought.

Mrs. Dawes, on the contrary, became visibly worse. It seemed as if the once active, indefatigable woman had no strength left to draw upon. She did not even ask after Jörgen; her correspondence she had quite given up.

Mary managed the property with the assistance of the overseer, and her father's money with the aid of a lawyer. She took lessons and studied. Twice a week she went to town.

The time passed thus until the beginning of November. Then Anders Krog received a letter from a near relation in Christiania, whose only child, a daughter, had just become engaged. He was particularly anxious that Mary should come and take part in the festivities to be held on this occasion. Several entertainments were to be given by both families concerned.

Mary was surprised at the pleasure with which the prospect suddenly filled her. The old Adam was not dead! She hummed cheerfully as she went about the house making her preparations. She was longing for new surroundings—and for new homage! It was as reparation she desired it; this she was obliged to confess to herself.

She had not been in Christiania many days before Anders received a letter proclaiming her praises in the strongest words in the language. It was not the engaged couple, but Mary, who attracted most attention at the balls; it was she who was distinguished and fêted—the young couple themselves being amongst her most devoted admirers! Her unique style of beauty, her charm of manner, her accomplishments, her tact, had made an indelible impression upon them all. They must be allowed to keep her a little longer.

Anders Krog sent the letter in to Mrs. Dawes, with the request that it should be returned soon. He spent most of the day reading it.

Next morning Mary came home. She went upstairs quietly to her father's room. He was shocked with her look. She was ill, she said; and this was plainly visible. She was not pale, but grey; her eyes were heavy with sleep, her voice was faint. She embraced her father long and tenderly, but would neither look at his letter nor tell him about her visit. She must go to bed and rest, she told him, as soon as she had seen Mrs. Dawes.

She did not stay half a minute with Mrs. Dawes, whom she left terribly anxious.

She slept all day, ate a little at supper-time, and slept again all night.

When she got up she looked much as usual, and was active and interested in everything. Overseer, gardener, and housekeeper came with their reports, and she went her usual rounds. Then she made her father happy again by coming smiling into his room.

She had come to tell him that there was nothing now to prevent her marrying at once. They would be quite well enough off. Her father managed with great difficulty to say that he had been thinking the same himself. His eyes and the one hand said more, namely, that nothing would please him better.

But when she told Mrs. Dawes, and added that she thought of going at once to Stockholm to propose it (Jörgen's name was not mentioned), Mrs. Dawes's usual perspicacity returned; she sat up in bed and began to weep bitterly. Then Mary's courage failed her; she threw herself on the bed and whispered: "It's only too true, Aunt Eva!" She wept as she had never wept in her life before. But as Mrs. Dawes's agitation was increased by this, she was obliged to raise her head and say: "Aunt Eva, dear, Father will hear us!" This subdued them a little. Then Mrs. Dawes told, through her tears, that this was her own story over again. Not until after her fiancé had induced her to go the same length did she discover what a despicable man he was.

"Then we were obliged to marry. You see now, child, what we women are; we never learn."

"Oh, if only you and Father had not insisted on bringing this man into my life!" moaned Mary. "My instinct warned me to keep him at a distance, but you deadened it." She added at once: "No, don't take it like that, Aunt Eva! I am not reproaching you and Father. Besides, there's no use in complaining now. There is only one thing to be done—to shut my eyes and take the plunge."

In this Mrs. Dawes entirely agreed with her. "Afterwards you will do as I did; when your reputation is saved, you will separate from him."

"No, that I shall not do. There will be something then that will bind us together. Good God! good God!" she moaned, clinging to her old friend and smothering her cry in the bed-clothes.

Mrs. Dawes sat helpless, holding her. "I don't understand this," she said.

Mary raised her head quickly: "Do you not understand? He did it on purpose to bind me. He knew me."

Then she threw herself across the bed again, miserable, despairing. Between her outbursts of weeping came the cry: "There is no way out of it! no way out of it!"

Mrs. Dawes had neither the strength nor the courage to seek for words to comfort such distress.

It took its free course, until the anger cooled. Mrs. Dawes could feel that another emotion was gradually taking the upper hand. Mary raised her head; in her eyes, red with weeping, was hatred.

"I thought that I was giving myself to a gentleman; I discovered that it was to a speculator." She rose slowly.

"Will you say that to him, child?"

"Most certainly not! Nothing whatever to that effect. I shall merely say that it is necessary we should marry."

Three days later a letter was brought in to Jörgen Thiis at the Foreign Office. It was from Mary. "I am at the Grand Hotel, and expect you to meet me there, outside the entrance, at two o'clock punctually."

He understood at once what this implied, and hurried off, for it was now a quarter to two. It did not strike him until he was on his way downstairs that their meeting was to be "outside the entrance"!

She did not wish to be alone with him in her room.

This altered his intentions. He ran up to his rooms and released from imprisonment a little black poodle puppy, a valuable animal, which he was training.

The middle of the road was filthy with slush and mud, and the dog was at once ordered to keep beside his master on the pavement, which was clean. After a few sprightly excursions he became obedient; he was afraid of Jörgen's thin cane.

Mary's erect figure was distinguishable from a long distance. She stood with her back to them, looking in the direction of the palace. Jörgen's heart beat violently; his courage was failing him.

Mary became aware of his approach by the dog's rushing up to her as to an old friend. She loved dogs; nothing but her constant change of abode had prevented her keeping one. And this was such a beautiful, healthy, well-kept animal, so entirely to her taste in every way, that she involuntarily bent down to take notice of him. As she did so she saw Jörgen. She drew herself up again at once.

"Is this your dog?" she asked, as if they had parted half an hour ago.

"Yes," answered he, taking off his hat respectfully.

Then she bent down again and patted the dog: "What a beauty you are! a real beauty! No—keep down!"

"Keep down!" came in a more peremptory tone from Jörgen.

Mary straightened herself again. "Where shall we go?" she asked. "I have never been in Stockholm before."

"We may as well go straight on. If we take the turning yonder we shall come to John Ericson's monument."

"Yes, I should like to see that." They walked on.

"Come here!" called Jörgen to the dog, indicating the spot with his stick. He was offended by Mary's not even having offered him her hand. The dog came dejectedly, but cheered up immediately, for Mary spoke to him and patted him again.

"I have been over in America," she said.

"Yes, I heard that."

"The 50,000 kroner of which you spoke were not in my father's books, which made me certain that he must keep a separate account of the money in America. This account I found. It showed me the necessity for going across and saving what could be saved. The main sum was, of course, hopelessly lost."

"What success had you?"

"I brought home with me the accumulated interest of all these years."

"The money had been well invested?"

"Better, I believe, than it could have been in Europe."

Here followed a short intermezzo. The dog had been off the pavement, and now received a few cuts with the cane. This made Mary indignant.

"Dear me! the dog doesn't understand."

"Yes, he understands perfectly; but he has not learned to obey."

They walked on quickly. "What is your intention in telling me this?" asked Jörgen.

"To show you that we can marry at once."

"How much is there?"

"About two hundred thousand."

"Dollars?"

"No, kroner. And the 50,000 besides."

"It is not enough."

"Along with the rest?"

"The 'rest' is hardly yielding anything at present. That you know."

Mary began to feel ill. He knew it by her voice when she said: "We have the timber to fall back upon."

"Which cannot be felled for three years; possibly not for four, or even five? That depends entirely on its growth."

Mary knew that he was right. Why had she mentioned it? "But—ten to twelve thousand kroner a year...?"

"Is not enough in our position."

Another intermezzo. There was no pavement here. They had come to a large, open space, thick with mud. Both had forgotten the dog. A fat, dirty ship-dog, also of the poodle tribe, had come on shore with some sailors, who were sauntering along in the same direction as Mary and Jörgen. With this welcome playfellow Jörgen's dog had joined company. Jörgen had the greatest trouble in inducing him to come back—dirty as he already was. As soon as Mary called too, he came boldly and joyfully. But a stroke with the cane awaited him, and called forth a howl.

"It is strange," said Mary, "that you cannot treat a nice dog kindly!" She was thinking of his cruelty to their neighbour's old Lapland dog.

Jörgen did not answer. But as soon as he felt sure that the dog was following meekly, he said: "Does Uncle Klaus know anything about this money?"

"I do not believe that any one knows about it except ourselves. Why do you ask?"

"Because it will be our best plan to speak to Uncle Klaus."

Mary stood still, astonished. "To Uncle Klaus?"

Jörgen also stood still. They looked at each other now.

"It will be to our interest," continued Jörgen.

"With Uncle Klaus——?" Mary stared. She did not understand him.

"For the sake of the family's honour he will do a great deal," said Jörgen, giving her a quick side-glance as he moved on.

She had turned ghastly white, but she followed. "Must we confide in Uncle Klaus?" she whispered behind him. A lower depth of humiliation there could not be.

"Yes, we'll do so!" he answered encouragingly, almost gaily. "Now he will not say 'No'!"

Had this, too, entered into his calculations?

He went closer to her. "If Uncle Klaus knows nothing about the American money, we shall get more—do you see?"

How well he had thought it all out! In spite of her disgust, Mary was impressed. Jörgen was a cleverer man than she had taken him for. Once he had the opportunity to develop all his gifts, he would surprise many besides herself.

She walked along, shrinking into herself like a leaf in too dry heat.

"You will manage this with Uncle Klaus yourself?"

"I shall go back with you now, as you may suppose. You need not have come. You had only to let me know."

Her head was bent and she was trembling. His superiority robbed her of her strength and courage; his words sickened her. As on a previous occasion, one foot refused to plant itself in front of the other; she could follow no farther.

Then she heard Jörgen call: "Come here, you little devil!" The dog again! His dirty scamp of a playfellow had once more tempted him from the path of duty.

There was something peculiar about Jörgen's voice when it commanded—it was subdued and sharp at the same time. The dog recognised it, but only looked round, irresolute. Being endowed with a happy frivolity of disposition, he rushed again merrily up to his comrade and went on with the game as if nothing had been said.

Mary stood learning a lesson. It was just underneath John Ericson's statue that this happened. She looked up at the statue, looked into John Ericson's kind, thoughtful eyes, until tears filled her own. She was utterly miserable.

Jörgen was engrossed with the dog. The animal's education was conducted on the principle that he must never be allowed to have his own will when it conflicted with his master's. "Come here, you little rogue," said Jörgen ingratiatingly. The dog was so surprised that he stopped in the middle of his game. "Good dog! come along!" He made one or two joyful bounds in Jörgen's direction; he remembered the good times they had had together—perhaps such a time awaited him now. But, whatever the reason, doubt seized him—he turned back and was soon between his dirty friend's paws again, both of them sprawling in the mud.

The passers-by stopped, amused by the animal's disobedience. This annoyed Jörgen. Mary knew it, and made an attempt to save the dog. Standing behind Jörgen, she said softly in French: "It is not fair first to coax and then to strike." Her words only made him more obstinate. "This is a matter you don't understand," he answered, also in French, and continued coaxing.

With the short-sighted trustfulness common to sweet-tempered puppies, the dog stopped in his game and looked at Jörgen. Jörgen, with his stick behind his back, advanced persuasively. He was furious at the laughter of the onlookers, but muffled his rage in soft words. "Come on, old fellow, come on!"

"Don't believe him!" shouted an English sailor. But it was too late. Jörgen had hold of one of the long ears. The dog howled; Jörgen must have pinched hard. Mary called in French: "Don't beat him!" Jörgen struck—not hard; but the terrified puppy yelled piercingly. He struck again—not hard this time either; it was done chiefly to annoy them all. The dog howled so pitifully that Mary could not bear to look in that direction. Gazing into John Ericson's good, kind eyes, she said: "These blows have separated you and me, Jörgen!"

Instantaneously he let the dog go and stood up. He saw her eyes flame; her cheeks were white; she held herself erect and faced him—above her John Ericson's head.

A moment later, and she had turned her back on him and was walking quickly away, with light, glad steps—the dog following.

The onlookers laughed, the English sailors derisively; Jörgen started in pursuit.

But when Mary saw that the dog was following her and not him, and that the creature's eyes sought hers to learn what she intended to do, the fear she had felt before turned into wild exhilaration. Such revulsions of feeling were not uncommon with her. She clapped her hands and ran, and the dog sprang along at her side, barking. The spell was broken, the disgrace was cast from her! Farewell to Jörgen and all his ways!

"That's what we are saying, my little rescuer, eh?" The dog barked.

She looked round to see Jörgen. He dared not hurry, for the sake of appearances.

"But we two dare, don't we?" Again she clapped her hands and ran, and the dog ran with her, barking.

Then she slackened her pace, and played with him and talked to him; Jörgen was so far behind. "You ought to be called 'liberator'; but that is too long a name for a little black puppy. You shall be called John—be named after him who looked at me and gave me courage." Off she and the dog ran again. "You follow me and not him! Well done, well done! That is what he whom you are called after did. He would have nothing to do with the slave-drivers; his friends were those who set free!"

Now they were round the corner. Jörgen was not visible. When he came to the hotel, he was told, though he had seen Mary go in, that she was not at home. He said that she had his dog. The waiter professed ignorance. There was nothing for it but to go. He had lost both her and the dog.

Up in her room Mary asked the dog: "Will you be mine? Will you go with me, little black John?" She clapped her hands to make him bark his joyful: Yes. The question of ownership was settled thus. A letter which came from Jörgen, probably on this subject, she burned unread.

She expected him to appear at the station, at the time when the train for Norway left, to claim his property. She drove boldly up with her dog at her side, washed, combed, perfumed. Jörgen was not there.

Mary slept all night with the dog at her feet, on her travelling rug.

But with morning came reflection. Now she was alone, alone with the responsibility.

Hitherto she had been forcing herself into the one narrow way of escape—to marry Jörgen at once, bear her child abroad, and after that—endure as long as she could.

But to marry the man she loathed, merely in order to save her good name—how inconceivable such a step now seemed to her! She had tried to take it, because she knew what those around her thought on such subjects, and because she occupied a peculiar position; upon festal garments a stain was unendurable.

But now she said "For shame!" at the thought of it—said it aloud. And the dog instantly looking up, she added: "Yes, John, it was 'to the dogs' I was going when I set off on this journey!"

But what was she to do now?

She knew what could be done. But two besides herself would be in that secret—Jörgen and another. This in itself was prohibitive. She could never again hold up her head proudly and independently—and to be able to do so was a necessity to her.

Well, what then?

As long as her journey and what it entailed had seemed to her to be imperative, for honour's sake inevitable, the idea of the last, the very last refuge had not suggested itself seriously.

Now it faced her in sad earnest!

She looked mournfully into the dog's honest eyes, as if she were searching for a way of escape from this too. She read in them the most unmixed happiness and devotion. Burying her face in his curls, she wept. She was so young still, she did not want to die.

For the first time she wept for herself, was sorry for herself. It did not seem to her that she had done anything to deserve this. Nor could she account to herself for the manner in which it had all come about.

The dog understood that she was unhappy. He licked her hands, looked up into her face, and whined to be allowed to jump up and comfort her.

She lifted him up and bent over him. Imagining that she meant to play with him, he began to snap at her hands. She let him have his way, and the two were soon engaged in a merry, babyish game, which lasted a long time, because John refused to be satisfied; every time she stopped, he began again.

Then she talked to him. "Little black John, you remind me of the negroes. You remind me that your namesake ransomed negroes from slavery. You have saved me from being enslaved. But it is a sorry deliverance, I can tell you, if I am not to have the right to live as well as you. Don't you think so too?" Then she began to cry again.

In Christiania she drove from one station to the other wearing a thick veil, the dog beside her on the seat. She saw none of her acquaintances. If they knew——!

Oh, that condemned and executed crow, which Jörgen wanted to pick up and she fled from—she had no idea how well she had seen it, seen the torn neck, the hacked body, the empty eye-sockets! The red wounds gaped at her; she could not get them out of her thoughts during this terrible drive.

It was winter now. She had not seen winter for many years. Dying, withered vegetation she had seen, but not winter's transforming power, not desolation decked in the fairest, purest white, with capricious variations where the landscape was wooded. The fjord was not yet ice-covered; steel-grey, defiant, hard, the sea came rolling up from every direction, like a hydra-headed monster challenging to combat.

Her imagination had been excited by the drive through the town; now the powers of nature took possession of it. All the more intensely did she feel her impotence. Could *she* accept any challenge to combat? Would *she* ever know the period of transformation? For her there was no course open but to die.

Whilst she was wrestling with these thoughts she suddenly saw her father's face. How could she live without telling him what was impending? And never, never would she be able to tell him! She could not even let him know that she had broken off her engagement. This alone would be more than he could bear.

What if, instead of speaking, she were to disappear? Good God! that would kill him at once.

During the rest of the journey she felt no more fear of others, none whatever for herself—it was all for him, for him alone!

She arrived in such an exhausted and miserable condition that she began to cry when she saw the house. There can have been few sadder walks than hers up to it. Even the dog's joyful antics when he reached firm ground could not distract her. She went straight to her own room to wash and change her dress, requesting that her father and Mrs. Dawes should be told of her arrival. Little Nanna went with her, to help her. The child played with the dog whenever she had an unoccupied moment; this annoyed Mary, but she said nothing.

She looked utterly worn-out, and it was only too evident that she had wept. But perhaps this was fortunate. Her father would understand at once that all was not well. If he were only able to bear it! She would tell him that she had had a long, fatiguing journey, and that Jörgen did not consider the means at their disposal sufficient for people in their position to marry upon. They must wait and see what Uncle Klaus would do.

If she cried—and she was sure to cry, so tired and heart-broken was she—it would prepare him for what was to follow. Oh, if he were only able to bear it!

But what else could she do? If she did not go to him at once he would suspect mischief, and feel alarmed, and that would be quite as bad for him.

She trembled as she stood at his door. Not only from anxiety for him—no, also because she must not throw herself down beside him, tell him everything, and weep till she could weep no more. How dreadful it all was!

But life is sometimes merciful!

Anders had not been told of his daughter's arrival, because he was asleep. The nurse had waited in the passage to let Mary know this when she came out of her room. Why did the woman not knock at the door and tell her? Simply because it was not natural to her to act thus. However, when Mary did come out, she was no longer in the passage, but half way downstairs. One of the servants was carrying up the invalid's dinner. The nurse, distressed at being unable to do this herself as usual, had thought that she would at least take it from her on the stairs.

Whilst she was doing this, Mary opened the door of her father's room. She stood still in the doorway, because the nurse, who had hastened up again, was whispering: "He is asleep, Miss Krog."

But the dog, understanding nothing, was in the room already, already had his paws on the edge of the bed and his face close to the face of the sick man, who was awaking—who awoke, with this black apparition staring into his eyes. The eyes opened wide with terror, gazed round the room, and met Mary's. She stood in the doorway, horror-struck, pale as death. Her father raised his head towards her; then the eyes became fixed and a far-away look came into them. The head sank back.

"He is dying!" cried the nurse behind Mary, setting down the tray and rushing forwards.

Mary would not believe it at first; but when she understood that it was true, she threw herself upon him with a heartrending scream. It was answered by one from Mrs. Dawes in the next room. The servants who hurried there found her lying unconscious. She recovered sufficiently to be able to stammer some unintelligible English words. The doctor said: "It will soon be all over with her too." Anders Krog was dead.

Mary clung to her reason as if she were grasping it with her hands. She must not, must not give way—must not scream, must not think. *She* had not killed him! She must listen to and remember what the others said, must give her consent to what they were proposing, which was to send for her father's sister. When she witnessed that sister's grief, she felt that she must not give way to her own. She must not, must not! "Help me, help me," she cried, "that I may not go mad!" And, turning to the doctor, she said: "*I* did not kill him, did I?"

The doctor ordered her to bed, prescribed cold compresses, and remained beside her. He, too, impressed on her the necessity of self-control.

Not till little Nanna brought the dog to her next morning, and the animal insisted on being taken into her arms, was she able to shed tears.

During the course of the day she improved a little. Her grief was alleviated by the heartfelt sympathy, often expressed in the most moving terms, which was conveyed to her by the numberless telegrams that arrived in town and were telephoned from there. All this sympathy for herself, admiration for her father, and intense desire to comfort and strengthen her, helped her greatly. From the incautious manner in which one of these telegrams was transmitted she learned that Mrs. Dawes, too, was dead. They had not dared to tell her. But the great and general sympathy helped her to bear this also. Now she understood how it was so great and general. Every one but herself knew that she had lost both, that she was alone in the world.

The message which touched her most came from Paris, and was as follows: "My beloved Mary,—Can it comfort you in your great sorrow to know that there is a resting-place here for you, and that I am at your service—to travel with you, to come to you, to do whatever you wish!—Yours unalterably, ALICE."

She knew who had sent Alice intimation.

Jörgen, too, telegraphed. "If I could be of the slightest service or comfort to you I would come at once. I am brokenhearted."

The same touching, reverential sympathy was shown on the occasion of the funeral, which was hastened on Mary's account, and took place three days after the deaths. Amongst the countless wreaths, the most beautiful of all was

Alice's. It was taken up to Mary—she wished to see it. The whole house was fragrant with flowers on that winter day, their sweet breath a message of love to those who slept there.

Mary did not go downstairs; she refused to see the coffins, or the flowers, or any of the preparations that had been made for the entertainment of friends who came from a distance.

More people came than the house could hold, and at the chapel there was a still larger gathering.

The clergyman asked if he might go upstairs and see Miss Krog. Mary sent him her best thanks, but declined the visit.

Immediately afterwards little Nanna came to ask if she would see Uncle Klaus. The old man had sent her a very touching telegram, in which he asked if he could not be of service to her in any way. And his wreath was so magnificent that, after hearing the servants' description of it, Mary had made them bring it, too, for her to look at.

She now answered: Yes. And in came the tall man, in deep mourning, gasping as if he had difficulty in breathing. No sooner did he see Mary standing by the bed, a figure of ivory draped in black, than he sank on to the first chair he could reach, and burst into loud weeping. The sound resembled what is heard when themainspring of a large clock breaks, and the whole machinery unreels itself. It was the weeping of a man who had not wept since he was a child—a sound alarmed at itself. He did not look up.

But he had an errand, so much Mary understood. He tried twice to speak, but the attempt only increased the violence of the weeping fit. Then, motioning despairingly, he rose and left the room. He did not shut the door, and she heard him sobbing as he went along the passage and downstairs, to go straight home.

Mary was deeply touched. She knew that her father had been the old man's best, perhaps his only friend. But she understood that it was not for him alone the tears had been shed; they told also of sympathy with her, and of remorse. Had it not been so, Uncle Klaus would have stayed beside the coffin.

The sweet-toned chapel bell began to toll. The dog, which had been kept prisoner in Mary's room all day, and was very restless, rushed to the window towards the sea, and put his fore-paws up on the sill, to look out. Mary followed him.

At that moment Uncle Klaus drove off. The singing of a psalm began in the rooms below, and the funeral procession issued from the house. The coffins were carried by the peasants from the neighbouring farms. When the first came in sight, Mary fell on her knees and wept as if her heart would break. She saw no more.

She flung herself across the bed. The strokes of the bell seemed to cut into her flesh; she imagined that she felt the stripes they raised. Her mind became more and more confused. She was certain now that her father, when he caught sight of her in the doorway, had guessed the truth, and that this had killed him. Mrs. Dawes had followed him, as she always did. Her love for Anders Krog was the one great love of her life. They were both here now. And Mary's mother, too, was in the room, in a long white robe. "You are cold, child!" she said, and took her into her arms—for Mary had become a child again, a little innocent child. She fell asleep.

When she awoke and heard no sound, outside the house or in, she folded her hands and said, half aloud: "This was best for us, for all three. We have been mercifully dealt with."

She looked round for the dog; she craved for sympathy. But some one must have taken him away whilst she was asleep.

No more was needed to make the tears flow again. Welling forth from the inexhaustible fountain of grief within, they poured down her cheeks and over the hands with which she was supporting her heavy head.

"Now I can begin to think of myself again. I am alone now."

THE CRISIS

WHEN Mary was visiting the graves next day, her grief was distracted by the following little occurrence.

It was Saturday, and the eve of one of the few Sundays in the year when service was held in the chapel. On such occasions it was customary to decorate the graves. As the farm to the right of Krogskogen had once formed part of that estate, its owners had their burial-place here. The peasant's wife had come with flowers to deck a new grave, and the old Lapland dog was with her. Mary's little poodle at once rushed at him fearlessly, and to the woman's and Mary's surprise the old dog, after cautious and minute inspection, made friends with the giddy youngster. Though he as a rule could not bear puppies, he quite fell in love with this one. He allowed his ears to be pulled and his legs to be bitten; he even laid himself down and pretended to be vanquished. This delighted Mary so much that she accompanied the woman part of the way home, to watch the game. And she was more than repaid for so doing. She heard warm praise of her father, and some of the anecdotes of him that were circulating in the neighbourhood at this time, and were ensuring him an honoured memory.

She thought as she walked home with her excited dog: "Am I beginning to resemble Mother? Has there always been in me something of her which until now has not had room to develop; something of her simple nature?"

This day brought two surprises.

The first was a letter from Uncle Klaus. He addressed her as: "My honoured and dear god-daughter, Miss Mary Krog." She had had no idea that she was his god-daughter; her father had never told her, probably did not know it himself.

Uncle Klaus wrote: "There are feelings which are too strong for words, especially for written words. I am no letter-writer; but I take the liberty of intimating to you in this manner, since I was unable to do it by word of mouth, that on the day when your father, my best friend, and Mrs. Dawes, your revered foster-mother, died, and you were left alone, I made you, my dear god-daughter, my heiress.

"My fortune is not nearly so large as is generally supposed; I have had great losses of late. But there is still enough for us both—that is to say, if your share is under your own management *and not Jörgen's*. I write on the supposition that you will now marry.

"Mrs. Dawes's will has been in my hands for many years, and I have had charge of her money. I opened the will yesterday. She has left everything to you. This means about 60,000 kroner. But the same holds good of this money as of your father's; it is for the moment yielding almost no interest.

"Your godfather,
"KLAUS KROG."

Mary answered at once:
"MY DEAR GODFATHER,—Your letter has touched me deeply. I thank you with all my heart.
"But I dare not accept your generous gift.
"Jörgen is your adopted son, and on no account will I stand in his way.
"You must not be angry with me for this. I cannot possibly act differently.
"In the matter of Mrs. Dawes's will, I shall come to a decision ere long, and shall then write to you again.

"Your grateful
"MARY KROG."

Whilst she was despatching this letter she heard a carriage drive up, and presently a card was brought in to her, on which she read: "Dr. Margrete Röy."

It was a little time before Miss Röy came in. She had been taking off her wraps. It was a cold day. The delay increased Mary's excitement, with the result that she trembled and turned pale as the tall, strong woman with the kind eyes entered the room. She saw the impression made by this on the kind eyes, which now poured forth all their compassion upon her. As if they had known each other for many years, Mary went up to her visitor, laid her head on her shoulder, and wept. Margrete Röy pressed the unhappy girl affectionately to her breast.

After they had seated themselves, she told her errand, which was to inquire when Mary intended to go abroad. Mary asked in surprise: "Have I spoken to any one about that?"

Miss Röy said that she had heard it from the nurse.

"Oh!" said Mary, "I have no idea what I said in the state I was in at that time. I have certainly given the matter no thought since."

"Then you are not going abroad?"

Mary sat silent for a moment. "All I can say is that I don't know. I have not yet made any plans."

Margrete Röy was embarrassed. Mary saw this, or rather felt it. "You also have perhaps had thoughts of travelling!" she said.

"Yes, and I wanted to know if I could be of any use to you. I should be happy to arrange my journey so that we could travel together."

"Where are you going?"

"I am going abroad to study—Paris first. The nurse told me it was there you meant to go," said Margrete, beginning to feel very awkward. Her wish had been to help Mary, but it seemed to her now that she was intruding.

"I appreciate your kindness," said Mary. "It is possible that I mentioned Paris. I don't remember. The truth is that I have come to no decision."

"Please forgive me, then. The whole has been a misunderstanding," said Miss Röy, rising.

Mary felt that she must not let her go, but her strength seemed to fail her. It was not until Margrete had reached the door that she managed to say: "I am coming to speak to you one day soon, Miss Röy." She said it in a low voice, without looking up. "I am not well enough to do it to-day," she added.

"I can see that. It is only what I expected; so I brought something with me for you—if you will only take it. It is the most invigorating tonic I know."

Mary felt all her sympathies go out to this woman. She thanked her heartily, adding: "Then, as soon as I am a little stronger, I may come?"

"You will be very welcome."

"Perhaps," said Mary, blushing, "you would not mind coming to me?"

"To your house in the market-place?" asked Miss Röy.

"Yes, to our house in the market-place. Though I ought no longer to say 'our' house!" The tears came again.

"You have only to let me know, and I shall come at once."

A week later Mary went to town—in the wildest November storm, the worst they had had in these parts. The fjords were not yet frozen over, so the steamer managed to reach town, but had to remain there.

Margrete Röy was much astonished at being summoned on such a day. It was to a warm, comfortable house she came, not the deserted one with the drawn down blinds which she was accustomed to see. She was conducted up an old-fashioned broad stair; the whole interior was in the style of the old town-houses of the beginning of last century.

Mary was in the farthest away of the suite of sitting-rooms, a red boudoir, unchanged since her mother's day. She was sitting on a sofa, beneath a large portrait of her mother. When she stood up in her black dress, pale and heavy-eyed under her crown of red hair, it struck Margrete Röy that she was the very image of sorrow, the most beautiful one that could be imagined. A solemn tranquillity surrounded her. She spoke as low as the storm outside permitted.

"I feel that you respect another's grief. I am also certain that you betray no secrets."

"I do not."

A little time passed before Mary said: "Who is Jörgen Thiis?"

"Who is he——?"

"I have several reasons for believing that you can tell me."

"You must first allow me to put a question. Are you not engaged to Jörgen Thiis?"

"No."

"People say that you are."

Mary remained silent.

"You have perhaps been engaged to him?"

"Yes."

"But," said Margrete quickly and joyously, "you have broken off the engagement?"

Mary nodded.

"Many will rejoice to hear it; for Jörgen Thiis is not worthy of you."

Mary showed no signs of surprise.

"You know something?" she asked.

"Doctors, Miss Krog, know more than they may tell."

"Yet I do believe that he loved me," said Mary, to excuse herself.

"We all saw that," replied Margrete. "He undoubtedly loved you better than he had ever loved before. Nor was it surprising," she added. "But when I lived in Christiania I knew a sweet young girl who at that time was the one love of his life! She allowed herself to be deeply moved by this, and as they could not marry, she gave herself to him."

"What did she do?" asked Mary, startled. Had she understood aright? The storm was howling so loudly outside that it was difficult to hear.

Margrete repeated distinctly and impressively: "She was a warm-hearted girl, who believed that she was doing right, as she was his one and only love."

"They could not marry?"

"It was not possible. So she gave herself to him without marriage."

Mary started up, but did not move forward. She was going to say something, but stopped.

"Do not be so startled, Miss Krog. It is nothing very uncommon."

This information lowered Mary considerably in her own estimation. She slowly seated herself again.

"You cannot have had any experience of this sort of thing, Miss Krog?"

Mary shook her head.

"In which case it surprises me that you were able to escape from Jörgen Thiis in time; *he* has had plenty."

Mary made no reply.

"We expected, especially after your father and Mrs. Dawes both became invalids, that you would have been married before autumn."

"We intended to be, but it proved impossible."

Margrete could not fathom what lay beneath this enigmatic answer; but she said, with a searching glance: "This, doubtless, added very considerably to his ardour?"

Mary trembled inwardly, but controlled herself.

"You seem to know him?" she said.

Margrete reflected for a moment, then answered: "Yes. I am older than you, older than Jörgen, too. But in Christiania I also, to my shame be it spoken, was infatuated with him. This he discovered—and tried to take advantage of." She laughed.

Mary turned pale, rose, and walked to the window. The wind was lashing the rain against the panes with ever-increasing force. She remained for a few moments gazing out into the storm, then came and stood in front of Margrete, agitated, restless.

"Will you promise me never to tell any one what we have spoken about to-day—under any circumstances whatever?"

Margrete looked at her in surprise. "You wish me to tell no one that you have asked me about Jörgen Thiis?"

"It is my express desire that no one should know it."

"Do you mean any one in particular?"

Mary looked at her. "Any one in particular?" She did not understand.

Margrete rose. "A man came to this town on purpose to tell you that Jörgen Thiis was not worthy of you. He came too late; but I think he deserves to know that you have discovered for yourself what Jörgen Thiis is."

Mary answered, eagerly: "Tell *him*. By all means tell *him*!... So that was why he came," she added slowly. "I am glad that you have told me. Because my other reason for wishing to see you was—" she hesitated a little, "the other thing I wanted to ask you was—to give my kind remembrances to your brother."

"That I shall do, gladly. Thank you for the message. You know what you are to my brother."

Mary looked away. She struggled with herself a moment, then said: "I am one of the unhappy people who cannot understand their own lives—cannot understand what has happened. I can find no clue to it. But something tells me that your brother has had his share in it."

She evidently wished to say more, but could not. Instead, she returned to the window and remained standing there again. The storm without called into the room with its thousand-voiced wrath. It was calling her.

"What a terrible storm!" said Margrete, raising her voice.

"I am rejoicing at the thought of going out into it," said Mary, turning round with sparkling eyes.

"You are never going out in this weather!" exclaimed Margrete.

"I mean to walk home," answered Mary.

"To *walk*?"

Mary came forward and placed herself in front of Margrete, as if she were about to say something wild and dreadful. She stopped short, but what she had not said rushed into her eyes, into her whole face, to her heart. She flung up her arms and with a loud groan threw herself back on her mother's sofa, and covered her face with her hands.

Margrete knelt down beside her. Mary allowed her friend to put her arms round her and draw her to her like a tired, suffering child. And she began to cry, as a child cries, touchingly and helplessly; her head sank on to Margrete's shoulder.

But only for a moment; then she sat up with a sudden start. For Margrete had whispered into her ear: "There is something the matter with you. Speak to me."

Not a word came in answer. Margrete dared not say more. She rose; she felt that it was time to go.

Nor did Mary do anything to retain her. She too had risen to her feet. They bade each other good-bye.

But Margrete could not help saying, as she left the room: "Do you really mean to walk——?"

Mary gave a nod which implied: "Enough has been said! That is my affair!"

Margrete closed the door.

The lamps were lit in the streets when Mary left the house. It was with difficulty she could keep her feet in the gusts that blew from the south-west, strengthened by compression between the houses. She had on a waterproof cloak and hood, firmly secured, and long waterproof boots. She walked as fast as she could. One thought alone remained to her after the conversation with Margrete Röy. But it united with the wind and the rain in driving her, lashing her on—the thought of Margrete's horrified eyes and pale face when she said: "There is something the matter with you; speak to me!" Good God! Margrete understood. They would all look at her like this when they heard. Thus terribly had she disappointed and wounded those who had believed in her. She felt as if she had them all behind her, as if it were from them she was fleeing—the flock of crows! She flew on, and had reached the outskirts of the town before she knew where she was. Here, beyond the last lamp, it was pitch dark; she had to wait a little before she could see her way. But what a pace she set off at then! The gale was coming half from behind, half from the side.

The judgment passed upon her was driving her out into the wide world—no, much farther than that! It seemed to her that at the moment when she first understood her position a packet had been given her, which she had not opened until now. She had felt all the time what was in it, but it was only yesterday she had opened it. It contained a large black veil, large enough for her to conceal herself and her shame in—the veil of death. But even this was given upon a certain condition—a condition she had known about since she was a child. For as a child she had heard the story of a grand-aunt of her own, who, in the hope of concealing that she had become pregnant during her husband's absence, walked barefooted upon an ice-cold floor, secretly, night after night, in order that she might die a natural death. It would never be known that she had brought it about herself, so there would be no occasion to ask why she had done it.

But some one had heard her pacing thus night after night, and the question was asked after all.

Things should be managed better this time! The weakness to which Mary had so unexpectedly given way in Margrete's presence was quite gone. Now she had the strength to carry out her purpose.

As if it were to be put to the test at once, something shadowy appeared at her side. It rose unexpectedly out of the darkness, so alarmingly near that she set off running. To her horror she seemed to hear through the roar of the storm that she was being pursued! Then she took courage and stood still. Whatever was following her stopped too. Mary moved on; it also moved on. "This will never do," thought she. "If I am not brave enough to face this, I am not brave enough to face what comes next." She thereupon turned and went straight up to the pursuing monster, which whinnied good-naturedly. It was a young horse, seeking in its desolateness the neighbourhood of a human being. She patted it and spoke to it. It was a messenger from life—the desolate was comforting the despairing. But, as the animal continued to follow her, she took it in to the next farm. She must be alone. The people at the farm were much astonished. They could not understand any one being out in such weather, least of all a woman! Mary hurried away from the light and out into the darkness again.

The little occurrence had strengthened her. She knew now that she had courage, and walked on quickly.

She was nearing the first headland round the face of which the road was cut. It either really was the case, or it seemed to her, that the hurricane was increasing. It must surely soon have reached its worst. To her it represented her own misery and shame. This thought strengthened her. It was not death she feared, but life.

She thought it all out again as she pressed on. She would not save herself by allowing her child to be killed, nor would she send it away to strangers and thus disown it; she could not live without self-respect.

If a suitor were to come—and doubtless as many would come now as in days past—should she begin by confessing? Or should she maintain a dishonourable silence? There was only one thing she could do with honour—die with her child. She felt incapable of anything else. But no one must have any suspicions. She must die of an illness; therefore an illness must be ensured that would end in death.

This much she owed to herself; for she was as certain to-day as on the evening when she went into Jörgen's room that her action was not one for which she deserved to be disgraced.

It had been a terrible mistake, that was certain; but the fault did not lie with her. There had no doubt been a considerable admixture of natural instinct in the feeling that prompted it; but even granting this, it was an action of which she was not ashamed. She owed it to herself to die with the undiminished sympathy of all who knew her; she also owed it to the companions who had recognised her as their leader. She had not disloyally forfeited their faith in her.

She was reaching the most exposed part of a headland now, and the struggle which began there unconsciously became to her a struggle to settle this question. It was as if all the powers of nature were trying to wrest her self-respect from her and procure her condemnation. The sea was open here, and from miles out the waves came rolling in, gathering force as they came. When they struck the cliff they leaped yards into the air. The largest of them lashed her with their highest jets. "Take that! Take that!" And the gale put forth all its strength in its endeavour to force her away from the hewn cliff. It seemed, moreover, to be trying, though her skirts were well protected by her cloak, to twist and tear them off her. "Stand naked in your shame, in your shame!"

But the raging waves did not frighten her into feeling herself guilty, nor did the gale succeed in blowing her against the parapet, and over it into the sea. She had to walk bent; she had even to stand still when the worst gusts came; but as soon as they were over she set off again, and held steadily on her way. "I will not part with my wreath of honour; I will die with it. Therefore *you* shall not have me!"

She rounded the point, and turned inland towards the low ground between it and the next headland. There had once been a landslip here; the piece of the cliff which had fallen lay as heaps of stones below, and through these the road now passed. Amongst the crumbling blocks by the wayside stood a slender birch, quite alone. Mary remembered it as she came up to it. Had it weathered such a storm uninjured? Yes, it was safe and sound. She paused beside it to recover her breath. It bent so low that every moment she thought: Now it must break! But up it came again as fresh as ever. She herself could not stand still, with such hurricane force was the gale blowing here; but the young birch, which was so tall and had such a spreading top and such a slender, swaying stem—it stood, quite alone.

She was thinking about this as she descended towards the level ground, when the gale suddenly lashed the rain into her face; each jet was a sharp arrow. "Ah, no!" she thought; "*this* would be what I should feel if I tried to face the storm which awaits me."

The lights from the little farmhouses, the only thing that she saw, proclaimed peace. But she knew that it was not for her.

She sped swiftly along the shore, but she was becoming tired now. One sign of this was that imagination began to take the upper hand; the reality disappeared in the semblance—in old mythical conceptions. As she toiled up and outwards to the next point, the sea was no longer sea, but hundreds upon hundreds of gaping sea monsters, roaring with desire. And raging aerial monsters with tremendous wings had promised those below to fling her out to them. With all the strength remaining to her she kept close to the rocky wall; but beneath it here there was a ditch, into which she fell and was wet through. More enemies still are abroad to-night, she thought, as she crawled out. Fortunately this headland was a narrow one; she soon reached the next stretch of level ground. Now there was only one more point to round. It was not to save her life that she was so unwilling to be blown into the sea, but to save her honour! If she were found in the sea, or disappeared altogether, they would say that she had sought death—and would try to discover her reason for doing so.

But now she heard through the darkness the bark of the old Lapland dog. It sounded quite near. She had been walking faster than she thought; she was close to his home. There were its lights!

The mere thought of meeting a living creature that cared for her moved her. She loved life, and she no longer believed that she was so unfit to live. This familiar voice calling to her through the darkness affected her as the sight of people on shore affects those clinging to a wreck.

As she passed the farm, the dog left his sentinel's post and came to be spoken to, wagging his tail and giving friendly little barks. Mary gave his wet coat three farewell pats and hastened on. She soon heard him bark again, but it was another, angrier bark. She involuntarily thought of Jörgen—and continued to think of him all this last part of the road, which, but for him, would have been sacred to her father. How many hundred times, beginning as a little child, she had walked and cycled with her father here! Now this place too had been spoiled by Jörgen. Never could she walk here again without *him*. Not a step further in her life could she take without him!

Involuntarily she looked heavenwards—to see nothing but clouds and thick darkness. She reached the last headland utterly exhausted, and rounded it without thinking at all, without any feeling that it was the last time, but also without fear.

Of what was before her now Mary was as certain as of the road beneath her feet, which was leading her through the Krogskogen fields to the landing-stage. It was so dark that her eyes, though by this time accustomed to the darkness, did not distinguish the white walls of the chapel until she was close to the landing-place. Her thoughts rushed to the graves in the churchyard, but deserted them again instantly in order to concentrate themselves on what she was about. She stepped on to the quay without hesitation and walked quickly along it. The gale did not threaten here, the rain no longer lashed her face; both had become subdued and friendly powers from the time she had set foot on Krogskogen soil, with its protecting ridge and islands. In other circumstances she would have felt relief and possibly peace in return to the shelter of her home—now every thought was blunted. Quite mechanically she hurried on. Mechanically she unfastened some of the buttons of her cloak to get at the key, mechanically inserted it in the key-hole and opened the door of the bathing-house. Not until she was standing inside in the pitch-darkness did her senses awake and feel alarm. When the remnant of south-west wind which was blowing here slammed the door, she shuddered. She felt as if she were not alone.

And now she must undress and go down the steps to become ice-cold—ice-cold! Then dress again and go home to fever, and to its consequences.

If the fever did not do what she expected of it, she had what would help. She had found it amongst Mrs. Dawes's stores. The blame would be laid on the fever.

But now that the moment had come for her to begin and undress, she shrank and shivered. It was the water, the ice-cold water she was shrinking from. There would likely be ice at the edge here, and she would have to walk over it with her bare feet. No, she would keep on her stockings; she could dry them afterwards, and no one would have any suspicion. But the ice-cold water ... what if she took cramp in it? No, she would keep herself in motion, she would swim. But what if she cut herself on the ice in coming out? She must keep on her underclothing too. But would it be dry by to-morrow morning? Yes, if she hung it near the stove. She would lock her door, and have everything in order before the maid came. If only she were in her right mind in the morning! She had never been ill; she had no idea what would happen.

Before falling into this long train of reflections, she had unbuttoned her waterproof. Now, instead of taking off the hood, as was natural, she began, without conscious intention, to unfasten her dress at the neck, where the locket with her mother's portrait hung. Her hands shook as she did it, and her body also began to tremble. She had not thought of the locket for many years, nor was she thinking of it now; the trembling had no connection with it. But the locket became, as it were, involved in the trembling. She must take it off. If only she did not forget it! She would make sure by putting it into her pocket at once.

Oh, horror of horrors! what did she hear? Firm steps on the landing stage, coming nearer and nearer. The trembling stopped; instinctively Mary fastened, first the collar of her dress, then her cloak—quickly, quickly. Who could have any errand here? It could not be to the bathing-house at any rate.

But it was straight there the steps came. The handle was seized, the door flew open, and the doorway was filled by a huge figure in a waterproof cloak. The hooded head was considerably higher than the door. An electric lamp threw light straight into Mary's face. She gave a wild scream as she recognised Frans Röy.

Such a feeling of faintness came over her that she was on the point of falling; but she was seized and carried out. It all happened in an instant. She heard the door banged; she was lifted and carried off. She could not say a word, nor did Frans say anything.

But before they had left the landing-stage she had come to herself again. Of this Frans was conscious; and presently he heard her say: "This is violence!" No answer. After a determined struggle to free herself, she repeated in a clearer, stronger voice: "This is violence!" No answer. But his free arm was put gently round her. She asked excitedly: "How do you come here?" Now he answered. "My sister told me." His voice embraced her as gently as his arm. But she struggled against both. "If your sister has any affection for me at all, or if you have, leave me alone!" He walked on. "Let me go, I say! This is shameful!" She struggled so vigorously that he was obliged to change his hold; but where she was she had to remain. With tears in her voice she said: "I allow no one to decide for me." Then he answered: "You may struggle your hardest, but I will carry you home. And if you do not obey me, I shall have you placed under restraint."

The words acted like a fetter of iron. She became motionless.

"You will place me under restraint?"

"I shall, for you have lost control over yourself."

Never since she could hear at all had she heard anything so silly as this. But she would not discuss the matter with him. She merely said: "And do you imagine this will be of any use?"

"I think so. When you see that we are doing everything in our power for you, you will give in to us, because you are good."

After a short silence she said: "I cannot accept help from any one who has not entire respect for me—" and she began to cry.

Then Frans Röy stood still and peered under her hood. "You don't imagine that *I* have not entire respect for you? Do you suppose that I would be carrying you now if I had not? To me you are all that is noblest and most beautiful. That is why I am carrying you. You may have done Heaven knows what wrong deed—*I* know that if you did it, it was from the noblest of motives. You can't act otherwise! If you have been deceived, if you have made a terrible mistake—why, I love you all the better!—for then you are unhappy—that I know. And perhaps now it may be possible for me, too, to help you. No greater happiness could befall me. I will leave you, if you insist upon it. I will marry you, if you can trust yourself to me. I will kill the fellow, if *that* is your wish. I will do anything whatever for you, if you will only be happy—for that is my chief desire."

He stopped short, but began again.

"When I set off after you this evening, I was in greater misery than I had ever imagined possible. She is going to throw herself into the sea, I thought. Of course I shall go after her. In this storm it means death to us both; but there is no help for that. Nor was that what distressed me. No, it was your unhappiness, your despair—the idea that you could believe yourself unworthy to live—you who could not act unworthily to gain life's highest prize! Never, never have I known a human being for whom I could answer as confidently. And I could not tell you this; I could not help you. I knew you; I dared not come near you. But I have been able to save you after all. For you cannot possibly wish to die now, after you have heard me?"

He had heard her sob; her arms were round his neck now, almost stifling his words. He let her slip slowly down. But she still held fast with the arm which was round his neck; and when she reached the ground she flung the other round it too, and laid her head upon his breast, sobbing—but with happiness now. He could feel the quick beat of her heart; it was the speed of joy.

The housekeeper in town had telephoned to Krogskogen that Miss Krog was walking home, in a worse storm than any one remembered, and had inquired again and again if she had arrived.

Nanna and the dog had been out on the steps several times, but the dog had never barked. Now he not only barked, but scampered off down the road.

The servants had been in the greatest anxiety. It did not seem to them at all remarkable that Mary's unhappiness and distress should have driven her out into the storm. Some such action as this hazarding of a life which she no longer valued had been an imperative necessity to her. Therefore now, when little Nanna rushed in calling: "Here she comes! here she comes!" they wept for joy. They had long had the rooms warm and hot food in readiness. Now they laid another cover, for Nanna had rushed in again to tell them that Miss Krog was not alone; she had heard a man speaking. The maids at once said to each other that Jörgen Thiis had come at last. "No," said Nanna; "it was not his voice; it was a strong man's!"

But the dog's joy at seeing Mary again was boundless. He barked, he yelped, he jumped right up to her face; there was no end to his demonstrations. When Frans Röy spoke to him, he went up to him at once, as to an old friend, but immediately returned to Mary. The little shaggy creature's ardent delight represented to her the joy of her home at seeing her again, saved. His was the greeting of both the dead and the living. This was what Mary felt. And she also felt that his happiness possibly preluded a re-awakening of her own, when she had succeeded in shaking off the impression of the horrors she had undergone.

When she entered the house, heralded by the dog, who was as wild with joy as ever, the three maids were all in the hall to welcome her, Nanna with them. They stopped short in their exclamations when they saw the enormous figure looming behind her; for in his waterproof cloak and hood Franz Röy seemed supernaturally tall. But it was only for a moment; then they broke out: "Oh, Miss, to think that you should have been out in such a storm! We have been terribly anxious. The housekeeper in town let us know. But we had no one to send to meet you, for there is a fire in the neighbourhood and all the men have gone off there. Thank God that we have you again, safe!"

Mary concealed her emotion by hastening upstairs. Her room was warm, her lamp was lighted.

"Is all this affection and care new? Or is it just that I have never noticed it before?"

The dog whined outside until she was obliged to let him in. He was so obtrusive in his gratitude that it was with difficulty she managed to change her clothes.

When she was doing her hair she remembered the locket with her mother's portrait. She took it from her pocket, and before fastening it on her neck again, looked at the portrait—for the first time for many years—and caressed and kissed it. Presently she lit a candle, and with it in her hand crossed the passage to her father's room. There she set it down, and going forward to his bed, bent over it and kissed the pillow. On coming out, she stopped at the door of the visitors' room. "In this room he shall sleep; then it can be opened again to-morrow; its hateful associations will be gone." A maid to whom she gave orders to light a fire told her that this had already been done, and taking Mary's candle, went in to light the lamp. Mary stood looking after her. "Have they really been like this all the time?"

The maid remained in the room, arranging it. Mary moved on towards the stairs. There she once more stopped. The dog, who had run down, came rushing up; he was determined not to lose her again. She stroked him gratefully; it was like a first little instalment of that gratitude with which her heart was full to overflowing.

"To-morrow—this evening I am too tired—to-morrow I will tell Frans Röy everything! Every single thing that has happened! Perhaps this will help me to understand it all myself."

With this brave resolve she walked downstairs, but stopped once more before she reached the foot. "Strange it is—most strange—but I feel as if I could tell the whole world!"

The dog was standing at the door of the Dutch room. He smelt Frans Röy there.

Mary followed him and opened the door. As she entered Frans exclaimed, as if he had had difficulty in keeping silence so long: "What a beautiful home!" Noticing the dog's continued attentions, he added: "And how much you are thought of in it!" His face lighted up.

"You are in uniform!" she exclaimed.

"Yes. I was at a wedding when I was sent for." He laughed.

The uniform had suggested a thought to Mary. With the dog tugging at her dress, she said, looking brightly up into Frans Röy's face: "It will not be the first time that a general of engineers has lived at Krogskogen."

Magnhild Dust

CHAPTER I.

THE landscape has high, bold mountains, above which are just passing the remnants of a storm. The valley is narrow and continually winding. Coursing through it is a turbulent stream, on one side of which there is a road. At some distance up the slopes farms are spread; the buildings are mostly low and unpainted, yet numerous; heaps of mown hay and fields of half ripe grain are dotted about.

When the last curve of the valley is left behind the fjord becomes visible. It lies sparkling beneath an uplifting fog. So completely is it shut in by mountains that it looks like a lake.

Along the road there jogs at the customary trot a horse with a cariole-skyds. In the cariole may be seen a waterproof coat and a south-wester, and between these a beard, a nose, and a pair of spectacles. Lashed to the back seat is a trunk, and seated on this, with her back to the cariole, is a full-grown "skyds"-girl, snugly bundled up in a kerchief. She sits there dangling her coarsely-shod feet. Her arms are tucked in under the kerchief. Suddenly she bursts out with: "Magnhild! Magnhild!"

Conveyance.

The traveler turned to look after a tall woman in a waterproof cloak who had just walked past. He had caught a glimpse of a delicately-outlined face, beneath a hood which was drawn over the brow; now he saw the owner standing with her forefinger in her mouth, staring. As he was somewhat persistent in his gaze, she blushed.

"I will step in just as soon as I put up the horse," called out the skyds-girl.

They drove on.

"Who was that, my dear?" asked the traveler.

"She is the wife of the saddler down at yonder point," was the reply.

In a little while they had advanced far enough to gain a view of the fjord and the first houses on the point. The skyds-girl reined in the horse and jumped down from the trunk. She first attended to the animal's appearance, and then busied herself with her own toilet. It had ceased raining, and she removed her kerchief, folded it, and stowed it away in a little pocket in front of the cariole. Then thrusting her fingers under her head-kerchief she tried to arrange her hair, which hung in matted locks over her cheeks.

"She had such a singular look,"—he pointed over his shoulders.

The girl fixed her eyes on him, and she began to hum. Presently she interrupted herself with,—

"Do you remember the land-slide you passed a few miles above here?"

"I passed so many land-slides."

She smiled.

"Yes; but the one I mean is on the other side of a church."

"It was an old land-slide?"

"Yes; it happened long ago. But that is where once lay the gard belonging to her family. It was swept away when she was eight or nine years old. Her parents, brothers and sisters, and every living thing on the gard, perished. She alone was saved. The land-slide bore her across the stream, and she was found by the people who hastened to the spot,—she was insensible."

The traveler became absorbed in thought.

"She must be destined to something," said he, at last.

The girl looked up. She waited some time, but their eyes did not meet. So she resumed her seat on the trunk, and they drove on.

The valley widened somewhat in the vicinity of the point; farms were spread over the plain: to the right lay the church with the churchyard around it; a little farther on the point itself, a small town, with a large number of houses, most of which were but one story high and were either painted white and red or not painted at all; along the fjord ran the wharf. A steamer was just smoking there; farther down, by the mouth of the river, might be seen a couple of old brigs taking in their cargoes.

The church was new, and showed an attempt at imitating the old Norse wooden church architecture. The traveler must have had some knowledge of this, for he stopped, gazed a while at the exterior, then alighted, went through the gateway, and into the church; both gate and door stood open. He was scarcely inside of the building when the bells began to ring; through the opening he saw a bridal procession coming up from the little town. As he took his departure the procession was close by the churchyard gate, and by this he stood while it moved in: the bridegroom, an elderly man, with a pair of large hands and a large face, the bride, a young girl, with a plump, round face, and of a heavy build. The bridesmaids were all clad in white and wore gloves; not one of them ventured to bestow more than a side glance at the stranger; most of them stooped, one was hump-backed; there was not one who could truly be said to have a fine form.

Their male friends lagged behind, in gray, brown, and black felt hats, and long frock coats, pea-jackets, or round-abouts. Most of them had a lock of hair drawn in front of the ear, and those who had beards wore them to cover the entire chin. The visages were hard, the mouths usually coarse; most of them had tobacco stains about the corners of their mouths, and some had cheeks distended with tobacco-quids.

Involuntarily the traveler thought of her in the waterproof cloak. Her history was that of the landscape. Her refined, unawakened face hung as full of yearning as the mountains of showers; everything that met his eye, both landscape and people, became a frame for her.

As he approached the road, the skyds-girl hastened to the wayside where the horse was grazing. While she was tugging at the reins she continued to gaze fixedly at the bridal procession.

"Are you betrothed?" asked the stranger, smiling.

"He who is to have me has no eyes yet," she replied, in the words of a proverb.

"Then, I suppose, you are longing to get beyond your present position," said he, adding: "Is it to America?"

She was surprised; that query was evidently well aimed.

"Is it in order that you may more speedily earn your traveling expenses that you have gone into the skyds line? Do you get plenty of fees? Hey?"

Now she colored. Without uttering a word in reply, she promptly took her seat on the trunk with her back to the stranger, before he had stepped into the cariole.

Soon they had neared the white-painted hotels which were situated on either side of the street close by the entrance to the little town. In front of one of these they paused. By the balustrade above stood a group of carriers, chiefly young fellows; they had most likely been watching the bridal procession and were now waiting for steamer-bound travelers. The stranger alighted and went in, while the girl busied herself with unstrapping the trunk. Some one must have offered her help, for as the traveler approached the window he saw her push from her a great lubberly boy in a short jacket. In all probability some impertinence had also been offered her and had been repaid in the same coin, for the other carriers set up a shout of laughter. The girl came walking in with the heavy trunk. The traveler opened the door for her, and she laughed as she met him. While he was counting out her money to her, he said,—

"I agree with you, Rönnaug, you ought to be off to America as soon as possible."

He now handed her two specie dollars as her fee.

"This is my mite for your fund," said he, gravely.

She regarded him with wide-open eyes and open mouth, took the money, returned thanks, and then put up both hands to stroke back her hair, for it had again fallen out of place. While thus engaged she dropped some of the coins she held in one half-closed hand. She stooped to pick them up, and as she did so some of the hooks in her boddice gave way. This loosened her kerchief and one end fell out, for a knot in one corner contained something heavy. While readjusting this she again dropped her money. She got off at last, however, with all her abundance, and was assailed with a volley of rude jests. This time she made no reply; but she cast a shy glance into the hotel as she drove the horse past, full trot.

It was the traveler's lot to see her once more; for as he passed down to the steamer, later in the day, she was standing with her back turned toward the street, at a door over which hung a sign-board bearing the inscription: "Skarlie, Saddler." As he drew nearer he beheld Magnhild in the inner passage. She had not yet removed her waterproof cloak, although the rain had long since ceased. Even the hood was still drawn over her head. Magnhild was the first to espy the stranger, and she drew farther back into the house; Rönnaug turned, and then she too moved into the passage.

That evening Rönnaug's steamer ticket was bought; for the sum was complete. Magnhild did not undress after Rönnaug had gone home late in the evening. She sat in a large arm-chair in the little low room, or restlessly paced the floor. And once, with her heavy head pressed against the window pane, she said half aloud,—

"Then she must be destined to something."

CHAPTER II.

SHE had heard these words before.

The first time it was in the churchyard that blustering winter day her fourteen relatives were buried,—all whom she had loved, both parents and grandparents, and brothers and sisters. In fancy she saw the scene again! The wind had here and there swept away the snow, the pickets of the fence stood out in sharp prominence, huge rocks loomed up like the heads of monsters whose bodies were covered by the snow-drifts. The wind whistled behind the little group of mourners through the open church porch whose blinds had been taken out, and down from the old wooden belfry came the clanging toll of the bell, like one cry of anguish after another.

The people that were gathered together were blue with the cold; they wore mittens and their garments were closely buttoned up. The priest appeared in sea-boots and had on a skin suit beneath his gown; his hands also were eased in large mittens, and he vigorously fought the air round about him with these. He waved one of them toward Magnhild.

"This poor child," said he, "remained standing on her feet, and with her little sled in her hand she was borne downward and across the frozen stream,—the sole being the Lord saw fit to save. To what is she destined?"

She rode home with the priest, sitting on his lap. He had commended her to the care of the parish, and took her home with him "for the present," in order to set a good example. She nestled up to his fur overcoat, with her small cold hands inside of his huge mittens, beside his soft, plump hands. And all the while she kept thinking: "What am I destined to, I wonder?"

She presumed that her mind would become clear on this point when she got into the house. But nothing met her eye here she had not seen before until she entered the inner room, where a piano which some one was just playing in the highest degree attracted her.

But for that very reason she forgot the thought she had brought in with her.

In this household there were two daughters, heavy-looking girls, with small round heads and long, thick braids of light hair. They had recently been provided with a governess, a pale, though fleshy person, with her neck more exposed and her sleeves more open than Magnhild had ever seen in any one before. Her voice sounded as though it needed clearing, and Magnhild involuntarily coughed several times; but this was of no avail. The governess asked Magnhild's name and inquired if she knew how to read, to which Magnhild replied in the affirmative. Her whole family had been noted for their love of reading. And then the governess proposed, still with the same husky after-tone in her voice, that she should be allowed to share the instructions of the little girls, in order to spur them on. Magnhild was one year older than the elder.

The mistress of the house was sitting by, engaged with her embroidery. She now glanced up at Magnhild and said, "With pleasure," then bent over her work again. She was a person of medium size, neither thin nor stout, and had a small head with fair hair. The priest, who was heavy and corpulent, came down-stairs after removing his gown; he was smoking, and as he crossed the floor, he said, "There comes a man with fish," and passed out of the room again.

The youngest girl once more attacked her scales. Magnhild did not know whether she should remain where she was, or go back to the kitchen. She sat on the wood-box by the stove tormented with the uncertainty, when dinner was announced in the adjoining room. All work was put aside, and the little one at the piano closed the instrument. Now when Magnhild was alone and heard the rattling of the knives, she began to cry; for she had not yet eaten a morsel that day. During the meal the priest came out from the dining-room; for it had been decided that he had not bought enough fish. He opened the window and called out to the man to wait until dinner was over. As he turned to go back into the dining-room he espied the little one on the wood-box.

"Are you hungry?" asked he.

The child made no reply. He had lived long enough among the peasants to know that her silence meant "yes," and so taking her by the hand he led her to the table, where room was silently made for her.

In the afternoon she went coasting with the little girls, and then joined them in their studies and had a lesson in Bible history with them; after this she partook of the afternoon lunch with them, and then played with them until they were called to supper, which they all ate at the same table. She slept that night on a lounge in the dining-room and took part the next day in the duties of the priest's daughters.

She had no clothes except those she had on; but the governess made over an old dress for her; some articles of old linen belonging to one of the little girls were given to her, and a pair of their mother's boots. The lounge she had slept on was removed from the dining-room, because it occupied the space needed for some shoemakers who were to "see the household well shod." It was placed in the kitchen, but was in the way there; then in the bed-room of the maid-servants, but there the door continually struck against it; finally it was carried up to the nursery. Thus it was that Magnhild came to eat, work, and sleep with the priest's daughters; and as new clothes were never made for her she naturally fell to wearing theirs.

Quite as much by chance she began to play the piano. It was discovered that she had more talent for music than the daughters of the house, so it was thought best that she should learn, in order to help them. Moreover, she grew tall, and developed a fine voice for singing. The governess took great pains in teaching her to sing by note; she did so at first merely in the mechanical way she did everything, later because the remarkable skill in reading at sight which her pupil developed under her guidance proved a diversion to them all in their mountain solitude. The priest could lie on the sofa (the place he most frequently occupied) and laugh aloud when he heard Magnhild running all sorts of exercises up and down like a squirrel in a tree. The result of this, so far as Magnhild was concerned, was that the young girl learned—not more music, as one might have supposed, but—basket-making.

The fact was that about this time there spread, like an epidemic among the people, the idea that skill in manual industries should be cultivated among the peasants, and propagators of the new doctrine appeared also in this parish. Magnhild was chosen as the first pupil; she was thought to have the most "dexterity." The first thing taught was basket-making, then double spinning, then weaving, especially of the more artistic kinds, and after this embroidery, etc., etc. She learned all these things very rapidly, that is to say, she learned zealously as long as she was gaining an insight into each; further development did not interest her. But as she was henceforth expected to teach others, grown people as well as children, it became a settled habit for her to repair twice each week to the public school where many were assembled. When anything had once become part of her daily routine she thought no more about it. The house that had given her shelter was responsible for this.

The mistress of the house made her daily regulation visits to the kitchen, cellar, and stables, the rest of the time she embroidered; the whole house was covered with embroidery. She might be taken for a fat spider, with a little round head, spinning its web over chairs, tables, beds, sledges, and carts. Her voice was rarely heard; she was seldom addressed by any one.

The priest was much older than his wife. His face was characterized by its small proportion of nose, chin, and eyes, and its very large share of all else belonging to it. He had fared badly at his examination, and had been compelled to support himself by teaching until, when he was advancing in years, he had married one of his former pupils, a lady with quite a nice property. Then he betook himself to seeking a clerical appointment, "the one thing in which he had shown perseverance," as he was himself in the habit of playfully remarking. After a ten years' search he had succeeded in getting a call (not long since) to his present parish, and he could scarcely hope for a better one. He passed most of his time in lying on the sofa reading, chiefly novels, but also newspapers and periodicals.

The governess always sat in the same chair in which Magnhild had seen her the first day, took the same walk to the church and back each day, and never failed to be ready for her duties on the stroke of the clock. She gradually increased in weight until she became excessively stout; she continued to wear her neck bare and her sleeves open, furthermore to speak in the same husky voice, which no effort on her part had ever yet been able to clear.

The priest's daughters became stout and heavy like their father, although they had small round heads like their mother. Magnhild and they lived as friends, in other words, they slept in the same room, and worked, played, and ate together.

There were never any ideas afloat in this parish. If any chanced to find their way there from without they got no farther than the priest's study. The priest was not communicative. At the utmost he read aloud to his family some new or old novel that he had found diverting.

One evening they were all sitting round the table, and the priest, having yielded to the entreaties of the united family, was reading aloud the "Pickwick Club."

The kitchen door slowly opened and a large bald head, with a snub nose and smiling countenance, was thrust in. A short leg in very wide trousers was next introduced, and this was followed by a crooked and consequently still shorter one. The whole figure stooped as it turned on the crooked leg to shut the door. The intruder thus presented to the party the back of the before mentioned large head, with its narrow rim of hair, a pair of square-built shoulders, and an extraordinarily large seat, only half covered by a pea-jacket. Again he turned in a slanting posture toward the assembled party, and once more presented his smiling countenance with its snub-nose. The young girls bowed low over their work, a suppressed titter arose first from one piece of sewing and then from another.

"Is this the saddler?" asked the priest, rising to his feet.

"Yes," was the reply, as the new-comer limped forward, holding out a hand so astonishingly large and with such broad round finger tips that the priest was forced to look at it as he took it in his own. The hand was offered to the others; and when it came to Magnhild's turn she burst out laughing just as her hand disappeared within it. One peal of laughter after another was heard and suppressed. The priest hastened to remark that they were reading the "Pickwick Club."

"Aha!" observed the saddler, "there is enough to make one laugh in that book."

"Have you read it?" asked the priest.

"Yes; when I was in America. I read most of the English writers; indeed, I have them all in my house now," he answered, and proceeded to give an account of the cheap popular editions that could be obtained in America.

The laughter of young girls is not easily subdued; it was still ready to bubble over when, after the saddler was furnished with a pipe, the reading was resumed. Now to be sure there was a pretext. After a while the priest grew tired and wanted to close the book, but the saddler offered to continue the reading for him, and was allowed to do so. He read in a dry, quiet manner, and with such an unfamiliar pronunciation of the names of the personages and localities introduced that the humor of the text became irresistible; even the priest joined in the laughter which no one now attempted to restrain. It never occurred to the girls to ask themselves why they were all obliged to laugh; they were still laughing when they went up-stairs to go to bed, and while undressing they imitated the saddler's walk, bowed and talked as he did, pronounced the foreign words with his English accent. Magnhild was the most adroit in mimicking; she had observed him the most closely.

At that time she was fifteen, in her sixteenth year.

The next day the girls passed every free moment in the dining-room, which had now been transformed into a workshop. The saddler told them of a sojourn of several years in America, and of travels in England and Germany; he talked without interrupting his work and with a frequent intermingling of jests. His narratives were accompanied by the incessant tittering of his listeners. They were scarcely aware themselves how they gradually ceased laughing at him and laughed instead at the witty things he said; neither did they observe until later how much they learned from him. He was so greatly missed by the girls when he left that more than half of their time together was occupied in conversation about him; this lasted for many days after he was gone, and never wholly ceased.

There were two things which had made the strongest impression on Magnhild. The first was the English and German songs the saddler had sung for them. She had paid little attention to the text, unless perhaps occasionally; but how the melodies had captivated her!

While singing hymns one Sunday they had first noticed that Skarlie had a fine voice. Thenceforth he was obliged to sing for them constantly. These foreign melodies of his fluttering thither from a fuller, richer life, freer conditions, larger ideas than their own, clung to Magnhild's fancy the entire summer. They were the first pictures which had awakened actual yearning within her breast. It may also be said that for the first time she comprehended what song was. As she was singing her interminable scales one day, before beginning her studies in singing from note, she came to a full realization of the fact that this song without melody was to her like wings beating against a cage: it fluttered up and down against walls, windows, doors, in perpetual and fruitless longing, aye, until at last it sank like the cobwebs, over everything in the room. She could sit alone out of doors with *his* songs. While she was humming them, the forest hues dissolved into one picture; and that she had never discovered before. The density, the vigor in the tree-tops, above and below the tree-tops, over the entire mountain wall, as it were, overwhelmed her; the rushing of the waters of the stream attracted her.

The second thing which had made so deep an impression on her, and which was blended with all the rest, was Skarlie's story of how he had become lame. In America, when he was a young man, he had undertaken to carry a boy twelve years old from a burning house; he had fallen with the boy beneath the ruins. Both were extricated, Skarlie with a crushed limb, the boy unscathed. That boy was now one of the most noted men of America.

It was his lot to be saved, "he was destined to something."

This reminder again! The thought of her own fate had heretofore been shrouded in the wintry mantle of the churchyard, amid frost, weeping, and harsh clanging of bells; it had been something sombre. Now it flitted onward to large cities beyond the seas, among ships, burning houses, songs, and great destinies. From this time forth she dreamed of what she was destined to be as something far distant and great.

CHAPTER III.

LATE in the autumn all three girls were confirmed. This was such a matter of course to them all that their thoughts were chiefly busied with what they should wear on the day of the ceremony. Magnhild, who had never yet had a garment cut out and made expressly for herself, wondered whether an outfit would now be prepared for her. No. The younger girls were furnished with new silk dresses; an old black dress that had become too tight for the priest's wife was made over for Magnhild.

It was too short both in the waist and in the skirt; but Magnhild scarcely noticed this. She was provided by the governess with a little colored silk neckerchief and a silver brooch; she borrowed the every-day shawl of the mistress of the house; a pair of gloves were loaned her by the governess.

Her inner preparations were not much more extensive than the outer ones.

The day glided tranquilly by without any special emotion. Religious sentiments at the parsonage, as well as elsewhere in the parish, were matters of calm custom. Some tears were shed in church, the priest offered wine and a toast at table, and there was a little talk about what should now be done with Magnhild. This last topic so affected Magnhild that after coffee she went out and sat down alone. She gazed toward the broad rocky path of the land-slide on the verdure-clad mountain, then toward the mighty mass of débris in the midst of the plain, for it was there her home had stood.

Her little brothers and sisters appeared before her, one fair, bright face after another. Her mother came too; and her melancholy eye dwelt lingeringly on Magnhild; even the lines about the mouth were visible. The fine psalm-singing of her mother's gentle voice floated around Magnhild now. There had been sung in church that day one of the hymns her mother used to sing. Once more, too, her father sat on the bench, bowed over the silver work in which he was a master. A book or a newspaper lay at his side; he paused in his work now and then, stole a glance at the page before him, or turned a leaf. His long, delicately cut face inclined occasionally toward the family sitting-room and its inmates. The aged grandparents formed part of the home circle. The grandmother tottered off after some little dainty for Magnhild, while the old grandfather was telling the child a story. The dog, shaggy and gray, lay stretching himself on the hearth. His howl had been the last living sound Magnhild had heard behind her as she was carried downward across the stream. The memory of that awful day once more cast over her childhood the pall of night, thunder, and convulsions of the earth. Covering her face with her hands, she burst into tears.

The saddler's ballads came floating toward her, bringing a sense of want with their obscure dream images. And there drifted past her a motley throng of those half-comprehended songs and the anecdotes upon which she had often placed false interpretations, until, exhausted by the thoughts, emotions, and yearnings of the day, with an aching void within and a dull feeling of resignation, she feel asleep.

In the evening Rönnaug, with whom they had become acquainted during the confirmation instructions, made her appearance; she was out at service in the neighborhood and had a holiday in honor of the occasion. She brought with her a whole budget of gossip concerning the love affairs of the parish, and the inexperienced girls sat with wondering eyes listening. It was she who caused the youngest girl to tear her new silk dress. Rönnaug could roll down hill with such incomprehensible speed that she was induced to repeat the feat several times, and this finally led the priest's daughter to try her skill.

Hereafter Rönnaug often dropped in of an evening when her work was done. They all took delight in her wild exuberance of spirits. She was as hearty and as plump as a young foal; she could scarcely keep the clothes on her back because she was all the time tearing them to tatters, and she had never-ceasing trouble with her hair, which would keep falling over her face because she never had it done up properly. When she laughed, and that was nearly all the time, she tossed back her head, and through two rows of pearly teeth, white as those of a beast of prey, could be seen far down her throat.

In the autumn Skarlie came again. There was a difference between the reception now given him and the former one. The three girls surrounded his sledge, they carried in his luggage, notwithstanding his laughing resistance, their laughter accompanied him as he stood in the passage taking off his furs.

Questions without number were showered like hail upon him the first time they sat with him in the work-room; the girls had an accumulation of treasured-up doubts and queries about things he had told them on his previous visit, and many other perplexing themes which they considered him able to solve. On very few topics did Skarlie hold the prevailing opinions of the parish, but he had a way of deftly turning the subject with a joke when pressed too closely for his precise views. When alone with Magnhild he expressed himself more freely; at first he did so cautiously, but gradually increased his plainness of speech.

Magnhild had never viewed her surroundings with critical eyes; she would now laugh heartily with Skarlie over the priest's last sermon, or his indolent life; now over the spider-like activity of the mistress of the house, because it was all described so comically. At the "fat repose" of the governess, even at the "yellow, round heads" of her young friends, Magnhild could now laugh; for the humor with which everything was delineated was so surprisingly original; she did not perceive that this jesting was by degrees undermining the very ground she stood upon.

The quite usual amusement in the country of teasing a young girl about being in love was, meanwhile, directed rather unexpectedly toward Magnhild; she was called "the saddler's wife," because she passed so much time in his society. This reached Skarlie's ears and immediately he too began to call her his "wife," his "tall wife," his "blonde wife," his "very young wife."

The following summer the priest's daughters went to the city for increased opportunities of culture. The governess remained "for the present" at the parsonage.

The saddler came once more in the autumn to complete his work. Magnhild was now, of course, more frequently alone with him than before. He was merrier than ever. One joke that was often repeated by him was about journeying round the world with "his young wife." They met with an immense number of traveling adventures, and they saw many remarkable sights, all of which were so accurately described by Skarlie that they attained the value of actual experiences. But the most ludicrous picture he drew represented the two tramping through the country: Skarlie limping on before with a traveling satchel, Magnhild following in a waterproof cloak and with an umbrella in her hand, grumbling at the heat, dust, and thirst, weary and heartily disgusted with him Then, having reached their journey's end, they rested in Skarlie's little home in the little town, where Magnhild had everything her own way and lived like a princess all the rest of her life.

It would be impossible to describe the countenance of the priest when the saddler appeared in his study one evening, and taking a seat in front of him asked, after a few cordial, pleasant remarks by way of introduction, whether the priest would object to his marrying Magnhild. The priest was lying on the sofa smoking; his pipe dropped from his mouth, his hand sank with it, his fat face relaxed until it resembled a dough-like mass, in which the eyes peeped forth as wholly devoid of thought as two raisins; suddenly he gave a start that set a quantity of springs beneath him to creaking and grating, and the book that lay upside down on his knee fell. The saddler picked up the volume smiling, and turned over the leaves. The priest had risen to his feet.

"What does Magnhild have to say to this?" asked he.

The saddler looked up with a smile.

"Of course I should not have asked if she were not likely to give her consent," said he.

The priest put his pipe in his mouth, and strode up and down the floor, puffing away. Gradually he grew calmer, and without slackening his speed, he observed:—

"To be sure I do not know what is to become of the girl."

Once more the saddler raised his eyes from the book whose leaves he was turning over, and now laying it aside, he remarked:—

"It is, you know, rather a sort of adoption than a marriage. Down yonder at my house she can develop into whatever she pleases."

The priest looked at him, took a puff at his pipe, paced the floor, and puffed again.

"Aye, to be sure! You are, I believe, a wealthy man?"

"Well, if not precisely wealthy, I am sufficiently well provided to get married."

Here Skarlie laughed.

But there was something in his laugh, something which did not quite please the priest. Still less did he like the tone of indifference with which Skarlie seemed to treat the whole affair. Least of all did he like being so taken by surprise.

"I must speak with my wife about this," said he, and groaned. "That I must," he added decidedly, "and with Magnhild," came as an afterthought.

"Certainly," said the other, as he rose to take leave.

A little while later, the priest's wife was sitting where the saddler had sat. Both hands lay idly open on her lap, while her eyes followed her spouse as he steamed back and forth.

"Well, what do you think?" he urged, pausing in front of her.

Receiving no reply, he moved on again.

"He is far too old," she finally said.

"And surely very sly," added the priest, and then pausing again in front of his wife, he whispered: "No one really knows where he comes from, or why he chooses to settle here. He might have a fine workshop in a large city—wealthy, and a smart dog!"

The priest did not use the choicest language in his daily discourse.

"To think she should allow herself to be so beguiled!" whispered the wife.

"Beguiled! Just the word—beguiled!" repeated the priest, snapping his fingers. "Beguiled!" and off he went in a cloud of smoke.

"I am so sorry for her," remarked the wife, and the words were accompanied by a few tears.

This touched the priest, and he said: "See here, mother, we will talk with her, both of us!" then strode heavily on again.

Ere long Magnhild stood within the precincts of the study, wondering what could be wanted of her. The priest was the first to speak:—

"Is it really true, Magnhild, that you have agreed to be the wife of this fellow, the saddler?"

The priest often used the general term "fellow" instead of a proper name.

Magnhild's face became suffused with blushes; in her whole life she could never have been so red before. Both the priest and his wife interpreted this as a confession.

"Why do you not come to us with such things?" asked the priest, in a vexed tone.

"It is very strange you should act so, Magnhild," said the mistress of the house,—and she wept.

Magnhild was simply appalled.

"Do you really mean to have him?" asked the priest, pausing resolutely in front of her.

Now Magnhild had never been accustomed to being addressed in a confidential tone. When questioned thus closely she had not the courage to give a frank statement of all that had occurred between her and Skarlie, telling, how this talk of marriage had commenced as a jest, and that although later she had had a misgiving that it was becoming serious, it was so continually blended anew with jests that she had not given herself the trouble to protest against it. How could she, with the priest standing thus before her, enter on so long a story? And so instead she burst into tears.

Well now, the priest did not mean to torment her. What was done could not be undone. He was very sorry for her, and in the goodness of his heart merely wanted to help her lay a solid foundation to her choice. Skarlie was a man of considerable means, he said, and she a poor girl; she certainly could not expect a better match, so far as that went. True, Skarlie was old; but then he had himself said that he designed rather a sort of adoption than a marriage; his only object was Magnhild's happiness.

But all this was more than Magnhild could bear to listen to, and so she rushed from the room. In the passage she fell to crying as though her heart would break; she was obliged to go up to the dark garret in order to avoid attracting attention, and there her grief gradually assumed definite shape. It was *not* because the saddler wanted her that she was in such distress; it was because the priest and his wife did not want her.

This was the interpretation she had put on their words.

When the governess was informed of the affair she differed entirely from the mistress of the house, who could not comprehend Magnhild, for the governess could comprehend the young girl perfectly. Skarlie was a man of fine mind and very witty. He was rich, jovial, rather homely, to be sure, but that was not of such great consequence down at the Point. And she adopted this tone in talking with Magnhild when she finally succeeded in getting hold of her. Magnhild was red with weeping, and burst into a fresh flood of tears; yet not a word did she say.

Somewhat curtly the priest now informed the saddler that as the matter was settled he might as well proceed with the preparations. The saddler desired this himself; moreover, he was now quite through with his work. Eagerly as he strove for an opportunity to speak with Magnhild, he even failed to catch a glimpse of her. He was therefore forced to take his departure without having an interview with her.

During the days which followed Magnhild neither appeared in the sitting-room nor at table. No one attempted to seek her and talk with her; the governess deemed it quite natural that in the face of so serious a step the young girl should wish to be alone.

One day the members of the household were surprised by the arrival through the mail of a letter and large package for Magnhild. The letter read as follows:—

In order to complete our delightful joke, dear Magnhild, I came down here. My house has been painted this summer, within and without, a joke which now almost looks like earnest—does it not?

Beds, household furniture, bedding, etc., are articles that I deal in myself, so these I can purchase from my own stores. When I think of the object I have in view, this becomes the most delightful business transaction I have ever entered into.

Do you remember how we laughed the time I took your measure in order to prove accurately how much too short in the waist your dress was, how much too wide across the shoulders, and how much too short in the skirt? Just by chance I took a note of your exact measurement, and according to it I am now having made:—

-        1 black silk dress (Lyons taffeta).
-        1 brown (cashmere).
-        1 blue (of some light woolen material).

As I have always told you, blue is the most becoming color that you can wear.

Such orders cannot be executed without some delay; but the articles shall be sent as speedily as possible.

For other garments that you may perhaps require I telegraphed to Bergen immediately upon my arrival here; such things can be obtained there ready-made. You will most likely receive them by the same mail which brings you this letter.

As you see (and shall further continue to see), there are sundry jokes connected with this getting married. For instance, I made my will to-day, and in it designated you as my heiress.

With most respectful greetings to the priest and his honored family, I now subscribe myself

Your most obedient jester,

SKARLIE.

Magnhild had taken refuge in the garret, with both the letter and the large package. She had plunged forthwith into the letter, and emerging from its perusal perplexed and frightened, she tore open the package and found many full suits of everything pertaining to feminine under garments. She scattered them all around her, blushing crimson, angry, ashamed. Then she sat down and wept aloud.

Now she had courage to speak! She sprang down-stairs to the priest's wife, and throwing her arms about her neck, whispered, "Forgive me!" thrust the letter into her hand, and disappeared.

The priest's wife did not understand Magnhild's "Forgive me!" but she saw that the young girl was crying and in great excitement. She took the letter and read it. It was peculiar in form, she thought; yet its meaning was plain enough: it indicated a sensible, elderly man's prudent forethought, and deserved credit. An old housewife and mother could not be otherwise than pleased with this, and she carried the letter to the priest. It impressed him in the same way; and he began to think the girl might be happy with this singular man. The mistress of the house searched everywhere for Magnhild, in order to tell her that both the priest and herself were of the opinion that Skarlie's conduct promised well. She learned that Magnhild was in the garret, and so throwing a shawl round her (for it was cold) she went up-stairs. She met the governess on the way and took her with her. Magnhild was not visible; they saw only the articles of clothing strewn over floor, chests, and trunks. They collected these together, discussed them, examined them, and pronounced them admirable. They well knew that such a gift was calculated to embarrass a young girl; but then Skarlie was an elderly man whose privilege it was to take things in a fatherly way. This they told Magnhild when they finally found her. And she had no longer the courage to be confidential. This was because the priest's wife, sustained by the governess, spoke what they deemed sensible words to her. They told her that she must not be proud; she must remember that she was a poor girl who had neither relatives nor future of her own. In the days which followed, Magnhild fought a hard fight in secret. But she lacked energy for action. Where could she have gained it? Where could she go since the priest's family had so evidently grown tired of her?

A little later there arrived a chest containing her dresses and many other articles. Magnhild allowed it to stand untouched, but the governess, who so well understood this bashfulness, attended to having it opened. She and the priest's wife drew forth the contents piece by piece, and not long afterwards Magnhild was trying on dress after dress before the large mirror in the family sitting-room. The doors were locked, the priest's wife and the governess full of zeal. Finally they came to the black silk dress, and Magnhild gradually ceased to be indifferent. She felt a blushing gratification in beholding in the glass her own form encompassed in beautiful fine material. She discovered herself, as it were, point by point. If it chanced to be the face, she had not before this day so fully observed that those she beheld at her side were without distinct outline, while hers—Her vision had been rendered keen by the sense awakened, in the twinkling of an eye, by a handsome, well-fitting garment.

This picture of herself floated before her for many days. Fearing to disturb it she avoided the mirror. Once more she became absorbed in the old dreams, those which bore her across the sea to something strange and great.

But the marriage? At such moments she thrust it from her as though it were a steamer's plank, to be drawn ashore after serving its purpose. How was this possible? Aye, how many times in the years that followed did she not pause and reflect! But it always remained alike incomprehensible to her.

She could neither be persuaded to put on one of the new dresses the day Skarlie came, nor to go out to meet him; on the contrary, she hid herself. Later, and as by chance, she made her appearance. With unvarying consistency she treated both the marriage and Skarlie as though neither in the least concerned her.

Skarlie was in high spirits; the fact was both the priest and his wife took pains to make amends for Magnhild's lack of courtesy, and he reciprocated in the most winning manner. The governess declared him to be decidedly amiable.

The next evening Magnhild sat in the dining-room arranging some articles belonging to the industrial school that must now be sent back. She was alone, and Skarlie entered softly and smiling, and slowly closing the door behind him took a seat at her side. He talked for some time on indifferent subjects, so that she began to breathe freely again; she even ventured at last to look down on him as he sat bent over smoking. Her eyes rested on the bald head, the bushy brows, and the extreme end of the snub-nose, then on his enormous hands and their very singular-looking nails; the latter were deeply set in the flesh, which everywhere, therefore in front also, encompassed them like a thick round frame. Under the nails there was dirt, a fact to which the governess, who had herself very pretty hands, had once called the attention of her pupils as a deadly sin. Magnhild looked at the reddish, bristling hair which completely covered these hands. Skarlie had been silent for a little while, but as if he felt that he was being scrutinized, he drew himself up, and with a smile extended to her one of his objectionable hands.

"Aye, aye, Magnhild!" said he, laying it on both of hers. This gave her a shock, and in a moment she was like one paralyzed. She could not stir, could not grasp a single thought except that she was in the clutches of a great lobster. His head drew nearer, the eyes too were those of a lobster; they stung. This she had never before observed, and she sprang hastily to her feet. He retained his seat. Without looking back Magnhild began to busy herself where she stood with another lot of the industrial work. Therefore she did not leave the room, but a little while later Skarlie did.

The governess decked her in her bridal finery the next day; the mistress of the house too came to look on. This gave her great pleasure, she said. Magnhild let everything be done for her without stirring, without uttering a word and without shedding a tear.

It was the same in the sitting-room. She was motionless. A feeling akin to defiance had taken possession of her. The men-servants and the house-maids sat and stood by the kitchen door, which was ajar, and just inside of it; Magnhild saw, too, the heads of little children. The deacon started the singing as the priest came down-stairs.

Magnhild did not look at the bridegroom. The priest touched on tender chords; his wife shed tears, and so too did the governess; but Magnhild's icy coldness chilled both him and them. The discourse was brief and dealt chiefly in mere generalities. It was followed by congratulations, and a painful silence; even the saddler had lost his smile. It was a relief when they were summoned to dinner.

During the repast the priest, desiring to propose a toast, began: "Dear Magnhild! I trust you have no fault to find with us,"—he got no farther, for here Magnhild burst into such convulsive weeping that the priest's wife, the governess, aye, even the priest himself became deeply affected, and there arose a long and painful silence. Finally, however, the priest managed to add: "Think of us!" But these words were followed by the same heart-rending weeping as before, so that no toast was drunk. What this really signified was not clear to any of those present, unless perhaps to the bridegroom; and he said nothing.

While they were at dessert one of the young girls approached the bride and whispered a few words in her ear. Rönnaug was outside and wished to say farewell; she had been waiting ever since the company had gone to table and could stay no longer. Rönnaug was standing on the back porch, benumbed with the cold; she did not wish to intrude, she said. She examined the bride's dress, thought it extraordinarily fine, and drawing off one mitten stroked it with the back of her hand.

"Yes, I dare say he is rich," said she, "but if they had given me a gown of silver I would not"—and she added a few words which cannot be repeated here, and for which Magnhild, her face flaming, administered a good sound box on the ear. The kerchief softened the blow somewhat, but it was seriously meant.

Magnhild returned to the dining-room and sat down, not in her place at the bridegroom's side, but on a chair by the window; she did not wish anything more, she said. It was of no avail that she was entreated to sit with the others at least until they had finished; she said she could not.

The departure took place shortly after coffee was served. An incident had meanwhile occurred which suppressed all emotion, of whatever nature it might be. It was that the bridegroom suddenly appeared, looking like a shaggy beast, carrying a fur cape, fur boots, a short coat, a hood, fur gloves, and a muff. He let them fall in front of Magnhild, saying with dry earnestness,—

"All these I lay at your feet!"

There burst forth a peal of laughter in which even Magnhild was forced to join. The whole bridal party gathered about the things which were spread over the carpet, and every one was loud in praise. It was evidently not displeasing to Magnhild either, in the face of a winter journey,—for which she had been promised the loan of a variety of wraps,—to have such presents lavished upon her.

In a few moments more Magnhild was attired in her blue dress, and she was enough of a child or rather woman to be diverted by the change. Shortly afterwards the new traveling wraps were donned, piece by piece, amid the liveliest interest of all, which reached its height when Magnhild was drawn before the mirror to see for herself how she looked. The horse had been driven round, and Skarlie just now came into the room, also dressed for traveling, and wearing a dog-skin coat, deer-skin shoes and leggings, and a flat fur cap. He was nearly as broad as he was long, and in order to raise a laugh, he limped up to the mirror, and, with dry humor in his face, took his stand beside Magnhild. There followed a burst of laughter, in which even Magnhild herself joined—but only to become at once entirely mute again. Her silence still hung over the parting. Not until the parsonage was left behind did she become again dissolved in tears.

Her eyes wandered listlessly over the snow-covered heap of ruins on the site of her childhood's home; it seemed as though there were that within herself which was shrouded in snow and desolation.

The weather was cold. The valley grew narrower, the road led through a dense wood. One solitary star was visible.

Skarlie had been cutting figures in the snow with his whip; he now pointed the latter toward the star and began to hum, finally to sing. The melody he had chosen was that of one of the ballads of the Scottish highlands. Like a melancholy bird, it flitted from one snow-laden fir-tree to another. Magnhild inquired its meaning, and this proved to be in harmony with a journey through the depths of a forest. Skarlie talked further about Scotland, its history, his sojourn there.

Once started, he continued, and gradually broke into such merry anecdotes that Magnhild was astonished when they stopped to rest; astonished that she had been able to laugh, and that they had driven nearly fourteen miles.

Skarlie helped her out of the sledge and ushered her into the inn, but he himself went directly out again to feed the horse.

A stylish looking young lady sat by the hearth in the guest-room warming herself, scattered over the benches around were her traveling-wraps; they were of such fine material and costly fur that Magnhild grew curious and felt obliged to touch them. The traveling-suit the lady wore, so far as material and style was concerned, made the same impression on Magnhild as she might have gained from a zoölogical specimen from another quarter of the globe. The lady's face possessed youth and a gentle melancholy; she was fair and had languishing eyes and a slightly-curved nose. Her hair, too, was done up in an unfamiliar style. Pacing the floor was a slender young man; his traveling boots stood by the hearth and his feet were cased in small morocco slippers, linedwith fur. His movements were lithe and graceful.

"Are you Skarlie's young wife?" inquired the hostess, quite an old woman, who had placed a chair by the hearth for Magnhild. Before Magnhild could reply, Skarlie came in with some things from the sledge. The bald head, half protruding from the shaggy furs, the deer-skin shoes, sprawling like monstrous roots over the floor, attracted the wondering gaze of the young lady.

"Is this your wife?" repeated the hostess.

"Yes, this is my wife," was the cheerful reply, as Skarlie limped forward.

The young man fixed his eyes on Magnhild. She felt herself growing fiery red beneath his gaze. There was an expression entirely new to her in his face. Was it scorn? The lady, too, now looked at her, and at the same moment the hostess begged Magnhild to take a seat by the fire. But the latter preferred remaining in the dark, on a bench in the farthest corner.

It was fully ten o'clock when the Point was reached, but every light there had been extinguished, even in the house in front of which the sledge stopped. An old woman, awakened by the jingling of the bells, came to the street door, opened it and looked out, then drew back and struck a light. She met Magnhild in the passage, cast the light on her and said finally, "I bid you welcome."

A strong smell of leather filled the passage; for the work-room and shop were to the left. The loathsome odor prevented Magnhild from replying. They entered a room to the right. Here Magnhild hastily removed her traveling-wraps;—she felt faint. Without casting a glance about her, or speaking to the woman who was watching her from behind the light, she then crossed the floor and opened a door she had espied on coming into the room. She first held the light in, then stepped in herself and closed the door after her. The woman heard a rumbling within and went to the door. There she discovered that one of the beds was being moved. Directly afterward Magnhild reappeared with the candle. The light revealed a flushed face. She looked resolute.

She now told the woman she had no need of her services.

The saddler did not come in for some time; for he had been seeing to the horse, which he had borrowed for the journey. The light was still on the table. There was no one up.

CHAPTER IV.

TWO years had passed since that evening, and the greater part of a third.

Magnhild was quite as thoroughly accustomed to the new daily routine as she had been to the old.

The priest visited her three or four times a year; he slept in the room over the workshop usually occupied by Skarlie when he was at home. During the day the priest visited at the captain's, or the custom-house officer's, or at the home of the chief of police. His coming was called the "priestly visitation."

There was chess-playing in the day-time and cards in the evening. The priest's wife and young lady daughters had also been seen at the Point a few times. In the lading-town there was scarcely any one with whom Magnhild associated.

Skarlie and she had taken one trip to Bergen. Whatever might there have happened or not happened, they never undertook another, either to Bergen or elsewhere.

Skarlie was more frequently absent than at home; he was engaged in speculations; the work-shop was pretty much abandoned, though the store was still kept open. A short time after her arrival, Magnhild had received an invitation from the school committee—most likely through Skarlie's solicitation—to become the head of the industrial school. Henceforth she passed an hour or two every day at the public school; moreover, she gave private instructions to young girls who were grown up. Her time was employed in walking, singing, and a little sewing; she did very little reading, indeed. It was tedious to her.

Directly after she came there, Rönnaug had appeared at the Point, and had hired out at the nearest "skyds" (post-station), in order to earn money speedily for the purchase of a ticket to America. She was determined to live no longer the life of an outcast here, she said.

Magnhild took charge of Rönnaug's money for her, and was alarmed to note how rapidly it increased, for she had her own thoughts about the matter. Now the ticket was bought, Magnhild would be entirely alone.

Many were the thoughts called forth by the fact that the journey across the sea to new and perhaps great experiences should be so easy for one person and not for another.

One morning after a sleepless night, Magnhild took her accustomed walk to the wharf to watch the steamer come in. She saw the usual number of commercial travelers step ashore; the usual number of trunks carried after them; but this day she also observed a pale man, with long, soft hair and large eyes, walking around a box which he finally succeeded in having lifted on a wagon. "Be careful! Be careful!" he repeated again and again. "There must be a piano in the box," thought Magnhild.

After Magnhild had been to school, she saw the same pale man, with the box behind him, standing before the door of her house. He was accompanied by the landlord of one of the hotels. Skarlie had fitted up the rooms above the sitting-room and bed-chamber for the accommodation of travelers when the hotels were full. The pale stranger was an invalid who wished to live quietly.

Magnhild had not thought of letting the rooms to permanent guests and thus assuming a certain responsibility. She stood irresolute. The stranger now drew nearer to her. Such eyes she had never beheld, nor so refined and spiritual a face. With strange power of fascination those wondrous eyes were fixed on her. There was, as it were, two expressions combined in the gaze that held her captive, one behind the other. Magnhild was unable to fathom this accurately; but in the effort to do so she put her forefinger in her mouth, and became so absorbed in thought that she forgot to reply.

Now the stranger's countenance changed; it grew observant. Magnhild felt this, roused herself, blushed, gave some answer and walked away. What did she say? Was it "Yes" or "No"? The landlord followed her. She had said "Yes!" She was obliged to go up-stairs and see whether everything was in readiness for a guest; she did not rely very implicitly on her own habits of order.

There was great confusion when the piano was carried up; it took time, too, to move the bed, sofa, and other articles of furniture to make room for the instrument. But all this came to an end at last, and quiet once more prevailed. The pale stranger must be tired. Soon there was not a step, not a sound, overhead.

There is a difference between the silence which is full and that which is empty.

Magnhild dared not stir. She waited, listened. Would the tones of the piano soon fall upon her ear? The stranger was a composer, so the landlord had said, and Magnhild thought, too, she had read his name in the newspaper. How would it be when such a person played? Surely it would seem as though miracles were being wrought. At all events, something would doubtless ring into her poor life which would long give forth resonance. She needed the revelation of a commanding spirit. Her gaze wandered over the flowers which decorated her window, and on which the sun was now playing; her eyes sought the "Caravan in the Desert," which hung framed and glass covered by the door, and which suddenly seemed to her so animated, so full of beautifully arranged groups and forms. With ear for the twittering of the birds in the opposite neighbor's garden and the sporting of the magpies farther off in the fields, she sat in blissful content and waited.

Through her content there darted the question, "Will Skarlie be pleased with what you have done? Is there not danger of injury to the new sofa and the bed too? The stranger is an invalid, no one can tell"—She sprang to her feet, sought pen, ink, and paper, and for the first time in her life wrote a letter to Skarlie. It took her more than an hour to complete it. This is what she wrote:—

I have let the rooms over the sitting-room and bed-chamber to a sick man who plays the piano. The price is left to you.

I have had one of the new sofas (the hair-cloth) carried up-stairs and one of the spring beds. He wants to be comfortable. Perhaps I have not done right.

MAGNHILD.

She had crossed out the words: "Now I shall have an opportunity to hear some music." The heading of the letter had caused her some trouble; she finally decided to use none. "Your wife," she had written above the signature, but had drawn her pen through it. Thus fashioned, the letter was copied and sent. She felt easier after this, and again sat still and waited. She saw the stranger's dinner carried up to him; she ate a little herself and fell asleep,—she had scarcely had any sleep the previous night.

She awoke; there was yet no sounds of music above. Again she fell asleep, and dreamed that the distance between the mountain peaks had been spanned by a bridge. She told herself that this was the bridge at Cologne, a lithograph of which hung on the wall near the bed-chamber. Nevertheless it extended across the valley from one lofty mountain to the other, supported by trestle-work from the depths below. The longer she gazed the finer, more richly-colored the bridge became; for lo! it was woven of rainbow threads, and was transparent and radiant, all the way up to the straight line from crest to crest. But crosswise above this, the distance was spanned by another bridge. Both bridges began now to vibrate in slow two-fourths time, and immediately the entire valley was transformed into a sea of light, in which there was an intermingled play of all the prismatic hues; but the bridges had vanished. Nor were the mountains any longer visible, and the dissolving colors filled all conceivable space. How great was this? How far could she see? She grew positively alarmed at the infinity of space about her and awoke;—there was music overhead. In front of the house stood a crowd of people, silently gazing at the upper window.

Magnhild did not stir. The tones flowed forth with extreme richness; there was a bright, gentle grace over the music. Magnhild sat listening until it seemed as though these melodious tones were being showered down upon head, hands, and lap. A benediction was being bestowed upon her humble home, the world of tears within was filled with light. She pushed her chair farther back into the corner, and as she sat there she felt that she had been found out by the all-bountiful Providence who had ordered her destiny. The music was the result of a knowledge she did not possess, but it appealed to a passion awakened by it within her soul. She stretched out her arms, drew them in again, and burst into tears.

Long after the music had ceased,—the crowd was gone, the musician still,—Magnhild sat motionless. Life had meaning; she, too, might gain access to a rich world of beauty. As there was now song within, so one day there should be singing around about her. When she came to undress for the night she required both sitting-room and bed-chamber for the purpose, and more than half an hour; for the first time in her life she laid down to rest with a feeling that she had something to rise for in the morning. She listened to the footsteps of her guest above; they were lighter than those of other people; his contact with the furniture, too, was cautious. His eyes, with their kindly glow of good-will, and the fathomless depths beyond this, were the last objects she saw distinctly.

Indescribable days followed. Magnhild went regularly to her lessons, but lost no time in getting home again, where she was received by music and found the house surrounded by listeners. She scarcely went out again the rest of the day. Either her guest was at home and she was waiting for him to play, or he had gone out for a walk, and she was watching for his return. When he greeted her in passing she blushed and drew back. If he came into her room to ask for anything, there ran a thrill through her the moment she heard the approach of his footsteps; she became confused and scarcely comprehended his words when he stood before her. She had, perhaps, not exchanged ten words with him in as many days, but she already knew his most trifling habit and peculiarity of dress. She noticed whether his soft brown hair was brushed behind his ears, or whether it had fallen forward; whether his gray hat was pushed back, or whether it was drawn down over his forehead; whether he wore gloves or not; whether he had a shawl thrown over his shoulders or not. And how was it in regard to herself? Two new summer dresses had been ordered by her, and she was now wearing one of them. She had also purchased a new hat.

She believed that in music lay her vocation; but she felt no inclination to make any kind of a beginning. There was enough to satisfy her in her guest's playing, in his very proximity.

Day by day she developed in budding fullness of thought; her dream-life had prepared her for this; but music was the atmosphere that was essential to her existence: she knew it now. She did not realize that the refined nature of this man of genius, spiritualized and exalted by ill-health, was something new, delightful, thought-inspiring to her; she gave music alone the credit for the pleasure he instilled into her life.

At school she took an interest in each scholar she had never experienced before; she even fell into the habit of chatting with the sailor's wife who did the work of her house. There daily unfolded a new blossom within her soul; she was as meek as a woman in the transition period, which she had never known. Books she had heard read aloud, or read herself at the parsonage, rose up before her as something new. Forms she had not noticed before stood out in bold relief,—they became invested with flesh, blood, and motion. Incidents in real life, as well as in books, floated past like a cloud, suddenly became dissolved and gave distinct pictures. She awoke, as an Oriental maiden is awakened, when her time comes, by song beneath her window and by the gleam of a turban.

CHAPTER V.

ONE morning as Magnhild, after making her toilet, went into the sitting-room, humming softly to herself and in joyous mood, to open the window facing the street, she saw a lady standing at the open window of the house opposite.

It was a low cottage, surrounded by a garden, and belonged to a government officer who had moved away. Vines were trained about the windows of the house partially covering them, and the lady was engaged in arranging one of the sprays that was in the way. Her head was encircled with ringlets, which were rather black than brown. Her eyes sparkled, her brow was low but broad, her eyebrows were straight, her nose was also straight but quite large and round, her lips were full, her head was so beautifully poised on her shoulders that Magnhild could not help noticing it. The open sleeves had fallen back during the work with the vines, displaying her arms. Magnhild was unable to withdraw her eyes. When the lady perceived Magnhild, she nodded to her and smiled.

Magnhild became embarrassed, and drew back.

Just then a child approached the lady, who stooped and kissed it. The child also had ringlets, but they were fair; the face was the mother's, and yet it was not the mother's, it was the coloring which misled, for the child was blonde. The little one climbed upon a chair and looked out. The mother caught hold of the vine again, but kept her eyes fixed on Magnhild, and her expression was a most singular one. Magnhild put on her hat; it was time for her to go to school; but that look caused her to go out of the back door and return by the same way, when she came home an hour later.

He was playing. Magnhild paused for a while in her little garden and hearkened, until finally she felt that she must go in to see what effect this music had upon the beautiful lady. She went into her kitchen and then cautiously entered her sitting-room, shielding herself from observation. No; there was no beautiful lady at the window opposite. A sense of relief passed over Magnhild, and she went forward. She was obliged to move some plants into the sunshine, one of her daily duties, but she came very near dropping the flowerpot into the street, for as she held it in her hands the lady's head was thrust into the open window.

"Do not be frightened!" was the laughing greeting, uttered in tones of coaxing entreaty for pardon, that surpassed in sweetness anything of the kind Magnhild had ever heard.

"You will allow me to come in; will you not?" And before Magnhild could answer, the lady was already entering the house.

The next moment she stood face to face with Magnhild, tall and beautiful. An unknown perfume hovered about her as she flitted through the room, now speaking of the lithographs on the wall, now of the valley, the mountains, or the customs of the people. The voice, the perfume, the walk, the eyes, indeed the very material and fashion of her dress, especially its bold intermingling of colors, took captive the senses. From the instant she entered the room it belonged to her; if she smelled a flower, or made an observation concerning it, forthwith that flower blossomed anew; for what her eyes rested upon attained precisely the value she gave it.

Steps were heard above. The lady paused. Magnhild blushed. Then the lady smiled, and Magnhild hastened to remark: "That is a lodger—who"—

"Yes, I know; he met me last evening at the wharf."

Magnhild opened her eyes very wide. The lady drew nearer.

"My husband and he are very good friends," said she.

She turned away humming, and cast a glance at the clock in the corner between the bed-room wall and the window.

"Why, is it so late by your time here?" She drew out her own watch. "We are to walk to-day at eleven o'clock. You must go with us; will you not? You can show us the prettiest places in the wood behind the church and up the mountain slopes."

Magnhild promptly answered, "Yes."

"Listen: do you know what? I will run up-stairs and say that you are going with us, and then we will go at once—at once!"

She gave Magnhild's hand a gentle pressure, opened the door and sped swiftly up the stairs. Magnhild remained behind—and she was very pale.

There was a whirling, a raging within, a fall. But there was no explosion. On the contrary, everything became so empty, so still. A few creaking steps above, then not another sound.

Magnhild must have stood motionless for a long time. She heard some one take hold of the door-knob at last, and involuntarily she pressed both hands to her heart. Then she felt an impulse to fly; but the little fair curly head of the child, with its innocent, earnest eyes, now appeared in the opening of the door.

"Is mamma here?" the little one asked, cautiously.

"She is up-stairs," replied Magnhild, and the sound of her own voice, the very purport of the words she uttered, caused the tears to rise in her eyes and compelled her to turn her face away.

The child had drawn back its head and closed the door. Magnhild had no time to become clear in her own mind about what had occurred; for the child speedily came down-stairs again and into her room.

"Mamma is coming; she said I must wait here. Why are you crying?" But Magnhild was not crying now. She made no reply, however, to the child, who presently exclaimed: "Now mamma is coming."

Magnhild heard the lady's step on the stair, and escaped into her bedroom. She heard the interchange of words between mother and child in the adjoining room, and then to her consternation the bedroom door was opened; the lady came in. There was not the slightest trace of guilt in her eyes: they diffused happiness, warmth, candor through the whole chamber. But when her gaze met Magnhild's the expression changed, causing Magnhild to drop her eyes in confusion.

The lady advanced farther into the room. She placed one hand on Magnhild's waist, the other on her shoulder. Magnhild was forced to raise her eyes once more and met a grieved smile. This smile was also so kind, so firm, and therefore so persuasive, that Magnhild permitted herself to be drawn forward, and presently she was kissed—softly at first, as though she were merely fanned by a gentle breath, while that unknown perfume which always accompanied the lady encompassed them both, and the rustle of the silk dress was like a low whisper; then vehemently, while the lady's bosom heaved and her breath was deeply drawn as from some life-sorrow.

After this, utter silence and then a whispered: "Come now!" She went on in advance, leading Magnhild by the hand. Magnhild was a mere child in experience. With contending emotions she entered the pretty little cottage occupied by the lady, and was soon standing in the midst of open trunks and a wardrobe scattered through two rooms.

The lady began a search in one of the trunks, from which she rose with a white lace neckerchief in her hand, saying: "This will suit you better than the one you have on, for that is not at all becoming," and taking off the one Magnhild wore, she tied on the other in a graceful bow, and Magnhild felt herself that it harmonized well with her red dress.

"But how have you your hair? You have an oval face and your hair done up in that way? No"—and before Magnhild could offer any resistance she was pressed down into a chair. "Now I shall"—and the lady commenced undoing the hair. Magnhild started up, fiery red and frightened, and said something which was met with a firm: "Certainly not!"

It seemed as though a strong will emanated from the lady's words, arms, fingers. Magnhild's hair was unfastened, spread out, brushed, then drawn loosely over the head and done up in a low knot.

"Now see!" and the mirror was held up before Magnhild.

All this increased the young woman's embarrassment to such a degree that she scarcely realized whose was the image in the glass. The elegant lady standing in front of her, the delicate perfume, the child at her knee who with its earnest eyes fixed on her said, "Now you are pretty!"—and the guest at the opposite window who at this moment looked down and smiled. Magnhild started up, and was about to make her escape, but the lady only threw her arms around her and drew her farther into the room.

"Pray, do not be so bashful! We are going to have such a nice time together;" and once more her attention was full of that sweetness the like of which Magnhild had never known. "Run over now after your hat and we will start!"

Magnhild did as she was bid. But no sooner was she alone than a sense of oppression, a troubled anxiety, wrung her heart, and the lady seemed detestable, officious; even her kindness was distorted into a lack of moderation; Magnhild failed to find the exact word to express what distressed her.

"Well? Are you not coming?"

These words were uttered by the lady, who in a jaunty hat, with waving plume, beamed in through the window. She tossed back her curls, and drew on her gloves. "That hat becomes you very well indeed," said she. "Come now!"

And Magnhild obeyed.

The little girl attached herself to Magnhild.

"I am going with you," said she.

Magnhild failed to notice this, because she had just heard steps on the stairs. Tande, the composer, was coming to join them.

"How your hand trembles!" cried the little one.

A hasty glance from the lady sent the hot blood coursing up to Magnhild's neck, cheeks, temples—yet another from Tande, who stood on the door-steps, not wholly free from embarrassment, and who now bowed.

"Are we going up in the wood?" asked the little girl, clinging tightly to Magnhild's hand.

"Yes," replied the lady; "is there not a path across the fields behind the house?"

"Yes, there is."

"Then let us go that way."

They went into the house again, and passed out of the back door, through the garden, across the fields. The wood lay to the left of the church, and entirely covered the plain and the tower mountain slopes. Magnhild and the child walked on in advance; the lady and Tande followed.

"What is your name?" asked the little girl.

"Magnhild."

"How funny, for my name is Magda, and that is almost the same." Presently she said: "Have you ever seen papa in uniform?"

No, Magnhild never had.

"He is coming here soon, papa is, and I will ask him to put it on."

The little girl continued to prattle about her papa, whom she evidently loved beyond all else upon earth. Sometimes Magnhild heard what she was saying, sometimes she did not hear. The pair walking behind spoke so low that Magnhild could not distinguish a single word they were saying although they were quite near. Once she gave a hasty glance back and observed that the lady's expression was troubled, Tande's grave.

They reached the wood.

"Just see! here at the very edge of the wood is the most charming spot in the world!" exclaimed the lady, and now she was radiant again, as though she had never known other than the most jubilant mood. "Let us sit down here!" and as she spoke she threw herself down with a little burst of delight and a laugh. Tande seated himself slowly and at a little distance, Magnhild and the child took their seats opposite the pair.

The little one sprang directly to her feet again, for her mother wanted flowers, grass, ferns, and moss, and began to bind them at once into nosegays when they were brought to her. It was evidently not the first time Magda had made collections of the kind for her mother, for the child knew every plant by name, and came running up to the group with exclamations of delight whenever she found anything her mother had not yet noticed but which she knew to be a favorite of hers.

Various topics were brought forward, some of which, although not all, were dwelt upon by Tande, who had stretched himself out on the grass and seemed inclined to rest; but from the moment an affair of recent occurrence was mentioned, concerning a wife who had forsaken her husband, and had eventually been cast off by her lover, he took zealous part, severely censuring the lover, for whom Fru Bang made many excuses. It was absurd, she said, to feign an affection which no longer existed. But at least it was possible to act from a sense of duty, Tande insisted. Ah, to duty they had bid farewell, the lady remarked softly, as she busied herself in decking Magda's hat with flowers.

Further conversation incidentally revealed that Fru Bang had been in the habit of mingling in the first circles of the land; that she had traveled extensively, and evidently had means to live where and how she pleased. And yet here she sat, full of thoughtful care for Magnhild, for Tande, for the child. She had a kindly word for everything that was mentioned; her fancy invested the most trifling remark with worth, just as she made the blades of grass she was putting into her nosegay appear to advantage, and managed so that not one of them was lost.

Tande's long pale face, with its marvelously beautiful smile, and the soft hair falling caressingly, as it were, about it, had gradually become animated.

The glowing, richly-tinted woman at his side was part of the world in which he lived and composed.

The spot on which they sat was surrounded by birch and aspen. The fir was not yet able to gain the mastery over these, although its scions had already put in an appearance. While such were the case grass and flowers would flourish—but no longer.

CHAPTER VI.

MAGNHILD awoke the next day, not to joyous memories such as she had cherished every morning during the past few weeks. There was something to which she must now rise that terrified her, and, moreover, grieved her. Nevertheless it attracted her. What should she pass through this day?

She had slept late. As she stepped into the sitting-room, she saw Fru Bang at the open window opposite, and was at once greeted with a bow and a wave of the hand. Then a hat was held up and turned round. Very soon Magnhild was so completely under the spell of the lady's kind-hearted cordiality, beauty, and vivacity that her school hour was nearly forgotten.

She was met by a universal outcry when she appeared at the school with her hair done up in a new style, and wearing a new hat and a white lace neckerchief over her red dress! Magnhild had already felt embarrassed at the change, and now her embarrassment increased. But the genuine, hearty applause that arose from many voices speedily set her at her ease, and she returned home in a frame of mind similar to that of a public officer whose rank had been raised one degree.

The weather was fine as on the preceding day. A little excursion was therefore decided on for the afternoon. In the forenoon Tande played. All the windows in the neighborhood were open, and Fru Bang sat in hers and wept. Passers-by stared at her; but she heeded them not. There was something passionately intense and at times full of anguish in his playing to-day. Magnhild had never before heard him give vent to such a mood. Perhaps he, too, felt it to be a strange bewilderment; for rousing himself he now conjured up a wealth of bright, glittering bits of imagery which blended into the sunshine without and the buzzing of the insects. This dewy summer day became all at once teeming with discoveries; in the street, now parched and dry, the particles of dust glittered, over the meadows quivered the varied tints of green where the aftermath had sprung up, and of yellow and brown where it had not yet made its appearance. There was everywhere an intermingling of gold, red, brown, and green in the play of the forest hues. The loftiest pinnacle of the mighty mountain chair had never been more completely bathed in blue. It stood out in bold relief against the glowing grayish tone in the jagged cliffs about the fjord. The music grew more calm; pain was uppermost again, but it was like an echo, or rather it seemed as though it were dissolved into drops which ever and anon trickled down into the sunny vigor of the new mood. The lady opposite bowed forward until her head rested on her arm, and her shoulders quivered convulsively. Magnhild beheld this, and drew back. She did not like such an exposure.

On the excursion that afternoon it again fell to Magnhild's lot to take the lead with the child; the other two came whispering after them. They found to-day a new tarrying-place, a short distance farther up the mountain than where they had assembled the previous day;—the lady had been weeping; Tande was silent, but he appeared even more spiritual than usual.

The conversation this time centred in the fjord scenery of Norway, and the depressing influence it must necessarily have on the mind to be so completely shut in by mountains. The various barriers in the spiritual life of the people were named; old prejudices, established customs, above all those regulations of the church which had became mere empty forms, hypocrisy, too, were all reviewed in the most amusing manner; the infinite claims of love, however, were freely conceded.

"See, there she is sitting with her forefinger in her mouth again," laughed the lady; this greatly startled Magnhild, and created a fresh flow of merriment.

A little while after this Magnhild permitted her hair to be decked by Magda with flowers and grass. She hummed softly to herself all the while, a habit she had acquired during the days when she was practicing reading notes at the parsonage. This time her irregular song took higher flights than usual, inasmuch as thoughts filled it, just as the wind inflates a sail. The higher she sang, the stronger her voice became, until Magda exclaimed:—

"There comes mamma."

Magnhild was silent at once. True enough there came the lady, and directly following her Tande.

"Why, my child, do you sing?"

In the course of the day they had fallen into the habit of using the familiar "du;" that is, Fru Bang used it, but Magnhild could not do so.

"That is the highest, clearest soprano I have heard for some time," said Tande, who now drew near, and who was flushed from having taken a few steps at a more rapid pace than usual.

Magnhild sprang to her feet, so hastily that there fell a shower of flowers and grass to the ground, at the same time putting up her hands to remove Magda's adornments from her hair, which called forth a bitter complaint from the little girl. Tande's words, appearance, and the look he now fastened on her had embarrassed Magnhild, and Fru Bang displayed most kindly tact in endeavoring, as it were, to shield her young friend.

It was not long before they were on their way home,—and they went at once to Tande's room to try Magnhild's voice.

Fru Bang stood holding her hand. Magnhild sang the scale, and every note was so firm and true that Tande paused and looked up at her. She was then obliged to admit that she had sung before.

A feeling of happiness gradually took possession of her; for she was appreciated, there could be no mistake about it. And when a little two-part song was brought forward and Magnhild proved able to sing the soprano at sight, and then a second one was tried and a third, such joy reigned in the little circle that Magnhild gained inspiration, which gave her a beauty she had never possessed at any previous moment of her life.

Fru Bang had a fine alto; her voice was not so cultivated as it was sympathetic; nor was it strong, but for this reason it was all the better suited to Magnhild's voice, for although the latter doubtless was stronger, Magnhild had never been accustomed to letting out its full strength, nor did she do so now.

As they gradually became more acquainted with the songs, Tande kept adding to the richness and fullness of the piano—the accompaniments.

The street had become crowded with people; such music had never been heard before in the little town. It was evident that a swarm of new ideas were let loose upon those heads. The thoughts and words of the ensuing evening were no doubt more refined than usual. Upon the children there surely dawned a foreboding of foreign lands. A drizzling rain was falling, the crests of the lofty mountains on both sides of the valley and surrounding the fjord were veiled, but towered up all the higher in fancy. The glorious forest hues, the placid surface of the fjord, now darkened by the rain, the fresh aftermath of the meadows, and not a disturbing sound save from the turbulent stream. Even if a wagon came along, it paused in front of the house.

The silence of the multitude without harmonized with the mood of those within.

When the singing at length ended, Tande said that he must devote an hour each day to instructing Magnhild how to use her voice, so that she could make further progress alone when he and Fru Bang were gone. Moreover, they must continue the duet singing, for this was improving to the taste. Fru Bang added that something might be made of that voice.

Tande's eyes followed Magnhild so searchingly that she was glad when it was time to take leave.

She forgot some music she had brought with her, and turning went back after it. Tande was standing by the door. "Thanks for your visit!" he whispered, and smiled. This made her stumble on the threshold, and overwhelmed with confusion, she came near making a misstep at the head of the stairs. She entered her sitting-room in great embarrassment. Fru Bang, who was still there waiting to say "Good-night!" looked at her earnestly. It was some time before she spoke, and then the greeting was cold and absent-minded. She turned, however, before she had proceeded many steps, and descrying Magnhild's look of surprise, sprang back and clasped her in a fervent embrace.

At no very remote period there had been an evening which Magnhild had thought the happiest of her life. But this—

When steps were again heard above she trembled in every fibre of her body. She could see Tande's expression, as he raised his eyes while playing. The diamond, cutting brilliant circles of light over the keys of the piano, the blue-veined hands, the long hair which was continually falling forward, the fine gray suit the musician wore, his silent demeanor,—all dissolved into the melodies and harmonies, and with them became blended his whispered "Thanks for your visit!"

At the cottage across the street it was dark.

Magnhild did not seek her couch until midnight, and then not to sleep; nor did he who was above sleep; on the contrary, just as Magnhild had retired he began to play. He struck up a melancholy, simple melody, in the form of a soprano solo at first, and finally bursting into what sounded like a chorus of female voices; his harmonization was exquisitely pure. Without being conscious herself of the transition of thought, Magnhild seemed to be sitting on the hill-side on the day of her confirmation, gazing at the spot where her home had stood. All her little brothers and sisters were about her. The theme was treated in a variety of ways, but always produced the same picture.

At school the next morning Magnhild was accosted with many questions concerning the preceding evening; among other things whether *she* had really taken part in the singing, *what* they had sung, about the other two, and whether they would sing often.

The questions filled her with joy: a great secret, *her* secret, was in its innermost depths. She felt conscious of strange elasticity. She had never made such haste home before. She was looking forward to singing with him again in the forenoon!

And she did sing. Tande sent word down by the sailor's wife that he expected her at twelve o'clock. A little before this hour she heard once more that melancholy, pure composition of yesterday.

Tande met her without a word. He merely bowed and went straight to the piano and then turned his head as before to bid her draw nearer. She sang scales, he gave suggestions as a rule without looking at her; the whole hour passed as a calm matter of business; she was thankful for this.

From her lesson she crossed the street to the lady. Fru Bang sat, or rather reclined, on the sofa, with an open book on her lap, and with Magda, to whom she was talking, in front of her. She was grave, or rather sorrowful; she looked up at Magnhild, but went on talking with the child, as though no one had entered. Magnhild remained standing, considerably disappointed. Then the lady pushed aside the child and looked up again.

"Come nearer!" said she, feebly, and made a motion with the hand that Magnhild did not understand.

"Sit down there on the footstool, I mean."

Magnhild obeyed.

"You have been with him?" Her fingers loosened Magnhild's hair as she spoke. "The knot is not quite right,"—then with a little caress, "You are a sweet child!"

She sat up now, looked Magnhild full in the eyes, gently raising her friend's head as she did so.

"I have resolved to make you pretty, prettier than myself. Do you see what I have bought for you to-day?"

On the table behind Magnhild lay the materials for a summer costume.

"This is for you, it will be becoming."

"But, dear lady!"

"Hush! Not a word, my friend! I am not happy unless I can do something of the kind—and, in this case, I have my own reasons into the bargain."

Her large, wondrous eyes seemed to float away in dreams.

"There, that will do!" said she, and rose hastily.

"Now we will dine together; but first we must have a short stroll, and in the afternoon a long stroll, and then we will have some singing and afterwards a delightful siesta; that is what he likes!"

But neither short nor long stroll was accomplished, for it rained. So the lady busied herself with cutting out Magnhild's dress; it was to be made in the neighborhood after Fru Bang's own pattern.

They sang together, and even longer than on the preceding day. A supply of songs for two voices was telegraphed for; a few days later the package arrived. During the days which followed most of the songs were gone through with the utmost accuracy. Every day Magnhild had her regular lesson. Tande entered into it with the same business-like silence as on the first day. Magnhild gained courage.

Wonderful days these were! Song followed upon song, and these three were continually together, chiefly at the lady's, where they most frequently both dined and supped. One day Fru Bang would be in the most radiant mood, the next tormented with headache, and then she would have a black, red, and brown kerchief tied like a turban, about her head, and would sit or recline on the sofa, in languid revery.

As they were thus assembled together one day, and Magda stood at the window, the little one said,—

"There goes a man into your house, Magnhild: he is lame."

Magnhild sprang up, very red.

"What is it?" asked Fru Bang, who was lying on the sofa with a headache, and had been talking in a whisper with Tande.

"Oh! it is"—Magnhild was searching for her hat; she found it and withdrew. From the open window she heard the child say: "A lame, ugly man, who"—

Skarlie was working this year on the sea-coast. A foreign ship had been wrecked there Skarlie and some men in Bergen had bought it; for they could repair it at a much less outlay than had originally been estimated. They had made an uncommonly good bargain. Skarlie supervised the carpentering, painting, and leather work of refitting the vessel. He had come home now after a fresh supply of provisions for the workmen.

His surprise on entering his house was not small. Everything in order! And the room filled with a pleasant perfume. Magnhild came—it was a lady who stood before him. Her whole countenance was changed. It had opened out like a flower, and the soft, fair hair floating about neck and drooping shoulders threw a lustre over head and form. She paused on the threshold, her hand on the door-knob. Skarlie had seated himself in the broad chair in the corner, and was wiping the perspiration from his bald head. As soon as his first astonishment was over, he said: "Good-day!"

No reply. But Magnhild came in now, and closed the door after her.

"How fine it looks here," said he. "Is it your lodger"—

He puckered up his lips, his eyes grew small. Magnhild looked at him coldly. He continued more good-naturedly,—

"Did he make your new dress, too?"

Now she laughed.

"How are you getting on?" she asked, presently.

"I am nearly through."

He had acquired the comfortable air of a man who is conscious of doing well in the world.

"It is warm here," said he; the sun had just burst forth after a long rain, and was scorching, as it can be only in September. He stretched out his legs, as far as the crooked one permitted, and lay back, letting his large hands hang down over the arms of the chair, exact pictures of the web-feet of some sea-monster.

"Why are you staring at me?" asked he, with his most comical grimace. Magnhild turned with a searching glance toward the window.

The room had become filled at once with the peculiar saddler odor which attended Skarlie: Magnhild was about to open the window, but thinking better of it stepped back again.

"Where is your lodger?"

"He is across the street."

"Are there lodgers there, too?"

"Yes, a Fru Bang with her daughter."

"So they are the people you associate with?"

"Yes!"

He rose, took off his coat, and also laid aside his vest and cravat. Then he filled his cutty with tobacco, lighted it, and sat down again, this time with an elbow resting on one arm of the chair and smoking. With a roguish smile he contemplated his other half.

"And so you are going to be a lady, Magnhild?"

She did not answer.

"Aye!—Well, I suppose I shall have to begin to make a gentleman of myself."

She turned toward him with an amused countenance. His chest, thickly covered with dark red hair, was bare, for his shirt was open; his face was sunburned, his bald head white.

"The deuce! how you stare at me! I am not nearly as good-looking as your lodger, I can well believe. Hey?"

"Will you have something to eat?" asked she.

"I dined on the steamer."

"But to drink?"

She went out after a bottle of beer, and placed it with a glass on the table beside him. He poured out the beer and drank, looking across the street as he did so.

"That's a deuce of a woman! Is *that* the lady?"

Magnhild grew fiery red; for she too saw Fru Bang standing at the window, staring at the half-disrobed Skarlie.

She fled into her chamber, thence into the garden, and there seated herself.

She had only been there a few minutes when she heard first the chamber, then the kitchen door open, and finally the garden door was opened by her husband.

"Magnhild!" he called. "Yes, there she is."

Little Magda's light curly head was now thrust out, and turned round on every side until Magnhild was seen, and then the child came slowly toward her. Skarlie had gone back into the house.

"I was sent to ask if you were not coming over to take dinner with us."

"Give greetings and thanks; I cannot come—now."

The child bestowed on her a mute look of inquiry, then asked: "Why can you not? Is it because that man has come?"

"Yes."

"Who is he?"

It was in Magnhild's mind to say, "He is my ——"; but it would not cross her lips; and so without speaking she turned to conceal her emotion from the child. The little one stood silently waiting for some time; finally she asked,—

"Why are you crying, Magnhild?"

This was said so sweetly: it chimed in with the memory of the whole bright world which was once more closed, that Magnhild clasped its little representative in her arms, and bowing over the curly head burst into tears. Finally, she whispered,—

"Do not question me any more, little Magda; but go home now, this way, through the garden gate, and tell mamma that I cannot come any more."

Magda obeyed, but she looked over her shoulder several times as she walked away.

Magnhild removed all traces of tears, and went out to make some purchases; for her larder was nearly empty.

When she returned home, and passed through the sitting-room, Skarlie was still in his chair; he had been taking a little nap; now he yawned and began to fill his cutty.

"Did you tell me the lady across the street was married?"

"Yes."

"Is *he* married, too?"

"I do not know."

"I saw them kissing each other," said he.

Magnhild grew very pale and then red.

"I have never seen anything of the kind."

"No, of course not; they did not suppose that I saw them either," said he, and began to light his cutty.

Magnhild could have struck him. She went directly to the kitchen, but could not avoid coming back again. Skarlie greeted her with,—

"It is no wonder they make much of you, for you serve as a screen."

She had brought in a cloth to spread the table, and she flung it right at his laughing face. He caught it, however, and laughed all the louder, until the tears started in his eyes; he could not restrain his laughter.

Magnhild had run back into the kitchen, and she stood in front of the butter, cheese, and milk she had ready to carry into the adjoining room,—stood there and wept.

The door opened, and Skarlie came limping in.

"I have spread the cloth," said he, not yet free from laughter, "for that, I presume, was what you wanted: eh?" and now he took up one by one the articles that stood before Magnhild, and carried them into the next room. He asked good-naturedly after something that was wanting, and actually received an answer. After a while Magnhild had so far recovered her composure as to set the kettle on the fire for tea.

Half an hour later the two sat opposite each other at their early evening meal. Not a word more about those across the street. Skarlie commenced telling of his work on the steamer, but broke off abruptly, for Tande began to play. Skarlie had taste for music. It was a restless, almost defiant strain that was heard; but how it brightened the atmosphere. And it ended with the little melody that always transported Magnhild to the home of her parents, with the fair heads of her little brothers and sisters round about. Skarlie evidently listened with pleasure, and when the playing ceased, he praised it in extravagant terms. Then Magnhild told him that she was singing with Tande; that he thought she had a good voice. She did not get beyond this; for the playing began anew. When it had ceased again, Skarlie said,—

"See here, Magnhild! Let that man give you all the instruction he will; for he is a master—and with the rest you need not meddle."

Skarlie was still in extraordinarily high spirits when, weary from his journey, he went up to the room over the saddler workshop to go to bed. He filled his pipe, and took an English book and a light up-stairs with him.

Magnhild thoroughly aired the room after him, opening all the windows as soon as he was gone. She paced the room in the dark for a long while ere she laid herself down to sleep.

The next morning she stole out of the back door to school, and returned the same way.

She found the whole school in a state of rejoicing over the news Skarlie had just brought, that a quantity of handwork for which he had undertaken to find purchasers in town had been sold to unusually great advantage. He had doubtless told her this in the course of the morning, but she had been so absorbed in her own affairs that it had made no impression on her. Scarcely was this theme exhausted when one of the young girls (there were both children and grown people in attendance at this hour) expressed her surprise at Magnhild's appearance, which was so different from that of the preceding days. The pupils inquired if anything was amiss. Magnhild did not wear the dress, either, that was so becoming to her, that is, the one given to her by the lady. It was hunch-back Marie, and tall, large-eyed Ellen who were the loudest of all in both delight and astonishment. Magnhild felt ill at ease among them, and took her departure as early as possible. As soon as she had reached home it was announced to her by the sailor's wife that Tande was expecting her. A brief struggle ensued; and then she put on the dress which became her best. She was received as she had been received yesterday, the day before, and every other day: he greeted her with a slight bow, took his seat at the piano and struck a few chords. She was so thankful for his reserve, and especially to-day, that she—her desire to show her appreciation failed to find utterance.

As she came down-stairs she saw Skarlie and Fru Bang standing by the lady's door, in close conversation; they were both laughing. Magnhild stole in unperceived and continued to watch them.

There was a changeful play of expression in the countenances of both, and herein they were alike; but here, too, the resemblance ceased, for Skarlie had never looked so ugly as he did now in the presence of this beautiful woman. Moreover, the smooth, glossy hat he wore completely covered his forehead, giving his face a contracted look; for the forehead alone was almost as large as all the rest of the face. Magnhild was conscious of him at this moment to the extreme tips of her fingers.

The lady was all vivacity; it flashed from her as she tossed back her head and set all her ringlets in fluttering motion, or shifted her foot, accompanying the act with a swaying movement of the upper part of the body, or with a wave of her hand aided in the utterance of some thought, or indicated another with an eager gesture.

The hasty, assured glances the two exchanged gave the impression of combat. It seemed as though they would never get through. Were they interested in each other? Or in the mere act of disputing? Or in the subject they were discussing? Had not Tande come down-stairs, their interview would scarcely have drawn to a conclusion that forenoon. But as he approached with a bow Skarlie limped away, still laughing, and the other two went into the lady's house, she continuing to laugh heartily.

"A deuce of a woman!" said Skarlie, all excitement. "Upon my word she could very easily turn a man's head."

And while he was scraping the ashes from his cutty, he added: "If she were not so kind-hearted she would be positively diabolical. She sees everything!"

Magnhild stood waiting for more.

He glanced at her twice, while he was filling his cutty from his leathern pouch; he looked pretty much as one who thought: "Shall I say it or not?" She knew the look and moved away. But perhaps this very action of hers gave the victory to his taunting impulse.

"She saw that there was light last night up over my workshop. I really thought she was going to ask whether"—

Magnhild was already in the kitchen.

At noon a wagon drove up to the door; Skarlie was obliged to go out into the country to buy meat for his workmen down on the sea-coast.

As soon as he was gone, the lady came running across the street. It was now as it ever had been. Scarcely did she stand in the room, shedding around her sweet smile, than every bad thought concerning her crept away abashed, and with inward craving for pardon, Magnhild yielded to the cordial friendliness with which the lady threw her arms about her, and kissed her and drew her head down caressingly on her shoulder. This time there was not a word spoken, but Magnhild felt the same sympathy in every caress that had accompanied every previous embrace and kiss. When the lady released her, they moved away in different directions. Magnhild busied herself in breaking off a few withered twigs from one of the plants in the window.

Suddenly her cheek and neck were fanned by the lady's warm breath. "My friend," was softly whispered into her ear, "my sweet, pure little friend! You are leading a wild beast with your child hands."

The words, the warm breath which, as it were, infused magic into them, sent a tremor through Magnhild's frame. The tears rolled down her cheeks and fell on her hand. The lady saw this and whispered: "Do not fear. You have in your singing an enchanted ring which you only need turn when you wish yourself away! Do not cry!" And turning Magnhild round, she folded her in her arms again.

"This afternoon the weather is fine; this afternoon we will all be together in the wood and in the house, and we will sing and laugh. Ah! there are not many more days left to us!"

These last words stabbed Magnhild to the heart. Autumn was nigh at hand, and soon she would be alone again.

CHAPTER VII.

THEY were up-stairs in the afternoon, standing by the piano singing, when they heard Skarlie come home and go into the sitting-room below. Without making any remarks about this, they went on singing. They sang at last by candle-light, with the windows still open.

When Magnhild came down-stairs Skarlie too had his windows open; he was sitting in the arm-chair in the corner. He rose now and closed the windows; Magnhild drew down the curtains, and in the mean time Skarlie struck a light. While they were still in the dark, he began to express his admiration of the singing to which he had been listening. He praised Magnhild's voice as well as the lady's alto, and of his wife's soprano he repeated his praise. "It is as pure—as you are yourself, my child," said he. He was holding a match to the candle as he spoke, and he appeared almost good-looking, so calm and serious was his shrewd countenance. But ere long there came the play of other thoughts. This indicated a change of mood.

"While you were singing her husband, the captain of engineers, arrived." Magnhild thought he was jesting, but Skarlie added: "He sat in the window opposite listening." Here he laughed.

This so alarmed Magnhild that she was unable to sleep until late that night. For the first time it occurred to her that Fru Bang's husband might be repulsive to her, and she considered the lady's conduct from this point of view. What if those two people really loved each other? Suppose it were her own case? She found herself blushing furiously; for at once Tande's image rose distinctly before her.

When she awoke the next morning she involuntarily listened. Had the tempest already broken loose? Hurriedly putting on her clothes she went into the sitting-room, where Skarlie was preparing to start off again. A portion of the articles he was to have taken with him had not yet arrived; he was obliged to go with what he had and come again in a few days. He took a friendly leave of Magnhild.

She accompanied him as far as the school.

Scarcely had she returned home than she saw a man with red beard and light hair come out of the house opposite, holding little Magda by the hand. This must be Magda's papa. The little girl had his light hair and something of his expression of countenance; but neither his features, nor his form; he was of a heavy build. They crossed the street, entered the house, and went up-stairs. Surely there could be no quarrel when the child was along? Magnhild heard Tande go dress himself, and she heard an audible, "Good-day! Are you here?" in Tande's voice.

Then nothing more, for now the door was softly closed. So filled with anxiety was she that she listened for the least unusual sound overhead; but she heard only the steps now of one, now of both. Soon the door opened, she heard voices, but no contention. All three came down-stairs and went out into the street where the lady stood waiting for them, in her most brilliant toilet, and with the smile of her holiday mood. Tande greeted her, she cordially held out her hand. Then the whole four walked past the house-door, and turned into the garden way to take the usual path across the fields to the wood and the mountains. At first, they sauntered slowly along in a group; later, the father went on in advance with the child, who seemed desirous to lead the way, and the lady and Tande followed, very slowly, very confidentially. Magnhild was left behind alone, overwhelmed with astonishment.

In the afternoon Magda came over with her papa. He greeted Magnhild with a smile and apologized for coming; his little daughter had insisted on his paying his compliments to her friend, he said.

Magnhild asked him to take a seat, but he did not do so at once. He looked at her flowers, talked about them with an air of understanding such as she had never heard before, and begged to be allowed to send her some new plants upon whose proper care he enlarged.

"It is really little Magda who will send them," said he, turning with a smile toward Magnhild. This time she was conscious that he was shyly observing her.

He looked at the pictures on the wall, the bridge at Cologne, the Falls of Niagara, the White House at Washington, the Caravan in the Desert, and "Judith," by Horace Vernet; examined also some photographs of unknown, often uncouth-looking men and women, some of them in foreign costumes.

"Your husband has been a traveler," said he, and his eyes glided from the portraits back to "Judith," while he stood stroking his beard.

"Have you been long married?" he presently asked, taking a seat.

"Nearly three years," she replied, and colored.

"You must put on your uniform so that Magnhild can see you in it," said the little girl; she had posted herself between her father's knees, now toying with his shirt studs, now with his beard. He smiled; certain wrinkles about the eyes and mouth became more apparent when he smiled, and bore witness of sorrow. Musingly he stroked the little one's hair; she nestled her head up against him, so lovingly, so trustingly.

He awoke at last from his revery, cast a shy, wondering look at Magnhild, stroked his beard, and said,—

"It is very beautiful here."

"When will you send Magnhild the flowers you spoke of?" interrupted the little girl.

"As soon as I get back to town," said he, caressing the child.

"Papa is building a fort," explained Magda, not without pride. "Papa is building at home, too," she added. "Papa is all the time building, and now we have a tower to our house, and all the rooms are so pretty. You just ought to see."

And she fell to describing her home to Magnhild, which, however, she had often done before. The father listened with that peculiar smile of his that was not altogether a smile, and as though to turn the conversation he hastily observed: "We took a short stroll up the mountains this morning (here the little girl explained where they had been) and then"—There was undoubtedly something he wanted to say; but a second thought must have flashed across the first.

He became absorbed again in thought. Just then Tande began to play overhead. This brought life to the countenance of Magda's father, a wondering, shy look stole over it, and bowing his head he began to stroke his little daughter's hair.

"He plays extraordinarily well," he remarked, and rose to his feet.

The next day the captain left. He might perhaps return later to meet the general of engineers, with whom he had to make a tour of inspection. The life of those left behind glided now into its accustomed channels.

One evening Magnhild appeared at Fru Bang's with a very carelessly arranged toilet.

As soon as the lady noticed this she gave Magnhild a hint, and herself covered her retreat. Magnhild was so much mortified that she could scarcely be prevailed upon to enter the sitting-room again; but amid the laughing words of consolation heaped upon her she forgot everything but the never-wavering goodness and loving forethought of her friend. It was so unusual for Magnhild to express herself as freely as she did now, that the lady threw her arms about her and whispered,—

"Yes, my child, you may well say that I am good to you, for you are killing me!"

Magnhild quickly tore herself away. She sought no explanation with words, she was by far too much startled; but her eyes, the expression of her face, her attitude, spoke for her. The door was opened, and Magnhild fell from surprise to painful embarrassment. Tande had, meanwhile, turned toward Magda, humming softly, as though he observed nothing; he amused himself by playing with the little one. Later he talked with Magnhild about her singing, which he told her she must by no means drop again. If arrangements could be made for her to live in the city,—and that could so easily be brought about,—he would not only help her himself, but procure for her better aid than his.

Fru Bang was coming and going, giving directions about the evening meal. The maid entered with a tray, on which were the cream and other articles, and by some untoward chance Fru Bang ran against it directly in front of Magnhild and Tande, and her efforts to prevent the things from falling proved fruitless, because the others did not come speedily enough to her aid. Everything was overthrown. The dresses of both ladies were completely bespattered. Tande at once drew out his pocket handkerchief and began to wipe Magnhild's.

"You are less attentive to me than to her," laughed the lady, who was much more soiled than Magnhild.

He looked up.

"Yes, I know you better than her," he answered, and went on wiping.

Fru Bang grew ashen gray. "Hans!" she exclaimed, and burst into tears. Then she hastened into the next room. Magnhild understood this as little as what had previously occurred. Indeed, it was not until months had elapsed that one day, as she was wandering alone through the wintry slush of a country road, with her thoughts a thousand miles away from the lady and the whole scene, she suddenly stood still: the full meaning of Fru Bang's behavior rushed over her.

Tande had risen to his feet, for Magnhild had drawn back in order not to accept any further assistance from him. That *she* could act so, and that *his* name was "Hans," was all that was clear to her at this moment. Tande slowly paced the floor. He was very pale; at least so it seemed to Magnhild, although she could not see very well, for it was beginning to grow dark. Should she follow the lady, or withdraw altogether? Magda was in the kitchen; she finally concluded to go to her. And out there she helped the little girl fill a dish with preserves. From the chamber which adjoined the kitchen she soon heard a low conversation and sobs. When Magda and she went into the sitting-room with the dish, Tande was not there. They waited so long for the evening meal that Magda fell asleep and Magnhild had to go home.

Not long afterward she heard Tande, too, come home. The next forenoon she sang with him; he appeared quite as usual. In the afternoon she met the lady by chance in the street, and she made sundry criticisms on Magnhild's improvising, which she had heard, a little while before, through the open window; at the same time she straightened Magnhild's hat, which was not put on exactly right.

Skarlie came home again. He told Magnhild that on a trip to Bergen he had traveled with Captain Bang.

There was a person on the steamer, he said, who knew about Fru Bang's relations with Tande and spoke of them. Magnhild had strong suspicions that Skarlie himself was that person; for after he had been home the last time she had heard allusions to these relations from Tande's woman-servant, the sailor's wife, and several others.

"The captain is good-natured," said Skarlie; "he considers himself unworthy to be loved by so much soul and brilliancy. He was, therefore, rejoiced that his wife had at last found an equal."

"You seem delighted," Magnhild replied, "you appear more disgusting than you"—She was just going to Fru Bang's, and withdrew without deigning to complete the sentence.

She was to accompany Magda to an exhibition to be given by an old Swedish juggler, with his wife and child, on the square some distance behind the house.

When Magnhild came in, the lady met her all dressed; she was going to the show, too. The explanation of this speedily followed; that is to say, Tande appeared to accompany them. He reported that the general had arrived.

Then they set off, Magda and Magnhild, the lady and Tande. A crowd of people had assembled, most of them outside of the inclosure, where they could pay what they pleased. Within the inclosure there were "reserved" places, that is, benches, and to these the lady and her party repaired.

The old juggler was already in his place, where, with the aid of his wife, he was preparing for the show. He bore a ludicrous resemblance to Skarlie, was bald, had a snub-nose, was large and strong-looking, and his face was not devoid of humor. Scarcely had Magnhild made this discovery than she heard Magda whisper to her mother,—

"Mamma, he looks just like Magnhild's husband."

The lady smiled. At the same moment the old juggler stepped up to them. Among the reserved places was one "especially reserved," a bench, that is, with a back to it. The old man was quite hoarse, and his language, so far as it could be comprehended, was such a droll mixture of Swedish and Norwegian, that those nearest laughed; and the clown-like courtesy of his manner also created a laugh, even among those at a distance. But so soon as the laugh began Tande stepped back a few paces. The lady went forward, and Magda and Magnhild followed.

The old juggler had a wife much younger than himself, a black-haired, hollow-eyed, sorrowfully thin person, who had the general appearance of having been unfortunate. There soon came skipping out of the tent a little lad with curly hair, sprightly eyes, and an air of refinement over face and form which he did not get from his mother, still less from the old clown. He was dressed as a jester, but was evidently anything else. He paused at his mother's side and asked her some question. He spoke in French. The lady, who was annoyed by Tande's foolish shyness, addressed the boy in his native tongue. The little fellow came forward, but merely to pause at a short distance and stand viewing her with an expression of dignified inquiry. This amused her, and taking out her purse she handed him quite a large coin.

"*Merci, Madame!*" said he, making a low bow.

"Kiss the lady's hand!" commanded the old man. The boy obeyed, with shy haste. Then he ran back to the tent, whence was heard the barking of dogs.

Suddenly there arose a commotion in the crowd behind those who were seated. A woman with a child three or four years old in her arms was trying to push her way forward. She could not stand and hold the child forever, she said; she wanted to sit down. She was quite as good as any one else present.

But there seemed to be no seat vacant except on the front bench. So to the front bench she went, to the great sport of the multitude; for she was well known. She was no other than "Machine Martha." Two years before she had come to the Point with a child and a large and a small sewing-machine, with which she supported herself, for she was capable. She had deserted her husband with an itinerant tradesman, who dealt, among other things, in sewing-machines. He had deceived her. Since then she had fallen into wretched habits of drunkenness, and had become thoroughly degraded. Her face was rough and her hair disheveled. Nevertheless, she still seemed to have sufficient energy left to raise a storm. She seated herself directly beside the lady, who shrank away, for Martha smelled strongly of beer.

The old juggler had noticed the involuntary movement the lady made. He was on hand at once, and, in a hoarse, rough voice, ordered Martha to take another place.

She must have been abashed herself by all the silk she had come into contact with, for she now got up and moved away.

As she was watching her Magnhild descried Skarlie. At his side Martha paused. Soon she came forward again. "I will sit there, I tell you," said she, and resuming her seat she placed the child on the bench beside her.

The old juggler left his preparations. He had grown angry. "You cursed"—here he must have remembered the fine company he was in, for he continued: "It costs money to sit here." He spoke Swedish.

"Here is a mark!" said the woman, holding out the coin as she spoke.

"Very well," said he, hoarsely; "but sit on another bench. Will the ladies and gentlemen please move closer together?" he begged of those on the nearest benches. Whether his directions were followed or not, Martha did not stir.

"The devil a bit will I move," said she.

"Let her stay where she is," whispered the lady.

"Not for any sum," replied the gallant old man. "These seats are reserved for the highest aristocracy," and he took hold of the child. But now Martha sprang up like one possessed.

"You Swedish troll!" cried she, "will you let my child alone?"

The crowd burst into stormy shouts of laughter, and encouraged thereby, she continued: "Highest aristocracy? Pshaw! She is a—she, as well as I." The word shall remain unwritten; but Martha looked significantly at the lady. A volley of laughter, and then, as at the word of command, the silence of the grave.

The lady had started up, proud and beautiful. She looked around for her escort. She wished to leave. Tande was standing not very far off, with a couple of travelers, who had begged to be presented to the well-known composer. The lady's flaming eyes met his. He gazed back at her intently. Every one was looking at him. But no one could penetrate his gaze, any farther than they could have penetrated a polished steel ball.

And yet, however unfathomable those eyes, there was one thing they said plainly enough: "Madame, I know you not!" And his refined, arched brow, his delicately-chiseled nose, his tightly-compressed lips, his hollow cheeks, aye, the glittering diamond studs in his shirt, the aristocratic elegance of his attire, all said, "Touch me not!" Over his eyes were drawn veil after veil.

It was all the work of a moment. The lady turned to Magnhild as though to call on her to bear witness. And yet no! There was no one in the world beside him and herself who could know how great was the offering that now was burnt, how great the love he now flung from him.

Again the lady turned toward him a look, as brief as a flash of lightning. What indignation, what a great cry of anguish, what a swarm of memories, what pride, what contempt, did she not hurl at him. Magnhild received the quivering remains as she turned to her to—aye, what should she do now? Her face suddenly betrayed the most piteous forlornness, and at the same time a touching appeal, as that of a child. The tears rolled down her cheeks. Magnhild, entering completely into her mood, impulsively held out her hand. The lady grasped it and pressed it so vehemently that Magnhild had to exercise all her self-control not to scream aloud. The poor, wounded, repulsed woman gathered together all her inward strength through this outward expenditure of force, and thus she became uplifted. For at the same time she smiled. And lo! across that part of the square where the tight rope was stretched and where spectators were forbidden to intrude, there strode at this moment two officers, seen by all; but how could admittance be refused to a general's cap? And such a one was worn by the all-powerful individual who, with long strides and wide-swinging arms, as though he were himself both commander and army, advanced with his adjutant on the left flank. Already from afar he saluted, in the most respectful manner, his captain's beautiful wife. She hastened to meet her deliverer. On the general's arm she was led back to her place, while he himself took a seat by her side. The adjutant fell to Magnhild's lot, after the lady had introduced them. The general stole many a glance at Magnhild, and the adjutant was all courtesy. This was almost the only thing Magnhild noticed. She was quivering in every nerve.

The lady sparkled with wit, sprightliness, beauty. But every now and then she would seize Magnhild's hand, and press it with remorseless energy. She strengthened herself in the reality of the moment. The bodily pain this caused Magnhild corresponded with the spiritual pain she experienced. She heard the adjutant at her side and Magda cry out in wonder. She, too, now saw several balls glittering in the air, and she saw a large one weighed by a spectator, and then cast into the air by the old athlete, as though it were a play ball, and caught again on his arm, shoulder, or breast; but at the same time she heard the lady tell the general that she would leave the next morning under his escort; she had been waiting for him since her husband could not come.

Magnhild well knew that all was now over: but would the end come as soon as the next morning? A loud outcry, coming chiefly from the voices of boys, cut through her pain. The old man had thrown the large ball into the air with both hands, and then quite a small ball, and continued to keep them in rapid motion for some time. To Magnhild the small ball represented herself; and the large one—? It was not in order to search for an adequate symbol, nor did she apply it, but everything became symbolic. The perpetual glitter of the balls in the air represented to her the icy glance which had just made her tremble.

"The old man is extraordinarily strong," said the adjutant. "I once saw a man in Venice with another man standing on his shoulders, who stooped and raised a third, and he worked his way up and stood on the second man's shoulders, and then, only think, they drew up a fourth, who managed to stand on the shoulders of the third. The first man walked about on the ground, carrying with him the other three, while the upper man played with balls."

"Were I to die at this moment," the lady was saying on the other side, "and the soul could forget everything here and have imparted to it a new series of wonderful problems, infinite vistas, so that enraptured discovery after discovery might be made—what could there be more glorious?"

"My imagination does not carry me so far," came in the general's firm voice. "I am ready to stake my life that to live and die in the fulfillment of one's duty is the greatest happiness a healthily organized human being can feel. The rest is, after all, of little consequence."

Here Magnhild received a feverish pressure of the hand.

"Applaud, ladies and gentlemen, applaud," said the clown, hoarsely and good-naturedly. This raised a laugh, but no one stirred.

"Why do not the dogs come out?" asked Magda, who heard the animals impatiently barking in the tent.

About the mountain peaks clouds crisped and curled; a gust of wind betokened a change in the weather; the fjord darkened under the influence of a swiftly rising squall. There was something infinitely sublime in the landscape; something awe-inspiring.

It began to grow cold. The people in the background felt hushed and gloomy. Now the clown's wife came forward; *she* was to go on the tight rope. The haggard, faded beauty wore a dress cut very low in the neck, and with short sleeves. The lady shivered as she looked at her, complained of cold feet, and rose. The general, the adjutant, and consequently Magnhild also, did the same; Magda alone, with looks of entreaty, kept her seat; she was waiting for the dogs. A single glance from her mother sufficed; she got up without a word.

They passed out the same way the officers had come in; not one of them looked back. The lady laughed her most ringing laugh; its pleasant tones rolled back over the assembled multitude. Every one gazed after her. The general walked rapidly, so that her light, easy movements appeared well at his side. The general's height invested hers with a peculiar charm; his stiff, martial bearing and figure heightened the effect of her pliant grace. The contrasts of color in her attire, the feather in her hat, an impression from her laughter, affected one man in the audience as he might have been affected by withdrawing music.

When the officers took their leave at the lady's door, she did not speak a word to Magnhild; she did not so much as glance at her as she went into the house. Magnhild felt her sympathy repulsed. Deeply grieved, she crossed the street to her own house.

Tande returned late. Magnhild heard him walking back and forth, back and forth, more rapidly than ever before. Those light steps kept repeating: "Touch me not!" at last in rhythm; the glitter of the diamond studs, the aristocratic elegance of the attire, the deep reserve of the countenance, haunted her. The lady's anguish groaned beneath these footsteps. What must not *she* be enduring? "That amidst the thunder and lightning of her suffering she should think of me," thought Magnhild, "would be unnatural." In the first moment of terror she had sought refuge with her young friend, as beneath a sheltering roof, but immediately afterward all was, of course, forgotten.

Some one came into the hall. Was it a message from the lady? No, it was Skarlie. Magnhild well knew his triple time step. He gave her a searching glance as he entered. "It is about time for me to be off," said he. He was all friendliness, and began to gather together his things.

"Have you been waiting for a conveyance?" asked she.

"No, but for the meat I ordered and had to go without the last time; it came a little while ago."

She said no more, and Skarlie was soon ready.

"Good-by, until I come again!" said he. He had taken up his things, and now stood looking at her.

"Skarlie," said she, "was it you who gave Machine Martha that mark?"

He blinked at her several times, and finally asked: "What harm was there in that, my dear?"

Magnhild grew pale.

"I have often despised you," said she, "but never so much as at this moment."

She turned, went into her bed-room and bolted the door. She heard Skarlie go. Then she threw herself on the bed.

A few bars were struck on the piano above, but no more followed; Tande was probably himself startled at the sound. These bars involuntarily made Magnhild pause. Now she was forced to follow the steps which began afresh. A new tinge of the mysterious, the incomprehensible, had fallen over Tande. She was afraid of him. Before this, she had trembled when he was near at hand; now a thrill ran through her when she merely thought of him.

The steps above ceased, and she glided from the unfathomable to Skarlie; for here she was clear. How she hated him! And when she thought that in a fortnight he would come again and act as though nothing had occurred, she clinched her hands in rage and opened them again; for as it had been a hundred times before, so it would be again. She would forget, because he was so good-natured, and let her have her own way.

A profound sorrow at her own insufficiency fell like the pall of night on her fancy. She burst into tears. She was unable to cope with one of the relations of life, either those of others or her own; unable to grasp any saving resolution. Indeed, what could this be?

The steps began again, swifter, lighter than ever. Once more Magnhild experienced that inexplicable, not unpleasant tremor Tande had caused in her before.

It had finally grown dark. She rose and went into the next room. At the cottage opposite there was light, and the curtains were down. Magnhild also struck a light. Scarcely had she done so when she heard steps in the hall, and some one knocked at her door. She listened; there came another rap. She went to the door. It was a message from the lady for Magnhild to come to her. She put out the light and obeyed the summons.

She found everything changed. All around stood open, already-packed chests, trunks, boxes, and traveling satchels; Magda lay sleeping on her own little hamper. A hired woman was assisting the maid in putting the room in order. The maid started up saying: "My lady has just gone into her bed-room. I will announce you."

Magnhild knocked at the door, then entered the chamber.

The lady lay on her couch, behind white bed curtains, in a lace-trimmed night-dress. She had wound about her head the Turkish kerchief which was inseparably associated with her headaches. The lamp stood a little in the background, with a shade of soft, fluttering red paper over it. She was leaning on one elbow which was buried deep in the pillow, and she languidly extended the free left hand; a weary, agonized gaze followed. How beautiful she was! Magnhild was hers again, hers so completely that she flung herself over her and wept. As though under the influence of an electric shock the sick woman sat up and casting both arms about Magnhild pressed her to her own warm, throbbing form. She wanted to appropriate all this comprehension and sympathy. "Thanks!" she whispered over Magnhild. Her despair quivered through every nerve of her body. Gradually her arms relaxed and Magnhild rose. Then the lady sank back among the pillows and begged Magnhild to fetch a chair and sit by her.

"The walls have ears," she whispered, pointing to the door. Magnhild brought the chair. "No, here on the bed," said the lady, making room beside her.

The chair was set aside again. The lady took Magnhild's hand and held it in both of hers. Magnhild gazed into her eyes, which were still full of tears. How good, how true, how full of comprehension she looked! Magnhild bent down and kissed her. The lips were languid.

"I sent for you, Magnhild," said she, softly. "I have something to say to you. Be not afraid,"—a warm pressure of the hand accompanied these words; "it is not my own history—and it shall be very brief; for I feel the need of being alone." Here the tears rolled down over her cheeks. She was aware of it and smiled.

"You are married—I do not understand how, and I do not wish to know!" A tremor ran through her and she paused. She turned her head aside for a moment. Presently she continued: "Do not attempt"—but she got no farther; she drew away both hands, covered her face, and flinging herself round, wept in the pillow. Magnhild saw the convulsive quivering of back and arms, and she rose.

"How stupid that was of me," she heard at last; the lady had turned round again, and now bathed eyes and brow with an essence which filled the room with perfume. "I have no advice to give you—besides, of what use would it be? Sit down again!" Magnhild sat down. The lady laid aside the phial and took Magnhild's hand in both of hers. She patted and stroked it, while a long, searching gaze followed. "Do you know that you are the cause of what happened to-day?" Magnhild flushed as though she were standing before a great fire; she tried to rise, but the lady held her fast. "Be still, my child! I have read his thoughts when we were together. You are pure and fine—and I—!" She closed her eyes and lay as still as though she were dead. Not a sound was heard, until at last the lady drew a long, long breath, and looked up with a gaze so full of suffering!

Magnhild heard the beating of her own heart; she dared not stir; she suppressed even her breathing. She felt cold drops of moisture start from every pore.

"Yes, yes, Magnhild;—be now on *your* guard!"

Magnhild started up. The lady turned her head after her. "Be not proud!" said she.

"Is there any place where you can now go?" Magnhild did not hear what she said. The lady repeated her question as calmly as she had spoken before. "Is there any place where you can now go? Answer me!"

Magnhild could scarcely collect her thoughts, but she answered: "Yes," merely out of accustomed acquiescence to the lady. She did not think of any special place of refuge, only that she must go away from here now, at once. But before she could move, the lady, who had been watching her closely, said,—

"I will tell you one thing that you do not know: you love him."

Magnhild drew back, swift as lightning, her eyes firmly fixed on *hers*. There arose a brief conflict, in which the lady's eyes, as it were, breathed upon Magnhild's. Magnhild grew confused, colored, and bowed her head on her hands. The lady sat up and took hold of her arm. Magnhild still resisted; her bosom heaved—she tottered, as though seeking support; and finally leaned aside toward where she felt the pressure of the lady's hand.

Then throwing herself on the lady's bosom she wept violently.

CHAPTER VIII.

WHILE he was still in bed the next morning there was brought to Tande by the sailor's wife a letter. It had a dainty, old-fashioned, somewhat yellow, glazed envelope, and the address was written in an unpracticed lady's hand, with delicate characters, of which those extending below the lines terminated in a little superfluous flourish, as if afraid of being round and yet with a strong tendency to become so.

"From whom can this be?" thought Tande.

He opened the letter. It was signed "Magnhild." A warm glow ran through him, and he read:—

HR. H. TANDE,—I thank you very much for your kindness to me, and for the instruction you have so generously given me. My husband has said that you have no room-rent to pay.

I am obliged to go away without waiting for an opportunity to tell you of this. Once more my best thanks.
MAGNHILD.

He read the letter through at least five times. Then he studied each word, each character. This epistle had cost fully ten rough sketches and discarded copies; he was sure of it. The word "Magnhild" was written with more skill than the rest; the writer must have had frequent practice in that early in life.

But with such trifling discoveries Tande could not silence the terrible accusation that stared at him from this letter. He lay still a long time after letting the letter drop from his hands.

Presently he began to drum on the sheet with the fingers of his right hand; he was playing the soprano part of a melody. Had it reached the piano, and had Magnhild heard it, she would surely have recognized it.

Suddenly Tande sprang out of bed and into the adjoining room. Stationing himself behind the curtain he took a cautious survey of the opposite house. Quite right: the windows were all open, two women were at work cleaning; the house was empty. Tande paced the floor and whistled. He walked until he was chilled through. Then he began to dress. It usually took him an hour to make his toilet, during which he went from time to time to the piano. To-day he required two hours, and yet he did not once go near the piano.

In the forenoon he took a long walk, but not to the spots they had all visited together. During this walk what had occurred began to assume a shape which made him feel less guilty than he had felt at first. The next day he scarcely felt that he was in the least to blame. Toward evening of the third day his conscience began again to trouble him; but on the following morning he rose from his couch ready to smile over the whole affair.

The first day he had twice commenced a letter to Magnhild but had torn up each effort. On the fourth day he found, instead of the attempted letter, a musical theme. This was capable of being developed into a complex, richly harmonized composition, full of magnificent unrest. Several bars of the simple, refined melody which had conjured up for Magnhild dreams of her childhood might be sprinkled through it. Could not the two motives be brought into conflict?

But as he failed to succeed to his satisfaction, Tande concluded that neither at this place nor it this time could it be accomplished. He remained at the Point one week longer, and then packing up his things he departed. The piano he left behind him, and the key with it. He set forth for Germany.

CHAPTER IX.

ABOUT five years had elapsed when one Sunday evening in spring, a party of young girls passed up the one large street of the coast town. They were walking arm in arm, and their numbers were continually increased; for the girls were singing a three part song as they went along.

In front of the saddler's house (which, by the way, was now without either sign-board or shop) they slackened their speed, as though they especially desired their singing to be heard here. Perhaps they also expected to see a face at one of the low windows; but they saw none and soon moved onward.

When the last of the party had disappeared, a woman rose from the large chair in the corner. She was scarcely more than half dressed, had down-trodden slippers and disheveled hair. As she knew that no one lived opposite and saw no one in the street, she ventured to approach the window, and resting her arm on the sash she bowed her head in her hand and became absorbed in thought. And as she stood thus she dreamily listened to the harmonies which ever and anon floated back to her.

This chorus was a reminder that Magnhild had once loved song and had believed that in it she had found her vocation. It was she who stood there, and who although, it was Sunday, or perhaps just because it was Sunday, had not thought it worth while to dress herself; it was six o'clock in the afternoon.

She was roused by the rattling of carriage-wheels from another direction. The steamer must have arrived. So accustomed was she to this one break in the desert-stillness of the town, that she forgot she was not dressed, and looked out to see who was coming. It proved to be two ladies; one with a child in her arms and a sunshade; the other with a fluttering veil, bright, eager eyes and a full face. She wore a Scotch plaid traveling suit, and as the carriage drove rapidly past she nodded to Magnhild, the travel-bronzed face all beaming; later she turned and waved her gloved hand.

Who in all the world could this be? In her surprise, which with her always gave place to embarrassment, Magnhild had drawn back into the room. Who could it be?

There was something familiar that was struggling in vain for the supremacy when the lady came running back toward the house. She moved on briskly in her light traveling costume, and now springing up the steps she soon stood in the door that was thrown open to receive her. She and Magnhild looked at each other for a moment.

"Do you not know me?" asked the elegant lady, in the broadest dialect of the parish.

"Rönnaug?"

"Yes, of course!"

And then they embraced.

"My dear! I am here solely on your account. I want to tell you that all these years I have been looking forward to this moment. My dear Magnhild!"

She spoke an intermixture of three languages: English, the dialect of the parish, and a little of the common book language of Norway.

"I have been trying to speak Norse only a couple of months, and do not succeed very well yet."

Her countenance had developed: the eyes glowed with more warmth than of yore; the full lips had acquired facility in expressing every varied shade of humor, friendliness, and will. Her form was even more voluptuous than it had formerly been, but her rapid movements and the elegant traveling suit she wore softened the effect. Her broad hands, which bore the impress of her working days, closed warmly about Magnhild's hand, and soon they were sitting side by side while Rönnaug told her strange experiences of the past four or five years. She had not wanted to write about them, for no one would have believed her story if she had. The reason why she had not kept her promise to write immediately upon reaching her journey's end was simply because even during the voyage she had risen from the steerage to the first cabin, and what had caused this promotion would have been misinterpreted.

When she sailed from Liverpool she was sitting forward on the gunwale of the large ship. A gentleman came up to her and in broken Norwegian claimed acquaintance with her, for just as she was sitting now, he said, she had sat a month before on the back of his cariole. Rönnaug, too, remembered him, and they talked together that day and many other days. After a while he brought a lady with him. The next day he and the lady came again and invited Rönnaug to go with them to the first cabin. Here the lady and she, with the aid of the gentleman, entered into an English conversation, which created much amusement. Others soon gathered about the group and the upshot of it all was that Rönnaug was compelled to remain in the first cabin, she really did not know at whose expense. She took a bath, was provided with new clothes from top to toe, several ladies contributing, and remained as a guest among the passengers. All were kind to her.

She left the ship with the lady, who proved to be an aunt of the gentleman who had first spoken to Rönnaug and at whose expense, as she soon learned, she had traveled. He afterwards had her provided with instruction and the handsomest support, and it was at his expense they all three took frequent long journeys together. For the past two years she had been his wife, and they had a child about a year old whom she had with her. And this child Magnhild must see—not "to-morrow," nor "by and by," but "now," "right away!"

Magnhild was not dressed. Well, then she must speedily make her toilet. Rönnaug would help her—and in spite of all resistance they were both soon standing in Magnhild's chamber.

As soon as Magnhild had begun to dress Rönnaug wandered about in the rooms. As she did so she asked one single question, and this was: why Magnhild was not dressed so late in the day. A long protracted "oh!" was the only answer she received. Rönnaug hummed softly to herself as she went out into the front room. By and by some words were uttered by her; they were English words, and one of them Magnhild heard distinctly: it was "disappointed." Magnhild understood English; during the past three winters Skarlie had read the language with her, and she could already read aloud to him from the American weekly paper, which, since his sojourn in America, it had been a necessity for him to take. She knew, therefore, that "disappointed" was the same as "*skuffet*."

There are times when a change occurs in our mood, inasmuch as the sun which filled the whole room suddenly disappears, leaving the atmosphere gray, cold, within and without. In like manner Magnhild was involuntarily seized with an indescribable dread; and sure enough, the next time Rönnaug came humming past the open door (she was looking at the pictures on the wall), she cast a brief side glance in at Magnhild; it was by no means unfriendly; but it was felt, nevertheless, by Magnhild, as though she had received a shock. What in all the world had happened? or rather, what was discovered? It was impossible for her to conceive. She cast her eyes searchingly around the room, when she came in after dressing. But she sought in vain for anything which could have betrayed what she herself would have concealed, or indicated what could have caused displeasure. What was it? Rönnaug's face was now quite changed—ah! what was it?

They set forth; both had grown silent. Even on the street, where there must be so much that was familiar, she who had but now spoken in three languages could hold her peace in them all. They met a man in a cariole, who was talking passionately with a younger man he had stopped; both bowed to Magnhild, the elder one with an air of indifference, the younger one with triumph in his pimpled face and flashing eyes. For the first time Rönnaug roused to interest. Although nearly five years had elapsed since she had served as "skyds" girl to the unknown man who had talked about Magnhild's destiny, and who had seen her herself in circumstances of which she was now ashamed, she recognized him at once. Hurriedly grasping Magnhild's hand, she cried:—

"Do you know him? What is his name? Does he live here?"

In her eagerness she quite forgot to use her mother-tongue.

Magnhild replied only to the last question:—

"Yes, since last winter."

"What is his name?"

"Grong."

"Have you had any conversation with him?"

"More with his son; that was he who was standing by the cariole."

Rönnaug looked after Grong, who at this moment drove briskly, it might almost be said angrily, past them.

They soon came to the second hotel on the right hand side; a maid servant was asked if a lady had stopped there with a child. They were shown up-stairs. There stood the lady who had accompanied Rönnaug. The latter asked her in English where the child was, at the same time presenting Miss Roland to Mrs. Skarlie, after which all three went into the adjoining room.

"Ah, we have a cradle!" exclaimed Rönnaug in English, and threw herself on her knees beside the cradle.

Magnhild remained standing, at a little distance. The child was very pretty, so far as Magnhild could see. Rönnaug bent over it and for some time she neither looked up nor spoke. But Magnhild saw that great tears trickled down on the fine coverlet that was spread over the cradle. There arose a painful silence.

Rönnaug rose to her feet at last, and with a side glance at Magnhild she went past her into the front room. Magnhild finally felt constrained to follow her. She found Rönnaug standing by the window. A carriage stopped at that moment in front of the hotel. Magnhild saw that it was drawn by three men. It was a new, handsome traveling carriage, the handsomest she had ever seen.

"Whose carriage is that?" asked she.

"It is mine," replied Rönnaug.

Betsy Roland came in and asked some question. Rönnaug went out with her, and when, directly afterward, she returned to the room, she went straight up to Magnhild, who still sat looking at the carriage. Rönnaug laid one arm about her neck.

"Will you go with me in this carriage through the country, Magnhild?" she asked, in English.

At the first contact Magnhild had become startled; she was conscious of Rönnaug's eyes, of her breath; and Rönnaug's arm encircled her like an iron bar, although there certainly was no pressure.

"Will you go with me through the country in this—in this carriage, Magnhild?" she heard once more, this time in a blending of the dialect of the parish and English, and the voice trembled.

"Yes," whispered Magnhild.

Rönnaug released her, went to the other window, and did not look round again.

"Is the carriage from America?"

"London."

"How much did you give for it?"

"Charles bought it."

"Is your husband with you?"

"Yes—ja," and she added, brokenly, "Not here; Constantinople—delivery of guns—in September we are to meet—Liverpool." And then she looked up at Magnhild with wide open eyes. What did she mean?

Magnhild wished to go. Rönnaug accompanied her down-stairs, and they both went out to inspect the carriage, about which stood a group of people who now fell back somewhat. Rönnaug pointed out to Magnhild how comfortable the carriage was, and while her head was still inside she asked,—

"Your rooms up-stairs, are they to let?"

"No, it would give me too much trouble."

Rönnaug hastily said "good-night," and ran up the steps.

Magnhild had not gone very far before she felt that she certainly ought to have offered those rooms to Rönnaug. Should she turn back? Oh, no.

This was one of Magnhild's wakeful nights. Rönnaug had frightened her. And this journey? Never in the world would she undertake it.

CHAPTER X.

WHEN she left her chamber after ten o'clock, the first object she beheld was Rönnaug, who was coming up from the coast town, and was on her way to call on Magnhild—no, not on Magnhild, but on the priest, the young curate, who lived at Magnhild's house, in the former saddler workshop. Rönnaug at the priest's? At eleven o'clock she was still with him. And when she came out, accompanied by the curate, a shy young man, she merely put her head in Magnhild's door, greeted her, and disappeared again with the curate.

Magnhild found still greater cause for wonder, for later in the day she saw Rönnaug in company with Grong. This wounded her, she could scarcely tell why. The following day Rönnaug called in as she passed by; various people were discussed whom it had entertained Rönnaug to meet, but not a word was said about the journey. Several days went by, and it was still not mentioned. Perhaps it had been given up!

But finally Magnhild began to hear about this journey from others: first from the sailor's wife who did the work of her house, then from the woman of whom she bought fish, finally from every one. What should she do? For upon no account would she consent to go.

Rönnaug told her that she was reading Norse with Grong, and also with the curate, in order that neither might have too much torment with her at any one time; she wrote exercises, too, she said, and laughed. In the same abrupt manner she touched upon sundry individuals and circumstances, mentioned them in the most characteristic way, and hurried on to something else. Magnhild was not invited to the hotel. Rönnaug often went by pushing her child in a little wagon she had bought; she would stop and show the child to every one she met, but she never brought it in to see Magnhild.

Rönnaug made the most extraordinary sensation in the town. It was no unusual thing at a sea-port town to see remarkable changes of fortune. Judging from the presents Rönnaug made, indeed from her whole appearance, she must be immensely wealthy, yet she was the most unassuming and sociable of all. Magnhild frequently heard her praises sounded; the young curate alone occasionally observed that she decidedly evinced that impatience which was characteristic of such a child of fortune.

But what then did Rönnaug hear about Magnhild? For it might be assumed beyond all doubt that if she did not question Magnhild herself she at least asked others about her. This was true, but she proceeded very cautiously. There were, indeed, but two people to whom she put direct questions,—the young curate and Grong.

The curate said that during the whole time he had been at the Point, and that was now nearly a year, he had neither heard nor seen anything but good concerning Magnhild. Skarlie was a person who was less transparent; according to universal testimony he had settled in this town merely to study the prevailing conditions and utilize them for his own benefit—"without competition and without control." He was sarcastic and cynical; but the curate could not deny that it was sometimes amusing to talk with him. The curate had never heard that Skarlie was otherwise than considerate to his wife—or rather his adopted daughter; for other relations scarcely existed between them. And the shy young curate seemed quite embarrassed at being obliged to give this information.

Grong, on the contrary, called Magnhild a lazy, selfish, pretentious hussy. She would not even take the trouble to tie up her stockings; he had noticed this himself. The hand-work she had started here had long since been left to a hunchback girl named Marie and a tall girl by the name of Louise. Magnhild occasionally taught them something new, yet even that was due not to herself but to her husband, who picked up such things on his travels and spurred her on to introduce them. Upon the whole, Skarlie was a capable, industrious fellow, who had breathed life into this sleepy, ignorant parish, and even if he had victimized the people somewhat, it could scarcely be expected that so much knowledge should be gained for nothing.

Magnhild's vocation? Bah! He had long since given up the idea of there being such a thing as a special destiny. In Nordland, many years before, he had seen an old man who in his childhood had been the only person saved out of a whole parish; the rest had been swept away by an avalanche. This man was a great dunce; he had lived to be sixty-six years of age without earning a farthing except by rowing, and had died a year before, a pauper. What sort of a destiny was that? Indeed, there were precious few who had any destiny at all.

Grong at this time was wretchedly out of humor: he had believed his gifted son to be destined for something; he lived for his sake alone—and the young man had accomplished nothing except falling in love. Rönnaug, who knew nothing of Grong's own experience, was shocked at his harsh verdict. Nor could she induce him to discuss the subject with her, for he declared point blank that Magnhild bored him.

So she once more sought Magnhild herself, but found her so apathetic that it was impossible to approach her.

If she would persevere in her design, there was nothing left for her but to resort to strategy.

In the most indifferent tone in the world she therefore one day announced to Magnhild that in a couple of days she proposed starting; Magnhild would not need to take much luggage with her, for when they stopped anywhere they could purchase whatever they required. That was the way she always managed.

This was about nine o'clock in the morning, and until twelve o'clock Magnhild was toiling over a telegram to her husband who had just announced to her his arrival at Bergen. The telegram was at last completed as follows:—

"Rönnaug, married to the rich American, Charles Randon, New York, is here; wants me to go with her on a long journey.—Magnhild."

She felt it to be treason when, on the stroke of twelve, she dispatched this telegram. Treason? Toward whom? She owed reckoning to no one. Meanwhile, in the afternoon, she went out in order that no one might find her. When she returned home in the evening a telegram was awaiting her.

"Home by the steamer to-morrow.—Skarlie."

Rönnaug sought Magnhild at eight o'clock the next morning: she wanted to surprise her with a traveling suit that was ready for her at the hotel. But it was all locked up at Magnhild's. Rönnaug went round the house and peeped in at the bed-room window whose curtain was drawn aside. Magnhild was out! Magnhild, who seldom rose before nine o'clock!

Well, Rönnaug went again at nine. Fastened up! At ten o'clock. The same result. After this she went to the house every quarter of an hour, but always found it fastened up. Then she became suspicious. At eleven o'clock she paid two boys handsomely to stand guard over the house and bring her word as soon as Magnhild returned.

Rönnaug herself stayed at the hotel and waited. It came to be one, two, three o'clock—no messenger. She inspected her guards; all was right. The clock struck four, then five. Another inspection. Just as the clock struck six a boy came running along the street, and Rönnaug, hat in hand, flew down the steps to meet him.

She found Magnhild in the kitchen. Magnhild was so busy that Rönnaug could find no opportunity to speak a single word with her. She was passing incessantly to and fro between kitchen, yard, and inner rooms. She went also into the cellar and remained there for a long time. Rönnaug waited; but as Magnhild never paused, she finally sought her in the pantry. There she asked her if she would not go with her to the hotel for a moment. Magnhild said she had no time. She was engaged in putting butter on a plate.

"For whom are you making preparations?"

"Oh!"—

The hand which held the spoon trembled; this Rönnaug observed.

"Are you expecting Skarlie by the steamer—now?"

Magnhild could not well say "No," for this would speedily have proved itself false, and so she said "Yes."

"Then you sent for him?"

Magnhild laid aside the spoon and went into the next room; Rönnaug followed her.

It now came to light how much good vigorous Norse Rönnaug had learned in the short time she had been studying, even if it were not wholly faultless. She first asked if this signified that Skarlie would prevent the journey. When Magnhild, instead of making any reply, fled into the bed-chamber, Rönnaug again followed her; she said that *to-day* Magnhild must listen to her.

This "to-day" told Magnhild that Rönnaug had long been wanting to talk with her. Had the window Magnhild now stood beside been a little larger, she would certainly have jumped out of it.

But before Rönnaug managed to begin in earnest, something happened. Noise and laughter were heard in the street, and ringing through them an infuriated man's voice. "And *you* will prevent me from taking the sacrament, you hypocritical villain?" After this a dead silence, and then peals of laughter. Most likely the man had been seized and carried off; the shouting and laughing of boys and old women resounded through the street, and gradually sounded farther and farther away.

Neither of the two women in the chamber had stirred from her place. They had both peered out through the door toward the sitting-room window, but they had also both turned away again, Magnhild toward the garden. But Rönnaug had been reminded by this interruption of Machine Martha, who in her day had been the terror and sport of the coast town. Scarcely, therefore, had the noise died away, before she asked,—

"Do you remember Machine Martha? Do you remember something that I told you about your husband and her? I have been making inquiries concerning it and I now know more than I did before. Let me tell you it is unworthy of you to live under the same roof with such a man as Skarlie."

Very pale, Magnhild turned proudly round with:—

"That is no business of mine!"

"That is no business of yours? Why you live in his house, eat his food, wear his clothes, and bear his name,—and his conduct is no business of yours?"

But Magnhild swept past her and went into the sitting-room without vouchsafing a reply. She took her stand by one of the windows opening on the street.

"Aye, if you do not feel this to be a disgrace, Magnhild, you have sunk lower than I thought."

Magnhild had just leaned her head, against the window frame. She now drew it up sufficiently to look at Rönnaug and smile, then she bowed forward again. But this smile had sent the blood coursing up to Rönnaug's cheeks, for she had felt their joint youth compared in it.

"I know what you are thinking of,"—here Rönnaug's voice trembled,—"and I could not have believed you to be so unkind, although at our very first meeting I plainly saw that I had made a mistake in feeling such a foolish longing for you."

But in a moment she felt herself that these words were too strong, and she paused. It was, moreover, not her design to quarrel with Magnhild; quite the contrary! And so she was indignant with Magnhild for having led her so far to forget herself. But had it not been thus from the beginning? With what eager warmth had she not come, and how coldly had she not been received. And from this train of thought her words now proceeded.

"I could think of nothing more delightful in the world than to show you my child. There was, indeed, no one else to whom I could show it. And you did not even care to see it; you did not so much as want to take the trouble to dress yourself."

She strove at first to speak calmly, but before she finished what she was saying, her voice quivered, and she burst into tears.

Suddenly Magnhild darted away from the window toward the kitchen door—but that was just where Rönnaug was; then toward the bed-room door, but remembering that it would be useless to take refuge there, turned again, met Rönnaug, knew not where to go, and fled back to her old place.

But this was all lost on Rönnaug; for now she too was in a state of extreme agitation.

"You have no heart, Magnhild! It is dreadful to be obliged to say so! You have permitted yourself to be trailed in the mire until you have lost all feeling, indeed you have. When I insisted upon your seeing my child, you did not even kiss it! You did not so much as stoop to look at it; you never said a word, no, not a single word, and you have no idea how pretty it is!"

A burst of tears again checked her flow of words.

"But that is natural," she continued, "you have never had a child of your own. And I chanced to remember this, otherwise I should have started right off again—at once! I was so disappointed. Ah! well, I wrote Charles all about it!" In another, more vigorous tone she interrupted herself with: "I do not know what you can be thinking of. Or everything must be dead within you. You might have full freedom—and you prefer Skarlie. Write for Skarlie!" She paced the floor excitedly. Presently she said: "Alas! alas! So this is Magnhild, who was once so pure and so refined that she saved me!" She paused and looked at Magnhild. "But I shall never forget it, and you *shall* go with me, Magnhild!" Then, with sudden emotion: "Have you not one word for me? Can you not understand how fond I am of you? Have you quite forgotten, Magnhild, how fond I have always been of you? Is it nothing to you that I came here all the way from America after you."

She failed to notice that she had thus avowed her whole errand; she stood and waited to see Magnhild rouse and turn. She was not standing near enough to see that tears were now falling on the window-sill. She only saw that Magnhild neither stirred nor betrayed the slightest emotion. This wounded her, and, hasty as she was in her resolves when her heart was full, she left. Magnhild saw her hurry, weeping, up the street, without looking in.

And Rönnaug did not cease weeping, not even when she had thrown herself down over her child and was kissing it. She clasped it again and again to her bosom, as though she wanted to make sure of her life's great gain.

She had expected Magnhild to follow her. The clock struck eight, no Magnhild appeared; nine—still no Magnhild. Rönnaug threw a shawl over her head and stole past the saddler's house. Skarlie must have come home some time since. All was still within; there was no one at the windows. Rönnaug went back to the hotel and as she got ready for bed she kept pondering on what was now to be done, and whether she should really start on her journey without Magnhild. The last thought she promptly dismissed. No, she would remain and call for assistance. She was ready to risk a battle, and that with Mr. Skarlie himself, supported by the curate, Grong, and other worthy people. She probably viewed the matter somewhat from an American standpoint; but she was determined.

She fell asleep and dreamed that Mr. Skarlie and she were fighting. With his large hairy hands he seized her by the head, the shoulders, the hands; his repulsive face, with its toothless mouth, looked with a laugh into her eyes. She could not ward him off: once more he had her by the head; then Magnhild repeatedly called her name aloud and she awoke. Magnhild was standing at the side of her bed.

"Rönnaug! Rönnaug!"

"Yes, yes!"

"It is I—Magnhild!"

Rönnaug started up in bed, half intoxicated with sleep. "Yes, I see—you—It is you? No, really you, Magnhild! Are you going with me?"

"Yes!"

And Magnhild flung herself on Rönnaug's bosom and burst into tears. What tears! They were like those of a child, who after long fright finds its mother again.

"Good Heavens! What has happened?"

"I cannot tell you." Another burst of passionate weeping. Then quietly freeing herself from Rönnaug's arms, she drew back.

"But you will really come with me?"

There was heard a whispered "yes," and then renewed weeping. And Rönnaug stretched out her arms; but as Magnhild did not fly into them, she sprang out of bed and took her joy in a practical way by beginning to dress in great haste. There was joy, aye, triumph in her soul.

As she sat on the edge of the bed, drawing on her clothes, she took a closer survey of Magnhild; the summer night was quite clear and light, and Magnhild had raised a curtain, opened a window, and was now standing by the latter. It was about three o'clock. Magnhild had on a petticoat with a cloak thrown over it; a bundle lay on the chair, it perhaps contained her dress. What could have happened? Rönnaug went to her parlor to finish dressing, and when Magnhild followed her, the new traveling suit was lying spread out and was shown to her. She uttered no word of thanks, she scarcely looked at the suit; but she sat down beside it and her tears flowed anew. Rönnaug was obliged to put the clothes on her. As she was thus engaged, she whispered:—

"Did he try to use force?"

"That he has never done," said Magnhild; "no, there are other things"—and now she became so convulsed with weeping that Rönnaug said no more, but finished dressing both Magnhild and herself as quickly as possible. She hastened into the bed-chamber to awaken her American friend, then down-stairs to rouse the people of the hotel: she wanted to start within an hour.

She found Magnhild where she had left her.

"No, this will not do," said she. "Pray control yourself. Within an hour we must be away from here."

But Magnhild sat still; it was as though all her energy had been exhausted by the struggle and the resolve she had just come from. Rönnaug let her alone; she had as much as she could do to get ready. Everything was packed, and last of all the child was wrapped in its traveling blanket without being roused. Within an hour they and all their belongings were actually stowed away in the carriage.

The world around them slept. They drove onward in the bright, dawning morning, past the church. The sun was not visible; but the skies, above the mountains to the east, were flushed with roseate hues. The landscape lay in dark shadows, the upper slope of the mountains in the deepest of deep black-blue; the stream, not a streak of light over its struggle, cut its way along, like a procession of wild, angry mountaineers, recklessly dashing downward at this moment of the world's awakening, without consideration, without pausing for rest, and with shrill laughter at this mad resolve and the success which attended it.

The impressions of nature, and the feelings Magnhild might otherwise have experienced during this journey away from the griefs of many years, over the first miles, as it were, of a new career in the sumptuous traveling carriage of the friend of her childhood,—all were lulled into a weary, vapid drowsiness. Her daily life had been for years one monotonous routine, so that the emotions of a single evening had completely exhausted her strength. She longed now for nothing so much as for a bed. And Rönnaug, bent on fully carrying out the wonders of contrast, was not content with traveling in her own carriage with two horses (when the ascent began she would have four), she wanted also to sleep in one of the guest-beds at the post-station where she had once served. This wish was gratified, and three hours' sleep was taken by them all. The hostess recognized Rönnaug, but as she was a person Rönnaug had not liked, there was no conversation between them.

After they had slept, eaten, and settled their account, Rönnaug felt a desire to write something with her own hand in the traveler's register. That was indeed too amusing. She read what was last written there, as follows: "Two persons, one horse, change for the next station," and on the margin was added,—

"Birds encountered us two, tweewhitt!'With *us* to tarry, think you, tweewhitt?'
"'We plan, we reason, no more, tra-ra!Each other we adore, tra-ra!'"

"What nonsense was this?" The rest of the party must see: it was translated into English for Betsy Roland. Now they remembered that as they drove into the station they had seen a carriage, with a gentleman and lady in it, driving quickly past them up the road. The gentleman had turned his face away, as though he did not wish to be seen; the lady was closely veiled.

They were still talking of this when they sat in the carriage and drove away, while all the people at the station had assembled to watch them. The travelers concluded that the verses must have been written by some happy new-married couple; and Magnhild, by one of those trains of thought which cannot be accounted for, called to mind the young couple, the gentleman in morocco slippers, and the lady with her hair so strangely done up, she had met at the next station, on her own wedding trip. This led her to recall her own wedding, then to think of what she had gone through in all these years, and of how aimless her whole life was,—aimless whether she looked into the past or into the future.

Day had meanwhile dawned in wondrous beauty. The sun had risen above the lofty mountains. The valley, although narrow, was so situated that it was thoroughly illumined by the sunshine. The stream now flowed in a narrower, more rocky bed, was white with foam where struggles arose, grass-green where they ceased, blue where there were overhanging shadows, and gray where the water formed eddies over a clay bottom. The grass here was filled with stubble, farther up it was studded with yellow cowslips, the largest they had ever seen.

The peaks of the mountains sparkled, the dark pine forest in the bosom and lap of the chain displayed such a wealth of luxuriance, that whoever viewed it aright must inevitably be refreshed. Close by the road-side grew deciduous trees, for here the pines had been cut down, yet ever and anon they pushed their way triumphantly forth from their vigorous headquarters in the background. The road was free from dust. On the outskirts of the forest grew mountain flowers, all glittering with the last dew-drops of the day.

The travelers had the carriage stop that they might pluck some of the flowers; and then they sat in the grass and amused the child with them; they wove garlands and twined them about the little one. A short distance farther up, where the stream had sunk so far beneath them that its roar had ceased to sound above all else, they heard the jubilant song of birds. The thrush, singly and in groups, swung from tree to tree, and its vigorous chirping had a cheering tone. A startled wood-grouse, with strong wing-beats, flew shrieking among the branches. A dog who followed the horses set chase to the red grouse; they shrieked, flapped their wings, hid in the heather, shrieked, started up again and sought a circuitous way back. They must have nests here. There was also a rich growth of birch round about this little heath.

"Ah, how I have longed for this journey! And Charles, who gave it to me!" The tears stood in Rönnaug's eyes, but she brushed them away, after she had kissed her child. "No, no tears. Why should there be any?"

And she sang:—

"Shed no tear! Oh shed no tear!The flower will bloom another year.Weep no more! Oh weep no more!Young buds sleep in the root's white core."

Keats.
"This is our summer trip, Magnhild! The summer travels in Norway. Now onward!"
But Magnhild bowed down and covered her face with her hands.
"All shall be well with you, Magnhild. Charles is so good! He will do everything for you."

But here she heard Magnhild sob, and so she said no more.

The sunny day through which they rode onward, the fresh, aromatic mountain air they inhaled, the sounds of jubilee which burst forth from the forest, blending with childhood's memories, became too much for Rönnaug. She forgot Magnhild and began to sing again. Then she took the child and chatted playfully with it and with Miss Roland. She was surprised by Magnhild's asking:—

"Do you love your husband, Rönnaug?"

"Do I love him? Why, when Mr. Charles Randon said to me: 'I will gladly provide for your education, Rönnaug; I hope you will let me have this pleasure,'—well, I let him have the pleasure. When Mr. Charles said to me: 'My dear Rönnaug, I am much older than you; yet if you could consent to be my wife, I am certain that I should be happy,'—well—and so I made him happy. And when Mr. Charles said: 'My dear Rönnaug, take good care of our little Harry, so that I may find you all in Liverpool in September, and your Norwegian friend with you,'—why, I determined that he should find us all in Liverpool in September, and little Harry well and hearty; and my Norwegian friend along, too!"—and she kissed the child and set it to laughing.

They changed horses at the next post-station. Magnhild and Miss Roland kept their seats in the carriage. Rönnaug got out, partly to re-visit familiar haunts, partly to make an entry in the register. That was her duty, she said. Presently she came back, laughing, with the register. Under the entry: "Two persons for the next station,"—indicating that these two persons were too much absorbed to even trouble themselves with the name of the next station,—were the following lines:—

"Love is all the budding flower,Perfect blossom, fruit mature.When breaking boughs no more endure,Then "stop!" is shrieked to Winter's power.Rather life to stop be driven;No alternative is given!"

Rönnaug translated it for Betsy Roland, and now various conjectures were expressed by them all, in both Norwegian and English. They agreed in supposing the writers to be two lovers, on a journey, under peculiar circumstances; but whether they were a newly-married couple, or merely lovers; whether theirs was a runaway flight, or whether they were simply actuated by exuberance of spirits over happily overcome obstacles, or,—oh! there were manifold possibilities.

Rönnaug wished to copy the verses, and Magnhild offered her a leaf from her pocket-book. As this was produced a letter fell from it. Magnhild was surprised, but she soon remembered that she had received the letter by mail the evening before, an hour after her husband's arrival. Wholly absorbed in her conflict with him, she had placed it for the time in her pocket-book. She never received letters, so she could not imagine from whom this could come. The two travelers from America did not notice that the letter bore a foreign stamp, but Magnhild saw this at once. She tore open the letter; it was written in a delicate hand, on fine paper, and was quite long. It was headed "Munich," and the signature was—did she read aright?—"Hans Tande." She folded the letter again, without knowing what she was doing, while the hot blushes spread over face and neck. The two others acted as though they had observed nothing; Rönnaug busied herself with copying the verses.

They drove rapidly on, and left Magnhild to her reflections. But her embarrassment increased to such a degree that it became positive torture to her to sit in the carriage with the others. She meekly begged to be allowed to get out and walk a little distance. Rönnaug smiled and ordered the coachman to stop,—they had just reached a level plain where the horses could rest a while. When the travelers had alighted, she took Magnhild by the hand and led her toward a thicket a few steps behind them.

"Come—go in there now and read your letter!" said she.

When Magnhild found herself alone in the wood she stood still. Her agitation had compelled her to pause. She peered about her, as though fearing even in this lonely spot the presence of people. The sun played here and there on the yellow pine needles that were strewn about, on the fallen decayed branches, on the dark green moss covering the stones, on the heather in the glades. Around her all was profoundly still; from the sunny margin of the wood there floated toward her the twittering of a solitary bird, the babbling of the child, and Rönnaug's laughter, which rang with the utmost clearness through the trees.

Magnhild ventured to draw forth the letter once more. She opened it. It was not folded in the original creases. She spread it out before her, and looked at it as an aged woman might gaze into the depths of a chest upon her bridal garments. A solitary sunbeam, breaking through the branches, played restlessly on the sheet, and was now round, now oblong. Magnhild saw within its shining ring one word, two words, more distinctly than the rest. "Great hopes—and failed!" were written there. "Great hopes—and failed." She read and trembled. Alas! alas! alas! Over and over again she read the words, and felt rich in expectation, in dread, in memories of bliss and of conflict; she could not sit still, she rose to her feet, but only to sit down again to fresh efforts. The ringing tones of Rönnaug's laughter broke upon her solitude, like a staff, which she grasped for support. She gained courage from Rönnaug's courage, and looked here and there in the letter, not to read, rather to find out whether she dare read. But she was too agitated to connect the broken sentences, and was led, almost unawares, to a continuous perusal. She did not understand all that she read. Still it was a communion; it was like the warm clasp of a hand. There was music wafted about her,—*his* music; she was once more in his presence, with the rare perfume, the look, the embarrassed silence, amid which she had experienced earth's highest bliss. The diamond cut its shining circlets over the piano keys, his white, refined hand played "Flowers on the Green." Wholly under his influence now, she became absorbed in re-reading the letter, comprehended it better than before, paused, exulted without words, read, while the tears trickled down her cheeks. She paused, without being aware of it, simply because she could not see, began again, without perceiving it, wept profusely, read on, finished only to begin anew—three, four, five times from beginning to end. She could read no more.

What had she not experienced during this perusal of thoughts and feelings she had had a thousand times before, and thoughts and feelings she had never dreamed of!

The first complete impression she gathered, in the humid forest shades, where she sat concealed from view, was like a shaft of quivering sunbeams. It was the foreboding which stole over her—it was not put into words, and yet it was breathed from every line (a thousand times sweeter so!) the foreboding, aye, the certainty, that he, yes, that he had loved her!—and the second was that he had at the same time been fully aware of her love, long, long before she had grasped it herself! and he had not hinted at this by so much as a look. How considerate he had been! And yet, what must he not have seen in her heart! Was it true? Could it be true?

Ah! it was all one! And yet amidst her grief the thought of being able to feel all this to the core as *he* had felt, was like the sun shining behind a misty atmosphere and gradually bursting through the layers of fog with thousands of undreamed-of light effects, above and below. How freely she could breathe again after the void, privation, brooding of many years.

Not until later did individual thoughts force themselves forward, then not fully until Rönnaug came to her. There was something labored in this letter; it read occasionally like a translation from a foreign language. But now for the *letter itself*:—

I have just returned from the south. I thought myself strong enough. Alas! The papers have doubtless informed you that I am ill; but the papers do not know what I now know!

The first thing I do in this new certainty is to write to you, dear Magnhild.

You will, of course, be painfully surprised at the sight of my signature. I awakened great hopes—and failed when they should have been fulfilled.

A thousand times since I have thought how impossible it would be for you to go to the piano and try over some song we three had studied together, or some exercise we two had gone through. A miracle would have been needed to compel you to do so.

A thousand times I have considered whether I should write to you, and tell you what I must now tell you, that this has been the deepest sorrow of my life.

You set me free from a once rich, but afterward unworthy relation, and this was my salvation. The germ of innocence in my soul was once more released. The entire extent of my emancipation, however, I did not realize so long as we were together.

And I repaid you for what you had done for me by desolating your life, so far as lay within my power. But I have also yearned to tell you what I now believe: our destiny upon earth is not alone what we ourselves have recognized it to be, not alone what we believe to be the main purpose of our existences. When you, without being yourself conscious of it, gave me a purer, higher tendency, you were fulfilling a part of your destiny, dear Magnhild. It was perhaps a small part; but perhaps it was also only an hundredth part of still more which you had done for many others without so much as suspecting it yourself.

Magnhild, I can say it now without danger of being misinterpreted, and also without doing harm; for you have become four years and a half older and I am going hence; indeed, I believe it will help you to hear it. Well, then, the innocence in your soul had become, amidst your peculiar circumstances, a moral atmosphere which in you, more than in any one I ever met, proclaimed itself to be a power. It was all the more beautiful because so unconscious in its manifestations. It was breathed from every manifestation of your bashfulness. It revealed itself to me not alone in your blushes, Magnhild; no, in the tone of your voice also, in the immediate relations you held with every one you had intercourse with, or looked upon, or merely greeted. If there were those in your presence who were not pure, you made them appear abhorrent; you taught even the fallen ones what beauty there is in moral purity.

You have the fullest right to rejoice over what I say. Aye, may it bring you more than rejoicing! It is not well to brood over a lost vocation, Magnhild, and the letters I receive from Grong lead me to suppose that this is what you are now doing. One who does not attain the first or greatest object of his ambition ought not to sink into listless inactivity; for do we not thus check the development of the thousand-leaved destiny of the tree of life? May not even disappointment be part of this?

(Five days later.)

Magnhild, I do not say this in self-justification. Every time I think of your singing I realize what I have repressed. It possessed a purity, untouched by passion, and that was why it moved with such exalting influence through my soul. The perfume of tender memories was in it, memories of my childhood, my mother, my good teacher, my first conceptions of music, my first yearning for love, or thirst for beauty. It also revived the first, pure tintings of life, those which had not yet become glaring, still less tainted.

I think of your singing artistically schooled, radiant with spirituality—what a revelation! And this I checked in its growth.

I bought while we were together some of the brooches made by your father. I showed them to no one. Under the circumstances it would have caused suspicion and consequent annoyance. But in those brooches I felt the family calling, Magnhild, the family work, which your talent should have further continued. In your father's work there is innocent fancy, patience, in its imperfections, as it were, a sigh of far more significant, undeveloped power.

Is all this now checked because your progress is checked, you who are the last of your family and without children? No, I cannot justify myself.

(I have been again compelled to lay aside my pen for many days. Now I must try if I can finish.)

Let not the wrong I did to you, and thereby, alas, to many both in the present and in the future, be used by you as an excuse for never making further progress! You can, if you will, give free scope to whatever power there is within you, if not in one way, in another. And do this now; do it, also, because I implore you! You can make the burden of my fault less heavy for my thoughts, now in the last hours of my life.

Aye, while I write this it grows lighter. The kindness you, in spite of all, surely cherishtoward me (I feel it!) sends me a greeting.

You will, so far as you can, rescue my life's work, where it failed to complete its efforts; you will build upon and improve, Magnhild!

You will, moreover, accept this request as a consolation?

(I could proceed no farther. But to-day I am better.)

If what I have written helps to open the world once more to you, so that you can enter in and take hold of life's duties; aye, if all that you have either neglected or only half performed can come to attain the rank of links in life's problem, and thus become dear to you,—then it will do me good; remember this! Farewell!

Ah, yes, farewell! I have other letters to write, and cannot do much. Farewell!

HANS TANDE.

(Eight days later.)

I copy in this letter to you the following lines from a letter to another:—

"It is not true that love is for every one the portal to life. Perchance it is not so for even half of those who attain *real life*.

"There are many whose lives are ruined by the loss of love, or by sacrificing everything to love. With some of them, perhaps, it could not have been otherwise (people are so different, circumstances excuse so much); but those whose existences I have seen thus blighted could unconditionally have gained the mastery over self and in the effort acquired a new power. Encouraged, however, by a class of literature and art whose short-sightedness proceeds from a maimed will, they neglected all attempts at gaining strength."

CHAPTER XI.

MAGNHILD and Rönnaug came arm in arm out of the wood where Rönnaug had finally been obliged to seek her friend, where so many confidences had been made, so much discussed and considered. They emerged into the open plain. How blue the haze about the mountains! And this was the frame for the pine forest, the surrounding heather, and the plain with Miss Roland and the child. The latter were sitting on blue and red rugs near the carriage. From this foreground the mother's eye wandered away more musingly than ever, and gained even stronger impressions of outline, light, color.

"The summer travels in Norway! The summer travels in Norway!" she kept saying to herself.

From the way in which she uttered these words it might be surmised that in the entire English vocabulary there was nothing which admitted of being repeated with such varied shades of meaning.

The two friends took a long ramble. Magnhild had become a new being to Rönnaug, her individuality enriched, her countenance illumined and thus transformed. For nearly five years Magnhild had been secretly brooding over her lost vocation, and her lost love, those two sisters that had lived and died together. At length she had opened her heart to another; thus something had been accomplished.

The horses were now hitched to the carriage, and the party drove on. The noonday repose of nature was not disturbed by so much as the rumbling of the wheels, for the carriage wound its way slowly over the mountain slopes.

At the next post-station the following lines were found in the register:—

"There met us croaking ravens on our way:We knew that Evil this to us did bode;We made no off'rings, though, as on we rode,To angry gods—the mild are fall of doubt.Why should we care? One God to us feels kindly.He is with us! And Him we follow blindly:—We laugh at all the omens round about."

These little verses began to affect the party like a chorus of birds.

But a joy to which we are unattuned is apt to jar; and here, moreover, the verses became prophetic, for the travelers had gone but a short distance when they gained a view of the church steeple on the heights where Magnhild's parents and brothers and sisters were buried, and of the stony ground in the mountain to the left where the home of her childhood had been situated.

This barren patch of stones always rose up distinctly in Magnhild's mind when she thought of her own life, whose long desert wastes seemed to lay stretched out before her like just such a heap of ruins. Here it faced her once more. It was some time before the consolation she had newly grasped could find expression, for she was haunted by so much that was unsolved, so much that was doubtful. She was now approaching the starting-point of the whole; from the brow of the hill the parsonage was visible.

It had been agreed that they should stop here. The carriage rolled down toward the friendly gard through an avenue of birch-trees. Rönnaug was giving Miss Roland a most humorous description of the family at the parsonage when suddenly they were all terrified by having the carriage nearly upset. Just by the turn near the house-steps the coachman had driven against a large stone which lay with its lower side protruding into the road. Both Rönnaug and Miss Roland uttered a little shriek, but when they escaped without an accident they laughed. To their delight Magnhild joined in their laughter. Trifling as had been the occurrence, it had served to rouse her. She was surprised to find herself at the parsonage. And this stone? Ah, how many hundred vehicles had not driven over it! Would it ever be removed, though? There stood old Andreas, old Sören, old Knut? There, too, was old Ane, looking out! From the sitting-room came the sound of a dog's bark.

"Have they a dog?" asked Magnhild.

"If they have," replied Rönnaug, "I will venture to say it came through its own enterprise."

Old Ane took the luggage, Rönnaug the child, and the whole party was ushered through the passage into the sitting-room, where no one was found except the dog. He was a great shaggy fellow, who at the first kind word relinquished his wrath, and in a leisurely way went from one to the other, snuffing and wagging his tail, then sauntering back to the stove, lay down, fat and comfortable.

A creaking and a grating could now be heard overhead; the priest was rising from the sofa. How well Magnhild knew the music of those springs! The dog knew it too, and started up, ready to follow his master. But the latter, who was soon heard on the groaning wooden stairs, did not go out but came into the sitting-room, so the dog only greeted him, and wagging his tail went back to the stove, where he rolled over with a sigh after his excessive exertion.

The priest was unchanged in every possible particular. He had heard about Rönnaug, and was glad to see her; his plump hands closed with a long friendly clasp about hers and with a still longer one about Magnhild's. He greeted Miss Roland and played with the child, who was in high glee over the unfamiliar objects in the room, especially the dog.

And when he had lighted his pipe and had seated the others and himself on the embroidered chairs and sofas, the first thing he must tell them (for it was just about a month since the matter had been successfully terminated) was that the "little girls" were provided for. There had been secured for each an annuity. It was really on the most astonishingly favorable terms. God in his inconceivable mercy had been so good to them. About the "Fröken" (so the former governess was usually called), they had had greater cause for anxiety. They had, indeed, thought of doing something for her, too, although their means would scarcely have sufficed to make adequate provision for her, and she had grown too unwieldy to support herself. But God in his inscrutable mercy had not forgotten her. She no longer needed an annuity. She had gone to make a visit at the house of a relative not many miles distant, and while there God had called her to Himself; the journey had been too much for her. This intelligence had reached the parsonage a few days before, and the priest was in great uncertainty as to whether a bridal couple would postpone their wedding for a few days.

"Thus it is, dear Magnhild, in life's vicissitudes," said he. "The one is summoned to the grave, the other to the marriage feast. Ah, yes! But what a pretty dress you have on, my child! Skarlie is truly a good husband to you. This cannot be denied."

The mistress of the house and her two daughters at length appeared. The moistened hair, the clean linen, the freshly ironed dresses, betokened newly-made toilets. They had not a word to say; the priest took charge of the conversation, they merely courtesied as they shook hands, and then, taking up their embroidery, sat down each on her own embroidered chair. One of the daughters, however, soon rose and whispered something to her mother; from the direction in which first her eyes then her mother's wandered, it might be concluded that she had asked whether the gauze covers should be removed from the mirror, the pictures, and the few plaster figures in the room. As the girl at once took her seat again, it must have been decided that the covers should not be removed.

"Tell me about the Fröken who is dead," said Magnhild.

With one accord the three ladies dropped their embroidery and raised their heads.

"She died of apoplexy," said the priest's wife.

They all sat motionless for a moment, and then the ladies continued their embroidery.

The priest rose to let the dog out. The animal departed with the appearance of being excessively abashed, for which the priest gave him much praise. Then followed a lengthy account of the dog's virtues. He had come to them three years ago, the Lord alone knew from where, and He alone knew why the dog had come to the parsonage; for the very next summer the animal had saved the "Fröken's" life when she was attacked on her accustomed walk to the church by Ole Björgan's mad bull.

The third great event, that old Andreas had cut his foot, was next detailed at quite as great length. The priest was just telling what old Andreas had said when he, the priest, was helping him to the couch, when the narrative was interrupted by an humble scratching at the door; it came, of course, from the dog. The corpulent priest rose forthwith to admit the animal, and bestowed on him kind words of admonition, which were accepted with a timid wagging of the tail.

The dog glanced round the room; observing that the eyes of the priest's wife manifestly rested with especial friendliness on him, he walked up to her, and licked the hand extended to him.

At this moment Magnhild rose, and abruptly crossing the floor to where the priest's wife sat, she stroked her hair. She felt that every one was watching her, and that the mistress of the house herself was looking up in embarrassed surprise,—and Magnhild was now powerless to explain what she had done. She hastened from the room. Profound silence reigned among those left behind.

What was it? What had happened? It was *this*: in the forenoon Magnhild had received a letter, as we know, and it had caused her to look with new eyes on the life at the parsonage.

The tedium seemed uplifted, and behind it she beheld a kindness and an innocence she had always overlooked. And she began to understand the character of that home.

There was not a word in the priest's narratives, from beginning to end, designed to call attention to the good he or any of his household had done. The listener was left to find this out for himself. But the dog had discovered it before Magnhild.

The dog returned thanks; had she ever done so? The thought had rushed over her with such force that it caused her to feel an irresistible impulse to express her gratitude. The universal astonishment caused by her effort to do so made her for the first time realize how unaccustomed her friends were to thanks, or indication of thanks from her, and she became frightened. This was the reason why she had left the room.

She took the road leading up toward the church, perhaps because it had just been mentioned. Her new views wholly absorbed her. Until now she had seen only the ludicrous side of the life at the parsonage. The members of the household had provoked, amused, or wearied her. But hitherto she had not been aware that what had just been praised in herself had been gained by her in this household whose influences had spread themselves protectingly over her soul, just as the embroidery was spread over the furniture in these rooms. Had all the weaknesses of the house served

Skarlie as a means to ensnare her, in this same house she had acquired the strength wherewith to resist his power until the present time.

If she had lived here without forming close relations with any one, the fault lay not alone in the monotonous routine of the house: it was due chiefly to herself, for even in the days of her life at the parsonage she had wrapped herself up in dreams. It must have required all the forbearance by which the family were characterized to bring her, notwithstanding all this, to the point she had reached. In any other family she would have been shown the door—dull, awkward, thankless as she had been.

Yes, thankless! Whom had she ever thanked? Aye, there was one—him who had done her the most harm but also the most good; for him she loved. But this could scarcely be counted.

But whom else? Not Skarlie, although he had been incessantly kind to her, even he. Not Fru Bang, and how kind she had been! Not Rönnaug; no, not Rönnaug either.

She was appalled. For the first time in her life she held true communion with herself, and she had done little else all her life than commune with herself.

Now she comprehended, although once before she had been startled by a passing thought of the kind; now for the first time she comprehended what it must have been to Rönnaug after having longed for so many years to tell her about the rich change in her own life, to show her her child, to bring her freedom and increased happiness; and then to find a person who did not even care to take the trouble to walk to the hotel, not a hundred steps distant, because, forsooth, it would necessitate her dressing herself.

She sat once more on the heights facing the ruins of the home of her parents; and she covered her face in shame.

From the thoughts to which this spot gave birth she did not escape until evening, weary in body and in soul.

When late in the evening she said good-night to Rönnaug, she threw her arm round her, and leaned her head against hers. But words refused to come; they are not easily found the first time they are sought.

CHAPTER XII.

THE next morning Rönnaug dreamed of singing; she still heard it when she awoke, and ere long she had so far collected herself as to consider whether it could really be Magnhild who was singing. This thought caused her to become wide awake and to leave her bed.

She scarcely waited to don her morning-gown before she opened a window. From the sitting-room, which was at the other end of the house, there came the sound of singing and a low piano accompaniment. The voice was pure and high; it must be Magnhild's.

Rönnaug made haste to complete her toilet and go down-stairs. She carried her boots out into the passage and put them on there lest she should awaken Miss Roland and the child. There was some one coming up the stairs. Rönnaug quickly put down her boots and stepped forward; for the head which was now displayed to her view was Grong's. What, Grong here?

He greeted Rönnaug with a keen, hasty glance, and, without a word, went into an apartment near hers.

Rönnaug sat listening to the singing while she put on her boots. It flowed so equally and calmly; unquestionably there was joy in it, but the joy was subdued—it might be called pure.

She remained still until Magnhild ended, and even then paused a little while. She finally went down-stairs. The door of the sitting-room was half open, which accounted for her having heard so distinctly. Magnhild had turned round with the piano-stool and sat talking with the two friends of her childhood, who had seats one on each side of her. She had been singing for them, it would seem.

They all rose as Rönnaug entered. Magnhild called her friend's attention to the clock. Verily, the hour hand pointed to ten. Magnhild had been up a long time—and singing.

The girls withdrew to carry coffee, eggs, etc., into the dining-room. As soon as Magnhild saw that she and Rönnaug were alone, she hastened to ask if Rönnaug knew that Grong was at the parsonage. Rönnaug told about having just met him.

"Yes," whispered Magnhild, "he is traveling in search of his son. Only think, the young man has eloped with the girl to whom he is betrothed! He is twenty years old, she about sixteen."

"So, then, the verses—?"

"Were of course by Grong's son. Grong is furious. He wanted to make a poet of his son, though!"

They both laughed.

The young man was really extraordinarily gifted, Magnhild further narrated, and for his sake his father had read extensively, besides taking long journeys with his son in Germany, France, Italy, and England. Plans had been made to give the young man an opportunity of gaining an impression of the scenery of his fatherland and of country life, but—pop!—the bird had flown.

Grong was now heard on the stairs, so nothing more was said. He gave the ladies a sharp glance as he entered, then began to pace the floor, as completely hidden by his beard as though it were a forest, and veiled by his spectacles as an image is veiled in a fountain.

They sat down to the late breakfast, and the priest's wife received them, one by one, with diffident friendliness. The priest had gone down to the school-house to attend a meeting.

After the meal was over, Grong, who had not opened his mouth for any other purpose than to eat and to drink, walked through the sitting-room and passage directly out to the door-steps. Rönnaug bravely followed; she wished to talk with him. He discovered this and made an effort to escape, but was overtaken and obliged to walk up the road with Rönnaug. When he heard what she wanted, he exclaimed:—

"I have been so confoundedly bored with this tall woman and her tiresome vocation, that you will find it impossible to get one word out of me. Besides, I am expecting my 'skyds.'"

He was about to turn away; but Rönnaug held fast to him, laughing, and brought him back to the theme. Before she had succeeded, however, in laying before him the necessary facts, he interrupted with,—

"The fact is she has no vocation whatever; that is the whole secret of the matter. Her singing? Tande so often wrote to me about her singing. Well, I have been listening to her singing this morning, and do you know what I think about it? Technical correctness, good method, pure tone, in abundance; but no fancy, no inspiration, no expression; how the deuce could there be! Had she had fancy, she would have had energy, and with her voice, her natural technical ability, she would have become a singer, whether there was a Tande or not, whether she had married a Skarlie or a Farlie."

Notwithstanding the harsh, blunt form in which this idea was framed, there might be sufficient truth in it to make it worth while to place Magnhild's history before Grong in its true light. Grong could not resist the fascination of a soul's experiences. He became all ear, forgetting both his ire and his "skyds."

He heard now about the Magnhild who would scarcely take pains to dress herself, and who let Skarlie do and say what he pleased, but who the moment Skarlie mentions Tande's name and hers together, in other words, invades her inner sanctuary, flees forthwith from him to America. Was there no energy in that?

He heard about the Magnhild who, checked in her highest aspirations, became wholly indifferent. The relations with Tande were fully explained. Grong, indeed, had been partially acquainted with them by Tande himself. Rönnaug also thought it right to inform Grong of the purport of Tande's letter; she could recall it perfectly, for it had made a deep impression on her.

What an impression did it not make on Grong!

How much it must have cost this man in his time to renounce what he had originally believed to be his vocation. And now to have to give up his hopes for his son? How could she and Magnhild have laughed at this—as they had done that same morning.

"Consolation in the idea that our calling is greater and more manifold than we ourselves are aware? Yes, for those who can blindly and without exercise of their own wills place themselves under subjection to the unknown guidance! I cannot do so!" He raised his clinched hand, but let it fall again. "Is it a crime to steer toward a definite goal, and concentrate one's will, one's responsibility upon its attainment? Look at yonder insect! It goes straight forward; it has a fixed aim. Now I crush it to death. See—thus!

"You should have seen my wife," he continued, presently. "She sped onward through life, with fluttering veil; her eyes, her thoughts sparkled. What was her goal? Just as she was beginning, with my aid, to comprehend her faculties, she expired. A meteor!

"I had a friend. What talents, and what aspirations! How handsome he was! When he was but little over twenty years of age, he fell during the siege of a Danish fortress, scarcely mentioned, scarcely remembered. A meteor!

"But what solicitude for existences which neither can nor will be of any use in the world. That fisherman in Nordland was the only person who was saved from destruction out of a whole parish. And he lived more than sixty years as stupid as the codfish he drew out of the sea.

"For the sake of others? For the advancement of one's fellow-creatures? For the good of posterity? Aye, aye, find consolation in all this, if you can! Before I shall be able to do so I must see the benefit of it for myself. The mole's life in the dark, with chance alone for its guide, is not a life that I could lead, even though I might have a certificate guaranteeing that light should dawn on me one day, that is to say, on the other side of the grave. I admire those who can be content with such a lot."

"In other words, you despise them!" interposed Rönnaug.

Grong looked at her, but made no reply.

Rönnaug was anxious to know how it was best to advise Magnhild. Grong promptly answered,—

"Advise her to go to work."

"Without definite object? Merely for the sake of work?"

He hesitated a moment, and then said,—

"I will tell you one thing, my good lady: Magnhild's misfortune has been that throughout her whole life she has had every want supplied, every meal, every garment. Had she been obliged to labor hard, or to bring up children, she would not have indulged so freely in dreams."

"So, then, work without definite aim?" repeated Rönnaug.

"There are so many kinds of aims," said Grong, peevishly,—and then he was silent. It was evident that he had been all round the circle and had returned to his wrath over what had befallen himself.

They had turned and were retracing their steps in the friendly birch avenue leading to the parsonage. The tones of a human voice were heard; they drew nearer, paused, and listened attentively. The windows were open, and every note rang out, clear and equal.

"Yes, there is purity in the voice," said Grong; "that is true. But purity is a mere passive quality."

They went on.

"Not technical skill alone, then?" queried Rönnaug.

To this Grong made no reply. He had fallen into a new train of thought. When they had reached the house, he roused himself.

"She and I are, both of us, I dare say, bearers of a half-completed family history. Nevertheless, her family dies out with her; and mine? Oh, all this is enough to drive one mad! Where is my 'skyds?'"

With these words he strode past the main building to the court-yard behind. Rönnaug slowly followed. The "skyds" had not yet arrived. Grumbling considerably, Grong sauntered up to the coach-house, whose doors stood open, and in which he saw Rönnaug's carriage. She joined him, and they discussed the carriage together. It was too light for a traveling carriage, Grong thought. One fore-wheel must already have been damaged, for it had been taken off. So, then, it depended upon the blacksmith how long the ladies would remain at the parsonage? But he would start without further delay; for there—at last—came the "skyds."

He bade her a light farewell, as though he were merely going to the next corner, and then went into the house for his luggage. Rönnaug, however, determined to wait until he came out again.

She had a kindly feeling for him. She earnestly hoped that the son's case was not so bad as the father now thought. There was so much unrest in Grong. Was not this caused by his having a great variety of "talents," but no one special talent? She had once heard Grong half jestingly make a similar assertion about another person. All these endowments, however, might be combined in one main tendency, of this Rönnaug felt sure. It might be the same in the case of Magnhild; but perhaps there was not sufficient talent there. Technical ability? Aye, if that were her chief endowment she could doubtless render it available in singing.

Rönnaug had failed to find the light she needed. This was truly discouraging; for counsel must be given, a resolution formed. She prayed God for her friend, and for this gloomy man now coming out of the house, accompanied by the priest's wife, who seemed to be the only person to whom he had said farewell.

"Present my greetings to my old teacher," he called down from the cariole, as he grasped the hand of the mistress of the house. "Tell him—tell him nothing!" and with this he whipped up his horse so suddenly that the "skyds" boy came near being left behind.

The priest's wife made some remarks about his surely being very unhappy, as she stood watching him drive away. While the ladies were still at the door, a woman came walking up the road toward them. She nodded and smiled at the mistress of the house as she passed on her way to the kitchen.

"You made your sale?"

"Yes."

"I thought so from your looks."

Then turning to Rönnaug the priest's wife said,—

"This woman, you may well believe, made Magnhild happy this morning."

"How so?"

"Why, she stopped here with her work on her way to the dealer, who makes purchases for a merchant in town. Just as she stepped inside Magnhild came down into the kitchen. When the woman caught sight of her, she eagerly addressed her—she is a great talker—and she began to cry and to talk, to talk and to cry, telling how poor she had been and how well off both she and her children now were. Magnhild, you know, for many years taught an Industrial School up in these mountains, and this woman was one of her aptest pupils. This hand-work, I can assure you, has spread rapidly here; there are scarcely any poor people to be found in our parish now."

"But Magnhild—was she glad?"

"She certainly must have been glad, for soon afterward we heard her singing. And the last time she was here—about four or five years ago—we could not persuade her to go near the piano."

Rönnaug now greeted Miss Roland, who was coming toward her with the child. A little later, as she was going through the passage to the sitting-room, the sounds of music once more floated out toward her. The priest's daughters were at the piano, singing a duet with feeble voices, one of which was more quavering than the other. They were drawling out,—

"All rests in God's paternal hand."

The door stood open. One of the girls sat at the piano, the other stood at its side. Magnhild sat facing them, leaning against the piano.

Peace radiated from the little hymn, because they who sang it were at peace. The small, yellow-haired heads above the stiff collars did not make a single movement, the piano almost whispered. But the sunshine, playing on the embroidered furniture and the embroidered covers, blended with the music a harmony from afar.

When they had finished singing, one of the girls told that a lady traveling that way had taught them the hymn, and the other, that her part had been arranged by the Fröken. Without uttering a word, without even changing her position, Magnhild held out her hand, which was clasped by the young lady nearest her.

At this moment voices were heard out of doors. The priest was approaching, accompanied by several men. As they stopped at the door-steps, Rönnaug entered the sitting-room. Soon a tramping of many feet was heard on the steps; the group at the piano rose, Magnhild crossed the floor to where Rönnaug stood. First the dog, then the priest, entered in solemn procession, and slowly following them came dropping in, one by one, six or seven of the farmers of the little mountain parish, heavy, toil-worn men, all of them. Magnhild pressed close up to Rönnaug, who also drew back a little, so that they two stood in front of the gauze-covered mirror. The priest said good-morning, first to Mrs. Randon, then to Magnhild, and asked how they were. Then the men went round the room, one by one, and shook hands with every one present.

"Call mother," said the priest to one of his daughters, and cleared his throat.

The mistress of the house soon appeared, and again man after man stepped forward, shook hands, and returned to his place. The priest wiped his face, stationed himself in front of the frightened Magnhild, bowed, and said:—

"Dear Magnhild, there is no cause for alarm! The representatives of our little parish chanced to assemble to-day in the school-house, and as I happened to mention that you were making a journey and had stopped at the parsonage on your way, some one said: 'It is due to her exertions that the poor-rates of this parish are so small.' Several others expressed the same sentiments. And then I told them that this should be said to your face; they all agreed with me. I do not suppose thanks have ever been offered to you, my dear child, either here or down at the Point, where the results of your work are even greater than here and have spread to the parishes on both sides of the fjord.

"Dear child, God's ways are inscrutable. As long as we can discern them in our own little destinies we are happy, but when we fail to see them we become very unhappy." (Here Magnhild burst into tears.)

"When you were carried downward by the landslide, with your sled in your little hand, you were saved in order that you might become a blessing to many.

"Do not scorn the gratitude of this humble parish: it is a prayer for you to the Almighty. You know what He has said: 'Inasmuch as ye have done it unto one of the least of these my brethren, ye have done it unto me.' May you realize this!"

The priest now turned toward his wife, and in the same solemn tone said,—

"Have refreshments handed to these men!"

He strode round among the latter with playful remarks, but the whole house seemed to shake beneath his tread. The more deeply Magnhild seemed moved the happier the priest was.

Magnhild felt a strong impulse to say something to him; for had she not found a refuge in his house, none of the results for which she had just received such unmerited thanks would have been accomplished. But the priest's impetuosity restrained her.

Refreshments were handed round; then the men once more shook hands with every one and withdrew, led by the priest, whose voice could be heard almost all the way to the school-house.

CHAPTER XIII.

IN the afternoon the mail from the Point arrived, bringing a letter for Magnhild. She was alarmed, and handed the letter to Rönnaug, who soon returned it to her, with the information that she need not be afraid to read it herself.

"You will see by this what your journey has already brought about," Rönnaug added.

The letter was from tall Louise.

DEAR MAGNHILD,—I was obliged to go up to your house to-day to ask for the pattern you had promised to explain to us. But I found only Skarlie at home, and he was not exactly—ah! what shall I call it? for I have never before seen so unhappy a person. He said you had gone on a journey.

I heard later that you were traveling with Mrs. Randon, and thinking it most likely that you are at the parsonage in the mountains I address you there. For you must not leave us, Magnhild, or if you do go away, you must come back to us again!

We have all of us plainly seen that you were unhappy; but as you said nothing, we did not like to say anything either. But can you not stay with *us*?

How shall we make progress with the new work which has just been introduced? We cannot understand it without some one to explain it to us. And there is the singing, too! Dear Magnhild, so many people thank me and Marie; she and I take the lead now, it is true, but we all know to whom we owe our excellent means of support, the good times we have together, and our opportunities for helping one another. Now that you have left us it seems very dreadful to think that we never did anything to give you pleasure, and that you do not really know us.

I can assure you we could do much for you in return for your kindness to us if you would only let us. Do not leave us! Or if you must, come back to us when your journey is over!

Your devoted, heartily grateful
LOUISE.

There was added to the letter an extremely neat postscript from Marie.

I was so grieved when Louise told me you had gone. She has more energy than I, poor hunchback. She has written and said what we all, yes, all of us, think of the matter.

But I have the *greatest* cause to write to you. What in the world would have become of me if you had not come to the school and made me skillful in work that is just suited to me. Without you I should have been a burden to others, or at least I should never have learned to take pleasure in work. Now I feel that I am engaged in something which is continually growing. Yes, now I am happy.

I have told you this at last. How often have I wished to open my heart to you, yet did not quite dare, because you were so reserved!

What delightful times we might have had together! But can we not have them yet?
Your
MARIE.

Postscript.—You may think I mean that you took no interest in us. No: I did not mean that. You were too patient with us for me to have any such thought. But it seemed as if you were indifferent to everything about you, people as well as all else; that is what I had in mind.

Cannot you, as Louise says, come to us? We will gather about you, as bees about their queen, dear Magnhild.

There is no better way to express what now happened to Magnhild, than to say that a new life-spring welled up within her. This help from what she had never thought of as anything but a pastime and a monotonous routine worked wonders. She felt that she must endeavor to deserve this devotion; she knew now what it was her duty to do.

She was walking and talking with Rönnaug in the court-yard. Evening was drawing nigh; the fowls had already sought shelter and were settling themselves cackling on the roost; the cows were being driven home from the pasture, and slowly passed by. The perfume of hay was wafted toward the ladies, ever and anon, for loads were being hauled into the barn.

Rönnaug was so sure of what she was doing that she did not hesitate to tell Magnhild what the same mail had brought her: it was a newspaper containing a telegram from Munich announcing the death of Tande. These tidings produced no further effect upon Magnhild than to make both her and Rönnaug pause for an instant and then walk on in silence. Tande had always been thought of as one very far away, and now he seemed nearer. What he had recently sent her for her guidance became more profoundly true than ever.

The first words she uttered were not about Tande but about Skarlie. Perhaps it would be best to send for him that they might have an explanation before she started on her journey. Rönnaug was not disinclined to agree to this; but she thought that she, not Magnhild, should attend to the explanation. In fact, there was nothing to say except to announce what Magnhild had resolved upon doing.

The conversation was spasmodic like their walk. All the people of the house were out making hay. Miss Roland and the child had also gone to the field. Magnhild and Rönnaug were about going there themselves when a boy came walking into the yard whistling, with his hands in his pockets. Seeing the ladies he stood still and stopped whistling. Then he took a stand on his right foot; the left heel he planted in the ground, and moved his leg in such a way that the sole of the foot stood erect and fanned the air.

Presently he drew nearer.

"Is it you they call Magnhild?" he asked, in the ringing dialect of the parish.

He addressed the question to the right one, who replied in the affirmative.

"I was sent to ask you to come down to our place, Synstevold; for there is a fellow there waiting to see you."

"What is his name?" asked Rönnaug.

"I was told not to tell," said the boy, as he planted his left heel in the ground again, fanned the air with his foot, and stared at the barn.

Rönnaug broke into the dialect as she asked whether the "fellow" was not lame.

"That is very possible," answered the boy, with a grin, and an oath.

Here Rönnaug ran to meet old Andreas who was just coming out of the barn with an empty hay wagon to go after another load; the rumbling of the wheels prevented him from hearing her call; but she overtook him.

"Was it you who took one of the fore-wheels from my carriage?" asked she.

"Fore-wheel of the carriage," repeated old Andreas. "Is it off? Stand still, you fool there?" he cried, giving the reins such a jerk that one of the horses started to move backward instead of forward, for it was a young horse.

But in the mean time Rönnaug had gained light on the question, and left Andreas. In slow English she told Magnhild what she believed she had discovered; she did not want the boy who was standing by to understand. Andreas drove on.

Magnhild laughed: "Yes, Skarlie has come. It is undoubtedly he!" and turning to the boy she said that she would accompany him at once.

Rönnaug tried to persuade Magnhild to remain where she was and let *her* go. No, Magnhild preferred to go herself. She was already on her way when Rönnaug called after her that she would soon follow herself to see how things were going. Magnhild looked back with a smile, and said,—

"You may if you like!"

So after a time Rönnaug set forth for Synstevold. She knew very well that Skarlie could offer nothing that would tempt Magnhild, but he might be annoying, perhaps rough. The fore-wheel was a warning.

There was perhaps no one to whom Skarlie was so repulsive as to Rönnaug. She knew him well. No one besides Rönnaug could surmise how he had striven, dastard as he was, to taint the purity of Magnhild's imagination, to deaden her high sense of honor. Magnhild's frequent blushes had their history.

What was it that so bound him to her? At the outset, of course, the hope that failed. But since then? The evening before, when the conversation had turned on the Catholic cloisters, the priest had remarked that Skarlie—who was a man that had traveled and thought considerably—had said that in the cloisters the monks prayed night and day to make amends for the neglected prayers of the rest of the people. That was the reason why people were willing to give their money so freely to the cloisters: it was like making a cash payment on the debt of sin.

Rönnaug had sat and pondered. Had not Skarlie hereby explained his own relations with Magnhild? It was his way of making payments on his debt of sin.

And so, of course, he grudged giving her up.

Had he but been harsh and impatient, Magnhild would immediately have left him. That was just the misfortune; he was a coward, and he could not bear to renounce her. He was very humble whenever he failed in his attempts to win her, and when he had been especially malicious he forthwith made amends by being as friendly and interesting as possible. And this was what had kept the ball rolling.

Amid these and similar reflections, Rönnaug took the way across the fields in order not to be seen from the place. The grass where she walked had not been mown; she trampled it mercilessly under foot, but she paused before a patch of flowers whose varied hues and leaves she could not help contemplating. Suddenly she heard voices. In front of her there were several willow copses through whose branches she espied the pair she was seeking.

There sat Skarlie and Magnhild in the grass, he in his shirt-sleeves and without a hat.

Half-frightened for Magnhild and utterly without respect for *him*, Rönnaug immediately stood guard. Concealing herself from view she took her post between two copses. Skarlie and Magnhild could be seen quite distinctly, for the space behind them was open.

"Then I shall certainly close up down at the Point, and I will follow you."

"You may if you choose. But spare me further threats. For the last time: I have resolved to go. I wish to travel in order to see and to learn. Some day I hope to return and teach others."

"Do you intend to come back to me?"

"That I do not know."

"Oh, you do know very well."

"Perhaps I do, for if you should lead a better life I presume I would come back to you; but I do not believe you capable of changing, and so I might just as well say at once that I shall not return to you."

"You do not know all I mean to do for you."

"What, your last will and testament again? Suppose we drop this subject now."

She sat twirling a flower, upon which she was intently gazing. Skarlie had placed his shorter leg under him; his face was all puckered up and his eyes stung.

"You have never appreciated me."

"No—that is true. I have much to thank you for which I have taken without thanks. Please God, I shall one day show my gratitude."

"Cannot we make it right now? What is it you want? To travel? We can travel; we have means enough."

"As I said before, let us drop this subject now."

He sighed, and taking up his cutty, he laid his forefinger over it. It was already filled; he produced a match-box.

"If you can smoke there is hope for you," said Magnhild.

"Oh! I am not smoking; it is nothing but habit,"—he drew a long sigh. "No, Magnhild, it is impossible for things to go well with me if you leave me. For that is about equal to closing up my house and driving me out into the world. The gossip of the people would be more than I could bear."

He looked now positively unhappy. Magnhild plucked several flowers; but if he expected an answer from her it was in vain.

"It is hard for those who have strong natures," said he; "the devil gains the upper-hand over them in many ways. I thought *you* would have helped me. One thing I must say: if we two could have had a right cozy home together, and a child"—

But here she sprang up quickly, and the flowers fell from her lap.

"Let us have no more of this! He who means to do right does not begin as you did. But in spite of the beginning you might perhaps still have—Yet how did you act? I say: let us have no more of this!"

She moved away a few paces and came back again with: "No, I was not to blame when I gave myself to you, for you promised that I should do and live precisely as I pleased. And I was such an inexperienced child that I did not in the least understand how you were outwitting me. But I did wrong when I heard how matters really were and did not at once leave you. Also when I failed to do so later. However, this is connected with many things about which we will not talk at present. All we can do now is to make amends, as far as we can, for the past. Give me up, and try to do your duty toward others."

"What do you mean by that?" His eyes blinked and his face grew sharp.

"I mean that you have outwitted others, so I have heard, for your own selfish ends. Try to make amends for your evil deeds, if you really desire improvement."

"That is not true. If it was, it is nothing to you."

"Alas! alas! There is little hope of improvement, I fear, in this as in other things. Aye, then, farewell! It shall be as I have said."

He looked up and distorted his face to a grin, making the eyes almost wholly disappear beneath the bushy brows.

"You cannot leave here without my consent."

"Oh!"

"Moreover, have you considered what you are doing? Are you right in the eyes of God?"

"You know very well what I think upon *this* subject."

"Pshaw! If you mean that talk about unholy marriages, it is sheer nonsense. There is not a word in the Bible about it. I have looked."

She stroked the hair from her brow. "Then it is written here," said she, and turned to go.

Skarlie began to get up. He was very angry.

Rönnaug felt the necessity of making haste, for now she was in danger of being seen.

Suddenly the three stood face to face.

Rönnaug went right up to Skarlie, in the sweetest, most amiable manner, heartily shook his hand, and said in English that she was delighted to see him, he had often been so extremely kind to her. Then she began to jest; she was at once insinuating and daring. Skarlie could not help laughing and offering some remarks, also in English; then Rönnaug said something witty to which Skarlie could retaliate; soon they were both laughing heartily. The impression made on him by this handsome, finely developed woman, transported him, as it were, before he was aware, to other scenes and spread a new train of thoughts over his spirit. The jesting became livelier. English alone was spoken, which particularly pleased Skarlie; and it put him in a good humor, too, tohave a chance of displaying his ready wit, of which he possessed an abundance. Finally, Rönnaug held him completely bound by the spell of her witchery, and thus made no unalloyed good impression on Magnhild, who was alarmed at this display of the powers Rönnaug had at her command. She wound her spell about him, with her look, her words, her challenging figure; but her eyes flashed fire, while she was laughing: she would have liked, above all things, to give him a good box on the ear! Women become wonderfully united when they have occasion to defend or avenge one another.

Amid the stream of conversation she gradually led the limping Skarlie round the willow copse, and when they stood on the other side she turned toward the copse which had concealed her while she was eavesdropping. Thrusting aside some of the branches, she asked Skarlie, with a laugh, if he would not be "gallant enough" to aid them in rolling home the wheel that lay concealed here. He could not possibly allow the ladies to do it alone, she said.

Skarlie heartily joined in her laughter, but showed no readiness to give her any assistance. He was in his shirt sleeves, he said; he must go after his coat if he was to accompany them to the parsonage.

Rönnaug assured him that his coat could be sent after him, and that he would find it far easier to roll the wheel without it. She went to work to raise the wheel unaided, shouting "Ahoy!" No sooner had she, with great effort, succeeded in getting it up, than it fell over again.

"It requires two to do this!" said she.

She once more stooped to take hold of the wheel, and while bending over it flashed her roguish eyes on Skarlie. His were irresistibly attracted to her face and superb form. The wheel was raised. Rönnaug and Skarlie rolled it forward between them, she skipping along on one side, he limping on the other, amid merry words and much laughter. Magnhild slowly followed. Rönnaug cast back a look at her, over the top of Skarlie's bald head; it sparkled with mirth and victory. But ere it was withdrawn, its fire was scorching enough to have left two deeply seared brown stripes on his neck and shoulders.

The distance was not very short. Skarlie groaned. Soon Rönnaug felt great drops of sweat rolling down from his face upon her hands. All the more swiftly did she roll. His sentences became words, his words syllables; he made a vigorous effort to conceal his exhaustion with a laugh. At last he could neither roll himself nor the wheel; he dropped down on the grass, red as a cluster of rowan berries, his eyes fixed in their sockets, his mouth wide open. He gasped to recover his breath and his senses.

Rönnaug called to old Andreas, who at this moment appeared on the road with a load of hay, to come and take the wheel. Then she drew her arm through Magnhild's, bowed and thanked Skarlie—still in English—"many thousand times for his admirable assistance." Now they could start the next morning early—and so, "farewell!"

From the road they looked back. The attitude of Andreas indicated that he was asking Skarlie how the wheel had come there. Skarlie made a wrathful movement of the hand, as though he would like to sweep away both the wheel and Andreas; or perhaps he was consigning them to a place where the inhabitants of Norway are very apt to consign their least highly-prized friends. The ladies now saw him turn his face toward them; Rönnaug promptly waved her handkerchief and cried back to him, "Farewell!" The word was echoed through the evening air.

The two friends had not proceeded many steps before Rönnaug paused to give vent to the residue of her wrath. She poured out a stream of words, in a half whisper. Magnhild could only distinguish a few of these words, but those she did make out were from the vocabulary of the old days of service on the road; they compared with Rönnaug's present vocabulary as the hippopotamus compares with the fly.

Magnhild recoiled from her. Rönnaug stared wildly at Magnhild, then composed herself and said in English, "You are right!" but immediately gave way to a new outburst of wrath and horror; for she was so forcibly reminded of the time when she herself crept along as best she could down among the slimy dwellers of the human abyss where darkness reigns, and where such as he down on yonder hill sat on the brink and fished. She thrust her hand into her pocket to draw forth Charles Randon's last letter, which she always carried about her until the next one came; she pressed it to her lips and burst into tears. Her emotion was so violent that she was forced to sit down.

It was the first time Magnhild had ever seen Rönnaug weep. Even upon the deck of the vessel on which she had set sail for America she had not wept. Oh, no, quite the contrary!

CHAPTER XIV.

THEY remained at the parsonage several days, for when it was announced that Magnhild was going with Rönnaug to America the good people were so startled that it was thought best to grant them time to become accustomed to the idea. Magnhild wished for her own sake, too, to pass a little time with them.

One day the ladies were all taking a walk along the road. Rönnaug and Miss Roland had little Harry between them, so they made but slow progress. From sheer solicitude for the child they all went quite out of the way of a large carriage which was overtaking them.

"Magnhild!" was called from the carriage, at the moment those walking had fully turned their faces toward it.

Magnhild looked up; a lady in black was smiling at her. Magnhild sprang directly toward her; the coachman stopped his horses. It was Fru Bang.

The lady drew Magnhild up to her and kissed her. A stout military man by the lady's side bowed.

The lady was thin. She wore a mourning suit of the latest style. Jet beads, strewed all over the costume, sparkled with every movement; from the jaunty hat, with waving plume, flowed a black veil which was wound about the neck. As from out the depths of night she gazed, with her glowing eyes, which acquired, in this setting, an especially fascinating radiance. Melancholy resignation seemed to command, as it were, the countenance, to hold sway over every nerve, to control the smile about the mouth, to languish in these eyes.

"Yes, I am changed," said she, languidly.

Magnhild turned from the lady to the stout officer. The lady's eyes followed.

"Do you not recognize Bang? Or did you not see him?"

His size had increased tenfold, the flesh resembling heavy layers of padding; he occupied at least two thirds of the carriage, crowding his wife, for one shoulder and arm covered hers. He looked good-natured and quite contented. But when one looked from his plump, heavy face and body back to the lady, she appeared spiritualized—aye, to the very finger-tips of the hand from which she was now drawing the glove.

Steadfastly following Magnhild's eyes, she stroked back from Magnhild's brow a lock of hair which had crept forward, and then let her hand pass slowly, softly over her cheek.

"You are in mourning?" asked Magnhild.

"The whole land should be in mourning, my child!" And after a pause, came a whispered, "He is dead!"

"You must remember that there is no time to lose if we would reach the steamer," said Bang.

The lady did not look up at her husband's words; she was busy with the lock she had just stroked back. Bang gave the coachman a sign, the carriage was set in motion.

"I am going to America," whispered Magnhild, as she descended from the carriage step.

The lady gazed after her a moment, then she seemed to grasp in its full extent what it implied that Skarlie's wife was going far, far away—what suppositions might be therewith connected and what consequences. For her face resumed somewhat of its old brightness, her frame regained its elasticity: at once she was on her feet, had turned completely round, and was waving her handkerchief. With what charming grace she did it!

Her husband would not permit the carriage to halt again. He contented himself with following his wife's example by waving one hand. The movement must have been accompanied by an admonition to sit down, for the lady disappeared forthwith.

The plume in her hat waved over his shoulder. More could not be seen; she must have let herself glide back into her place.

DUST.

CHAPTER I.

THE drive from the town to Skogstad, the large gard belonging to the Atlung family, with its manufacturing establishment on the margin of the woodland stream, at the usual steady pace, might possibly occupy two hours; but in the fine sleighing we had been having it could scarcely take an hour and a half. The road was a chaussée running along the fjord. All the way from town I had the fjord on the right-hand side, and on the left broad fields, gently sloping down from the heights and dotted with villas and gards, surrounded by hedges of trees and having avenues leading to them.

Farther on, the heights became mountains, and rose more abruptly from the shore; here, too, they became more and more rugged, and at last had no other growth than the pine forest, from the uppermost ridge all the way down to the fjord, forest, forest, far as the eye could reach. This belonged to Skogstad; the factory on the Skogstad River prepared the raw material.

The Atlungs were of French descent, having settled here in the times of the Huguenots, and were people of plain origin who had bettered their condition by marrying into the once wealthy and influential Atlung family, taking its name, which sounded not unlike their own.

I thoroughly enjoyed the drive. It had recently been snowing, and the snow still lay on the trees; not a breath of wind had left its traces in the wood. On the other hand, it had been thawing a little, which the deciduous trees that here began to press forward farther down toward the road could not tolerate; the sole covering they wore was the new-fallen snow of the morning.

Between both the white landscape and the snow-laden air, the fjord appeared black. It was not far to the opposite side, and there still loftier mountains loomed up, now also white, but of that subdued tint imparted by the atmosphere.

Where I was driving the sea lay close up to the edge of the snow, only a few sea-weeds, some pebbles, and in some places not so much as these, separated the two forms and hues of the same element—reality and poetry, where the poetry is just as real as the reality, simply not so enduring.

As soon as I had advanced as far as the forest, this attracted my undivided attention. The fir-trees held great armfuls of snow; in some places it had been showered around; nevertheless there was still so much uncovered that a shimmer of dark green overspread the whiteness of the entire forest. On a nearer view it could be seen that the single uncovered branches were thrust forth, as it were, defiantly, and that the red-tinted lower boughs had pierced the snow-drifts.

Higher up mighty trunks were visible, most of them dark, although some of the younger ones were brighter: taken all together an assemblage of well-laden giants, and this gave an air of solemnity to the thicket. The foremost trees, which were low enough not to impede the view, and which while growing had been disfigured either by man or beast, perhaps too by the storms (for they had borne the brunt of these), had not the regular shapes of the others; they were more gnarled, affording the snow an opportunity to commit what ravages it chose among them. Their lowest branches were in some places quite bowed to the ground, often making the tree appear like an unbroken mass of white; others were fantastically transformed into clumsy dwarfs, with only upper parts to their bodies, or into sundry human forms, each with a white sack drawn over the head, or a shirt that was not put on right.

Alongside of these awkward figures I noticed small clusters of deciduous trees, over which but the faintest suspicion of snow was spread; a single one, which stood apart from the rest, looked as though its outmost white branches, as they grew finer and finer, gradually flowed into the air; then there were young spruce trees which formed pyramid upon pyramid of regular layers of snow. Close down by the sea, where there were more stones, might now and then be seen a bramble bush. The snow had spread itself on every thorn, so that the bush looked as if it were strewed over with white berries.

I rounded a naze with a crag upon it, and here is where Skogstad proper begins. The ridge recedes and is broken by the river. Again we see gently sloping fields, and here lies the gard. The river flows farther away; the red roof and a row of buildings alongside become visible. On either side of the gard lie the housemen's places with their surrounding grounds, but they are separated from the gard by fields on the one side and by a wood or park on the other.

At the sight of the park I forgot all that had gone before. Originally it was intended to slope down to the sea; but the stony ground had evidently rendered this impossible, and so the trees on the lower square had been felled; but in the course of years, instead of pine woods a vigorous growth of deciduous trees had shot up. These, being of the same year's growth, were of an equal height, and extended all the way up to the venerable pine trees in the park. The effect of the delicate encircling the ponderous, the light opposed to the heavy, the low and perpetually level at the foot of the upward-soaring and powerful, was very fine.

The eye reveled in this, searching for forms; I would combine a hundred branches in one survey, because they ran parallel in the same curve, at about the same height; or I would single out one solitary bough from the rest and follow it from its first ramification through the branches of its branches to the most delicate twig,—a distended, transparent white wing, or a monstrous fern leaf strewed all over with white down. Then I was compelled once more to cease following the forms and turn to the colors; the unequal coating presented an infinite variety.

I turned my back on my traveling companion, the fjord, and wound my way up to the gard. Where the park ended, the garden began, and the road followed this in a gradual ascent. Once there had been a wood here also, and the road had passed through it; but of the wood there was left but a few yards, on either side, thus forming the avenue. Large, old trees were about being replaced by young ones, whose growth was so dense that in some places I could not see the gard I was driving toward. But the snow-romance followed, decking the sinking giants with white flags, powdering the young and fresh ones, and playing Christmas masquerade with the deformed ones.

CHAPTER II.

THE impressions of nature play their part in our anticipations of what we are about to meet. What was there so white and refined in the experience that awaited me here?

She was not clad in white, to be sure, the last time I saw her, the bright attractive being whom I was now to meet again. On her wedding journey, and in Dresden, some nine years previous to this time, we had last been together. True, she was dressed in gala attire every day—a whim of the young bridegroom, in his blissful intoxication; but most frequently she wore blue, not once did she appear in white; nor would it have been becoming to her.

I remember them especially as they sang at the piano, he sitting, because he was playing the accompaniment, she standing and usually with her hand on his shoulder; but what they sang was indeed white, at least it was always of the character of a more or less jubilant anthem. She was the daughter of a sectarian priest, and they had just come from the parsonage and from the wedding feast. Since then I had heard of them from time to time at the parsonage, and from that source I had received repeatedly renewed urgent entreaties to visit them the next time I was in their vicinity. I was now on my way to them.

I had heard the dwelling-house spoken of as one of the largest frame buildings in Norway. It was gray and immensely long. No Atlung had ever been satisfied with what his predecessor had built, and so the house had had an addition made to it by every generation and a partial remodeling of the old portions, so far as it was necessary to make these correspond with the new. I had heard that many and long passages (concerning which at festal gatherings rhymes without end were said to have been made) endeavor to unite the interior in the same successful or unsuccessful manner as the out-buildings, sloping roof, balconies, and verandas attempt to keep up the style of the exterior. I have heard how many rooms there are in the house, but I have forgotten it.

The last addition was made by the present owner, and is in a sort of modernized gothic style.

Behind the dwelling the other buildings of the gard form a crescent, which, however, protrudes in rather an unsightly manner on one side. Between these and the dwelling I now drove in order to alight, according to the post-boy's advice, at a porch in the gothic wing. I did not see a living being about the gard, not even a dog. I waited a little but in vain, then walked through the porch into a passage, where I took off my wraps, and then passed on into a large bright front room to the right. Neither did I see any one here; but I heard either two children's voices and a woman's voice, or two female voices and one child's voice, and I recognized the song, for it was one that was just then floating about the country, the lament of a little girl that she was everywhere in the way except in heaven with God, who was so glad to have unhappy children with Him. It sounded rather strange to hear such a lament in this bright, lively room, filled with guns and other sporting implements, reindeer horns, fox skins, lynx skins, and similar substantial objects, arranged with the most exquisite taste.

I knocked at the door and entered one of the most charming sitting-rooms I have seen in this country, so bright its outlook on the fjord, so large it was, so elegant. The brightly polished wooden panels of the wall were relieved by carved wooden brackets, each bearing a bust or a small statue; the stylish furniture was in every direction gracefully distributed about on the Brussels carpet. Moody and Sankey's dreamy melody flowed out over this like a white or yellow sheet. This hymn belongs to a collection of Christian songs which are among the most beautiful that I know; but it made the same impression here as if beneath this modern room there was a crypt from the Middle Ages where immured nuns were taking part in ceremonies for the dead, amidst smoking lamps, and whence incense and low chanting, inseparably blended, stole up into the bright conceptions and cheerful art of the nineteenth century.

The singing proceeded from one woman and two boys, the elder of the latter seven years old or a little more, and the younger about six. The woman turned her face toward the door, and paused quite astonished at my entrance; the boys were gazing out of the window, and did not look at her; they were wholly absorbed in their singing, and therefore they continued a while after she had ceased.

Of these two boys the one resembled the father's family, the other the mother's; only the mother's eyes had been bestowed on them both. The elder of the boys had a long face, with high brow and sandy hair, and he was freckled like his father. The younger one had his mother's figure, and stooped slightly because the head was set forward on the shoulders. But in consequence of this his head was usually thrown somewhat backward in order to recover its equilibrium. The result of this again was that the lips were habitually parted, and then the large, questioning eyes and the bright curly hair encircling the fine arched brow were exactly like the mother's. The elder one was tall and thin, and had his father's lounging gait and small, outward turned feet. I observed all this at a glance, while the boys walked across the room to the table by the sofa, as their companion left them. She had advanced, after a moment's hesitation, to meet me; she was evidently not sure whether she knew me or not. On hearing my name, she discovered with a smile that it was only my portrait she had seen, the portrait in the album, a souvenir of the wedding journey of the heads of the house. She informed me that Atlung was at the factories, and would be home to dinner, that is to say in about an hour, and that the mistress of the house was at one of the housemen's places I had seen from the road; it seemed that there was an old man lying at the point of death there.

She made this announcement in a melodious, although rather feeble voice, and with a pair of searching eyes fastened on me. She had heard something about me. I had never thought that I should see one of Carlo Dolci's madonnas step down from a frame to stand in a modern sitting-room and talk with me, and therefore my eyes were certainly not less searching than hers. The way the head was poised on the shoulders, its inclination to one side, the profile of the face, and beyond all else the eyes and the eyebrows, indeed, the bluish green head kerchief, which was drawn far forward, imparting to the pale face something of its own hue—altogether a genuine Carlo Dolci!

She walked noiselessly away, and left me alone with the boys, whom I at once attacked. The elder one was named Anton, and he could walk on his hands, at least, almost; and the younger one informed me that his name was Storm, and told me a great deal more about his brother, whom he regarded with unqualified admiration. The elder, on the other hand, assured me that his brother Storm was a very bad boy sometimes; he had recently been caught at some of his naughty tricks, and so papa had given him a flogging that same day; Stina had told papa about it. Stina was the name of her who had just left us.

After this not very diplomatic introduction to an acquaintance, they stood one on each side of me and prattled away about what at present was working in their minds, with most extraordinary force. They both now told me, the elder one taking the lead and the younger following with supplementary details, that yonder at one of the houseman's places, past which I had driven, lived Hans, little Hans; that is he *had* lived there, for the real, true little Hans was with God. He had come to the gard to play with the boys almost every day; though sometimes they too had been over at the housemen's places, which I soon perceived were to the boys the promised land of this earth. Then one evening, about a fortnight since, Hans had started to go home at dusk; it was before the snow came, and in the park, through which he had to pass, the fish pond lay spread before him so smooth and black. Hans thought he would like to slide on it and he climbed up from the path on to the pond, for the path ran right along it. But that same day there had been a hole cut in the ice for the people to fish, and they had forgotten to put a signal there, and so little Hans slid right into the hole. A child's cry of distress had reached the gard; the milkmaid had heard it, but only once, and she had not thought very much about it, for all the boys were in the habit of playing in the park. So little Hans had disappeared and no one could say where he was. Then the ice was cut away from the pond and they found him; but the boys were not allowed to see him. They had, however, been permitted to be present at the funeral with all the little boys and girls of the factory school. But Hans was not buried in the chapel where grandfather and grandmother lie; he was buried in the churchyard. Oh, what beautiful singing they had had! The school-master had sung bass with them, and the old brown horse had drawn Hans, who was in a white painted coffin that papa had bought in town, and there were garlands of flowers on it. Mamma and Stina had arranged them. All the children got cakes before they started and currant wine. And the song was the one the boys had just been singing; Stina had taught it to them. Hans had been very poor; but now he had all he wanted; he was with God; it was only the coffin that was put in the ground. What was in the coffin? Why, it was not the real Hans that was there, for Hans was quite new now. Angels had come down to the pond with everything that the new Hans was to wear, so that he did not feel cold in the pond; he was not there. All children who died went to God, and that together with a hundred thousand million very small angels. The angels were all round about us here too; but we could not see them because they were invisible, and Hans was now with them. The angels could see us, and they were so kind to us, especially to children, and they always wanted to have very unhappy little children with them; that was the reason why they took them. It is ever and ever and ever so much nicer to be with the angels than to be here. Yes, indeed, it is, for Stina said so. Stina too would rather be with the angels than here; it was only for mamma's sake that Stina did not go to them, for mamma would be so lonely without her. All angels had wings, and now Hans's father was lying ill, and he would soon be with Hans. He also would have wings and be a little angel and fly about here and wherever he himself chose—right up to the stars. For the stars were not only stars, they were as large, as large, when we got up to them, as large as the whole earth, and that was enormously large, larger than the largest mountain. And there were people on the stars, and there were many things that were not here. And that same afternoon Hans's father was to go right to God, for God was up in heaven. They would like so much to see Hans's father get his wings; but mamma would not let them go with her. And Hans's father had already become so beautiful, as he lay in his bed, that he almost looked like an angel. Mamma had said so; but they were not allowed to see him.

Stina made her appearance as they came to the last words; she bade them come with her and they obeyed.

A door stood open to the left; I could see book-shelves in the room to which it led, so that I presumed the library must be there. I felt a desire to know what the father of these boys was reading just then—provided that he read at all. The first thing I found open on the desk, by the side of letters, account-books, and factory samples, was Bain. And Bain's English friends were the first books my eyes beheld on the nearest shelves. I took out one, and saw that it had been much read. This accorded with what I had heard of Atlung.

Just then bells were heard outside. I thought it must be the mistress of the house returning, and put back the books in the same order I had found them. In so doing I disarranged some behind them (for the books stood in two rows), and I felt a desire to examine also these that were hidden from view, which took time. I did not leave the library until just as the lady was entering the front door.

CHAPTER III.

FRU Atlung was evidently glad to see me. She had a singular walk; it seemed as though she never fully bent her knees; but with this peculiar gait she advanced hastily toward me, grasped my hands with both of hers, and looked long into my eyes, until her own filled with tears. It was, of course, the wedding journey this look concerned, the most beautiful days of her life;—but the tears?

Fru corresponds to the German Frau, and means Mrs.—Translator.

Nay, unhappy she could not be. She was so thoroughly the same as she was formerly, that had she not been somewhat plumper, I could not—at all events, not at once—have detected the slightest change. The expression of her countenance was exactly the same innocent, questioning one, not the slightest suggestion of a sterner line or a change of coloring; even the hair fell in the same ringlets about the backward thrown head, and the half parted lips had the same gentle expression, were just as untouched by will, the eyes wore the same look of mild happiness, even the slightly-veiled tone of the voice had the same childlike ring as of yore.

"You look as though you had not had a single new experience since last we met," was the first remark I could not help making to her.

She looked up smiling into my face, and not a shadow contradicted my words. We took our seats, each in a chair that stood out on the carpet, near the library door; our backs were turned to the windows, and thus we faced a wall where between the busts and statues that rested on the carved wooden brackets, there hung an occasional painting on the polished panels.

I gave an account of my trip, received thanks for coming at last. I delivered greetings from her parents, of whom we talked a little. She said she had been thinking of her father to-day, she would have been so glad to have had him with her; for she had just come from a dying man, whose death-bed was the most beautiful she had ever witnessed. Meanwhile, she had assumed her favorite position, that is to say, she sat slightly bowed forward, with her head thrown back, and her eyes fixed on the upper part of the wall, or on the ceiling. As she sat thus, she pressed one finger against her open under lip, not once, but with a constant repetition of the same movement. Now and then the upper portion of her body swayed to and fro Her eyes seemed to be fixed; they did not seek my face, either when she asked a question or when she received an answer, unless something special had attracted her from her position. Even then she would promptly resume it.

"Do you believe in immortality?" she asked, as though this were the most natural question in the world, and without looking at me.

But as I was surprised, and consequently compelled to look at her, I perceived that a tear was trickling down her cheek, and that those open eyes of hers were full of tears.

I felt at once that this question was a pretext; it was her husband's belief she was thinking of. Therefore I thought I would spare her further pretexts.

"What is your husband's opinion of immortality?"

"He does not believe in the immortality of the individual," replied she; "we perpetuate ourselves in our intercourse with those about us, in our deeds, and above all in our children: but this immortality, he thinks, is sufficient."

Her eyes were fixed as before, and they were still full of tears; but her voice was mild and calm; not a trace of discontent or reproach in the simple statement, which doubtless was correct.

No, she is not one of the so-called childlike women, I thought; and if she has the same innocent, questioning expression she had nine years ago, it is not because she has been without thought or research.

"You talk, then, with Atlung about these subjects, I suppose?"

"Not now."

"In Dresden you seemed to be thoroughly united about these things; you sang together"—

"He was under father's influence then. Besides, I think he was not quite clear in his own mind at that time. The change came gradually."

"I saw some books, that are now placed behind the others."

"Yes, Albert has changed."

She sat motionless, as she gave this answer, except that her finger continued its play on the under lip.

"But who, then, attends to the education of the children?" asked I.

Now she turned half toward me. I thought for a while that she did not intend to answer but after a long time she did speak.

"No one," said she.

"No one?"

"Albert prefers to have it so for the present."

"But, my dear lady, if no one teaches them, at least one thing or another is told to them?"

"Yes, there is no objection to that; and it is usually Stina who talks with them."

"And so it is left entirely to chance?"

She had turned from me, and sat in her former attitude.

"Entirely to chance," she replied, in a tone that was almost one of indifference.

I briefly related to her what Stina had told the boys about the life beyond the grave, about angels, etc., and I inquired if she approved of this.

She turned her face toward me. "Yes; why not?" said she. Her great eyes viewed me so innocently; but as I did not answer immediately the blood slowly coursed up into her face.

"If anything of the kind is to be told to them," said she, "it must be something that will take hold of their childish imaginations."

"It confuses the reality for them, my dear lady, and *that* is the same thing as to disturb the development of their faculties."

"Make them stupid, do you mean?"

"Well, if not exactly stupid, it would at least hinder them from using their faculties rightly."

"I do not understand you."

"When you teach children that life here below is nothing to the life above, that to be visible is nothing in comparison to being invisible, that to be a human being is far inferior to being an angel, that to live is not by any means equal to being dead, *is that* the way to teach them to view life properly, or to love life, to gain courage for life, vigor for work, and patriotism?"

"Ah, in that way! Why, *that* is our duty to them later."

"Later, my dear lady? After all this dust has settled upon their souls?"

She turned away from me, assumed her old position, stared fixedly at the ceiling, and became absorbed in thought.

"Why do you use the word dust?" she began presently.

"By the word dust I mean chiefly that which has been, but which now having become disintegrated, floats about and settles in vacant places."

She remained silent a little while.

"I have read of dust which carries the poison from putrified matter. You do not mean that, I suppose?"

There was neither irony nor anger in the tone, so I failed to understand at what she was aiming.

"That depends on where the dust falls, my dear lady; in healthy human beings it only creates a cloud of mist, prejudices which prevent them from seeing clearly; if there be stagnation this dust will oftentimes collect an inch thick, until the machinery is thoroughly clogged."

She turned toward me with more vivacity than she had yet shown, and leaning on the arm of her chair brought her face nearer to mine.

"How did you happen upon this idea?" asked she. "Is it because you have seen how much dust there is in this house?"

I admitted that I had seen this.

"And yet the chambermaid and Stina do nothing else but clean away the dust, and I did nothing else either at first. I cannot understand it. At home at my mother's, there was nothing I heard so much about as dust. She was always busied about father with a damp cloth; he was constantly annoyed because she would disturb his books and papers. But she insisted that he gathered more dust than any one else. He never left his study that she was not after him with a clothes-brush. And later it came to be my turn. I was like my father, she said I accumulated dust, and I never could dust well enough to satisfy her. I was so weary of dust that when I married a Paradise seemed in prospect because I thought I should escape this annoyance and have some one to dust for me. But therein I was greatly in error. And now I have given it up. It is of no use. I evidently have no talent for getting rid of dust."

"And so it is very singular," she continued, as she sank back in her chair, "that you too should come with this talk about dust."

"I hope I have not hurt your feelings?"

"How can you think—?" and then, in the calmest, most innocent voice in the world, she added: "It would not be easy to hurt the feelings of any one who had lived nine years with Albert."

I became greatly embarrassed. What possible good could it do for me to become entangled in the affairs of this household? I did not say another word. She too sat, or rather reclined in her seat, for a long time in silence, drumming with her fingers on the arms of her chair. Finally I heard, as from far away, the words: "Butterfly dust is very beautiful, though." And then some time afterward there glided forth from the midst of a long chain of thought which she did not reveal, the query, "refracted rays—the various prismatic colors—?" She paused, listened, rose to her feet; she had heard Atlung's step in the front room.

I also rose.

CHAPTER IV.

THE door was thrown wide open, and Atlung came lounging in. This tall, slender man, in these capacious clothes that showed many a trace of the factories he had been visiting, bore in his face, his movements, his bearing, the unconcerned ease of several generations.

The gray eyes, beneath the invisible eyebrows, blinked a little when he saw me, and then the long face broadened into a smile. His superb teeth glittered between the full, short lips, as he exclaimed: "Is that you!" He took both my hands between his hard, freckled ones, then dropping one of them threw his arm around his wife's waist. "Was not *that* delightful, Amalie? What? Those days in Dresden, my dear?"

When he had relaxed his hold, he made eager inquiries about myself and my journey,—he knew I was to make a short trip abroad. Then he began to tell me what occupied *him* the most, and meanwhile he strolled up and down the room, took up one article between his fingers, handled it, then took up another. He did not hold any little thing as others do with the extreme tips of his fingers; he firmly grasped it in his hand so that his fingers closed over it. In conversation, too, it was just the same: there was a certain fullness in the way he took up each subject and flung it away again at once for something else.

His wife had left the room, but returned very soon and invited us to dinner. Just at that moment Atlung was sauntering past the piano, on which was open a new musical composition, whose character he described in a few words. Then he began to play and sing verse after verse of a long song. When he was through, his wife again reminded him of the meal. This probably first called his attention to her presence in the room.

"See here, Amalie, let us try this duet!" he cried, and struck up the accompaniment.

Looking at me with a smile, she took her place at his side and joined in the song. Her somewhat veiled, sweet soprano blended with his rich baritone, just as I had heard it nine years before. The voices of both had acquired that deeper, fuller meaning which life gives when it has meaning itself; their skill, on the other hand, was about the same as of old.

Any one who but a moment before might perhaps have found it difficult to understand how these two had come together, only needed to be near them while they sang. A lyric abandonment of feeling was common to both, and where there was any difference of sentiment they were perfectly content to waive it. They floated onward like two children in a boat, leaving the dinner behind them to grow cold, the servants to become impatient, the guest to think what he pleased, and the order of the house and their own plans for the day to be upset.

In their singing there was no energy, no school, no delicate finish of style of this simple number, which, moreover, they were doubtless singing for the first time; but there was a smooth, lazy, happy gliding over the melody. The light coloring of the voices blended together like a caress; and there was a charm in the way it was done.

They sang verse after verse, and the longer they continued the better they sang together, and the more joyously. When finally they were through and the wife, with her somewhat labored step, walked into the dining-room on my arm, and Atlung sauntered on before to give Stina the key to the wine-cellar, there was no longer any question in Fru Atlung's eyes, only joy, mild, beautiful joy, and her husband warbled like a canary bird.

We sat down to table while he was still out, we waited an interminable time for him; either he had not found Stina or she had not understood him: he had gone himself to the cellar and had returned so covered with dust and dirt that we could not help laughing. His wife, however, paused in the midst of her laughter, and sat silent while he changed his clothes and washed.

He swallowed spoonful after spoonful of the soup in greedy haste, regained his spirits when his first hunger was satisfied, and began to talk in one unbroken stream, until suddenly, while carving the roast, he inquired for the boys. They had had their dinner; they could not wait so long.

"Have you seen the boys?" he asked.

"Yes," I replied, and I spoke of their extreme artlessness, and what a strong likeness I thought one bore to his and the other to his wife's family.

"But," he interposed, "it is unfortunate that both families have comparatively too much imagination; there is an element of weakness in it, and the boys have inherited their share from both families. A very sorrowful occurrence took place here about a fortnight since. A little playfellow was drowned in the fish-pond. What the boys have made out of this—of course, with Stina's aid—is positively incredible. I was thinking about it to-day. I have not said anything, for after all it was extremely amusing, and I did not want to spoil their intercourse with Stina. But, indeed, it is most absurd. See here, Amalie, it would almost be better to send them away to school than to let them run wild in this way and get into all kinds of nonsense."

His wife made no reply.

I wanted to divert his attention, and inquired if he had read Spencer's "Essay on Education."

Then he became animated! He had just settled himself to eat, but now he forgot to do so; he took a few bites and forgot again. Indeed, I should judge we sat over this one course a whole hour, while he expatiated on Spencer. That I who had asked if he had read the book in all probability had read it myself, did not trouble him in the least. He gave me a synopsis of the book, often point after point, with his own comments. One of these was that even if as Spencer desires, pedagogics was introduced into every school, as one of its most important branches—most people would nevertheless lack the ability to bring up their own children; for teaching is a talent which but few possess. He for his part proposed to send the boys, as soon as they were old enough, to a lady whom he knew to possess this talent and who also had the indispensable knowledge. She was an enthusiastic disciple of Spencer.

He spoke as though this were a matter long since decided upon; his wife listened as though it were an old decision. I was much surprised that she had not told me of it when we were talking about the children a little while before.

I do not now remember what theme we were drifting into when Atlung suddenly looked at his watch.

"I had entirely forgotten Hartmann! I should have been in town! Yes, yes—it is not yet too late! Excuse me!"

He threw down his napkin, drank one more glass of wine, rose and left the room. His wife explained apologetically that Hartmann was his attorney; that unfortunately there was no telegraphic communication between the gard and the town, and that unquestionably there was some business that must be settled within an hour or thereabout.

It would take an hour at least to drive to town, if for nothing else than to spare the horse; at least an hour there; and then an hour and a half back, for no one would drive such a long distance equally fast back and forth with the same horse. I sat calculating this while I finished eating, and became aware at the same time that my coming was most inopportune. Therefore I resolved that after coffee I too would take my leave.

We had both finished and now rose from the table. My hostess excused herself and went out into the kitchen, and I who was thus left alone thought I would look round the gard.

When I got out on the steps in front of the porch, I was met by a burst of loud laughter from the boys, immediately followed by a word which I should not have thought they would take in their mouths, to say nothing of shouting it out with all their might, and this in the open yard. The elder boy called it out first, the younger repeated it after him.

They were standing up on the barn bridge, and the word was addressed to a girl who stood in the frame shed opposite them, bending over a sledge. The boys shouted out yet another word, and still another and another, without cessation. Between each word came peals of merriment. It was clear that they were being prompted by some one inside of the barn door. The girl made no reply; but once in a while she looked up from her work and glanced over her shoulder—not at the boys but at some one behind the barn where the carriage-shed was situated.

Then I heard the sound of bells from that direction. Atlung came forth, dressed for his trip and leading his horse. Great was the alarm of the boys when they saw their father! For they suddenly realized, though perhaps not distinctly, what they had been shouting,—at least they felt they had been making mischief for some one.

"Wait until I get home, boys," the father shrieked, "and you shall surely both have a whipping."

He took his seat in his sledge and applied the lash to his horse. As he drove past me, he looked at me and shook his head.

The boys stood for a moment as though turned into stone. Then the elder one took to his heels with all his strength. The younger followed, crying, "Wait for me! Say, Anton, do not run away from me!" He burst into tears. They disappeared behind the carriage-shed; but for a long time I heard the sobbing of the younger one.

CHAPTER V.

I FELT quite out of spirits, and determined to leave at once; but as I entered the sitting-room my hostess was seated on the large gothic settee or sofa, near the dining-room door, and no sooner did she perceive me than she leaned forward across the table in front of her and asked,—

"What do *you* think of Spencer's theory of education? Do you believe we can put it into practice?"

I did not wish to be drawn into an argument, and so merely answered,—

"Your husband's practice, at all events, does not accord with Spencer's teachings."

"My husband's practice? Why, he has none."

Here she smiled.

"You mean he takes no interest in the children?"

"Oh, he is like most other men, I suppose," she replied; "they amuse themselves with their children, now and then, and whip them occasionally, too, when anything occurs to annoy them."

"You believe that husband and wife should have equal responsibilities in such matters?"

"Yes, to be sure I do. But even in this respect men have made what division they chose."

I expressed a desire to take my leave. She appeared much astonished, and asked if I would not first drink coffee; "but, it is true," she added, "you have no one to talk with."

She is not the first married woman, I thought, who makes covert attacks on her husband.

"Fru Atlung!" I said, "you have no reason to speak so to me."

"No, I have not. You must excuse me."

It was growing dusk; but unless I was greatly in error, she was almost ready to weep.

So I took my seat on the other side of the table. "I have a feeling, dear Fru Atlung, that you desire to talk to some one; but I am surely not the right person."

"And why not?" she asked.

She sat with both elbows on the table, looking into my face.

"Well, if for no other reason, at least because such a conversation needs to be entered into more than once, because there are so many things to consider, and I am going away again to-day."

"But cannot you come again?"

"Do you wish it?"

She was silent a moment, then she said slowly: "As a rule, I have but one great wish at a time. And it was fully in keeping with the one I now have that *you* should come here."

"What is it, my dear lady?"

"Ah, that I cannot tell you, unless you will promise me to come again."

"Well, then, I will promise you to do so."

She extended her hand across the table with the words: "Thank you."

I turned on my chair toward her, and took her hand.

"What is it, my dear lady?"

"No, not now," she replied; "but when you come again. You must help me—if you believe it to be right to do so."

"Of course."

"Because you, I know, think in many particulars as Atlung does. He will listen to *you*."

"Do you think so?"

"He will not listen to me, at all events."

"Did you ever make an effort to be heard?"

"No, that would be the worst thing I could do. With Atlung everything must come as by chance."

"But, dear me! I noticed that on the whole you seemed to hold most blessed relations with each other."

"Yes, to be sure we do! We often amuse ourselves exceedingly well together."

I had a feeling that she did not wish me to look at her, and I had turned away, so that I sat with my side to the table as before. The twilight deepened about us.

"You remember us, I dare say, as we were in Dresden?"

"Yes."

"We were two young people who were playing with life; it had been very amusing to be engaged, but to be married must be still more diverting, and then to come home and keep house, oh! so immensely entertaining; but not equal to having children. Well, here I am now with a house which I am utterly powerless to manage, and two children which neither of us can educate; at least Atlung thinks so."

"But do not you try to take hold?"

"Of the house, do you mean?"

"Well, yes, of the house."

"Dear me! of what use would that be? I usually get a scolding when I try."

"But you have plenty of help, I suppose?"

"Yes, that is just the misfortune."

I was about to ask what she meant by this when the dining-room door was noiselessly opened; Stina entered with the lamps. She passed in and out two or three times; but the large room was far from being lighted by the lamps she brought in. Meanwhile, conversation ceased.

When Stina was about to leave, Fru Atlung asked for the children. Stina informed her they were being searched for; they were not on the gard. The mother paid no further attention to this, and Stina left the room.

"Who is Stina?" I asked, as the door closed behind her.

"Oh, she is a very unhappy person. She had a drunken father who beat her, and afterwards she had a husband, a bank cashier, who also became a hard drinker and beat her. Now he is dead."

"Has she been here long?"

"Since before my first child was born."

"But this is sad company for you, my dear lady."

"Yes, she is not *very* enlivening."

"Then most surely she should be sent away."

"That would be contrary to the traditions of this house. An older person must always take charge of the children, and this older person must live and die in the family. Stina is a very worthy woman."

Again the subject of our conversation came noiselessly into the room; this time with the coffee. There was upon the whole something ghost-like about this blue-green Carlo Dolci portrait flitting thus over the rugs in the large room, where she was searching for a shade for the lamp on the coffee table, as though it were not dark enough here before. The shade was, moreover, a perforated picture of St. Peter's at Rome.

Stina departed, and the lady of the house poured out the coffee.

"And so you men are going to take from us the hope in immortality, with all the rest?" she abruptly asked.

To what this "all the rest" referred, I was allowed to form my own conjectures. She handed me a cup of coffee and continued,—

"When I was driving this morning to the other side of the park to visit the dying man, it occurred to me that the snow on the barren trees is, upon the whole, the most exquisite symbol that could be imagined of the hope of immortality spread over the earth; is it not so? So purely from above, and so merciful!"

"Do you believe it falls from the skies, my dear lady?"

"It certainly falls down on the earth."

"That is true, but it comes also from the earth."

She appeared not to want to hear this, but continued,—

"You spoke a little while ago of dust. But this white, pure dust on the frozen boughs and on the gray earth is truly like the poetry of eternity; so it seems to me," and she placed a singing emphasis on the "me."

"Who is the author of this poetry, my dear lady?"

She turned on me her large eyes, now larger than ever, but this time not questioningly; no, there was certainly in her look.

"If there is no revelation from without, there is one from within; every human being who feels thus possesses it."

She had never been more beautiful. At this moment steps were heard in the front room. She turned her head in a listening attitude.

"It is Atlung back again!" said she, as she rose and rang for another cup.

She was right; it was Atlung, who as soon as he had removed his out-door wraps opened wide the door and came in. His attorney, Hartmann, had grown anxious and had come to meet him. Atlung had attended to the entire business with him on the highway.

His wife's questioning eyes followed him as he sauntered across the floor. Either she did not like his having interrupted us, or she noticed that he was out of humor. As he took the coffee cup from her hand, he recounted to her his recent experience with the boys. He did not mention any of the words the little fellows had shouted out with such jubilant merriment; but he added enough to lead her to surmise what they were. And while he was drinking his coffee, he repeated to her that he had promised them a whipping; "but," said he, "something more than the rod is needed in this case."

As she stood when she handed him the cup, so she remained standing after he had finished his coffee and gone. Terror was depicted in both face and attitude. Her eyes followed him as he walked about the room; she was waiting to hear this something else which was more than the rod.

"Now I will tell you what it is, Amalie," came from across the room, "the boys must leave to-morrow at latest."

She sank slowly down on the sofa, so slowly that I do not think she was aware that she was seating herself. She watched him intently. A more helpless, unhappy object I had never seen.

"You surely think enough of the boys, Amalie, to submit? You see now the result of my humoring you the last time."

But if he goes on thus he will kill her! Why does he not look at her?

Whether she noticed my sympathy or not, she suddenly turned her eyes, her hands, toward me, while her husband walked from us across the floor; there was a despairing entreaty in this glance, in this little movement. I comprehended at once what was her sole wish: this was the matter in which I was to help her.

She had sunk down on her hands, and she remained lying thus without stirring. I did not hear sounds of weeping; probably she was praying. He strode up and down the room; he saw her; but his step kept continually growing firmer. The articles he picked up and crushed in his hand, he flung each time farther and farther away from him, and with increased vehemence.

The dining-room door slowly opened. Stina appeared again, but this time she remained standing on the threshold, paler than usual. Atlung, who had just turned toward us, stood still and cried: "What is it, Stina?"

She did not reply at once; she looked at the mistress of the house, who had raised her head and was staring at her, and who at last burst out: "What is it, Stina?"

"The boys," said Stina, and paused.

"The boys?" repeated both parents, Atlung standing motionless, his wife springing up.

"They are neither on the gard, nor at the housemen's places; we have searched everywhere, even through the manufactory."

"Where did you see them last?" asked Atlung, breathless.

"The milkmaid says she saw them running toward the park crying, when you promised to give them a whipping."

"The fish-pond!" escaped my lips before I had time to reflect, and the effect upon myself, and upon all the others, was the same as if something had been dashed to pieces in our midst.

"Stina!" shouted Atlung,—it was not a reproach, no, it was a cry of pain, the bitterest I have ever heard,—and out he rushed. His wife ran after him, calling him by name.

"Send for lanterns!" I cried to the people I saw behind Stina in the dining-room. I went out and found my things, and returning again, met Stina, who was moving round in a circle with clasped hands.

"Come now," said I, "and show me the way!"

Without reply, perhaps without being conscious of what she was doing, she changed her march from round in a circle to forward, with hands still clasped, and praying aloud: "Father in heaven, for Christ's sake! Father in heaven, for Christ's sake!" in touching, vigorous tones; and thus she continued through the yard, past the houses, through the garden, and into the park.

It was not very cold; it was snowing. As one in a dream, I walked through the snow-mist, following this tall, dark spectre in front of me, with its trail of prayer, in and out among the lofty, snow-covered trees. I said to myself that two small boys might of course go to the fish-pond in the hope of finding God and the angels and new clothes; but to spring into a hole if there was one, when there were two of them together—impossible, unnatural, absurd! How in all the world had I come to think of or suggest such a thing? But all the sensiblethings one can say to one's self at such a moment are of no avail; the worst and most improbable suppositions keep gaining force in spite of them; and this "Father in heaven, for Christ's sake! Father in heaven, for Christ's sake!" which soughed about me, in tones of the utmost anguish, kept continually increasing my own anxiety.

Even if the boys had not gone to the fish-pond, or if they had been there and had not dared jump into the water, they might have tumbled into some other place. The father of little Hans was to receive wings that afternoon; might not they, with their troubled hearts, be sitting under a tree somewhere waiting for wings to be given them? If such were the case, they would freeze to death. And I could see these two little frozen mortals, who dared not go home, the younger one crying, the elder one finally crying too. I positively seemed to hear them—"Hush!"

"What is that?" said Stina, and turned in sudden hope. "Do you hear them?"

We both stood still; but there was nothing to hear except my own panting when I could no longer hold my breath. Nor was there anything resembling two little human beings huddled together.

I told her what I had just been thinking about, and drawing near me she clasped her hands, and, in tones of suppressed anguish, whispered: "Pray with me! Oh, pray with me!"

"What shall I pray for? That the boys may die, and go to heaven and become angels?"

She stared at me in alarm, then turned and walked on as before, but now without a word.

We followed a foot-path through the wood: it led to the fish-pond, as I remembered from the story about little Hans; but we had to go more than half the length of the park in order to reach the latter. Through a ravine flowed a brook, and here a dam had been made. It was large so that the fish-pond had a considerable circumference. We had to step up from the foot-path in order to reach the edge of the pond. Stina continued to walk in front of me, and when she had climbed the bank and could see the pond and the two parents standing on it, she kneeled down, praying and sobbing. Now I was sorry for her.

When I also stood upon the bank and saw the parents, I was deeply affected. At the same time I heard voices in the wood behind me. They came from the people with the lanterns. The flickering light of the four lanternsthat, subdued by the falling snow, was shed over human beings, the snow itself, the lower trunks of the trees, and the shadows into which some individuals in the party and some of the trees and certain portions of the landscape occasionally fell, all became fixed forever in my memory with the words I at that moment heard from the pond: "There is no hole in the ice!"

It was Atlung's voice, quivering with emotion. I turned and saw his wife on his neck. Stina had sprung up with an exclamation which ended in a long but hushed: "God be praised and thanked!"

But the two on the ice still clung together, with some difficulty I climbed down from the bank and crossed to where they stood; the wife still hung on Atlung's neck and he was bowed over her. I paused reverently at a little distance; they were whispering together. The light shed by the lanterns on the pond was the first thing that roused them.

"But what next? Where shall we seek now?" asked Atlung.

I drew nearer. I now repeated to the parents, although more cautiously, what I had already said to Stina, that perhaps the children were sitting somewhere under a tree, waiting in their distress of mind for compassionate angels, and in that case there would be danger of their being already so cold that they would be ill. Before I had finished speaking, Atlung had called up to those on the bank: "Had the boys their out-door things on when they were last seen?"

"No," replied two of the by-standers.

He inquired if they had their caps on; and here opinions differed. I insisted that they did have them on; some one else said No. Atlung himself could not remember. Finally some one declared that the elder boy had his cap on, but not the younger one.

"Ah, my poor little Storm!" wailed the mother.

Among the people on the edge of the pond there were some who wept so loud that they were heard below. I think there were about twenty people, side by side, about the lanterns.

Atlung shouted up to them: "We must search the whole park through; we will begin with the housemen's places." And he came toward the bank, climbed up and helped his wife up after him.

They were met by Stina. "My dear, dear lady!" she whispered, beseechingly; but neither of the parents paid any attention to her.

I stared into the ravine below us. To look down on snow-laden trees from above is like gazing on a petrified forest.

"Dear Atlung! will not you call?" begged the wife.

He took a position far in advance of the rest; all became still. And then he called aloud through the wood, slowly and distinctly: "Anton and little Storm! Come home to papa and mamma! Papa is no longer angry!"

Was it the air thus set in motion, or did the last flake of snow needed to break an overladen branch fall just then, or had some one come into contact with such a branch; suffice it to say, Atlung received for an answer the snow-fall from a large bough, partly at one side, partly in front of us. It gave a hollow crash, rousing the echoes of the wood, the bough swayed to and fro, and rose to its place, and snow was showered over us. But this swaying motion finally caused all the heavy branches to loose their burdens; crash followed crash, and snow enveloped us; before we knew what was coming the nearest tree had cast the burden from all its branches at once. The atmospheric pressure now became so great that two more, then five, six, ten, twenty trees freed themselves, with violent din, from their heavy loads, sending an echo through the wood and a mist as from mighty snow-drifts. This was followed by cluster after cluster of trees, some at our sides, some at a long distance off, some right in front of us; the movement first passed through two great arms, which gradually spread into manifold divisions; ere long the whole forest trembled. The thunder rolled far away from us, close by us, now at intervals, now all at once, and seemed interminable. Before us everything was surrounded by a white mist; this loud rumbling of thunder through the wood had at first appalled us; gradually as it passed farther on and grew in proportion it became so majestic that we forgot all else.

The trees stood once more proudly erect, fresh and green; we ourselves looked like snow-men. All the lanterns were extinguished, we lighted them again, and we shook the snow from us. Then we heard in a moaning tone: "What if the little boys are lying under a snow-drift!"

It was the mother who spoke. Several hastened to say that it could not in any way harm them, that the worst possible result would be that they might be thrown down, perhaps stifled for a little while; but they would surely be able to work their way out again. There was one who said that unquestionably the children would scream as soon as they were free from the snow, and Atlung called out: "Hark!" We stood for more than a minute listening; but we heard nothing except a far-off echo from some solitary cluster of trees that had just been drawn into the vortex with the rest.

But if the boys were in one of the remote recesses of the wood, their voices could scarcely reach us; on either side of us the edges of the ravine were higher than the banks of the pond where we stood.

"Yes, let us go search for them," said Atlung, deeply moved; as he spoke, he went close to the brink of the pond, turned toward the rest of us who were beginning to step down, and bade us pause. Then he cried: "Anton and little Storm! Come home again to papa and mamma! Papa is no longer angry!" It was heart-rending to hear him. No answer came. We waited a long time. No answer.

Despondently he returned, and came down on the path with the rest of us; his wife took his arm.

CHAPTER VI.

WE reached the edge of the wood, and then our party divided, keeping at such a distance apart that we could see one another and everything between us; we walked the whole length of the wood up and then took the next section down, but slowly; for all the snow from the trees was now spread over the old snow on the ground; in some places it was packed down so hard that it bore our weight, but in other places we sank in to our knees. When we assembled the next time, in order to disperse anew, I inquired if after all it were likely that two small boys would have the courage to remain in the wood after it had grown dark. But this suggestion met with opposition from all. The boys were accustomed to be busied in the wood the whole day long and in the evenings too; they had other boys who constructed snow-men for them, forts and snow-houses, in which they often sat with lights, after it was dark.

This naturally drew our thoughts to all these buildings, and the possibility of the boys having taken refuge in one or other of them. But no one knew where they were situated this year, as the snow had come so recently.Moreover, they were in the habit of building now in one place, now in another, and so nothing remained but to continue as before.

It so happened that Stina walked next to me this time, and as we two were in the ravine, and this was winding in some places, we were brought close together, and had no locality to search. She was evidently in a changed frame of mind. I asked her why this was.

"Oh," said she, "God has so plainly spoken to me. We are going to find the boys! Now I know why all this has happened! Oh, I know so plainly!"

Her Madonna eyes glowed with a dreamy happiness; her pale, delicate face wore an expression of ecstasy.

"What is it, Stina?"

"You were so hard toward me before. But I forgive you. Dear Lord, did not I sin myself? Did not I doubt God? Did not I murmur against the decrees of God? Oh, His ways are marvelous! I see it so plainly—so plainly!"

"But what do you mean?"

"What do I mean? Fru Atlung has for the last half year prayed God for only one single thing. Yes, it is her way to do so. She learned it of her father. Just for one single thing she has prayed, and we have helped her. It is that the boys may not be separated from her; Atlung has threatened to send them away. Had it not been for what has happened this evening he would surely have kept his word; but God has heard her prayer! Perhaps I too have been an instrument in his hands; I almost dare believe that I have. And the death of little Hans, yes, most certainly the death of little Hans! If those two sweet little souls are sitting and freezing somewhere, waiting for the angels, oh, the dear, dear boys, they surely have these with them! Do you doubt this? Ah, do not doubt! If the boys are made ill—and they most surely will be ill—it will be most fortunate for them! For when the father and mother sit together beside the sick-bed, oh, then the boys will never be sent away. Never, no never! Then Atlung will see that it would be the death of his wife. Oh, he sees it this evening. Yes, he unquestionably sees it. He has already made her a solemn promise; for the last time we met, she gave me a look of such heartfelt kindness, and that she did not do a little while ago. It was as though she had something to say to me—and what else could it possibly be in the midst of her anxiety than this? She has discerned God's ways, she too God's marvelous ways. She thanks and praises Him, as I do; yes, blessed be the name of God, for Jesus Christ's sake, through all eternity!"

She spoke in a whisper, but decidedly, aye, vehemently; the last, or words of thanksgiving, on the contrary, with bowed head, clasped hands, and softly, as to her own soul.

We drifted apart, although now and then we drew near together again, when the ravine obliged us to do so, and all attempt at searching on our part ceased.

"There is one thing I need to have explained," I whispered to her. "If everything from the time of the sorrowful death of little Hans has happened in order that Atlung's boys may remain with their mother; then this great fall of snow we have recently seen and heard must be part of the whole plan. But I cannot see how?"

"That? Why that was simply a natural occurrence; a pure accident."

"Is there such a thing?"

"Yes," replied she; "and it often has its influence on the rest. To be sure, in this instance I cannot see how. It is a great mercy though, that I can see what I do. Why should I ask more?"

We peered about us; but we felt convinced that the boys were not in the ravine. What I had last said seemed to absorb Stina.

"What did *you* think about the snow-fall?" asked she, softly, the next time we were thrown together.

"I will tell you. Shortly before we came out into the park, Fru Atlung had been saying to me that the hope of immortality descended from heaven on our lives, just as hushed, white, and soft as the snow on the naked earth"—

"Oh, how beautiful!" interposed Stina.

"And so I thought when the shock came, and the whole forest trembled, and the snow fell from the trees with the sound of thunder,—now do not be angry,—that in the same way the hope of immortality had fallen from the mother of the boys, and you and all of us, in our great anxiety for the lives of the little fellows. We rushed about in sorrow and lamentation, and some of us in ill-concealed frenzy, lest the boys had received a call from the other life, or lest some occurrence here had led them to the brink of eternity."

"O my God, yes!"

"Now we have had this hope of immortality hanging over us for many thousand years, for it is older, much older than Christianity; and we have progressed no farther than this."

"Oh, you are right! Yes, you are a thousand times right! Think of it!" she exclaimed, and walked on in silent brooding.

"You said before that I was hard toward you, and then I had done nothing but remind you of the belief in immortality you had taught the boys."

"Oh, that is true; forgive me! Oh, yes indeed!"

"For you know that you had taught them that it was far, far better to be with God than to be here; and that to have wings and be an angel was the highest glory a little child could attain; indeed, that the angels themselves came and carried away unhappy little children."

"Oh, I beg of you, no more!" she moaned, placing both hands on her ears. "Oh, how thoughtless I have been!" she added.

"Do not you believe all this yourself, then?"

"Yes, to be sure I believe it! There have been times in my life when such thoughts were my sole consolation. But you really confuse me altogether."

And then she told me in a most touching way that her head was no longer very strong; she had wept and suffered so much; but the hope of a better life after this had often been her one consolation.

Atlung's mournful call, with always the same words, was heard ever and anon, and just at this moment fell on our ears. With a start we were back again in the dreadful reality that the boys were not yet found, and that the longer the time that elapsed before they were found, the greater the certainty that they must pay the penalty of a dangerous illness. It continued to snow so that notwithstanding the moonlight we walked in a mist.

Then a cry rang through forest and snow from another voice than Atlung's and one of quite a different character. I could not distinguish what was said; but it was followed by a fresh call from another, then again from a third, and this last time could be distinctly heard the words: "I hear them crying!" It was a woman's voice. I hastened forward, the rest ran in front of and behind me, all in the direction whence came the call. We had become weary of wading in the heavy snow; but now we sped onward as easily as though there were firm ground beneath our feet. The light from the lanterns skipping about among us and over our heads, shone in our eyes and dazzled us; no one spoke, our breathing alone was heard.

"Hush!" cried a young girl, suddenly halting, and the rest of us also stood still; for we heard the voices of the two little ones uplifted in that piteous wail of lamentation common to children who have been weeping in vain for long, long hours and to whom sympathy has finally come.

"Good gracious!" exclaimed an elderly man,—he well knew the sound of such weeping. We perceived that the boys were no longer alone; we walked onward, but more calmly. We reached and passed the fish-pond, and came to a place a little beyond the ravine, where the trees were regular in their growth; for the spot was sheltered and hidden. The weeping, of course, became more distinct the nearer we approached, and at last we heard voices blended with it. They were those of the father and mother, who had been the first to gain the spot. When we had reached an opening where we could see between the trees into the snow, our gaze was met by two black objects against something extremely white; it was the father and mother, on their knees, each clinging to a boy; behind them was a snow fort, or rather a crushed snow house, in which, sure enough, the boys had sought refuge. When the lanterns were brought near, we saw how piteously benumbed with the cold the little fellows were: they were blue, their fingers stiff, they could not stand well on their feet; neither of them had on caps; these no doubt lay in the heap of snow, if the boys had had them with them at all. They replied to none of the tokens of endearment or questions of their parents; not once did they utter a word, they only wept and wept. We stood around them, Stina sobbing aloud. The weeping of the boys, and the lamentations, questions, and tokens of endearment of the parents, together with the accents of despair and joy, which alternately blended therewith, were very affecting.

Atlung rose and took up one child; it was the elder one. His wife rose also, and gathered up the other in her arms. Several offered to carry the boy for her; but she made no reply, only walked on with him, consoling him, moaning over him, without a moment's pause between the words, until she made a misstep and plunging forward fell prostrate on the ground over her boy. She would not have help, but scrambled up with the boy still in her arms, walked on, and fell again.

Then she cast a look up to heaven, as though she would ask how this could happen, how it could be that this was possible!

Whenever I now recall her in her faith and in her helplessness, I remember her thus, with the boy in front of her stretched out in the snow, and she bending over him on her knees, tears streaming from the eyes which were uplifted with a questioning gaze toward heaven.

Some one picked up the boy, and Stina helped his mother. But when the little fellow found himself in the arms of another, he began to cry: "Mamma, mamma!" and stretched forth his benumbed hands toward her. She wanted to go to him at once and take him again in her arms, but he who carried the child hastened onward, pretending not to hear her, although she begged most humbly at last. They had scarcely come down on the footpath before she hastened forward and stopped the man; then with many loving words she took her boy again in her arms. Atlung was no longer in sight.

I allowed them all to go on in advance of me.

But when I saw them a short distance from me, enveloped in snow between the trees and heard the weeping and the soothing words, I drifted back into my old thoughts.

These two poor little boys had accepted literally the words of the grown people—to the utter dismay of the latter! If we were right in our conjectures (for the boys themselves had not yet told us anything and would not be likely to tell anything until after the illness they must unquestionably pass through); but *if* we were right in our conjectures, then these two little ones had sought a reality far greater than ours.

They had believed in beings more loving than those about us, in a life warmer and richer than our own; because of this belief they had braved the cold, although amid tears and terror, waiting resolutely for the miracle. When the thunder rolled over them, they had doubtless tremblingly expected the change—and were only buried.

How many had there been before them with the same experience?

CHAPTER VII.

I LEFT Skogstad at once, and without taking leave of the parents, who were with their children. I got a horse to the next station, and was soon slowly driving along the chaussée. The snow which had fallen made the road heavier than when I had come that way. A few atoms still swept about through the air but the fall was lightening more and more, so that the moonlight gradually gained in force. It fell on the snow-clad forest, which still stood unchanged, with fantastic power; for although the details were lost the contrasts were striking.

I was weary, and the mood I was in harmonized with my fatigue. In the still subdued moonlight the forest looked like a bowed-down, conquered people; its burden was greater than it could bear. Nevertheless, it stood there patiently, tree after tree, without end, bowed to the ground. It was like a people from the far-distant past to the present day, a people buried in dust. Yonder "heaven-fallen, merciful snow"—

And just as all symbols, even those from the times of old, which mythology dimly reveals to us, became fixed in the imagination, and gradually worked their way out to independence, so it was now with mine. I saw the past generations enveloped in a cloud of dust, in which they could not recognize one another, and that was why they fought against one another, slaying one another by the millions. Dust was being continually strewed over them. But I saw that it was the same with all those who were wounded, or who must die. I saw in the midst of these poor sufferers many kind, refined souls, who in thus strewing dust were rendering the highest, most beautiful service they knew, like those priestly physicians of Egypt, who offered to the sick and dying magic formulas as the most effectual preventive of death, and placed on the wounds a medicine, the greater part of which was composed of mystic symbols.

And I saw *all* the relations of life, even the soundest, strewed over with a coating of dust, and the attempt at deliverance to be the world's most complete revolution, which would wholly shatter these relations themselves.

And as I grew more and more weary and these fancies left me, but what I had recently experienced kept rising uppermost in my mind, then I plainly heard weeping in among the snow-flakes that were no longer falling; it was the boys I heard. They wept so sorely, they lamented so bitterly, while we tenderly bore them from dust to more dust.

I passed through the forest and drove along its margin up to the station. When I had nearly reached this I cast one more look downward over the tree-tops, which were radiant in the moonlight. The forest was magnificent in its snowy splendor.

The majesty of the view struck me now, and the symbol presented itself differently.

A dream hovering over all people, originating infinitely long before all history, continually assuming new forms, each of which denoted the downfall of an earlier one, and always in such a manner that the most recent form lay more lightly over the reality than those just preceding it, concealing less of it, affording freer breathing-space—until the last remnants should evaporate in the air. When shall *that* be?

The infinite will always remain, the incomprehensible with it; but it will no longer stifle life. It will fill it with reverence; but not with dust.

I sat down in the sledge once more, and the monotonous jingle of the bells caused drowsiness to overcome me. And then the weeping of the boys began to ring in my ears together with the bells. And weary as I was I could not help thinking about what further must have happened to the two little fellows, and how it must appear at first in the sick-room at Skogstad, and in the surroundings of those I had just left.

How different was the scene I imagined from what actually occurred!

I could not but recall it when, two months later, I drove over the same road with Atlung and he related to me what had taken place. I had then been abroad and he met me in town.

And when I now repeat this, it is not in his words, for I should be totally unable to reproduce them; but the substance of his story is what follows.

The boys were attacked with fever, and this passed into inflammation of the lungs. From the outset every one saw that the illness must take a serious turn; but the mother was so sure that all had come to pass solely in order that she might keep her boys, that she inspired the rest of the household with her faith.

However serious the illness might be, it would only be the precursor of happiness and peace. While yet in the wood she had obtained a solemn promise from her husband that their children should not be sent away; but that a tutor should be engaged for them who would have them continually under his charge. And by the sick-bed, when through the long nights and silent days they met there, Atlung repeated this promise as often as his wife wished. She had never been more beautiful, he had never loved her more devotedly; she was in one continual state of ecstasy. She confided to Atlung that from the first time, about half a year before, he had declared that the boys must go away, she had prayed the Lord to prevent it, prayed incessantly, and in all this time had prayed for nothing else. She knew that a prayer offered in the name of Jesus must be granted. She had prayed in this way several times before in regard to circumstances which seemed to herself to be brought into her life under the guidance of faith, brought into it in the most natural way. This time she had called her father to her aid and finally Stina; both of them had promised to pray only for this one thing. It did not seem to occur to her for a moment that there was another way of gaining her point, for instance, as far as lay within her power, and as far as her faith permitted it, to study Atlung's ideas on education, and to endeavor to persuade him to unite with her in an attempt, that it might be proved whether they were equal to the task. She started from the standpoint that she was utterly incompetent; what, indeed, was she able to do? But God could do what He would. This was his own cause, and that to a far higher degree than any other matter concerning which he had granted her prayers, and so she was sure He would hear her. Every occurrence, every individual who came to the gard, was sent; in one way or another everything must be a link in the chain of events, which was to lead Atlung to other thoughts. When she told Atlung this, in her innocence and her faith, he felt that, at all events, there was no human power which could resist her. He was so completely borne along in the current of her fancies that he not only became convinced that the boys would recover, but he even failed to perceive how ill she was.

The long stay in the park, without any out-door wraps and with wet feet, the overstrained mental condition and long night vigils, the pursuit of one fixed idea, without any regard to its effect on herself, being so wholly absorbed in it that she forgot to eat, indeed, no longer felt the need of food—wholly robbed her of strength at last. But the first symptoms of illness were closely united with her restless, ecstatic condition; neither she herself, nor the rest of the household paid any heed to them. When finally she was obliged to go to bed, there still hovered over her such joy, aye, and peace, that the others had no time for anxiety. Her feverish fancies blended in such a way with her life, her wishes, her faith, that it was often not well to separate them. They all understood that she was ill and that she was often delirious, but not that she was in any danger. The physician was one of those who rarely express an opinion; but they all thought that had there been danger he would have spoken. Stina, who had undertaken the supervision of the sick-room, was absorbed in her own fancies and hope, and explained away everything when Atlung showed any uneasiness.

Then one noon he came home from the factories, and after warming himself, went up-stairs to the large chamber where the invalids all lay, for the mother wanted to be where the boys were. Her bed was so placed that she could see them both. Atlung softly entered the room. It was airy and pleasant there, and deep peace reigned. No one besides the invalids, as far as he could see at first, was in the room; but he afterwards discovered that the sick-nurse was there asleep in a large arm-chair, which she had drawn to the corner nearest the stove. He did not wake her; he stood a little while bending over each of the boys, who were either sleeping or lying in a stupor, and thence he stepped very softly to his dear wife's bed, rejoicing in the thought that she too was now peaceful, perhaps sleeping; for he did not hear her babble which usually greeted him. A screen had been placed between the bed and the window, so he could not see distinctly until he came close to her. She lay with wide-open eyes; but tear after tear trickled down from them.

"What is it?" he whispered, startled. In her changed mood he saw at once how worn, how frightfully worn, she was. Why, in all the world, had he not seen this before. Or had he observed it, yet been so far governed by her security that he had not paid any attention to it. For a moment it seemed as if he would swoon away, and only the fear that he might fall across her bed gave him strength to keep up.

As soon as he could he whispered anew, "What is it, Amalie?"

"I see by your looks that you know it yourself," she whispered slowly, in reply; her lips quivered, the tears filled her eyes and rolled down her cheeks: but otherwise she lay quite still. Her hands—oh, how thin they were; the ring was much too large on her finger, and this he remembered having noticed before; but why had he not reflected on what it meant?

Her hands lay stretched out on either side of the body which seemed to him so slender beneath the coverlet and sheet. The lace about her wrists was unrumpled, as though she had not stirred since she was dressed for the morning, and that must now be several hours since.

"Why, Amalie," he burst out, and knelt down at her bedside.

"It was not thus I meant it," replied she, but in so soft a whisper that under other circumstances he could not have heard it.

"What do you mean by 'thus,' Amalie? Oh, try once more to answer me! Amalie!"

He saw that she wanted to reply, but either could not, or else had thought better of it. Tears filled her eyes and trickled down her cheeks, filled her eyes and were shed again, her lips quivered, but as noiselessly as this occurred, just so still she lay. Finally she raised her large eyes to his face. He bowed closer to her to catch the words: "I would not take them from—you," spoken in a whisper as before; the word "you" was uttered by itself, and in the same low tone as the rest, encompassed with a tenderness and a mournfulness which nothing on earth could exceed in strength.

He dared not question further, although he failed to understand his wife. He only comprehended that something had occurred that same forenoon which had turned the current of life to that of death. She lay there paralyzed. Her immobility was that of terror; something extraordinary had weighed her down to this speechless silence, had crushed her. But he also comprehended that behind this noiseless immobility there was an agitation so great that her heart was ready to burst; he knew that there was danger, that his presence increased the danger, that there must be help sought; in other words, he comprehended that if he did not go away himself, his face as it must now look was enough to kill her. He never knew how he got away. He can remember that he was on a stairway, for he recollects seeing a picture that his wife herself must have hung up, it was one representing St. Christopher carrying the child Jesus over a brook. He found himself lying on the sofa in the large sitting-room, with something wet on his brow, and a couple of people at his side, of whom one was Stina. He struggled for a long time as with a bad dream. At the sight of Stina his terror returned. "Stina, how is it with Amalie?" The answer was that she was in a raging fever.

"But what happened this forenoon while I was absent?"

Stina knew nothing. She did not even understand his question. She was not the one who had attended Fru Atlung in the forenoon; she had watched in the night, and then the patient's fever fancies were happy ones, as they had again become. Had the doctor been with her in the forenoon? No, he was expected now. He had said yesterday that to-day he would not come until later than usual. This indicated a feeling of security on the doctor's part.

Had Fru Atlung spoken with any one else? If so it must be the sick-nurse. "Bring her here!" Stina left the room. Atlung also sent away the others who had assembled around him, he needed to collect his thoughts. He sat up, with his head between his hands, and before he knew it he was weeping aloud. He heard his own sobs resounding through the large room and he shuddered. He felt sure; oh, he felt but too sure, that he would sit here alone and hear this wail of misery for weeks. And in this sense of boundless bereavement, her image stood forth distinctly: she came from her bed in her white garment and told him word for word what she had meant. Her prayer to God had been to be allowed to keep her boys, and now this had been granted in a terrible way for she was to have them with her in death. It was this which had paralyzed her. And the beloved one repeated: "I did not mean it thus, I would not take them from—you."

But how had this idea suddenly occurred to her? *Why* was her security transformed into something so terrible?

The sick-nurse knew nothing. Toward morning the dear lady had fallen into a slumber, and this had gradually become more and more calm. When she awoke rather late in the morning, she lay still a little while before she was waited on. She was excessively weak; the housekeeper helped care for her. Not a word was said to her about her condition, not a single word. She had not spoken herself, except once; it was after she had had a little broth, then she said: "Oh, no, never mind!" She lay back and closed her eyes. Her attendants urged her to take some more; but she made no reply. They stood a little and waited; then they left her in peace.

As the evening wore on, the fever increased; by the doctor's advice she was carried into the next room. She understood this to mean that she was being borne into Paradise, and while they were moving her, she sang in a somewhat hoarse voice. She talked, too, now, without cessation; but with the exception of that hymn about Paradise there was nothing in her words which indicated that she remembered anything that had occupied her thoughts in her moments of consciousness. All was now happiness and laughter once more. Toward morning she slept; but she woke very soon, and at once the unspeakable pain she had had before came over her, but at the same time came also the death-struggle. Amid this she became aware that the beds of the boys were not near hers. She looked at Atlung and opened her hand, as if she would clasp his. He understood that she thought the boys had gone on before and wanted to console him. With this cold little hand in his, and with its gentle pressure through the struggle with the last message from this receding life, he sat until the end came.

But then, too, he gave way wholly to his boundless grief. The responsibility he felt for not having attempted to draw her into his own vigorous reading and thought; for having left her to live a weak dream-life; to bear the burden of the housekeeping and the bringing up of the children, but not in community of spirit and will, partly out of consideration for her, partly from a careless desire to leave her as she was when he took her; for having amused himself with her when it struck his fancy to do so, but not having made an effort to work in the same direction with her,—this was what tormented his mind and could find no consolation, no answer, no forgiveness.

Not until the following night when he was wandering about out of doors, beneath a bright starlit sky, came the first soothing thoughts. Would she under any circumstances have forsaken the ideas of her childhood to follow his? Were not they an inheritance, so deeply rooted in her nature that an attempt to alter them would only have made her unhappy? This he had always believed, and it was this which ultimately determined him to live *his* life while she lived hers. The image of his beautiful darling hovered about him, and the two boys always accompanied her. Whether it was because of his own weariness, or whether his self-reproaches had exhausted themselves and let things speak their own natural language—his guilt toward her and toward them was shifted slightly and spread over many other matters, which were painful enough; but not as these were.

What these matters were, he did not tell me; but he looked ten years older than before.

The doctor sought an interview with him the next day, and said that he felt obliged to tell him that if he had not pronounced his wife's condition dangerous it was because he had felt sure that she would recover. Her own happy frame of mind would help her, he thought. But something most have happened that forenoon.

Atlung made no reply. The doctor then added that the boys were past all danger; the elder one, indeed, had never been in any.

Atlung had not yet for a moment separated mother and boys in his thoughts. During their illness he felt with her that they must live; for the last twenty-four hours he had been convinced that they must follow her in death. He could not think of the mother without them.

And now that he must separate them, the first feeling was—not one of joy: no, it was dismay that even in this matter the dear one had been disappointed! It seemed as though she were living and could see that it was all a mistake, and that this last mistake had needlessly killed her.

The two little boys, clad in mourning, were the first objects we met on the gard. They looked pale and frightened. They did not come to meet us, nor did they return their father's caress.

In the passage Stina met us; she too looked worn. I expressed my honest sympathy for her. She answered calmly that God's ways were inscrutable. He alone knew what was for our good.

Atlung took me with him to the family burial-place, a little stone chapel in a grove near the river. On the way there, he told me that every time he tried to talk confidentially with the boys and endeavor to be both father and mother to them, his loss rushed over him so overwhelmingly that he was forced to stop. He would learn with time to do his duty.

The sepulchral chamber was a friendly little chapel, in which the coffins stood on the floor. The door, however, was not an ordinary door, but an iron grating which now stood open; for there was work going on in the chapel. We removed our hats, and walked forward to her little coffin. We did not exchange a word. Not until after we had left it and were looking at the other coffins and their inscriptions, did Atlung inform me that his wife's coffin was to be placed in one of stone. I remarked that in this way we would eventually have more of our ancestors preserved than would be good for us. "But there is reverence in it," he replied, as we walked out.

There was warmth in the atmosphere. Over the bluish snow, the forest rose green or dark gray and the fjord was defiantly fresh. Spring was in the air, although we were still in the midst of winter.

Printed by Amazon Italia Logistica S.r.l.
Torrazza Piemonte (TO), Italy

55557647R00170